To Gloria

Feel free to share this.

With affection.

BRITISH
AMERICAN
PUBLISHING

BRENNAN'S POINT

DANIEL LYNCH

BRENNAN'S POINT

BY DANIEL LYNCH

British American Publishers, Ltd.

This novel is a work of fiction. Names, characters, places and incidents either are the product of the author's imagination or are used fictitiously. Any resemblance to actual events or locales or persons, living or dead, is entirely coincidental.

93 92 91 90 89 5 4 3 2 1

Library of Congress Cataloging in Publication Data

Lynch, Daniel, 1946—
    Brennan's Point / by Daniel Lynch.
        p. cm.
    ISBN 0-945167-03-2 : $19.95
    I. Title.
PS3562.Y417B7   1988
813'.54—dc19   88–17725
                                                      CIP

To Nellie, Anna and Donna;
essentially, three of a kind

BOOK 1

Chapter 1

Outside the night was awash in winter drizzle. Inside, Liam Brennan was drunk. The wetness was commonplace, but the drunkenness was not, nor was the anger that had prompted it.

When he had begun drinking in the early evening, his rage had been a towering thing. He had shaken with it, close to exploding. Now, with the clock approaching ten, the immense quantities of ale he had poured down his throat had begun to extinguish his anger, cooling it to glowing embers.

He emptied his glass and stared with vacant eyes. To hell with them, he thought. To hell with Da and Mother and especially to hell with Donal. As Liam sat and brooded at a corner table in McCarthy's Pub in 1908, he realized suddenly that his glass had gone dry. He motioned for another. The devil take them all, he said to himself, and welcome to them.

The argument, as always, had been trivial—on the surface, at least. His brain fogged in by now, Liam couldn't remember precisely what words had begun it or who had uttered them, Donal or himself. He could recall that by the time the day's work had been done, and Liam and Donal had secured their father's shabby fishing boat to its berth at the shaky old dock that jutted out into the Shannon Estuary, they had been close to blows.

Donal was older, bigger. But Liam, at twenty, was a rugged, rawboned youth who could hold his own in a fight and had held his own in entirely too many, which was one of the reasons Donal was his mother's favorite and Liam was her constant target for criticism. Like all Irish mothers, Margaret Brennan had prayed her younger son would become a priest. Instead, she found that she had borne a raucous and spirited pub brawler.

Her husband, wiry little Kevin Brennan, had watched as the dispute between his sons grew. At first he had said nothing and merely went about his work. But as their voices rose and the prospect of physical conflict grew more likely, he finally had jumped from the deck of his boat to the dock and stepped in between his towering sons, pushing them rudely apart. He had stared them both into submission. Donal had faltered first, turning away, muttering. Liam had responded by stalking off to the pub, where he had been drinking and sulking for hours now, resentment festering in his soul.

This rivalry between him and Donal had to end, he knew. They were grown men now, and it was past time for them to make the peace; only Liam lacked the patience to find a way, and Donal lacked the will. Liam seethed at the situation.

Now, however, his temper was at last beginning to ease, partly because of the ale and partly because Michael Kelly and Tim Gallagher were beginning to sing. They were seated on rude, wooden chairs by the hearth where a peat fire was glowing, and where Kelly had brought his mandolin. They were playing now, easing into serious music. Liam was beginning to relax in anticipation. Kelly and Gallagher were men of his own age who came to McCarthy's almost nightly to sip poteen and sing the old songs of County Clare that had made this area famous throughout Ireland. Kelly possessed a rich baritone, and Gallagher's voice was a pure tenor. They had sung together since childhood in the church choir. Liam listened with growing pleasure as their voices blended in a rendition of "The Isle of Innisfree." He leaned back in his chair, put his calloused hands behind his head and closed his eyes as the music flowed over him.

"Milseacht," he whispered to himself in Gaelic.

"Sweet, did you say, Liam Brennan?" Peggy McCarthy asked.

She placed another glass of ale on the table before him. At her words, Liam opened his eyes and smiled up at her. To Peggy, flirting was part of her job as a serving girl in her father's pub, but with Liam she had never had to make a special effort. She had loved him as long as she could remember, but it was only on nights like this, when he had barely a leg under him, that Peggy could provoke a response. She only wished that his warmth toward her would, just once, endure past closing time.

Tonight, Liam picked up his ale, looked at her and smiled. "There's a throne in heaven for you, Peggy McCarthy," he said, taking a deep drink.

Peggy made a face and said, "A lot you know of thrones in heaven, Liam Brennan. You know of fishing and boats. You know of drinking, there's no doubt of that, and the good nuns have seen that you know of reading and ciphering and some of the old language. But on the subject of crowns in heaven, you're surely no expert, and that's a blessed fact."

Liam, his glass at his lips, suddenly shot out his free hand and caught her waist firmly. "An evening in your lovely arms, Peggy Darlin'. That's heaven enough for me."

He tried to pull her close, but Peggy, feigning annoyance but giggling with delight, pulled away with practiced skill.

"Enough with your scandalous talk, Liam Brennan," she said mockingly, "my da will box your ears for you, and there'll be justice in it."

Liam cast a glance across the room at McCarthy, Peggy's father, who was serving drinks behind the bar. Even in the relatively crowded pub, McCarthy stood out half a head over everyone else. In his late forties, with arms like tree trunks, he had a deeply furrowed brow and the barrel chest of a born bone-crusher. He'd ousted Liam from the place more than once.

Liam looked at the bar and its customers for a long moment, then he turned back to dark-haired Peggy, charmingly lush in her prime years. She had, he noted, made no effort to move away from him.

"Your da is far too busy seeing to the needs of our betters to worry about so frivolous a thing as your virtue, Peggy Darlin'," he said thickly.

Peggy cast an eye back toward the bar and saw that two youngish men, each dressed in tailored tweeds uncommon to the village of Labasheeda, had settled into seats at the far end. Peggy frowned. She knew them and noted with disdain that her father had already begun fawning over them. Everything about his manner and carriage underwent a sudden transformation from proud publican to deferential servant. She turned back to Liam.

"And he should be," she scolded him, her mood shattered. "Would you want that the big lord's sons should become feisty in me da's pub? Then we'd know trouble, wouldn't we?"

Liam reached out and grabbed her wrist. This time he pulled her down on the bench next to him. His grasp was rougher than usual. He glared across the pub at the new customers.

"The devil take the English bastards," he said quietly, letting go of her wrist.

Peggy elbowed him rudely in the ribs, whispering, "Hush, Liam. You've a foolish tongue to speak so of the big lord's sons when they're close enough to hear."

Liam continued to glare at them for a moment or two. Then he turned to Peggy, his expression suddenly softened.

"I'll tell you of trouble, Peggy Darlin'," he said, "trouble is the likes of me, penniless and hopeless, nursing a broken heart over the likes of you." He leaned close to her. "Meet me tonight in the loft out back after closing."

She elbowed him again, not gently. "Why do you mock me so, Liam Brennan?" she demanded in hurt tones. "Are you without a heart as well as a brain?"

Liam leaned over in the dim light of the peat fire and nuzzled her neck. "I've no heart at all. You've broken it for me for all my days. I'll have to go to confession tomorrow, Peggy McCarthy, because I lust for you deep in my sinful soul."

That was too much for Peggy. She pushed him away and jumped up, her face reddening. "Then burn, Liam Brennan," she hissed, "I'll not be trifled with."

Liam sighed and lifted his pint. "No," he said, "and that's the pity of Ireland, that her women won't be trifled with—not even by their husbands." He took a deep drink.

Peggy put her hands on her ample hips and looked down at him, her face split by an evil grin. "So, it's a proposal of marriage, is it?"

Liam suddenly spat ale across the table in front of him. He coughed and looked up at her. "Peggy Darlin'," he said quickly, "your da has raised a literalist."

Peggy reached down and wrapped her hand around his glass. "That's about what I thought I'd hear from a carouser and a womanizer. I ought to pour this over your thick head."

Liam laughed and leaned back. "Go serve your fine English lordlings, Peggy Darlin'. They're bound to show you more respect than a carouser and a womanizer like me."

Peggy shook her head at him. "You're an evil man and bound for no good." Then her face softened, and she flashed him a shy smile. "But I'll forgive you if you ask politely."

Liam bowed his head. It was an exaggerated gesture. "Your forgiveness, good woman. The drink and your beauty have robbed me of my gallantry and good sense."

Peggy sighed and turned to walk back to the bar; as she did Liam reached out and caressed her round behind. She knocked his hand aside and danced lightly away, smiling and trying to hide it. Liam watched her bounce away, fighting her way through the small knot of customers in the pub. As she bent over one table on the other side of the room, one of the young Englishmen at the bar turned in his seat and looked at her. They were only a few feet apart, and the man suddenly reached out, as had Liam, and pulled the girl close.

"Well, Cecil," he said to his brother in drunken, Oxford-accented tones, "look what we have here, eh?"

Cecil leaned forward unsteadily. "I say. Pretty thing."

Peggy struggled to break free, and there was nothing coquettish in her manner. At the same time, she had no wish to offend these men. Her eyes were large and round, and her voice quavered with uncertainty.

"Please, My Lord," she said. "I have patrons waiting."

"Yes," William said with a grin, "but waiting for what, my dear? That's the question."

The music suddenly died, and the dozen or so men gathered in the little pub grew silent, their pints sitting untouched before them.

Trouble, McCarthy concluded, hurrying to the end of the bar. Two drunken Englishmen, the sons of the big lord at that, manhandling an Irish girl in a village pub late at night. In the Ireland of 1908 it didn't do to batter Brits, and McCarthy knew that someone would decide to do just that unless the publican restored order immediately. For the ten-thousandth time McCarthy complained silently to God for sending him a flighty daughter instead of a son.

"Now, My Lords," he said in his best placating tone, "this little lass is my very own child, and she has her work to be about."

Peggy squirmed to break free from her captor's embrace, but she was careful also to avoid hurting him. "My Lord, please," she said, "I have work."

It might have ended there, but the Englishmen were too drunk to grasp the gravity of the situation. The one called Cecil turned to McCarthy. "And what might this work for the patrons consist of?" he demanded, slurring his words.

Cecil and his brother William laughed. Off in the corner Liam Brennan suddenly rose. He stood six feet and two inches, and he weighed more than thirteen stone, all of it bone and muscle toughened by a lifetime of hauling heavy nets full of whitefish. Liam pushed through the tightly knit group of patrons and moved next to the Englishmen.

"Let her go, you British bastard," he rasped.

McCarthy motioned Liam away, fruitlessly. William's smile wavered only slightly. Casually, he turned his head toward Liam and said evenly, "Would you be kind enough to repeat that please, my good man?"

"I'm not your good man," Liam shot back, his big fists clenched, "I'm my own good man and none other's."

Peggy's eyes widened. "Liam, this is my own affair . . ."

From behind the bar, McCarthy was motioning frantically for Liam to step away.

"Liam, eh?" the Englishman said. "That's my own name—William. Only it's Liam in your own barbaric tongue, isn't it, my good man?"

Liam reddened visibly, and a muffled grumbling arose from around the pub. But William, drunk as he was, seemed not to note the growing hostility around him.

"And the last name?" he inquired of Liam. "Pray tell, what is your family name, my good man? That would be a useful piece of information."

And so it would, Liam knew. It would, no doubt, result eventually in his arrest and a week or two in the gaol for disturbing the peace.

"Let loose the girl," he said evenly, "then you can have my last name. Not before."

William smiled. He was a handsome man in his midtwenties, well scrubbed, neatly dressed and clean cut. He let go of Peggy suddenly and she jumped back into the bunch of customers who had crowded in on the confrontation. William's eyes met Liam's evenly, then he said, "There you are. And the last name again, if you will?"

Liam said nothing and without warning drove a red-knuckled fist straight into the Englishman's face. The sharp impact of the blow knocked William off his stool. He hit the floor hard. The customers scuttled back to provide room for the battlers, and Liam could hear Tim Kelly cheer.

McCarthy rushed around the bar, intent on preventing mayhem, but by then Cecil had leaped at Liam. Cecil was not a large man, and Liam caught him by the throat with one great hand. He pushed him back over the bar and struck him half-a-dozen fierce, hammering blows full in the face. William, his nose bleeding and his smile long gone, clambered to his feet as Cecil slipped limply off the bar to the rough floor.

William unleashed a roundhouse blow at Liam that caught the fisherman high on the forehead. William's second punch was harder but wild. Liam stepped inside it and drove a hard right to the Englishman's middle. William bent over in pain, and Liam rammed a knee into his face, snapping him upright, then he hammered him to the floor. The brawl ended when McCarthy hurdled Cecil's prostrate form and grabbed Liam from behind, pinning his arms to his side.

"Stop it, Liam Brennan," McCarthy hissed in his ear, "stop it before you're a murderer as well as a fool."

For a moment, his blood hot, Liam struggled against McCarthy's grasp. The publican's great muscles flexed, and Liam found himself immobilized. Then his head cleared as he surveyed his handiwork. William was rolling weakly on the floor, bleeding from a cut over one eye and from his nose. Cecil, however, was moving not at all. The full impact of what he had done suddenly sank in on Liam, and his knees nearly failed him.

"What's done is done," he told McCarthy quietly.

The publican let him go. Liam looked about him. The faces of McCarthy's patrons, so alight with pleasure just a moment before, were now solemn. All were acutely aware of the identities of the victims and what that meant for Liam. He felt Peggy's hand clutching at his own.

"Liam," she whispered, looking down with horror at Cecil's motionless form, "you're done a terrible thing here. A terrible thing."

"I did what I wished to do. I wish I could do it again."

McCarthy took Liam's arm and led him roughly to the door. The patrons stood aside for him, and several reached out and slapped his back as he went by. "Well done, lad," Liam heard Gallagher say in his high, sweet voice. "The bastards had it coming."

"Flee while you can, lad," McCarthy told him, then pushed him outside and shut the door hard behind him. For a moment Liam stood unmoving, trying to get his bearings. Then he heard the door open behind him, and Peggy McCarthy slipped out.

"You're a grand fool, Liam Brennan," she said, "to do what you did for me. But you can't stay lollygagging here in front of me da's pub. Off with you."

"My da will help me," Liam muttered to himself.

"None can help you now," Peggy told him. Impulsively, she threw herself into his arms and pressed her lips to his in a wet, passionate kiss. She stayed with him for a long moment then pushed him back.

"I'll never forget you," she whispered, "even if they stretch your neck on the courthouse steps in Ennis."

He squeezed her hand. "And little chance of that there'll be," Liam Brennan told her.

* * * *

Labasheeda was built on a slope that led to a bay on the Shannon. It occupied twenty-six shabby acres, was home to four hundred souls and was older than recorded history. Two Celtic ruins occupied its outskirts, their function long forgotten.

The Brennan cottage was a three-room affair four hundred feet above the Shannon. The house in which Liam Brennan had been born and lived all his life had a dirt floor, a fireplace that was the source of all heat and the scene of all cooking and a privy close to the rear door. Liam shared this house with his brother, his parents and his two teenaged sisters.

As Liam reached the house and slipped inside, he could see his parents asleep in the corner of the best room in their ancient, steel-framed bed, their features distinct in the orange light thrown off by the peat fire. Kevin Brennan lifted his head as Liam entered.

"It's me, Da," Liam whispered. "Come outside. We have to talk."

Kevin Brennan looked over his shoulder at the bulky figure of his wife, Margaret. Her breathing was slow and measured. He slipped out from beneath the covers and moved outside the house to join his son.

Kevin was a small man, and he was lean and hard and nimble. He looked up at Liam. "What have you done?" he asked simply.

Liam told the story quickly and accurately, omitting no detail. Kevin listened in silence.

"You can't stay in Labasheeda," he said finally. "We need to get you to Limerick."

"I'm sorry, Da," Liam told him. "I lost me head."

Kevin Brennan sighed. "Perhaps it was meant to be."

* * * *

Liam's escape had been a neat thing, he reflected. Within moments of his brief talk with his father outside the Brennan cottage, Kevin and Donal had emerged from the house.

Then they were off, the three of them, in the boat across the Shannon, with Kevin at the helm and Liam and Donal rowing to aid the light nighttime breeze. They had made Tarbert on the Shannon's southern shore just before daybreak, and Kevin had somehow obtained a pony cart on the docks. Liam had been ordered into the back of the cart and covered with a blanket. "Hush ye, now," Kevin had hissed at him.

Liam wasn't sure how long he lay hidden beneath the blanket; the motion of the cart and the ale he had drunk at McCarthy's had lulled him to sleep. Eventually Kevin reached back and pulled the blanket off him, and Liam emerged to a bright, rare, sunlit morning that made the dewy countryside gleam.

"Where's Donal?" he asked.

"Gone back with the boat, if he hasn't sunk it already going into the bay in the dark. I told him to stay out in the open water until dawn, but you know Donal."

Liam nodded. "How'll you get back?"

Kevin Brennan smiled, a rare occurrence. "In my fine pony cart, of course. I bought the thing at the dock in Tarbert, from a fish merchant."

Liam was stunned. "You bought it? With what?"

"With some gold I've kept for emergencies."

"And now the gold is gone, and you're stuck with a cart you've no use for."

Kevin shook his head. "You're like your mother when it comes to money—always counting every pence like it was the last one on Earth. Well, never you mind. I'll sell the thing in Ennis or Kildysart, and probably at a profit, and I'll walk the rest of the way home. For now, we'll ride like the gentry. Stop your worrying about my pocketbook. God knows you've worries enough of your own."

"How long will I have to stay in Limerick, Da?" he asked. "When do you think I'll be able to come back home?"

Kevin looked down the dirt road ahead of them. "You'll stay in Limerick only a short while," he said after a moment, "then you'll be going to Cork, and then to a ship and then to Australia or America where you'll be safe."

"Da!" Liam said in shock. "You mean I'm not coming home?"

Kevin's eyes stayed on the empty road ahead. "You've smashed the skulls of two English lordlings," he said, "and over the likes of Peggy McCarthy at that. If you've killed one of them, as you suspect, they'll hang you, Liam. Have no doubt of that. And, if you've only bruised their pride, you'll still spend time in the gaol, perhaps years there."

"I'll never go to their damned gaol," Liam said hotly, "I'll die first. I swear it."

"Then you'll go to sea," Kevin said curtly.

"But why, Da?" Liam insisted. "Why can't I wait a little while in Limerick and come home later?"

Kevin was silent for a long time, then he said, "Because I'll die soon enough. And when I do, the boat goes to Donal. That's why. He's the eldest son, and it's his right. If you stay, Liam, you'll end up working for hire on other men's boats or for hire in the big lord's fields—not that he'd have you after what you did last night to his sons. No, you have to leave." He looked hard at his younger son. "You would have had to leave even if this had never happened."

"Da . . . ," Liam began.

"Hear me out," Kevin snapped. "From the day Donal was born into this world as the elder son, the boat has been his, and you've been the one who would have to leave. I've never told either of you. I didn't tell him because he wanted it so badly that it was poisoning the feelings he should have had for you. I didn't tell you, Liam, because I couldn't bear to see the pain in your eyes, as I'm seeing it now. When I die, Donal must use the boat to support your mother until she joins me and then to support your sisters until they leave home. And then he'll have his own wife and children, and there'll be none left over for you. Believe me when I say you're the fortunate one, Liam. Because wherever you go— Australia or America or New Zealand—you've a chance for a better life than Donal will ever have. He's a slave to his obligation, and you'll be a free man. That's why you were the one who went to school while Donal worked with me on the boat. That's why you can read and write and do the ciphers, because you were always the one who would have to make his way in the world."

Liam listened to the words now, accepting their terrible logic and finality.

For Ireland in 1908, Limerick was a metropolis. More than one hundred and thirty thousand souls inhabited the ancient city, about five percent of the island's entire population. To Liam, it was an incredibly busy and noisy place. He, who had grown up in a tiny village where no one was a stranger, was struck by the sight of people passing one another in the street without exchanging greetings or in any way acknowledging the other's existance. At the rail station Kevin bought Liam a ticket to Cork. Then the two of them sat aboard the cart in silence, puffing their pipes and awaiting the train. Finally Kevin knocked out his pipe and reached into his coat pocket. He brought out a bulging cloth pouch.

"Take this, lad," he said, "you'll need it."

He dropped the heavy sack into Liam's outstretched palm, and Liam heard the unmistakable clink of coins.

"What's this, Da?"

"Your mother's fortune," Kevin told him. "Or, at least, a good part of it."

"Da!" Liam said in shock, "I can't take this. What'll the girls use for their fortunes?"

Kevin waved off Liam's protests. "There'll be enough left," he said. "Already Gerry Donovan is making a terrible fool of himself over your sister Kathleen. The young dunce is so in love that I doubt he'll complain over a few less coins in her fortune. And Anna—well, you know that Anna has made sounds about the convent for years. Now she's told your mother and me that she means to do it the coming spring or the next. She'd make a fine nun, with her gentle ways and her shyness. And the church will take her without a dowry. None of my children will want for the sake of a few gold coins, Liam, least of all you, who's going off in the world."

Liam had seen the fortune only once, years before, hidden deep in the chest of drawers in the cottage's best room. He knew that it consisted of ancient gold coins from Britain and dubloons recovered by his ancestors after Spanish soldiers had lost them after reaching shore following the sinking of the great Armada centuries before. His mother's fortune had consisted of nearly a hundred such coins, and Liam guessed from its heft and feel that the sack in his hand contained at least half that number and probably more.

"Da," he began, "I can't . . ."

"Hush with you," Kevin commanded. "There, your train is coming."

A huge black locomotive was pulling up to the platform, all gushing steam and hissing and clanking of enormous metal parts.

"There she is, lad," Kevin told him, "you'll be in Cork in an eye's blink."

Liam felt the tears well in his eyes. "I can't leave you, Da," he muttered. "Don't make me go."

"Yes, you can, lad. Yes, you can."

"I love you, Da," Liam told him.

Kevin stood back and looked up at his son. The old man was smiling and weeping at the same time. "And I love you, Liam," he choked out, his fingers digging into Liam's forearms. "I love you as no man has ever loved a son."

Chapter 2

In winter frost clutched hard at the earth's heart in upstate New York. It dug its fingers a full yard into the soil and held tight until the spring thaw. Then, as the sun's warm rays broke through naked tree branches, the ice began to move. The result was frost heave, which pushed the soil upward and sometimes split it open like an overripe grape.

Frost heave was the bane of the railroad in colder climates. At its worst, it loosened the spikes that connected the rails, tearing them from their moorings. So, in the spring, trains laden with strong-backed laborers were sent out to inspect the tracks and heal the wounds inflicted by the frost.

In May of 1911 Liam Brennan rode on such a train. It consisted of a soot-encrusted locomotive, a freight car full of tools and work materials and a battered caboose that housed the work crew. The little train chugged along a stretch of worn track many miles west of Albany, where Liam had lived nearly three years in a railroad workers' boardinghouse on Sheridan Avenue near the red-roofed capitol building.

It was early morning, and the engine, which was built for vastly heavier loads, was pulling easily. The crew had been riding the rails for four days now, moving steadily westward, swinging sledges, driving spikes, laying new track where the old had been crippled by the frost. They would end up in Buffalo and return by a different route, pounding steel and fixing the track as they went. The men had slept soundly in the caboose the night before. They were drinking strong coffee and stronger tea and eating bread for breakfast when the train ground to a halt.

"All right," the foreman called out, "here's the spot." He was a burly man named Slaughter, and he was past forty, which made him old for this sort of work. Few railroad laborers had gray hair. They were mostly young men who, if they were lucky, would move into jobs in the round-house as they grew older. Or, they would move into the locomotives as firemen or engine tenders or, eventually, engineers, eating steam and coal dust when their arms and backs were no longer strong enough to swing the sledge or lift the rails.

If they were not lucky, their hearts would burst one day as they swung the sledge, or they would fall prey to the ailments of exhaustion, like pneumonia. And there were always the accidents. Railroad widows and orphans were common. Fully one-third of this crew was made up of boys in their teens who had taken over the jobs of their dead fathers to support their mothers and younger brothers and sisters.

Slaughter was a rarity for another reason: he wasn't Irish. He wasn't even Italian, as some of the newer laborers were. He was also secure enough in himself to keep his distance from his charges, as he felt he needed to do to maintain authority, especially on two-week-long jaunts like this one when everyone slept in the same caboose, ate the same food and smelled one another's sweat at close quarters.

"Come on, now," Slaughter said, "down with you."

The men climbed down from the caboose and stretched in the sunlight. Liam, the subforeman, was the third man out. The work had widened and broadened his arms and shoulders. He was twenty three now, reddish-haired by birth and reddish-skinned from the sun, taller by inches than most of his fellows and powerfully built.

He had arrived in New York and had immediately been drafted into service by a railroad crew boss waiting on the dock to snare immigrants. To his surprise he had found life in the fraternity of railroad workers to his liking. It was hardy, painful, dirty work—digging, lifting, hauling and dragging up to fourteen hours a day, six days a week. But it was a man's work.

The fact was that virtually every Irish family was a matriarchy, and the family headed by Kevin Brennan in Labasheeda had been headed by him in name only. Kevin had, his entire life, deferred to Margaret. She had ruled the house with her daughters as ministers and Kevin and Liam as minions. Donal had occupied the prized position of crown prince, although he had never realized it and had accepted his special status only as his due.

The same situation had been the rule rather than the exception in every home in the village, which explained the popularity of McCarthy's pub. In many a household in Labasheeda, a man who wished to drink a pint or two or puff thick, black tobacco in his pipe was not permitted to do so at home. So off he'd go to McCarthy's. And throughout the villages and cities of Ireland, men would go off nightly to pubs like McCarthy's for the same reason.

It was no accident, then, that the corner tavern evolved in American cities as an institution particularly entrenched where there were many

Irish. For an Irishman the pub was a place to be with men, to pursue male pursuits forbidden in homes ruled almost without exception by women.

Slaughter moved along the line of men climbing down from the caboose, his movements brisk and businesslike. He motioned to the stretch of track ahead of the locomotive.

"The winter's done its work on that rail and another two lengths ahead," he said. "You can see it. Brennan, you take your boys, get your tools and some rail out of the boxcar and replace those two pieces. Drive down any loose spikes. The rest of us will go on ahead and see what other damage we find. When you're finished up here, bring the train down and catch us."

Liam nodded. "That we will. All right, lads. Get your gear. There's track to be laid."

Liam's crew opened the boxcar and climbed in. They came out with crowbars, shovels, sledges and spikes. It took six of them to free the first bent and rusted rail. They carried it across the tracks and dropped it down the side of the incline. It slid noisily down the gravel bank, settling at the bottom on a bed of dead leaves.

Liam brushed off his hands. "Now the replacement," he told his crew.

The work crew reentered the supply car and emerged with a length of shiny new sixty-pound rail, fresh from the steel mills of Buffalo. They positioned it carefully, fitted the spikes and began driving them. The sound of metal striking metal rang musically through the wooded countryside.

Liam stepped back as the hammers swung to check the line of the track. As he did, he saw Sean Flaherty, a boy of sixteen on his first work crew, drive a spike ineptly as it was held by Mike Carroll, another teenager with only limited experience. Liam shook his head. The Flaherty lad was barely large enough to swing a nine-pound hammer, much less the twelve-pounder he had chosen.

"Flaherty, you great fool," Liam chided good-naturedly, "that's not how you drive a spike. You sent it in at an angle like that and the first train over it will knock it loose."

Liam moved in and replaced Carroll, who looked relieved. "Here, lad," Liam told Flaherty, "you've got to make the man who positions the spike hold her up straight for the first swing—like this. Then you've got to give her a fearsome whack, not one of those love taps you were giving her."

Flaherty smiled sheepishly. He wanted to do well, needed to, in fact, if his mother and younger sisters were to continue eating regularly. Several weeks before, his father, Patrick Flaherty, had fallen beneath the wheels of a speeding freight car. Sean Flaherty, the heir to his father's position on the laboring crew, valued Liam's instruction. He knew that his survival on the crew depended on it.

"Come on, now," Liam urged him, "let me see what you're made of, lad."

Flaherty lifted the hammer high and swung. It was a good swing, brought down from high over his head. It went straight and true. As the sledge began its descent, Liam heard Slaughter call his name from down the track. He reacted instinctively, turning his head and body toward the sound. In so doing, he moved the hand that held the spike ever so slightly, and Flaherty's sledge drove the flesh mercilessly against the top of the sixty-pound rail.

Liam cried out in shock and fell backward on the ties. He sat up immediately, clutching the hand. He had heard and felt the bones of his left hand crack and break. Only a few seconds after the impact, the hand was swelling. Young Flaherty, his jaw agape, dropped the sledge and dropped to his knees beside Liam. Then the pain hit—exploding in Liam's hand like a bomb. His red face turned redder.

All work had stopped. Slaughter, who had been leading his own crew back to the train after finding a nearby rail that needed replacement, was at Liam's side only seconds after he saw his assistant fall back on the ties. They met one another's gaze, and each knew what was at stake. A one-armed laborer was an unemployed laborer.

"Let me see your hand, Liam," Slaughter ordered.

The foreman examined the hand carefully. It was not an uncommon wound, and he knew how to determine the seriousness of the blow Liam had sustained. He moved Liam's fingers, and then stopped when he saw his face turn ashen beneath his sunburn.

"It's smashed, you know," he told Liam gently. "Smashed good and proper, too."

"I can still work."

Slaughter shook his head. "I don't think you can swing a sledge with one hand. I don't think you can use a shovel with one hand. Do you?"

Liam was silent for a moment. Then, quietly, he said, "No."

Slaughter stood up. "All right, then. We've got a day's work to be done, Liam. We'll transfer you down the line to the Boydstown and Ringlesport line, and they'll get you to a doctor to see what can be done about that hand. But you're off the crew for now. There's nothing I can do for you."

Liam nodded. "I understand."

Slaughter turned to the knot of laborers that surrounded them. Their faces were universally grim. The incident had reminded them all of their vulnerability. One moment of inattention and you had a smashed hand like Liam Brennan or you were mincemeat on the rails, like Sean Flaherty's da.

"Get him into the caboose and make him comfortable," Slaughter told his crew. He turned back to Liam, "After you can see a doctor, you can use your railroad pass to get back to Albany.

Liam said nothing. Flaherty and Carroll helped him to his feet and half carried him back to the caboose. They helped him inside, and Flaherty put him in a bunk and covered him with a blanket.

"Liam, I'm sorry, man," he said. "Truly I am. I'd give anything to take back that swing."

With his good hand, Liam reached out and patted the boy on the shoulder. "It's all right, lad. It wasn't my drinking hand, after all."

Carroll scampered over to his own bunk and came back with a pint bottle of rye whiskey, which he gave Liam.

"Here," he said, "drink this while you lie there. It'll dull the pain."

During the next hour, Liam drank most of the bottle in silence, listening to the ring of sledges striking spikes, of men grunting and cursing with effort. He could almost hear the sweat fall. After a while the throbbing pain in his swollen hand began to dull and he drifted off to sleep, the music of laboring his lullaby.

＊ ＊ ＊ ＊

James Frazier gently brought Liam's hand to rest on the crisp, linen-covered corner of his examining table. He was a solemn man in his late thirties who looked every bit the country doctor he was.

"A nasty wound," Dr. Frazier said. "You have several broken metacarpal bones, Mr. Brennan, and as near as I can determine, fractures of at least two of the phalanges. I'm going to have to set as many of these bones as I can manage, and then you're going to have your hand in a cast for a while."

"When can I go back to work?"

Frazier shook his head. "As a railroad laborer, not until the cold weather rolls around again. What else can you do?"

Liam shrugged. The effects of the rye whiskey had long since worn off, but the pain had been eased considerably by the several slugs of laudanum Frazier had produced and poured down Liam's throat when he saw how much his patient was suffering.

"I've worked on the railroad nearly four years, but I was a fisherman in Ireland. I saw a big lake here when I came in on the train."

Frazier nodded. "That's Iroquois Lake. It's one of the Finger Lakes.

We folks here in Lakeside are on one end and Ringlesport is on the other end, thirty miles away."

"Why do they call them that?" Liam asked. "The Finger Lakes?"

"They lay in a row, like fingers on a hand" the physician said. "The Seneca Indians believed that they were formed by the fingers of the Great Spirit. Actually, they're the leavings of an Ice Age glacier. Iroquois isn't the biggest of them, but she's the prettiest."

"It's a fine, big body of water. Is there any commercial fishing here?"

Frazier shook his head. "If anybody in Lakeside wants a fish for supper, they go down to the village dock and throw in a line. It's possible you might be able to find work on one of the steamers that work the lake—as long as you don't have to use this hand too much and if you know how to handle a big boat's helm."

"My da's boat was seven meters, she was, more than twenty feet. I sailed her in many a rough sea."

"Well, then," Frazier said, "when the cast dries, go down to the dock and check around. There might be something. If you get a job at the dock, you can probably sleep on the boat. But if you can't line anything up, come on back here and you can spend the night on the couch over there. My wife and I'll put a good meal into you, too."

Liam was surprised. "That's kind of you. I hope I don't have to take you up on the offer."

"Listen," Frazier said with a grin, "you won't be the first to sleep on that couch, if it comes to that. And you won't be the first accident victim that Elizabeth and I've fed, either."

"Still," Liam told him, "it's a nice thing you've offered, and I won't forget it."

Not quite two hours later, Liam walked out of Frazier's little office, one hand encased in a still-damp cast and the other clutching the seabag in which he habitually carried his small store of personal possessions while out on the rails with the work crew. Aside from what he had on his back, Liam owned only a razor, several sets of underwear, some additional work clothes, one good suit of dress clothes and a pair of shiny leather shoes.

He was a bit lightheaded from the effects of the laudanum, and as a result he was in an inappropriately gay mood. He began to whistle softly and then to hum to himself a popular song that seemed to fit his current situation almost perfectly.

"All alone," he hummed softly, "all alone, nobody here but me. Parlor's nice and cozy, everything is rosy . . ."

Rosy? he thought suddenly. Rosy, indeed. Here I am without a job and a hand like a piece of raw beef inside this cast. Brennan, you fool, he told himself, your brain's gone soft. Rosy, is it? Thus sobered, he headed for the village dock.

For all its status as the seat of Lake County, Lakeside was home to only a few thousand people. All in all, Liam thought as he walked through the village toward the dock, it was a pretty place, a peaceful slice of Americana shaded by tall, old trees and cooled by the breeze off the lake. He couldn't help but compare Lakeside to his birthplace, Labasheeda, with its mean little whitewashed houses and less than a single block of commercial development. No, Lakeside wasn't Labasheeda, but it wasn't Albany, either—Albany with its delightful sin strip along Green Street and its raucous nightlife near State and Pearl. No vaudeville here, he thought. And not a fancy restaurant in sight.

Lakeside's municipal dock was a big, T-shaped affair that stretched a good one hundred and fifty feet out into the clear water, and its main section was built to accommodate carriages and freight wagons. The dock had the capacity for dozens of boats, among them the six commercial steamers, several of which rolled gently at berth, bow-first. The steamers were huge boats, by inland standards, the smallest one at berth at least fifty feet long, and the largest closer to a hundred.

But it was neither the dock nor the steamers that prompted Liam Brennan to stop in his tracks. It was the view of the lake. It took his breath away. It stretched behind the boats into, it seemed, infinity. Liam could not see the other end of the lake, which faded off miles away to meld with the sky, but he could see the great hills rising up like a living lip from the shoreline and dissolving into the horizon. Atop the hills, which glowed a lush and healthy green in the sunlight, floated enormous clouds, like celestial balls of cotton, casting moving and clearly defined shadows over the water and the hillsides.

He stood there and drank it in. Liam Brennan, raised in one of the world's most beautiful spots, had never seen anything quite so lovely as Iroquois Lake on that glorious spring afternoon in 1911. He had no idea of how long he stood there, unmoving and feeling more at peace than he could recall, when he heard a voice call him.

"You, there," the voice bellowed, "who do you think you're gawking at?"

Liam realized that the voice was directed toward him. It came from an enormous, white-shirted man on the deck of the nearest steamer. It was a large, white vessel whose name, the *Iroquois Queen*, was painted proudly on her prow in graceful black letters. The man's face was sheathed in bushy muttonchop whiskers, and he was tall and round. He reminded Liam immediately of William Howard Taft, although not quite so fat and a good many years younger. Liam put the man in his early forties.

"Forgive me, sir," Liam told him, "I wasn't gawking at you. I was gawking at this fine and lovely boat—and a darlin' thing she is. Could you tell me where I might find the captain?"

The fat man's face softened behind his whiskers. "You're talking to him. Capt. Henry Baddington, at your service. What can I do for you, my friend?"

Liam walked over to the edge of the dock and looked up at Baddington, who was several steps higher on the deck. "I'm wondering if you could use an extra hand."

Baddington motioned to the fresh cast. "You look as though you could use an extra hand yourself."

"I'm an able pilot—one good hand or two, and I can do my share of lifting, if it comes to that, cast or no cast."

"I'm my own pilot," Baddington told him, "and there's not a better one on the lake. There's certainly not another I'd trust my boat to. What need do I have of you?"

Liam smiled slightly. "You wouldn't even have talked to me this long if you didn't have some need for a hand who can pilot your boat. Don't you ever get sick, man? Wouldn't you like a day off now and again?"

Baddington threw back his head and burst into raucous, good-natured laughter. Liam suddenly liked the fat man.

"Come aboard," Baddington said to him.

Liam walked down the dock and up the vessel's gangplank. Baddington came around to meet him. Up close, the steamer captain was even rounder than he had appeared from below, but he was far shorter. Liam towered over him.

"What's your name?" Baddington demanded. "How'd you hurt your hand?"

"Liam Brennan, Sir. A sledgehammer blow by a careless lad has put me off the railroad—and some carelessness of my own, if the truth be told."

"You really can pilot a boat?" Baddington asked. "If you lie to me, I'll know right off, the minute you take the helm."

"I've never piloted a steamer," Liam admitted, "but I've piloted fishing boats in waters more treacherous than these."

Baddington nodded and produced the stub of a cigar from his vest pocket. He lit it with a wooden match and blew out a cloud of blue smoke.

"You know," he said, "this is seasonal work. The lake freezes over in the winter with ice two feet thick, and I spend my winters by the fire, living off my earnings in glorious relaxation, while my crew scatters."

"I expect that by that time I'll have the use of my hand back, and I can go back to the railroad. You should know, sir, that I can read and do ciphers, and I can help with the bookkeeping as well as the piloting."

Baddington puffed on his cigar stub. "All right. The pay is five dollars a week and food when we're on the water, Brennan. That's less than the railroad pays, I know, but if I decide to let you near my books you'll see for yourself that it's all I can afford."

"I'll need a place to sleep," Liam told him.

"There's always room in the hold. We'll be sailing on an excursion at seven tonight with a couple of hundred swells from Boydstown. Be here at seven on the dot, and we'll see what kind of pilot you are. If you sink my boat, I'll smash your other hand for you, along with every other bone in your body."

Liam laughed, but Baddington did not.

"I'll be careful with your fine, big boat," Liam told him.

* * * *

Liam walked back to Dr. Frazier's office, told him of his good fortune and thanked him for his help. Frazier wished him well and cautioned him to protect his hand. Then Liam strode two doors away to one of the village's two banks and made arrangements to have the contents of his safety deposit box at the Albany Savings Bank transferred to the Lakeside Trust Company. From the bank, he walked down the street and around the corner and finally found what he was looking for, a small cafe.

He entered and bought a copy of the village's weekly newspaper, the *Lakeside Journal*, which he read assiduously as he downed an early dinner. It was a far cry from Albany's papers, the *Times Union* and the *Knickerbocker Press*, but it passed the time as he ate. Then he walked back to the dock and climbed up to the wheelhouse of the fat man's steamer.

"You're early," Baddington told him. "Well, it gives you time to see the boat."

For the next twenty minutes Baddington led Liam up and down the *Iroquois Queen*, introducing him to the other crew members as they arrived. They seemed pleasant enough, but Baddington was clearly the only qualified seaman on board with the possible exception of a crusty, middle-aged man named Brady, the chief engineer.

"She's a lovely vessel," he told Baddington.

"Well," the fat man said, "she should be. She was built back in '94 by A. W. Springstead over in Geneva, and they did good work."

As they made their way back up to the wheelhouse, Liam asked, "How big is she?"

"The *Queen*," Baddington said, motioning below to the deckhands to let the milling passengers on the dock come aboard, "is ninety three feet—a beam of seventeen, and she draws six and a half."

"What's her displacement?"

Baddington nodded approvingly and said, "She displaces a hundred and fifty tons. The engines are condensing engines with a thirty-inch bore and a five-foot stroke, each powered by its own steam boiler. She'll crank out two hundred horsepower in each engine."

The excursion crowd came aboard as Baddington questioned Liam about his experience with big boats. Liam told him the truth. At seventeen, furious at Donal over some matter he couldn't now recall, he had left his father's boat and signed on for nearly a year on a vessel nearly as large as Baddington's excursion boat. The fishing vessel, the *Mermaid*, had fished the Atlantic off the Shannon, and Liam had learned how to handle her under power from her mate, a man named Clifford who had taken a liking to the him. The *Mermaid* had gone down in the mouth of the Shannon during a wild October storm—luckily while Liam had been home ill. The accident had taken the lives of six men—one of them was Clifford—and Liam's father had forbidden him to sign aboard another oceangoing vessel.

Still, Liam had learned how to handle a big boat under power, and he knew that training was going to come in handy here.

After the crowd came aboard Baddington flipped off the cover to the engine room tube and barked, "All right, Mr. Brady, fire her up." Then he turned to Liam, as the *Iroquois Queen*'s huge engines churned into life. "All right, Mr. Brennan," he said. "Take her out. Now we'll see what kind of pilot you are."

Liam checked out the window to be sure that all the lines had been freed, then he flexed his one good hand and grasped the wheel. He leaned over the tube and snapped, "Reverse, one eighth."

The engines surged, and the *Iroquois Queen*'s great sidewheels began to turn clockwise. The vessel pulled away from the dock, spewing water from the wheels, and out into the wide open lake with Liam's hand on the wheel, holding her steady. When he felt she had backed out far enough, he said into the tube, "Ahead, one quarter."

The sidewheels came to a sudden halt. Then they changed direction, moving counterclockwise, and the big boat moved ahead. Liam spun the wheel to the starboard, and the *Iroquois Queen* began her turn to the right. The turn came more slowly than Liam had estimated, and the boat missed the dock by a scant fifteen feet before she came about and headed out into the lake. Liam made a mental note to allow more latitude in future turns. The boat was broad, and she had a wider turning radius that he had imagined. He was careful, though, to hide his miscalculation from Baddington. He leaned over the tube as the boat came about and said, "Ahead, one half."

The *Queen's* big engines whined, and he could hear her enormous gears clank as the vessel picked up speed. Baddington, who had been watching carefully and silently from the rear of the wheelhouse, stepped up to Liam's side. "You came close to taking the bow off my steamer," he said.

"I was twenty feet from the dock," Liam told him.

"Fifteen, maybe," Baddington shot back, "but far enough, after all."

Every weekend the *Iroquois Queen* ran—one excursion on Friday night, one each Saturday afternoon and evening, and one Sunday afternoon. The evening cruises attracted a younger, raucous crowd from neighboring cities and towns who drank heavily and partied from the moment the boat left dockside until it returned. The daylight excursions attracted older couples or families, usually with young children.

Liam found that he enjoyed the daylight cruises much more than those in the evenings, not only because the work was less worrisome, but because he found the scenery of the lake and its shoreline unparalleled by anything in his experience. As a passenger on excursion vessels like the *Iroquois Queen*, he had cruised up and down the Hudson. The river had, despite its beauty, lacked the grandeur of the view offered by Iroquois Lake. He had also taken an excursion once on a steamer on Lake George, some sixty miles north of Albany. Although he had been awed by the rugged loveliness of the Adirondack wilderness surrounding pristine Lake George, he had somehow found it less inviting than this gentler landscape, which was part virgin forest, part farmland and part civilization. The boat also stopped on the day cruises at two hotels along the lake, the Iroquois Hotel and another inn called the Shoreline, down near the lake's Ringlesport end, some thirty miles out of Lakeside.

Liam found it all remarkably pleasant, and he found the work agreeable. He slept soundly at night in his hammock, snug in the ship's hold. Baddington let him pilot virtually all the weekend cruises, while the captain mingled with and entertained the passengers, resplendent in his white captain's coat. Baddington reserved for himself, however, the routine work of piloting the vessel during the week, picking up passengers at the hotels and crops at the docks of a half-dozen steamboat stops at the larger farms around the lake.

During the third week of Liam's employment on the *Iroquois Queen*, Baddington called him to the wheelhouse one sun-drenched afternoon as the boat chugged down the middle of the lake at three-quarter speed. Baddington gave Liam the helm and settled his considerable bulk into a chair along the rear of the wheelhouse. "My back is giving me trouble," he complained. "I have to sit down for a while."

Liam, at the helm and silently grateful for Baddington's immense girth and bad back because it gave him the chance to pilot the boat, said nothing. The captain stood up after a while and walked around the cabin, stretching, his hands pressing at his lower spine. Rubbing the small of his back, the fat man looked out over the water.

"A fine lake," he said, almost to himself.

"I've never seen anything like it, Henry," Liam told him, looking around through the windows, marveling at the landscape and the stunning blueness of the water. The relationship between the two men had progressed to the first-name stage in only days. "It looks a bit like the Shannon, only the hills rise higher from the shore, and the beach here is rocky slate. The Shannon is that way in some places, but it's marshy in most. Henry, why are the fields different colors up there on the mountain? They're like that all around the lake."

Baddington's eyes followed Liam's finger. "Different crops," he explained. "Most of the farmers here, as you've seen, grow fruit or vegetables to send by rail to Boydstown or Rochester. Or they grow grain for their milk cows. But more and more of them are growing grapes for the wineries. That's vineyard up there, that deep green patch you can see next to the summer wheat."

"What wineries?" Liam asked.

"There are three or four of them on the lake, now, all down near the Ringlesport end. The wineries grow some of their own grapes, but they also buy a good many from the farmers. It's getting to be a good cash crop."

Liam said, "I would have thought it would be too cold here to grow grapes and make wine."

Baddington shrugged. "Apparently it is. None of the wineries make very good wine—not compared to the foreign stuff."

Liam studied the patchwork quilt of fields rising up the mountainsides on either side of the lake. "The vineyards are pretty, though," he said, gazing up at them as they shone like dark emeralds in the sunlight.

* * * *

On a warm morning in late July, after Liam had been working on the *Iroquois Queen* for several months, he came up on deck from his hammock in the hold to find out who was shouting and swearing so loudly that the racket had awakened him. Rubbing his eyes, Liam looked down on Baddington and three crewmen on the dock below, locked in what seemed like mortal combat with a large, chestnut gelding. The animal's eyes were rolling wildly, and he was resisting the fevered efforts of the four men to pull him aboard the *Iroquois Queen*.

The steamer often transported livestock between farm and railhead, but seldom did the loading of a single animal require the efforts of four men. As he stepped down the gangplank to the dock, Liam smiled at the efforts of his colleagues to drag the beast up the gangway to the lower deck. The horse was pulling back on the rope attached to his halter. He was neighing shrilly and sending out dangerous kicks, which the crewmen dodged carefully and which Baddington, his great bulk both an asset and a hindrance in such an operation, was managing to evade only through divine intervention.

"What's this?" Liam said, laughing.

Baddington ignored the question and leaped at the horse's head. The fat man grasped the animal's halter with one hand and twisted the horse's left ear with the other. The pitching, rearing animal came to a sudden halt, and Baddington and the other deckhands held tight to the horse, all gasping and sweating. The horse, immobilized by the twisted ear, stood twitching. Its eyes were rolling with fear and showing white around the edges.

"It's a demon of a horse, is what it is," Baddington gasped out. "Here, Russell, you grab his ear like this and try to keep him still. I've got to catch my breath."

Russell moved in gingerly next to the horse and grabbed its halter and ear as Baddington released them.

"I'd grab him by the balls, if he had any," Russell muttered, "a good horse calms down once he's gelded."

"It's the water," Baddington gasped, sinking unceremoniously to his rump on the dock. He was aware that the crews of other steamers were calling out good-natured taunts at his discomfiture, but he was too tired and too preoccupied to retort.

"Ride him around for a while, Henry," one of the other captains called out. "That'll tire him out quick enough."

"He's afraid of the water," Baddington told his crewmen, "and he won't go up the gangplank. The goddamn beast is going to kick holes in my boat if I take him aboard when he's this crazy."

Liam sat down on the dock next to Baddington. "A pretty thing, he is," Liam said. "What are we doing with him?"

"We're taking him out to the Weidener farm," Baddington said. "He was brought in by rail car. The railroad people came to my house last night, and they said the owner wanted him shipped this morning. Then, this morning, they brought him here and made me sign papers for him and then they told me he'd kicked out the side of a boxcar. They wouldn't even stay around to help us get him on board. Do you know anything about horses, Liam?"

Liam shook his head.

"I know about horses," Russell said, still grasping the animal's ear and halter firmly. "We had horses on the farm, but they were work horses, and they did what they were told. This is a fancy riding horse, and he's going to do what he goddamn well pleases. I say let's blindfold the bugger. Maybe if he can't see the water he won't be afraid of it."

"He's not that stupid," Baddington shot back.

"You'd be surprised at how stupid a horse is," Russell said. "Just because they're big, that don't mean they're smart. They got little tiny brains about the size of fish brains."

"All right," Baddington said finally, "put a blindfold on him, and we'll give it a try."

Liam stood up and pulled off his shirt. As the crewmen held the animal firmly, he moved in and tied the shirt over the horse's eyes and face. Instantly, the animal relaxed.

"Well, I'll be damned," Baddington said.

"I told you," Russell said. "They got no imagination. If a horse can't see something or hear it nor smell it, then as far as he's concerned it just ain't there, even if he just seen it a second before."

"Let's get him on board before he gets worked up again," Baddington said.

To the cheers and taunts of the other steamer crews they led the now docile animal up the gangplank and onto the lower deck.

"Put him in the forward hold," Baddington said, "and tie that blindfold down good."

Baddington went aboard, breathing hard and wiping the sweat off his brow and the dust from his clothing. Liam went down to his sea chest, put on another shirt and joined the captain on the upper deck.

"Where did you say we're taking the animal?" he asked.

"To the Weidener farm," Baddington said. "Christian Weidener bought that goddamned beast for his daughter. We'll drop it off this afternoon when we pick up his lettuce and dairy products."

Liam nodded. The Wieidener farm was just a touch more than eight miles up the shoreline from Lakeside. It was a regular stop. Liam knew well by now the point of land that jutted a hundred feet out from the beach into the lake. Weidener had a large dock built off the end of the point into deep water, one of only two dozen or so docks on the lake built in water deep enough to accommodate the big steamers. Liam had seen Christian Weidener before as he had stood on the dock watching his produce go aboard. He was a big man with a sour expression. He would occasionally greet Baddington, but the crewmen were beneath his notice.

"Why didn't they just go in and pick up the horse at the railroad station?" Liam asked.

"God alone knows," Baddington said crankily. "Nobody knows why Christian Weidener does anything. He's a gloomy German, and he talks to damned few people. All I know is what the railroad people told me last night—that there'd be this horse for me to deliver to his place, and that it would be expensive and we should treat it carefully. Now I've got an insane beast down in the forward hold who'll probably bust loose and jump overboard in the middle of the lake and drown. That happened once, you know. Not to me, but to one of the other captains a few years back. A Holstein bull just jumped overboard and drowned. The owner was fit to be tied."

Baddington leaned back against a bulkhead and lit a cigar. "I can understand why a man would buy a breeding bull, even if it was crazy. But why a man would buy an animal like that horse is beyond me, especially for his daughter. Christian's got no sense at all when it comes to Helga."

"I didn't know he had any children," Liam said. "He's the only one I've ever seen at the dock."

"She's there all right, and if you ever get to see her you'll see why Christian pampers her so. He'll certainly have his chance to shower money on her over this. Wait until he sees my bill for what I just had to go through."

Foster and Russell came topside. Foster assured Baddington that the blindfold was fastened on the horse good and tight and that the animal appeared calm in the forward hold. In another ten minutes the *Iroquois Queen* was ready to begin her run along the lake.

"Take her out Liam," said Baddington, still flushed from his unaccustomed exertion. He sat down in the wheelhouse chair, barely moving as Liam piloted the *Queen* away from the dock. In another minute the boat was chugging up the lake.

Only a few minutes out of Lakeside, Liam spotted something unusual. "What's that out there, Henry?" he asked.

Baddington stood up and looked out over the water. Off the *Queen's* port bow, moving toward them at an unusually high speed, was another steamer. She was of a sleeker, more modern design than the *Queen*; there were no paddle wheels along her sides and her hull was trimmer. Baddington kept his eyes glued to the steamer as it drew nearer, frowning deeply behind his muttonchops.

"Now there's a vessel for you," Liam said.

"Not for me, she isn't," Baddington snorted. "That's the *Aurora*. She's been in drydock in Ringlesport to have her engines reworked. She's the newest and biggest boat on the lake. I guess she'll be back at work this weekend, and that'll hurt our excursion business. She's supposed to do twenty knots now, with that work on her engines, but I don't believe it. No steamer afloat can do twenty knots."

"She's making good time."

"Not twenty knots, she isn't," Baddington shot back. "Her captain is a nasty son of a bitch named Parker Gillis. He's a new man on the lake, a New Englander. He's been bragging that he and his shiny new boat will take business away from me and the other steamer captains, and he might be right. You saw what our excursion business was like when his boat was in drydock. She has a steel hull. A steamer should be made out of honest wood, not steel like a goddamn locomotive."

The Aurora was bearing down on them now, cutting neatly through the water, and Liam examined the boat as Baddington talked.

"She looks big," Liam offered.

"She's big, all right. She's one hundred and fifteen feet with a twenty-seven-foot beam. Big as hell, she is. Three hundred and twenty horses of deisel power, with the work that's been done on her in Ringlesport. That's why I don't believe the claim of twenty knots. The *Queen* has eighty more horses, and I can't get her above seventeen knots without the boilers threatening to blow. And the *Queen* displaces twenty five percent less than that metal tub. Two hundred tons for an inland boat. Can you believe it?"

Liam eyed the Aurora, then he said, "She has a prop where we have paddle wheels. That might make a big enough difference in efficiency to give her the speed."

Baddington shook his head. "Not three knots' worth—not with the difference in horsepower."

They watched as the *Aurora* passed gracefully fifty yards off their port bow, all white paint trimmed in royal blue. Liam could see a man in the wheelhouse, whom he assumed to be Parker Gillis. The *Aurora*'s horn blasted a loud, perfunctory greeting. Baddington reached up and pulled the cord of his own steam whistle, which cried out in a voice markedly higher and weaker than the *Aurora*'s rich baritone. Then the bigger boat's stern glided by, and left the *Iroquois Queen* rolling gently in her wake.

Baddington watched the larger vessel slice through the water on its way back to its berth at the Lackside village dock. "You know," he said slowly, "when this boat was built it cost not quite sixteen thousand. Gillis spent sixty five thousand on his tub not two years ago, and a couple of thousand more this year reworking his engines."

The *Iroquois Queen* made several stops on its morning run before she nosed, under Liam's hand, up against Christian Weidener's dock just before noon. Liam called down the tube for Brady, who worked the engine room, to kill the engines. Then he walked out on the upper deck and looked up at the farm on the hillside rising off the lake.

Christian Weidener certainly was a planter, he thought. Of that there was no doubt. Past the shoreline and the trees beyond the beach, across the road and up the hillside above the big, white farmhouse, the mountain exploded into a patchwork quilt of fields. Summer wheat waved in the breeze off the lake; apple and pear trees were laid out in neat orchards, and corn sprang up four and five feet high, awaiting the harvest. Higher up, a few vineyards basked in the rich summer sun. Farther down the mountainside toward the village Liam could see a white barn and open pasture where Holsteins grazed. The farmhouse was a two-story clapboard structure freshly whitewashed under a green, gabled roof. Ornately carved woodwork decorated the sweeping front porch. The house stood snug under an umbrella of shade trees, commanding a stunning view of the lake.

Closer to the water, on the lake side of the road, a small and ancient fishing shack, clearly much older than the main house, nestled against the steeply rising bank. Two rowboats were pulled up on the rocky beach. On the dock at the end of the point, where the *Iroquois Queen* was moored, sat wooden crates filled with lettuce, boxes of eggs and a dozen steel ten gallon containers of milk. Already Russell and Brady and the others were taking them on board as Baddington stepped down the gangplank and greeted Christian Weidener.

Weidener wore a light blue work shirt and tan work pants. His skin was burned red by the sun. His hair, exposed as he removed the hat and wiped his brow, was half blond, half gray and sparse in the front. The farmer's face was deeply lined, and his watery blue eyes seemed frozen in an expression of melancholy.

Baddington and Weidener exchanged papers. Then Baddington came back on the boat, climbed to the wheelhouse and told Liam to stow the documents in the tiny office on the upper deck. As Liam came back out on deck, he saw the front door of the farmhouse on the hill burst open and a woman come flying out, her golden hair billowing behind her.

"Who's that," he asked Baddington as he gestured toward the figure, "running down the hill like a madwoman?"

"Christian's daughter, Helga. She's in a hurry to see her new riding horse, I'd imagine. She's welcome to the damned thing, just as soon as I get the dock cleared off."

Liam said, "We ought to get him off the boat before he gets feisty again."

Baddington shook his head vigorously. "No. Wait until the dock is clear and all that produce is stowed away. This time you can help Foster and Russell and the others. I don't want to get within fifty feet of that animal."

Liam looked up and over the landscape looming on the hill above them. "A nice farm," he said.

Baddington lit a cigar. "Well kept," he observed. "Christian is an orderly man. Not the friendliest fellow you'll ever meet, mind you, but a solid sort just the same."

"How long has he owned this place?" Liam asked.

"Oh, I guess he came here fifteen years or so ago, with his little girl. This property was owned by the Wrights then, and it wasn't much more than that house there and woods and some pastureland, and not much of that cleared. The Wrights were dairy people, mostly. Christian came in here with cash money back in the late nineties, made them an offer on this land here, and the Wrights snapped it right up. Now that Christian has cleared most of the land and made a pile of money from the lumber got some good crops going, I guess the Wrights wonder if they did the right thing."

Liam looked up the slope toward the vineyards. "I see he's one of your grape growers."

"Mostly dairy products and fruit," Baddington said. "And lettuce and tomatoes and stuff like this down on the dock. That's where the money is in farming. But Christian does do some contract growing for the wineries."

But by now Liam was hardly listening. Instead, he was watching Helga Weidener scamper across the road, down the wooden steps that ran beside the shack leading down to the beach, then out the point of land to the dock. She arrived breathless. She was a ruddy, healthy-looking blonde in her late teens. She wore a white summer blouse and a blue skirt under an apron. A pretty girl, he noted, mostly because of her coloring, which was spectacular. Her jaw was a little big, and so was her mouth, and she was too tall and rugged for his taste, built like her father. But pretty, still, he thought. Her vivid blue eyes gleamed up at the upper deck from the dock.

"Captain," she called to Baddington, "you brought my horse, I hope."

Baddington leaned over the rail, grinning through his muttonchops. "I did, indeed, Helga. He's in the forward hold."

"Can I see him?" Helga called out, and without awaiting an answer she ran up the gangplank to the *Queen*'s lower deck.

"Just be careful," Baddington called down to her as she came aboard and disappeared from view beneath the deck on which both Baddington and Liam were standing. Baddington leaned his ponderous bulk over the rail and cupped one hand next to his mouth. "He might be a bit wild from the trip," he called after her.

"I'd better get the beast out of there," Liam said. He started down the stairs to the lower deck, and as he did he heard the hatch to the forward hold slam open. He felt a sudden flutter of alarm. "Oh, Jaysus," he muttered to himself, a sense of foreboding arising in him. He danced lightly down the steps to the lower deck, his brow knitted and his lips tightly set. Baddington waddled after him, his cigar thrusting out of his muttonchops. On the dock, an expression of concern flashed across Christian Weidener's face. He started up the gangplank, but Liam, dropping to the lower deck from the fourth step, shot right by the farmer as he came on board. As Liam walked briskly toward the forward hold, he heard the horse's startled neigh. Liam broke into a sprint. The foolish girl has pulled off the blindfold, he thought.

Immediately the forward hold echoed with the sound of the chestnut gelding's thrashing about. Liam reached the open hatch only a heartbeat later, in time to see the horse half rear as the terrified, wide-eyed girl, her only means of escape blocked by the huge, lunging animal, flattened against the bulkhead. Liam's shirt, that had been used as a blindfold back on the village dock, lay in a tattered heap on the floor.

The horse was unsure of its surroundings, and its nerves were frayed from the boat ride. He pranced and jumped wildly inside the hold. A stray hoof could smash the girl's leg or her skull. Liam leaped into the small room and grabbed frantically for the horse's halter. The animal threw back its head as Liam's hand closed on the leather strap. Liam, all one hundred and ninety-five pounds of him, was lifted off his feet and spun in a quarter circle as the gelding struggled to shake free.

Still holding the halter tightly, Liam felt his feet touch the deck for a fraction of a second as the horse reared straight up this time, pulling him with him. Liam found himself in the air, pressed against the horse's hot side, looking up at its wildly rolling eye. "Damn you," Liam shouted at the animal, a mingled current of anger and fear surging through him.

Then the horse came down. Liam's feet slammed onto the deck, and the big animal pulled sideways immediately, causing Liam to lose his grip on the halter and fall headlong onto the hard deck.

As he struggled to rise, the breath knocked out of him, he never saw the gelding's left front hoof as it shot out in his direction.

Chapter 3

He saw only white.

At first, the image was vague and fuzzy, and Liam struggled to bring it into focus, only his eyes were not cooperating. The mass of white before him seemed limitless, stretching out forever. What was that? he wondered.

From somewhere on his left, a feminine voice rang out, "He's waking up."

Liam turned his head toward the sound, and as he did the room came into focus. He realized immediately that he had been staring up at the ceiling of a large bedroom, and that Helga Weidener had been sitting in a chair near the door. As he looked over at her, she rose and came to him.

"You lie still, now," she said, putting her palm to his forehead.

Liam started to sit up, but as he did his head exploded into pain so intense that he was forced to shut his eyes and fall back with a grimace against the pillow.

"You see, Papa," Helga was saying, "he's trying to sit up. He's going to be all right." She smiled at Liam.

As Liam's vision cleared, he recognized that Helga wasn't alone in the room with him. He recognized Dr. Frazier. Liam began to sit up again, but Frazier put a hand on his shoulder and gently held him down.

"Easy, there, Mr. Brennan," the doctor said, "let's take another look at that wound." Frazier put his hands atop Liam's head and probed. Liam winced at this new pain, sharper than the one that reverberated dully through his head. "You took a nasty bump there," the doctor told him. "How does it feel?"

"Ow," Liam said. "It feels better when nobody's fooling with it."

Frazier laughed and took his hands away. "How's your stomach feel?" he asked.

Liam pondered the question. "Empty."

"Any nausea?"

"No, I don't think so."

"Dizziness?" Frazier asked. "Double vision?"

"I have both, I think. I have trouble seeing much beyond where your head is. Everything is blurred past that distance."

Frazier looked into Liam's eyes with a small instrument that resembled a little funnel with a handle at the end. He looked into each ear, then listened to Liam's heart and took his pulse. He took his blood pressure as well. Throughout this procedure Helga looked on over the physician's shoulder. Liam looked up at her at one point and managed a weak, self-conscious smile, which she returned.

After several more minutes of poking and probing, Frazier finally stood up. Now Liam could see the physician's face more clearly, and he could see Christian Weidener standing next to him. Liam hadn't noticed the big farmer slip through the door.

"He seems to have a slight concussion, Christian," Frazier said. "It's difficult to say how bad it might be, but it seems minor. About the only thing you can do with these things is see how they develop. My guess is that he'll be all right with a little bed rest."

Weidener looked down at Liam. "So," he said, in a thick Germanic accent, "now what do we do with him?"

"I'd keep him in bed for a few days," Frazier told Weidener. "Feed him liquids and a generally bland diet. If he holds it down, fine. When the double vision and the blurriness he's experiencing go away, let him up and have him walk around a bit. He should be fully recovered in no more than a week, I'd say. Two at the most. I'll come back and see him in a week or so."

Liam's mind had been drifting. It suddenly occurred to him that he was still the topic of conversation.

"I can't stay here," he broke in. "I have a job."

"And you'll still have it when you're better," Frazier told him. "Henry Baddington thinks the world of you. He'll stop by tomorrow, and I'm going to stop by his house in Lakeside tonight and tell him that a horse's hoof was no match for a thick Irish skull. But you've been unconscious for about six hours, you should know, and you can't go back to work for a while."

Liam looked around him. He was in a comfortably furnished room fitted with floral wallpaper. He could see through the window that the sky outside was darkening.

Helga said, "You stay right here, Mr. Brennan, in my Papa's bed."

To Liam, it sounded distinctly like an order from someone used to giving them. Apparently, it struck Christian Weidener the same way.

"And just where do I sleep, little one?" he asked.

"You sleep in my bed, Papa. I'll sleep on the sofa in the parlor or out on the swing on the porch. It's going to be a warm night."

"I can't take your bed, Sir," Liam said.

"No choice is being offered either of us, it would seem. Helga has ruled. Like her mother, she is. And I don't mind so much. I'll sleep elsewhere for a while. I must to the fields go early, in any case."

"I wouldn't feel right."

"Maybe tomorrow we move you," Christian Weidener said. "There is the fishing shack at the foot of the point."

Frazier turned to Weidener. "I'll be on my way now, Christian, if you'll have my carriage brought around."

"You won't stay for dinner?"

"No," Frazier said, "thanks anyway. Elizabeth will have something warm for me. You take it easy, Mr. Brennan. A concussion is nothing to fool with. You heard my instructions, and if you've got any sense you'll follow my advice. Of course, if you had any sense you wouldn't have taken on that horse in such close quarters to begin with."

"I'll walk you out, Jim," Christian Weidener told Frazier, and the two men left together.

Helga moved up to where Frazier had been sitting on the bed next to Liam. Against the growing shadows in the room, her face and pale hair seemed almost luminous. Liam was amazed at how clearly he could smell her perfume and the soapy residue from the clean linens on the bed. His sense of smell seemed to be heightened dramatically.

"I'm grateful for what you did," she told Liam. "I was very foolish to run into the hold the way I did. It was childish to get so excited."

"Where's your horse?" Liam asked her. "I hope I didn't do him any harm, hanging off him like that."

"It was more the other way around. He's in his stall in the horse barn now, just as calm as can be. The boat ride terrified him. A good riding horse always has spunk. We should have gone into Lakeside and picked him up at the railroad station, but Papa was so busy . . ."

"How did you get the horse off the *Queen?*"

"Oh," she said, "I certainly didn't do it. I got out of the hold just before you got kicked in the head. One of the other crewmen came in and dragged you outside. Then they put a blindfold over my horse's face, and he calmed down right away when they got him on solid land. I took him up to the barn by myself. Do you drink coffee?"

"Tea," Liam said, "when I can get it."

She stood up. "I'll make you some. And some hot soup."

She danced out of the room. Liam lay against the heavy down-filled pillow and looked around him. Christian Weidener's bedroom was larger by a third than the main room of his parents' cottage in Labasheeda. His eyes fell on a photo of Helga that adorned a marble tabletop near the bed. It was a formal portrait, taken not too long ago. It failed to do her justice, he thought. It didn't capture the creaminess of her skin, nor the spun gold of her hair, and it unfairly emphasized the thickness of her mouth. She was not a classic beauty, he conceded, but in person, sitting next to the bed, she had intoxicated him with her vibrance and warmth. Liam, aware of the foolishness of the thought and not caring in the slightest, found himself unaccountably angry with the anonymous photographer who had taken the picture. He stared at it for a long time, smitten and groggy. When Helga came back to the room with the tea and soup on a tray, he was asleep.

* * * *

Shortly after dawn Liam awoke, ravenous. He checked the clock in the corner of Christian's bedroom, and he realized that he had slept more than eleven hours. It had been nearly twenty hours since he had last eaten. Even as the thoughts passed through his mind, Helga pushed open the bedroom door and entered, all smiles and crisp apron, with a tray of food. She brought a pot of strong tea, pancakes and sausage. Liam ate as if he were starving, while she sat beside his bed, watching appreciatively.

"Well," she said, "you're getting better fast, if your appetite is any indication."

"Truly, I'm starved," Liam told her as he swallowed.

"I love the way you talk."

Liam smiled self-consciously. "The brogue, you mean. I'd have thought it would be mostly gone by now, after a few years in this country. Of course, most of the people I was with on the railroad had brogues as thick as mine."

She cocked her head. "You want to get rid of it? Why?"

"In America, a brogue makes a man stand out. There are those who assume that an Irishman won't eat meat on Friday but drinks whiskey for breakfast."

Helga laughed. "That's very funny."

"Not if you're on the receiving end. Now it's time for me to vacate your father's room. Where am I going?"

"Down to the shack. That's the little building near the dock, the one at the foot of the point. There are a couple of bunks there, and you'll have company. John Hardy has use of the place. He's getting pretty old now, and mostly what he does is fish in the mornings to bring in food for us and the other men. He can be cranky, but I think you'll get along."

"For as long as I'm here," Liam said, "I'm sure we will."

Liam was shaky when he got up. He felt his head spin, and Helga reached out and caught him. She was a large woman, and strong, and she held him upright until the pain subsided and his head cleared. As the cobwebs faded away, Liam became aware of her warm body pressing against him, her arms wrapped around his middle and of her perfume.

"Will you be all right now?" she asked.

"God only knows," Liam said, and they both knew he wasn't referring to his health. Helga's eyes met his only briefly, then they were off and down the stairs, out the hallway, out over the front porch and down the path to the road. All the while Liam was leaning against her for support, and for all he knew he might really have needed it.

She led him into the shack and settled him into a bunk along one wall. The little house was shabby and cluttered, with rough wooden walls, an unfinished and dusty floor and no ceiling but naked beams swathed in spiderwebs beneath the wood-planked roof. There was a tiny kitchen, a main room that doubled as sitting and sleeping quarters and a tiny bedroom used for storage, flush against the bank of the hill. A large, grease-encrusted black stove dominated one wall, and next to it was a sink with a hand pump to bring in lake water.

"Where's my new neighbor?" Liam asked Helga as she pulled the covers up around his chin.

"Still out on the lake. He'll be in before long. The fish don't strike much past early morning."

Liam yawned. "It's foolish," he told her, "but I feel sleepy again. I've just slept around the clock."

Helga stood up. "Dr. Frazier said that's a symptom of a concussion. You just go back to sleep and let yourself get better. He said that sleep is better than anything we can give you."

"So it is," Liam said, already drifting off.

"I'll be back with your lunch," she said. He could hear her voice fading off. The door to the shack closed softly, as did Liam's eyes.

Sometime later Liam found himself mysteriously transported to Saint Patrick's Church in Labasheeda, a large, cruciform building that overlooked the Shannon. Father McBride was saying mass. Liam was eleven years old, on his knees, an altar boy again, watching the sun slice through the stained-glass windows to wash the interior of the church in shades of blue and red and yellow. Liam stood in front of the priest, looking up at him, passing him the chalice. Then Father McBride was looking down at him, his image blurred. He was holding something to his chest, something large and thick and silvery, shining in the light. Liam strained to

see it, and then the fog was clearing and he could make it out. It was
. . . a fish.

Liam's eyes shot open. He began to sit up with a start. The pain
coursed through his head like a bolt of lightning. He fell back against
the bunk and opened his eyes again. Standing over him was not Father
McBride inexplicably holding a fish but a bent old man in filthy overalls,
a rumpled plaid shirt and a crushed hat. He was all stink and bristles,
his face creased and tanned. He was saying, "I know who you are. You're
the deckhand who got himself kicked in the head yesterday by that
goddamn horse Helga got herself, ain't you?"

"I am," Liam said, the soft sound of his own voice inflicting unspeakable pain on the inside of his head. "My name is Liam Brennan.
You must be Hardy."

"What're you doin' here?" Hardy demanded. "You were up in the
big house, I thought."

"I've been told that I'll be staying here a few days until this knot on
my head goes down and I can go back to work."

Hardy dropped his fish into the sink and put his horny hands on his
hips. "This is my place, y'know. Been mine for years. Nobody ever stays
here but me."

"I know," Liam said, "but this is where they put me. What kind of
fish do you have there, Mr. Hardy?"

Hardy turned to the sink and pulled up the stringer. It took two
hands, because hanging from it was a collection of huge, silvery creatures
as much as two feet long. "Lake trout. Got six of the bastards this mornin'."

"Fine fish," Liam said.

Hardy detached one from the stringer, put down the rest and held
up his trophy lengthwise in front of him. "This one here, he's the biggest.
He'll go eight'r nine pounds."

Liam whistled in genuine appreciation. "I've not seen a fish so large
since I left the Shannon."

Hardy dropped the fish back into the sink, where it landed with a
dull slap. "Those're nothin'. This was a bad day. Evil weather movin' in,
and that spooks the lakers. There's trout in this lake that go up to twenty
pounds—maybe twenty-five'r thirty, some of 'em. Big bastards. Live way
down deep, where the water's cold."

Hardy's hostility had vanished as he had begun to talk about fishing.
He chuckled as he told Liam, "There ain't no better fisherman on Iroquois
Lake'n John Hardy. That's 'cause I know how lakers think, is why."

Liam watched the old man stand up and begin to move around the
shack as he spoke. His chest was swelled out a bit, and although he was
bent from arthritis, he actually managed to strut as he spoke. Liam

suppressed a smile. Hardy went over to the sink and looked appreciatively at his fish. Then he turned to Liam. "I'll take you out in the rowboat some morning'n show you a little bit about how it's done," the old man said. "There's a special rig used here in the finger lakes. I'll show you some things." Then the old man's eyebrows rose. "But I still won't show you everything."

As Hardy cleaned and filleted his fish, Liam drifted back to sleep. He awakened late in the day, with beams of weak sunlight shining into the shack's windows. Hardy was nowhere to be found. Stiffly, Liam rose. He cleaned himself up in the sink, shaved for the first time in thirty-six hours and then wandered out on the dock to watch the sunset. He had been standing in private silence for several minutes before he heard the sound of a horse's hooves clopping on the wooden planking of the dock behind him. He turned to find Helga riding toward him, towering over him on her new horse.

"How's your head this afternoon?" she asked, looking down.

"Fine, no thanks to this creature here."

Liam reached up and rubbed the horse's velvet muzzle. The animal moved into him and nuzzled him gently.

"It's calm he is now," Liam said, "now that he's done his worst to me poor head." He stroked the horse's face. "You foolish beast. I'm your friend. I'll kick you in the head one of these days, and we'll see how you like that."

Helga swung down off the horse. She was wearing jodphurs and riding boots. Liam tried not to stare, but a woman in pants wasn't all that common.

"See," Helga said, stroking the big animal's neck, "Ajax is sorry. That's what I've decided to call him."

"He should be," Liam said. "Did the *Iroquois Queen* dock here today?"

"It did, and you slept right through it all. Captain Baddington got off the boat and went into the shack and looked at you. He said you must have a head like an anvil. Then he steamed off toward Ringlesport. He'll be by next week to bring us supplies and pick up some crops. He'll pick you up then."

"I'm sorry I missed him," Liam said.

"So was he. But he didn't have the heart to wake you, and he didn't have time to wait for you to wake up on your own. He dropped off your possessions. They're in the shack."

Liam shook his head and rubbed the back of his neck. "I've been sleeping too much. I feel sluggish."

"A good dinner will fix you up," Helga told him. "Climb up on my brave steed, and I'll lead you up to the big house."

Liam looked at Helga and the horse, and he flushed slightly. "I can walk."

"It's not an easy climb," Helga warned him, "and Dr. Frazier left us strict orders that you weren't to overexert yourself. You have to ride, not walk. Now, get on the horse."

Seeing it more closely, Liam realized that the Weidener house was no larger than a good-sized farmhouse. It was furnished with sturdy, overstuffed chairs and sofas and heavy oaken tables. The walls were painted in subdued colors or covered with muted floral wallpaper. The building itself seemed to date back at least a century.

Christian Weidener was sitting in the parlor. He was dressed in work clothes as he had been the day before, but he had traded in his work boots for a pair of slippers to avoid leaving marks on the thick oriental carpet that sprawled across the dark, wooden floor.

Dinner was excellent. Liam, Helga and Christian sat at a round table and dined on fried lake trout fillets with applesauce and peas and thick slices of freshly baked bread. Christian served a white wine from a bottle with no label. For dessert they had coffee, a pot of tea for Liam and a carrot cake dripping with white, buttery icing. The cook, Minnie, was a fat, solemn woman of about sixty, and as she cleared away the dishes Liam sat back contentedly and told her, "Good food is the best medicine in the world. I feel like a new man."

"My food'll cure anything," Minnie said. "And if it doesn't, then at least you'll die with a full belly."

Helga went over to a hutch along the wall and produced a humidor. "Cigar, Papa?"

Christian, who had said little during the meal, nodded silently and took a thick, black cigar.

"Cigar, Mr. Brennan?" Helga asked.

Liam produced his pipe. "I have this," he said, stuffing it with tobacco from his pouch.

Helga brought out two ashtrays from a drawer of the hutch and sat back down. "I like the smell of pipe smoke," she said.

"And cigar smoke, too, I hope," Christian said. "What, I ask myself, is a cigar without brandy?"

Helga caught the hint and went into the kitchen, emerging a moment later with snifters of brandy for the men and a glass of sherry for herself. Christian pulled contentedly at his cigar and sipped his brandy. Then he said, "Tell me about yourself, Mr. Brennan."

Liam did. He began with Ireland, omitting mention of Peggy McCarthy, and ended his story with the incident the day before with Helga's horse. Christian listened intently, his pale blue eyes expressionless.

Then he said, "Tell me, what are your plans in this country? Are you going back to the railroad?"

"Truthfully, sir," Liam said, "I don't know. I'm nearly twenty-four years old, and I suppose I ought to have firmer plans, but I don't. I can't ever remember being happier than I've been working on the *Iroquois Queen*. And Captain Baddington keeps telling me there's no life more worthwhile than being a steamboat captain on the lake. But I wouldn't want to stay a deckhand forever, and he also tells me that the cost of a boat is high now. The new one on the lake, the *Aurora*, cost a fortune to build, he told me."

"And it will never earn back what it cost," Christian said. "The days of the steamer are nearly done now."

"Why do you say that?"

"The automobile will finish them," Christian said, sipping his brandy. "As autos and roads get better, there will be no reason for the steamboats. Already some of the farmers on the lake are buying trucks and transporting their own goods."

Liam nodded. "There's always the railroad, then."

"Ya," Christian said, "the railroad is here, but those who own it will not sell it, even if anyone had enough money to buy it. And besides, the automobile will hurt the trains in years to come as it will hurt the steamboats. If you decided to stay here, your best move would to be to buy some land of your own and farm it. Otherwise, you must work for someone else. There is no shame in that, but there is no future either."

Liam said nothing for a moment, digesting the older man's words. Then he said, "You have a disturbing talent, Sir, for getting to the heart of a a matter. Well, You've brought the decisions I face into focus for me. I know nothing of farming. My people have been fishermen for generations."

Christian's eyes narrowed through his cigar smoke. "A farmhand you want to be?"

"No," Liam said, "but I don't want to be a deckhand on a steamboat or a railroad laborer either—not forever."

"Do you really like the lake country so much?" Helga broke in.

Liam sat back and thought for a moment before answering. "Yes, I do, I think. I've been nowhere I liked better, not even Ireland. It's more alive here than it was back home."

Christian stubbed out his cigar. "Perhaps you could come watch the work on the farm tomorrow. There is work for farmers mainly in the spring, when we plant, and from late July on, as we prepare to harvest. In the winter, we do nothing. I read in the winter. Do you read, Mr. Brennan?"

"As much as I can."

"Who are your favorite authors?" Christian asked.

Liam's eyebrows rose slightly in surprise. Then he said, "I like Dickens very much. Britisher or no, he could tell a story. Kipling, too, with the same reservation. In this country, I've developed an affection for Mark Twain."

"He wrote most of his work near here," Christian said, "in a city not far away. Who else?"

"The last book I read was Dreiser's *Sister Carrie*. I know it was considered a little sordid, but I liked it, nonetheless."

Christian nodded appreciatively. "I see you read a bit. I wouldn't have expected that a man who did the work you do . . ."

". . . you mean a man who works with his hands?"

Christian smiled slightly, not in the least self-conscious. "Yes, that is what I meant, I suppose. My point was that perhaps you would not mind farming in a place like this as much as you think. You are used to working hard with your body. You would have your winters free to read. And winters can be long here." He stood up abruptly. "I think I will go to my room now to read some before going to bed. I must rise early to watch the preparations for the harvest. The early apples we are picking tomorrow. Perhaps you would like to see the harvest, Mr. Brennan?"

Liam rose. "Yes, that might be interesting. Good night, sir. I'm deeply appreciative of your hospitality. You've been very generous."

Helga said, "I'll walk Mr. Brennan back to the shack."

"Please, call me Liam. And there's no need to walk me all the way down the hill. I can find my way."

"Nonsense, Liam," she said firmly. "It's dark outside. I know the path, and you don't. Besides, it wouldn't do if you were to fall and bump your head again."

Christian was already at the stairs. "Good night," he said, and went upstairs.

The night was chilly and moonless, the path shrouded in blackness.

"Take my hand," Helga said, "or we'll be separated."

Her hand was warm and dry in the blackness. "How will you get back?" he asked her.

"I know every inch of this path," she assured him from the darkness. "I could get back in my sleep."

"Your father is an interesting man."

"My father is a wonderful man. He knows everything. He can do anything. He's stubborn, and he keeps to himself too much, but he's remarkable in many ways."

"What happened to your mother, if you don't mind my asking?"

"I don't mind," Helga said, as they reached the road. They walked slowly, their footing secure now, but she kept hold of his hand. "My mother died years ago. We were in Germany then. Papa was heartbroken. He and my mother had loved each other since they were small children. We had a farm and a small winery on the banks of the Rhine, and everything reminded him of Mama. So he sold out and came to this country when I was little. He tried to buy a farm along the Hudson, north of New York City. It reminded him of the Rhine. But the land there was too expensive, so we came here. I was very young, and I don't remember Germany. This is home, and it's beautiful."

"The lake country is lovely," Liam agreed, "I've never seen anything to rival it."

"My father says that, too. He says it looks like northern Switzerland, around Lake Luzerne. Only it's newer here—fresher and cleaner."

"Why was he asking me all that about what I'm going to do with my life and what I read and so forth?"

"Perhaps he was curious about you."

"I gathered that," Liam told her. "But why?"

"I suppose," Helga told him, her face veiled by the night, "that when you began to speak about your experiences you weren't what he had expected. My father has made a study of English, trying to learn to speak it well. He still has lapses in grammar, and his accent will never go away; but he understands the language, and he was impressed with the way you use it. You don't talk like a deckhand or a railroad laborer."

"Because I read?"

"Papa is impressed by a man with a mind," she told him. "He admires a man who reads and entertains serious thoughts."

Liam shrugged. "I suppose I ought to be flattered."

"No," Helga said. "You shouldn't be flattered by my father's interest in you. You should, however, be flattered by my interest in you."

Before Liam could respond to that unexpected statement, Helga had dropped his hand and melted against him, searing him through their clothing. Liam wrapped his arms around her and pressed his lips against hers in the darkness. Her mouth opened beneath his, and the power of her perfume swept over him again, as it had that first day. He was startled by the heat of her and by her softness. His hand moved to her hair, stroked it, became entwined in it. He kissed her lips, her cheeks, her eyes, her forehead. He buried his face in the nape of her neck, her hair brushing against his cheek, and touched his lips to her ear. He pressed himself against her, and to his surprise she pressed back, her hips driving into him. He felt her breath coming in short gasps. Automatically and without thought, Liam closed one large hand over her breast. Her own hand closed over his and pressed it tightly against her.

Then Helga pulled away suddenly, leaving him dizzy and cold where she had warmed him only a moment before. Her hand reached out in the darkness and gently touched his cheek. Her fingertips ran over his lips as lightly as breath.

"Good night, Liam," she said, and her voice was bright with mirth. "The shack is right behind you."

Liam turned and saw that they had stopped right next to the shadowy outline of the steps leading down to the shack. He turned back to Helga, but she was gone. He couldn't see her, but he could hear the crunch of her departing footsteps on the dirt road.

"Good night," he called out.

"Sleep well," her voice came back.

He turned and stood at the top of the stairs. His head was swimming from the embrace. Liam had known women, some intimately, but never before could he recall one who in just a few moments of such limited contact had left him so weak in the knees.

You won't sleep much tonight, Liam me lad, he told himself, as she knows full well.

* * * *

Liam came awake to a harsh knock on the shack's door. John Hardy stirred uneasily then turned his face to the wall, grunting in his sleep. The door swung open and Christian Weidener loomed up against the lake beyond in the dim light of predawn.

"I said last night I would show you something of the work of the farm," Christian said. "This is the time of day that work begins."

Liam, his eyes red, yawned. He vaguely recalled that he might have expressed a polite interest in observing the work on the farm. Certainly, at this time of day, it had little appeal for him. "Let me get my pants and my boots on."

In a moment, Liam and Christian were on their way up the hillside. They stopped at the kitchen of the big house, where Minnie gave them each a mug of steaming coffee and a piece of hot breakfast cake she had just pulled from the oven. Then, as the sun peeked over the top of the mountain, the two men went back outside. For the next half hour they toured the farm on foot, up and down the hillside, with Christian obviously moving more slowly than his accustomed rate of speed out of deference to Liam's injury. Finally they stopped at a high point on the hillside with a commanding view of the lake and the farm nestled on its shores.

"We have about four hundred hectares here," Christian told him, "much of it is still woods, especially down by the beach. We grow apples and pears in those orchards up there, and we grow corn and other vegetables in those fields over there. That up there is wheat, and over there is buckwheat. I have cows too—twenty Holsteins. Years ago I convinced the man I bought this land from to throw in all the lakefront so I could water them. On the day we did business I spoke English not so well as I knew how, so he thought he was swindling the poor foreigner into paying him so much for worthless lakefront and all this wooded land. But I cleared much of the land in the first five years and made back the cost by selling the trees as lumber. I made the land pay in another five, and someday the lakefront will be worth more than all the cleared land. Now all the people in this place know one thing about Christian Weidener: they know he is not so big a fool as they thought."

From their vantage point on the rocky outcropping they could look down on most of Christian's holdings. The harvest of the early apples was beginning in earnest. A crew of women from the village had arrived by wagon to pick them. Liam looked up behind him at the rows of vineyard along the uppermost reaches of Christian's land.

"These grapes," he said, "when will they be harvested, too?"

Christian shook his head. "Not for many weeks will the grapes be ready. These I harvest myself, with a crew of my own choosing and with great care."

"Where do you sell the grapes?"

Christian pointed to a carpet of vineyard. "Those are table grapes. They are sold like the rest of the fruit. But those up higher, those are the grapes from which I make my wine."

"You have a winery here?"

"It is there," Christian said, pointing to a squat, stone building down on the road several hundred yards from the big house. Liam had seen the building from the lake, but he had assumed it was a storage facility.

"The building looks unused," Liam said.

"I use it. But no one else goes near it. It was once a barn. In there I have built a laboratory of sorts, and I have some bottling equipment and a cellar I had dug back into the hillside. But still my wine is not ready to sell, not even after more than fifteen years of work. When the wine is right, if God wills it, I will sell wine better than any made around this lake—as fine as any in Germany or France or Italy. This is my dream, a fine winery on this land."

Liam looked down the hillside at the little winery. Its roof was made of dark green shingles, and with its shell of brownish stone it was a forbidding little building. "Is this good country for wine?" he asked,

"Captain Baddington says the wine from this region isn't very good because of the long winters. Doesn't that hurt the grapes?"

Christian's stern face broke into a small smile. "You had some of my wine last night, at dinner. What did you think of it?"

Liam shrugged. "It seemed very good to me."

"That is because you know nothing of wine," Christian said flatly. "It is not so good, not yet; but, listen to me, these winters do not hurt the grapes if you are a good vineyardist and if you understand how to use the water from the lake. The secret to growing grapes in cold climates is having water nearby, and a sloping hill leading down to it."

"I don't know anything about growing anything. How does the lake protect the grapes from the cold?"

Christian removed his hat, and the wind across the hillside blew the gray-blond wisps of hair atop his head into disarray. He looked up at the vineyard above and behind them. Then he said, "Large bodies of water like the Rhine or the Hudson or this big lake keep the heat of the summer, and as they cool the warm air rises up the slopes. It extends a growing season that would be too short, otherwise." Christian kicked loose some soil, picked it up and let it flow through his fingers. "Then, too," he went on, "this is fine soil for grapes. It is stony and rich in minerals. The soil is volcanic and soft, and the grape roots can penetrate far below the frost level for food and underground water. In the winter, the snow forms a thick blanket over the earth, and it insulates the roots from the cold. I tell you that all factors considered, there is no place on earth like this for growing fine wine, especially whites."

"Then why is the wine produced here so ordinary?"

"Ordinary?" Christian snorted. "It is worse than ordinary most of the time. It is because this is a young industry here. In Germany we have been making wine for a thousand years and longer. Here the first grapes for wine were not planted until eighty years ago, and then by a clergyman who grew grapes as a hobby. What do churchmen in this country know of wine? The monks of Europe, some of them know. But not here. It took twenty years after the first grapes were planted here before Andrew Reisinger started the first winery, and all that has come after is still very new. No, there is much work to be done. First you must find the right grapes to grow best in this place. Then you can make the right wine. I will not sell wine that is inferior."

Liam was entranced by Christian's enthusiasm. He would never have guessed that the older man had this much passion in him. "What do you mean, the right grapes?" Liam asked.

"You must find the right grapes for this soil," Christian explained. "All the grapes of Europe that make the fine wines are members of a single species, *vitis vinifera*. There are thousands of varieties of *vinifera*, but none of them can grow in North America because they have a soft, pulpy root that is especially vulnerable to a North American louse called phylloxera. No, here the only root that can survive phylloxera is the root of the native American grape. The most common species of that is *Vitis labrusca*. The problem is that *labrusca* grapes do not make such good wine."

"Was the wine we had last night made from a *labrusca* grape?" Liam asked.

"Yes. It was a catawba. This is a common wine made here." Christian shrugged. "It will not make you ill, but it is not very good. But, look up there, I have *vinifera* growing in that vineyard. There I have Riesling and Gewürztraminer growing in this soil."

"How did you do that? Won't that louse get them, that . . ."

". . . Phylloxera. No, they are safe from phylloxera. This is because I have done something that no one else has done here. I have sent to Europe for cuttings from *vinifera* vineyards, and when they arrive here I graft them onto the root stock of *labrusca*."

"And it worked?"

"It seems to be working," Christian said cautiously. "It was done once before, in reverse. You see, back in the 1870s a French vineyardist thought it might be interesting to plant American grapes in European soil. What he did not know was that bringing American grapes to Europe would also bring the phylloxera. The louse devastated the vineyards of Europe. It swept through France and into the Rhine and Rhone river valleys. All the grapes of Europe were threatened. Something had to be done, and a few vineyardists—my father among them—began grafting *vinifera* onto *labrusca* root stock. No one knew what would happen. It was assumed that the grapes from such a marriage would be the grapes of the root stock, but it turned out not to be the case. The *vinifera* thrived. So it is true that today all the vineyards of Europe are producing *vinifera* grapes from *labrusca* roots imported from this region. If great wine can be produced from this marriage in Europe, why cannot great wine be produced from the same marriage here? This is the question I asked myself, and this is the question I have been trying to answer all these years. Each year I buy more imported *vinifera* vines from a nurseryman in Fredonia named George Josselyn, and every year I graft more of them on my vines. Each year my wine grows better. Now it has become good enough to be called—as you put it—ordinary."

Liam looked up at the vineyard above him and shook his head. The thought that had gone into it, the complexity of it all had never occurred to him.

"Let us go up to the vineyard," Christian said.

They climbed the hill to the rows of trellises high on the slope. The plants were suspended from wires attached to posts at each end of the trellis. They were planted lengthwise on the hill in terraces that climbed the slope. The green grapes hung in fat bunches amid the darker green leaves. Liam took one bunch in his hand and held it gently. "It sounds like a long process," he said.

"I have been working on this fifteen years," Christian told him. "When I am ready, I will open the Weidener Winery and produce the finest Gewürztraminers and Rieslings in the world. This is the place for it to be done, and this I promise you I will do."

Liam watched Christian as the older man surveyed his vineyard with pride and affection.

"It sounds exciting," Liam said to him, intruding on his reverie. "It gives me a new perspective on farming."

Christian looked at him. "Farming, bah! That is for farmers. The cattle and the food crops are necessary. They pay for all this. But this vineyard is what is important. When I was a young man, my father sent me to study at the Geisenheim wine school. I learned much there about wine growing and a little something, too, about the making of wine, although I was stronger in the growing—always stronger there. I am putting that to use here. There will come a day . . ." Christian's voice trailed off. He reached out a large, worn hand and lovingly stroked a bunch of fat grapes. Then, as the morning wind ruffled the leaves of the vines, he put his straw hat squarely on his head and turned to Liam. He seemed almost embarrassed at revealing so much of himself. "Come," he said, "the harvest goes on, and I must watch."

Liam followed him down the hillside.

Chapter 4

The *Iroquois Queen*, water churning white about her bow, nuzzled up to the dock at the end of the point. Liam came running out of the shack and reached the dock as Baddington eased his great bulk down from the upper deck to the Weidener dock.

"Well," Baddington chuckled, "there's proof that there's no substance on earth as hard as an Irishman's head. How are you feeling?"

"Like a pup," Liam told him. "I've been fed and treated like a damned prince."

"Well, now," Baddington said, "it's time you gathered up your gear and climbed on board. I've got crop pickups and deliveries to make."

"I can't go without running up to the big house to say my farewells."

"Snap to it, boy," Baddington said, glancing at his pocketwatch, "I'm on a schedule."

Liam sprinted up to the big house. His week's rest at the Weidener farm had completely renewed him, and he moved with ease and grace up the hill from the beach. As his feet hit the path in front of the house, Helga came out on the porch from the kitchen, her hands and apron bathed in flour.

"I heard the whistle," she said, her face set in stone. "You're leaving now?"

"Leave I must," Liam told her.

"When will I see you again?"

"Soon. I'll be by here on the *Queen* by and by. Perhaps I can rent a carriage and we can go riding on my next day off."

"Yes," she said, "I can see you once a week, and we can wave to each other, you from the pilot's cabin and me from the dock. It won't really be the same, will it, Liam?"

Liam was nonplussed. "No," he began awkwardly, "but . . . ."

Helga cut him off with a cold glare. "Papa is in the back. You should say goodbye to him."

51

"Helga . . .," Liam pleaded.

Her blue eyes were like ice. "Your boat is waiting." She turned without another word and walked to the other end of the porch, her back to him. Liam looked down the hill toward the dock, where Baddington was motioning to him to hurry. Liam ran around to the rear of the house. There he found Christian nailing new planking on the back steps. The older man looked up at him.

"Captain Baddington is here, Mr. Weidener," Liam said. "I was wanting to thank you for your hospitality and your kindness."

"So, then," Christian demanded, the smile vanishing, "you're really going to leave us, after all? Sit down, Liam."

"I'm afraid Captain Baddington is waiting."

"Captain Baddington has kept me waiting often, as my crops rotted in the sun on the dock. For me he can now wait a little. Sit down."

Liam settled onto the back steps.

"Have you thought of what we spoke of?" Christian asked. "Have you thought of your future?"

Liam thought for a moment before he answered. "Aye, sir," he said. "That I have, more than before, certainly. I think you're right about the steamboats, that their time is coming to an end. But for now, that's my work, and I take pleasure in it."

"And when winter comes? There'll be no steamboats on the lake until next spring."

"Then I don't know," Liam conceded. "The more I consider it, the less I'm interested in returning to swinging a sledge on the railroad until I lose an arm or a leg. I'm beginning to think I might be becoming accident prone, with that hammer blow I took and that kick from Helga's horse. It sounds superstitious, I know, but people believe in fairies where I grew up, and some of it must have rubbed off."

"So stay here," Christian said simply.

"Sir?" Liam said.

"Stay here. Work for me."

"I know nothing of farming."

"And you care less—for the corn and the cows. Is this not right?"

Liam nodded.

"And the grapes?"

"Well, Sir, no, not the grapes. The work with the grapes sounds interesting, and that's a fact."

"This is wine country, Liam. There is a future for a young man who learns wine growing and winemaking. I will teach you, if you like. There is much to learn, and you are a smart young man."

Liam stood and began to pace in front of the steps. He turned toward

Christian. "May I ask you why, sir? Why are you offering me this job? You seem to have more than enough help to run the farm."

Christian stood up as well and put his hands on his hips. "Because you gave me my daughter when she might have been taken away from me, and I feel it is only proper that I give you something else in return. Also, this growing of wine is not an easy task, and I am growing older as my vineyards grow larger. I need a man to help me in the vineyard with the planting and the pruning and the repair of trellises. In addition, let me say that this making of wine is a task of great joy and complexity. Growing and making wine is an art—a thinking man's art—and two heads are better than one in such a matter. I have need of someone with whom I can talk. Helga has no interest. She is a woman, after all. That is why I make you this offer. Do you understand?"

Liam thought it over for perhaps fifteen seconds. He thought of the railroad, of the lake, of Helga. Vivid images passed through his mind. Then he answered, "Yes."

Christian beamed and slapped him on the back. "Goot," he said. "You will continue to sleep in the shack. This will be difficult work, and there will be much of it. For this I will pay you eight dollars each week, and your shelter and food will be supplied you."

"That's fair," Liam said. "I've no fear of work. I'll be going down to the dock now, and speaking with Captain Baddington."

"Go, then," Christian said, and picked up his hammer.

Liam walked around the house to start down the hill. As he passed the front porch, he saw that Helga was still standing there, looking out over the lake and down at the steamer at the dock. Their eyes met, and hers were wet with tears. Liam was touched.

He stopped, put his hands on his hips and looked at her with mock sternness. Then he said, "You should know, Helga Weidener, you spoiled brat of a girl, that I'll be staying underfoot."

Helga's eyes brightened. "You're staying?"

Liam nodded. "That I am. I'm to work the grapes with your father."

Helga ran down the steps and threw herself in his arms. She kissed him enthusiastically. "Liam," she said, her hands holding his face, "I'm so happy. I'm sorry I was so nasty to you. I'm ashamed of myself. It's just that I didn't want you to leave me."

Liam took her hands and squeezed them. "I'm happy, too, if the truth be told. It's a fine opportunity, truly."

Helga stepped back, still holding his hands, and smiled mischievously. "Aye," she said, mimicking his brogue, "that it is."

Liam laughed. He spun her about and smacked her backside smartly.

"Now off with you," he said. "I must have a word with Captain Baddington."

Baddington was chewing the stub of his cigar as he saw Liam approach empty-handed.

"Henry . . .," Liam began.

But Baddington cut him off. "You don't have to tell me, boy. You're staying here. Well, I can't say as how I blame you. She's a pretty girl."

"Oh, it isn't that, Henry. Mister Weidener needs help here on the farm, and . . ."

". . . And he can't manage another day without the assistance of a man who's never worked on a farm a day in his life," Baddington laughed, his voice thick with sarcasm.

Liam's eyebrows rose.

Baddington chuckled and put an arm over Liam's shoulders. "Now I've offended you, boy, and I'm sorry. But listen to me and pay attention to the advice of a more experienced man—remembering, as you do, that experience is the name men give to their mistakes, and that I've made my share and more. This girl is the center of her father's life. You just make sure you don't end up being treated like her prize riding horse up there. Don't you get kicked in the head again."

Liam shook his head. "I'll miss working for you, Henry. And I'll miss your pretty boat, too."

Baddington laughed. He shook Liam's hand and went aboard the *Iroquois Queen*. He climbed up to the wheelhouse and shouted down the tube for the boilers to be brought up to pressure. Liam watched from the dock as the crew made ready to depart. Baddington came out on the upper deck. "Take care of yourself, now," he called down. Then he disappeared into the wheelhouse. The *Queen's* whistle blasted twice. Then, amid the clanging of bells, two great white clouds billowed up from the high twin stacks. The huge sidewheels turned once, then twice, then they began their steady beat, churning the lake's water white beneath them. Baddington backed the *Queen* away from the dock, out into deeper water, and turned her prow toward Ringlesport. The wheels reversed, and the boat surged forward. Liam watched the *Iroquois Queen* as she disappeared down the lake.

* * * *

"This vineyard," Christian said, "will be ready in a few days for harvest."

Liam nodded. They were standing high on the hillside in the vineyard that overlooked the apple orchard, where the leaves were beginning to change into their fall colors. It was late morning in early October, and the air was chilly.

"This year, the harvest will be done by the two of us," Christian said. "The table grapes can be harvested by the work crew. But I will not trust the ones from which we will make wine to them."

"I've never harvested any crop," Liam said, "much less wine grapes."

"There is a first time for all things. Now, you come with me. I show you something."

Christian marched off, and Liam followed several paces behind. After several months of living and working at the Weidener farm, Liam had grown accustomed to following Christian while the older man marched relentlessly up and down the hillside, through the fields and orchards and vineyards, in and out of the big house and the little winery. So far Liam had done little but listen and perform specific tasks for him, such as cleaning and readying the pressing equipment and swabbing out vats and casks in the winery. He had managed to strike up a nodding acquaintance with the other men who worked on the farm, Jim Heller, a cheerful man of about Liam's age who came from the village daily to tend the dairy herd; and Sam Gilmore, a burly, middle-aged man who came with Heller to do odd jobs. Both men were friendly enough, but they remained somewhat distant, unclear as to what Liam's role on the farm might be. He shared their confusion to no small degree, because his primary tasks thus far had been to listen to Christian talk and to endure his silences the rest of the time. Liam had a vague notion that he was not earning his keep, and this troubled him. On the other hand, there were the hours with Helga, and those troubled him not at all.

Liam and Christian reached the end of a trellis, and Christian turned and pointed down the row of vines hanging over the wires.

"There," he said. "See that?"

Liam looked down the row. "I'm not sure what I'm looking at."

"You're looking at a well-planted vineyard," Christian told him. "I'll tell you in a moment how you can tell. And a well-planted vineyard is the first step toward good wine, because without good grapes your wine will not be good. It takes four years before even the finest vineyard, begun with skill and care, can produce good grapes for wine. Unless you plant well, you will waste those years and you will have to start again. I know this; I have had to plow under vineyards that were not planted properly."

Liam nodded. "I understand. I'm listening."

Christian turned and pointed to the forest beyond the trellises. "Do you see those trees there? If those trees are cleared away, the field that is left will be a good place for a vineyard. The hill slants, and that means good drainage. The soil is of sufficient depth to encourage good rooting.

You must look for good soil somewhere between three and six feet down. Understand?"

Liam nodded.

"Good," Christian said. "Now, the first thing that must be done is to clear several hectares of this forest. You must cut down the trees, and then you must harness the workhorses and pull out the stumps. Then the trees must be cut into vineyard posts and into firewood, and the stumps must be dragged by the horses down to that bluff and rolled down the bank the rest of the way into the lake. If you work quickly, this will take you until just before the snow flies, even with the help I will give you from Heller and Gilmore. All this will be difficult work."

"I told you, I'm not afraid of work."

Christian smiled slightly. "This is good, because there is much for you not to be afraid of. Then, if the ground has not grown too hard, you must plow a series of drainage ditches—an irrigation system—and there are chemicals to put in the soil. Again, much work."

"Go on," Liam said.

Christian looked appraisingly at the stand of trees. "Then there is winter, and nothing can be done here when the soil is frozen like rock. This is when I will teach you to make wine from the grapes we will harvest next week from that vineyard over there. It is very complicated."

But Liam was less interested at that moment in the arcane process of making wine than he was in the prospect of creating a vineyard. His eyes were on the forest. "Tell me what we'll do here in the spring," he said.

"The spring," Christian said, eyeing Liam carefully. "So, in the spring you must lay out the vineyard in rows. Here you will have several hectares—no, let us talk in terms of acres; we must be good Americans and use American measurements. With the slant of this slope, it would make sense to plant in rows that run at right angles to the hillside. By planting in such a way, you reduce soil erosion. Also, irrigation is better, since the water spreads more easily. Understand?"

Liam nodded.

"Good. Now, you want rows as long as you can make them. This makes it easier for the harvesting to do. Also, by making long rows, you will need fewer end structures to support the wires, and this saves money. Now, this is the most important part."

"Which is?"

"How far apart do you make the rows?"

Liam shrugged. "A meter or two, I suppose."

"Hah!" Christian snorted. "You are wrong. Look here at the distance between the rows in this vineyard. These are four feet apart. This I did wrong. I have learned that in the soil of this place, vines should be planted precisely eight-and-one-half feet apart *precisely*. If they are planted closer, like these here, your yield per acre will be too low. Your vines will fight one another for nutrients in the soil, and you will end up with fewer grape tons per acre."

"How many tons per acre is considered good?"

Christian held up a hand in restraint. "In a moment I will tell you that. First, how far apart do you set the posts in each row?"

This time Liam studied the existing vineyard carefully before responding. "I'd say a little less than a meter."

"You place the posts precisely two feet apart—no closer, no farther. Understand?"

"I understand. Two feet."

"Now I tell you about tonnage," Christian said. "It depends very much on the variety. Some varieties are more productive than others. But, generally, if you plant well you should get about thirty-two hundred vines per acre. And if each vine lives and prospers, you should get thirty-two thousand pounds of grapes from that acre, which means sixteen tons of juice. This translates into one hundred eighty bottles of wine per ton, or twelve hundred cases."

Liam tried, unsuccessfully, to imagine twelve hundred cases of wine. "That's an enormous amount. And from a single acre? Have you ever gotten that much?"

"No," Christian admitted, "never that much. But when my vineyards are planted properly, and when I develop varieties of wine that will both produce good wine and stand up to this climate, then I will produce twelve hundred cases per acre. This I promise. Now, about the planting in the spring."

"Yes," Liam said. "Tell me about that."

Christian lifted his arm and motioned toward the forest, imagining that the trees were already cut down and that the field was already cleared. "In the spring, you must mark out the vineyard. You must use a series of stakes to tell you where you will set your posts and set up your rows. The positioning of these stakes is crucial. They are guides for planting. Then you must fit out the soil."

"What does that mean?" Liam asked.

Christian said, "This means clearing the vineyard of rocks—as much as is possible in this soil, which breeds rocks as I wish it would breed grapes. This means raking and kneeling in the dirt and carrying away rocks on your back. My legs and back have the arthritis in them after the winter, and I can no longer do this as I used to. It is hard, dirty work."

"All of it sounds like hard, dirty work," Liam commented.

Christian smiled his half smile. "But you are not afraid of it; is that not so?"

"No," Liam said. "I'm not afraid of it."

"Good. Then, after the vineyard is fitted out, we will dig up some of the *labrusca* roots in the old vineyard and transplant them into the new one. Then the plants come. I have ordered many *vinifera* plants from Germany and France to be delivered this spring. I have ordered Chardonnay and Riesling for whites and Cabernet Sauvignon from France for red wine, even though I have had terrible luck with reds here. We will trim them and moisten them when they arrive, and we will graft them onto *labrusca* vines that you have transplanted. And next year I will receive more varieties, and more the next, and I will make wine from all of them. And, when the wine is right, I will put my labels on the bottles and I will sell it. But not before it is right."

"After they're planted, what then?"

"We must wait three years before the first harvest," Christian told him. "But we will not be doing nothing while we wait. In the first year of growth, we will not tamper with the vines. They will begin to develop, and they will grow one or two or perhaps three shoots per vine. Our enemy here will be weeds. The vineyard must be free of them, because weeds rob the young vines of critical soil nutrients, and young vines are very vulnerable. Here, with plants from European vines grafted on them, they will be even more vulnerable, and we must protect them. We must guard them in that first year from insects and deer and from birds, so they must be watched daily. We must shoot the deer who come here to feed and hang their insides in a bag on the end posts to frighten away other deer. The smell of blood will do that. Next winter, we will plant oats or rye between the rows."

"Why would we plant something that would compete with the vines?" Liam asked.

"Grapes are not like other fruit," Christian explained. "They like to keep on growing, right into the winter. It is critical to know when to stimulate growth and when to hold it back. The oats and rye will hold it back by competing for soil and nutrients. Then, the second year, that is when the real work comes. The second year, you must erect the posts to support the vines. You will, from the trees you cut down, make for me about two hundred and twenty-five posts for each acre. These will be set aside to dry. The best posts are from locust trees, and I will show these to you so you will know them. Then, after you have driven the posts into the ground, you must erect the trellis."

"You mean put up wires like those?"

"Ya," Christian said. "Some of the trellises will have two wires running the length of the row; some three. All that depends on the variety of the grape."

"How long are the posts supposed to be?" Liam asked.

"About eight, maybe ten feet. You must use a sledge hammer and drive them deep into the ground. You must staple the top wire of the trellis to the post between four and six feet from the ground. The end posts must be very strong, because they support the entire structure. You must drive them to at least two feet in depth to hold them; four feet is better, although it is more difficult. For a two-trellis system, you will need nearly ten thousand feet of wire. This is very expensive."

Liam said, "What happens when the wire begins to sag? How do I keep the wire tight in the wind when the plants are weighted down by snow?"

"A good question," Christian responded. "Come here and look." He led Liam to the end of an existing trellis and pointed to the pulley arrangement that held the wire. "You must erect pulleys on the end posts. The wires must be kept tight. You must check and adjust them twice a week. This is very important, especially when winter is gone, because the grapes must have sun. The vines must stand erect so the fruit will get the light."

Liam nodded solemnly. The magnitude of planting and growing an acre of grapes was sinking in on him now. "And after that?"

"After that," Christian said, "then comes the pruning, the training, the shoot positioning and so forth."

"What does that involve?"

"You will learn," Christian told him, "that and more. Then comes the tying, the suckering and a thousand other tasks and decisions that will affect vine and crop sizes. Of this, pruning is perhaps the most important."

"Why?"

"Because if you prune too much, you have too little crop. If you prune too little, you have too many clusters of grapes, and this has the same effect as pruning too much. You will have smaller grapes, and you will diminish the size and strength of the entire vine."

"What then?" Liam asked.

"Then you harvest and make wine," Christian said, "and that is the hard part—the making of wine. The rest, all this, it is hard work, and it requires thought. No winery can succeed without someone who has the skill to grow fine grapes. But the making of wine, that is not merely a skill. It is art. It is chemistry. It is precision. It is temperature control. It is blending and bottling properly. It also takes an instinct that most men do not possess, no matter how much schooling they have had."

Liam was silent. It seemed to him that Christian might have, in that last statement, revealed more of himself than he had meant to. There was a moment of awkward silence between them, then Liam said, "There's a lot to learn, and a lot to do. I can see why you decided you might need an assistant."

"Ya," Christian told him, "you can see one reason. There are others, but you will learn about them when the time is right. It is not just the growing that requires more than one man now; it is also the making of the wine."

Without warning, Christian turned and started down the hill at a brisk pace. Liam, taken a bit aback, ran after Christian and fell into step beside him.

"Where are we going now?" Liam asked.

"To the toolshed. To get you an ax. You have trees to cut down to make me a vineyard, and it will be light for many hours yet."

* * * *

Summer departed and, unexpectedly, came back later that year. In early November, with the trees stark and naked against the leaden sky, a blanket of warm air enveloped the lake country and hovered over it for weeks. For Liam, the unexpected gentleness of the weather was a blessing. It reminded him of Ireland at the same time of year, but, more important, it gave him desperately needed time to finish clearing land for the new vineyard.

Working long days with Christian's hired men and sometimes with Christian himself, who was capable of prodigious amounts of physical labor when his arthritis was dormant, Liam had mounted the operation to take down the trees with axes and two-man saws.

As the trees were felled, they were sawed into ten-foot lengths, stripped of their branches and pulled down the hill to a level spot just above the existing vineyards to dry. The branches were chopped into firewood and removed by wagon.

It was hard, brutal work, and Liam knew that a snowfall would halt their efforts, leaving nothing else to be done in the new vineyard until spring. That, Christian warned, would set back the planting schedule and they could lose as much as a year in getting the new vineyard into operation.

So it was that Liam often was on the job before the others and often stayed until the last little bit of daylight had departed. Most days he brought with him a sandwich and a thermos of tea made up hurriedly in the predawn shadow of the shack. While Heller, Gilmore and Christian, when he worked with them, would go down to the big house for lunch, Liam would wolf down his meal at the worksite and continue with the chopping and sawing through the meal hour.

By the time late November rolled around, the trees had been cut and removed and the workmen were pulling out the stumps. The smaller ones came out with only some digging and some urging of the two big plow horses who occupied the barn stalls next to Helga's prize riding horse. The larger stumps, however, required the use of dynamite, and Liam was nervous about the explosive. Heller was an expert with it, but he too treated it respectfully. The first time they blasted a large stump free of the earth, Liam watched it fly four feet into the air in a storm of dirt and pebbles.

"The damned stuff scares the hell out of me," he confided to Heller.

"Me, too," Heller told him. "But it sure beats digging those goddamn things out with picks and shovels."

On an overcast day late in the month, the temperature a blazing fifty or so beneath thick clouds, Liam swallowed the last of his sandwich and went back to work digging out a particularly obstinate elm stump. Heller and Gilmore worked on an even larger stump, swearing at it ferociously as they pushed while the horses pulled against their harness. All three men were naked to the waist despite the chill, and each was covered with a patina of sweat.

With a mighty shove from Heller and Gilmore, and an equally spirited effort on the part of the plow horses, the larger stump finally broke loose. Heller stood up and wiped his brow with the dirt-encrusted back of his hand.

"Well," he gasped, "that takes care of that son of a bitch. I'm going down to the house and see what's for lunch. You fellas coming?"

Liam, digging at the roots of his elm stump, didn't bother to look up. "I just had something to eat. I'm going to get this goddamned thing out of the ground before I go anywhere. You two go on ahead."

Heller pulled on his shirt and a denim jacket over that. "You're a madman, Liam. Come down and have a cup of coffee, anyway. It'll still be here after lunch."

"I know," Liam said, leaning one shoulder against the stump and testing it. "That's what I'm afraid of. If I don't have it out by the time you get back, we'll have to use the dynamite."

Heller shrugged. "Have it your own way," he said. Then, as he turned to walk down the hill to the big house, he saw Helga riding up on Ajax, a picnic basket hanging off the saddle. Heller grinned at the sight and turned back to Liam.

"Here comes something for somebody," he said, "and it ain't for me."

Gilmore looked down at Helga galloping up the hill on Ajax and laughed out loud. "Looks like a picnic basket for two. There's three of us here, and with her that makes four. You fellas go on down to the house, and I'll eat my lunch up here with Helga. How's that sound?"

Heller chuckled while Liam stood up from his stump and smiled sheepishly. Helga's obvious affection for him could have been a source of dissension between him and the others, but Heller and Gilmore had understood from the beginning that Liam's relationship with the Weideners was not their own. Moreover, Liam was likeable enough and he did more work than the two of them put together. These men, who worked with their hands, respected that. Even John Hardy, who viewed both Heller and Gilmore as newcomers and would not deign to speak to them, was beginning to show signs of warmth toward Liam, who was glad of it. He liked John Hardy, crude, crusty exterior and all, and he detected a core of profound sadness in the old man.

Helga rode over the crest of the hill and into their midst, glowing in the crisp air, her hair falling around her shoulders. She wore a pair of men's dungarees, as she often did when riding, and as she reined in Ajax she greeted Liam with a smile.

"It's lunchtime, slavedriver," she said to him. "Why don't you let Jim and Sam take a break and see what Minnie has put together down at the big house?"

Liam reached for his shirt. "Me, too?" he asked.

Helga stuck out her tongue at him. "I thought I'd share lunch with you up here," she said, "unless you have a better offer."

"Well," Heller said, "I guess that makes it official. Come on, Sam. Let's go down the hill and see what Minnie's cooked up for us."

Heller and Gilmore walked off down the hill, and Helga swung down off her horse. She held up the picnic basket.

"It was nice of you to bring this for me," Liam told her as he slipped on his shirt. He began to remove the harness from the two big workhorses.

"I didn't bring it for you," Helga told him, "I brought it for us. I haven't seen much of you in weeks now. You're always up here on the hill cutting down trees all day."

Liam hobbled the plow horses and set them free to graze. He went over to Ajax, slipped off the animal's tack and hobbled the gelding with a length of rope to keep him from wandering off. All the while, Helga was talking.

"It's a good thing that I'm not overly sensitive," she told him, "otherwise I'd think you didn't want to see me."

"Helga . . .," he began.

"Well, today there's no excuse. There is just the two of us here, and you're stuck with me for the next hour or so, at least. Now, where should we eat?"

Liam rubbed his back. It was chronically sore lately. "Ordinarily, I'd say let's go down to the lake and eat on the dock, but I wouldn't have the energy to come back up the hill. Let's just go back here in the woods."

Helga led the way into a stand of high pines overlooking the vineyard Liam was preparing. She found a soft spot carpeted in pine needles under a roof of dark green branches above, and she sat down. She began going through the picnic basket.

"So," she said good naturedly, "you haven't answered me. Have you been avoiding me, Liam?"

He dropped to the earth beside her. They were sheltered beneath the pine branches, and the light breeze through the grove of pines had a lemon scent to it.

"Hardly that," he told her, "but you know I promised your father I'd have the vineyard cleared and prepared before the snow flies. A few more days, maybe a week or a bit more, and all the stumps will be out."

"I hope so. Now, I've brought you some chicken sandwiches and some hard-boiled eggs, and there's a bottle of wine for us to share."

"Your father's wine?"

"Yes. I went down in the cellar of the winery and found a white. It was made last winter from grapes in the lower vineyard. He says it's not very good, but it tastes fine to me. On the other hand, all wine tastes pretty good to me."

"Me, too," Liam admitted. "He's promising to teach me the wine-making process this winter—if I get this field cleared on time."

She laughed. "He'll teach you whether or not the field is ready. He's anxious to teach somebody. He tried to teach me years ago, but it all bored me. He needs somebody to listen to him about his wine, and it wasn't going to be me."

Helga distributed the food, and Liam found, to his surprise, that he was still hungry, even after the sandwich he had consumed only a few minutes before. He downed three hard-boiled eggs in a row, barely taking time to chew.

"You'll choke to death," Helga warned him, pouring wine into a goblet she had brought from the dining room cabinet. She passed the glass to Liam. He sipped it, then took a gulp of it. The eggs were sticking to the inside of his mouth. The wine refreshed and warmed him as it went down. He held out the empty goblet, and Helga refilled it.

"This tastes fine to me," he said.

"Not to Papa, though. Cheers."

Liam, the food settling in his stomach, leaned back against the bole of a tall pine. "He's a strange man, your father."

"In what way do you find him strange?"

"He's . . .," Liam began, then he sat up and mustered his thoughts before going on. "There's a coldness to him sometimes. He can be very distant. I can't explain it."

"Perhaps you're right," Helga said thoughtfully. "I guess I've never seen it the way you might. He's always quite open and warm with me. He adores and spoils me, as I'm well aware."

"So is everyone," Liam said, smiling.

"Hush," Helga told him. "But with other people . . . maybe it was my mother's death."

"How did she die?"

"Childbirth. Having me. She wasn't built for it, I guess. She was a little woman, and her hips were too narrow, or something. It's made him, I don't know, build sort of a wall between himself and other people, all except me. You know, he's completely alone except for me. He had no family left in Germany. He has no close friends, just people he does business with. And I don't think he's been in bed with a woman since I was born." She reddened slightly after those words. "I hope I'm not shocking you, talking about things like that. You must think I'm terrible."

Liam laughed pleasantly. The two glasses of wine he had consumed so quickly had relaxed him, and he felt warm and flushed. "About men and women?" he said. "I don't think that's so terrible."

"But I suppose it shouldn't be spoken of so freely," Helga said, averting her eyes slightly.

"Why not? It happens. Or else how would we all get here?"

Helga smiled self-consciously. "You're taunting me now. And besides, not all men seem to need women that way."

"No? And what, my Darlin', makes you such an expert on the topic?"

Helga drained her wine glass and poured another. "I just think that some men don't seem to need it so much. Priests, for example. They don't have women in that way. Even you, now that I think about it. You don't seem to need it. You haven't left this farm in two months."

"As I am well aware," Liam told her. He found, to his discomfort, that the tone of the conversation was arousing him somewhat.

"So," Helga said, smiling triumphantly, "there's my proof."

"That I don't need women? That's no proof at all."

Helga turned toward him and suddenly leaned over. With her face no more than an inch from his, and the smell of her perfume wafting into his nostrils, she smiled again, and this time the look in her eyes was pure mischief.

"Do you, Liam?" she asked. "Do you need women in that way?"

This time Liam reddened.

"Helga," he said awkwardly, sensing that he was losing control of both the conversation and himself, "this is nothing we should be talking about this way."

Then, quite suddenly, Helga's joke ended. She came into his arms, as she had that night in the darkness on the road below. He fell back on the bed of pine needles and pulled her atop him as their lips met. Liam felt her press against him, and he felt himself stirred unexpectedly and fiercely. His hands traveled over her without any protest on her part, all thought gone from both of them. He was touching her through her clothing, pressing against her, feeling the heat of her against his hand through the denim. Then, after a moment, she was up and kneeling astride him, looking down at him, her face flushed, her pale hair in disarray and her eyes clouded with a smoky, smouldering look. Her hands traveled to the top of her dungarees and unfastened them.

Liam, his last vestige of reason asserting itself, managed to say, "Helga, this isn't wise . . .,"

"I love you, Liam," she said, unfastening her blouse.

Her breasts came free as she cast the blouse aside. Liam's hands went to them, his thick fingers caressing her pink nipples as she took in her breath sharply. Then he cast away all reason. He rose up to pull her close to him again, the blood rushing in his ears, his head pounding. He rolled her over gently and pressed her back against the carpet of pine needles. As he put his hand down the loose top of her blue jeans, Helga's eyes closed tightly.

"Yes," she said softly. "Like that. Yes."

Liam pulled off her dungarees and ripped at his own clothing. He saw her eyes on him as his own nakedness came free. She reached for him, touching it with eager fingers. He knelt between her widespread legs, stroking her breasts, her midsection, marveling at her beauty. Then, with no further thought—with nothing that resembled thought—he slipped into her, felt her hips begin their natural movements, felt her warmth and wetness envelope him.

Helga's fingers dug into his shoulders. "Yes . . . like that . . . like that . . ."

Chapter 5

Liam had miscalculated on the vineyard. It took him fully two-and-a-half weeks before the last stump was pulled out in a hail of dirt and pebbles. By that time the uncharacteristic warmth that had arrived in November had departed. The last of the work had been carried out in bitter cold, with Liam, Heller and Gilmore wearing coats and gloves and freezing as they strained, especially in the early morning hours before the sun rose high enough to provide any heat at all.

As the roots of the last stump came free, leaving the field as stark and bare as a moonscape, Jim Heller took off his knit cap and tossed it high in the air. Then he sank to his buttocks on the cold dirt.

"Thank God," he gasped, his words frozen in the air as he uttered them. "That's the end of it. Now I can go back to my cattle barn and take it easy for the winter."

Despite the cold, Liam flushed slightly at mention of the cattle barn. It had been there, high in the loft and on a bed of dry hay, that he and Helga had made love only the week before. It had been a hurried, frantic coupling, markedly different in tone from their first session up in the grove of pine trees. It had been conducted amidst the stench of cattle dung and the odor of the musty barn, leaving them both feeling a trifle soiled and awkward with one another as they lay naked in the straw, clutching one another to escape the chill.

"We have to stop this," Liam had told her. "We're risking too much. I work every day with your father, and sometimes I'm overcome with guilt at what I'm doing with his daughter every time he turns his back."

"I don't feel any guilt at all," she had told him. "I love you. You love me. I want you inside me, as a part of me. This is what people do when they love each other."

"I love you too, Darlin'," he said, "but it's not right—not with you."

She sat up, turning her bare back to him. "Don't talk like that, Liam. Don't make me feel like I'm a whore."

He clutched her close to him as they both shivered in the cold of the cattle barn. "Hush, hush. Don't talk that way. I love you with all my heart and soul. I've never felt this way before."

And he hadn't. Liam wanted simply to be with her every moment. Yet he knew that if he was with her he would be so intoxicated by her sensuality that he would be unable to resist the urge to take her and revel in the soft warmth of her body. He knew he had to bring his desire for her under control before disaster struck them both.

That day in the cattle barn he had held her close, feeling her tears run down his naked shoulders, and he had told her that the two of them had to regain their senses.

"We'll get caught if we don't stop," he said, "perhaps even by your father. I'm going to finish the work in the vineyard. I'm going to work myself until I can't move. I can't see you this way again, Helga—not for a while."

And so he had finished the vineyard, working ferociously, with so much energy and fierceness that Gilmore and Heller had been amazed. He had dropped almost ten pounds in two weeks, straining against the stumps, pushing, pulling and digging. When the last stump was pulled free, Liam collapsed against it like a rag doll, his chest heaving in exhaustion. He and Heller didn't move for several minutes. Then Heller stood up and stretched his aching muscles.

"We've done it, Liam," he said. "We've got the goddamn thing cleared."

Liam nodded dully. "We've got it cleared," he said. Then, without another word, he staggered down the hill to the shack to sleep, which he did fitfully for nearly twelve hours. The following morning, he rose in the darkness of the shack and washed while Hardy snored on in his bunk. Liam dressed and briskly walked to the winery. He found Christian in the laboratory, hunched over a desk in the corner of the room, lost in thought.

"I'm here to learn about winemaking," Liam told him.

Christian, brow furrowed, looked up. "The field is finished?"

Liam nodded. "All cleared as of yesterday. It's just waiting for next spring."

"Good," Christian said. "I will check it later. Now, about this making of wine. You will not learn this in a day or even in a year. Perhaps not in a lifetime. It has become clear lately to me that I may not have learned how to do it properly in all these years. I have made seventy different varieties of wine these past fifteen years, using some of the finest grapes that Europe could produce. None of what I have made has approached what my father made on the banks of the Rhine. I have not yet achieved the proper balance in this place, and I have exhausted my knowledge and my patience."

Liam said, "I don't know what your father made, but the wine you've made that I've tasted . . ."

"Is adequate," Christian said in a voice tinged with exasperation. "It is as good, I suppose, as any that is made in this place—in these Finger Lakes. I could, if I so desired, stop the selling of my grape harvest to the big wineries and begin producing my own wine to sell. But I did not want to make wine that was merely adequate when I came here, and this is merely ordinary. I do not know of a way to make it better."

The depth of Christian's dejection was almost absolute, Liam suddenly realized. The older man's stony wall of reserve was, for the first time and for the moment at least, broken down. Liam found himself somewhat embarrassed at witnessing it even as he was consumed with an urge to to ease Christian's intense disappointment.

"More experimentation is what it needs," he finally got out. "More time."

Christian shook his head wearily. "You are young. It is easy for you to talk of more time; it has no meaning for you. But for me it is different. For a man past forty-five, time could end in the next moment. I cannot count on more time to perfect my wine. What can be done must be done now."

Liam walked across the lab and stood next to him. "Christian, you're disappointed today. You're entitled to a bad day. Tomorrow, things will look better to you."

Christian sighed and produced a small cigar from his shirt pocket. He lit it and sat back down at the desk, leaning back against the window.

"No," he said slowly. "I have given this much thought. On the Rhine, building on what my father and grandfather had learned about winemaking there, I could have made great wine. My grapes are fat and my harvest is rich. But I have not mastered the magic of the laboratory here, the actual business of winemaking, its chemistry—not with the differences in the way grapes grow in this soil and this climate."

Liam said, "What are you going to do?"

Christian stood up once again and began pacing the room. "There are three courses open to me. I can abandon the winemaking entirely and continue as a contract grower for the big wineries. This is not enough for me. Or, I can sell this wine I produce now and debase my family name, make it stand in this country for only the adequate and the ordinary. The third thing I can do is to import a winemaker from Europe—a young man, like yourself, who is better trained than I am, who knows the latest techniques. This I can also do, and if he manages to make fine wine in my winery, from my grapes, it will be an accomplishment in which I can share."

Liam nodded. Clearly, this had been on Christian's mind for some time. He had thought it through. Liam knew that he was being asked for his advice, and the realization flattered him.

"Can you do this?" Liam asked. "Do you know where you could find a winemaker?"

"I believe I could," Christian said. "I could work through a broker in New York who could find me such a man in Germany or the south of France or, perhaps, in Italy. If I am ever going to make wine good enough to put out under the Weidener name, as my family did in Germany, then it looks very much as though I must do this. And if I am going to do it, I ought to do it quickly—this winter."

"From what you've told me, though, even with the sort of man you're looking for, it could take years to make the sort of wine you're after. What will you do with that cellar full of wine you already have?"

Christian shrugged. He had thousands of bottles in the cellars beneath the winery. "Perhaps I will eventually have labels made up and sell it," he said, "but not under my family name. It is just taking up space now, and the space is not needed for anything else."

The two men were silent for a while, then the big German said, "You must not worry about what will become of you if I bring in a winemaker from Europe."

Liam laughed. "I'll be no more worried about myself than I was when I came here."

"Do not worry," Christian assured him, "a winemaker is a creature of the winery. He makes wine, but he seldom understands the whole business. Nor do most of them want to. That you will know. Already you show a feel for the growing, and you will learn enough of the winemaking that, like me, you cannot be fooled. And you will learn also of the distribution and sale of the final product and the buying of grapes from the contract growers, when that time comes. There will be enough for you to learn and do to be able to help me, even if I am able to import the best winemaker in Europe."

"That's good to hear, Christian," Liam said, "and it's generous of you."

"Not entirely generous," Christian said dourly. "If the winemaker we bring in happens to be a German, then I will have someone with whom I can deal concerning this winemaking. But I may have to take an Italian or a Frenchman. An Italian perhaps would be bearable. But a Frenchman?

They make very fine wine, but I have never met a Frenchman I could abide."

* * * *

Less than a month after the conversation between Christian and Liam in the winery, and just after the new year's celebration of 1912, a letter came from Christian's New York broker that he had found a young and superbly trained winemaker willing to take the position. He was Henri Le Barnot of Bordeaux. The broker warned in his letter that Le Barnot's current employer considered him enormously talented but also enormously temperamental. The broker stressed that Le Barnot's credentials were, however, impeccable.

Christian, seated behind the desk in his study in the big house, read the letter aloud to Liam. "What did I tell you?" he said. "A typical Frenchman."

* * * *

John Hardy had taken the wagon into town for supplies, and Liam was sitting in front of the warm stove in the shack slogging through a book of John Donne's poetry from Christian's library when Helga came in the door. She was wrapped in a thick shawl against the cold. As she entered, Liam jumped to his feet and rushed over to her. He kissed her cheek.

"Hello there, Helga Darlin'. Come down to keep me company, have you?"

Helga's face was set sternly. "I thought I'd have to. You haven't worked too hard at keeping me company lately."

He turned away from her. "If the truth be told, I've been struggling to avoid the near occasion of sin, as the prayer says. I'm afraid of being too close to you, for fear it'll happen again. I have too much feeling for you to continue using you badly, Helga. Truly I do. Forgive me. I'm doing the best I can."

Helga threw off her shawl and walked to the stove to warm herself. "Liam," she said, her back to him, "let's get married."

Liam was stunned. He walked over and stood behind her. Then he put his hands on her shoulders and gently turned her face to his.

"Do you mean that?" he asked her.

Helga smiled self-consciously. "I was hoping you would ask first. When you didn't, I figured that it was up to me to take the first step. Why else would I say it? I love you."

Liam looked down into her face, then he turned and walked back to the window. The lake was nearly frozen now, and the sunlight glinted off it with a harsh glare. "You know I love you, Helga. Don't doubt that for a moment. But . . . well, I've never planned to marry until I had something of my own—a boat or a piece of land. Men marry late in Ireland, Helga, after they've established themselves and they can afford to support their wives and little ones."

"This isn't Ireland," she reminded him. "How long do you expect me to wait? Or is it that there isn't any need to marry me, now that you've already had everything I have to give you?"

He turned and looked at her. "Helga . . ."

"Liam," she broke in, "do you love me or not?"

"I do. But it's not enough, Helga. Not until I've begun my life—begun a real livelihood—can I marry. Not until I've begun something."

She smiled at him again, but it was a smile without warmth or mirth. Her eyes were cold and frightened. "You've already begun something. I'm carrying your child, Liam."

He felt his stomach turn over. He stammered, "H-How . . .?"

"The usual method," Helga said crisply. "There's no doubt. I think it might have been that very first time, up in the woods."

"Sweet Jesus," he muttered.

"I'm already starting to strain against my clothes," Helga said, and now her voice contained a plaintive note. "If you love me, please for God's sake don't leave me alone like this."

He swept her into his arms then, holding her tightly, kissing her forehead and cheeks. She was racked with sobs, and she collapsed against him.

"I could never leave you alone," he told her. Never for a second."

Helga clung to him tightly. "I knew you wouldn't," she said, her voice muffled against his chest.

* * * *

It took them two days before they could bring themselves to face Christian. Liam would have waited longer, so great was the deep sense of betrayal he felt. But Helga argued that she couldn't hide her swelling middle forever, especially not from the sharp-eyed Minnie.

Standing outside the polished door to Christian's library on a cold, forbidding afternoon, Liam had taken special care to look presentable. He was clean-shaven and dressed in his best shirt and good woolen trousers. Helga knocked on the door. They could hear the sound of Christian shuffling papers and moving in his chair. "Come in."

Christian was sitting behind his desk, which was strewn with papers and ledgers, doing the farm's accounts. In the winter, when he seldom worked outdoors, Christian's wardrobe underwent a transformation. For outdoors work in warm weather, he routinely wore work shirts and dungarees. But in the winter, inside the house, he dressed more elegantly. Today he wore a crisp white linen shirt without the dress collar, a hand-knitted blue sweater, gaberdine trousers and leather slippers.

Christian watched them enter, hand in hand, and his eyebrows immediately raised. "So? What is this?"

"Liam has something to say to you," Helga said, squeezing Liam's hand tightly.

Liam just blurted it out. "Helga and I want to get married, Christian."

For a moment, Christian's face remained impassive. Then he stood up and came around the desk to face them. He leaned back against the desk top and folded his arms in front of him.

"So," he said, "I suppose this was to be expected."

Liam had not expected enthusiasm, but neither had he expected the stony expression that had settled on Christian's face.

"We want your blessing, Papa," Helga said.

Christian's eyes went from Helga, to Liam, then back to Helga. "There is little I can say," he said slowly. "I knew something was brewing when you begged me to let him stay. I had hoped this infatuation of yours would pass. But it has not, and now you want to marry this man who has nothing. I cannot approve, Helga."

"Papa . . .," Helga began.

But Christian held up a hand and cut her off. "No, you have come to me and said this, and now I must say what is in my heart. I had hoped for better for you. There have been other young men with property of their own. You have rejected their advances, and you have gone out of your way to encourage the advances of this man. This I do not understand, and I do not approve of this marriage."

Christian turned to Liam. "You are a fine young man, but you have not proven yourself, and you know that. I am a reasonably wealthy man, and I had hoped that the man Helga would marry would be of comparable position. It is not wrong to want the best for one's children. This is not a personal offense, Liam. You understand?"

Helga reddened visibly, and her blue eyes narrowed. "How could he understand, Papa, with what you've said?" Her voice grew loud and shrill. "This is what I want, Papa. I want Liam."

Liam squeezed her hand to quiet her. "I do understand," he told Christian. "You want what I would want for my own daughter. But this must be done, Christian. Helga and I must marry."

"Liam . . .," Helga said, her voice tinged with alarm.

Liam turned to her. "He must be told. He'll know soon enough, anyway."

Christian's face suddenly darkened. He stood up straight and dropped his hands to his sides. "Know what?"

Liam turned to him. "Helga is carrying a child, Christian, my child—"

The blow caught Liam high on the left cheekbone. He had tried to block it, but it had come too quickly. He managed only to pull his head far enough to one side so that the punch missed his jaw.

The force of the blow, born of pure rage, drove Liam across the room and over a leather armchair next to the fireplace. He hit the floor hard, his head striking the hardwood at the edge of the oriental carpet.

Helga clutched at Christian. "Papa, stop! It wasn't Liam's fault."

Christian shook her off and advanced on Liam, who was getting up, his head spinning and pounding and a red welt already across his cheek. As Christian came toward him, Liam raised his hands to defend himself. Helga was grasping for Christian, her voice frantic. "No, Papa! No!"

Christian stopped and looked down at Helga, who now was clinging tightly to his arm. He turned back to Liam. When he spoke, his voice was low and filled with menace, his eyes were blue ice. "I took you into my house. I fed you my food—!"

"And I betrayed you," Liam said softly, rubbing at his cheek. "I'll spend a lifetime regretting breaking faith with you. But for now, I love Helga, and I'll do whatever I can to make up to you for this, Christian. Of all men, I've cared most for your respect."

"Respect?" Christian spat. "You can do this and talk to me of respect?"

"Papa," Helga wailed, her face awash with tears.

Christian turned on her, and for the first time since he had been at the farm, Liam saw Christian's ice-cold anger directed toward his daughter. She saw it, too, and she cowered before it.

"Get out," he hissed at her. "Your future husband and I have business to discuss."

Helga stood frozen, still shocked by the events of only a few seconds before.

"Get out!" Christian bellowed.

With an anguished howl, Helga fled from the room and upstairs. As she did, Minnie appeared in the hallway. She looked up after Helga, then she looked into the study and caught Christian's baleful glare.

"I'll mind my business, Mister Weidener," she told Christian, and went back into her kitchen. Christian closed the door and turned to Liam.

"So," he said in a low voice, "this was your way to make your fortune—to marry it instead of earning it."

Liam flushed instantly. "No. I want nothing from you that I haven't earned."

"Hah!" Christian said. "It is very clear . . .!"

'Nothing is clear, Christian," Liam said, feeling a surge of the temper that had forced him out of Ireland. "Not to you, and certainly not to me. But that's a discussion for another day. For now, I want to know this: How many acres do you own?"

Christian, by the door, glared menacingly. "What has this to do with anything?"

"We're doing business, if you insist on putting it on this basis. How many?"

Christian looked carefully at Liam, his expression a mixture of curiosity and hatred. "In corn," he began, I have—"

"In grapes, damn it," Liam snapped. "That's all that counts."

"I have nearly one hundred and fifty acres in grapes," Christian said.

"And you contract sell what? One forty or so?"

"About."

"How many acres of timber?"

"Another two hundred. In other crops I have . . ."

"I'll buy the two hundred," Liam told him curtly, "plus the acre I just cleared. I don't care about the other crops. I'll buy it all outright, before the marriage. And I'll buy the fishing shack as a home for me and Helga and our child. We'll have our own roof over our heads, not yours."

Christian looked at him for a moment, then he burst out laughing. "You? Buy? With what?"

"With this," Liam told him. Then he reached into the rear pocket of his trousers and tossed the pouch of gold coins his father had given him across the room, where it landed on Christian's desk. It hit with a thump and a jangle.

"That's gold," Liam said. "Those coins have been passed down through my family for generations. They're hundreds of years old. I had them appraised in Albany two years ago, and their value to a collector is worth many times what the gold they're made of would fetch. I know what they told me they were worth at the time, but you can go into Rochester, find your own expert and have them appraised yourself. I'll live with whatever figure you come up with. In any event, they're yours. In addition to that, I have one thousand, two hundred and fourteen dollars and seventeen cents in the Lakeside Trust Company that I saved from my years on the railroad. That money, and the money from the gold coins, are both yours. Anything else that you figure I owe you can come out of my salary, for as long as it takes. I'll take just enough for me and Helga and the baby to eat on. I'll clear the land myself, on my days off. I don't want a thing from you, Christian."

Christian gazed at the pouch on his desk. Then, an expression akin to amazement on his face, he looked back to Liam. He opened his mouth to speak, but Liam raised a hand and cut him off.

"I'm not finished, Liam told him. "Before I marry Helga, you have to do something else. You must draw up a will, or redraw whatever will you might have. It has to say this: anything you own at the time of the marriage, except what I'm buying from you, must be passed on at the time of your death—in its entirety—to Helga or her surviving children. Nothing is to go to me that I haven't paid for. I don't care how it's worded. Work that out with your lawyer, but that should be the sense of it. Nobody will be able to say that Liam Brennan got a rich man's wife with child to get his hands on her father's property. And one more thing, Christian. Unless such a will is filed before the marriage, there will be no marriage. I'll pack my bags and leave alone."

Christian's eyebrows rose in surprise.

"I'd rather have the child grow up thinking me a cad than a fortune hunter," Liam said. "That's the bargain. Do you agree?"

Christian was silent for a long moment, digesting what he had heard. Then he said, "I agree. It will be as you say."

"We'll have to move quickly," Liam said. "As it is, the baby will be born more than two months early."

Christian moved around behind his desk and hefted the pouch.

"I will have my lawyer here tomorrow," Christian said. "It appears that I misjudged you."

Liam looked down at the floor. His speech had drawn off his anger.

"I misjudged myself as well," he said quietly. "I behaved like a fool with Helga, and I'm ashamed of it. Now we'll have to make the best of it—all three of us."

"Four," Christian corrected, "there will be four of us very soon."

Chapter 6

The wedding, to Liam's relief, was a Catholic ceremony, held in Saint Michael's Church in Lakeside. Not that Liam was particularly devout; but he was relieved that he had not been forced to inform his parents that he had not been married by a priest.

As it happened, however, the Weideners were also nominal Catholics, which came as something of a shock to Liam, who had assumed that all Germans were Lutherans. Not only that, and for reasons not even Helga could fathom, Christian Weidener was also a faithful and generous financial supporter of Saint Michael's, although he seldom worshipped there or anywhere else. As a result, the red-faced Irish priest, Father Maloney, was effusively solicitious of the big German farmer. The ceremony was something of an event for both the church and the village as well. It was attended by everyone with any connection to the farm, including Hardy, who had been astounded when Liam asked him to serve as best man.

"You must be joking," Hardy had said, coughing madly after swallowing a wad of tobacco in his shock. "I'm old enough to be the bride's grandfather. I can't be no goddamn best man at a wedding like this."

"And who else would I ask?" Liam had responded. "You're not much, John Hardy, and that's a blessed fact, but you're the closest thing I've got to a friend on this farm."

Hardy had shaken his head. "What about that fat steamer captain, Baddington?"

Liam had smiled and put a hand on the old man's shoulder. "John," he had said, "I'm asking you."

So, shaved and dressed in a suit Liam had bought for him, a surprisingly younger looking and respectable John Hardy stood in the sacristy of Saint Michael's Church looking out over the guests—at Minnie in a floral print dress and black straw hat, at Heller in a suit jacket and open shirt and at the others who had trekked to the church from the village and its environs on a bleak, frigid winter day.

Dr. Frazier was there in a somber brown suit, along with his pudgy, bubbling wife. Their eldest daughter, Ellen, who was a few years younger than Helga, had been selected as the maid of honor. Henry Baddington attended with his wife, a quiet, tiny woman who contrasted sharply with the steamboat captain. Where he was dark, she was fair; where he was loud and boisterous, she was painfully shy.

Also in attendance were Thomas Allen, who operated Lakeside Mills, a prosperous wheat-, oat-, and buckwheat-milling operation; Emmett John-stone, the president and chairman of the board of Lakeside Trust Company; John B. Coughlin, owner of Coughlin's Hardware and Farm Supply in the center of the village; William B. Waterman, who managed the local offices of the Lakeside and Boydstown Railroad; Spencer King, Lakeside's only dentist, and all their wives.

In addition, the county court judge attended and all four of Lakeside's lawyers were on hand with their spouses. Abner Wright, the crusty old farmer from whom Christian had bought his land a decade and a half earlier, sat stiffly in a rear pew with his wife, both of whom were profoundly uncomfortable at even witnessing a Catholic ceremony. They were sur-rounded by a dozen of the lake's most prosperous farmers and their wives, all dressed in unaccustomed suits and formal dresses.

Christian had also invited the winery people with whom he did business. He had also invited the other steamboat captains, and they all sat in one spot in the church with the exception of Foster Gillis, owner and captain of the *Aurora*, whom they shunned.

Peter Day, owner of the Lakeside Hotel, was not on hand for the ceremony. He was busy at his establishment two blocks away preparing for the wedding luncheon, which would be held in what passed for the hotel's ballroom. That was an oversized dining room on the second floor that overlooked the village dock and the gray-green water beyond.

To Liam, the ceremony seemed to shoot by in a flash, then he and Helga were walking down the aisle of Saint Michael's Church and forming a brief receiving line in the vestibule with Christian, Hardy and Ellen Frazier. Then it was off to the reception. The meal at the Lakeside Hotel was about half over before Peter Day and his waiters managed to pass out all the bottles of wine to the tables. When that was done, Christian stood up at the head table and tapped his glass with a fork. The room quieted as the guests turned to listen to the father of the bride speak.

"I must have your attention, please," Christian said. "I wish to propose a toast." He raised his glass high. "To my daughter Helga and her husband Liam—a lifetime of joy."

Everyone drank, and there was a smattering of applause from around the room. Christian held up his hand again and waited for the silence to return.

He said, "Wait, there is more. You must all know this—that when I die my family name will die with me. I have no sons to carry it on, although the blood will be there, and that is what is important. In a few years, therefore, I plan to begin producing my own wine under my own name—Weidener wines. In this way, I will carry on my family's name and work from Germany. However, this wine which you are now drinking will go on sale commercially this spring, and it will be a regular line produced by my winery. This wine, however, will be produced under another label."

Christian reached down to the table and held up one green bottle. He pointed to the label. "On this very special day," he announced, "we are drinking Brennan wine."

It was an assemblage of guests who had grown up in wine country, and the room erupted into applause and cheers. Liam was astounded. On such a day, he hadn't bothered to look at the labels on the wine bottles placed on the table. His eyes had been filled with Helga, radiant on her wedding day, and with the spectacle of the wedding, which had something of a dreamlike quality for him. Now, as the guests turned toward him, he turned the bottle in front of him so he could read the label. He saw, printed in plain, black letters on a white background

BRENNAN WHITE TABLE WINE
100% NEW YORK STATE
12% ALCOHOL BY VOLUME
Produced and bottled by
Weidener Vineyards
Lakeside, New York

Liam stood up and walked over to Christian. The two men shook hands, which sparked more applause. Then the meal resumed, and Liam took Christian off to a corner of the room for private conversation.

"Christian, I've not the words to express my feelings. It's truly over-whelmed I am."

Christian waved away his comments. "It is nothing to become excited about. This wine with your name on it is merely ordinary. We both know that."

"But still . . ."

Then, to Liam's everlasting surprise, Christian suddenly smiled and wrapped a heavy arm around the younger man's shoulders. "Liam, I must treat you now as I would treat my own blood. You are my Helga's husband. You know that the time has come for me to put wine on the market. But I will not put my name on any wine that is not the best, and what I have already made must be sold under some name. So, why not yours?"

"Even so, I'm deeply touched."

"This is part of my wedding gift to you and Helga. Always, the Weidener winery will produce two brands—the Weidener brand for the finer wines and the Brennan brand for the lower-priced wines."

The other part of their wedding gift, as Liam was well aware, was their wedding trip to New York—three days and nights at the Waldorf Astoria. Helga was enthralled by the prospect of the trip, but Liam knew that this gift of the wine was by far the more important to Christian, and it was more important to Liam as well.

Christian eyed Liam carefully. "Be kind to my daughter, Liam. This is all I ask in return. We . . . we got off badly at the beginning, but you behaved with honor in the matter of the land and the will. I want the hard feelings between us to be forgotten."

"Forgotten it is," Liam told him.

* * * *

The Lakeside train station was nestled in snow and bathed in afternoon sunlight. The heaviest snowfall of the season, all sixteen inches of it, had come late, only two days before, and the village was still digging out.

Liam walked into the station and looked around. He was running late. Not all of the road from the farm had been clear, and it had taken the horse and carriage considerably longer to negotiate it than he had planned. He checked the wall clock and frowned. The train had long since left, and the question was, Liam asked himself, Where is my passenger?

Then Liam saw him. He was standing on the other side of the huge, black stove in the center of the station house. He was wrapped in a bulky, woolen, ankle-length coat with a fur collar, and on his head was a neat black derby. Beneath the derby and around his neck, the man wore a heavy woolen scarf. Liam had failed to spot him at first because he was so small that the stove had hidden him from his view. The man was not much more than five feet tall, and he was circling the stove in an effort to warm himself. The way he walked in spurts and held himself stiff and still in front of the stove's heat before moving away again in tiny, mincing steps reminded Liam of a bird. He walked across the station house to greet him. "Mister Le Barnot?" he queried, as he drew near.

The little man turned toward him and looked up. Henri Le Barnot, the new winemaker, was no more than Liam's age and possibly a year or two younger. He sported a thin and dandyish moustache grown, Liam suspected, over a very long period of time, because the rest of his face was so smooth that he probably had to shave no more than three or four times a week. His dark eyes were like raisins against his pale skin.

"This is me," Henri Le Barnot said, extending his hand in greeting. "You are Mr. Weidener, no?"

"No," Liam said. "I'm Liam Brennan, Mr. Weidener's son-in-law. He sent me in to pick you up."

Le Barnot turned to a tiny woman sitting on the bench behind him. The delicate, fur-draped figure with flaxen hair and enormous blue eyes was as tiny for a woman as Le Barnot was for a man. She stood up and hurried over to them as soon as the Frenchman's eyes fell on her. Le Barnot said, "This is my wife, Annette. She speaks no English, but she will learn. Annette learns very quickly in all matters."

"Hello," Liam said to her, bowing slightly and extending his hand. Annette Le Barnot smiled winningly, took the outstretched hand and curtsied.

"'Allo," she said.

"Your English is very good," Liam told the Frenchman.

Le Barnot waved away the compliment. "In Europe, many people speak two or three languages or more."

"Not in Ireland. That's where I'm from."

The little Frenchman shrugged extravagantly. "Ah, well," he said, "Ireland is Ireland, after all."

For a moment, Liam wasn't sure if he should be offended, but there was no time to ponder the question because Le Barnot was already off and outside on the platform near the tracks gathering his luggage. Liam took one look at the vast array of suitcases and trunks and knew immediately that he would have to return the next morning to pick up the bulk of the luggage in the big farm wagon. They took what they could fit into the carriage and left the rest sitting on the platform.

"This will be safe here?" Le Barnot inquired.

"No one ever steals in Lakeside," Liam explained. "The village is so small that if you tried to steal something and use it for yourself everybody would know that you'd stolen it."

Annette sat flanked by Henri and Liam as they drove out of town. Liam pointed out the lake as they neared it.

"Very nice," Henri said. "My furniture will arrive later in the week from New York. We must pick that up as well."

"Your furniture?"

"But of course. Annette must have her things in her new home."

This time it was Liam's turn to shrug. "Well, if it comes I'll get it out to the farm."

They were outside the village in just a few moments, driving along Lakeside Road. Less than a mile out of town the first of the snow-shrouded Lakeside vineyards came into view. Henri studied them with great interest from his seat in the carriage.

"It is amazing," he said, huddling in his enormous coat, "this cold. Have you ever looked at a map of the world?"

Liam turned toward the Frenchman. "Once or twice," he said dryly.

"This wine district is on virtually the same latitude as the wine districts of France and Germany," Le Barnot said through chattering teeth, "yet it is so cold here. It must be very difficult to make wine in this country."

"That's why Christian sent for you. He can't get it the way he wants it. He hopes you can."

"If it can be done, I can do it."

Liam shook his head and lit his pipe. "Nobody can fault you for confidence; I'll give you that."

"It is true. I am a genius."

"A genius, is it?"

The little Frenchman nodded and shrugged again. "Well, not in all matters. But in this making of the wine, I am a genius. The problem is that in the south of France there are many, many men who have genius at making wine."

"That's not one of our problems here."

"I know," Henri said. "I have tasted wine from this part of the world. How much farther now?"

"Several miles yet."

The little Frenchman shivered and put his arm around his wife to warm them both. "This cold is unspeakable," he muttered.

The temperature was down to around ten degrees. During the next few miles, the biting wind off the frozen lake even got to Liam, who had grown accustomed to it, so all three were relieved when the carriage pulled off the road and stopped in front of Christian Weidener's white house overlooking the barren, snow-covered lake. As Liam pulled the horse to a halt, Christian came out onto the porch and walked down the steps. Helga, her pregnancy showing, came out after him. Christian helped Henri and Annette down from the seat while Liam unloaded their bags.

Christian took Henri's hand and shook it vigorously. "Mister Le Barnot," he said, "I am Christian Weidener. This is my daughter, Helga, and you have already met her husband. We welcome you to our home. Please come inside and warm yourselves by the fire. Then Helga will show you to your residence. We have had built a small house near the winery building. The foundation was dug and sunk before the ground froze, and the house is very comfortable. Not so big, but nice. I hope it is to your liking. If not, we can have modifications made to it when the warm weather comes."

Henri wrapped his arms around himself for warmth and looked up the hillside behind the house. "I should like first to look at the vineyards," he said, gazing up the snow-covered slope, "and then I must examine the winery."

Christian and Liam exchanged glances. Christian turned back to Henri. "But first a glass of schnapps or brandy, to drive away the chill? Then we can go up to the vineyards."

Henri shook his head vigorously. "No. My Annette, she will go inside to warm herself. I must first see the vineyards. I have come a long way to see this."

"Let me get my coat," Christian said curtly. "I must go with you."

Liam took the Le Barnots' bags to their house and unloaded them in the living room. The little house was already furnished with goods Christian had bought in Boydstown, and Liam wondered with some amusement what Christian's reaction would be when he learned that Henri had brought his own furniture from France. Especially, Liam reflected, considering that part of the arrangement had included Christian's pledge to pay all moving and travel expenses. Liam wondered idly what it cost to move a house full of furniture from Bordeaux, France, to Lakeside, New York, and chuckled inwardly at the thought of the expression on Christian's face when he found out.

Liam drove the carriage to the barn. He had put the horse in its stall when he saw Christian and Henri coming down the hillside, their breath forming long plumes of steam. Liam went around behind the house and met them.

"And now the winery, if you please," Henri said.

Christian pointed down the road. "It is down there."

Without another word, Henri began trekking off in the direction Christian had indicated. Christian and Liam followed along behind.

"What did he do in the vineyard?" Liam asked.

Christian scowled. "He examined the way the vineyards are laid out. He looked over the trellis structures. Then he looked at the vines, and he dug through the snow with his bare fingers and scraped loose some of the soil. He rubbed that between his fingers."

"What did he say?"

Christian's scowl deepened. "Not a word."

In the winery, Henri went through each room slowly and carefully, his obsidian eyes intense and alert. Christian and Liam followed, describing each piece of equipment and its function. In the cellar, Henri asked to sample a bottle of red and a bottle of white. Liam opened two bottles and produced glasses from the rack along the wall. Henri sniffed each cork in its turn, sniffed each glass of wine and then sampled each, allowing the wine to swirl around in his mouth. "Now," he said to Christian, "tell me how you make this wine."

Christian stared at the young Frenchman for a moment. Then he cleared his throat and began. The harvest, he explained, was carried out at specific periods, all the grapes picked by hand. The grapes were transported by cart to the winery to be crushed by the two large, hand-operated presses Christian had bought so many years ago. The refuse left in the press, called pumice, was returned to the fields for use as fertilizer. The juice was then run through cloth filters to remove any remaining bits of skin or stems.

It was then placed in several huge vats made of white oak. There it would sit for up to three weeks, depending on the temperature of the room. The ideal temperature, both men knew, was sixty-five degrees. If such a temperature could be maintained precisely, the juice would be properly fermented in only ten days. But Nature was seldom so kind in the Finger Lakes, and the initial process varied depending on the weather, Christian's judgment and the performance of the natural yeast in the grape juice, which was slowly changing the sugar in the juice to alcohol.

During this period, a winery worker, which meant Liam, was required to regularly stir the mixture with a wooden paddle to keep a hard cap from forming on the juice.

At a certain point in the process, fermentation would be halted at Christian's judgment by a dose of sulfur dioxide. At that point the oak vats would be emptied and the wine moved to redwood vats. These second vats were more porous than the oak, and they permitted air from the wood to enter the wine and cause the natural aging process to be carried out more quickly. Then, after aging the red wines he made from six months to a year and the whites and rosés from three to six months, Christian would bottle his wine.

"The difficulties here," Christian explained, "are knowing when to halt the fermentation process and how long to age the wine in the redwood vats. In Germany, I had no problems with such things. But here, this is where my process needs refining."

Henri nodded, deep in thought. "How well do you clean the first vats, the ones of oak, after the juice is removed?"

"I clean them," Liam broke in. "They're scrubbed down clean after every batch of juice."

"Do you clean them with sulfur dioxide?" Henri demanded.

Liam and Christian exchanged glances.

"We clean them with water and brushes," Christian said, "just as we clean the aging vats."

"There was a time," Henri said, "when no one used sulfur dioxide for anything but stopping the fermentation process. But we have learned in France that the wood of the fermentation vats retains traces of juice from previous batches, and even in the cleanest vats such fermented juice can tend to affect the outcome of succeeding batches."

"But surely," Christian said, "if the vats are cleaned carefully enough . . ."

Henri raised one finger, like a schoolmaster lecturing a slow pupil. "There are tiny fragments of juice that cannot be seen by the naked eye. Perhaps in Germany in very old, hardened vats and using methods and grapes that have been in place for years this is not a factor. But here, with new wood and much experimentation necessary, I think it might be. Besides, in Germany most good wineries now use sulfur dioxide to clean the vats. Then they scrub a second time and make the sulfur dioxide go away."

Christian shook his head. "I did not know," he mumbled.

"Also," the little Frenchman went on, "you must be careful with sulfur dioxide. If you have too heavy a hand, it can affect the finish of the wines, as it has of those I tasted. That edge they have is from the sulfur dioxide. Too sharp. It is most ideal, in the finest of wines, to use no sulfur dioxide at all, to let the fermentation process end naturally."

"But that is so haphazard," Christian argued. "Sugar content varies from grape to grape—"

"So it is not possible to determine the precise sugar content of the total of the freshly crushed juice, no? And if there is too much sugar you must use sulfur dioxide to stop fermentation early. And if there is too little you must add sugar to increase alcohol content. Is this not so?"

Christian nodded silently.

"This is true," Henri said, "but there are ways around it. As the time for harvest comes around, you go into the vineyard every day with your laboratory equipment and you take hundreds of tiny juice samples from hundreds of grapes. You mix the samples together and test for average sugar content. When the sugar has reached the level you want and no more, then you harvest immediately and crush only bunches you have already sampled. In this way you can let fermentation die naturally without having to kill it with sulfur dioxide."

"That would be expensive," Christian argued. "You would produce very limited quantities."

"Very limited quantities of the finest quality," Henri said, "which you could sell for a much higher price, because the wine would have no hint of sulfur dioxide in it. There would be only the natural flavor of the grape. You do this of course, only with the finest grapes. And you must age this wine longer and more carefully. Also, do you now add yeast in the fermentation process?"

Christian shook his head. "No, we add some sugar when the alcohol content is coming out too light, and we add the sulfur dioxide when it is coming out too heavy. That is all."

Henri Le Barnot raised one eyebrow. "There is a technique, Mr. Weidener, in which the winemaker adds sulfur dioxide immediately to stop the action of the natural yeast altogether and then adds his own yeasts to better control the fermentation process."

Christian's face was expressionless. "Much has changed since I learned my trade," he said quietly.

Henri nodded. "In the winery much has changed. I shall need things here. I shall need to order special yeasts and equipment for a real chemical laboratory—much equipment, and it will cost much money. We shall also begin to think of more vats, and perhaps more room in the winery as time goes on."

Christian's lips tightened slightly as Henri wandered over to a window and stared up at the snow-covered fields. "You have fine vineyards," he said appreciatively, "as fine as any I have ever seen. You are a master vineyardist, Mister Weidener."

"The planting never changes," Christian said. "That I do as I learned from my father, and there was never a better vineyardist than he."

Henri spun about. "You know," he said, "a man with your vineyard skills, you might be able even in this climate to grow champagne grapes here—Pinot Noir and Pinot Chardonnay, perhaps."

Christian shook his head. "I experimented years ago with a French Colombard, but the crop was poor."

"It is just as well," Henri said with a hint of disdain in his voice. "French Colombard makes execrable champagne."

"I don't think we should talk now of sparkling wine," Christian said, his eyebrows flying together. "If you know what you are talking about, it would seem that we have enough to do without trying to make sparkling wine."

Henri walked over from the window and placed a hand on the bigger man's shoulder.

"You are quite right, sir," he said, "there is much to do. But these are magnificent vineyards, and I am certain I can produce fine wine here. I am honored that you brought me here from France." Then he stood on his toes and to Liam's amusement and Christian's utter shock unexpectedly planted a kiss on Christian's cheek.

"Come," Henri said, stepping back and smiling broadly, "let us go back to your house for some of that fine brandy you spoke of."

Then the little Frenchman turned and walked out the door as Christian reached up and rubbed roughly at his cheek. Liam looked at Christian, whose face was dark with consternation.

"Frenchmen," the German muttered.

* * * *

Henri Le Barnot's presence at the Weidener farm changed virtually everything about the rhythms and routines of life in the winery. Where Christian's decisions had dominated, Henri's word became law. Under the Frenchman's guidance, Liam undertook a detailed and meticulous cleaning of the fermenting vats, scrubbing them with a sulfur dioxide solution, day after day. The wine that had occupied them had already been moved to the aging vats, and Henri complained bitterly that there was little he could do, therefore, with the juice from the previous harvest.

"My real work must wait until this coming fall," he told Liam and Christian. "The damage has already been done to what was pressed."

It soon became clear that Henri and Christian would not get along. Henri was impulsive and outspoken, and he was critical of almost every aspect of Christian's winemaking process. This infuriated Christian, who kept his temper in check only because the Frenchman knew his business. He was perfectly willing to benefit from Henri's store of knowledge in the arcane art of winemaking, but he could not bring himself to like the man, and he made no real effort to do so.

"You deal with him," Christian told Liam. "I will not talk to this man."

So Liam did, learning much about winemaking in the process. Christian had already taught him the basics, but under Henri's guidance, delivered in the manner of an impatient teacher tutoring a hopeless pupil, Liam began his graduate course in winemaking.

"It will take many years before you know even the simplest things," Henri assured him. "There is so much to know, so much to understand. And, when you have learned all the technical information, there is still one more thing to learn, and that is the one thing no one can teach you. Instinct. You must develop a feel for the wine if you are to become a real winemaker. This is what distinguishes the great winemaker from one who is merely ordinary. You must know instinctively when to halt the aging. You must have the instinct to know when to let the fermentation go on a touch longer, to know how the yeast is behaving and how to help it or compensate for it. There are many, many nuances in winemaking, and they are what making truly fine wine is all about."

"How will I learn these things?"

"Perhaps you will not," Henri told him. "Christian never did."

Henri and Annette had settled into their cottage on the slopes overlooking the winery and the lake. With the exception of only a few items, the furniture Christian had bought for them was moved out to make room for the elegant pieces Henri had transported from Bordeaux. At a loss as to what to do with the furniture he had bought for the Le Barnots, and which they had rejected, Christian ordered that it go into the shack, where Hardy was still in residence while Liam did what he sworn not to do: occupy his wife's bedroom in the big house.

"I don't want all this stuff here," Hardy complained as Liam began moving in the new furniture and moving out the junk. "I got this place looking the way I like it."

"John," Liam told him, "you're going to have to start living like a human being. And you've got to stop spitting tobacco juice on the floor. If you ruin the new rug, Christian will have your hide."

Helga and Annette, meanwhile, had begun something of a friendship. It was limited by Annette's difficulty in learning English. That problem was rooted in the fact that no one on the farm spoke particularly good American English. Christian's English was heavily accented, and his occasional lapses into Germanic grammar could leave everyone confused, especially Annette. The hired help, especially Minnie and Hardy, all mangled the language on a regular basis. All this left Annette hopelessly baffled and slow to converse with anyone but Helga.

Nonetheless, they were young married women who felt a strong need to communicate on matters no one else could understand or appreciate, and before long they had begun to converse in a mixture of English, French and sign language.

Liam, meanwhile, was working six-day weeks at the winery and around the farm. On the seventh day he was up on the frozen hillside clearing the first of the two hundred acres he had bought from Christian. By late March he had chopped down a good many of the trees and, using the big workhorse, Prince, had moved them to the line separating Christian's land from his. He stacked the trees into piles for cutting into firewood and trellis poles in the spring. The problem Liam faced now was clearing the stumps of those trees when the ground was frozen. There was only one solution. As much as it disturbed him, Liam began to use dynamite.

On an otherwise quiet Sunday morning in early March of 1912, Henri Le Barnot's sleep was broken by the dull roar of dynamite from the hillside above. He came awake with a jolt. Annette, sleeping beside him, rolled over irritably and pulled the covers over her head.

"My God, what is that?" Henri demanded in French.

"I am sure I do not know," said Annette from beneath the covers. "Go back to sleep and it will go away."

Only a few minutes later, however, the winter air was split by the roar of another explosion, and Henri leaped out of bed. "There is a war going on, my love," he said, hurriedly getting into his clothes.

Henri followed the sound and found Liam high on the hill, pulling out the remains of a large oak stump with the aid of the big bay workhorse.

"Hey," Henri called out, "what are you doing? Those horrible explosions could wake up dead people."

Liam looked up from his task. "Clearing this land. Sorry about the noise, but the ground is frozen like rock, and it will be for a few more weeks, at least. I need to use dynamite."

Henri looked around at the sight of nearly a full acre of stumps sticking up from the snow-covered ground like nails in a whitewashed board.

"That's too big a job for one man," he said. "You should have help."

"I'll take help from no man on this land," Liam told him, "not until I can hire my own help with my own money. This is special land."

"What makes it so special?"

Liam said, "Because this is where the champagne grapes will be planted; the ones you were talking about your first day here."

"But Christian has said he is not interested in Champagne."

"This isn't Christian's land," Liam told him, "it's mine. On this land, it's not up to Christian. And how come you call it champagne and he calls it sparkling wine? What's the difference?"

"There is no difference," Henri said. "There are those who will not call sparkling wine champagne unless it is grown and produced in the Champagne region of France. This is very important to the French government and to many wine people in France. It is not so important to me, but Christian is very much a conservative man in matters of wine."

"And other matters as well."

Henri nodded. "I am not sure I can make good champagne here. You must know that."

Liam shrugged. "So? It's worth a try, isn't it? You know something? I've never tasted champagne."

An expression of shock spread over Henri's face. "You jest with me," he accused.

"No, I haven't—truly."

"Come with me," Henri ordered.

Liam unhooked the horse and walked him down the hill behind Henri. He left the animal tied to a tree outside the winemaker's house and went inside. The interior of the little house was a French palace, filled with delicate and lovely period furniture. Annette was in the kitchen wrapped in a thick robe, cooking. She greeted Liam with a smile and a nod, then she and Henri began conversing in rapid-fire French. Annette left the kitchen and returned a moment later with a bottle of champagne and two delicate, tulip-shaped glasses with long stems. Henri popped the cork expertly and poured each glass half full.

"Here," he said, holding one of the glasses out to Liam. "Drink."

Liam reached for the glass, but Henri said, "No. Hold it by the stem, thusly. If you hold it up here, your hand will warm the glass and warm the wine. Champagne should be drunk cold."

Liam took the fragile crystal stem in his big, horny fingers. He sipped the wine carefully, as he had been taught, then he smiled broadly.

"This is marvelous," he said. "What makes it bubble so?"

"God," Henri explained, sipping from his glass. "God made champagne. And then he showed man how to make it. But champagne is a gift from God even more special than other wines."

Liam, amused, smiled and took another sip. "God made champagne?"

"It is not a joke," Henri said solemnly. "About four hundred years ago, a monk in the Abbey of Hautvillers, near Espernay, went down into the cellar to check on his wine. He discovered that some of it had turned to champagne, which no one had ever heard of. The monk spent many years learning how to duplicate what God had done for him in that first batch of wine. Finally, he did, and many think that the champagne that now bears his name is the finest in the world. His name was Dom Perignon. Have you heard of him?"

"I'm afraid not."

Henri rolled his eyes. "Name of a name," he said in French. Then, switching back to English, he said, "My God, where have I brought myself?"

Liam laughed. "Well, what do you expect? This is the first time I've tasted champagne. It won't be the last, though."

Henri grinned. "It is magnificent. Have you had breakfast?"

"Just some coffee. I came out early to get some work done."

"Annette," Henri said. Then, in French, he told her, "Breakfast for my friend and myself." He turned to Liam and said in English, "A champagne breakfast." Henri refilled both their glasses.

Twenty minutes and two glasses later, Annette placed plates in front of them. Liam cut into his food and tasted it carefully.

"What is this?" he asked.

"A crepe," Henri explained, "with some cheese inside and a light wine sauce. My Annette's father, he is a chef for a rich man in Bordeaux."

"It's like a thin pancake."

"One could say that, but it would not be wise to say it in a good restaurant in Paris."

Liam took a sip from his freshly refilled glass. Then he said, "You know, I think we're going to get along."

"But of course," Henri laughed. "Champagne makes great friendships."

* * * *

Helga awakened in the blackness of the bedroom, coming slowly out of a dream in which her midsection had been aflame. As she awoke she realized that the sleep was gone but the pain was not. It knifed through her like hot steel.

"Liam," she called out.

He came awake instantly. "What is it?"

"I don't know. I feel a pain."

Liam struggled with the matches on the night table and finally managed to light the kerosene lamp there. In the golden lamplight, Helga's face was waxy and pale.

"Is it the child coming?" he whispered, touching her moist brow.

"No," she whispered through clenched teeth. "It can't be that. It's only March."

Helga put her hand under the cover. When she withdrew it, blood gleamed from her fingertips. "I shouldn't be bleeding down there," she said.

Liam felt a bolt of sheer terror flash through him. "Where does it hurt?"

"Here," she said, touching her body near her bulging middle. She blanched suddenly as a wave of pain passed over her again. "Liam, it really hurts. I'm afraid . . . I really am afraid that the baby is coming. Oh, God. Get Papa—please?"

Liam began pulling on his dirty work clothes. They were laying in a heap where he had dropped them after a brutally hard day on the hillside. With the softening of the ground under the ever-warming sun, he had been working at an exhausting pace.

"I'm going to get someone to go into the village to get Dr. Frazier," he said. "Don't worry. We'll have the doctor here soon."

Helga reached out to him, her fingers digging into his shirt sleeve. "Please," she said weakly, "get my fath—"

But her words were interrupted by a sharp knock at the door. Christian, without waiting for an invitation, threw open the door. He was in his trousers and an undershirt, and his feet were bare on the icy wooden floor. His face was creased with concern. "I heard sounds," he said. "Helga, are you all right?"

She struggled to sit up. She reached out for Christian, who sat on the bed next to her. "Papa, my middle hurts. I'm frightened."

Christian took her hands in his and gently pushed her back on the pillow. His gnarled hand brushed back the sweat-soaked hair that had fallen in her eyes. "There," he said softly. "There."

Liam said, "I'm going to wake Hardy and have him go for the doctor."

Christian looked up at him. With his head and eyes, he motioned for Liam to go into the hall. Liam did, and in a moment Christian followed. He quietly closed the door behind him.

"Trust no one to go for the doctor," he said in a low voice filled with alarm. "Go yourself."

Liam shook his head vigorously, the terror rising in him but accompanied now by a surge of anger. "Hardy can go. I want to be with her. She needs me."

"Hardy," Christian sneered. "He is an old man, and he is probably sleeping off a drunk even as we speak. Do you trust him with your wife's life?"

Liam's temper died as quickly as it had flared. Christian was right.

"I'll go," he said simply.

Liam took Ajax and tied the big gelding to the rear of Frazier's buggy for the return trip. The house on Iroquois Lake was fully lit when they reached it. Henri was pacing in the parlor, and Christian came downstairs when he heard the front door open and close.

"She is in very bad pain," Christian told Frazier.

"Well, let's see her," the doctor said.

All three men followed the doctor upstairs, where they found Helga in bed with Annette bathing her brow with a cold towel. Frazier knelt next to Helga, put his hand on her middle through the sheet and another on her forehead. He looked at her carefully and took her pulse with his pocketwatch. He opened his bag and pulled out a stethoscope and some other, more esoteric instruments. Then he turned to the crowd gathered at the bedside.

"I'm going to have to go up under this nightgown," the doctor said. "I think you men should leave."

"Is it the baby?" Christian demanded, making no move to leave.

Frazier turned around, and his face was stern. "I think so. If it is, it's coming too damned early. Now you men get the hell out of here. I want

Mrs. Le Barnot to help." He turned to Annette. "Put on a big pot of water and boil it. I want to sterilize my instruments."

Annette, uncomprehending, shook her head, but Henri rattled off the instructions in French. She nodded and ran off downstairs.

"Now everybody get out," Frazier said. He turned to Helga, and in gentler tones, said, "You're in good hands, Helga. I've delivered more babies than any other doctor in the lake country."

Liam, Christian and Henri went downstairs. They settled into the chairs and sat, saying nothing, for a few moments. Then Henri said, "He seems like a good doctor, this man."

"He is, Liam said. "He's taken care of me for everything from a broken hand to a kick in the head."

"This is not a kick in the head," Christian snarled.

Liam looked over at his father-in-law and was startled to see on his face an expression that combined anger, fear and even traces of hatred.

"Christian, we're all afraid . . .," Liam began, but then he let his voice trail off. This was not time to argue. Christian, he knew, was half mad with fear.

Christian turned his face toward the fireplace and maintained complete silence for several hours as Annette ran up and down the stairs at Dr. Frazier's bidding. Finally, as the sky outside began to lighten with the bright rays of dawn, Frazier appeared on the landing overlooking the parlor. Christian, Liam and Henri rose as a group as the physician came down the stairs, his back bent in weariness and his face drawn. His bag was in his hand. A piece of blood-stained white towel stuck out its top. The bag was too full to be closed properly.

Christian's face was white, bloodless. "Is she . . .?"

Frazier put down the bag next to the fireplace and laid a hand on Christian's shoulder. "Helga's fine, Christian."

Liam saw Christian suddenly go limp, as though all his bones had dissolved. The older man sank back into his chair, his face buried in his hands. *"Danke Gott,"* he said.

"The child?" Liam whispered.

Jim Frazier turned to Liam, his expression grave. He motioned toward his medical bag, and Liam understood instantly.

"The child lived for only a few moments, Liam," Frazier said gently. "It was far too early in the pregnancy."

Liam felt a surge of dizziness hit him. He walked over to the fireplace. He put his arms on the mantel and his face into his arms, and he stood there for a moment, gathering his thoughts, fighting the swirling in his head and the growing pit of sorrow in his middle. Henri came up behind him. "I am sorry for you, my friend," he told Liam.

"Maybe the child had something wrong with it," the physician said. "Maybe if it had gone to term it would have been an idiot or a cripple or blind. These things are generally blessings in disguise, Liam, although it's hard to believe that now, I know."

"At least Helga is all right," Christian said from his chair, "that is what is important."

"Was it a boy or a girl?" Liam demanded.

"It makes no difference," Christian said.

But Frazier, looking into Liam's face, knew it did. "It was a boy, Liam."

Liam moaned softly. "A son . . ."

"One more thing," the doctor said, staring into the fire Liam had built during the period of silent waiting. "In my judgment, you should think very carefully about permitting Helga to become pregnant again."

The full impact of those words took a moment to register on Liam.

"Why?" he demanded. "What are you saying?"

Frazier sat down in a chair near the fire. He was exhausted. "She's not built right for childbearing. Her pelvic girdle is too small. It's possible that it contributed to this miscarriage. I can't say for sure. But I can tell you this: I don't think she could have carried that child to term in any event. The pressure of an infant near full term would be terribly painful for her, and the bone structure surrounding her birth canal would make a normal birth virtually impossible."

Liam shook his head in disbelief. "This can't be. Helga is a big girl . . ."

"Not down there, she's not," the doctor said. "She's like a child in her pelvic structure."

"Can't she have a baby if you give her an operation and take it?"

But then Christian was up and out of his chair, looming over them. "No one will cut into my Helga," he said.

Liam jumped to his feet, and the two big men were nose to nose. "She's my Helga, too, and we want a baby together."

"Do you want to kill her?" Christian demanded.

Liam shook his head in exasperation. "What a foolish thing to say, Christian."

"I watched her mother die giving birth to her. We had been warned, too, but we took the chance. I traded my wife for a child. I will not trade my daughter for a grandchild. I will not permit it."

"There'll be no such trade," Liam shot back hotly, "and it's not your decision, Christian. It's ours—Helga's and mine."

"You live on my land," Christian thundered, "under my roof."

Liam was dangerously close now to losing all control. "Then we'll leave your goddamned roof and your farm," he bellowed. "I'll not have you or anyone else tell me that there'll be no Brennan sons on American soil."

They might even have come to blows had not the doctor leaped from his chair and come between them at that instant. He put a calming hand on one shoulder of each man.

"Gentlemen, please," the physician said. "Your wife—and your daughter, Christian—is lying upstairs after a terrible ordeal. I've sedated her, but you'll wake her up with this kind of shouting. This has been a difficult and emotional night, and it's not the best time to discuss the future. What's important now is Helga's recovery, and she'll need both of you to help her."

Liam spun on his heel, turned and stalked to the other side of the room. Christian took a deep breath and said, "Of course. I must apologize. Jim, you must stay with us for breakfast."

"I wish I could, but I have other patients to worry about, and they have to be able to reach me. The youngest Wright girl is expecting any day now, and so is John Coughlin's wife. And it'll be her fifth, so it'll come fast."

"Then I'll have John Hardy drive you home. You can sleep in the buggy. He can sleep in your barn for a few hours and then hitch a ride back."

Frazier shook his head. "Don't worry yourself about it, Christian. You have problems enough of your own. Besides, I'd be afraid that if John Hardy slept in my barn the cow wouldn't give milk for a week. I'll get home all right. Even if I go to sleep, the horse knows the way."

The doctor began to pull on his heavy coat, and from across the room Liam said, "Doctor, you could take a baby if it came to that, couldn't you?"

Frazier buttoned the old, frayed, woolen greatcoat, the veteran of many night calls in the winter. "It could be done, Liam. She'd have to go into the hospital down in Boydstown, and that's sixty miles away. And even with all the drugs we have now, there'd always be the danger of infection after the surgery. Some doctors like to cut people open for just about anything, but I'm sort of old-fashioned that way. I say don't operate on anybody unless you absolutely have to, to save their life. But, yes, she could have a child that way. As to whether I'd recommend it . . ., well, maybe one of those Boydstown doctors would. I'd have to give it a lot of thought."

The doctor put on his derby and picked up his bag. "I'd say it's a decision you should think about carefully. But not tonight. Or, this morning, rather."

Christian glared at Liam. "We will not talk of this now," he ordered.

Liam met Christian's gaze with a glare of his own. "All right. We'll not talk of it now. The doctor is right there. But we'll think of it, sure enough."

Then, as Dr. Frazier said his goodbyes to Henri and an exhausted Annette, Liam walked slowly upstairs, feeling Christian's eyes boring holes in his back. He entered the bedroom to find Helga asleep in the dim light of the single kerosene lamp. Liam pulled a chair close to her bed and looked down at her. Her face was peaceful but sallow. Her breathing was even. Good God, he thought, what she's been through this night. He took one of her cold hands in his, and Helga stirred. She mumbled. Liam leaned close to her, brushed back her hair and kissed her chilled and still-moist forehead.

Helga mumbled again, her eyes still closed, her head rocking slowly from side to side. "Papa," she said in a whisper. "I hurt."

Liam's eyes filled with tears. They welled up, blinding him, but they did not roll down his cheeks. They clung to his eyes, blurring the world for him, burning. He reached down and cradled Helga's head in his arms.

"Hush, Darlin'. Hush, now. I'm here. I'm here."

"Papa . . .," Helga mumbled.

"Yes, Darlin'," Liam said, his voice choked, "it's Papa here to care for you. Now sleep. Go to sleep."

And she did.

Chapter 7

Minnie and Annette babied Helga shamelessly, and they fed her so well that within a few days she was complaining that she soon would have to borrow from Minnie's wardrobe.

What Helga needed most was sleep, and Liam moved back to the shack so she could rest undisturbed. He spent hours at her bedside, reading to her and holding her when she wept, which was often. Dr. Frazier had warned that it would be weeks, perhaps longer, before her normal emotional state reasserted itself.

Christian, too, spent considerable time at Helga's bedside, but never when Liam was there. The two men avoided one another whenever possible, and their brief business conversations were barely civil. Liam felt certain that the wall erected between them the night Helga lost the baby was there to stay.

Liam also suspected that between Helga and Christian were ties he couldn't properly appreciate. Christian had married off his daughter, but he had not even begun to let her go. He seemed to feel as strong a proprietary interest in her as ever, and he felt that his status as father outweighed Liam's far more recent role as husband. This seemed especially true now, when the reason for the sudden marriage had ceased to exist.

The situation was helped not at all, Liam realized, by the fact that Liam and Helga had continued to share Christian's home instead of starting one of their own. He resolved to tell her, when her health had improved, that she faced a choice—to move into the village with him or stay at the farm while he moved himself. But even as he considered giving her such an ultimatum, he rejected it. He was not prepared to have his bluff called.

Thus, the problem with Christian defied Liam's ability and will to resolve it. Christian certainly would not decide whether Liam and Helga would try to have more children. That, Liam believed deeply, was a matter between him and his wife.

These thoughts were in Liam's mind constantly, yet it never occurred to him to share them with Henri, who had become a close friend, or Hardy, with whom he was now living and for whom he had come to feel great affection. Liam often envied Helga her capacity to share her intimate thoughts with close friends like Annette. The realization that Helga had confidantes and that he was instinctively unwilling to reveal his own doubts and fears to another man, especially one whose esteem he valued, made Liam suspect that there somehow was a flaw in the male nature.

Before the miscarriage Liam had once asked Helga, "Do you tell Annette everything?"

"Not everything, no. But most things."

"Why do you need to talk to her at all when you have me to talk to now?"

Helga had laughed. "Don't be foolish, Liam. I couldn't talk to you the way I talk to Annette, even though we have such a hard time communicating."

"Why not?"

"You're a man," she explained.

Liam had shaken his head in mystification. "Does Annette tell you everything?"

"Of course she does."

He had no such sounding board for the immense grief he felt over the death of his son. That's how he thought of the tiny, lifeless, bloody creature that Dr. Frazier had carried from the big house that dawn in his medical bag. God knew what had happened to it. Liam tried not to think about that.

From the moment Helga had announced her pregnancy, Liam had been convinced she was carrying a son. The thought had warmed him and spurred his maniacal efforts in clearing the forest above the house to build a legacy and a livelihood for his unborn son. Once it was clear that Helga would survive the miscarriage, he had found himself almost overcome with grief and anger at the loss of the child. That was responsible for much of his resentment toward Christian, who seemed to view the miscarriage as a blessing because it had saved Helga from the ordeal of childbirth and because it now provided him with a reason why she should never give birth.

Liam's mind was awash with anger, grief and self-pity. The only thing that could sufficiently relieve his sense of loss would be a new child to take the place of the one who had been lost to him.

One night, in the shack with Hardy, Liam said, "John, you told me once that you were married and that your wife's still alive. Can you tell me, what went wrong?"

Hardy's eyebrows raised as he stared at the flames in the open stove and pondered the question. "It's hard to remember, it was so long ago. I guess it was Nancy's mother that done it."

"Nancy was your wife?"

"Nancy is my wife," Hardy corrected. "Still is. We never got no divorce. She'll be my wife 'til one of us dies, and I guess that ain't far off now. I'm past seventy now, and Nancy's damn near as old. Pretty soon now, one of us is going to be free of the other."

The old man was silent for a long moment. Then he said, smiling, "She was a pretty little thing. Looked like a little bunny rabbit—all big brown eyes and white teeth. Don't know which shined more—them eyes or the teeth when she smiled. I married her when I was just past twenty and she was just fifteen, and I left her when I was past thirty, I guess. Haven't seen her twice in more than forty years."

"What could make a man stay married for fifty years and not see his wife for forty of them?" Liam asked.

"I told you," Hardy said. "It was her mother. After we got married, we moved in with her ma. Nancy's mother—now, there was a woman for you. Big, she was, like an elk—tall, rangy, mean eyes. She could give you a look that would make milk go sour."

"Is she dead now?"

"Just barely," Hardy said. "Didn't die 'til about three years ago, old as hell. Kept living on out of sheer meanness. Nancy agreed with her mother on everything. So I just up and left one day. The hell with both of 'em, I said."

"Any children?"

"Four. Two boys, two girls."

Liam puffed thoughtfully on his pipe. Then he said softly, "John, how could you leave your children?"

Hardy looked over at Liam. The light of the fire inside the stove danced in the old man's eyes.

"Well," he said slowly, "they didn't think nothing much of me. Heard their mother and grandmother saying day after day what a no-account I was. They started to think that way, too. One day my son Horace—he was troublesome, Horace—he busted up a fly rod I had, and I was whipping him for it. I must have told him a hundred times to keep his hands off that fly rod. I was giving it to him with my belt across his backside when Nancy and her mother come out in the yard and started beating me with pots and pans and brooms and calling me a drunk and all. And I hadn't had nothing to drink that day. Not a drop. So I just up and walked out. Never regretted it for a second, neither." Hardy looked back into the fire, remembering. "A man's got a right to some respect in his own house, even if it ain't his own house, if you know what I mean."

"Where are they now?" Liam asked.

Hardy pulled on the bottle again. "Well, Nancy, she's still in the same house we lived in with her ma. Big white house across from the courthouse, with a picket fence around the yard. My sons and daughters are all grown. Beverly lives on a little farm down near Boydstown, married to a railroad clerk. Florence lives in Lakeside with her mother. She never got married. She's got to be in her forties now, an old maid. James got himself killed in Cuba, back in '98. That was the only time I was ever in that house again, for his wake and funeral."

"How about Horace?"

"Oh, Horace lives just outside Lakeside. He's got a nice farm over on the other side of the lake. Not as big as this one, but a real nice place. Good vineyards. Got sort of a pretty wife and a bunch of kids. Very respectable fellow, Horace. Came as something of a surprise to me, I'll tell you. He sure was a hellion as a youngster."

"And except for the funeral of the other son, you've never seen any of them since you left?"

Hardy pulled on his bottle and when he answered his words were beginning to slur.

"Well," he said thickly, "that ain't quite right. I'd go back once in a while and look in on them when they was growing up. Never let them see me, though. I'd just sit on the courthouse steps, watching them from a distance playing in the yard, swinging on the swing I built and hung from a big horse chestnut tree. Stuff like that. I'd see them, though."

"Why didn't you go over and talk to them?"

"They didn't want me to," Hardy said, his voice growing hoarse as he spoke. "They wanted me to leave them be, and that was fine. I just wanted to see them now and again, that's all."

Without warning, Hardy suddenly started to sob. Tears streamed down his stubbled cheeks like a waterfall. "I used to think," he choked out, "they're so goddamn beautiful. How did living things like that come out of something like me?"

"John . . .," Liam said, profoundly uncomfortable.

Hardy wiped at his eyes with a filthy sleeve. "Horace don't even know me today—what I look like now. When he sees me in town, he just figures I'm one of the old drunks you see down near the courthouse, all retired and sitting there all day with nothing to do. Sometimes when I see him in town, I just follow after him, careful-like, so he don't see me, and I watch him. He's a tall man, Liam, taller than you, even. There's nothing like a son, Liam, goddamn it. Having a son is like having a second chance in life. A son can be what you wished you could have been. That's what James was to me—a hero like I would have liked to have been. That's what Horace is to me, even though he don't know it— even though he don't even know me when he sees me."

Hardy wept for a long time after that, and finally Liam stood up and went over to the old man. He put his arm around Hardy and pulled him to his feet. The old man was no heavier than a bag of dry leaves. "You've had too much to drink, John," Liam said. "You should get some sleep now."

In only a few moments John Hardy was in deep slumber. His snoring came hard and loud. Liam, in his own bunk on the other side of the room, lay in darkness, deep in thought.

"A son," Hardy had said. "There's nothing like a son."

The next morning, Liam rekindled the fire, bundled himself up against the morning cold, left the shack and ran up the hill. He burst through the back door and into the kitchen. Minnie was at work over the stove.

"Hang up your coat and sit down," she told him. "Now that you're finally up, I'll start Helga's breakfast. You sit down and have a nice cup of coffee, and her food'll be fixed so's you can take it up to her in a few minutes."

Liam kept his coat on. "I'll just take a quick cup of coffee down to John Hardy first. He had a rough night."

Minnie frowned in disapproval. "Let me guess why. I'll put some cream and sugar in it. Two lumps. That's the way he likes it."

Liam took the steaming mug down the slope and entered the shack. The fire in the wood stove had already raised the temperature inside the building to the point where it was bearable. Liam warmed his hands at the stove for a moment, then he put the cup on top of it and went over to wake Hardy.

"Wake up with you now, John," he said, shaking the old man. He drew back his hands and froze. For a long moment, he was motionless. Slowly, his heart pounding, he put a finger to the old man's cheek. It was, as he had known it would be, as cold as stone.

When he climbed the hill again and entered the kitchen, he was as pale as marble.

"What's the matter with you?" Minnie said in alarm. "Are you sick?"

Liam slumped in the chair at the kitchen table and stared ahead of him blankly.

"John Hardy's dead," he said. "He died in his sleep."

Minnie raised a hamlike fist to her mouth, and for the briefest of seconds her eyes grew large. Then she bit her lower lip and quickly poured a mug of coffee for Liam and one for herself. She sat down at the table across from him.

"Here," she said softly. "Drink some coffee."

Liam buried his face in his hands and breathed deeply.

"Don't grieve like that, Liam," she told him. "John Hardy has been dead since before you were born."

"Minnie, he had a wife and children, all grown up."

Minnie nodded. "A wife in Lakeside, and a daughter living with her and another daughter living down near Boydstown. And Horace, the farmer."

Liam looked at Minnie for a long moment. She knew he was looking, and she said nothing. Then she turned and met his gaze evenly. "I wasn't always old and fat," she said, "and he wasn't always what he was when you came here. And it was all a long time ago. Take him to his wife, Liam. He's always belonged to her."

Liam left the kitchen without another word. He went into the barn and hitched Prince to the farm wagon, drove the wagon down the path to the road and parked it beside the shack. Then he went inside, wrapped John Hardy in his blanket and carried him up the wagon. He arranged the blanket from the bunk to hide the body, then he went inside to gather Hardy's meager personal posessions.

In the bottom drawer of the dresser, he found a box of old photographs. There was a formal portrait of an incredibly young John Hardy in a suit and high collar standing behind a seated young woman and four young children. There also was an old and faded photo of Minnie, badly frayed at the edges. Liam studied it. Clearly she had not always been old and fat. That photograph would stay here.

Finding the big white house across from the courthouse was not difficult. Liam pulled Prince to a halt in front of the house. He got down and walked up on the front porch. He knocked on the door, and in a moment an elderly woman opened it. She wore rimless glasses, and her gray hair was pulled back severely.

"Nancy Hardy?" he asked.

"Yes."

"My name is Liam Brennan. I'm from the Weidener Farm. I . . . I have your husband's body in that wagon out there. He died last night, in his sleep."

Nancy Hardy's pinched face remained expressionless. Her eyes dropped for just a moment, then she looked up at Liam. She came out on the porch into the bitter cold wearing only her house dress and an apron, and she walked out to the wagon with Liam following behind. Nancy

Hardy pulled back the blanket and stared impassively at John Hardy's face for a long time, perhaps a minute or more.

"Mother?" came a voice from the doorway of the house. "What is it?"

Liam turned and saw a middle-aged woman there, a younger version of the mother, right down to the rimless spectacles.

"It's your father," Nancy Hardy said, not looking up and almost to herself. "He died last night."

Florence Hardy gasped and disappeared instantly from the doorway. Her mother turned to Liam. "Please take him to the McMartin Funeral Home. That's down to the end of this street and around the corner, two squares down."

"I know where it is."

"Good. Tell Mr. McMartin I'll be along directly, as soon as I'm dressed properly."

"Yes, Ma'am."

"Thank you, Mr. . . ."

"Brennan, Ma'am. John was my friend."

"Mr. Brennan. Thank you for bringing John home."

Liam debated the matter in his mind for only a moment, then he said, "He spoke of you last night, Ma'am. It was the last thing he spoke of before he died."

She turned away. "Please, don't tell me about it."

Then, without another word, Nancy Hardy walked stiffly back into her house and closed the door behind her.

* * * *

Baddington delivered the *vinifera* cuttings four days later. They arrived in wooden crates, swaddled in dirt from France. Liam examined them and was disappointed. "They don't look so special. They look no different than the *labrusca* vines."

"They are different," Henri assured him. "If *vinifera* of these varieties take to our native root stock, even you will taste the difference in the wine they produce." He looked at one dry cutting closely. "If they take. That is the question."

The arrival of the cuttings and the coming of warm weather meant a dramatic increase in the farm's volume of work. The heavy work on any farm is largely confined to warm weather, but this was especially true of the Weidener farm, where grapes had become more and more of a major cash crop.

With Hardy gone, someone also had to take over his role as a procurer of meat for the farm. So Liam took over John Hardy's chores as fisherman and hunter. He would be on the lake virtually every morning fishing for trout for the table, and he shot a deer in early May when he found that the graceful animals had invaded his new vineyards high on the hillside. Liam had stood alone in the vineyard, over the corpse of the doe he had shot, and said, "You'll not feed from these vineyards. If I have to kill every blessed deer in the lake country, you'll not ruin these grapes."

Henri became Liam's frequent companion on the fishing trips on the lake and on fly-fishing expeditions later in the day to the streams that ran down the hillside to the lake. There they would take brook trout and small rainbows. Henri could not, however, develop a taste for the killing and butchering of deer. Despite that, the two men were together much of every work day, caring for the new *vinifera* vines and working in the winery, bottling the wine from last fall's pressing.

Christian grew more and more distant from them both. He left the business of the new vineyards and the winery to the two of them. Instead, he concentrated on the business aspects of distributing his production, his dairy farming and his other crops. He withdrew totally from the business of winemaking, leaving that strictly in Henri's hands. He oversaw the maintenance of his own vineyards, but he steadfastly refused to ask for Liam's help in that task. Liam noted also that the older man really had no need of that help. Liam often wandered through Christian's vineyards and compared them to his own, and he found that Christian's were invariably neater, that his plants grew better and stronger, than his overall management of his vineyards was still superior to Liam's. From that, Liam concluded that Christian had not taught him everything.

Only once did Liam go to Christian for help. In one section of his vineyard, the new vines from Europe grafted on native American vines simply were not doing well, and he couldn't figure out why. He sought out Christian in the fields one afternoon, swallowed his pride and asked his father-in-law's advice.

"It's the soil there," Christian told him. "It won't support that particular variety. The root stock you selected is too delicate."

"What can I do? How can I grow those grapes in that soil?"

"Perhaps you cannot," Christian said.

Liam was infuriated by Christian's attitude. The older man seemed to take pleasure in Liam's misfortune, and Liam turned without another word and walked away, angry at himself for making himself vulnerable to Christian's scorn.

"You could try pulling out the root stock and replacing it," Christian called after him.

Liam turned around. "What do you mean replacing it?"

Christian shrugged. "Your root stock is Niagara. If it is not taking well to the soil there, pull it out and replace it with another variety of *labrusca*—Concord, perhaps. That is the definitive variety of *labrusca*. Then remove the grafts you have put on the Niagara vines and graft them onto the Concord. That might work."

Liam eyed him carefully. "I'll try it."

Christian's idea worked, and Henri was much impressed.

"Christian is a grower," he told Liam. "He is a fine grower, and I envy him that talent."

"And he envies you yours," Liam said. "That's why you can never be close."

"And what does he envy in you?" Henri demanded. "Why cannot you and he be close."

Liam shook his head. "Helga," he said simply. "He'll never forgive me for taking Helga away from him. That wouldn't bother me so much, I suppose, if I really had her. As it is, she's at least as much his as mine. More, these days."

Henri didn't press the matter, and Liam didn't elaborate. He and Henri talked of many things: their work, the art of fishing, the state of the world as the presidential election of 1912 rolled around. They never, however, talked about Helga and the way she seemed to have changed recently. She was still warm toward Annette, and she was always polite and friendly toward Henri. As her health returned, however, she began going into the village more often or simply riding Ajax by herself for long hours. Although Annette and Helga were still friendly and Liam and Henri were fast friends, the social combination of Liam and Helga and Henri and Annette had faded.

The relationship between Liam and Helga had grown strained, and as the summer drew to a close and the farm prepared for the harvest, Liam was acutely aware that he and Helga had not made love since her miscarriage nearly six months before. She was pleasant toward him. When he had cleaned up the shack she had moved into it with him, but she repulsed his every advance, leaving him wounded and baffled.

He kept all this to himself. But it made him utterly miserable. After so many months of stoic silence he finally turned to Henri late one afternoon as they worked in the winery, sampling some of the wines, and said, "How long have you been married now, Henri?"

Henri sensed that his friend was troubled. He set aside his glass. "Four years," he replied.

"Are you happy?"

Henri shrugged expansively. "Who would not be happy with my Annette? She is a saint, a treasure beyond price."

"Then why no children?"

"Perhaps God meant for me to create only the wine. If so, then I will create the finest wine that can be made, and that wine will be my children."

Liam groped to express his thoughts. "Do you and Annette . . ., well, have you tried to have children? Forgive me if I'm asking something that's none of my business. Just tell me to be quiet."

Henri laughed. "I have no secrets—not from you, my friend. This you must know by now. Are you asking if Annette and I make love? My friend, what a question to ask a Frenchman."

"And still no children?"

Henri shook his head sadly. "No, and I am sure we are doing it correctly."

"Henri," Liam said suddenly, "You're my friend, you know, my best friend."

"And you are a friend to me," Henri said, touched. "I have no others in this country—certainly not that Hun of a father-in-law you have."

"The doctor," Liam began, "he said that Helga . . ."

"Should have no children. I know. Annette has told me."

Liam's eyebrows raised. "Annette?"

"Women are not like men, my friend, They tell one another everything. And it is a good thing, too. Otherwise we men would find out nothing."

"Henri, I don't know what to do. How can I live with a woman without . . .," Liam's voice trailed off.

Henri shook his head in sympathy. "I do not know. It is a terrible problem." He took down a bottle of wine and filled glasses for them both. "Perhaps some wine will make it seem less serious."

"I'm afraid to go near her. She's so lovely, and I'm afraid I won't be able to keep from . . ."

"My friend, you are upset. Do you know how I can tell? You cannot finish a thought. Or perhaps that is just your Irish shyness, speaking of matters so intimate. Have no fear of confiding in me. Your words will go nowhere."

"Not even to Annette?" Liam asked.

Henri sat back in his chair and sipped from his glass. "I will tell you what my father told me. He said that a wise man encourages his wife to tell him everything. He, in turn, tells her nothing except that she is the joy of his life. The women love to talk, and that is all they really want to hear from us, in any case."

"I'm miserable, Henri," Liam admitted.

"As I would be in your place. God has given you a great burden to bear."

They talked and drank for several more hours, all thought of work dismissed. Henri talked of his boyhood in Bordeaux—of the jolly, vibrant, elfin creature who was his mother. She was a woman, Liam realized as he heard Henri speak of her, who must have been a precise duplicate of Annette.

Liam talked, too, about his own family and life in Labasheeda. When he told Henri the circumstances surrounding his flight from Ireland, Henri was shocked. "You killed a man?" he said.

Liam nodded. "It was the drink. I've written letters home for years, and I've asked them how the big lord's sons were after we fought. But in none of the letters I've received back from home have they answered that question. To me, that's answer enough."

They drank and talked until the shadows in the winery had grown so deep that they could hardly see one another across the table. They were about to leave when Annette came storming into the building. In a stream of angry French, she berated Henri for sitting there drinking and missing dinner. Henri tried to stiffly maintain his dignity throughout the exchange, but he was swaying on his feet, and it was a lost cause. He apologized vigorously as Annette stalked out of the winery. Henri shrugged to Liam and followed after her, weaving dangerously.

Liam finally rose unsteadily and made his way out to the road. It was a moonless, starless evening. He came lurching into the doorway of the shack to find Helga sitting in the wicker rocking chair on the far side of the sitting room, reading. She glared at him as he staggered in.

"Good evening to ye, wife," Liam said, his brogue as thick as it had been the day he had stepped off the boat in New York. "Have you food for your husband, who's been slaving away in the winery 'til this late hour?"

Helga turned her eyes back to her Jane Austen novel. "You were drinking at the winery," she said coldly. "You can hardly stand up. You stink of wine, Liam."

"If I stink of wine," he said slowly, "then it's a fine smell, because it blots out the stench of sorrow."

"Sorrow?" Helga said, leaping up and snapping the book shut. "You're the cause of all the sorrow around here. I wish I'd never seen you. My father was right from the start. You're a nothing and a nobody."

When Liam answered, his voice was low. It contained a note Helga didn't recognize.

"I am what I am," he told her evenly, "and I have no shame in it. At least I'm a man in my own right, not tied to the apron strings of a parent."

She reddened then, and her voice rose. "You're no man," she told him, her face a sneer. "You're not one-tenth the man my father is, and you never will be. You spend all your time up on that hillside, trying to match your vineyards with his. You can't even plow a field properly. I've heard him say it."

A flash of red erupted in Liam's head, back behind his eyes. He felt the blood rush into his face, making it red and hot. He crossed the room in two long strides and grabbed her wrists firmly. Helga looked up at him with an expression that combined surprise, rage and fear.

"I know one field I can plow," he told her. "It's lain fallow long enough."

He bent down and swept her up in his arms. Helga was tall for a woman, and solidly built, but Liam was a big man in his prime and hardened from years of demanding physical work. She was no more than a toy in his hands, and her struggles might have been those of an infant. He carried her into the little bedroom and threw her roughly on the bed. Helga struggled to get up, but he pushed her down and pinned her to the covers. For a long moment neither of them moved. Then Liam freed one of her wrists, and he took his hand and wrapped his fingers gently in her blonde hair. She shook her head, trying to dislodge his hand. Then he bent down over her and brushed his lips across her cheek. His other hand went to the back of her neck, stroking it, kneading it gently. It had been many months, but he recognized its meaning when he felt Helga suddenly draw in her breath sharply. Liam dropped a hand to her breast. She looked up at him. "You bastard," she whispered.

Then she wrapped her arms around his neck and pulled him down on top of her.

Despite Liam's need, they found themselves making slow and deliciously leisurely love. It was marked by gentle caresses, sighs and soft groans in the darkness. Liam's hard hands were as soft on her flesh as breath. Their hips undulated in a slow-motion dance as they sank more deeply into one another. When the urgency came upon them both, their pace quickened to a frenzy. They called one another's name until the sounds became unintelligible cries of mutual need. They ended almost precisely together, Helga driving her pelvis against Liam, bearing down on him and searing his skin as life surged out of him into her in thick, liquid ribbons. It seemed to Liam that it would go on forever, until he was empty forevermore. Then, clutching one another as the waves lapped at the slate shore of the point, they slept.

In the morning, Liam awoke to sunlight streaming in the front windows. He turned and looked at Helga beside him, her golden hair spread like newly cut wheat over the linen pillowcase. He bent over and nuzzled her neck. He could feel her stir. "Helga . . .," he said.

Then she was up and out of bed, giving him the briefest flash of her naked form as she grabbed the blanket and wrapped herself in it. She stalked from the little bedroom without a word. Liam was up after her immediately, as bare as on the day of his birth. He caught her in the sitting room and spun her about. He tried to hold her close, but Helga pulled away roughly.

"No more, Liam," she said. "Never again. Never."

She ran into the kitchen, and he could hear the sound of her noisy weeping through the doorway. For only a moment, Liam considered running in after her. But he knew from her manner that the effort would be doomed to failure. He turned and went back into the bedroom and began to gather up his clothes.

Nothing has changed, Liam told himself. Not a blessed thing has changed.

* * * *

It was six weeks later that Liam, working in the vineyard, saw Christian storm out of the back door of the big house and start up the hillside toward him.

Liam continued his work. He was examining the bulging green berries of his crop, the bunches of grapes growing fat on the vines. He examined them and caressed them with affection. This first crop of *vinifera* grapes would be exceptionally fine. Now, if Henri could make good on his boasts—if he could make wine from these grapes even a fraction as good as that produced in Europe—the winery would take a huge leap forward. Liam looked with satisfaction at the round bunches. The crop was growing well. Until harvest, he could do no more.

He heard Christian's footsteps in the loose soil behind him, and he turned toward the older man. Christian's face was a startling purple, and his brow was deeply furrowed. It took Liam a moment before he realized that Christian's expression and color were the signs of a fierce rage, the worst Liam had ever seen in his father-in-law. But by the time he had become aware of Christian's frame of mind, a hard punch had been unleashed at Liam's face.

Liam responded purely on instinct. That afternoon in Christian's study when the big German had knocked him all the way across the room was a vivid memory, burned into Liam's brain forever. This time when the blow came, he was ready. He stepped into it, as he had done fully half a hundred other times on the railroad, and he threw up his left arm at the same time. His block rendered Christian's blow harmless. At the same time, Liam threw a punch of his own. He put his weight behind it, and he delivered it with velocity. Liam's fist caught Christian squarely in the midsection. He felt it drive in deep, forcing the older man's breath from him like a bellows. Christian grunted and crumpled to his knees. Liam leaped back, his fists clenched and ready.

"You're a madman, Christian," he roared at the figure on the ground choking for breath. "You're insane, is what you are. Why would you go and jump me like that?"

Christian coughed and gasped for air. Liam, calmer now, took a deep breath of his own and reached down to help him to his feet. Christian waved him away and knelt for a moment, his face almost blue. Then he choked out, "You've killed Helga. She'll die because of you, you son of a bitch."

"What are you talking about, man? Have you gone daft?"

Christian sank down to a sitting position. As he rested there in the dirt, skin pale and his grayish-blond hair awry, he seemed smaller and older than Liam had ever seen him. He felt a sudden surge of guilt at having struck the older man, a sensation that vanished with Christian's next words. "You bastard," he muttered. "She is with child again. She told me how you forced her, raped her, may you rot in hell."

For a moment, Liam was too stunned to move. He simply stood there, jaw agape. Then the impact of his father-in-law's words sank in on him, and Liam turned, leaving Christian sitting in the dirt, and walked down the hill toward the big house. Halfway down, he began to run. He stormed up the back porch steps and inside. Liam found her sitting by the fireplace, her eyes red and damp with tears. "Is this true?" he asked her.

Helga's eyes were alight with pure hate. "Yes, it's true. You know it's true. Where's Papa?"

"Up on the hill, in the vineyard. He's all right. Why didn't you tell me first?"

"Tell you?" she said, bursting anew into tears. "Why? So you could rejoice in what you've done to me?"

Liam dropped to his knees beside her. As always when he came in from the fields and found himself close to her with her pink blondeness and crisp, clean-smelling clothing, Liam felt crude and dirty. Now, under these circumstances, the sensation was even more pronounced. He put one soiled hand over her clean one, and she pulled her hand free as though she had been caressed by a snake.

"It's cause for rejoicing," he told her, "for both of us. Helga, you mustn't let your fears rob you of the joy of producing a child. There's no reason to fear. There are fine doctors in the hospital in Boydstown. They'll care for you properly."

Helga sprang up and ran across the room. She whirled toward Liam.

Her face was contorted with fear and outrage. "I'll die, Liam," she shrieked at him. "This will kill me, like it killed my own mother. And it's your fault. If you'd just let me alone . . ."

"I couldn't. I love you too much. And I love the baby we have coming. I want you to love it, too."

"I hope it dies," she shouted at him. Then, to his shock, she began beating herself in the midsection with her clenched fists. Liam's eyes grew wide with alarm. He leaped at her, grabbing her wrists in his big hands.

"Let me go!" she shrilled at him. "I want to kill it before it can kill me."

Liam wrestled her gently but firmly into a chair, tightening his grip on her wrists until she stopped resisting. "Stop this!" he ordered sharply. "You can't do this."

Helga relaxed then. She sank back into the chair, sobbing uncontrollably. "All right," she said through her tears. "Let me go. I won't kill it. I don't have the courage."

He released her and stepped back, looking down at her. Helga glared up at him, and the naked hatred in her eyes was so intense that he was forced to turn away from it. "But it's over between us, Liam Brennan," she said quietly. "You leave this farm. You leave today."

Liam was silent for a long moment. Then, slowly, he shook his head. "I'll not leave now, Darlin'," he told her. "You can't drive me away while you're carrying this child. No power on earth could make me go now."

"My father can make you go," she hissed at him.

"No," Liam said calmly. "He has no power over me. I own a part of this place, and I own you, too. You're my wife, not his. And I'll not tolerate another attack on me. I'll defend myself. You tell him that, although I suspect he knows it already."

"Then live here," she said, "but live alone. I'm moving back into this house, to my old bed, and I'll sleep in it alone. This marriage is finished."

"You'll feel differently when you feel the life moving inside you," he finally said. It was weak and lame, and he knew it.

"I'll never feel differently, about you or this child. If it's born alive, I want you to take it with you and go away forever. I don't want you, and I don't want your child."

Liam felt himself go limp then, as though all the bones in his body had dissolved under the weight of her attack. He was suddenly bone weary, as tired as he had ever been. "As you will," he said to her.

"Go away, Liam," she told him. "Leave me alone."

Liam turned and dragged himself toward the door. As he did, he saw Christian standing there. Christian, clearly, had heard it all. The older man was dirty from the fields, and his face was still deathly pale from the blow he had absorbed. He stepped aside to permit Liam to leave the parlor, and Liam dragged himself by as though he were weighed down by a burden heavy beyond comprehension. As he passed Christian, their eyes met. "Nicely done, Christian," Liam said softly.

Christian's face was expressionless. "I wish you had never come here."

Liam brushed by him and walked out on the porch. He walked stiffly down the path to the road and down the steps to the shack. There he broke out a bottle of John Hardy's ferocious homemade applejack and drank until he fell into a deep, sodden sleep.

This time, Helga began to show very early. By the three-month mark she was conspicuously swollen and uncomfortable, much larger than she had been during her first pregnancy.

Liam was concerned about her health, and made several attempts to open a dialogue with her when he saw her in the kitchen of the big house or outside. But she would simply gather up her book or her sewing and walk away as though he didn't exist. Liam and Christian avoided each other at all times.

By the time the harvest was over and the pressing of the wine was complete, Helga was enormous. Liam was worried. Finally he went to Christian. "She'll have to go to the hospital soon," Liam told him.

"We're going to Boydstown by train on Friday. Jim Frazier has made all the arrangements with the hospital there."

"And you weren't going to tell me?"

"You are not involved," Christian said coldly.

"You're wrong on that. I'm the father, and I'm very much involved. And I'm going with you."

"Helga does not want to be near you."

"Christian" Liam said, "she was near me long enough to conceive the child, and she'll be near me for the trip to Boydstown and until this baby is born."

Henri drove the three of them by buggy to the Lakeside train station early on Friday morning. It was a typical early December day in Lakeside. The weather was raw and gray and the air was speckled with snow flurries. Helga was bundled in a heavy coat and scarf, her face the color of curdled milk. When they boarded the train for the hour-long journey to Boydstown, Liam sat alone and Helga and Christian sat side by side across the aisle. In Boydstown Heights, just outside the city, the remaining color was suddenly drained from Helga's face. She dug her fingers into Christian's arm.

"Papa," she whispered, "something just happened."

Christian notified the conductor, and before Liam was fully aware of what was happening Helga was being guided back to the caboose where

she could lie down in privacy. Liam saw Christian take her by the arm
to the end of the coach car, and he put down his newspaper and followed.
"What is it?" he demanded of Christian. "I want to be with her."

"She does not want you."

Liam ended up standing on the platform outside the caboose in the
bitter cold as the train clanked its way into Boydstown's railyards. Liam,
shivering violently, could see through the misty glass into the caboose.
Helga was stretched out on a bunk with Christian kneeling beside her,
holding her hand and talking to her. Her teeth were digging into her
lower lip. As the train pulled into Boydstown Station, Liam could see her
suddenly convulse and shut her eyes tightly in agony.

"Papa!" she shouted out, her voice carrying through the glass out to
Liam on the platform. "Oh, Papa! Papa! Papa! Papa!"

Chapter 8

At 9:33 P.M. on December 7, 1913, Helga Weidener Brennan gave birth by caesarian section to a five-pound, nine-ounce girl in Boydstown General Hospital. The child was small but healthy and vigorous. She was named Helen Christine Brennan by her father, who provided the office of the county registrar of vital statistics all relevant information about the parents and their predecedents. The mother emerged from the operation in satisfactory condition. Both the child's father and maternal grandfather spent the next eleven days in residence in separate rooms in Boydstown's finest (and only) downtown hotel. During this period, the child's father and grandfather exchanged not a word. Also during this period the child's father visited her mother twice daily, but their conversations were perfunctory on every occasion.

When Helen Brennan was twelve days old, the four of them returned home. Henri met them with the buggy at the Lakeside train station. Liam held his infant daughter in his arms during the buggy ride out to the farm. Helga and Christian talked during the trip, but they virtually ignored Liam. The tone of the trip seemed so bizarre to an outsider that Henri, sitting in front with the reins in his hands, merely shook his head and mumbled to himself in French. When the buggy reached the house, Christian helped Helga down and then immediately went inside the big house to start a fire. Henri drove the buggy to the barn, and Liam, the baby in his arms, found himself standing on the front porch in the cruel December cold facing his wife. "Well," Liam said, "what now? Do you take the child with you or do I take her with me to the shack?"

For the first time since he had learned she was pregnant a second time, Liam saw Helga waver. "Can you feed her, Liam?" Helga asked quietly.

Liam looked down into the face of the sleeping Helen, heavily wrapped against the cold. "I'll figure it out. I can water down cow's milk, and

115

tonight I can feed it to her from my finger. Tomorrow I'll go into the village and get some baby bottles. I'll find a way."

Helga stared at Liam and the child for a long time. He could see what he would have described only as torment in her eyes, and he couldn't fathom in more detail what might be going on behind them. "Liam," she said at last, "I see you there with the baby, and I'm filled with feelings I can't explain."

"What sort of feelings?"

"Feelings that things are very wrong. Feelings that they ought not to be wrong. Not after all that's happened."

"They don't have to be," Liam said to her. "You're alive and well, and you're the mother of a beautiful child. We made her, Helga, and we're a part of her forever."

Helga shook her head. Tears welled up in her eyes. "I'm so confused," she said.

Liam stepped close to her, so close they were almost touching. He could feel the warmth radiating off her face.

"Come with me and our daughter to our home," he said, nodding toward the shack down at the foot of the point. "You have to decide quickly. We can't keep Helen out in this cold."

"Come inside with me," Helga said. "We can talk there."

Liam shook his head. "I'll never enter that house again. Not with him there."

"He's my father, Liam, and he loves me."

Liam opened his coat and snuggled the sleeping Helen against his body. "I'm your husband, and I love you, too. There comes a time when a man leaves his mother and a daughter her father and they begin their own life together. There'll come a day when this darlin' creature in my arms will leave me, and when she does I expect her to go to her husband with all her love, given freely and none held back. That time is long past due for you, Helga. Come to me as my wife, completely and without reservation, or I'll take my child and be gone within a fortnight. I won't stay, not like this."

Helga's expression was anguished. "Liam," she pleaded, "he's my father."

"Choose," he said simply.

Helga's eyes dropped to the gray wood of the porch floor. She stared at it for a few moments, wordless and motionless. Then she lifted her head, reached out and took Liam's arm. "Let's go home," she said.

As they walked down the path to the road and then down the steps to the little house on the beach, Christian watched from the sitting room window. When they entered the shack, he moved to the rocking chair by the fire he had just built, lit a cigar and sat there for a long time, staring into the flames.

Liam, Helga and Helen remained in the little house by the lake for several days, not emerging once that anyone noticed. They were undisturbed, although Annette and Minnie were consumed with curiosity about the baby. But it was as though everyone understood that whatever was going on in the shack was private and crucial to the future of the family, the farm and the winery. So no one intruded on them, certainly not Christian, who went about his work in the winery and in his study speaking to no one except when absolutely necessary.

All Henri and Annette knew for sure was that serious discussions were under way in the little house by the lake and that Christian had been shut out of them. On the evening of the second day, after Henri returned home from his chores at the winery and Annette was serving him a fine dinner of chicken in brown sauce, she suddenly announced, "I am going down to the shack to see Helga's baby."

Henri dropped his fork on the polished wooden floor. "You will do no such thing," he snapped indignantly.

"And why not?" Annette demanded. "Is Helga not my friend? Is Liam not your friend? Should we not insist on the right of friends to view the child? Did not you get a glimpse of the child when you picked them up at the train station? Why should not I see the baby as well?"

Henri was sputtering. Such a show of defiance from Annette was unheard of. "Are you insane, woman?" he bellowed at last. "You know of their problems. Are they not entitled to their privacy?"

"But Henri," she pleaded, "I want to see the little baby."

"Soon enough," he said, pleased to be back in command once again. "When they are ready, you will see the child."

She nodded, accepting the wisdom of his words, but distraught nonetheless. So it was with great joy that several days later, while sipping coffee with Minnie in the kitchen of the big house, that Annette spied Helga coming up the path clutching a warmly wrapped bundle in her arms.

"Helga!" Annette cried.

Helga, a shy smile on her face, came up the steps. "I've brought something for you to hold," she told Annette, transferring the bundle to her friend's arms.

Inside the warm kitchen, Annette and Minnie fussed and carried on over the baby while Helga, smiling placidly with pride and satisfaction, brewed herself a cup of tea.

"She has your eyes," Minnie pronounced, "and your coloring, too."

"Maybe," Helga said, "but she has her father's disposition. She weeps and wails constantly."

"Well," Minnie said, reluctantly passing the child back to a beaming Annette, "you can't let her get away with that. I know. I've raised my own babies up until they were grown. She's got to learn that you ain't going to jump every time she lets out with a whimper."

Helga laughed. "I know. Don't tell me; tell Liam. He's up out of bed a half-dozen times a night, holding her and rocking her. I told him he's going to spoil her, but he does it anyway."

Minnie reached over and stroked little Helen's silken cheek. "Well," she said, "when they're real little like this, I guess it's all right. Aren't you the little darling, though."

"Minnie," Helga said, "what are you planning for Christmas dinner?"

Minnie shrugged her massive shoulders. "What I always make, I guess. A turkey roast."

"If Annette and I help you, could we do something very special this year?"

Minnie sniffed, "My turkey roast is always special."

"I know it is," Helga said, "but I'm thinking of a gigantic feast— turkey and venison and some ham. And chestnuts and dressing and brown bread and corn bread and whipped potatoes and rolls and dumplings. And maybe we can make some of those potato pancakes Papa likes so much. And some pies and cakes. And Annette can do something with the vegetables with those sauces she makes. What do you think?"

Minnie put her hands on her ample hips. "Why?"

"Because this Christmas will be a special occasion. It's Helen's first, and I want a good party, so maybe Papa and Liam will make up. Liam is willing now."

"Well," Minnie said, "we'll try it, and good luck. But I'm going to need a lot of help for the next couple of days.

Both Helga and Annette agreed, and one morning as Christmas drew near Liam found himself left alone in the little house with Helen and a bottle of milk and instructions to summon Helga only if she were really needed. Then Helga was off up the hill to assist Minnie and Annette in preparation for the feast. In another hour Henri was at the door with a prized bottle of French champagne from his diminishing stock.

"I have come to see my godchild," he announced.

Liam laughed. "She's nobody's godchild yet, but when she's christened formally nothing would please us more than if you and Annette were the godparents."

"Had we not been asked," Henri said gravely, "we would be back in Bordeaux by springtime."

"So," Henri said later, after he and Liam had toasted the baby several times, "Annette told me that Helga is overflowing with joy."

"So am I," Liam assured him. "Helga and I've been sitting here, alone with the baby, just talking. Getting her out of that hospital and away from Christian is what made the difference."

"You cannot keep her from her father forever."

"I don't want to. But I needed her alone here for a while, with no outside influences. If you want the truth, I'm more sympathetic to Christian than I had been. I think I have some understanding of why he behaves as he does."

"Yes, you can understand a man's behavior and still object to that behavior. The question is, What happens now?"

"I'll do my best to make my peace with him," Liam told Henri.

On Christmas day Helga, Annette and Minnie spent the morning in the kitchen struggling over the old coal stove preparing more food than a regiment could consume. Minnie wasn't worried about excess; she knew that whatever wasn't eaten could be stored until July, if necessary, in the icehouse.

Just before noon Christian came in from the winery and stuck his head through the kitchen door. "So," he said, "all this for Christmas dinner."

"Yes, Papa," Helga said as she rolled buttery dough for the pie crust. "You go upstairs and wash and shave and get into your best suit. This will be a special dinner."

"Helga," he pointed out patiently, "there has been little time this year for a celebration. There is no tree, only a few presents . . ."

"We all have each other," Helga said, "and now there's one more of us. You get dressed."

"Helga . . .," Christian began.

"If you're going to stand there," Minnie told him, "you can come in here and mash down those potatoes. That's a job for a strong back."

Christian's brow furrowed. He closed the door, and in a few seconds they heard his heavy tread on the stairs.

"That's what I figured," Minnie muttered, pulling the huge potato masher from the bottom cupboard.

At two in the afternoon, Christian was sitting in the parlor in a well-pressed suit of gray wool engrossed in a worn copy of the *Saturday Evening Post*. Minnie opened the door to the dining room, and he looked up. In the dining room, Helga was seated at her usual place. The table groaned with the weight of all the food, a steaming bounty unlike any Christian had ever seen in this house. Henri, in a collar and tie, sat demurely next to Annette on the far side of the table, and a place had been set for Minnie, who normally ate her meals alone in the kitchen.

"Dinner, Mr. Weidener," Minnie said from the doorway, and she sat down.

Christian frowned and took his customary spot at the head of the table. He looked over the feast spread before him. In the center of the table was Minnie's golden turkey, flanked by a clove-studded ham and a roast of venison covered with white grape sauce and surrounded by an assortment of side dishes, sauces and several bottles of Brennan wine.

"You should say grace, Papa," Helga said.

Christian studied the table. One chair was conspicuously empty, although a place had been set in front of it. "Where is your husband?" he asked gravely. Then, almost as an afterthought, "And where is the child?"

Helga lowered her eyes. "Liam and the baby are down at the shack," she said quietly. "I saw no sense in bringing them here if they would disturb you."

Christian stared out over the table, and then he leaned back in his chair. For a long moment he drummed his fingers on the table. "So," he said with visible irritation, "we are going to celebrate Christmas here with an empty chair, and it is my doing. Is that it?"

No one spoke.

Christian stood up suddenly and tossed his napkin on his empty plate. "All right," he said in a brittle voice, "I will go get them." He stepped away from the table, but as he did Liam threw open the kitchen door and stood there in his wedding suit, Helen in his arms. "Well," he said, "I'm glad you said that. A man could lose his mind watching food like this go by to the table. They wouldn't give me a scrap."

Their eyes met, Liam's bright with mirth and Christian's hard, glassy and unfathomable. For a long moment they stared at one another. Then Liam crossed the room in two long strides and deposited Helen in Christian's arms. "Here," he said, "I've been holding her since we got back from Boydstown. Let her pee on you for a change." Then he slid into his chair, leaving Christian standing with the baby in his arms and an expression of profound surprise and discomfort on his face.

Helga motioned to his chair. "Sit down, Papa," she ordered, smiling, "we're all starving."

Christian, the child in his arms, settled uncomfortably into his chair. As he did, Helen's tiny hand reached up and clutched at his nose. Christian pulled back his head and as he did, Helen's other hand latched firmly onto his ear. There was laughter from around the table, which died instantly as Christian's eyes came up blazing. Then his face took on a peculiar look. He stared down at the baby. "She did wet on me," he

announced, and then he suddenly broke into a great bellow of laughter—
the first that Liam had ever heard from him. Helga and Liam exchanged
relieved glances across the table. In an eyeblink, Henri was pouring wine
into everyone's glass.

"A toast," Henri proclaimed, raising his glass high, "to the newest
Brennan and the newest Weidener."

Christian, holding Helen tightly with one arm, lifted his glass with
the others. He drank deeply and set it down again. Then he looked up.
"She really did wet on me," he said solemnly, and this time everyone
laughed.

* * * *

When spring came and the ice broke up on the lake, the steamboats
resumed their routes. *Iroquois Queen*'s first delivery of the season brought
the new *vinifera* cuttings, and Liam hurriedly ran up the bank to bring
Henri down to the dock. Henri examined them with care. "Most of them
are in fine condition," he said. "The others . . ., well, we have enough
to graft onto the *labrusca* vines. These are the ones, I think, with which
we can do something special."

"Yes?" Liam said.

"Yes," Henri responded. "You know, I am beginning to think we
might make champagne here after all."

The arrival of the champagne cuttings spurred Liam's efforts to clear
his land. He had fallen behind badly after Helen's birth. Although he
and Christian were on civil, if not cordial, terms at this point, Christian
maintained his skepticism about trying to make champagne. "You expect
too much from the land," he told Liam. "This experiment will fail, and
if you put too much of yourself into it, it will break your heart."

Nonetheless, Liam worked feverishly at pulling out the remaining few
stumps from the land he had set aside for next year's new vineyard. They
were mostly the remains of old oaks, thick trees with deep roots that
defied his efforts with pick and shovel and those of the workhorses. He
was forced to use dynamite, which had always made him nervous.

All it took was one carelessly cut fuse, a slip on wet grass as he ran
away after lighting it and too little time to either make it to safety or
back to the fuse to snuff it out. The result was a two-foot chunk of rock-
hard oak root launched from the ground by the explosion with the velocity
of an artillary shell. It smashed into Liam's ankle as he ran desperately
toward cover, shattering it like china and knocking him completely off
his feet to be showered by a rain of shattered hardwood, dirt and small
rocks. He managed to half-crawl, half-hop to Henri's house, swearing

horribly but actually not ungrateful that he was still alive. When Annette answered his knock, the ankle was swollen to more than twice its normal size in his blood-filled work boot.

Christian and Henri loaded Liam into the wagon. As they transported him to Doctor Frazier's office he consumed a sizeable portion of a bottle of rye whiskey to ease the immense pain, and by the time he arrived in Lakeside he was nearly numb. Henri and Christian held him down while Frazier set the ankle and wrapped it in a solid plaster cast.

"He'll be an invalid for the rest of the summer," Frazier told Christian as Liam slept peacefully in a haze induced by alcohol and medication. "I can't say he won't have a bit of a limp afterward, either, when everything heals. If he does, I can break it again and reset it, although I don't think it's worth the bother unless it's a real bad limp."

So it was that three weeks later, Liam was sitting on the porch of the shack and looking out over the lake, Helen sleeping in his arms, when the *Iroquois Queen* rounded the point under a great plume of white smoke.

Liam turned in his chair, his ankle moving slightly in the cast and prompting him to sink his teeth into his lip. "Helga," he called out, "steamer's coming."

Helga came out onto the porch, drying her hands on her apron. Helen had been awakened by Liam's voice. Disturbed, she began to howl as Helga approached. Helga sighed and picked her up, cradling her close and calming her. "I guess one of us ought to get Papa," she said.

"One of us should. It won't be me, not with this boulder on my foot. Give me back the baby."

"I will not," Helga said, grinning. "She's coming with me."

By the time Helga returned from the big house with Christian in tow, the *Queen* was snugly tied up at the dock, and the crew was unloading seed and tools. Henry Baddington, a good twenty pounds heavier this spring, was in earnest conversation with Liam.

"I was just telling Liam," he said, "there's big trouble brewing in Europe. Might be a war, according to the New York papers."

"Between who?" Christian asked.

Baddington shook his head. "I can't quite figure out who. Everybody over there, I guess. I read it all in the New York papers a couple of days ago. You see, this Austrian duke—"

"Archduke Ferdinand?" Christian broke in.

"That's the fellow. He was visiting some place called Sarajevo, wherever the hell that is, and somebody shot him dead—right in his motorcar. They killed whoever shot him, but the Austrians are mad as hell at the Serbians, and there's talk that Germany and France and Belgium are going to get into it. I don't know who's going to be fighting who, but it all sounds pretty nasty to me."

Christian nodded, his expression grim. "It will be. If Europe goes to war with modern weapons, it will be terrible. The Kaiser cannot permit a thing like this to go unpunished."

"I wonder," Liam mused, "how deeply the Irish will get involved. If the British are dragged in, they'll conscript more Irish to fight their war for them. You can be sure of that."

"The British are very fortunate," Christian said. "There is a ribbon of sea to protect them—and the Irish—from whatever happens on the continent. Even if the British become involved, they will not be invaded."

"I wouldn't be too sure," Liam countered. "I read the other day in the *Post* that they can fly machines over the English Channel from Europe. It's no different than flying over dry land."

"A war in this day and age will be fought with machine guns and cannon," Christian responded, in the tone he habitually reserved for matters of absolute certainty. "No one will ever fight a war with flying machines—not in my lifetime or yours."

"That Hearst paper down in New York was speculating that if Britain gets into it we'll have to get into it ourselves," Baddington said.

"I doubt that," Liam said. "It's too far away. Besides, I can't see Wilson leading anybody to war for any reason, good or bad. He's not Teddy Roosevelt."

"On that we agree," Christian said.

"Finally," Liam added, and both men smiled slightly. Their peace was precarious at best, but a small joke could strengthen rather than threaten it.

Baddington, sensing a dynamic at work with which he wasn't completely in tune, suddenly shifted direction. "Listen, forget all that. I've got some real big news. I'm finally going to fix that bastard Gillis. I'm going to race the *Queen* against that steel tub of his."

"Race?" Christian said. "What is this madness?"

"Nothing mad about it, Christian," Baddington said. "Ten days from now, the *Queen* and the *Aurora* are going to take off from Lakeside for a race the length of the lake, all the way down to Ringlesport. The winner collects a thousand dollars from the loser."

"A thousand dollars?" Helga blurted out. She had been sitting silently throughout the earlier conversation about the possibility of war in Europe, but a steamer race at home with a thousand-dollar bet attached was vastly more interesting.

"Where's the wager money going to come from?" Liam asked.

"Well, Baddington said, "he's got a thousand in cash just as pocket money. As for me . . . well, I've put in three hundred and forty dollars. That's every cent of cash money I have in the world. I could take out a loan against my boat or my house, but I'm hoping to get the rest elsewhere."

"Where is elsewhere?" Christian asked quietly, suspecting that he already knew the answer.

Baddington smiled sheepishly through his muttonchops. "That's one of the reasons I wanted you to know about this, Christian. I'm asking interested parties, like yourself, if they're interested in investing in this little wager. It's a sure thing, mind you, and you get a free ride on the *Queen* during the race. That's one of the conditions—each boat has to be carrying a full load. It'll be the excursion voyage to end all excursion voyages. People are going to be talking about this for years. I'm asking most people for a hundred."

"That's a lot of money," Christian said, shaking his head slowly.

"But for you, Christian," Baddington added immediately, "I'd say fifty. You're a regular customer, after all. And you'll get it back plus another fifty when I win the race."

"Oh, come on, Papa," Helga teased, "it's not that much money. Besides, it'll be fun."

Christian frowned. "Well, for fifty, I can't see why not."

Baddington took his hand and shook it vigorously. "It's like having your money in the Bank of America, Christian. Wait and see."

"Henry," Liam told him, "if you push those steam boilers for thirty miles all the way down the lake you're likely to pop a seal on one or both of them. The *Aurora's* deisel powered. She won't have that problem."

"I'll put in fifty dollars, Captain," Helga volunteered.

"Helga!" Liam said in surprise.

"I have money of my own, Liam. Besides, I get a free ride, don't I, Captain?"

"And you'll add a lot of beauty to the boat, Helga," Baddington said, beaming.

"Christian," Liam pleaded, "tell her how much fifty dollars is.

But the older man merely permitted a small smile to play about the corners of his mouth. "This is your wife, Liam," he said, his tone decidedly amused, "I no longer have control over what she does or does not do."

Liam frowned deeply, and his gaze moved back and forth between his wife and his father-in-law. "And so," he said finally, "it would seem that she'll do precisely as she pleases."

Helga leaned over and kissed Liam lightly on the cheek. "Haven't I always?" she asked, smiling.

* * * *

The morning of the race Helga rose early. She put up her blonde hair and put on a pretty green dress with a pleated white front. She donned her wide-brimmed straw hat, the one Liam thought looked so nice on her. It was festooned with artificial flowers and a small bluebird peeking out of the foliage. Then she bent over Liam as he lay in bed watching her and kissed him goodbye. He caught a whiff of the perfume that had so intoxicated him at their first meeting.

"Have fun," he whispered, careful to avoid waking Helen in the next room. "I love you."

"I love you, too. Take good care of Helen for me."

"We'll be watching from the porch as the boats go by," he told her softly.

Helga left the shack quietly and put on her shoes on the front porch. A few minutes later, as he lay dozing, he heard the buggy come down the drive and pass the shack, the horse's hooves clopping on the hard-packed dirt road.

The race was scheduled to begin at ten, and if they got off on time they would be passing the point out front not more than a half hour after that, Liam knew. As he scrubbed himself down this morning and heated water for his shave, he realized that he was falling into a bad mood for no precise reason he could isolate or define. He fought to shake it off, and his mood improved somewhat when Henri and Annette appeared on the porch to watch for the *Iroquois Queen* and the *Aurora*.

"I have never ridden the steamerboats," Annette said, then added reprovingly, "Henri did not want to go to this race today."

"The ride from France was enough for me," Henri explained. "When you are in a boat as big as a building you should not be tossed around. The deck should be steady, like land. But it is never so. It unsettles me."

Minnie arrived about ten minutes later, carrying a pot of steaming coffee in one hand and a basket of her sugar rolls in the other. She and Annette set up the food on the porch table, then Minnie went into the shack and emerged with cream and sugar and Helen.

"She's such a little doll," Minnie said, clucking happily as the infant explored the vast folds of the old woman's face with her tiny fingers.

Precisely as she spoke, a tower of thick, white smoke became visible over the trees of the bluff between the farm and Lakeside. Henri spotted it and pointed excitedly. "There they are."

For a moment the audience on the porch was silent, watching the plume of smoke billow over the trees. Then a boat broke into sight around the bluff.

Liam shielded his eyes from the sun's glare and squinted out over the lake. The boat was several miles away, but as he studied its lines and the way it moved through the water, he recognized the craft immediately.

"There's one of them," Annette cried out.

"That's the *Aurora*," Liam told her. "That's bad. She's got a good lead—a very good lead for so early in the race."

In only a moment a second plume of smoke appeared over the trees, and a little later the *Iroquois Queen* came chugging around the bluff, her sidewheels churning and throwing water as she labored against the heavy waves. As the vessel came into sight, Henry Baddington extended his greetings to the residents of the Weidener Farm. He let loose with a long, powerful blast on his boat's whistle that rolled across the lake and up to the hill beyond. The *Queen* was well behind now, and the whistle blast had the ring of empty bravado. Liam could imagine the frenzy into which Baddington must have worked himself already.

"The other boat is moving very quickly," Henri said, studying them both as they drew near.

"Gillis has too much of a lead," Liam said grimly, "the pattern is set. There's no way Baddington can catch him. I'm afraid Christian can kiss goodbye to his fifty dollars. Helga, too, for that matter."

In the wheelhouse of the *Iroquois Queen*, Henry Baddington's face was a vivid red, and his jaw was set tightly beneath his muttonchops as he stood next to his pilot, Fred Russell. The bulky steamboat captain leaned over the pipe to the engine room and flipped off its cap. "What's the matter with you dumb sons of bitches down there?" He roared into the pipe. "Can't you get any more out of those engines? We're getting our goddamn asses whipped."

Down in the engine room Baddington's chief engineer stepped to the pipe. His name was Wilbur Brady, and he was not a man to be bullied and he was not in the mood to tolerate one of Henry Baddington's temper tantrums. This foolish damn race hadn't been Wilbur Brady's foolish damn idea. "We're mighty close to the red line on those boilers, Henry," he shouted back into the tube over the sound of thumping machinery, "and we got twenty miles or more to go. The boilers won't hold under this pressure for that kind of distance."

Baddington could feel his blood nearing the boiling point. "I'll be right down, you lazy little bastard. I'll show you how to do it, if I have to."

Baddington chugged down the steps to the lower deck and headed sternward to the engine room through the surging crowd of passengers. As he did, he bumped squarely into Helga, who was leaning on the rail and who stumbled back into her father's arms. Baddington, flustered, stopped to take her hand and pat it in apology. "Sorry about that, Helga," he said, "I'm in a hurry."

"Things do not look good, Henry," Christian said needlessly.

"They'll look better when I've put the fear of God into that engine crew," Baddington promised.

The fat captain moved along, pushing his way through the passengers. The boat carried fully a hundred and fifty passengers today, and the atmosphere was decidedly festive. He found his way to the engine room and pushed open the door. The small, wiry Brady and his assistant, a hulking teenager named Horner, looked up from their work as the captain came in and slammed the door behind him. Brady was furious. He pointed a grease-stained finger at Horner throwing wood into the firebox and at the needles registering pressure from the twin boilers. "Look for yourself," Brady bellowed. "She ain't got nothing more to give."

"She's got to have more," Baddington shouted over the roar of the fire and the machinery, "We're losing, goddamn it."

Brady shook his head in exasperation. "See for yourself. That's all there is."

Baddington examined the pressure gauges closely. The needles were quivering nervously just below the red danger line. The heat of the little room was intolerable, and he was already soaked with sweat beneath his heavy captain's coat. He turned to Brady, towering over the little man.

"Then tie down the safety valves," he ordered. "We've got to have more steam."

Brady was aghast. "Tie down the valves? You're crazy, Henry. We can't tie down the valves. This ain't worth dying for."

"You dumb little bastard," Baddington roared at him, "if we lose this race we might as well jump overboard and drown ourselves. Gillis'll own all the excursion business on the lake. There won't be a scrap left over for the rest of us. Do you want to starve or do you want to do what you're supposed to be able to do—get me twenty knots out of these boilers."

Brady was angry, but he was also shaken. He had never seen Baddington so agitated. "Nobody can get twenty knots out of these boilers in a headwind like this, Henry," he said, "they're damn near twenty years old."

Baddington's jaw set hard. "I'll show you how to get twenty knots."

He walked over to the side of the engine room, digging through the pile of tools and grease and scrap there until he brought forth a length of stout rope. He pulled his pocket knife from his coat and neatly sliced two lengths of cord from it. Then, calmly, he tied down the safety valves of each engine. He turned to Brady and Horner, who were standing motionless, astounded at what the captain had done.

Baddington pointed toward the firebox. "Pour more wood in there. And pour about three barrels of tallow in each boiler."

"Tallow?" Brady shouted.

"Tallow!" Baddington roared back. "We need a hotter fire. That's why we carry tallow to begin with, isn't it?"

"Not when the fire's already this hot," Brady said.

"Pump it in there," Baddington ordered, "we've got no reason to save it now. Do it! That's an order, Wilbur."

Brady took a deep breath. Then he turned to Horner, who was clearly terrified and waiting for his boss's instructions. "Let's do it," Brady said quietly.

The three of them quickly wheeled out the barrels of tallow from the storage next to the engine room and carried in a new load of wood. Brady put on heavy gloves and opened the firebox door. Fingers of flame leaped out at them. The firebox extended a full six feet inside the door, and its light was so intense that none of them dared look directly into it.

"Throw it all in," Baddington ordered.

Brady and Horner complied. They tossed in all three barrels, dancing back each time from the sparks that shot back into the engine room. They followed with a hefty load of pine wood, and then Brady slammed the door. Orange flame flared around its edges with evil energy as the tallow and pine wood caught, driving the three of them to the rear of the room. Then Baddington braved the awesome heat and moved forward to stand by the gauges, eyeing them carefully. They began to crawl upward, past the red mark, well into the danger range. Baddington stepped over to the pipe to the wheelhouse.

"Russell," he called out, "what's our speed?"

"We're up to nineteen, Captain," Russell's voice came back through the tube. "No, it's twenty now. Hot damn, we're up to twenty."

Baddington turned toward Brady, an expression of deep satisfaction on his face.

"There," he said, "I told you she had more in her. Now keep her up to this speed. And I don't care if you have to throw this fool in," he motioned toward Horner, "to make grease. Keep that pressure up."

Brady shook his head, his face like death. "Henry," he said quietly, "you're a goddamn madman."

"She can take it," Baddington said. "This is the best boat that ever sailed on this lake."

Baddington stormed out of the engine room and on deck. The cooler air outside hit him like a cold towel, and the sweat encasing his huge frame turned to an embrace of ice. He climbed the steps to the upper deck. His breathing was labored from his excitement and his exertions. He found Russell still at the helm, stoically guiding the *Queen* into the headwind. The *Aurora* was directly ahead, but the gap between the two craft had narrowed noticeably. Baddington put his hamlike hand on Russell's shoulder.

"I wonder what that bastard Gillis is saying to himself now," he said with a grim smile.

The *Iroquois Queen's* burst of speed was clearly visible from the porch of the shack. As the bulkier boat narrowed the gap, both vessels were directly off the point, clearly outlined against the hill rising on the far side of the lake.

"Look," Annette said, "they are not so wide apart now."

Liam leaned forward in his chair. "No, Henry's gaining. You can see it." He leaned back and lit his pipe. "I don't know how he's getting that kind of speed out of that old tub."

It took several more minutes, and by the time it happened the boats were some distance down the lake toward Ringlesport. But a cheer went up from the porch of the shack and the deck of the older boat as the *Iroquois Queen* pulled abreast of the trimmer hull of the *Aurora* and slipped past her on the starboard side. It was a stunning sight from the porch, one none of them would ever forget—the two shining white boats chopping through the rolling expanse of blue lake with its churning whitecaps, the great sidewheels of the *Queen* spinning in a blur.

In the engine room of the *Iroquois Queen*, Wilbur Brady wiped his sweaty brow with the back of a soot-stained glove. He had heard cheers from on deck even over the crashing, thumping music of the engines, and he knew the *Queen* had forged ahead. He turned to Horner, who was deathly pale beneath his dusting of soot, grease and sweat. Both men stood looking at one another in the hellish heat of the engine room. Then Brady motioned to the firebox door. "Open her up again," he told Horner, picking up a load of wood to feed the fire.

Horner's eyes rolled. He glanced at the pressure gauges.

"Wilbur . . ." he began.

"Oh, hell," Brady told him. "We're out in front now. We got to stay there. Henry's a blowhard, but he ain't nobody's fool."

The boats were nothing more than distant specks on the lake's horizon when the onlookers on the shack's porch saw it. A long, thin tongue of red-yellow flame licked out of the bowels of the *Iroquois Queen*. The flame rolled slowly and majestically across the surging whitecaps of Iroquois Lake. It was a second or so later before the thunderous roar of the explosion reached the shack. The flames surged out of the boat hundreds of feet up into the clean, summer air. Then, as the sound died away and the plume of the explosion turned from a pillar of flame to rolls of thick, black, oily smoke, hundreds of bits of wood and metal and bone and flesh that had been carried up by the blast stopped their leap skyward. They hung there in the sky for the briefest moment, then hurtled back to the shattered, smoking hull of what had been the *Iroquois Queen*.

From the porch of the shack nearly two miles away, Liam Brennan's eyes widened at what he knew would be the most conspicuous element of his nightmares for the rest of his life. "Sweet Jesus," he whispered.

Chapter 9

The enormity of the *Iroquois Queen* tragedy was unmatched in lake country history. In all, more than fifty souls were lost outright. Among the dead were a state senator, his wife and two small children; a high-ranking aide to the Catholic bishop of the Archdiocese of Rochester; the mayor of Lakeside, his wife and their eldest grandchild, age six; a group of students from Iroquois College, an expensive girls' school located on the lake just outside Lakeside, and seven Carmelite nuns from Boydstown. All but a few of the corpses sank with the boat's charred hull to the lake bottom, one hundred and eighty feet down, and could not be recovered. The bodies of Christian, Helga and Baddington were among them.

A special ward for survivors was set up at Lakeside Hospital, and the railroad made special runs to take those more seriously injured to the bigger hospitals in Rochester and Boydstown. Some of the injuries of the burn victims were incredibly painful, and Jim Frazier exhausted his supply of laudanum in the first few hours. He switched to injections of morphine until that, too, was gone on the second day. But by then most of the patients who were suffering most severely had died. Other doctors came in from Ringlesport and surrounding communities to help him. Frazier went four days and nights without sleep before he collapsed with what was later diagnosed as a mild heart attack.

The sinking of the *Iroquois Queen* meant the end of the steamboat era on Iroquois Lake. Life would be vastly different on the lake from now on, Martin Hooper, the editor of the *Lakeside Journal*, observed one day over lunch to John Coughlin, the hardware store owner.

"We're going to need better roads around the lake," Hooper said. "We might even give some thought to a trolley line from here to Ringlesport."

"Write an editorial on it, Martin," Coughlin advised. "Everybody'll read it, but nobody's going to want to pay for it. They'd rather spend their money on a motorcar."

Things already were dramatically different at the Weidener farm. While Henri continued his work at the winery and Gilmore continued to care for the cattle, while Minnie and Annette took over caring for Helen and Heller continued to perform odd jobs around the property, Liam simply retreated to the shack and stayed there, a virtual hermit.

Worse than his silence and self-imposed solitude was Liam's drinking. He appeared at the winery only to bring out bottles to take back to the shack. Henri began to keep count, and he realized that Liam was drinking as many as eight to ten bottles of wine in a single day.

Sleep was the problem. It would come to Liam only if he drank himself into a stupor, and so he did every night. He would awaken always within a few hours, and then he would drink some more until he again fell asleep. In the morning he would awaken ill, his heart and head pounding with every step he took, and he would drink in the morning to slow his heartbeat and ease his pain. And so it went, day after day, night after night, for months. Henri was powerless to stop it. Liam simply ignored him.

"Mister Brennan?"

The voice came from the doorway of the shack. Liam, lying on the davenport, opened his eyes and looked toward it. He saw the silhouette of a tall man dressed in a suit and a homburg. He was carrying a briefcase. Liam sat up.

"I stopped at the house up on the hill," the man said. "They told me I'd find you down here. May I come in?"

"Who're you?" Liam demanded, his voice a hoarse croak.

"I'm William Stewart. I'm your late father-in-law's lawyer. We met at your wedding a few years ago. My sympathies, Mr. Brennan, on your loss."

The lawyer had an owlish expression behind his pince-nez glasses, which were attached about the back of his neck by a navy blue ribbon. Liam opened the door and stepped unsteadily out onto the porch. The late morning sun assaulted his eyes. The contrast between the two of them was startling—Stewart in his stiff white collar and blue suit, Liam in overalls and work boots, a filthy plaid shirt, unshorn and unshaven, carrying a half-empty bottle of Brennan white table wine.

"Do you mind if I sit down?" Stewart asked, motioning to the rocking chairs and the little table at the front of the porch. He had determined which chair was upwind, and that was the one he had his eye on.

"Go ahead. Would you be wanting a drink? There's a glass inside, somewhere."

"No, thank you," Stewart said, settling purposely into the upwind chair, putting his briefcase on the little table and opening it. He dug through his papers while Liam settled into the other chair, the wine bottle nestled in the crook of his arm, like a baby.

"Well," Stewart said, smiling somewhat nervously as he went through his papers, "I guess you want to know why I'm here."

Liam merely looked at him, saying nothing. Then he shrugged and gazed out over the lake.

"Actually," Stewart said, "I'm here about the will."

Liam said nothing.

"Mr. Weidener's will," Stewart explained.

Liam's gaze moved from the lake to Stewart's face. "So?"

"Well, it's just that the surrogate's court is getting a bit impatient. There are papers to be signed and so forth. Inheritance taxes, you understand."

"So sign what has to be signed."

"I'm afraid I can't, Mr. Brennan. I have no power of attorney. Only you can sign them."

"Sign what?" Liam said irritably. "I didn't inherit anything. Christian and I discussed that."

"That's true," Stewart said, glad for the opportunity to explain everything and be on his way. "These documents are quite specific that you're to inherit none of Mr. Weidener's holdings, although they do specify that some land had already been transferred to you before his unfortunate death."

"That land was bought and paid for," Liam said. "I gave Christian a down payment in cash and gold, and he got every nickel of the proceeds of my last two grape crops. That account is clear."

"Yes, but you're the legal guardian of your children, and they and any further issue from you will inherit equally. So there are documents you must sign, Mr. Brennan. I've brought them along."

Liam frowned. His brain wasn't working clearly, he knew. "I don't understand."

"Well, it's all in the terms of the will Mr. Weidener had my father-in-law draw up several years ago. It states explicitly that all your children are to share the farm in common."

"I have only one child—a baby daughter."

"Well, that simplifies matters. The point here is that you'll have to act as your daughter's guardian until she reaches her majority, administering the affairs of the estate and so forth."

Liam rubbed the stubble on his chin. "Let me make sure I understand all this. Christian said that all my children are to share in the farm?"

"Yes," Stewart said, digging through the papers, that's my understanding of what's here."

"But he meant all my children with Helga."

Stewart looked at the will. "Well, that's not how it's worded. The phrase used here is 'all children produced by Liam Brennan and his legal wife.' "

"But he meant with Helga," Liam insisted.

"My late father-in-law drew up these papers, Mister Brennan. I wasn't involved. I can't say if he meant what you say he meant. I can only go by the document he executed. And the language of the instrument would seem to include any and all issue you produce in a legally valid union."

For the first time in months, a smile played across Liam's lips. "Bastards can't inherit, is that it?"

"No. Not according to the terms of this will."

So that's it, Liam thought. That was what Christian had been thinking of. He had been convinced—or, at least, suspected—that at some point in the marriage Liam would take up with other women and perhaps produce illegitimate offspring. In his old-world way, with his ingrained reverence for land and for blood, Christian had taken steps to protect Helga's children from any child of Liam's born on the wrong side of the blanket. Liam laughed again and shook his head. Even in death Christian was reproaching him.

"Well," he said wearily, "it makes no difference."

"Be that as it may," Stewart pressed, "there are papers here you have to sign to assure proper distribution of the estate."

Liam put his face in his hands, rubbing his eyes. He felt the tightness in his chest returning. He looked up at Stewart, and no hint of humor remained, ironic or otherwise. "Mr. Stewart, if I were to sign these papers, is there a chance then that you might go away and leave me alone?"

Finally, Stewart permitted himself to take offense. He stiffened in his blue suit. "An excellent chance, Mr. Brennan," he said.

Liam stood up. "Well then, let's go up in my late father-in-law's study where there's pen and ink—I have none here, I'm afraid—and sign these papers by all means. Then, Mister Stewart, you can be on your way."

And not a moment too soon, Stewart thought.

The farm was rapidly becoming a shambles. Minnie lived alone in the house at night because the baby slept at Henri and Annette's and Liam was locked in the shack, drunk. By mid-August Henri had found it no longer possible to continue paying the two hired men from his own pocket. The winemaker himself was finally forced to take on the care of the chickens and horses and the other livestock. Thus, life at the farm went on thanks to Henri's dedication and determination, although Annette found herself suffering an ever-growing list of complaints about life in general from her volatile little husband.

The fact remained, however, that by fall no plans had been made for the harvest. Apples and pears were ripening on the trees, and Henri knew from his chemical tests on the *vinifera* grapes that unless the harvest was scheduled soon there would be no wine to make that year. The grapes would become overly sweet and rot on the vines, or the excess sugar would disrupt his carefully laid plans for the fermentation process. He had gone to Liam on several occasions to outline the problem and plead for a solution, but Liam had listened only halfheartedly and, on one occasion, had actually fallen asleep while the winemaker was talking.

Henri accepted the situation and tried to make the best of it. He understood that Liam's soul was in crisis. But Annette's patience, usually an item of wonder to all knew her, was finally beginning to wear thin. "Henri," she told him one morning at breakfast, "we cannot go on this way. You must do something."

Henri held out his hands in a gesture of helplessness. "What do you suggest, my love? I can only do what I have always done. I make wine. And," he added in disgust, "I milk cows and feed chickens and slop pigs. This, too, must be done."

"Henri, you have not been paid in months. We have no money left after what you gave the others."

"So?" he said. "We have all we need here—a fine house to live in, food in abundance. I have my work."

She sat down at the table in their little kitchen and looked him in the eye. "And we have a child who is not ours."

Henri looked away. "What would you have me do?"

Annette reached over and took her husband's hand. She squeezed it gently. "Henri, I do not want to go back to Bordeaux."

"Nor do I," he told her.

"Then you must find some way to reach Liam. You must do this."

Henri sighed deeply. "I know," he said to his wife. "I know."

After he ate, Henri put his dishes in the sink for Annette to wash and walked to the shack on the point. He found Liam sprawled asleep, snoring loudly. The shack reeked of unwashed clothes, sour wine from the empty bottles strewn about and spoiled food from the wide-open icebox in the kitchen. Liam was foul with dirt, and the place stank with his odor, too. He had vomited during the night and was lying in it. Henri took in the scene with sadness and disgust. He went over to the kitchen sink and filled the mop bucket with cold water pumped by hand from the lake. He went back into the bedroom and poured the icy water over Liam, who awakened sputtering. "You are repulsive," Henri told him, tossing the bucket in the corner of the bedroom, where it landed with a smash.

"Wh-What?" Liam said, rubbing at his eyes and the water that streamed down into them from his unkept hair.

"You sicken the stomach," Henri said.

Liam sat up quickly, a mistake on his part, and immediately put his head in his hands. All the demons in hell were dancing inside his skull.

"Go away, Henri," he rasped out.

"I will not go away," Henri bellowed so loudly that Liam winced. "Is this how you honor your wife's memory? Is this how you show how much you loved Helga? The time for mourning is past. You have a farm to run. You have wine to make. You have responsibilities to others." Henri reached down, grabbed Liam savagely by the hair and pulled his head up. "You have a daughter."

Liam, much bigger than the little winemaker, pulled away easily, but the effort drained him. He fell back on the bed.

"Leave me alone," he said. His voice was a plea.

Henri sat down beside him. "To do what? To drink until your brain is numb? I have your child, my friend. Do you want me to run away with her?"

A flash of fear appeared in Liam's eyes. "You wouldn't do that."

Henri laughed then. It was a mirthless laugh, bitter and angry. "Would I not, though? I will not have children of my own. I know this, after all these years. What is to keep me from fleeing back to France with your child? You? This is a joke. You are too drunk even to stand."

Liam struggled to rise, but the pain in his head was too severe now. He sank back on the filthy bed, his chest heaving. "You're my friend, Henri," he choked out. "How can you torture me like this?"

"Because there is no choice," Henri told him. "The time has come to put an end to this sickness that has taken you. You must be a man. You should fall on your knees and thank God for your daughter, my friend. You have more than I will ever have, and it is difficult not to hate you for it."

"You have Annette."

"And you have Helga's memory, and a child that will give you love every day, as she would have, had she lived."

Liam shook his head. Then, very quietly, he began to weep. The tears poured down his dirt-stained face, into his ragged beard. Then Liam was sobbing noisily, all the agony in his soul pouring out of his eyes, choking him. He wept for a long while as Henri sat beside him on the filth-encrusted sheets. Then Henri put out a small hand and touched Liam's shoulder.

"No more of this, my friend," he said gently. "No more. You must promise me."

"How can I raise a child?" Liam wept. "I can't even take care of myself."

"Hire a woman to raise it," Henri told him, "to teach her properly how to be a woman. I do not want my Annette raising your child, my friend. Every day she holds it and cares for it and loves it, and she knows she will never have one of her own, and it breaks her heart. You cannot do this to my Annette. Anything else I could permit from you because you are my dearest friend. But not this pain you inflict on my Annette."

Liam sat up then. It was an enormous struggle, but he managed it, and he moved awkwardly to the edge of the bed, his face buried in his hands.

"You're right, Henri," he said, struggling to end the flood of tears. "I've got to get myself together. But I don't know how. I feel these pains all over my body. My heart feels like it's going to break loose of its moorings sometimes. I should have been the one with her—not Christian."

"He was not with her either," Henri said. "We all must die alone, no matter how close we are in life to others. You must live your life, Liam. You breathe. Your heart beats. You have no other choice."

Liam wrapped his brawny arms around his little friend and clutched at him, holding him close, almost cracking Henri's ribs. "Help me, Henri."

Henri felt tears of his own spring into his eyes. He patted Liam's broad back. "I will do all that I am able to do," he said.

* * * *

"Yes," the young man said, "may I help you?"

Katherine looked down at him. He was barely out of his teens—a proper young secretary who looked forward to moving up in the firm after he finished his apprenticeship. "I have an appointment with Mr. Merrill," she said. "My name is Katherine Cooley. I received a note about a position as a governess."

"He's expecting you. Please follow me."

Amos Merrill sat behind a gleaming desk. He rose as she entered. "Miss Cooley," he said with a smile, "please sit down."

Katherine did so. The young receptionist departed as Merrill settled his considerable bulk into his swivel chair. He was a red-faced, balding man who, she guessed, was considerably younger than his appearance, which made him seem forty. "And how are you today?" Merrill said, smiling beneath his walrus moustache.

"Very fine, sir," Katherine said. "Thank you for inquiring."

Amos Merrill leaned back and surveyed her. The voice was pleasant with a soft, southern accent. What he saw was a very plain young woman,

quite thin and severe in appearance, ill at ease but covering it up with
a skilled show of calm that he could discern only because he had spent
fifteen years of studying witnesses and juries. In that time, Merrill had
learned that appearances did, indeed, tell all; that a careful study of a
person's manner revealed a great deal about his or her soul. Merrill
decided at once that Katherine Cooley was a strong, independent woman.
He was a radical man for his time and place; he liked that. "Well, Miss
Cooley," he said, "let's talk a bit."

"Very well. Perhaps you could start by describing the family that's
considering employing me."

Merrill adjusted his eyeglasses. "At this point, I'm afraid not," he
said. "At the end of this interview, if I judge that you might be fit for
this position, I can then provide you with the name and the location of
the family. And then, of course, the family will want to speak to you
themselves."

Katherine sat back in her chair. "Very well."

"Why don't we begin with the reason you left the employ of Congressman Gordon."

Katherine met his gaze evenly. The reason for her departure several
weeks before from the impressive estate of Congressman J. Arch Gordon
was well enough known to the matrons of Boydstown. "I found conditions
in that household unsatisfactory," she said simply.

"I wonder if you could be a bit more specific."

It was possible he didn't know, Katherine mused. Perhaps men didn't
discuss these matters as freely as she had imagined.

"I presume that this conversation will be held in the strictest confidence," she said.

Merrill nodded. "It will be, rest assured."

"The congressman made what I considered to be improper advances
toward me, sir," Katherine said. "This happened on several occasions,
and finally I resigned, citing personal reasons."

"Personal reasons?"

"That's correct, sir."

"Then the congressman doesn't know the real reason for your resignation?"

Katherine smiled slightly. "He knows, sir. Mrs. Gordon, however, does
not. Nor would I wish her to. I say this to you because I would expect
that at a certain point you'll want to check her as a reference, and I'd
hate to have this come out. She idolizes her husband, sir, as do the
children, and the last thing I'd want to be responsible for, even indirectly,
would be to sully his image in their eyes."

Merrill drew deeply on his cigar. "I see. Then you were perfectly willing to sacrifice your job to prevent that from happening?"

Katherine nodded. "My first obligation is to the children, Mr. Merrill. They revere their father, as they should."

"I see," Merrill said. "Well, Miss Cooley, I suppose I should ask you a good many more questions. But you speak quite well, and I've already checked your educational credentials. Your references from Washington are in order. And the characteristic my client is most definite about is that the woman have a strong feeling for children. You seem to have that in abundance. So . . ."

"Yes, sir?" Katherine said.

Merrill told her, "The first thing you'll have to do is take the train to Lakeside . . ."

By the time she was nineteen, Katherine Cooley had been to normal school in her native Maryland and was trying to find proper work for a genteel young lady as a teacher or a governess. It was obvious to her, and it had been reinforced by her attractive, older, married sisters and her stern, humorless mother, that she'd be hard-pressed to find a husband with her pale looks, imposing intellect and cool manner.

"A man likes a woman he can feel comfortable with," her mother told her. "That ain't you, with your high-falutin' ways. You never laugh. You have to flatter a man, keep him full of himself."

"As you did with Daddy, I suppose," Katherine had replied.

"That's what I mean. You've got an evil tongue, Katherine."

"I come by it naturally," Katherine had said.

"I won't be spoken to like that in my own house," her mother had thundered.

"So I'll leave," Katherine had replied calmly.

And leave she did. She had gone to an employment agency in the nearby District of Columbia, and within days she found herself interviewing for a job as governess for the children of a member of President Taft's cabinet. She had stayed with the cabinet member's small children for several years. Then Taft had left office, replaced by the Democrat Wilson, and the cabinet member and his family had moved back to Illinois.

Katherine then found herself in the employ of Congressman J. Arch Gordon, a short, genial, middle-aged man with a much younger, much richer wife and two small children. Actually, Katherine's reputation as a fine governess and teacher had been formidable enough to land her any number of jobs in Washington, but she had been persuaded to accept the position with the Gordons when she learned that Gordon represented the southern tier of New York State in Congress. He lived in Boydstown. Intrigued by the prospect of living in the north for a while, Katherine had readily accepted the post, even though the Gordon children showed every sign of being impossibly spoiled and even though she hadn't liked the glint in the congressman's eye.

It had taken her more than a year to civilize the Gordon children. During that time, she developed a genuine friendship with their mother, a simple and somewhat scatterbrained woman named Charlotte whose family owned teak forests in Korea, gold mines in Montana and tin mines somewhere else. The family's routine consisted of regular pilgrimages to Washington, where they maintained an elegant townhouse on Capitol Hill; to Cape Cod, where they owned an unpretentious, thirty-room "cottage" in Marstons Mills, and, of course, at home in Boydstown, a twenty-eight-acre estate on the edge of town, the centerpiece of which was a monstrous English tudor mansion with slate floors in the library and foyer and the most modern indoor plumbing.

Katherine enjoyed her work and the luxurious atmosphere in which she performed it. The only problem was the congressman himself, a jovial lecher whose primary delight in life was running his hands under the skirts of female employees.

"Sir," Katherine had said angrily the first time it had happened to her, "you must not do that."

"And why not?" grinned J. Arch Gordon.

"Because it's improper, Sir," Katherine had replied, red-faced, "it's shameful."

"I suppose it is," the congressman conceded. "Still, if you'd only stand still you might find you enjoy it."

Katherine, however, was truly horrified by such conduct, and the day finally came when she gave in to the temptation to fight back against the abuse. The congressman made one advance too many, and Katherine disabled him with a knee to his groin. Then, as the congressman knelt in the library of the Boydstown mansion, clutching his privates, she had marched in to the mistress of the house and resigned, citing personal reasons she was unwilling to discuss.

"Oh my, Katherine," Charlotte Gordon had wailed, "whatever will we do without you? Mr. Gordon will be positively crushed."

Katherine had replied, "I wouldn't be at all surprised if he's crushed already."

She had then been faced with the choice of returning to Washington or staying on in Boydstown, which she had grown to like. Washington was home, but to return there without a job would have been to admit failure, if only temporarily, to her mother and sisters, which she had no inclination to do.

She had been prudent with her salary, saving most of it because she had had no real needs that had not been supplied by the Gordons. A comfortable room and meals had come with the job in exchange for virtually twenty-four-hour service on her part. She finally decided to take a rented room in a good section of Boydstown, to discreetly circulate her name among the better families in town and see what developed. When her money ran low, she could always take the flyer back to Washington.

That had been her condition when she had been contacted by Amos Merrill—who had heard of her through his wife—and she had been so far above the other possible applicants that hers was the only name Merrill had forwarded to William Stewart, who then forwarded it to Liam at the Weidener farm.

A week later, Katherine found herself in the study of the big house facing a haggard-looking man whose jaw was blurred by a three-day growth of beard. She could smell the liquor on his breath across the desk. Yet he listened to her tell her story with genuine interest, and his questions, delivered in a soft and appealing brogue, were politely phrased, although probing, as she had expected.

"One last question, Miss Cooley," he said as the interview drew to a close. "How old are you?"

"I'm twenty-four, sir," Katherine told him. "I don't smoke. I drink only moderately, and I have no regular gentlemen friends."

Liam laughed. "You answered several questions."

"I assumed that was information you considered pertinent, sir," she told him.

"It is, I suppose. I have no quarrel with smoking by women, you should know. As for gentleman friends . . . well, you can see how isolated we are here."

"And I presume you have no objections to drinking, either?" she said, and Liam didn't miss the edge to the remark.

"In a governess I'd object to it, yes," he said somewhat curtly. "But you've already made it clear that you're not given to excesses, haven't you?"

Katherine nodded. "I hope I've made that clear, yes."

Liam leaned back in Christian's chair and studied her for a moment. "Well, you've answered all my questions with a great deal of candor, Miss Cooley. I can't think of anybody else I'd rather see charged with bringing up my daughter to be a proper lady. I don't know what salary you'd be looking for . . ."

Katherine was not at all sure she wanted this job. Certainly the money would not be the deciding factor.

"The Gordons paid me ten dollars a week and room and board," she said.

"Yes," Liam said. "Well, you'd certainly want a raise, wouldn't you? How about twelve dollars?"

Katherine eyed him levelly. "Ten dollars would be more than sufficient, Mister Brennan. But before I decide, I would have to meet the child. It's possible she won't like me."

"Helen likes everybody," he said, "but come along."

He led her through the house and upstairs to Helga's old room, where Helen lay sleeping. Liam opened the door a crack, then he put his fingers to his lips. He and Katherine slipped into the room and stood over the sleeping infant. Helen clutched a small, stuffed bear. Her short, silken golden curls spread over the sheet, surrounding her tiny head like a halo.

"That's my darlin'," Liam said in a soft, hoarse whisper. He put a calloused hand down inside the crib and stroked the child's hair with great gentleness.

Katherine, standing off to one side and to the rear, looked at him, this big, sad, drunken man so desperately in love with the sleeping infant. She felt as though a huge, burning bubble had settled in her throat and chest. "I'd be pleased to accept the job, Mister Brennan," she said quietly.

* * * *

Indian summer visited the lake country that year. The first chill of autumn came and went suddenly to be replaced by a glorious interlude of warmth for the fall harvest. The sun hung over the sloping, hillside fields of the Weidener farm like a slice of lemon, and confused wild flowers in the fallow meadows burst forth in new, brightly colored petals.

Katherine, walking with the infant Helen through the rows of grapevines, was sure she'd never seen anything quite so lovely. Settled in Helga's old room, with Helen in the master bedroom and Liam once again living in the shack, she soon began to feel more at home than she ever had anywhere else. The broad, shining expanse of lake and rolling mountains was breathtaking, and she had struck up a warm and instant friendship with Annette Le Barnot, who was teaching her French. Katherine had also, to everyone's surprise, made a startling hit with Minnie, who seemed to sense instinctively that her prim and proper exterior masked an unusual warmth and depth of character and a whim of steel that Minnie both shared and admired.

"That's one fine young girl," Minnie told Annette one morning over coffee. "She's in love with that little baby in a way Helga never was, God forgive me for saying it."

Annette nodded. "And Liam too, I think."

"Oh," Minnie had said, "go on with you. Liam?"

Annette winked. "We French, we miss nothing."

Minnie pondered the proposition for a moment. "Could be," she said finally. "Mightn't be a bad thing. He's going to drink himself to death young unless somebody straightens him out."

Liam was, in fact, drunk by nightfall every day. He was working hard supervising the harvesting crews and clearing his own land each morning. He had begun again to rise before dawn daily to row out on the lake to catch trout for meals. Sometimes Henri, who was developing a genuine passion for trout fishing, went with him despite the demands of the season. But by lunch Liam had already consumed a serious amount of alcohol. By dinner if he wasn't quite drunk he was very near it. He was putting on weight in an unhealthy way, in a roll around his formerly trim middle, despite his regimen of physical exercise. Moreover, his color wasn't good. He spent every day outdoors, yet he was developing a definite pallor.

He took his only full meal of the day, dinner, with Katherine, Henri, Annette and little Helen in the dining room of the big house. Then he would go down to the shack after putting Helen to bed and brood and drink.

One night, after Henri and Annette had left for their house and Minnie had retired to her small room off the kitchen, Liam came downstairs from his nightly ritual of rocking Helen to sleep and reached for his coat. Katherine, who was sitting and reading in Christian's old chair near the fireplace, looked up. "Leaving so soon, Mr. Brennan?" she said.

Liam, his jacket in his hand, looked over at her in surprise. He always left the big house at this time. "There's much to be done tomorrow," he said. "We've three more days of harvesting, at the very least."

Katherine said, "Is the weather here always so gentle this time of year for the harvest?"

"Hardly. This is a rare, God-sent Indian summer. It's given us more time. We got off to a late start this year."

Katherine lowered her book. "Where did that term come from, I wonder."

"Indian summer?"

"Yes."

Liam settled into the rocking chair next to her, in front of the fire she had built to ward off the night chill. "Well, I was told once that it goes back to colonial days, when the Indians were raiding settlers. They would usually halt raids for the winter and the settlers knew they were safe until it got warm again. And then when summer came back again for a few weeks this time of year, they knew that the Indians would be back for blood one more time before the snow flew. I wouldn't imagine that the phrase had a particularly happy ring to it in those days."

They sat there for a moment, peering into the orange flame. Then, after a brief silence, Liam began to rise.

"Well . . ." he began, planning to say good night.

"What sort of Indians lived around here?" Katherine asked suddenly.

Liam sat back again, somewhat confused. He studied the young woman beside him. The light from the fire played off the curves and hollows of her face and neck. Liam, watching, noticed for the first time that her eyes were large and luminous with the firelight dancing in them. She looked almost pretty, sitting there like that. "Iroquois," he told her. "Around here the dominant Iroquois tribe was the Senecas. They were the politicians. The greatest of the Seneca leaders was a famous orator named Red Jacket. He was born in a village that used to be located down the lake a bit. Tell me, why are you asking me all these questions? Is there some reason you don't want me to go?"

Katherine looked at him. It was a direct question, and she decided it deserved an equally direct answer. "I think, Mr. Brennan," she said slowly, "that it might be in your own interest to spend more time in this house at night, after dinner, perhaps drinking coffee or tea. If my presence disturbs you, I'd be more than happy to retire to my own room. But you shouldn't spend so much time alone in that little house at night. It's not good for you."

Liam stood up. "I appreciate your concern, Miss Cooley," he said coldly, "but I'm a grown man fully capable of making decisions about how I'll live my life."

"Perhaps you are. But there's a little girl upstairs who's already without a mother. If you keep drinking the way you are, she'll be without a father soon enough as well."

Liam was flabbergasted at the woman's brass. "Who're you to talk to me that way?" he demanded harshly.

Katherine shrugged. "Who do I have to be? It doesn't take anybody special to see what you're doing to yourself."

Liam threw his jacket on the floor in rage. "I hired you to care for my daughter. I didn't hire you to give me advice on my drinking habits or any other aspect of my personal life."

Katherine stood up calmly and closed her book, placing it neatly on the table next to her. "Your personal life, sir, seems to have no other aspects."

Liam turned bright purple.

"My one concern," she went on in a level tone that wavered only slightly, "is the well-being of that child upstairs, Mr. Brennan. That's the responsibility you've given me, and I'd be remiss if I failed to speak out in this matter. I don't know what you were like before my arrival here, although I'm told you were a kind and gentle man, devoted to your family. But now you seem to have become a self-centered drunkard whose idea of a good time seems to be sulking and drinking himself into oblivion. You have your reasons, I'm sure, but the point I'm making is that a reason for doing something does not necessarily constitute a valid justification for doing it. Good night, sir."

Liam began to respond, but he was so furious that the words came out in a halting sputter. Before he could form a comprehensible sentence, Katherine turned and marched upstairs. He heard the door to her room close and suddenly found himself standing alone in the sitting room. At that moment, Minnie, in a robe and slippers over her flannel nightgown, came in from her room in back of the kitchen.

"I heard some shouting, Liam," she said, "are you all right?"

He bent over and picked up his jacket from the floor. "Apparently not," he snarled. Then he walked out the door and down to the shack.

Once inside, he stoked up the fire. Indian summer or no, the nights were getting chilly. He poured himself a half-cup full of John Hardy's applejack and sipped at the fiery liquid. It didn't taste right to him, and he went out on the porch and threw the liquor into the lake. Goddamn that woman, he thought, she had a tongue that could trim a hedge.

It was hours before he got to sleep.

* * * *

Liam did not discharge Katherine Cooley, although he was tempted to after their clash in the sitting room. He had spent a considerable amount of time and effort in finding her, and there was no debating that she was good for Helen, who was already beginning to toddle unsteadily and utter words Liam found unintelligible but that Katherine found perfectly clear. Moreover, Liam didn't question the motive behind her speech, nor, in fact, its accuracy.

For her part, Katherine viewed Liam as a tragic figure. She had seen the photographs of Helga that were all over the house, and she had been awed by the dead woman's beauty, so startling in contrast to her own plain features. Katherine thought, however, that she had seen in the photographs the slightest hint of something she didn't care for. She couldn't put it into words. She had seen in the eyes a vague indication that Helga had perhaps occupied the center of her own world to a startling degree. This deduction had been confirmed, more or less, in conversations with Minnie and Annette, who, although they had felt great affection for Helga, had not been blind to her faults. Nonetheless, Katherine felt enormous sympathy for Liam and for herself as well, aware as she was of the remote likelihood that she could ever inspire such devotion in a man. Still, she thought, there was the child. Regardless of his loss, Liam owed it to Helen to be the best Liam Brennan possible, and that he certainly was making no effort to be.

So both Liam and Katherine decided independently to make no further reference to the events of that night, to put it behind them without prejudice. But then, several weeks later, there came a night when Liam failed to come up from the shack for dinner. Henri, Annette and Katherine ate in awkward silence, broken only occasionally by Henri's attempts at wit. The meal was eaten quickly, and Henri and Annette left without coffee, pleading general exhaustion.

Minnie came in from the kitchen, and Katherine helped her clear the table, wrap up the leftover food and wash the dishes. Then Katherine brewed a cup of tea. She sipped it as she sat in front of the fireplace, and she waited until long past the hour that Liam usually chose to rock Helen to sleep. Then she went upstairs. Helen was lying in her crib, a stuffed toy firmly in her grasp. Katherine wrapped Helen snugly against the night chill, then stroked her flaxen hair, so much like Helga's hair in the photographs.

After a little while, Katherine went downstairs and threw a coat over her shoulders. Minnie had retired for the evening, and Katherine was careful not to disturb her. She lit a kerosene lamp, and followed the path from the big house, across the dirt road and down the wooden steps to the lake level, finding herself outside the door to the shack. She rapped loudly on the door. No answer. She rapped again.

Standing there, with the stars glittering over the lake behind her and a gentle wash of waves rolling up over the slate beach, Katherine could not say why she had come down from the big house. At first she felt a surge of anger at Liam, whom she was sure was lying dead drunk on the other side of the door, oblivious to any of them, including Helen. But later, as the silence had hung over the dinner table, she had begun to feel a vague sense of uneasiness, as though something was terribly wrong. Such intuitions came seldom to Katherine, and they were not always accurate when they did. But she did not discount them, as a man would have done. And now, rapping fiercely on the door of the shack and breaking the hush of nightime on the lakefront, she was torn between anger and fear—anger at Liam for what he had done and at herself for lowering herself to coming here and fear that something was very much wrong inside the shack.

At last she heard a stirring inside the darkened building, then she heard lumbering footsteps and the door flew open. Liam hung against it, his eyes blinking in the lantern's glare.

"What?" he asked dully. "Who is it?"

Katherine said, "It's me, Mr. Brennan. I came to see if you were all right. When you didn't come up for dinner, we were worried, and . . ."

Then Katherine's lips tightened. In the lantern's dim light, Liam was tilting precariously. His breath was sour with wine. His eyelids were at half-mast, as though he were dozing as he stood there. Liam Brennan, she realized, was extremely drunk. He grinned sheepishly and lurched out onto the porch. "I'm fine, fine," he told her, his words slurring. "Pretty night."

Katherine was enraged. She felt as foolish as she had ever felt. She watched Liam stagger in the weak light. He went down the steps to the beach, then weaved out to the point and onto the dock that jutted out into the water. Furious, her lantern held high, she followed. "I can see that you're fine," she fumed. "I should have known that you'd be fine."

"Look at that sky," Liam said, pointing in the general direction of the canopy of stars that covered the lake. "Where have you ever seen stars like that, now tell me?"

Katherine began to respond, but she realized that she was so angry now that speech had failed her. She spun on her heel and started back up the point to the steps. She could hear the hushed lapping of the waves against the rocky beach. Then, as she started up the steps to the porch, she heard another sound. It was unmistakably the sound of Liam Brennan hitting the water with a mighty splash. Katherine turned on the steps and held the lantern high, but all she could make out was the dim outline of the dock against the somewhat lighter shade of the lake. "Mr. Brennan?" she called out.

His answer was a muffled gurgling and a mighty splashing in the deep water off the point.

Katherine ran nimbly back down the stairs and out onto the dock. She held the lantern over the churning water. She could see Liam just beneath the surface, struggling feebly, a growing cloud of red staining the blackness around him. Katherine knew immediately what she had to do.

The water was an icy shock that took her breath away. She approached from the rear, grasping his hair with one hand, reaching for the dock with the other. Katherine pulled at the dock, and then she felt the bottom beneath her stockinged feet. She dug in her feet and yanked Liam hard by the hair. In a moment, she was dragging him up on the beach next to the dock. Once a substantial portion of his body was out of the water, it became impossible for her to move him another inch.

In the flickering light of the kerosene lantern on the dock, she examined him. Liam lay there coughing violently, spitting up water in all directions and gasping weakly for air. On the left side of his forehead, just above the eye, blood was seeping from an ugly inch-long gash. It looked to be an eighth of an inch or more in depth, but the blood was already beginning to coagulate after contact with the icy water. Katherine guessed that he had struck his head on the dock as he toppled into the water.

Coughing and retching, Liam pulled himself to a sitting position in the shallow water. He coughed again, clearing his lungs this time. He put his hand to his head wound, and his fingers came away bloody. "Good God," he mumbled, "what happened to me?"

Katherine shivered in the night chill, her wet clothing hanging on her like an enormous cold compress. "Can you walk?"

"Yes, he told her. "I manage to hurt myself in some foolish way on a regular basis. This year I've managed to do it twice, and we've months to go before 1915."

"You're a careless man, Mr. Brennan," she told him, "careless with just about everything and everyone."

Liam didn't argue. He merely leaned heavily on her as he staggered up the point and into the shack.

A fire blazed in the fireplace, and she deposited him in the wicker rocker in front of it, dripping water in a huge puddle beneath the chair. Liam lay back, his eyes closed. He was still coughing up some water. The head injury could be something to worry about. For a moment Katherine debated going to get Henri to take Liam into town to the doctor, but she rejected the idea almost immediately. It was almost impossible for a drunk to hurt himself seriously in a fall, she supposed, especially a fall into water, and the wound didn't look that bad. She went into the bedroom and found a blanket. She came out and wrapped it around him. He was asleep already, his breathing calm now, relaxed and regular. Katherine looked at him and shook her head wearily. He could stay in his wet clothes for all she cared. She certainly wouldn't take them off of him. She rather hoped he'd catch pneumonia, or a bad cold at least.

The shack was a disaster with clothing and dirty dishes all about. Katherine hustled about, compulsively stacking dirty dishes in the sink, tossing soiled clothes into a pile in the corner and gathering up a dozen or so empty wine and applejack bottles. Those she deposited in the trash. But she was shivering now in her sopping wet clothes. She moved closer to the fire, her lips blue and her teeth chattering. She knew she would have to leave and get back up to the big house, but her coat and shoes, which she had shed before jumping into the lake, were out on the dock. The thought of making her way up the hill wet, coatless and barefoot had no appeal for her. She would be the one who would end up with pneumonia if she tried that.

Only one sensible course of action was open to her. She went into the little bedroom and looked through the closet. There she found Helga's clothing, undisturbed since her death. Katherine tried to put on a pair of Helga's shoes, but they were much too large. She stripped off her own wet clothing and tried to put on one of Helga's slips and a dress. But again, the difference in their respective sizes was too great.

Finally, Katherine settled for wrapping herself in one of Helga's robes, which hung on her like a tent. She took her own soaked, dripping clothes, wrung them out over the sink and arranged them on the stone hearth. She had no choice but to stay in the shack until they dried sufficiently for her to put them back on and make her way up to the big house, an enterprise she hoped wouldn't take long.

She was shivering uncontrollably, and her skin had the bluish-gray tinge that comes with a marked dropped in body temperature. She found a bottle of wine in the kitchen, washed out one of the glasses on the counter and poured herself a half-tumbler full of Brennan white dinner wine. It went down smoothly and warmed her as it did. She refilled the glass. Then she settled herself into the rocker next to Liam, who was snoring loudly, and waited for the fire to do its work on her clothes.

The wine was loosening her up, and she felt the shivering begin to ease. The warmth of the fire was like heaven to her. Soon her shivering stopped completely. After a while, she reached down and touched her dress, which was spread out on the hearth. It was still wet, but slowly it was drying from the heat of the blaze.

Another hour or so, Katherine thought, settling back in the chair and wrapping herself snugly in the thick robe.

* * * *

"Coffee?" Liam asked.

Katherine awakened with a start. "Oh," she said. Then she looked around her. The fire was still blazing. It obviously had been replenished. But it was no longer night. Dawn sunlight shone through the windows of the shack, and Liam was looming up in front of her, his left eye swollen and blue black around the cut over it. He was dressed in a robe of his own, and he was smiling down at her.

"I must have fallen asleep," she said needlessly.

"And stayed asleep," he told her. "When I came awake a half hour or so ago, I stumbled around here building up the fire again, and I made enough noise, I'm sure, to wake the dead, but you slept on. How do you feel?"

Katherine stood up. She was stiff, and her back ached immediately. "Dear God," she moaned. "You should never go to sleep in a chair."

"Coffee?" Liam repeated.

"Please. No sugar."

"And no cream either, I'm afraid. I don't use either, so I keep none here."

Katherine merely nodded and took the cup of steaming black coffee from him. She ached in every bone of her body from spending the night in the wicker rocking chair. Her hair had dried as she slept, and it hung limply around her face and shoulders. Wrapped in Helga's enormous robe and her hair in such wild disarray, Katherine was sure she looked the perfect fool. "I have to get dressed and get back up to the house. Minnie will be looking for me, and Helen has to be fed."

"I'm sure Minnie is feeding her," Liam said. "Have some coffee first. Besides, your clothes are still damp on the underside. I checked them before I woke you up. You have to turn them over, you know, if you want to dry them out completely."

She looked at him. Except for the bruise, he appeared none the worse for wear after last night's adventure. In fact, she was forced to admit, he looked considerably better than she felt, and she had touched barely a drop. "You're going to have a terrible black eye," she told him. "It's already all puffed up."

"The wages of sin. I have only the vaguest memory of what happened."

"You were drunk. You fell into the lake and hit your head on the dock on the way in. I had to pull you out."

Liam smiled. "That much I do remember. What I don't remember is what you were doing here in the first place."

"I thought perhaps something had happened to you when you failed to appear for dinner and to say goodnight to Helen. You've never missed putting her to bed before."

Liam's eyebrows rose in amusement. "You mean to say you were worried about me? Is that it?"

Katherine flushed momentarily. Ordinarily she could more than handle Liam Brennan's attempts to discomfort her. But here, looking as she looked and dressed as she was dressed, she felt at a distinct disadvantage. "I . . . well, yes. I suppose I was. It was a perfectly natural reaction."

"I'm touched," he told her.

Katherine could not be sure if he was mocking her or making the statement in sincerity. Either way, she found the remark annoying. "Don't be," she said curtly. "I don't find drunkards touching or amusing, even when they're sober and sorry the next morning."

"You're a hard woman, Katherine Cooley," Liam told her.

"Mister Brennan, my father was a wonderful man. He was brave and charming and handsome. But in his later years he drank too much. He didn't drink the way you do, thank God, but he drank enough to depend on it. It made him weak. I don't find weakness in a man particularly appealing or amusing."

Liam sat down in the rocker and sipped his own coffee. "I suppose that from a certain perspective, what happened to me last night might be viewed as amusing. And you jumping in the lake fully clothed . . . well, I wish I'd been alert enough to commit the sight to memory. I'm sure it must have been difficult for you to maintain that marvelous composure . . ."

He was mocking her now, Katherine knew. There was no doubt about it. She began to frame an acid-tinged response. It was on her lips, ready to fly. But then, to her shock and to Liam's as well, she suddenly burst into tears. It was so unlike her that both of them were stunned. Katherine struggled to bring herself under control. The half-filled coffee cup slipped from her fingers and bounced off the wooden floor. She tried to speak, but the tears and the sobbing had overwhelmed her, and she turned away.

Liam, slightly astounded, stood up and walked over to her, standing behind her, towering over her. She was such a tiny woman, he thought, at least eight inches shorter than Helga, and small boned, like a bird. "I'm sorry," he said softly. "I didn't mean to upset you."

She whirled on him, her face red and contorted, and the tears streaming down it in rivulets. "Oh no," she said angrily. "Of course not. You never mean to hurt anybody, do you? But you do, you know. You've hurt Henri and Annette, who're your friends, although God knows why. You've hurt Minnie deeply. You should remember that she suffered some loss herself when your wife and her father died. She'd raised your wife from childhood. I've discussed it with her, although I know that hasn't occurred to you. And most of all, you've hurt Helen. You ignored her for months, as though she didn't exist. Last night you weren't there for her again. Your speciality is hurting people, Mr. Brennan. You seem to have a rare talent for it."

"And you?" he asked gently. "I've hurt you, too?"

"Yes," she said, her head high. "And me."

"How have I hurt you, Katherine? Tell me that, please."

She brushed by him. "Where are my clothes? I'll wear them wet. I don't care."

"They're still almost soaked through," Liam told her. "I'll get dressed and go up to the big house and get you some dry stuff. You'll never fit into anything of Helga's. She was twice your size."

"Never mind," Katherine snapped, gathering up her damp things from where they lay on the hearth.

Liam opened his mouth to speak. But at that moment a knock came at the door. Katherine and Liam exchanged glances—hers confused and angry and his apologetic. Then Liam went to the door and opened it a crack. Katherine heard Henri's voice from the porch.

"My friend," he said, "are you all right? We were worried about you when you did not come up to dinner last night. My God, what happened to your eye?"

By this time Henri had pushed himself fully into the doorway, and his glance went over Liam's shoulder to Katherine, standing next to the hearth in Helga's huge robe, her hair hanging loose. Momentarily, a look of consternation passed over Henri's face. Then it was replaced by a broad and knowing grin. "Forgive me," he said. "I am so sorry. I did not mean to disturb you. Or you, Katherine. I will be gone now."

"Come in, Henri," Liam said. "We're just having some coffee. We had quite an adventure here last night."

"Liam," Henri said disapprovingly, "a man does not discuss such adventures—particularly when the lady is present. My God, you Irish! Excuse me now. The wine awaits my attention." Then, with a wink and a smile—and before Liam could utter another word—Henri was gone, out the door and up the steps to the road.

Liam, coffee cup in hand, stepped out on the porch and shouted after him, "You've an evil mind, Henri Le Barnot."

"Of course," Katherine heard Henri shoot back. "All this is in my evil mind. I will see you later, my friend. Or, perhaps not. That, too, I would understand."

Liam stood on the porch for a moment, watching Henri go up the steps. Then he sighed and stepped back inside and closed the door. Katherine rolled her eyes heavenward and sank down to the hearth.

"Well," Liam said in an amused tone, "I'm afraid you're a marked woman now, Katherine."

"My God!" Katherine said in utter exasperation. "I won't be able to show my face. I've never been so mortified. Why did I ever come down here? I must have been out of my mind."

"Well, it's not so bad," Liam said, shrugging good-naturedly, "it's only Henri. He's right, though. In Ireland, a man and a woman who are found in this sort of circumstance ought to be married."

Katherine's face felt as though it was on fire. "You find all this quite amusing, don't you?"

He shrugged. "I'm not sure there's any recourse but to find some humor in the situation. You know, I've finally figured out what it is about you that bothers me."

"That bothers you about me?" she said in disbelief. "And what, pray tell, might that be?"

He came over and sat beside her on the hearth. "I've never seen you laugh. In fact, I've never seen you show the slightest shred of genuine emotion until just a moment ago. It becomes you."

Katherine's crimson face turned even redder. She turned away.

Liam said, "I guess I'd better get dressed and get up to the house and get you some clothes. I apologize if I've embarrassed you with what I've said, but it's true, you know."

Katherine turned and looked full into his face. "You're a strange man," she said quietly.

"Not so strange. Just weak flesh. Too weak, I'm afraid, but I'll try to do better."

He smiled at her. The effort virtually closed his injured eye. "Oh, and by the bye, when your hair is loose like that, falling down around your shoulders, it softens your face. It . . . well, it shows you to be a rather pretty woman when you unbend a bit."

Katherine flushed mightily now, but she also smiled, despite herself. "This is quite ridiculous," she told him.

"Life is ridiculous, or haven't you noticed. This, I think, is rather less ridiculous than most of it."

Then, slowly and with great gentleness, Liam Brennan raised one big hand and touched her chin with it. He lifted up her head and kissed her. It was not a passionate kiss. It was a loving gesture, and Katherine felt herself melting with it. It lasted a long while, and she never moved, did not breathe. When it was over, he stood up wordlessly and went into the bedroom to dress. Katherine continued to sit on the hearth, the fire warming her back through the oversized robe, listening to him as he whistled to himself in the bedroom. She put her fingers to her lips where he had touched her. Not many men had touched her there, and none ever with the capacity to so move her. As she thought that, a few more tears rolled down her cheeks. But this time they were good tears.

* * * *

Katherine Cooley and Liam Brennan were married on a cold, gray day in late January of 1915. It was, in contrast to Liam's first wedding, a relatively quiet affair, as was fitting less than a year after the untimely death of his first wife. It was presided over in the sitting room of the big house by Father Maloney, who would have preferred to have held it in the church but who acceded to Liam's request. A little altar was erected in the sitting room near the fireplace, and the small number of guests were seated in chairs rented from the Lakeside Hotel.

Although the guest list was considerably shorter than it had been for the wedding Christian had orchestrated, some of those who had been attendance for the wedding of Liam and Helga were on hand for his wedding to Katherine. Among them were Dr. and Mrs. Frazier and their daughter Ellen, Helga's maid of honor who herself was scheduled to marry in the spring and move to New York, where her husband-to-be practiced medicine.

"How do you think it looks?" Liam had asked Ellen a week before the wedding when he had bumped into her in town. "Is there talk about my remarrying so soon?"

"Don't be silly, Liam," she told him. "If you were fifty years old there might be talk. But you're a young man, and you and Helga weren't married all that long. Besides, the whole village knows how much her death devastated you."

"They know about the drinking, you mean."

Ellen shrugged. "It's a small town. But everybody is glad you're over that now, and Lakeside wishes you well. Especially me, and I was Helga's friend."

Aside from the Fraziers, Liam invited some of the town's leading families, excluding those whose only contact with the family had been through Christian. Also in attendance were several area farmers whom Liam had met through the grape growers' association, including the Young and Roach families. They owned land toward the lake's Ringlesport end and were now selling grapes to the Brennan Winery as contract growers. Congressman and Mrs. Gordon had been invited, but the congressman sent his regrets and those of his family, which came as no surprise to Katherine and caused her no pain. She took the refusal of her own family to attend, however, somewhat harder, even though she had suspected that her conversion to Catholicism would ensure their absence from the proceedings.

The wedding itself was significant for two reasons: it joined Liam and Katherine together in a union each needed desperately, and the guests and their respectful attitude marked Liam's official entry into the community of important people in Lakeside. Regardless of the intricacies of Christian's will, which were known around town the moment it was admitted to probate, Liam was nonetheless an important property owner in the local scheme of things. He was the operator of a new and growing winery and a bona fide member of the lake country establishment both on the strength of his holdings and the force of his personality. He was also better liked as a man than Christian had been.

After the ceremony and near the end of a sumptuous buffet dinner catered by Peter Day's staff at the Lakeside Hotel, Henri, who had served as best man while Annette had been matron of honor, rose and clinked a spoon against his wine glass until all conversation halted. "A toast," he said, "to Liam and Katherine—happiness, peace, long life and fulfill-ment."

All the guests downed their wine along with the bride and groom. Liam set his glass carefully on the table next to him and looked down into Katherine's eyes, a signal flashing between them. As he did, Jim Frazier approached and made small talk for a few moments. Then a waiter came over and offered to refill their glasses. Liam put his hand over the top of his glass. "None for me," he said quietly. "I've had enough to drink."

And so he had. For the rest of his days, Liam Brennan, grape grower and winemaker, never touched another drop.

Chapter 10

By 1916 Liam had settled firmly into the structure of Lakeside. His farm was large and reasonably prosperous. He had expanded his dairy herd and his plantings of barley, buckwheat, corn and other crops, not so much because farming interested him but because he needed the profits from those crops to underwrite the expensive work Henri was doing in the winery.

Liam was a careful money manager who negotiated good deals with Lakeside Trust when borrowing for seed and fertilizer. He kept his costs down by engaging in enormous amounts of physical work himself. As a result, within a few years he was a rarity for a farmer—a man who still had cash in the bank when spring rolled around.

Liam was active in the Grange, a member of the Lakeside Elks lodge, served on the township zoning board and even found his opinion solicited whenever the Lake County Republican Committee was about to slate candidates for public office. His farm, which until Christian's death had been referred to throughout the community as "the Weidener place," came to be known as "the Brennan place" in fairly short order.

Moreover, as private boating picked up on the lake, the point of land that jutted out from Liam's beach began to take on an identity of its own. The Lakeside Yacht Club, a collection of merchants and professional men whose zeal for sailing bordered on madness, issued updated charts of the lake in 1916. In so doing, they formalized popular nicknames for various points along the shoreline. The charts referred to the finger of land that extended from Liam's beach as Brennan's Point.

Before long the name began to be applied to the entire property. Whenever Bill Stewart, the lawyer, drove out to the farm with papers for Liam to sign, he routinely told his secretary he could be found for the next few hours at Brennan's Point. When it became Liam's turn to host the Elks annual picnic on his property, the flyers that were distributed to the membership specified that the picnic of 1916 would be held at Brennan's Point.

When America finally entered the war in Europe in April of 1917, Liam Brennan was twenty-nine years old and the father of two children. To his delight, Katherine had become pregnant shortly after their marriage and had given birth to a son, Kevin, late in 1915. Liam could see no point in the conflict, and he was a thoroughly Americanized rural Republican now, not a supporter of Woodrow Wilson, on whom he blamed the whole bloody business.

Yes, he conceded in political debates with the other grape growers and the other members of the Village of Lakeside Planning Board, it was true that a German submarine had sunk the British liner *Lusitania* at a cost of nearly twelve hundred lives, one hundred and twenty-eight of them American. But it was also true, he pointed out, that the German embassy had warned Americans to avoid British vessels, and it couldn't be disputed that the ship had been carrying forty-two hundred cases of cartridges and other British military supplies. Moreover, he was skeptical that this would be the war to end all wars, as the Europeans had promised. "I'm sure that somewhere down the road they'll find something else to fight about," he said often. "They always have."

Had Liam been called upon to serve, as nine million other men between the ages of twenty-one and thirty were called, he would have gone without question. But he was not called, and there was a valid question as to whether he could have passed the physical in any event. His ankle had never quite healed properly from the accident with the dynamite several years before. Liam walked with a slight but noticeable limp, especially in cold and wet weather, that might have rendered him unfit for service had the question ever arisen.

Also, there was talk in Lakeside—discreet talk, because no one wanted to offend him—that because his first wife had been born in Germany his sympathies were understandably with that nation in any conflict with the British. And, in truth, this analysis was not far wrong. Liam was not overly enthusiastic about being on the same side as the British Empire, regardless of the opponent's character.

Once America was in the war, however, Liam followed the clash with great interest. He bought a mail subscription to the *New York World* and read avidly of the adventures of "Black Jack" Pershing and the trials of Lloyd George and Clemenceau. He watched closely the autocratic behavior of Bernard Baruch as Wilson's War Industries Board chairman. Liam bought his share of Liberty bonds and then some, and he commiserated with Henri over the havoc that was being wreaked on the Frenchman's homeland.

Liam was moderately amused at the way the French ace Georges Guynemer and Germany's Red Knight, Baron Manfred von Richthofen, demolished Christian's prediction about the future of aerial warfare. The newspapers were filled with esoterica concerning the Fokker DR-1, the British Sopwith Camel and the American Curtiss JN-4D, the last developed by a genius who lived and worked not far from the farm, Glenn Hammond Curtiss, who was at that time the most famous man in the lake country. The nation's newest hero was the American ace Eddie Rickenbacker, whose German ancestry served as no impediment to his skill against the Kaiser's pilots.

Despite all this, life on the farm and throughout the lake country was little affected by the carnage in Europe. The trout still struck, the grapes still grew, the deer still wandered carelessly about the mountain slopes as though they were immortal.

No matter how distant the war from New York State's wine-growing region, however, a national movement was afoot that hit very close to home. Prohibition, the noble experiment, sent fingers of fear clutching at many a heart in the wine district.

Liam was one of a delegation of winemakers and vineyardists who made a trip one Sunday afternoon to Boydstown to confer on the issue with Congressman Gordon. The congressman received the delegation in the study of his enormous tudor mansion, and he listened politely as they presented their case. Then he sat behind his gleaming desk, shaking his head slowly, finally lifting it up and saying, "Gentlemen, I wish I could offer you more encouragement, but I can tell you honestly that my vote won't mean a hoot in hell on this issue. The country is going dry, and there's not a damned thing I can do about it. If I could, rest assured I'd vote your way."

"Does that mean," Liam asked, "that you're not going to vote our way?"

Gordon looked up. "You're Mr. Brennan; is that right?"

Liam nodded. "I am."

Gordon said, "I believe I had the pleasure of employing your wife some years ago, before your marriage." It was a question, although not worded as such, and Liam nodded again.

"Well then, Mr. Brennan, I suspect you have some knowledge of the sort of man I am, although you and I don't know one another personally. I'll be candid with you. If I thought my oposition would be a factor in this, I'd gladly vote against the amendment. But the fact of the matter is that it won't, and you should understand that I'm being subjected to serious pressure from the dry forces who are going to win this dispute in any event. I will tell you now, gentlemen, that I'm with you. I see no inherent evil in the consumption of alcohol. I've been known to imbibe a bit myself. But what we're talking about here is a fiercely controlled lobby, and it's a terrible force in this lower end of my district. I can't see the point in opposing a movement like this when my opposition will make no difference in the outcome. I'm voting for the amendment, and I hope you'll understand why."

Roach, one of Liam's contract growers, stood up. He was uncomfortable in his suit and tie and was red-faced even when he wore overalls. Now his cheeks were a vivid crimson. "Let me make sure I've got this straight," he said. "You're with us, but you're voting against us?"

"That's right, sir," Gordon said. "It would be a futile act of political suicide to do anything else. The fact is that whether you and I agree with it or not, there's a misguided crusading spirit that's swept over the country, a result, no doubt, of the foolish foreign war President Wilson has involved us in. The Senate has already passed this amendment, and I'm told on absolute authority that an enormous majority of my colleagues in the House will go along. With the sort of pressure to which I've been subjected in my district, I'd be a fool to vote against it, and I'm not going to."

"Even if you oppose it personally?" Roach demanded angrily. "Where are your convictions, man?"

The congressman leaned back and stroked his chin. "In this case, sir, the sentiment is so overwhelming that I can see no course open to me except voting the views of what I perceive to be a hefty majority of my constituents. If I don't, I can expect to be turned out in the 1918 elections in favor of a man who really agrees with Prohibition. Would you prefer that? I can see no reasonable course of action except to let this madness run its course, as I'm sure it will in due time."

Liam stood up from his chair. "You realize, of course, the effect this amendment will have on the wine-growing and winemaking industry of this state. It'll destroy the work of a lifetime for many of us—the work of generations for a good many more."

Gordon shrugged. "I sympathize with your plight, but there's nothing I can do about it. I wish there were."

"So do I, Congressman," Liam said, and he led the group of disgruntled wine growers and winemakers from the huge study with its rows of leather-bound classics and its slate floor, leaving J. Arch Gordon sitting alone at his desk.

It happened just as Gordon had predicted. The House of Representatives acquiesced to the dry lobby so without so much as a whimper. The state legislatures quickly followed suit. The ingrained Puritanism of the American conscience was in full revolt. The women had, at long last, gotten the vote, and a good many of them were vetoing the drinking habits of their husbands, fathers, brothers and sons.

As the doughboys returned home from the forests and fields of a bloodstained Europe, they found themselves unable to buy a legal drink from Boston to San Francisco. Predictably, they responded by buying bathtub gin, bootlegged beer and smuggled Canadian whiskey.

None of this did much good for domestic producers of fine wines. In 1917 New York State produced and sold nearly ten million gallons of wine. Several years later, the wineries of the state and the nation were dying. In New York only the winemakers with other interests, like Liam's farm, with its dairy, grain and fruit production, had any chance of survival. Those farmers who had given over all their acreage to vineyards were lost. Prohibition rendered seventy-five thousand acres of New York State vineyards worthless.

Although his crop and dairy production protected him, Liam plotted and schemed to keep his small winery going even on a reduced scale without ravaging his bank accounts. Finally an idea came to him. One morning he appeared at the winery and dragged Henri out into the waiting buggy.

"Where are we going?" Henri asked.

"To church," Liam said.

The church turned out to be not a church at all but the office of the chancellor of the Archdiocese of Rochester, a bulky, balding Irish immigrant, who saw them without an appointment.

"What can I do for you, gentlemen?" the monsignor asked.

"I think I can do something for you, Monsignor," Liam told him. "I'm here with a business proposition for the archdiocese."

Monsignor Malloy smiled slightly as Liam spoke. "I'm being pitched by a countryman, I see. What county, Mr. Brennan?"

"Clare, Monsignor."

"Lovely, lovely. I'm a Dublin man, myself."

"A city man is too smart to be pitched by a bumpkin from Clare," Liam said, "and you a priest to boot. I'll have to tread carefully, I can tell."

"What are you pitching, Mr. Brennan?"

"Wine, Monsignor. Sacramental wine. Where do you buy it now for all the churches in the archdiocese?"

Monsignor Malloy shrugged. "It comes in free from California. It's made by a friary there, somewhere near San Francisco. Can you do better than that?"

"Who pays transportation costs?"

"We do."

"You can have my wine for the altar at cost," Liam said, "less if you insist on it. I'll take a loss if I have to. I promise I'll come in cheaper than whatever you're paying now."

Monsignor Malloy pondered the proposition. "I'd have to look at the figures."

Liam nodded to Henri, who opened the small suitcase Liam had brought along and produced a bottle of Brennan red table wine. He pulled out a glass and poured it half full for the monsignor.

"This is a red," Henri explained, "not our best."

Monsignor Malloy sampled it. "Is this what you'd be giving us at cost?" he asked.

"It is," Liam told him.

"Done," said Monsignor Malloy.

That accomplished, Liam could breathe more easily. Although his vineyard had grown to nearly sixty acres in grapes, much of that given over to delicate European varieties whose yield was relatively low as he experimented with planting, pruning and harvesting techniques, it still made up only 15 percent of the farm's total acreage. As a result, he had never relied heavily on the winery for income as did the contract growers for the big wineries like Taylor and Gold Seal. The deal with the arch-diocese would reduce his losses as Henri continued his work through Prohibition.

Moreover, at the beginning of the 1920s, prospects for the American farmer, with the exception of wine grape growers, seemed generally bright. Wartime prices had been high. Although they could be expected to drop somewhat, Liam fully expected that American markets in Europe would be rich for years until the continent recovered from the war's devastation and resumed production of its own food. Much of Liam's production was purchased by cooperatives who sold it abroad in those first years after the war, and his dairy business was primarily a regional one. He fed his cattle on his own corn and winter grain, and a growing pattern of electrification in the cities meant that fruits and vegetables he raised could be kept in homes for longer periods and therefore would be more in demand.

So, while other wineries failed and vineyardists lost their land, Liam's basic farming interests permitted him to keep his going, although at a dramatically curtailed rate of production and at a heavy loss that he offset with his food crops. He minimized the losses by heavily pruning the vines to keep down the crop and thereby reduced harvesting and bottling costs. He had enormous storage facilities constructed at the winery to accommodate the bottles he wasn't able to dispose of through sale to the archdiocese, export to Canada and some modest sales to a Rochester bootlegger. Someday, he was sure, he would be able to sell this wine on the open market in America, and the pent-up demand would mean premium prices for it. For now, though, he could hang on with the revenues of his other production and even continue planting new vineyards.

In the early part of the Roaring Twenties, a social revolution that had only a tangential impact on isolated rural communities like Lakeside, men like Congressman Gordon were actively seeking ways to cement relations with the agricultural community through a series of federal laws that broke up packing company monopolies, exempted farm cooperatives from the Sherman Antitrust Act and put a stop to monopolies and price manipulation in the grain market. Congress passed other laws calling for the federal purchase of surplus grain and cotton at high prices, and it began making low-interest loans to farm cooperatives as foreign markets began to dwindle. Liam approved heartily of all these actions, although he objected strenuously to government sanction of organizations like the American Federation of Labor and took great satisfaction in the diminution of its power during the twenties. In addition, he opposed government aid to any segment of the population except farmers. In all other forms of government subsidy he discerned the specter of creeping socialism.

The only action President Wilson took with which Liam agreed was the ill-fated attempt at creating a powerful League of Nations to ensure peace in Europe. When it became clear that the league would be toothless, Liam was disturbed, especially when he saw his young son playing on the beach with Billy Frazier, the son who had been born late in life to a somewhat astonished Jim Frazier and his wife.

"Look at them," he told Katherine as they watched the two boys skipping flat pieces of the slate beach across the waves. "In another generation there'll be another war to fight in Europe, and Kevin and Billy there will be just the right age to fight in it. It's a terrible mistake Henry Cabot Lodge has made."

Katherine said, "Who knows what'll happen twenty years from now? You're such a pessimist, Liam."

"A man can make informed guesses. My guess is that it'll happen all over again—only worse."

The person most disturbed at the coming of Prohibition was Henri, whose skill and painstaking efforts were beginning to bear fruit in the quality of his wine. He had been convinced that the lake country could produce a superior champagne. And now that he had begun to make several grades of it from the varieties of *vinifera* grapes that Liam had imported and nurtured with such care, the champagne could not be sold.

Henri was in a perpetual state of depression, alternately railing in a fine Gallic rage at the dry lobby and brooding glumly in surly silence.

Liam had been fascinated by the process of making champagne. He had followed Henri through every step as he cast his spell over the grapes.

The grapes at Brennan's Point were always harvested by hand, although Liam had begun to mechanize other parts of the operation. Henri insisted on hand harvesting because he was terrified that the grapes would be damaged or bruised and thus affect the outcome of the carefully thought-out chemical processes he had developed. Liam put together a special crew of several dozen grape harvesters whom he supervised himself. They were mostly women from the village who were brought out to the farm daily for the harvest in a new Ford truck Liam had purchased and was learning to drive at great risk to life, limb and public safety throughout the lake country.

Once the grapes were picked high on the hillside and placed in bushelbaskets, they were delivered by that same truck and a wagon drawn by an aging and considerably calmer Prince to the winery building. There they underwent processing by top-grade equipment that Henri had obtained from failed wineries through the region. The grapes went through a hand press, and the juice was poured into a large copper kettle, mixed carefully with meticulously measured amounts of juice from other *vinifera* varieties and, in some cases, blended with sugar syrup and yeast. The mixture was heated to clarify it, then bottled and corked with a hand pump to ferment in the bottle. Some of the mixtures, which Henri called curvée, were fermented as still wine in the usual manner; but much of it went for the various grades of champagne. Henri experimented with champagne made from a single grape variety, such as Pinot Chardonnay, and from a variety of blends. He varied the yeasts, the amount of sugar added and the fermentation times and temperatures. At any given moment, he was making as many as a dozen different varieties and grades of champagne, none of which could be sold.

Once bottled and corked, the bottles were moved into what he called tierage, where bottles were left at an angle on wooden racks for anywhere from six months up to several years, depending on the type and quality of champagne Henri was trying to create.

In tierage the yeast would ferment the sugar into alcohol. When spent, the yeast would settle on the side of the bottle. After a specified period the bottles were removed and the yeast knocked loose by hand. The bottles were then moved to riddling racks, where they rested with the mouths pointed downward at a forty-five-degree angle, the sediment in each bottle gathering in its neck.

There they would sit for up to three weeks, until the sediment had settled firmly near the cork. Henri would give each bottle a quarter turn daily, twice a day for some varieties, to aid in clearing the wine. Then, in the depths of winter, the bottles would be removed. They would be taken outside and placed upside down in the snow and left there until the snow froze the sediment. Each bottle would then be uncorked and the solid block of sediment would blast out of the bottle. Liam erected a small wooden target next to the winery, and he and Henri would conduct marksmanship contests with frozen clots of sediment as they uncorked the bottles.

With the sediment removed, Henri would then move each bottle to the dosage machine. Dosage was a mixture of old wine and sugar syrup used to sweeten the champagne. The amount of dosage varied with Henri's plans for that particular bottle. The final corking was then performed with natural corks imported from Spain that were softened in hot water. Henri then supervised the addition of wire caps to hold the corks in place.

Under ordinary circumstances much of the wine would then be labeled, packed in wooden cases and shipped to market by truck and then rail. But these days, it was simply stored in cases in the winery's cellar, each bottle bearing a simple label in Henri's own elegant hand marking its vintage and other pertinent information. It was the sight of these cases rising up to the ceiling of the storage cellars that broke Henri's heart. Admittedly, much of the champagne was merely ordinary, the byproduct of the winemaker's experimentation. But some of it, a special concoction that had been made with the finest grapes, aged for years and treated with the greatest of care, Henri was sure could stand up to any champagne produced in the world. And it couldn't be sold. He was desolate.

One day, as they finished their work at the winery, Liam threw a thick arm around his friend's small shoulders. "The day will come, Henri," he said. "This madness can't last forever."

"Who would have ever thought," Henri said sadly, "that such madness could ever begin."

* * * *

In summer the Brennans often left the big house on hot nights and slept in the shack to enjoy the cooling night breezes off the lake. For Liam, the shack was so full of memories and emotion that he always dreamed when he slept there, although he could seldom recall those dreams when he awakened.

On a steamy August night in 1925 Liam lay in bed only a few feet from the gentle waves of Iroquois Lake and dreamed for the first time in years of the Shannon. He dreamed of his father at the helm of his fishing boat, of casting nets over brackish water, of the smell of peat and the taste of stout and the rich green of the fog-shrouded fields. He dreamed, strangely enough, of the *Iroquois Queen*, side wheels churning gently, nosing into the Labasheeda dock on the Shannon. Then the image faded and Liam slept soundly. In the morning, he awakened feeling closer to Ireland and the family he had left there, particularly his father, than he had felt in years.

It was only weeks later that Liam learned that his father had died that very night. "He had been feeling poorly for some weeks," Donal wrote in his cramped hand,

> and he had been complaining of weariness. Then one day as we pulled in the nets, he complained of a terrible pain in his chest. He laid down on the deck for a while and seemed to come out of it, although he was a terrible gray color, like a statue. That night he went to bed early. When Ma tried to wake him in the morning she realized that he was gone.
>
> So now it falls to me to care for our mother. Kathleen's husband, Gerry Donovan, is thinking of emigrating to Australia. Even with the Republic now, there is little opportunity for a man here. And with Anna in a convent in Galway, I am the one left with the responsibility. I suppose I should be thinking of marrying myself, but I wonder if I am not too old now, and there is Ma to consider. I do not know how she would take to a new woman in the house.

The letter went on in that vein for several more paragraphs and ended with a not-too-subtle plea for the fine landowner in America to send money for his mother's maintenance.

Liam, sitting at the kitchen table of the shack, buried his face in his hands and wept. After a while, Katherine, in from a swim, heard him and came in and took the letter, reading it quickly. She locked the door to the porch and led Liam to the tiny bedroom.

They made love with passion and gentleness. He pressed into her, clutching her near him. After a while, he slept fitfully in the midafternoon, and she held him close and stroked his hair.

It was a moment, one of many in their marriage, that would always linger in her memory: a bittersweet summer afternoon when she had comforted her husband; when she had performed a spouse's task.

Katherine knew that afternoon marked a seminal event in her marriage. It marked the day when Liam became hers, utterly and completely, for the rest of his days. It was the day she moved into the vacant spot in his heart that had, until that moment, been occupied securely by his most beloved parent. Now there was Katherine; only Katherine.

* * * *

On the Fourth of July, 1926, the Brennans were gathered, in family tradition, near a bonfire on the point. Around the lake's darkened shoreline other such fires blazed across the inky water.

Helen and Kevin played with sparklers, running up and down the beach and up and down the hillside as well. At one point, the children took their sparklers up the path to the big house. Helen turned to Kevin in the darkness and proposed a plan that both children knew violated the law that governed such gatherings. She said, "Let's go up to the big house and get some cake from the icebox."

Kevin shook his head in the darkness. "We're not supposed to go up to the big house without grownups."

Helen made a face at him. The family was living, as always, in the shack for the summer. Most of the big house was closed off and would remain that way until fall. "Come on," she urged.

"Nope," said Kevin.

It always baffled and angered Helen that she was forced to live by a set of rules that made no sense to her; rules set by adults who seemed constantly to be plotting and scheming to prevent her from wringing every last drop of fun out of anything. It also disturbed her that in recent months she had seemingly lost her ability to bend Kevin to her will. Until just the past year or so he had obeyed her as he obeyed Mother and Poppy, never questioning for a moment the authority and leadership her two extra years had conferred on her. She resented his growing refusal to follow her lead, and their constant bickering was a source of annoyance to Katherine and Liam. "Sissy," she said to him finally.

"Am not," Kevin said.

"Then let's go up to the big house and get some cake."

"No. We're not supposed to."

"Baby," Helen taunted, hurling at her younger brother the ultimate insult of childhood.

Kevin jumped to his feet, pulling himself up to his full four feet, four inches in height. "Don't call me that!" he shouted angrily. "I'll tell Mommy and Poppy."

Helen pondered the threat. If Kevin were to go into detail about the cause of their dispute it could have undesirable repercussions.

"Never mind then, sissy," she said, struggling to maintain the upper hand without pushing Kevin into carrying tales. "I won't do it, then. But I won't sit with you any more, either."

She turned and scampered up the path in the darkness.

"Helen," she heard Kevin call out unsteadily. She giggled to herself. She knew her little brother had a deathly fear of being left in the dark.

"Helen," he called out again.

"You stay right there," Helen said, "until I'm not mad any more. Then I'll come and sit with you again—if you stop being such a little pill."

There was a moment's silence from Kevin. Then she heard him say, "All right. Get over being mad fast, okay?"

She made her way up the rest of path then she entered the darkened house through the door off the back porch. Helen knew every inch of the kitchen better than she knew any other room in the place, even her own bedroom on the second floor. The kitchen of the big house was the center of family life, deserted only during the months of warmth that came in summer.

She found her way to the stove and got a wooden match from the box on the side. She came back to the kitchen table and found a kerosene lantern sitting in the middle. She held the lamp in her hand and opened the valve to permit the fumes to rise into the lamp's glass bonnet. Then she lit a match, striking it on the rough surface on the side of the lamp as she had seen the grownups do hundreds of times.

The only problem was that Helen Brennan was not a grownup, she was an eleven-year-old child on an errand of mischief. Her inexperience with the task at hand, the nearly complete darkness of the kitchen and her own nervousness at her forbidden activity combined to spell disaster. The match flared into life just in front of her eyes, startling her. She dropped the glass-topped lamp on the kitchen floor where it smashed, sending kerosene spreading across old, dry floorboards. Then Helen, frightened by the sound and the certain knowledge that she had made a spectacular mess, compounded the error by letting the still-burning match slip from her fingers.

The kitchen floor leaped into flames. Terrified, Helen flattened herself against one wall as they licked at the wooden kitchen table. In an eyeblink, it too was burning. Then the flames were crawling up the kitchen walls, catching the curtains Katherine had made. They shriveled and withered under the flickering embrace of the hungry fire. Helen's eyes grew huge with shock and fright. The fire was blocking her path to the rear door now, consuming everything in the kitchen. She could see the paint on the ceiling blister and blacken in the light, and the intense heat of the blaze seared her. She could hear glass crack and shatter from the heat. Helen screamed.

From the beach, Henri spotted the flames. He had been looking up casually toward the vineyards when he saw the fire burst through the windows along the side of the house. He stood up from his canvas chair, his eyes huge. *"Mon Dieu,"* he whispered.

Liam heard him gasp, looked at his shocked face and followed his gaze up the hillside. Then, before the women knew what was happening, Liam and Henri were sprinting away from them, running like madmen back along the point toward the hillside.

Katherine, in laughing conversation with Annette and Minnie, turned toward them as they began to run, saw the house ablaze on the hillside and felt her heart turn over inside her breast. "The children . . .!" she cried out.

Liam and Henri raced up the steps next to the shack. With his longer legs, Liam took the lead. Running across the road and up the path to the burning house, he nearly bowled over little Kevin, who was running down the path, terrified by the towering flames. Liam caught the boy in his big hands. "Where's Helen?" Liam demanded.

Kevin could hardly speak. "Inside . . ."

By the time Liam reached the big house, fully one-half of the lower floor was in flames. The weathered, dry, frame building was more than a hundred years old, and it was going up like a torch. The back of the building was totally engulfed. Liam ran up the front porch and threw open the door. Smoke poured out in billows, driving him back several steps. "Helen!" he called out into the smoke.

A tiny, terrified voice answered him. "Poppy . . ."

Liam ripped off his work shirt and fashioned a mask. He went into the building on his stomach to avoid the smoke. Helen, miraculously, was just a few yards inside the door, wandering the hallway blind and lost. Liam grabbed her, pulled her down to him and crawled out to the porch, his eyes smarting and tearing, his lungs bursting. When he felt his feet go over the threshold, he stood up and staggered down the steps and out into the night air away from the house. The others were there, and Katherine grabbed frantically at Helen. The child was coughing and crying piteously.

Liam rubbed at his own tearing eyes. "Is she burned?"

"No," Katherine said, regaining her composure, "I don't see any burns on her."

"We'd better get farther back," Henri warned.

The little group moved off back down the hill, away from the heat. Katherine held the sobbing Helen close to her with one hand and led the half-blind Liam with the other. When they reached the road Liam quickly counted heads. There was Katherine clutching the weeping Helen. Kevin stood beside her, his eyes wide. Minnie was there, her jaw agape as she stared up at the towering flames engulfing the big house. Henri and Annette stood in the dirt road next to her. That was everybody. Liam said a silent prayer of thanks. He knelt next to Helen. "Are you all right, Darlin'?"

"I'm all right, Poppy," Helen said in a whimper. "I couldn't see in there. I couldn't get out."

"Hush," Katherine said, "you're with us now. You're safe."

"You know that we will never let anything happen to you, little one," Henri told her.

The roof caved in with a crash, and sparks rose up and out of sight.

"I wonder if the barn is safe," Liam said.

"There is no wind to carry the sparks," Henri told him, "but I will get the horses out, just to be safe. And I will move the truck over to our house." Then he was gone, up the hill to the barn behind the big house, Annette at his heels.

The five of them left moved silently down off the road, down the stairs to the beach and the porch of the shack. High on the hillside, the big house was a flaming pyre.

"It'll burn for days," Katherine said. "Thank God we weren't in it."

"It could have been a lot worse," Liam said, putting his arm around her. "Minnie, are you all right?"

At the question, Minnie's legs gave out. She managed to make it to one of the rockers on the shack's porch before she sank down, her considerable bulk hitting the chair's seat with a thump. She looked up, and her expression was one of horror and exhaustion. "I've had enough," she said simply. "I'm too old for all this."

* * *

"With a view like this house'll have, Crowley said, "you'll definitely want a porch. It won't be that expensive."

"At this point," Liam said dryly to Katherine, who was sitting beside him, "I can't imagine that the cost of a porch would make much difference."

Howard Crowley was a smallish, fussy man in wire-rimmed spectacles. He was the best architect in Rochester. Two weeks after the fire he and the Brennans were sitting at a sunlit table outside the shack studying Liam's painfully drawn plans for a new house to replace the one that had been reduced to charred embers up on the hillside. The fire had destroyed some important papers in the study, a few momentos and photographs with sentimental meaning and all the family's winter clothing. But because the family's belongings and the farm's papers had been spread between the big house, the shack and the winery, they had lost nothing they couldn't replace before cold weather came. The crucial question was what to do now about erecting permanent living quarters.

Liam faced two choices: expand the shack or have a new house built on the hillside to replace the old one. It was an easy decision.

To begin with, Liam had never been overly fond of the big house. That was one reason he had moved his family into the shack every summer. To him the big house had been a constant reminder that he was living on Christian Weidener's property, and everything in the house had reminded him of Christian, from the drab, overstuffed furnishings and the Weidener family photographs on the walls to the gloomy, dark woodwork and the oppressive study where Liam had done his accounts. There had not been a room in the big house that had not been alive with ghosts for Liam, and except for the expense and inconvenience he knew the fire would cause him, he had felt not the slightest shred of regret as he had watched flames consume the structure.

Yet, at the same time, he had liked the house's location with its sweeping view of both the lake from the front and the vineyards climbing up the hillside from the back porch. Moreover, he knew that if the shack were expanded, he and his wife and children would be forced to live in squalor for months, dodging workmen and tripping over building supplies. Also, because of the steepness of the bank at the rear of the little house and the small area of building space on the beach in front of it, an expanded version of the shack would have to be constructed on as many as four cramped levels to provide the family with adequate living space in colder weather. In addition, the rear of the house would butt up directly against the road. As motor traffic increased, the noise would become unpleasant.

Finally, the insurance money and the growing success of Liam's dairy herd made it feasible to rebuild the big house slightly higher on the hill and farther off the road in a stand of tall pines, with an even more commanding view than the old house had enjoyed. The new house could be erected about one hundred and thirty feet above the level of the lake, giving its occupants a view that wouldn't be blocked in summer by the tops of the trees that lined the shore. Liam was determined, moreover, to build this house properly, with every modern convenience the old house had lacked.

So he called in Crowley and spread out the rough drawings of what he was after. The house would be three stories high, built of native stone on the first floor and wood on the two upper stories. The larger and more convenient layout included a spacious sitting room in the front and a parlor behind that, the two separated by a thick sliding door. There would be a study for Liam at the rear of the house with a fine view of the vineyards up the hillside; a large dining room and a monstrous kitchen.

There would be no room off the kitchen for a cook/maid, as was traditional in large houses of the period, because Minnie had announced her retirement after the trauma of the fire. "I hate to leave you, Liam," she had said, "but I can't start over again in a new house. I'm too old. I'm moving in with my niece in Lakeside. You can come visit me, and I'll have her bring me out here now and again."

He had leaned down and kissed her cheek. "I don't know how we'll get along without you, Minnie."

"You've got two women in that kitchen even without me," she had said. "Now they can do things their way. I love them both, and they love me, but they won't miss me in that new kitchen, I promise you."

The sleeping quarters, therefore, would be limited to the second floor, which would consist of one very large bedroom for Liam and Katherine in the front, overlooking the lake, and three smaller bedrooms, one each for the children and the last for guests. The third floor would contain a spacious attic that would be divided into a storage area and an enormous winter playroom for the children.

The new house, which was eventually built over the summer of 1926, was to be wired for electricity during construction, a feature that Liam had been planning to have installed in the old house after power lines had been strung along the lake the year before. He had delayed on electrifying the house because of the effort and expense involved, but the cash from the fire insurance made cost no longer a factor. Of all the features in the new house, none pleased Katherine more than the electricity. It would ease the household workload immeasurably, and it would make it possible to refrigerate food in warm weather.

Moreover, because of electricity, the new building would have a luxury unheard of when the old house had been constructed not long after the War of 1812, indoor plumbing. Liam was eagerly looking forward to the day when he could take an axe to the outhouse situated behind the rubble of the old house. He also planned an electric pump to bring up water from the lake to flush toilets, wash dishes and fill bathtubs, replacing the hand pumps that had been in use throughout the old house. The new house also would contain a hot water heater; no more boiling water on the kitchen stove for baths or for laundry.

Liam planned the house with two bathrooms—one off the master bedroom and the other at the head of the upstairs hallway. Each, he resolved, would contain a massive tub with clawed feet, and the master bedroom would, in addition, have a showerhead mounted over the tub, just like people enjoyed in the cities.

Made possible by electricity, a central, forced-air heating system hooked to a new coal furnace was also to be installed. Liam had grown to detest the repulsive and inefficient radiators that had occupied conspicuous corners throughout the old house.

All in all, Liam was tremendously pleased with his plans for the house, not just because of the design but because this would be a Brennan house, with no Weidener ghosts looking on. So, even though the total cost exceeded what he had realized in fire insurance, and he had been forced to take a ten-year mortgage to finance the difference, Liam was enthusiastic about the project.

His plans for the new house had been put together after laborious research into the great houses of America at the tiny Lakeside Public library. It would not, of course, be a great manor house in the American tradition, but it would be a roomy, comfortable structure that would be the fruit of his labor and his imagination. That was why he bristled slightly when Crowley, looking over the plans, told him he needed a porch on this place. "There's already a porch in the plans," Liam said, frowning. Surely his drawings had not been so crude that a man couldn't recognize a porch.

Crowley shook his head and said, "No, you don't understand. You've allowed for a one-story porch across half of the house, but you have to recognize that the building will command a spectacular view. The porch from which that view will be visible should be spectacular as well."

"What do you have in mind?" Liam asked him.

Crowley opened his briefcase and produced a sheaf of sketches. "This," he said.

Liam picked up the new plans, drawn with the architect's fine touch and elegant printing. He saw immediately that his basic plan had been untouched, but that the exterior of the house was dramatically different. In place of Liam's simple porch, Crowley had come up with an elegant two-tiered porch that ran the length of the house. The austere second-story windows that Liam's plans had called for had been replaced by French doors leading out from the two front bedrooms to the upper level. Instead of the New England-style appearance Liam had given it, Crowley's plans called for a building that looked more than a little like a Virginia planter's residence, with four large pillars in front. It was almost as though a Greek temple had been lifted up and transported to the hillside to look down on Iroquois Lake. Liam wasn't sure he liked it. "Katherine," he said softly, "what do you think?"

Katherine was entranced. The design tugged at her Maryland roots. "Oh, Liam," she said breathlessly. "It's lovely. It changes the house completely."

"That it does," he said, gazing at the modifications in his beloved design.

Crowley said, "I admit it's a bit different in appearance than what you had drawn, but it leaves your plans for the interior just about intact. You were after a larger and more comfortable version of the sort of pre-Victorian buildings you see all through this part of the country. But if you look in Lakeside and some of the other villages in the area, you'll see that this sort of Greek Revival architecture was quite popular in small towns in upstate New York until the last half of the 1800s, so it won't really be out of place. And in this location, this house will be stunning."

Liam snorted. "I'm beginning to think, Mister Crowley, that Harry K. Thaw shot the wrong architect."

"Oh, stop," Katherine said, laughing, "it's just that a house like this offends your old-world sense of propriety. I really think it's lovely. Will it be much more expensive?"

"Not much," Crowley said; "if you have it put on as original construction, you always get it cheaper."

"All right," Liam said, staring at Crowley's drawings. "But if you do this, you ought to add a couple of dormers on the roof to give it more balance."

Crowley looked at Liam in genuine surprise, then he studied his plans silently for a moment. He looked up. "You know," he said, his tone conveying just the slightest hint of annoyance, "that's just what it needs. I wish I'd thought of it."

* * * *

"Now," Liam told his children as the Brennans milled with the crowd on the Lakeside village dock, "what you'll be seeing is something you'll never see again on this lake. You're going to see a big steamboat move out from the dock under power. You'll see her go out into the deep water. And when they get her out deep enough, they're going to sink her."

Kevin was horrified. "Why?"

Liam gazed over the heads of other Lakesiders gathered for the occasion. It was a warm June day, and the Brennans had been in their new home since the previous October. This was their first warm-weather outing, and Liam's face grew solemn as he was flooded with memories. "Because she's a dinosaur," he said. "She was built to carry crops and supplies to and from the railhead, only now a motor truck does it faster.

And with everybody owning a boat of their own, and a good many of those with outboard motors, there's not much excursion business left for the big boat's owner. She's the last of the big steamers, and there's no work for her. So they're going to take her out into the lake and let her slip down to her grave."

Helen looked up at the big steamer, rocking gently in the waves in her berth. Foster Gillis had cared for her lovingly, and the *Aurora* was as elegant as ever. "That's so sad," she said.

Liam felt a lump come into his throat as she uttered the words. "It's God's way," he told her, his voice suddenly thick. "Everything has its day, and then something new comes along and the old things have to die and make way for the new. It's the same way with people, Darlin'. Nothing is different with people."

That was enough for Katherine. Most of the time she found Liam's sentiment touching, but this went beyond maudlin. "Stop that, Liam," she ordered. "You'll just frighten them. They're too young."

Kevin stared at the big boat long and hard. "Some things are forever, aren't they, Poppy? The lake is forever, isn't it?"

Liam nodded slowly. "Yes. The lake is forever. And the grapes. They'll outlast me and you and a good many others. You watch now, Darlins', they're taking her out."

The *Aurora*'s engine gurgled into life. As it did, the Lakeside Free Academy band began to play, breaking into an off-key version of "She May Have Seen Better Days," which struck Liam as an odd choice for the occasion but one not without a certain touch of irony.

The skeleton crew cast off the dock lines for the last time. Then, as Foster Gillis, up in the wheelhouse, pulled the *Aurora*'s whistle cord defiantly, the big boat slowly began backing away from the dock. She moved out into open water. Then Gillis brought her about neatly as the band played with renewed fervor. The water churned and boiled white at the *Aurora*'s stern as she moved to a point about a hundred yards off the dock. There she came to a halt.

As the crowd on the dock watched, the crew cut the engine and disappeared down inside the hull while the *Aurora* drifted. In a moment, Foster Gillis and his three crewmen hurried back topside and climbed down the ladder to a waiting rowboat lashed to the *Aurora*'s stern. They cast off the line, and as Gillis settled into the small boat's rear seat, looking over his shoulder at the *Aurora*, they began rowing back to the dock. They were perhaps seventy yards from the *Aurora* when the timed blast went off deep inside her.

Liam could see the huge hole appear in the steamer's hull. A finger of fire pointed through it, then pulled back inside. The sound of the explosion deep within the ship's guts came out muffled and dull. Liam had expected the *Aurora* to die with a mighty roar. Instead, it was more like a prolonged belch. Then she was suddenly listing hard to starboard as the water poured into her by the ton.

The *Aurora* died quickly. In just a moment she had flipped over completely on her side, the startling blue of her lower hull protruding from the lake almost obscenely, like the naked thighs of an injured woman who lacked the strength to keep her skirts down as she lay wounded. In less than a minute, she was gone. As she slipped soundlessly beneath the waves of Iroquois Lake, the band music faltered and died raggedly. The crowd gathered on the dock was strangely silent as a great blast of wind rolling in off Iroquois Lake burst suddenly through it, blowing off hats and mussing hair.

It's her soul, Liam thought. It's her bloody soul sweeping over us. But he would never reveal that thought, not even to Katherine.

BOOK 2

BOOK 2

Chapter 11

In later years Helen would always assert that she'd despised Jack at first sight. "I couldn't stand him," she would say. "He had a sort of look that told everybody that he thought he was really something."

And Jack, on those occasions when there was peace between them, would laugh and say, "Well, you looked to me as though you had been knocked for a loop."

"I had—literally. And it was your fault."

"There's no shortage of things that are my fault, is there?" Jack would reply, ending all discussion on the topic until it came up again.

In fact, both recollections were accurate. Helen had been knocked for a loop—literally. And it had, in a matter of speaking, been Jack's fault.

On a gentle spring morning in 1935, Helen, twenty-two years old and acknowledged as the grand belle of the lake country, came bouncing into the kitchen. Katherine and Annette were sitting at the big, round kitchen table drinking strong tea in the relaxing hours just after their husbands had gone off to work. Helen was dressed in slacks and a short-sleeved blouse a trifle too light for the season. Early June mornings in the lake country tended to be crisp.

"What would you like for breakfast?" Katherine asked.

Helen opened the icebox and inspected its contents with disinterest. "Just some milk. I'm getting too fat."

"Hah," Annette said, "you are a skinny marink."

Helen laughed. "A skinny what?"

"Marink. A skinny marink."

"That's French, Dear," Katherine explained.

"Is English," Annette said indignantly. "Marink—as in skinny."

Helen shrugged. Annette's English was always mysterious. "Well, anyway," she said, "I won't have time for more than milk. I'm going on a picnic; I'll get enough to eat there."

Katherine's eyebrows raised slightly. "With John Coughlin's boy again?"

179

Helen frowned. It never ceased to annoy her that her mother insisted on referring to all her friends as someone's son or daughter. It was as though they had no identities of their own. Helen's own identity, by implication, was similarly threatened. "Good God, no," she said. "Bucky Coughlin? I can't stand him. Just the girls. Lily Johnstone and Becky King. We're going to drive down to Watkins Glen. Dr. King gave Becky a new car for graduation."

"No boys, then?" Annette asked in disbelief.

"Tante Annette," Helen said, "you don't need boys to have a good time."

"In France, we always did," Annette offered.

"What kind of car did Becky's father get her?" Katherine asked.

"A convertible with a rumble seat. It's really snazzy."

"What is snazzy?" asked Annette, for whom American slang was a constant puzzle.

"It's a pretty car," Helen explained.

"Oh," Annette said, committing the word to memory for misuse at a future date.

Katherine said to Helen, "I'm sure that if you wanted to learn how to drive, your father or Kevin would teach you. And if you went to work in Lakeside, your father might even buy you a car of your own."

Helen had heard it all before. Get a job. Learn to drive. "I don't need to learn how to drive," she responded. "That's what men are for."

Katherine, mildly irked by the response, opened her mouth to speak, but as she did a horn sounded outside. Helen dived for her sweater and purse. "There's Becky now," she said, kissing both Katherine and Annette on the cheek.

"Take a jacket," Katherine called out in a pleading tone as Helen scurried off. But the only response was the sound of the screen door slamming and footsteps banging down the front steps. Annette laughed.

"She is so snazzy," Annette said. "Oh, to be young again, knowing what I know now."

"She is gorgeous, isn't she?" Katherine mused.

"She is much prettier than her mother was," Annette said, "and Helga was a pretty woman."

Katherine sat down and sipped her tea. "It's not good, you know— that sort of beauty. It carries Helen. She could have gone to college like Kevin or Becky King, certainly to business school. Do you realize, Annette, that she's been out of high school four years this month? And she hasn't gotten a job. She's not serious about any boy. She does very little work around here. I'd love it if I could get her to pay attention long enough to learn to cook something." Katherine sighed and smiled self-consciously. "There I go again."

Annette nodded sagely. The two women had grown close over the years. They spent day after day alone in the kitchen, working as a team to run the house, provide the meals and care for the two young children who were now grown and needed a different sort of care altogether.

In Katherine, Annette found someone to whom she could communicate the deep thoughts, desires, dreams and disappointments that Henri was more and more inclined, as he grew older, to dismiss as baseless feminine complaints. To Katherine, Annette was the sisterly companion she had never had, a wise and compassionate sounding board and a constant source of sly humor and side-splitting malapropisms. Annette also was the gentlest of souls, seemingly incapable of real anger, devoid of malice in any form, content with whatever situation in which she found herself. Katherine revered her and envied her disposition.

"Why do you not speak to Liam?" Annette asked.

"He won't do anything. Liam protects her and cares for her as though she were made of crystal. To be honest, a little unhappiness might just be what she needs to prepare her for life, real life, I mean, out in the world. She needs to understand that happiness isn't just the absence of misery. And Liam is completely blind where Helen is concerned."

Annette smiled slightly. "As you are with Kevin?"

Katherine nodded. "I admit it. And that makes me too vulnerable to speak to Liam on the topic of Helen, doesn't it? So, we go on. I do hope she finds herself while she's still young enough to adjust. She's so secure here at the Brennan's Point."

"You are a wart of worry," Annette said.

"A worrywart," Katherine corrected.

"I said this thing," Annette said.

Katherine was silent for a moment, staring over her tea, off into space. Then: "Annette, you don't think it's jealousy, do you?"

Annette was puzzled. "What?"

Katherine groped for the words. "You don't think I'm so afraid for Helen—so critical of her—because she's so pretty? I sometimes ask myself if that's not really what's going through my head—that she's so beautiful that she can get away with just about anything, and I've always been so plain that I could never get away with a thing. I hope that's not it."

Annette shook her head slowly. "How could you think this thing about yourself? Is not true."

"Well, I hope not. I do worry about her. And I love her like she's really mine."

Annette shook her head. "Katherine, you are such a bucket of fuss."

The road along the lake was exquisite in early June. The lake rolled restlessly under dazzling blue skies, and the trees were newly alive with fresh green, their branches waving in the warming air. Becky King was at the wheel of her new convertible. "Aren't you cold back there?" she demanded of Helen, back in the rumbleseat. "Your hair is getting all blown."

"It's the Jean Harlow look," Helen said. "Don't you think it's becoming?"

Becky looked back toward the road ahead. "You'd look becoming if it was shaved off," she said dryly. "That's all right. We like you in spite of your faults."

The term "we" included Lily Johnstone, seated in the front with Becky. They were Helen's two best and most devoted friends.

Helen said, "I was told just before you picked me up that I'm getting too skinny. And," she added after a moment, "that I should get a job."

"Well," Lily Johnstone said, "maybe you should. Honestly, Helen, I don't know how you spend your time all day."

Helen laughed. "Don't worry about me. Come this fall, you'll have little brats crawling all over you in that classroom and I'll be comfortably at home, living the life of a lady of leisure. So, there."

"I want to teach," Lily said defensively. "It's important to me."

"Well, Helen said, "not having to get up every morning and having to do something is important to me."

"Oh?" said Becky. "And what is this important task you're saving yourself for?"

"I don't know," Helen mused. "I've been thinking about going to New York and trying to get a job in the theater."

Lily was entranced. "The thee-uh-tah? Really?"

"Why not?" Helen said. "I might be able to do it. I can sing. Even Kevin admits that, and he doesn't give me credit for anything."

Becky sighed. "Or me either. And I wish he would."

Helen shook her head. "I wish I could figure out what you find so attractive about Kevin."

"He's your brother," Becky pointed out. "You're not supposed to see."

Helen shrugged. "Well, anyway, when I'm a star, you can all come and visit, and I'll introduce you to Clark Gable if you behave yourself and treat me with the proper deference. You can tell your little first-graders all about it, Lily."

Lily said nothing, but Becky turned her head slightly to respond, which turned out to be a mistake because the car was entering a curve. Sitting squarely in the middle of the road on the far side of the curve was a battered panel truck. Becky caught it out of the corner of her eye.

Her fingers clutched the wheel and she spun it hard. The tires squealed, and the car roared off the dirt road and onto the rough shoulder. It bounced over the ragged grass beyond and came to a halt in a shower of flying pebbles and dust. Becky clutched her chest and took a deep breath.

"Are you all right?" she gasped.

Lily, shaken, said, "I think so."

Becky's temper flared. "What sort of idiot would park like that right in the middle of the road?"

Becky twisted in the seat and saw that the idiot was running toward the car. He was a young man, strikingly handsome, if a bit short. He ran up to Becky's side of the car, his expression tense. "Is everybody all right in here?" he asked.

Becky was livid. "We were almost killed. Is that your truck? Whatever possessed you to park it so it sticks out in the road like that?" she demanded. "Don't you know people drive on this road?"

The young man's face took on an amused expression. "Some people drive on it," he said, "and some people apparently pilot low-flying planes along it. From your speed when you came around that curve, I'd say you were one of those."

Becky was steaming. "You've got a lot of nerve. You park your truck so it's sticking out in the middle of the road and almost kill us, and then you insult my driving."

The young man smiled. "Then let me apologize. Never let it be said that I in any way impugned the reputation of a lovely young lady—even her driving skills. I apologize."

Becky wanted to stay angry, but it wasn't working. "What's your name?"

"Jack Ryan," he said. "I'm really sorry about the truck. I parked it so I could go over there and get a photograph of that sailboat out in the middle of the lake. I was only going to be a second, and I didn't expect a car to come along. There's not much traffic on this road. And what's your name, if you don't mind my asking?"

Becky didn't, not at all. "I'm Becky King, and this is my friend, Lily Johnstone. This girl back here is Helen Brennan."

Jack Ryan's face took on a curious expression. "In the back? I hate to be the one to inform you, but there isn't anybody in the back."

Becky's head spun around. "Helen? My God, the rumble seat is down! Helen is trapped in there."

It took Jack Ryan only a second to twist the handle and open the rumble seat. Helen popped out, with a dazed expression and hair awry.

"Are you all right?" Lily asked with alarm.

Helen was shaky. "I . . . I think so. What happened?"

Jack Ryan took one look at Helen, and his smile broadened. "I'm afraid it was my fault. I was parked in the middle of the road."

"I had to swerve to keep from hitting him," Becky explained, "The car went off the road, and the rumble seat must have come down on you."

Helen rubbed her skull. "And hit me on the head," she said, rubbing her wound. "It was the strangest thing that ever happened to me. When the car swerved, that was the last thing I remember. Then I opened my eyes, and it was all dark. I thought I was dead. I thought I was in a casket and they'd buried me alive by mistake."

Becky shuddered. "God, what a terrible thought to have. You don't look so good. Maybe we should take you back home."

Helen shook her head. "I do have a bump. Maybe I should go back home."

Jack broke in. "I'll tell you what. Since this is all my fault, I'd be more than happy to take Helen home." He turned toward Helen, smiling broadly. "It is Helen, isn't it? It would be the least I can do."

Becky, looking at Helen and feeling events slipping away from her, said, "Well . . ."

"Please," Jack said. "Let me do it."

Becky looked at Jack and then at Helen. Even dizzy from the bump on her head, Helen was a vision. Becky had competed with Helen all her life, and she had never won except in the areas that counted for nothing, grades and the regard of other girls. Becky sighed silently. Her eyes met Helen's, and Becky surrendered, as usual.

Helen managed a weak smile. Her eyes turned toward Jack. "All right. But please, drive slowly."

By the time Jack and Helen arrived back at the big house overlooking the lake, Helen's headache had vanished, and her spirits had improved considerably. She recounted the incident to a worried Katherine and Annette while Jack apologized profusely and convincingly. By the time the women's fears were allayed and Jack's regret about the entire incident was conveyed, Liam had come in for lunch, which meant that the whole adventure had to be recounted again under his stern and disconcerting gaze. By then, of course, the food was ready and Jack had to be invited to stay for lunch, which he accepted without hesitation.

During the meal Liam spoke little. He spent much of the time watching Jack Ryan captivate the women with small talk. As he had grown older, Liam Brennan had become more solemn, his mind often occupied with the responsibilities of his business and worries about his children. Also, after years of settling into life in a peaceful place where little changed from year to year, he had developed a wariness of strangers. So, although he was moderately impressed with this young man's obvious facility in ingratiating himself with the female members of the household, Liam couldn't decide if he liked Jack Ryan. He was in no hurry to make up his mind.

After listening to Jack hold forth on the virtues of the table wine served with lunch (an assessment Liam shared) and the merits of Franklin D. Roosevelt (an assessment Liam did not share), Liam finally said, "Just what was it you were doing out there on that road?"

"Taking pictures," Jack told him. "I'm a photographer in Boydstown. I saw a sailboat out on the lake with the wind in its sails, and I thought it would make a great shot for the studio window. It will, too."

"Do you have your own studio?" Katherine asked.

Jack Ryan laughed. "Not yet. I'm working for Silvertone Studios in Boydstown. I'm the number-two man. Then again, it's only a two-man studio. But I should get this studio for my own before long. My boss is only a few years from retirement."

"You have family in Boydstown?" Katherine asked.

"I have more family than just about anybody you can imagine. I'm the second oldest of eight."

"How old are you?" Liam asked.

"Poppy," Helen said in annoyance, "the questions you ask. You're so nosy."

Liam's eyebrows raised. "I didn't realize that anyone's age might constitute a deep, dark secret—not a man's age, anyway."

"It doesn't," Jack said, smiling. "I'm twenty-four."

Liam nodded. "Do you read much?"

"Incessantly," Jack told him. "It's my one real source of recreation. I had to drop out of school my senior year. These are hard times, and my father needed help supporting the family, so college was out of the question. I've tried to make up for what I missed out on."

"Have you read Dickens?" Liam asked.

"Everything but *Oliver Twist*," Jack said. "I know my mother will give me that book for my birthday. She knows the gaps in my reading. So I haven't bothered to buy it."

"Who are your favorite writers?" Liam asked, suddenly recalling a similar conversation he had held light years before with Christian Weidener. The memory made him slightly uncomfortable.

Jack's brow furrowed slightly. "I love Dickens, but my tastes are fairly eclectic. Dashiell Hammet does detective stories I like very much. I admire Faulkner. Fitzgerald is a bit heavy for me, and I think his stories move slowly, but I love his characters. My father introduced me to his stuff."

Liam nodded. "Your father sounds like an interesting man. What does he do?"

"He works on the railroad. He's an engineer."

Liam was silent for a moment. "Your father wouldn't be Jim Ryan, would he?"

Jack nodded. "He certainly would. Do you know him?"

For the first time, the hint of a smile passed over Liam's face. "I did, years ago. I worked on the railroad before I married Helen's mother. I remember Jim Ryan very well. He used to fight professionally, didn't he?"

"So he tells everybody who asks," Jack said, "and most people who don't."

Jack Ryan ended up spending the day at Brennan's Point and eating dinner with the entire ensemble, which included Henri and Kevin, who was home from Cornell that weekend, where he had just finished a rocky second year. After dinner, the Brennans gathered around the piano, and Jack surprised everyone by playing with some skill, although he couldn't match the performance Kevin delivered after his years of lessons. "The nuns never taught me that well," Jack admitted. "Sister Benedict told me when I was a kid that she'd teach me if I continued to practice, which I did, but Kevin's teacher was better."

Helen walked him to his truck in the darkness and lingered outside nearly a half hour before Liam and Katherine, listening to the radio in the living room, heard the truck start up and head off down the road. Helen came into the house, her face flushed slightly, and Liam looked up.

"You spent a lot of time out there," he said to Helen.

"We were talking."

"Yes," Liam said. "He seems to do that well."

Katherine, her practiced ear catching the note of disapproval, said, "Liam, I thought he was very nice."

After Helen went upstairs, Katherine said, "She seems to be quite taken with that young man."

Liam grunted and picked up his book. "He's a fine talker. That and a nickel will get him a cup of coffee."

Several days later, a five-dollar basket of flowers arrived at the house from Krause's Florists in the village. It was not for Helen, but for Katherine. With it was a note.

"Dear Mrs. Brennan," it read, "I want to thank you and your husband for the hospitality and kindness you showed me after my thoughtlessness nearly deprived you of a daughter. My photograph of the sailboat, it turned out, was underexposed. But despite that, meeting you and your family made my trip to Lakeside well worthwhile."

Katherine was entranced. "Isn't he a nice young man?" she beamed to Liam.

He only grunted.

* * * *

It was merely a matter of time after that, as Liam had known it would be.

All Helen's previous suitors had been known to Liam, if not as individuals then as someone's son or nephew or grandson. He had found that linkage reassuring, just as he found his rather tenuous connection with Jack Ryan through his long-ago acquaintanceship with the young man's father better than nothing. Liam sensed that if he knew the young man courting his daughter came from a family to whom his own opinion had some value, that gave him a measure of control over the fellow that he would not have enjoyed otherwise. Liam was uncomfortable about the match between Helen and Jack Ryan in no small part because Jack was a Boydstown boy and not from a Lakeside family.

In 1935, Liam Brennan was forty-seven years old and comfortable. His winery had survived Prohibition, and the pent-up demand for good wine after repeal had enabled him to increase his acreage in grapes until they now made up nearly forty percent of the revenue of Brennan's Point. Although agricultural prices were generally off by the middle of the Depression, the prices of liquor, beer and wine were up. As Liam had survived Prohibition by depending on his food crops, so too was he surviving the Depression by increasing dependence on his winery. He was, in fact, even prospering, although he no longer was able to enjoy the cash reserve he had enjoyed in his early years.

By any standard, especially those of the Depression years, he was a successful farmer and winemaker. He was a member of the school board and a regular contributor to the Lake County Republican Committee's annual fund drives. He occupied a seat on the board of the Lakeside Trust Company. He was an officer in both the Grange and the Grape Growers Association, and he had served one term as exalted ruler of the Lakeside Elks.

He seldom attended mass, but he did make his Christmas and Easter duties and made quarterly contributions to the parish as well, so he was considered a member in good standing. He had been approached as a candidate for the county legislature, which he declined, and he was a trustee of the library. It had been a long time since anyone in Lakeside had provoked a serious disagreement with Liam. The life he had lived and the atmosphere in which he had lived it were not conducive to instilling empathy in a man like Liam. He knew he shouldn't be distrustful of Jack Ryan simply because the younger man had not been born and raised in Lakeside, but he was and that was that. Liam Brennan could— and sometimes chose to—feel pretty much any way he felt like feeling.

He hadn't given much real thought to his aversion to Jack Ryan. He hadn't felt the need to examine it closely. Had he done so, he would have been forced to admit that no small part of it was the young man's easy, disarming style. Liam had always gotten along with other men, but Jack possessed a warmth and wit Liam had never had. He was an endless repository of interesting trivia and gossip, of humorous stories and esoterica of all kinds. He was a smooth and entertaining talker whose great gift was his capacity to capture the imaginations of others. He was, in short, a great many things that serious, stoic Liam Brennan had never been and always envied. He was also, Liam suspected, something else distinctly less appealing.

Jack Ryan, Liam suspected, was lazy, although he had no hard evidence of it. To Liam, there was no greater sin.

It was clear that Jack possessed a fine intellect, far better than Helen's or his own or even Katherine's, but Liam had the feeling that it was intelligence virtually never applied to its fullest. The boy (as Liam persisted in calling him) had an encyclopedic memory, spouting statistics and obscure facts gleaned from this magazine or that book or a years-old radio speech. Liam, who thought in the beginning that Jack didn't know what he was talking about half the time, once wandered through the Lakeside Library after a board of trustees meeting to look up an especially arcane nugget of knowledge on European history that Jack had thrown out casually during one of his vastly entertaining monologues. Liam was startled and more than a little irritated to discover that the boy had been absolutely right.

"A boy with a memory like that could have a scholarship to any college in America, Depression or no Depression," Liam growled to Katherine. "He hasn't even finished high school."

"He had to go to work. He comes from a big family."

"He doesn't work now," Liam argued. "He takes pictures for pennies a week."

"Taking pictures is work, Liam. He's a photographer."

"Taking pictures isn't work," Liam shot back, exasperated, "not any more than Kevin playing piano in bars is work."

This was a sore point between them. The previous year Kevin had made a case at the dinner table one night for more spending money. Liam, wealthy in land but short of hard cash, had argued that he provided his son with all the money he needed but not enough to distract him from his studies. Kevin had responded by getting a part-time job in an Ithaca bar near Cornell as a piano-playing bartender. Liam had been angry. Katherine had defended Kevin's initiative. "Call it play if you like," she had shrugged.

"It is play, damn it. Is the boy going to spend his whole life playing? Is that what Helen wants for herself?"

"She says he makes her laugh. Don't you remember when you told me you'd never seen me laugh? You were right, you know. I never laughed much at all until I fell in love with you. Then I felt gay and lightheaded all the time."

He sighed and shook his head. "That doesn't have anything to do with anything."

Katherine walked over to where he was sitting at the kitchen table. She bent down and kissed his cheek, then she pressed his head against her breast and held him. "It has everything to do with everything, Liam Brennan," she told him.

Liam shared his reservations about the match between Helen and Jack only with Katherine and Henri.

"Your problem, my old friend," Henri said, "is that no one on this earth is good enough for your daughter."

"And what's wrong with that?" Liam shot back.

Henri grinned. "Christian Weidener would understand perfectly."

So, when Jack came to Liam one Saturday afternoon as he walked the fields, seeking out Helen's father for the traditional man-to-man conversation, it was no great surprise to Liam.

"I have every reason to expect I'll be able to open my own studio sometime this year," Jack said. "It'll mean that Helen and I can start out with something of our own—our own business."

Liam, striding through the rows of vines almost expressionless, wearing a gray fedora low over his face, merely grunted.

"I know this is a difficult thing for you, Mr. Brennan," Jack told him. "I expect that if I have a daughter, it'll be a difficult thing for me, too. But I love Helen, she loves me, and we're right together. We can have a good life."

The boy is handling this very well, Liam thought, and that didn't surprise him. "I won't say no," he told him, "it wouldn't do any good anyway, I suppose. So I'll only say this: Helen is her mother's daughter. I mean Helga, not Katherine. Helen has had just about everything her own way, always. She's as happy and as much at peace with life as anyone could be. She expects to remain happy. Do you understand what I'm saying?"

Jack nodded. "If she's not happy, it won't be because I haven't done everything in my power to keep her that way. I think I can do that, Mr. Brennan. And so does Helen." Jack hesitated for a moment, then he said, "You're right. We're going to get married whatever you say. We've talked about it. But I know that Helen won't feel the way she deserves to feel unless you give us your blessing. I'm asking you for it."

Liam lit his pipe slowly, inhaling the acrid smoke and blowing it out in a slender plume. Then, with a low sigh, he stuck out one gnarled hand. "You've got it," he said gruffly.

* * * *

Peter Baldwin had disliked Kevin Brennan on sight, and the favor had been returned. Neither of them could explain it adequately. Peter Baldwin, the tall, trim patrician from New Jersey, had no use for outgoing, athletic Kevin Brennan, the farmer's son. They disliked one another's looks, manners and outlooks on life. From the day they had signed up as pledges together at Theta Kappa Rho the animosity between the two had been unremitting, and it was held in check only by the fraternity's rigid social order.

So it was that Kevin Brennan and Peter Baldwin found themselves locked into a perpetual state of emnity that they were obligated to hide. The dislike crystallized over the years as they became juniors, and it took the form of a bitter rivalry. Baldwin was the better student, but Kevin was the better athlete. While Baldwin made dean's list every semester, Kevin, who had been outstanding in high school football and baseball, led the fraternity teams to victory in intermural competition. They even competed occasionally for the same girls, but that competition was never genuine. The moment the girl in question tilted one way or the other, the losing party would immediately withdraw from the contest, claiming loss of interest in the prize.

The Theta Kappa Rho house was a stately white frame building located on a tree-lined street on the hillside just below the main Cornell campus. It overlooked Ithaca and the vast splendor of Cayuga Lake, another of the Finger Lakes. After dinner on Fridays, pledges were obliged to roll out kegs of beer from the storeroom behind the kitchen, tap them and be prepared to serve and clean up after the brothers.

On such a Friday night shortly after the harvest of 1935, Peter Baldwin did a surprising thing. He got royally drunk and challenged Kevin to an arm-wrestling match at the dining room table. This challenge was immediately recognized for the momentous event it was, because it marked the first time that Baldwin had become venturesome enough to challenge Kevin on his own turf. Kevin, who was far less drunk than Baldwin, was amused. "Are you sure you want to do this, Pete?" he asked smugly. "You might break a nail, or something."

"Try me," Baldwin shot back through a smile that looked as though it had been painted on his face.

"Where's Billy?" Kevin inquired, looking around. "He wouldn't want to miss this."

Billy Frazier was the son of Dr. James Frazier of Lakeside and Kevin's closest friend since childhood. They had played high school football together, ended up going to the same college and, of course, pledged the same fraternity. They had been roommates for the past three years.

"He's been gone for hours, Brennan," someone called out. "You're too drunk to notice."

Kevin laughed. "Well, he's going to be sorry he missed this. Come on, Pete. Let's see what you can do." Which, predictably, turned out to be not much. Kevin slammed Baldwin's hand to the table in less than five seconds.

Baldwin reddened with anger and embarrassment. "Two out of three," he muttered thickly.

"Let's put some money on it," Kevin grinned, pulling out his wallet and slapping a ten-dollar bill on the table.

The action brought guffaws from around the room.

"Come on Baldwin," somebody called out. "You said two out of three. Now put up or shut up."

Baldwin, realizing that he had made a fool of himself, shook his head. The trick now, he decided, was to extricate himself from all this as gracefully as possible. "Nope," he grinned. "It's one thing to get drunk, but I don't see any reason why it should cost me money." He stuck out his hand to Kevin. "You're the winner."

Kevin, surprised and suspicious, took the outstretched hand.

"You're going to find a way to get even, aren't you?" Kevin said to Baldwin quietly and through a forced smile.

Baldwin smiled coldly over the handshake. "Sooner or later."

Kevin shook his head and took Baldwin's hand. "Better luck next time." Then he turned around and announced loudly. "You can count on that goddamn Frazier to miss anything interesting."

As the drinking contest extended into the evening, Kevin found himself short of the thick black cigars he had come to favor during college. He went up to his second-floor room for more and found Billy Frazier, fully clothed, asleep on his bed. Standing in the doorway, Kevin muttered, "Well, for Christ's sake." He rolled Billy over. Billy's eyes blinked and he came awake. He sat up, and as he did Kevin saw that his nose had been bloodied and his lower lip was the size of a sausage. "Jesus," he said. "What happened to you?"

Billy shook his head. "I stuck my nose where it shouldn't have been, I guess." he said. "How do I look?"

Kevin sat down next to Billy and examined his wounds. "Like you've been hit by a truck," he pronounced. "You might need stitches in that eye."

Kevin went to his shaving kit and brought out an alum stick and some bandaids. He began ministering to his friend's wounds.

"You ought to wash this out," he said. "Jesus, I hope we can clean you up before Helen's wedding next weekend. You'll scare hell out of everybody."

"Especially my mother," Billy said. "Ow! Go easy there."

"So what happened?"

"Do you know the Empire Supper Club?"

"I know it. I played piano there one weekend last year. That can be a rough place."

"You're telling me," Billy said. "I went down there to have dinner with this girl, only she didn't show up. So I had a couple of drinks while I was waiting, and after a while another girl I know came over and asked me to do a favor for her."

"Who were the girls?"

"The first one I don't even know," Billy said. "She was a fix-up. The second one was a girl named Jane Fellows. She used to go out with a guy I know in the premed society. She's a local girl, works in town. Anyway, she told me she was out with a fellow who was starting to scare her a bit. He's a professional boxer named Young Roberts. She said he was getting drunk, and she asked me if I'd sit with her for a while and maybe this fellow would leave her alone."

Kevin frowned. "And you did it?"

Billy shrugged. "Well, I was drunk. I still am, or all this would hurt something fierce. When this fellow Roberts came over and tried to take Jane back, I told him to shove off, and we ended up going outside."

"Serves you right," Kevin said, administering a bandaid to a ragged, half-inch gash over Billy's right eye. "A boxer? You must have been really tanked up."

"He's only a lightweight. I thought I could handle him, but he's real fast. I tried to fight him at long range. If I'd just have tackled him like we did in football and taken him down I think I could have taken him. By the time that occurred to me, though, I was on my behind in the alley behind the club and he had dragged Jane back inside. So I got up and walked home. I think my bloody nose ruined this shirt."

"This girl, what's her name, must be really something for you to risk a beating like this."

"She is," Billy grunted. "I don't think she had any interest in me, though. Linemen never get the really first-rate girls. They go for you backs. That shows how drunk I am, that I would admit that."

Kevin stood up. "Just go to sleep. Tomorrow morning you're going to wish you were dead."

Billy was asleep in five minutes. Kevin sat in a chair by the bed and quietly smoked one of his beloved cigars. He looked down at Billy's battered face, and the longer he sat there, the angrier he become.

If he'd had less to drink, or more, he wouldn't have done it; but finally Kevin slowly stubbed out the cigar and went to the closet. He slipped on a jacket and left the room. It was a fifteen-minute walk down the hill to the Empire Supper Club, and when Kevin entered, the crowd was already thinning out. Kevin went immediately to the bar. The bartender was a smallish, bald-headed man.

"Is there a fellow in here named Young Roberts?" Kevin asked.

The bartender cocked his head. "Who wants to know? And why?"

"He had an argument tonight with a friend of mine."

The bartender frowned. "You college kids and your arguments. Now look, any trouble you want to have, you have it outside. Otherwise I sic the cops on you."

Kevin nodded. "There won't be any trouble in here. You just point him out, so I'll know him, and then send him out to meet me in the back. Tell him I'm a friend of the guy he beat up tonight and that I'm alone."

"Are you alone?" the bartender demanded. "Not that he'll give two damns in hell. He'd fight an army just for fun."

"No army. Just me."

The bartender laughed. "Then you're going to get the shit beaten out of you. That's him over there, in the blue suit. I'll tell him you're waiting out there."

Kevin looked across the floor of the club. Young Roberts was standing near a table close to the bandstand. He was a few years older than Kevin, and his face was sharp-edged. He looked rather ordinary, although the young woman at the table with him definitely was not. She had long, tawny hair, and she was wearing a bright red dress.

Roberts walked around the table and sat down. Kevin watched as the boxer moved, saw a hint of beery unsteadiness, but also saw that Young Roberts moved with a natural grace and economy of motion that conveyed real power. Nobody to fool with, Kevin thought.

"I'll be out back," he told the bartender, and left.

Outside in the alley, Kevin positioned himself along the wall right next to the door. He had only a moment to wait, then the door came open and Young Roberts stepped out into the alley. He didn't see Kevin at first, and by the time he did Kevin had grabbed him by the arm with his left hand and had driven a hard right hand downward into the smaller man's face.

Roberts went down.

Then he got right back up, which had not been part of Kevin's plan. Robert's nose was bleeding, but he seemed unhurt otherwise.

"There," Kevin said. "I just wanted to introduce myself. I'm Kevin Brennan, and I figure we're even now for what happened to my friend."

Young Roberts laughed. Kevin weighed more than 200 pounds to Roberts's 135, but Billy Frazier had been even bigger.

"I don't figure we're even," the boxer said.

Kevin shrugged. This was what he had come here for. "So let's go," he said.

In just the first few seconds, it became clear to Kevin that he would lose, and badly. Roberts could hit, and he moved like mercury, always a split second ahead of Kevin's punches; always a split second before his attempts to dodge. The smaller man fired short, explosive punches, delivered in rapid, professional combinations. When a sharp hook to Kevin's middle doubled him up, Roberts was there to straighten him up with an uppercut. When Kevin threw a jab, Roberts slipped under it and drove a right into his face. After thirty seconds, Kevin had yet to land a punch and Roberts had yet to miss one. At the end of a minute of swift, nearly silent fighting in the alley, Kevin's face was swelling and he was beginning to see double images.

It was then that Kevin just grabbed the boxer by a sleeve, pulled him close and then drove him into the brick wall of the Empire Supper Club, his big shoulder right underneath the smaller man's breastbone. When Roberts hit the wall, the breath was forced out of him with a loud, whooshing sound. With breath, Roberts could move beautifully, like a ballet dancer. Without it, he couldn't move at all, and Kevin's big fist nailed him once, twice, and he went down.

Roberts got to his knees, gasping for breath and one eye closed, but still desperate to fight. Kevin, using his greater strength and size, grabbed the lightweight by the neck, lifted him off his feet and pressed him against the wall. Then, holding the boxer with his left hand, Kevin methodically beat him in the midsection with the right, finishing off with a punch flush on the chin. Then he dropped Roberts to the pavement and stepped back, reeling and his chest heaving. Roberts was rolling on the ground, grunting.

Kevin lurched off toward the back door. As he reached for it, the door opened and the woman who had been sitting at Roberts's table stepped into the alley. She looked at Kevin, then over at the prize fighter, who was sitting up against the wall, thoroughly beaten. "You beat him up," she said to Kevin. "Good. The bartender told me you might be able to do it. That's what I wanted to see."

Roberts saw the girl, then rolled over on his side, away from her. Kevin, in pain but still surging from the encounter, looked at the woman closely. She was no more than twenty and stunning. "Bloodthirsty little thing, aren't you?" he said. "Why did you ever go out with a creep like this to begin with?"

She shrugged. "It seemed like a good idea at the time. He was all over me tonight, whispering horrible things to me. I was really scared. I was going to have to let him take me home pretty soon."

Kevin nodded. "And you let Billy get beaten up because of your mistake."

"I didn't mean for anything like that to happen," she said defensively. "I didn't think Billy would actually fight him. I told Billy he was a professional."

Jane Fellows looked at Kevin's face. She reached into her purse and produced a handkerchief. "You're hurt, too. Here, take this."

"I'm going to get blood on it."

"I have others. Let's go inside and get some water so you can wipe off your face."

Inside, seated at a table in the corner, Kevin began to realize just how hard he had been hit. One lip was swelling, and one eye was nearly closed already. In the morning, he thought, I'm going to look worse than Billy, and I supposedly won the fight.

Jane dabbed at his eye with a wet handkerchief. "I feel awful about this," she said. "You may not believe it, but I don't always get myself into situations like this."

Roberts had staggered back into the club and was seated on a bar stool, surrounded by friends who were looking their way.

"If we stay here," she said, "you'll have more trouble. I have a car. Let's go somewhere else."

Jane got her purse and they left. They ended up at another bar closer to campus, sitting in a booth while a radio in the corner blasted out Cab Calloway. They made small talk over a couple of beers. Jane told him she was originally from Boydstown.

"What are you doing in Ithaca?" Kevin asked her.

"Waiting tables. There's no work in Boydstown. There's a Depression on, or haven't you heard. I guess it doesn't much affect college boys who can afford to go to Cornell. But it affects working people. I had a friend who could get me a job in a roadhouse, so I took it. Only I quit the other night."

"How come?"

"The owner was propositioning me every ten minutes."

"What are you going to do with yourself now?"

She shrugged. "Get another job. I have a few dollars saved up. Maybe I'll take a few weeks off."

Kevin lit one of his cigars. "How would you like to go to a party next weekend?"

She made a face. "A college boys party?" she asked, with more than a touch of disdain in her voice.

"No," he told her, "my sister's wedding. You'll enjoy yourself. You can come as my date."

Jane shook her head. "I don't think so."

"Hey," Kevin told her. "You're going."

* * * *

Peter Day, the hotel proprietor who had so elegantly catered the reception for both Liam's weddings, did not cater Helen's. He lay in Saint Peter and Paul's Cemetery, only a few yards from Minnie's resting place, and his hotel had been converted into apartments. This reception was held at Brennan's Point and catered by an Italian restaurateur from Boydstown who owned a summer home on the other side of the lake.

As the car caravan arrived from the church, Kevin leaped out of Billy Frazier's Model A, issued instructions to the band and then broke into a spectacular rendition of the big apple with the lovely girl he had brought as his date, whom no one had met as yet.

During a break in the music, Kevin brought Jane and Billy over to his parents.

"Pop, I'd like you to meet Jane Fellows." Kevin motioned to Billy. "You already know this reprobate."

"I don't even know the word," Liam said. "How are you, Jane? How did you get hooked up with these two? And Billy Frazier, what happened to your face?"

"I hit somebody's fist with it, Mr. Brennan. Next time I'll try it the other way around."

"It works better that way," Liam agreed. Then he looked closely at Kevin. "You look as though something of the sort happened to you."

"Intermural football, Pop," Kevin said. "Listen, Jane will be staying overnight, in Helen's room, if you don't mind."

"Not at all," Katherine said. "We're delighted to have you."

Jane smiled nervously. "Thank you, Ma'am. I know I'm putting you out . . ."

Katherine laughed. "After all this, a houseguest is no trouble at all, believe me."

Jane was formally introduced to Helen later in the day. By that time the newlyweds had changed their clothes and were preparing to leave on their wedding trip. They were delayed by well-wishers as Kevin and Billy and several others decorated Billy's Model A, which he had loaned the newlyweds when Jack's truck had failed to start at the church. Kevin slipped an explicit and bawdy list of wedding night instructions into an envelope and hastily addressed it to "The Amateurs" before placing it on the seat. Then, pelted with more rice, Jack and Helen slipped into the Model A and put-putted off down Lakeside Road.

Just outside Lakeside, Helen said, "Do you know what we're coming up to?"

"Yes, I do. This is the spot where we first met."

"Where you tried to kill me."

"Where we met and I knocked you for a loop."

"And you did—literally," Helen sighed, snuggling close to him.

Chapter 12

Kevin had spent his first two years at Cornell studying just enough to get by and spending the rest of his time enjoying the life of an Ivy League playboy. The bulk of his final two years was spent as Jane Fellows's lover. After six months of dating, Kevin simply moved in, hoping his family wouldn't find out. Jane didn't much care whether her family knew. "Not that they're likely to find out," she said one cold winter night in bed with Kevin. "I haven't seen my old man in eight years, not since he took off one night after a fight with my mom."

"I ought to meet her," Kevin said. "I don't think it would be wise to marry you without meeting your mother first. She might be colored, for all I know."

Jane sat up in bed. "Marry me?"

He shrugged. "Why not? You like the way I play the piano. If ever there was a good reason to marry somebody . . ."

Jane turned away, her face pale.

"Hey," Kevin said, sitting up and pulling her toward his embrace. "Come on. I thought it would make you happy. Don't you want to become an honest woman?"

"I do. But will your folks accept me? Your father scares me to death."

"He tries like hell to scare everybody. You're the only one who falls for it."

"What about law school?" Jane asked. "I thought you were going to be a lawyer."

"I have no interest whatsoever in becoming a lawyer. That's Pop's idea. I can't imagine spending my life going to real estate closings and drawing up wills. And that's all a lawyer does in Lakeside."

"You want to live in Lakeside? Kevin, that's such a small town."

"And Ithaca's a metropolis, I suppose. Anyway, it's nothing to worry about until May, when I graduate."

199

"Kevin, I don't know how I'd fit in with your family. They're rich, and my family is . . . well, they're seedy."

"My family has its seedy origins," he told her. "Pop got out of Ireland one step ahead of the cops. He doesn't have all that much money either, not in cash, anyway. I don't think he could lay his hands on more than five thousand dollars if he had to tomorrow—not without selling off something."

Jane laughed. "All I know is I saw where you live, and that's rich in my book."

Jane worried deeply about the manner in which she was viewed by Liam and Katherine. Although they were unfailingly courteous toward her, she nonetheless felt they were keeping their distance. At Helen's wedding and during several of the weekends Kevin had taken her home with him, she had felt Katherine's cool, appraising gaze on her. Jane had sensed that Katherine viewed her as a disconcerting development in a well-thought-out plan that involved Kevin going through law school, then marrying a Lakeside girl and settling down to a peaceful life as a country squire. As much as Katherine's constant observation disturbed her, Jane found Liam's aloofness nearly as bothersome. Jane was left with the impression that Liam never quite approved of anyone, of her least of all.

While she had little education, Jane had a quick mind and sharp instincts. She had learned how to speak fairly cultured American English by watching movies, which were her passion. She had learned how to dress and use makeup by modeling herself shamelessly after Katherine Hepburn, whom she viewed as the embodiment of all that was proper in a modern woman. Jane worked tirelessly at coming across as the sort of woman who might have gone to college and, if she hadn't, certainly could have and hadn't missed a thing by not being there.

In her heart, though, she knew it was all a fraud. It was her clear impression that both Katherine and Liam had seen through her facade, and she fiercely resented both of them for it. Jane Fellows had struggled since her teens to keep her demons locked tightly inside, to carve out a place in a hostile, judgmental and unforgiving world. She was determined to climb up even as she was convinced she would fall back, no matter how fierce her struggle. When she suspected that someone had somehow found a window into her soul, she regarded that person with horror. A marriage to Kevin, she realized, would make it impossible for her to avoid people she was convinced had found her out.

At the same time, Jane loved Kevin. He was the vindication of all her efforts, and he made her feel good in ways she hadn't imagined before she met him. The decision to marry him could be put off only a little longer. His parents were pressing him for postgraduation plans. On one of Kevin's weekends home, during his final semester at Cornell, his father entered the winery and found Kevin turning champagne bottles in the riddling racks. Liam was, to his surprise, struck by the resemblance of his son to his dead father. "You're bigger," Liam said. Kevin, startled, jumped at the sound. "You're bigger," Liam went on, "but the ghost of my Da moves with you. Except for the size and the coloring, you're him all over again in manner and carriage."

"Pop, do me a favor. The next time you find something profound you want to tell me, don't sneak up behind me in a quiet wine cellar to do it. You scared me out of ten years' growth."

"I didn't mean to. I was looking for Henri. Have you seen him?"

Kevin frowned. "He's locked in the lab, playing with one of his formulas. I asked him to let me in to watch him, but you'd think I was a spy from Great Western. Pop, why's he so secretive?"

"It's his nature, I suppose. You shouldn't let it trouble you."

"It's hard to avoid letting it trouble me. If I'm going to learn wine-making, I have to find a way to persuade him to teach me. I'm upset over this, Pop. I have a right to learn."

Liam nodded. He brought out his pipe and filled it slowly with tobacco. It was an unconscious ritual he followed as he thought. He put the pipe in his mouth without lighting it. Then he said, "You're serious about the wine, then—even after all this time? You'll not do the other?"

"If you mean law school, no. What I want is right here, Pop, in this winery, on this land."

"It's this girl, isn't it?"

"Yes and no. If you're asking if Jane is part of what I want, the answer is yes. If you're asking if I'd want something besides the wine if there was no Jane, the answer is no. I'm cut out for this. I can't do anything else without going crazy. Do you understand what I'm saying to you?"

"Your mother will take this hard," Liam said. "I hope you've thought this through."

"I have. You'll have to help me with Mother. You'll have to help me with Henri, too. He has to teach me."

Liam smiled ruefully. "Why should he teach you? He'd never teach me."

Kevin and Billy Frazier took their degrees in ceremonies at Cornell in May 1936. A party was held in a banquet room in an Ithaca hotel by the Brennans and the Fraziers for the new graduates, their friends and a number of friends of the families who had made the ninety-minute journey from Lakeside.

Billy Frazier was scheduled to go to medical school in Cleveland in

the fall, and Kevin was expected to begin work at the winery and in the
fields as soon as he got home. It had been pretty much accepted, although
not formalized with an announcement in the Lakeside newspaper, that
Kevin and Jane would be married that summer, toward the end of August,
before the harvest began. Plans called for them to move into the shack,
which Katherine was already refurnishing and cleaning up. Katherine was
even a little anxious for the wedding to take place once she became aware
that Kevin and Jane had been living together for nearly two years. She
had visions of the bride going down the aisle with the swelling fruit of
that cohabitation visible enough to be a topic of gossip throughout Lakeside.

"It's bad enough that they've been shacked up," she said to Liam.
"Let's get them married before Kevin has a pregnant fiance on his hands—
and on ours."

In contrast to Helen and Jack's lavish wedding, the nuptials of Kevin
Brennan and Jane Fellows were subdued. Billy Frazier served as best man,
and Jane asked Helen to be matron of honor. The new couple spent a
week honeymooning in New York City, then settled into life in the shack.
Kevin went to work in the winery, learning the growing and business
end of the winery from his father and struggling to get Henri to initiate
him into the mysteries of the laboratory. Kevin was delighted with the
way his life was turning out. He wished, though, that Jane would begin
to feel more at home at Brennan's Point. "Aren't you happy?" he asked
her one night as they sat on the porch of the shack, gazing out at the
summer moon over the lake.

Jane took his hand, kissed it and held it to her. She looked at him
and smiled. "I'm fine," she said.

* * * *

What Helen liked least about being married to Jack was his working
on weekends. It meant not only that she spent all week by herself in
their Boydstown apartment, but Saturdays as well. As winter broke and
she felt spring fever setting in, she decided to visit Brennan's Point by
herself. Kevin and Jane drove down to Boydstown to pick her up.

She picked an unreasonably cold, raw day in April, and the heater
in Kevin's second-hand Buick was balky. Helen, in a skirt and a linen
coat too light for the fortiesh temperatures, shivered in the back seat. As
they rolled out of Boydstown and onto the road that would take them
through Montour Falls and then Watkins Glen and then to the road which
led to Lakeside, Kevin reached into the glove compartment and produced

the flask he had carried with him to every Cornell football game for four years. He reached back over the front seat and handed it to Helen.

"Take a shot of this," he told her. "It'll warm you up."

Helen did. She felt the fiery liquor roll down her throat and she coughed. "That's horrible," she gasped. "How is everything at the point? Are Mommy and Poppy all right?"

Kevin shrugged behind the wheel. "Same as always. Mom has put on a bit more weight, but then again, so has Pop. He's taking things a bit easier now that I'm around, and it's showing. Henri still won't help me learn anything about making wine, but I'm doing a lot of reading on my own, and Pop is teaching me the business end and a little about the growing. I won't let him teach me a thing about basic farming. I told him he ought to get rid of all but a few of the cows and plant more vineyard. I think he will next year. Wait until you see the shack. Jane has done a fabulous job with it."

"Your mother has done a fabulous job," Jane said, unenthusiastically.

Kevin glanced over at her. "You've done as much as she has."

"I've followed orders," Jane said.

"How's Annette?" Helen asked quickly.

"Annette is like always," Kevin told her, "a saint. I don't know how she puts up with that nasty old Frenchman."

"Henri's bark is worse than his bite," Helen said.

"Well," Kevin said, "maybe I can talk Doctor King into fixing Henri's bark the next time he works on his bite. That fellow Becky married has turned out to be a jerk, by the way. He got into the Elks because of who his father-in-law is, but nobody can stand him. Not even Henri."

"Oh, Kevin," Jane said, "I think Henri is kind of cute."

"So does Pop. I guess I'm the only one who's never been able to see his charm."

"Neither did my grandfather," Helen said, "or so I'm told. What else is going on?"

"Well," Jane said coyly, "I'm about three months overdue on my period, and I'm starting to get worried."

"What?" Helen said, delighted. "You're pregnant?"

"Either that or she can't count," Kevin volunteered.

"Who do you suspect, Kevin?" Helen asked innocently. Both women laughed uproariously while Kevin, for once the victim, merely shook his head.

"The baby is due next fall," Jane said. "Dr. Frazier hasn't given me a date yet."

"I'm going to be an aunt," Helen squealed. "Marvelous."

"How about you and Jack?" Jane asked. "What's taking you so long?"

"Oh, I don't know. Money is so tight with the new studio and all. If business doesn't get better, I'll have to go to work pretty soon."

"Well," Jane said, "don't wait too long. I think everybody should have their kids when they're real young—eighteen, say. When you're eighteen, it's a lot easier than when you get up into your twenties. I can't imagine how girls have babies when they're in their thirties."

"How do you feel?" Helen asked.

"Awful. You can't see it under this coat, but I look like I'm going to have a gorilla."

Kevin reached an arm over Jane's shoulders, pulled her close and squeezed her. Helen could see Jane's face reflected in the mirror on the dashboard. Her cheeks were flushed with healthy color, a side effect of the pregnancy, she was sure. Helen felt a surge of jealousy and a sudden draft. She shivered in her light linen coat.

"Kevin," she said, "would pass that flask back here again? I'm turning blue from the chill."

* * * *

Jack had a good location for his studio, right inside the Main Street entrance of a big Boydstown department store, but he found that the space set aside for his laboratory wasn't sufficient. He was forced to rent more space in the rear of a small downtown store to set up a proper laboratory. It was an added expense piled on top of money he had already borrowed to buy cameras, tripods, an enlarger and printing easel, a lab timer and paper, film and chemicals. All in all, with the rent for the lab space coupled with the rent for the space in Hoffman's department store and the cost of paying off the bank loan, what Jack managed to clear from the business simply wasn't enough for them to live on.

"I can't do more than I'm doing," he told Helen. "I'm shooting all day and developing and printing all night. It's the double rent that's killing me right now—that and the bank loan. Once that loan is paid off, we'll be sitting pretty. But for now, you're going to have to find a job."

"Where can I work?" Helen asked him. "I've never done anything."

"How about a factory job? They're doing some hiring at Potter's."

Helen groaned. Potter's was a large firm on Boydstown's northern outskirts that manufactured industrial filters and machine parts. Helen had ridden by the plant every time she journeyed up to the lake. It was huge and forbidding, a steam-shrouded mountain of dirty brick and pipes and smokestacks belching day and night. "Oh, Jack," she said wearily. "What would I do in a place like that?"

"Look, I'm not telling you what to do. You can do what you want.

But I could use the help. And you're the one who complains about the phone calls."

The phone calls. Helen shuddered at the mention of the phone calls. From the day of their marriage, Jack had paid all the bills. Helen had neither the organization nor the inclination to manage the household accounts. She had never handled money and never wanted to. But, periodically, there would come a phone call from the telephone company or the electric company or the landlord, politely inquiring about an overdue check. More often than not, Helen answered the calls because Jack was working long hours and was seldom home, and she never had a response as to why the check was late. The phone calls left her in terror that someone on the party line had heard the conversation and would know that she and Jack were having money problems. They also left her frightened that she would pick up the phone some day and find that service had been cut off. She had visions of the house being plunged into sudden darkness as the electric company cut off service. Her darkest fears revolved around the sheriff suddenly appearing to evict them from their home for nonpayment of rent. Whenever such a call came, Helen would stammer out a promise that the bill would be paid immediately, then she would run downtown, find Jack and implore him almost hysterically to pay the bill before something terrible happened. He would always calm her, speaking in a low, soothing voice, and assure her that he had merely forgotten to mail the check, that he would run off on his lunch hour and take care of the whole thing. Then the phone calls would stop until the next month. The phone calls horrified Helen even more than the prospect of working at Potters, if that was really the choice she faced. "Maybe I'll catch the bus up there tomorrow and apply," she said quietly.

She did, and she got a job on the assembly line. And she liked it.

The Potter plant employed hundreds. Helen, who had always treasured routine, found the predictability of life on the assembly line reassuring. She knew what would happen next, how it would happen and what was expected of her. She also found herself enjoying the camaraderie of life on the line. She got a good shift, working almost precisely the hours Jack was open at the studio during the week, and she was left with her evenings free to oil color the prints Jack made as part of his portrait business. The starting wage at Potter's wasn't handsome by any means, but it made up the difference between Jack's income and the family expenses and left a little over for recreation and some nice clothing for Helen and a battered, third-hand Dodge.

More to the point, the money Helen brought in meant that the phone calls stopped. For Helen, that alone made it all worthwhile.

On Sundays they would alternately head to the Ryan house for dinner with Jack's family or drive up to Brennan's Point. Jack would often use the trips to the lake to take photos of the lake or the stunning scenery that surrounded it for display in his studio at Hoffman's. He was often tired, but business was slowly improving.

That summer Helen was assigned to a later shift to cover for a vacationing coworker. She didn't relish working until midnight, but she welcomed the prospect of having her days free for a week. Helen didn't tell Jack about the shift change. Her plan was to surprise him for lunch the first day.

When that day rolled around, Helen was awakened around ten by a nice woman from the telephone company, who pointed out that the check hadn't yet come in. Helen said she was sure her husband had sent in the payment and that she would mention it to him at lunchtime, just in case it had slipped his mind. If it had, she assured the woman from the phone company, she'd get her husband to write a check and she'd deliver it herself that afternoon. The call left Helen slightly unnerved. She drank a beer, which relaxed her.

She then showered and breakfasted and called Brennan's Point to talk to Katherine for twenty minutes. Then she got dressed carefully and walked downtown. When she got to the store and the studio shortly before noon, she was surprised to find it closed.

"He's at lunch," Helen was told by the woman at the nearby perfume counter. "He won't be back until two or three."

Helen glanced at the clock on the store wall. "It's not even noon."

The woman shrugged. "Jack takes long lunches."

Helen's eyes narrowed. "Where does he eat, do you know?"

The woman nodded. "Yep. He eats every day at Kenny Schick's, down at Main and Water."

Helen found Jack there, at the counter of Schick's Diner, engaging in banter with Kenny Schick, who was a jovial, fortiesh man with what Liam would have called, disparagingly, a gift for gab.

"What are you doing here?" Jack asked. "Don't you have a job any more?"

"I'm working the late shift this week. I came down here to surprise you and get you to take me to lunch. But I can see you're already at lunch. They told me at the store that you'd be here for a couple of hours."

"Not today. I've got too much to do. Sit down. Kenny makes a great cheeseburger, don't you, Kenny?"

"They made it sound like you take two-hour lunches a lot," Helen said.

"Lunchtime is usually slow, and I got in real early this morning. I had to get out of there for a while."

"How long do you plan to hang around here?" Helen demanded.

Jack's mouth grew tight. "As long as I feel like hanging around. What I do is my business, Helen. I don't tell you how to spend your lunch hours."

"I turn over every penny I make to you, and I spend my lunch hour in the cafeteria at the plant."

"What do you want me to do," Jack demanded, "go out to Potter's cafeteria to eat lunch?"

"I want you to stop hanging around here and get back to work," Helen said. "It's not like we can't use the money."

The conversation was attracting attention around the diner, and Jack was both embarrassed and furious. "I'll worry about the money."

"I wish you'd worry more about it," she told him. "I got a call from the telephone company this morning. I told them you'd sent in the check. Did you?"

"I'll drop it off this afternoon on the way home from work."

"Give it to me. I'll drop it off now."

"My checkbook is back at the studio," he said. "I'll take care of it."

"Jack," she said, "I can't live this way. I don't know when you're at work. I don't know what's been paid and what hasn't. In my house this never happened. Things were always taken care of."

"Look," he told her, "you're not living in your parents' house now. You're living in your own house, and this is the real world, not some fairyland. In the real world, sometimes not everything goes the way you'd like it to. I said I'd take care of the phone bill today, and I'll take care of it. So don't worry about it."

She started to break in, but he cut her off with an angry gesture. "And I'll run the studio, too," he told her. "You know what time I go in, and you know what time I get home at night. You've seen me up half the night processing and printing. It's not like I'm loafing. So if I want to take an hour-and-a-half lunch, so what? Now, what do you want for lunch?"

"Nothing. I'm not hungry. I just want you to go back to work."

Jack looked at her for a long moment, and she dropped her own eyes under his harsh gaze.

"All right," he said finally. He put a dollar bill on the counter. "Kenny, I'm square here."

Then Jack got up and walked out of the diner without another word, leaving her there. After a moment, Helen got up and left. She walked home, took off her clothes and got into bed.

Where she cried.

* * * *

The lake was different on different days.

Sometimes the water was a crisp blue under sunny skies filled with cotton-candy clouds. At other times it was a sweeping expanse of rolling slate gray under billowing thunderheads. At still other times, it was an angry plain of restless energy, topped by frothing whitecaps. When the sun went down it was often a still black mirror reflecting the pinpoints of starlight from the clear night sky. On cloudy nights it was a field of smooth, inky velvet.

But Jane Fellows Brennan found in Iroquois Lake one enduring constant that touched her unfailingly at the deepest level. Whatever else it might be on a given day, Jane knew that the lake was also something else, always.

It was boring.

The lake was boring. The vine-covered mountains surrounding it were boring. The shack, even redecorated, was boring. Her in-laws, stolid Liam and his prissy, fault-finding wife, were boring. And Jane, she knew, was boring, too. Boring and ugly and fat with child. And her husband didn't seem to care.

Once settled into his routine at the farm and winery, Kevin had immediately begun to grow away from her. He had become much more a part of the family from which he had sprung than the family he had chosen—his new wife. He had become preoccupied with the winery, with his daily conflicts with Henri. He left early; he came home late and tired. And all he talked about was wine. If Jane heard him utter the words "sugar content" one more time she would put her head in the oven.

At Cornell Kevin had enjoyed himself, and during his last two years that had meant spending virtually every second with Jane, tending to her needs and cheering her in her down moods. Now, as a young married man with a child on the way and feeling the weight of family responsibility for the first time, Kevin was less jovial, more prone to moodiness and private worry over business.

The onset of Jane's pregnancy had made her far more mercurial. The swelling of her trim middle was a constant source of concern to her. She gave little thought to what her life would be like after the baby came. That was not her way.

Now, on a warm September day as she watched thunderheads roll in over the lake from Ringlesport, Jane stubbed out her cigarette and glanced at the clock. It was nearly noon, and Kevin would be home soon. Sometimes he ate lunch at the big house, in the kitchen with his mother and Annette. Other times he worked through lunch in the laboratory on those rare occasions when Henri, consumed with curiosity about the chemical characteristics of a particular vintage, was willing to use Kevin as a lab assistant. But today he would be home. Jane had made a point at breakfast of asking him to eat lunch with her. "I get lonely," she had pouted.

"Why don't you go up to the big house and see Mom and Annette?" he had demanded. "They'd love the company." Jane had merely grunted noncommittally. She had tried that, and she had found herself an uncomfortable third wheel there. The two older women had been together for so long that they communicated in a verbal shorthand that consisted of references to past events with which Jane had no acquaintance and to people she had met only once or twice or not at all.

Jane's interest in housekeeping was severely limited. Her one passion, movies and movie stars, was never brought up. They hardly ever listened to the radio, although Jane knew that Annette sometimes tuned at night into to the French-language stations that beamed erratically across Lake Ontario from Quebec.

The one topic they all could discuss was pregnancy and child rearing, the one topic Jane had steadfastly avoided, despite her current condition. To her, pregnancy was an unpleasantness.

So, except for a few obligatory hours a week spent at Sunday dinner and other family events at the big house, Jane found excuses to stay at home in what everybody persisted in calling the shack, although it certainly wasn't that any more. Moreover, it was Jane's home, and she found the term offensive. She had lived in a few shacks in her time, and she knew the difference even if these rich farmers didn't.

Jane sighed and got up to make herself a fresh pot of coffee. As she did, she heard Kevin's heavy footsteps coming down the stairs from the road. She threw herself into his arms when he came through the door. "What'll you have for lunch," she demanded cheerily, "food or me?"

Kevin laughed and kissed her. He pushed by her and went to the refrigerator for a bottle of beer. "I'm bone-dry," he told her. "This ought to be a good harvest, if we ever get it going. The Aurore ought to be ready by this weekend if I can get Henri to give the okay."

"That means you'll start the harvest and the pressing this weekend?" Jane asked. "And that means twelve or fourteen hours a day, seven days a week, until you're finished?"

Kevin caught the edge in her voice. "Well," he said slowly, "these are the six weeks we work for all year. After everything is picked and pressed, it's all Henri's until next spring. Pop can sit back and relax, and I'll be on short days trying to get Henri to teach me more about being a winemaker."

"So for six weeks I just won't see you, is that it?"

He shrugged. "We'll have all winter to snuggle together."

"Six more weeks and I'll be so fat I'll be able to snuggle with myself."

He took her hands and kissed them. "I think you look terrific."

"Don't try to cheer me up. I'm all weepy, and I want to enjoy it."

"What are you weepy about? You're going to be a mommy."

"In two months. Now I'm just a blimp." Jane put her arms around Kevin and clung to him, pressing against him with her huge belly. "I'm so fat and ugly. And I'm lonely. And I'm scared about this baby."

"Scared?" he said. "What's to be scared of?"

"That's easy for you to say. I'm scared of the pain."

"Oh, come on," Kevin said. "It can't be all that bad."

"How do you know? When's the last time you had a baby?"

"Billy told me a medical school story about childbirth pain. There's this girl who goes to her doctor and she tells him she's scared silly about the pain. She says she wants him to give her some idea of how bad it's going to be, you know, so she can prepare herself. Well, he tells her, it's pretty tough to describe. But she keeps pushing him. So finally the doctor tells her to take her upper lip between her thumb and forefinger, like this, see?"

Jane was more than a little suspicious. "And . . .?"

"Then he tells her to pull it over the top of her head," Kevin said, grinning broadly.

Jane was livid. "Kevin, that's the most insensitive thing I've ever heard."

Kevin was nonplussed. "I'm only trying to make you laugh."

Jane would not be placated. "I don't think it's a damn bit funny. You get out of here and go back to your goddamn grapes."

"I thought you were going to feed me," he said.

But Jane was pushing him, and hard, toward the door.

"Get your mother to feed you," she said, her voice shrill. "Get out and leave me alone."

She pushed him through the door and out onto the porch as he protested, then she slammed the door and locked it. Kevin knocked on the door.

"Let me in," he said.

"Drop dead," Jane shouted at him through the door.

Kevin ate lunch at the big house. Down at the shack, Jane wept bitter tears of apprehension and loneliness.

* * * *

It was a stunningly good harvest.

Since the end of Prohibition Liam had devoted an ever-greater portion of his land to vineyard, primarily to the production of European hybrids. The dairy herd was down to a few cows. Cornfields had been sowed under to provide more room for the grapes.

The hybrids had been developed in Europe by a painstaking method of cross-pollination that often involved as many as fifteen or twenty thousand attempts to come up with the perfect variety. Liam had planted heavily in Aurore, which was the product of no fewer than 5,279 such cross-pollinations. The Seyval Blanc he had planted was the result of 5,276 such efforts.

The hybrids had flourished under his gentle hand, and the plump, gleaming berries, bursting with juice, had been harvested in record quantities. The wine they had begun to produce was vastly better than anything ever before sold under either the Brennan or Weidener labels, and now he had an immense quantity of juice on which Henri would work his magic over the winter.

"A good year," Henri said. "A very good year. Perhaps the best ever."

Liam, standing next to his winemaker, looking over the enormous fermenting vats that dominated the winery's first floor, nodded. "Could be," he said. "You know, it seems like only yesterday that we were close to starving. It's hard to believe things are going so well."

"That's because I'm in the business now," Kevin said. "You just needed a creative, energetic young genius who'd kick the place into shape."

Henri snorted. "I would feel better if we had one fewer young genius and one more European contest for our wines. This damnable war has made it impossible to win the sort of credentials we deserve with our wines—especially our whites and our champagnes. They would do well against the best the continent has to offer, and who knows it?"

Kevin said, "With all the other problems the war in Europe is causing, I can't say I'm too worked up because the European wine contests are shut down. Hitler is causing bigger difficulties than that."

"When he takes England," Liam said, "all will stabilize."

Kevin looked at his father in disbelief. "You don't really believe that, do you, Pop? You don't really think Roosevelt will let Hitler invade England."

Liam sighed. "No, probably not," he conceded. "If we'd been able to throw Roosevelt out last year, though, it wouldn't be a problem now."

"For that reason alone," Kevin said, "I'm glad he won."

"As am I," Henri broke in. "And I will be happier yet when America enters this war and liberates France from this madman."

"He's no madder than Churchill," Liam said. "I feel sorry about France, Henri, and I'm truly sorry we can't send our wine abroad this year for the international competition. This would certainly be the year for it. But if Hitler took England, the European situation would stabilize and things would get back to normal in no time."

Henri shook his head wearily. "My friend, you let your hatred of the British blind you. This Hitler is evil incarnate."

Liam shrugged. "He's a politician with a good army, that's all."

"And he'll send his army after us next if he manages to take Britain," Kevin broke in. "That's why Roosevelt has to get us into this war. Frankly, I think he'd have done it already if he wasn't such a politician himself."

Liam looked at his son in surprise. "Are you so interested in going off to fight for the British, you with a child coming any day now? Why should I want my son off in some foreign war to save the British monarchy? Whatever else Hitler might do if he takes England, he's said he'd free Ulster, and that's enough for me. It's not our business, anyway."

Kevin shook his head. "It's more our business every day. Say what you want about the British and Ireland, you'll get no argument from me there; but this country has cultural and historic ties with England that Roosevelt can't ignore."

Liam rolled his eyes at Kevin's statement. "The American flag first flew in open defiance of British tyranny. That's how little you know of cultural ties and history."

"How can you talk like this?" Henri shouted, his fist clenched over his head for emphasis. "This maniac is raping France. And we all have read of this business with the Jews. What is this man doing with the Jews?"

"I don't know," Liam said. "Probably nothing much. For all we know, it's all a lot of British propaganda. The thought of my son fighting a war for the sake of England sickens me. I pray it doesn't come to that."

Henri sighed deeply. "What will be will be," he said. "We are just poor winemakers."

Liam grinned. "Not so poor after the past few years, and especially after this harvest. There's something about a Depression that makes people want to drink more wine."

Kevin said, "Maybe a war would have the same effect."

"Well, then," Liam said, spreading his arms expansively, "let the war begin."

Annette appeared in the doorway. She never came to the winery, which Henri considered his private domain, and her appearance was cause for alarm.

"Annette," Henri said sharply. "What is the matter?"

Annette was nearly breathless. She obviously had run all the way from the house to the winery, clutching her skirts in her hands. "Jane," she said. "Her pains begin."

Kevin turned white. "I'll get the car." He turned to run out the door, but Liam caught his arm in a strong grip. "I'll get the car," he said calmly, "and I'll drive. You get your wife."

Kevin nodded. "All right, Pop. But hurry up."

Liam smiled at his son. "I hope it's a boy who grows up to give you orders."

* * * *

Susan Cecilia Brennan was born on October 14, 1941. It was a gloomy day, and she gave her mother a difficult time. Jim Frazier, wiping his lined brow after the delivery and leaning back exhausted in his chair in the small office the hospital provided him, said it was because Jane had not been able to relax.

"She just wouldn't let it happen to her," Frazier told Kevin and Liam as he lit a Lucky Strike from a green pack. "She wouldn't let her instincts take over."

Jane was a full twenty-four hours recovering from the delivery. When Kevin saw her almost immediately after she was wheeled out of the recovery room, she was ashen and shaken.

"You did it," he told her, squeezing her hand. "The baby is beautiful. She looks just like you."

"The doctor. He had to cut me . . . down there. What if it doesn't heal right?"

He smiled at her. "I'll give you an appraisal at the earliest possible opportunity. As soon as you're up to it, we'll conduct a test run."

She turned her head. "Jesus, don't even talk to me about that."

Susan was the model child, in marked contrast to her father, Katherine noted. She slept soundly and went on a regular schedule almost immediately. When she came home with Jane a few days later, she found herself under the tender care not only of her mother but also of her doting grandmother and Annette, who held the child by the hour and cooed soft French lullabies to her.

Henri and Liam were no better. Jane was surprised and pleased to see Liam's shell of reserve break down. At one point, as he rocked the child in the chair in the corner of the living room in the shack, she saw his eyes fill with tears as some private thought passed through his mind and touched his heart. Jane found herself touched by this exhibition, which Liam thought had gone unobserved.

Katherine had called Helen in Boydstown immediately after the baby was born. By that Sunday the entire family had gathered at Brennan's Point to welcome Susan to the clan in style. Katherine and Annette prepared a succulent feast, and Liam broke out bottles of his best wine. Kevin played the piano and sang, and Helen performed for the family as she had not done in years, her fine, soprano voice mixing with Kevin's rich baritone. Jane, for the first time, had felt very much a part of the proceedings, and she enjoyed them immensely. In the afternoon, she retired to the study to breast-feed Susan, and Helen came along.

"So," Jane said, "when are you and Jack going to have one?"

Helen shook her head. "I don't know. You know, the studio isn't really going great guns yet. And we've got that loan to pay off. If I don't keep working for a while, we're going to be in trouble. She's so adorable. Can I hold her?"

Jane handed her the baby. "Look at me," Jane said, patting her middle. "I can't get this to go away. I thought that once the baby was out, that would be it."

"It takes a while, I guess," Helen said. "Babies smell so nice."

"When they're splashed with talcum powder, they do. There are times when they don't smell so nice, believe me. You ought to see how my bubbies have swelled up. I hope they don't end up sagging, with her pulling on them the way she does."

"I love her so much," Helen said.

"Me, too," Jane said. "I just don't want another one right away."

* * * *

Annette burst from the kitchen, her face white.

"Terrible," she said, "a horrible thing has happened."

The Brennan family was gathered for Sunday dinner, this one special because it marked Helen's twenty-ninth birthday. They all stopped their talking and stared at Annette, who was literally trembling.

"Annette," Katherine said with alarm. "What's the matter?"

"The radio in the kitchen," Annette stammered. "I was trying to get my station from Quebec, and I hear this man saying this terrible things . . ." Then, unable to transmit her thoughts in English and so agitated that she had to get them out, Annette loosed upon the gathering a barrage of French that left them mystified.

Henri listened to her intently, then he stood up, crossed the living room and turned on the radio. The announcer's voice came in clearly.

". . . on U.S. Pacific bases that took a toll of at least 101 American military dead, more than 300 wounded and uncounted civilian and naval casualties. A report from Honolulu, not confirmed by the War Department in Washington, stated that 350 were killed when a bomb made a direct hit at the Army's air base, Hickam Field . . ."

The group in the living room of the big house exchanged worried glances. Then, as the voice continued, all eyes were riveted on the radio.

"President Roosevelt, just moments ago, called Congress into extraordinary joint session at 12:30 Eastern Standard Time tomorrow to hear him deliver a special message, presumably seeking a declaration of war against Japan. Congress appeared overwhelmingly in favor of the move. Japan's surprise dawn attack on American Pacific outposts welded factions into a spirit of unity recalling the days of April 1917 . . ."

"Oh, my God," Katherine said, her hand going to her mouth and her eyes wide in horror.

"Hush!" Henri snapped. "Listen . . ."

"Britain's land, sea and air forces based on Singapore were engaged in violent fighting with Japanese troops and ships that carried out a large-scale invasion on the strategic Malayan Peninsula. The invaders succeeded in putting parties ashore at several points . . ."

Jack stood up and slapped his hands against his thighs. "That rips it. We're in it now."

"Quiet!" Henri ordered.

"The British Parliament was called into special session at 3:00 A.M. tomorrow—that's 9:00 A.M. Eastern Standard Time—to hear a government statement which everyone agreed would be a declaration against Japan to coincide with similar action by the United States . . ."

"And look at who we're in it with," Liam roared out. "God help us, it's happening all over again, only worse this time."

Henri, leaning over the radio to catch every word, looked up pleadingly. "Does not anyone want to know what is happening to this world? I must have silence."

"In Berlin, the German government referred this afternoon to hostilities in the Pacific as 'clashes' and referred to President Roosevelt as 'war incendiery.' Germany, obligated under the three-power pact to go to Japan's assistance if Japan is attacked, failed to clarify that nation's intentions. Meanwhile, Radio Tokyo reported that Germany will declare war on the United States within twenty-four hours, and Japanese planes were reported attacking the city of Davo on the Philippine island of Mindanao, where the largest Japanese colony in the Philippines is located. Several lives were lost in that raid, with some estimates running as high as fifty. In Washington, Senator Tom Connally of Texas said—"

Liam flipped off the radio. "I've heard enough," he said, his face flushed. "We've all heard enough. We can listen to Roosevelt tomorrow. The war is still a long way off, and we're here as a family tonight."

Kevin shook his head. "You're kidding yourself, Pop. It's not that far off. Bucky Coughlin is in the Navy, and his father told me the other day when I was in the hardware store that Bucky is out in Pearl Harbor. If the Japanese hit Honolulu and the army base there, you can bet they hit the fleet, too."

"I didn't really think it would happen this way," Jack said. "Well, I guess it's time to make some plans."

Helen's eyes widened. "What do you mean?" she demanded. "What sort of plans?"

Kevin looked at her. "We're at war, Helen, or, at least, we will be after tomorrow when Roosevelt asks Congress to declare war on Japan. Then Germany will declare war on us, and—"

"And Roosevelt will have what he wants," Liam broke in, "war with Germany. I wouldn't be surprised if he did something to provoke the Japanese into attacking."

"Nonsense," Henri snapped. "I think I will volunteer."

"Henri, you are too old," Annette said. "They would not take you."

Henri bristled. "I am barely fifty. They will take everyone. They must. This is America."

"Well," Jack said, "we'll see if they take me with a history of asthma. If I can keep them from listening too closely to my lungs, I should be all right."

The gathering broke up very shortly after that. Jack and Helen soon took their leave, and Henri and Annette walked back to their house. Kevin gathered up the sleeping Susan while Jane wrapped herself in her thick winter coat. They walked down to the shack and Jane put the baby to bed while Kevin puttered in the kitchen. When she came out of the small bedroom, she found that Kevin had begun a fire and opened a bottle of champagne. He pulled her next to him on the sofa and held her close as the flames in the hearth crackled.

They were silent for a long while, looking into the flames, sipping their champagne and listening to the icy wind blast across the frozen lake out front.

Finally, Kevin said, "I imagine there's a real panic at Cornell right about now. If I know my fraternity, everybody is getting set to go down tomorrow morning and join up. They might as well. They'll just get drafted anyway."

Jane looked up at him. "That's what *you're* thinking, isn't it?"

"That's right. The smart thing to do is get in as early as you can. I'd like to go in as a flyer, but if I wait to get drafted there'll be a long line of fellows lined up for flight training."

"But you wouldn't have to go," Jane argued. "They'll take single men first, won't they?"

"Probably. At first, anyway. But then, after a while, they're get to the married men, then to the men with one child. If things get real tough, Henri might get to be a soldier yet."

Jane shuddered. "It won't get that bad. It can't."

"That's what Pop thought. Bucky Coughlin might be dead tonight—Bucky Coughlin, from Lakeside. We played high school football together. We even got laid for the first time together—him and me and Billy—with this hot-to-trot honey from Ringlesport." Kevin was silent for a moment. Then he said, "Jane, I'm going down to Boydstown tomorrow, and I'm going to enlist."

She jumped up instantly. "I knew it," Jane shouted. "I knew it, I knew it, I knew it. I knew you were going to say that."

"It's the only thing that makes any sense."

"It doesn't make any sense to me. It doesn't make any sense to our baby. And it doesn't make any sense to your father. I heard him tonight. So did you."

Kevin laughed out loud. "Oh, all of a sudden my father makes sense to you. There's a switch."

Jane glared at him. "Kevin," she said slowly, "if you go off to fight in some silly war somewhere—Tahiti, maybe—I'm not going to hang around here. I hate it here even when I have my husband around. I won't stay. I mean it."

Kevin reddened. "Jane, the whole goddamned country is going to go. They'll just draft me sooner or later. Besides which, I want to go. It's my duty."

"And you're going to beat Hitler all by yourself? They can't do it without the great Kevin Brennan?"

He sighed wearily. "I've explained this the best way I know how. You'll be fine. You have a nice house to live in. You'll have no money worries. You'll have help with the baby. You're going to be well taken care of."

Jane shook her head vigorously. "I'll lose my mind if I have to live here without you. I couldn't stand it."

Kevin put down his cigar. He reached up, took her hands and pulled her back down on the sofa with him. "All this is happening at a bad time, I know," he said. "Doctor Frazier said you'd have some bad ups and downs after the baby came, and you're having one. This is a bad situation, but it's not the end of the world."

"I'm telling you how I feel," she said, her face pressed against his chest. "Take me seriously, Kevin. Please."

"I do take you seriously. Now you have some faith in me. This will all work out all right. I love you, and I love the baby we made together, and I love the life we're going to have together until we're both a hundred and three."

He held her for a long time while the logs in the hearth crackled. After a while, he realized that she had been weeping and that she had cried herself to sleep in his arms. Kevin moved out from under her and covered her with a blanket. He moved to the rocking chair, refilled his empty champagne glass and relit his cigar. He stared into the fire for a long time, thinking.

He wondered what it would be like to go to war.

Chapter 13

Under most circumstances the jeep ride through the English countryside would have been pleasant. For once, the thick, shroudlike cloud cover that seemed to hover over Britain had lifted. Sunlight splashed over trees and meadows like a scene from a Renoir painting.

But Kevin's driver was a surly Oklahoman with little to say, and Kevin was thinking about home more and more now as his tour of duty abroad drew to a close. At the lake, he knew, this was the loveliest time of year, and lately he had been consumed by homesickness stronger than anything he had experienced since those first few months in Kansas. He sighed deeply. Agreeing to take on this chore, playing bombing instructor to the Limeys, had been a mistake, he was sure. If so, it hadn't been his first where the war was concerned.

That had been letting Jane and his father talk him out of enlisting immediately after Pearl Harbor. Why enlist, they had argued, when this whole thing could be over in a year? You have a wife and child. You won't have to go right away. Wait and see what happens, they had advised him. Maybe you won't have to go at all. Jack didn't have to go, they pointed out, thanks to his history of asthma. And Jack didn't have a baby to worry about.

Kevin, like a fool, he later told himself, had listened. The result had been that by the time he finally enlisted in the fall of 1942, after the harvest, of course, he found that it was too late to get into pilot training. He had to content himself with becoming a bombardier if he wanted to serve in the air corps.

By the time Kevin finished training in Kansas and got to England with the Eighth Air Force, the Germans had put up solid defenses against allied bombing. As a bombadier on a B-17, Kevin had found himself in the most bitter aerial combat of the war.

He was assigned to a crew in which the pilot was an Ohio farm boy of twenty-one and the copilot was a year younger. Early in the war a flight crew averaged fewer than ten missions before it was split apart by death. The rate of survival for the first six or eight missions was roughly one in three. Beyond that, a flyer was statistically dead. The flight crews responded to the incredible pressures of their work by drinking heavily and partying relentlessly when they were on the ground. They picked up talismans and lucky charms to carry with them in the air. Kevin became attached to a particular flight jacket, and he wore it constantly, convinced that he was doomed if he wore anything other than the fleece-lined leather jacket with the rip under the left arm.

Finally the jeep pulled in front of a quonset hut in the headquarters compound of the RAF's 27th Bomber Group. Kevin flagged down a passing airman. "Hey, pal," he said, "where do I find Flight Captain Farrington?"

The airman pointed to a large building across the compound. "I'd say he's probably in the briefing," he said in a thick cockney accent. "That's over there."

"Thanks."

The briefing room was jammed with flyers sitting with their backs to the door as Kevin entered. A trim RAF colonel was on the dais using a pointer to indicate locations on a large map that hung over the far wall.

"Thunderstorms are moving across the Rhine today," he was saying, "but they'll be pretty much cleared up by several hours before dawn. That'll give us time to get in and out and back into safe air space before it's too bright up there."

"What about the cloud cover, Sir?" asked a flyer in the back, a short distance from where Kevin was standing.

The colonel tapped the map with his pointer. "Moderate all the way over and back along this route, we expect. You can count on a thin layer from between—oh, say—twenty-five hundred to about eighteen thousand feet. There might be some stratocumulous about three thousand feet or so, in patches, but nothing that should impede bombing accuracy."

And nothing that should impede flak, Kevin thought to himself. His own preference was for heavy cloud cover all the way over and back and a clear, open patch of pure sunlight directly over the target. In twenty-five missions he had enjoyed such conditions precisely once.

"And the target, Sir?" another flyer asked.

"Trout," the colonel said.

"Very good, Sir."

Kevin leaned over to a flyer sitting near the door. "What's trout?" he whispered.

The flyer turned around. He was a strikingly handsome man about Kevin's own age. His hair was sandy and cut short, and he sported a trim little moustache. He looked at Kevin and grinned. "It's a fish, you twit," he said aloud, and other flyers in the area chortled.

The colonel looked over the heads of the flyers in front and said with only a hint of irritation, "Is there some problem there in the rear? Speak up, please."

Heads turned and bodies shifted in their chairs. Kevin, profoundly uncomfortable, said, "Sorry, Sir. No problem. I apologize for the interruption."

The colonel eyed him cooly. "You're one of the Americans we've borrowed, are you not?"

"Yes, sir. I'm Captain Brennan from the Eighth Air Force. I just this minute arrived, and they sent me in here. I was trying to find out what trout is. I asked this gentleman here."

The colonel nodded. "That's Flight Captain Farrington, Captain Brennan. He commands the ship you'll be flying in."

Kevin's blood ran cold at the words. Flying? He'd have to fly?

"I suppose," the colonel went on, "he told you that a trout is a fish, am I correct?"

"Yes, Sir."

"I suspected as much," the colonel said, as the men around the room chuckled lightly. "That's one of our old and not terribly amusing jokes here, for new men. Actually, trout is the code name for the city of Cologne, which is our target for tonight. Trout is a fine target, although we usually take more pleasure in bombing whitefish. That's Berlin."

"Thank you, Sir," Kevin said, casting a sideways glance as the grinning Farrington.

"You're quite welcome," the colonel said. "I wonder if we might continue now."

Kevin reddened. "Please do, Sir."

The colonel turned back to his map. "Thank you very much, Captain Brennan. Now, the weather alternative will be this site in the Ruhr. We don't expect to have to divert from our planned destination, but one never knows. You may pick up your target files from Lieutenant Allen. H-hour will be at zero-two-hundred. Best of luck, chaps."

The colonel stepped down from the dais, put down his pointer, put on his hat and marched smartly from the room, past Kevin. As he did, the flyers snapped to attention. Then Lieutenant Allen, in the front of the room, began handing out the target files, and the men began milling about, laughing and talking. Farrington stood up and stuck out his hand to Kevin. He was still smiling, and the smile was infectious. Kevin felt his irritation vanish as he took the Englishman's hand.

"Hello, Yank," Farrington said. "Welcome aboard. I hope you've been on a bombing run before."

Kevin frowned. "My share. I've never bombed a fish, though."

Farrington reached out and grabbed another man from the milling mob. "Good," he said. "This is Hedley, our bombadier. He's the chap you'll be teaching how to use that blasted bombsight they put in my ship this morning. Hedley, old man, this is Brennan. Say hello nicely, now, as you've been taught."

Hedley, who looked as though he might have shaved a total of a half dozen times in his life, grinned boyishly and stuck out his hand. "A pleasure," he said in a thick, Yorkshire accent. "I'm told this new sight is really something special."

"How old are you?" Kevin asked.

"Eighteen. But I'm working on nineteen. Oh, there's someone I have to see. Excuse me, please."

Hedley walked off to another group of airmen, and Farrington, his smile still intact, turned to Kevin. "I'm afraid you offended him, just a little," the Englishman said.

Kevin lit a cigar. "Sorry. I'm used to flying with kids, but nobody who looks that young. He looks like he might be fourteen."

Farrington laughed. "He does at that. But he's a good chap, and he's a fine bombadier. He's had forty-two missions, you know."

Kevin was stunned. "Forty-two? That kid?"

"Oh, yes," Farrington said. A tour with us is sixty. Of course, we've been bombing at night, which isn't quite as rough as the daytime precision bombing you chaps have been doing. Still . . ."

"How many missions do you have?" Kevin asked.

"I'm well into my second tour, now. I think I have a hundred and ten or so."

Kevin shook his head in disbelief. "Well, what's the casualty rate in this outfit?"

"Oh," Farrington said, "about five percent, a bit below the rate for you Yanks. According to the numbers, I've been dead for quite some time now. So has Hedley, actually, since he's flying with me. But I haven't told him because he might lie down if he finds out."

Kevin shook his head. "Flying with you guys is going to be an experience."

Farrington slapped him on the back. "So it shall, Yank. Come along, now. Let's get your gear stowed away."

* * * *

Farrington's big Stirling Mk 1 bomber was battered but well cared for. It reeked of fresh oil, and its Plexiglas nose was scarred and pitted from the impact of ten thousand minute fragments of flak. The aircraft's condition was testament to the skill of its crew, and Kevin Brennan had been flying bombing missions long enough to realize the value of an experienced pilot and crew in a proven, meticulously maintained plane over a green crew in a gleaming new bomber fresh off the assembly line.

Farrington's bomber took off precisely on schedule. Kevin was given a quick introduction to the other five members of the crew as they boarded, and he paid special attention to Farrington's flight engineer, Brownwell. The flight engineer was a solemn, well-knit man in his early twenties, a railway worker before the war, Farrington said. Brownwell's duties consisted of assisting on takeoffs and supervising fuel changeover, a task that could go horribly wrong if not handled properly. He was also expected to fix anything that could go wrong with the aircraft in flight, from a loose windscreen bolt to a dead engine.

Kevin had taken careful measure earlier of Farrington. A pilot had to be not only technically competent, but he also needed the capacity to stay cool and to respond faithfully to Kevin's instructions once the plane was over the target and the bombadier took command of its movements, issuing orders into his microphone for the pilot to move the plane this way or that, as the situation demanded. Farrington was witty, outrageous and affable. Whether he had the necessary nerve was open to question in Kevin's mind.

The third man Kevin studied carefully was the boyish Hedley, who might have gotten all the way through puberty but probably not, Kevin decided. He studied the young Yorkshireman not so much because his performance was as essential to Kevin's survival as that of the pilot and the flight engineer, but because teaching Hedley was, after all, Kevin's purpose in being aboard this plane in the first place. As the Stirling droned along in formation with a sky full of other British aircraft, Kevin and Hedley huddled tightly together in the plane's Plexiglas nose, a space designed for one man, while Kevin offered instruction in the use of the new Winthrop bombsight.

It was bitter cold in the nose. Communication was difficult because the crew had gone on oxygen at ten thousand feet, just as the formation pulled past the British coastline.

"The charm of this thing," Kevin told Hedley, shouting to be heard through his mask and over the engines, "is that you can use it from higher up than the sights you've been using. You get the same accuracy from twenty thousand feet that you guys have been getting at ten, provided it's clear enough at that altitude to see the target. The other thing is that the sight automatically adjusts for crosswinds, more or less."

"But how's the visibility through the sight?" Hedley shouted back.

Kevin said, "I think it's better. Listen, I'll drop tonight, and you watch. Then we'll do some ground training, and you can try some drops with it next time we're up."

Hedley nodded. "How long will you be with us, Yank?"

"Eight weeks is what my orders say. I think it's about four weeks longer than necessary, but I guess that'll give me more time to see London."

"Well, if you're going to do that, make sure you do it with Willie. He knows every bloody inch of London, all the good spots and the bad as well, if you get my meaning."

"Willie? You mean Farrington?"

Hedley laughed. "That's Baronet Farrington, if you please. Willie's a ruddy nobleman, he is. But he's a real rounder when it comes to the birds and the brew, Willie. He'll show you around proper."

It was a long flight, and the two men fell into silence, because conversation was so difficult. It was, as the colonel had promised at the briefing, a clear night; a good night to attack, a bad night to be dodging flak. The stars were arrayed like Christmas lights in the sky above. They shone down on aircraft in the formation. Engines flashed fire from their exhausts. Kevin studied his target file while Hedley kept an eye out for birds. A bomber crew lived in fear of many things when over their target. But here, in the blissful night air over the English Channel, the only thing to fear were stray flights of gulls, who could blast through a windscreen like cannonballs and who could kill an engine that happened to cut through a flock of them. After a while Kevin got bored and went up to the flight deck. Farrington and Brownwell sat in their seats, bathed in red light from the dials.

"A smooth flight so far," Kevin said.

"So far," Farrington said. "The old bucket is holding together all right."

Brownwell frowned and checked his instruments. "We'll see. The generator on number two wasn't at its best this morning. I found a wiring fault, but she's still reading a bit low. Try to take it easy on us tonight, eh, Yank? If you have to take some flak on this run, please try to take it in the port engines. Maybe we'll end up with a matched set."

Kevin studied the control panel for a moment, feeling the restlessness that always affected him as his plane approached the target.

Farrington said, sensing the American's unrest, said, "Why don't you go take a look at all those lovely bombs you'll be dropping?"

"Good idea," Kevin said.

Mostly, the Stirling carried five-hundred-pound general-purpose bombs. They were notoriously unreliable. A good third of them would fail to explode, which, under certain circumstances, could create the necessity for a second, incredibly dangerous run over the freshly hit target, if the target were important enough. The American five hundred pounders were vastly more dependable, Kevin knew, and he looked upon these bombs with deep suspicion.

Kevin also found some two hundred and fifty pounders interspersed in the bomb line, and, at the end, a single enormous eight thousand pounder crammed full of high explosives. This bomb could leave a crater half the size of a city block. It was a handy device if you lacked the time to aim.

These were the weapons he would be serving up to the Germans tonight. He knew that they, in turn, would be serving up weaponry of their own in the form of flak and fighters. Kevin sighed and made his way back to the Stirling's Plexiglas nose. He squeezed in beside Hedley, who was studying the target file.

"Went to look at the bombs, did you?" Hedley asked.

"Yep. This baby sure holds a lot of them."

"She'll hold fourteen thousand pounds worth. Jerry always knows when we've been there."

"When do the guns get tested?"

"Not until we're well over the Channel. We had a complaint a few weeks back that a stray slug did away with some chap's prize Guernsey, so we've orders now to test the guns out as far as possible."

Kevin, who knew what a prize Guernsey was worth, nodded. "Makes sense."

Hedley was as good as his word. The fourteen guns were tested, one at a time, a few minutes later. The plane rocked with each burst. Not much later, flying at maximum altitude, the formation passed over the continental coast and encountered its first flak. The plane was rocked and shaken but emerged unscathed. The German fighters came next, but they hit the far end of the formation. Farrington, following the action over his radio, reported that the Germans had been engaged by the British fighter escort. The formation settled into standard flight routine as it approached its target. As it came in on Cologne, the formation moved to a predetermined attack configuration, with the aircraft coming in at different altitudes to confuse the flak. Kevin moved into position in the Plexiglas nose, his hands sweaty even in the bitter cold. He clenched and unclenched his fists. Towers of flak around Cologne were clearly visible now. From his front-row seat he saw the first of the Stirlings swoop down. A moment later the first of the marker bombs exploded, illuminating the target for the rest of the formation. It was time.

Farrington's voice came over the intercom.

"We're going in, Yank," he said. "She's all yours now."

Kevin's mouth was dry. "I'm ready."

* * * *

Flak was all around them now, towering spires of light and smoke erupting about the Stirling as she began her run. Kevin kept his eye glued to the bombsight, his nervousness giving way to the training and experience he had undergone, his brain taking control from his instincts. He watched through the sight as the flak rocketed upward, bursting in ugly, black puffs in groups of four with a dull, thudding sound ending each time in a sharp, piercing crack. Its progress measured through the bombsight, the plane seemed to be creeping over the landscape, moving at a crawl, while the flak boomed upward and past them. The crosshairs converged over the target Kevin had seen in aerial photographs. He pressed the button.

Eight bombs fell from the open bomb bay door. The Stirling, suddenly four thousand pounds lighter, bumped upward like a bobber on a fishing line. Kevin felt the upward surge, and as the lines on his sight intersected, he let the rest of his bombs go, including the eight thousand pounder. The plane shuddered and pulled upward as though it had been torn loose from some invisible mooring line anchoring it to the earth far below.

Then came the scary part.

For the next fifteen or twenty seconds, the Stirling had to fly straight and level, a perfect target for the flak, as the crew waited for one of the bombs to explode over the ground. That was the photoflash bomb, a huge cannister of phosporous that generated millions of candlepower, enough to illuminate the target area for the cameras bolted underneath the Stirling. Kevin closed his eyes as the plane flew on smoothly. Seventeen, eighteen, nineteen . . .

"There it is!" Hedley called out as the photoflash bomb went off.

Kevin opened his eyes and saw through the Plexiglas nose a wall of flak rising up in front of them. He shut the bomb bay doors and screamed into his facemask: "Turn hard left and take her up!"

Farrington obliged with a passion. The old Stirling flipped over on one wing, and its nose went high. Kevin heard the plane's superstructure creak ominously and the four engines howl in protest. He felt himself pushed by G forces to one side, flattened against Hedley at the rear of the bombadier's compartment. The Stirling's moving parts screamed in agony at the strain, and flak explosions nearby rattled its aged bolts. Then

Farrington leveled it out, and Kevin and Hedley collapsed against one another, gasping for breath. Kevin took a deep breath, sweating despite the chill of the altitude. Then, out of one eye, he spied another spire of flak directly in their path.

"Right! Right!" he screamed into the microphone in his facemask.

Farrington obeyed instantly, and the process was repeated in reverse. Kevin and Hedley bounced about roughly in the Plexiglas nose. Then, suddenly, they were out of it, flying toward cloud cover, slipping into a blessed cloud and still climbing. Kevin heard the tail gunner's voice on the intercom.

"A direct hit, damn it all! A direct hit, Willie—right in their bloody teeth."

Kevin heard Farrington chuckle on the intercom. "You did all right, Yank."

Kevin rolled off Hedley, leaving the smaller man gasping for breath, and slumped against the bulkhead. "You, too," he muttered into his mask.

Then they were out of the cloud, and there was flak all around them.

"Jesus Christ!" Kevin shouted, peering out through the nose into the bursting shells, at death all around them. "Left, goddammit! Left!"

Left it was. The Stirling wrenched around in a merciless spin, and Kevin felt himself floating in thin air. He could feel the plane diving, and he saw blobs of inky smoke envelope the nose. His back was plastered back against the rear of the compartment as the plane plummetted, and his insides wrapped themselves around his backbone. He heard cries of dismay through the intercom from all over the plane. His heart was thumping like a hammer on an anvil. More flak loomed ahead.

"Climb!" he screamed to Farrington, and the pilot did just that. The Stirling dipped once and started back up, Kevin's face plastered against the Plexiglas, his body sodden with slimy sweat, his throat a raw and burning tunnel as he screamed his frenzied instructions. He could hear the engines whine in pain, overheating and sucking up oil to keep cool. He felt the plane miss a step as a piece of flak roared through the nose only inches from his head. How long the Stirling continued its crazy climb he could never determine. He knew only that eventually the climb slowly leveled off, and then he could see stars through the nose, and he could feel the frigid air pouring into the plane through fist-sized holes on either side of the bombing compartment. He lay on the bottom of the compartment, next to the bombsight, gasping for breath. He cast a furtive glance at the ashen-faced Hedley, his eyes opened to the size of saucers, mouth working like a fish out of water.

"You all right?" Kevin grunted.

Hedley nodded shakily. He made motions with his hands that said he was fine, merely speechless for the moment. Then Farrington's voice, disgustingly cheery, came through the intercom.

"Well, surprise," he said, "we're not dead. A close thing, eh?"

Kevin coughed. His burning throat was agony. "You should be clear now," he rasped, formally returning control of the aircraft to the pilot.

"Well, chaps," he heard Farrington say, "the hell of it is that we'll have to do it all over again in another night or two."

* * * *

It was inevitable that competent, jovial Kevin Brennan would become fast friends with competent, gregarious Willie Farrington.

From that first mission, they had one another's professional respect. Kevin applauded Farrington's skill as a pilot that brought them through that first mission and a half-dozen more with not a scratch. And Farrington, for his part, became quickly aware that he was carrying a superior bombadier, one with a steel-nerved capacity for intense concentration under heavy fire and whose hand-to-eye coordination was so extraordinary that he soon had the best hit record in the squadron. Kevin publicly chalked up that record to the Winthrop bombsight, but he knew better, and so did Farrington.

The fact was that Kevin dropped bombs better than he had ever done anything. It was a talent Farrington prized, and one Kevin tried not to think about. Somewhere in this war, Kevin knew, there were men who killed other men face to face, in honest combat. But he killed men—and perhaps women and children, too—from a distance with a technical skill with which he had been born. He knew he faced as much danger as any infantryman, but he couldn't overcome the suspicion that his brand of mechanized warfare, delivered from two miles in the sky, was dishonorable, cowardly and unworthy of a warrior. It wasn't a conviction he pondered at great length.

Such subtleties were lost on Farrington. He was a direct man, not given to pastel shades of thought. Willie Farrington was twenty-eight, precisely Kevin's age. He was movie-star handsome and so wildly and irresponsibly courageous that Kevin was perpetually astounded at him. He was also hilariously funny, with a flagrantly disrespectful attitude toward all authority and a biting wit that exposed the essential absurdity of virtually every value the RAF revered. He was a drinker who chased women shamelessly. He endured hardship with a wink and a joke. He professed not to have a single principle in life. He found the world endlessly amusing. Kevin had never met anyone he liked so much.

Farrington, for his part, found Kevin amusing, more so than the various and sundry other aspects of life, which were a perpetual source of entertainment to him. Farrington routinely doubled over with laughter as Kevin hammered away at the piano and bellowed obscene songs in the officers' lounge. He was delighted by Kevin's limitless capacity for all-night drinking bouts and carousing. He was entranced by Kevin's store of jokes, puns and shaggy dog stories. And he was baffled by Kevin's tendency to politely excuse himself from the company of the women with whom the RAF flyers routinely came into contact. Farrington was a tireless joker, drinker and lover. In Kevin he found his match in the first two departments, but he was baffled by his new friend's unwillingness to participate in the third. He knew Kevin had a wife and a child, but it never occurred to him that Kevin was celibate out of deference to them. Nothing could have struck Farrington as more ridiculous.

In fact, however, Kevin was scrupulously faithful to Jane. He hadn't even bothered to promise her that he would be, and he had no idea if she really expected him to take his marriage vows so literally, especially under the circumstances. But despite his cynicism and his outward disrespect for conventional values, Kevin was Liam Brennan's son in many ways. One of those ways was his view of duty and obligation. Kevin viewed life as a series of bargains. He had taken vows when he got married in exchange for certain benefits, and it never occurred to him that there might be an acceptable excuse for breaking them even when he was three thousand miles away and putting his life on the line on an average of twice a week. He was tolerant of his friends' marital indiscretions, but he felt no right to indulge in them, whatever the situation in which he found himself.

Farrington observed Kevin's behavior but didn't struggle to analyze it. He regarded it as a minor affliction in a man who otherwise seemed to have a solid grip on himself. Such sexual abstinence was rare, but not unheard of. And Farrington learned a good deal about Kevin's former life during drinking bouts conducted in pubs and clubs throughout London. Kevin told Farrington about his Irish father and southern mother, about his life in the lake country, about his wife and child and his sister and her marital problems. Farrington, in turn, volunteered information about his own life prior to the war. Among other things, he confided to Kevin, he was unconscionably rich. He wasn't actually a British nobleman, contrary to rumors in the squadron. The family title was actually held by his uncle Cecil, who was a minor baronet, a member of the House of Lords and something of a friend of Churchill's. Willie had attended public school and Oxford, and before the war he had worked briefly as a barrister, finding the profession lucrative, which didn't matter to him, and terribly dull, which did. Willie had been married briefly to a distant cousin, but it hadn't worked out, thanks to Willie's thirst for diverse feminine companionship. He and his wife had parted amicably when the war broke out. It almost seemed, he told Kevin, that Hitler had begun it all merely to save Willie from an unhappy marriage, and Farrington found it difficult to hate an enemy who had rescued him from so bitter a fate.

Nonetheless, he flew missions against Jerry with great enthusiasm. He had, he assured Kevin, never had so much fun, and he was actually considering staying in the RAF after the war. For a man of his social background, he pointed out, military life was not uncommon. While the officer class in the American military was primarily middle class, in Britain the officer class as often as not sprang from the upper rungs of society, and Willie would fit in nicely. "I'll probably end up a bloody field marshal if I live through this," he told Kevin.

"You hardly seem the type," Kevin said over his drink.

"Well," Farrington told him, "you're not what I have in mind when I think of a typical American farmer. Aren't you supposed to be wearing overalls and have a buckwheat cake sticking out of your mouth? Honestly, Brennan, you're not at all right for the role."

Kevin and Farrington flew together for four weeks, an average of two missions a week. Sometimes they were lucky enough to fly with the lead squadron, which meant they dropped marker bombs and got out of harm's way before the flak became genuinely heavy. More often, however, they flew near the middle of the formation, which meant dropping high-intensity bombs and feverishly dodging flak all the way out of the target zone. Only once did they fly at the tail end of the formation, and that was the worst. The German gunners had zeroed in on the incoming aircraft. On that mission, the Stirling lost an engine and had to hobble back to Britain in a cloud of smoke.

By the end of the four-week period, Hedley had taken over the bombing, and he was developing real talent with the Winthrop sight. Kevin knew his usefulness to the RAF was reaching an end, but he had another month to go on his orders, and he liked the nights in London. They almost made it worth flying the missions.

* * * *

One afternoon, as they emerged from debriefing, Farrington suddenly clutched Kevin's arm and said. "How would you like to go to the countryside for a few days, old boy?"

Kevin shrugged. "Sounds fine to me. Where are we going?"

"To the ancestral family estate, of course. Every Englishman has one, you know. Don't you ever go to the cinema?"

Kevin lit a cigar and puffed on it. "The question, it seems to me, is where will we get a staff car?"

"No, no, old man," Farrington said. "The question is, where will we get a plane? And, luckily, I've solved that thorny problem by calling in an old debt from a chap in operations who had a marvelous weekend not long ago with a certain young lady of my acquaintance. I've gotten us an observer plane for the next few days. A bit small, perhaps, but airworthy, I should think."

"We're flying? Where is this place, Scotland?"

"Hardly," Farrington laughed. "It's my Uncle Cecil's summer home in the west of Ireland."

Kevin was ecstatic. "Ireland? That's fabulous. I've been wanting to get over to Ireland ever since I got to the British Isles, but I could never get enough time together. Where in Ireland is your uncle Cecil's?"

Farrington smiled sheepishly. "Well, actually I'd hoped to keep it something of a surprise. But, if you must know, it's not too far from Ennis, in County Clare."

"That's right near the village where my father was born and raised."

"So I recall you saying. That's why I thought you might enjoy this little jaunt. I was going to make it anyway. Uncle Cecil and I are rather close. He was quite a rogue in his youth, or so I'm told, so we have that in common. It'll have to be a fast trip, I'm afraid. I have to have the plane back by Saturday afternoon."

"When do we leave?"

The flight was rough despite the fact that Farrington kept the little aircraft just below the cloud cover. But Kevin's nervousness vanished when he saw Ireland appear on the horizon. Farrington dipped to no more than a thousand feet in going over Kilkenny and even lower as they went over Limerick. Then the little plane was over a finger of sea that cut into the island. Kevin recognized it from the maps.

"Look," he said. "There's the Shannon down there."

"I'd be damned concerned if it wasn't down there," Farrington grinned. "That is, after all, where it's supposed to be."

"You British all have dishwater in your veins," Kevin told him. "That down there is where my ancestors lived."

"Yes, well, everyone's ancestors had to live somewhere, old boy."

* * * *

Farrington brought the plane down in a large field that was bordered by stone fences and marked at one end by a good-sized white stucco house with a thatched roof. Sheep scattered in terror as the little aircraft touched down. Farrington killed the engine, and the two men climbed out. "There he comes," Farrington said, pointing toward the house.

Kevin saw a white-haired figure burst out of the house, through a gate in the fence and begin heading toward them at a fast clip.

"Poor Uncle Cecil," Farrington said. "I didn't tell him we were coming. He's enraged that we frightened his bloody sheep."

There was no doubt that the sheep had been frightened. They were careening around the field in a flock, climbing over one another and crying out piteously.

Uncle Cecil drew near. He was a short, chunky man carrying a thick walking stick and wearing a gray sweater and baggy gray slacks. He recognized Willie, and he shook his head as he reached them.

"Damn you, Willie," he said, "you've terrified the blasted sheep again. They'll be bleating for hours now. Why didn't you tell me you were coming?"

"Because I knew you'd make it a point not to be in, Uncle. Now you have no choice but to let us impose on your hospitality, such as it is."

"Harumph," Cecil said. "And for how long, may I ask? Aren't you supposed to be fighting a war or some such thing instead of gallivanting around Ireland in what is, no doubt, a stolen airplane?"

"Borrowed," Farrington said. "And when you see Winnie next, please be kind enough to tell him how grateful I am for its use."

"Harumph," Cecil said again. "I know what that means. Well, don't think you'll be able to use my influence to get out of trouble. I'll advise them to let you escape and shoot you in the back—with my blessing. And who's this poor chap hopelessly under your unhealthy influence?"

"Uncle Cecil, this Capt. Kevin Brennan, U. S. Army Air Corps."

Kevin stuck out his hand. "How do you do, sir?"

Cecil took it warmly. "Well enough, I suppose, for a man who's just watched his prize sheep terrorized by a flying lunatic—and for the third time this year, isn't it, Willie? In any event, I was just sitting before the fire sipping some brandy. I suppose there's no way to avoid inviting you two in to have some with me."

"Actually," Farrington said, "I was thinking more along the lines of dinner, Uncle, even though you set a notoriously poor table. It is about that time, you know."

"A poor table, is it?" Cecil said. "Well, we'll just have to let Mrs. Murray know so she can prepare for four. Claire is here this week with me, you know. She motored into Ennis, but she ought to be back soon. Being an innocent child with questionable taste in some matters despite her flawless upbringing, she'll probably be glad to see you, Willie. For some unearthly reason, she tends to regard you as amusing, although I must confess that I can't see it at all."

"Claire is my cousin," Farrington told Kevin. "She's quite charming and, luckily, bears no resemblance whatever to Uncle Cecil, here."

Kevin smiled broadly. "I take it," he said, "that you two do this sort of thing quite a bit."

"Oh, constantly," Cecil said with a grin. "With Willie's father gone now, Willie has made it his mission in life to preserve my humility. For my part, I feel a similar obligation."

"A lost cause, I'm afraid," Farrington said. "And you have so much about which to be humble, Uncle."

"Damn," Cecil said. "It's starting to rain again. Get your bags, you fellows, and we'll continue all this next to a warm fire. Are my sheep safe with a stolen airplane in their midst, I wonder? Listen to the buggers bleat. Quiet, you wooly nuisances."

The house was good sized and comfortable, but not at all opulent. It was smaller by far, for example, than the house in which Kevin had grown up. The furnishings were old, worn and comfortable. The seat of an overstuffed chair near the parlor hearth seemed to have been worn over the years into the shape of Cecil Farrington's rear end. A faded coat of arms hung over the mantel, and paintings and photographs of Farrington's long-gone ancestors were hung throughout the house. He settled in the chair and informed his hatchet-faced housekeeper that there would be two more for dinner. Then he poured brandies for Kevin and Willie while he resumed his good-natured jibes with his nephew. After a while, the conversation grew more serious, dominated by talk of the war and of politics. Cecil had begun questioning Kevin about his life in America and his impressions of England when Claire Farrington came in. She was a pretty, dark-haired woman of perhaps twenty. She greeted Willie warmly, with a hug and a kiss, and she offered Kevin her hand politely. They had all settled back down in front of the fire when Mrs. Murray came in and announced that dinner was served, so the party transferred itself to a snug dining room. The food was only fair, but Cecil broke out a respectable bottle of Swiss red wine.

As he poured, Cecil said, "You were talking, Captain Brennan, about America—or, at least, your part of it. I've seen New York, Philadelphia and Washington, of course, but very little else. It's such a large country, isn't it? Where, precisely, are you from?"

"New York State. But a long way from New York City. My family operates a farm. It's mostly vineyard at this point, and a winery. My father happens to be from this region of Ireland."

"That's why I brought Brennan here, Uncle," Farrington said. "I thought he'd enjoy seeing the land from which he sprung, as it were."

Cecil frowned. "Such as it is," he said. "Ireland's a wretched place."

"Father!" Claire said in a shocked tone. "What a perfectly dreadful thing to say when you love this estate so. If Ireland's so horrible, then why don't you simply sell this place and buy another in Ulster, or in Britain?"

Cecil turned to Kevin, smiling sheepishly. "She knows I won't, of course. We've been here on this land for better than three hundred years. And the Free State was kind enough to let me keep it when the change went through back in '22. I've come here every summer of my life, and so has Claire, and I'll never leave willingly." He turned to Claire. "But I do sometimes wish, my dear, that the crown had seen fit to create the baronetcy in Britain. It would have simplified matters immeasurably. In any event, Captain Brennan, we'll have to see to it that you see your father's birthplace tomorrow. Just where is it, by the way?"

"It's a village called Labasheeda."

"Oh, yes," Cecil said. "Picturesque little place, down the Shannon. Not too far, actually."

"It's quite close," Claire said. "I'd be more than happy to drive you and Willie there in the morning."

Farrington shook his head. "No thank you. Let Brennan go rooting about for his relatives by himself. Having me at his side will certainly open no doors for him. Aside from which, I wouldn't feel this trip was justified unless I'd properly thrashed my uncle in a game or two of chess. I gather you still play as shabbily as last time, Uncle?"

"Well enough to hold my own against impudent children, I dare say."

Claire said, "Then it'll be just the two of us, Captain."

"Call me Kevin, please. And there's no need to put yourself out, Miss Farrington."

"Claire, if you're to be Kevin."

"Claire, then. If there's a car around that I could borrow, I can find my way."

"It's not that simple," Claire said. "The roads are poorly marked or, in many cases, not marked at all. Labasheeda is on the lower road between Kildysart and Kilrush, and the odds of you finding it on your own are slim. Even with precise directions, you'd be likely to lose your way."

"Aside from which," her father broke in, "driving in the west of Ireland can be a dicey experience for an American. We're left-hand drive here, just as in Britain. Perhaps you've mastered our system already, but it takes quite some getting used to for an American. And the car is right-hand drive to boot."

Kevin said, "Well, I don't want to get lost. I have to admit, I'm anxious to see the place and look up my people. My father talks about Labasheeda constantly."

"How long ago did he leave?" Cecil asked.

"He left in 1908—and in something of a hurry. He belted out a couple of young Englishmen and took a powder for New York the same night."

Cecil's brow furrowed. "And where did all this take place? Not in a pub, certainly?"

"Yes, sir. In the public house in Labasheeda."

Cecil leaned back in his chair and stared at Kevin for a long moment. "I'll be damned," he said finally. "I'll absolutely be damned." Cecil Farrington leaned forward. "Unless I'm very much mistaken, I was one of those young Englishmen your father 'belted,' Captain Brennan. And my older brother William, Willie's late father, was the other."

Farrington's eyebrows rose sharply. "Surely you're joking, Uncle. I never heard of any such incident."

"I'm not at all joking. It's an extremely memorable incident—drunk as your father and I were and behaving deplorably, as you might imagine. I seem to recall that there was a barmaid involved. It was hardly the sort of adventure one discusses extensively with one's children, Willie, but I remember Captain Brennan's father vividly. He was a tall, lean fellow with red or brown hair. I can't recall precisely. I do recall that he had a particularly vicious right hand."

Kevin said, "Mostly red then, I suppose. Mostly gray, now. And he's not as lean as he used to be."

"Father," Claire said, "You must tell us all about it."

Cecil smiled ruefully. "There's very little more to tell. William and I were barely out of our teens, out for a bit of frolic. We ended up in a village pub, where we drank entirely too much and made complete boors of ourselves. And we got our comeuppance from Captain Brennan's father. We came back home here, and your grandfather was justifiably outraged at our appearance and what we had gotten ourselves into. He ordered us both back to London for the rest of the summer."

"Did you contact the authorities?" Kevin asked.

"Good heavens, no," Cecil said. "Our father would have been mortified."

Kevin leaned back in his chair. "My father was always convinced that he had seriously injured one of you, maybe even killed somebody. You're telling me that he really didn't have to leave Ireland at all? That nobody was after him?"

Cecil shook his head. "Not a soul was after him, my good fellow.

No one was seriously injured—except in their pride, of course. Losing a pub brawl is hardly the sort of thing you report to the authorities."

"He'll just fall over when I write him about this," Kevin said.

Cecil chuckled. "Please tell him also, if you will, that I'm usually a much tougher nut to crack than I was that night."

* * * *

The sheep moved leisurely along the dirt road, bleating in soft tones, their woolly hindquarters bobbing in synchronization, like trained dancers as they wandered aimlessly along in harm's way. Claire Farrington, moving slowly into the flock in her black Austin sedan, peered up and over the hood of the vehicle. She blasted the horn, but the sheep only bleated a bit louder.

"Please keep your eyes open on the left there," she said to Kevin. "I can't see over the bonnet, and I'd hate to run over one of the poor little darlings. They're really so incredibly stupid."

Kevin surveyed the situation, sighed and got out of the car.

"Move it, you dumb bastards," he said, moving into the flock and kicking at their behinds with the loafers he'd brought from Britain, along with other civilian attire. The sheep bleated in protest, but they began to move to the sides of the road. Kevin motioned over his shoulder to Claire, and she moved forward. Kevin led the way, pushing, shoving, kicking and swearing, and then the Austin was through the flock and he climbed back into the little car.

"Jesus," he said, as Claire laughed merrily, "you were certainly right. Between the lack of road signs and the goddamn sheep every two hundred yards, I'd have ended up God knows where. How much farther?"

The car crested a hill. "Not too far now," she told him. "There's the Shannon."

Kevin saw it at the bottom of the hill, perhaps three quarters of a mile away, a ribbon of mist-shrouded water, the land beyond only faintly visible through the haze. He was struck by how much the Shannon resembled the lake on a hazy day. It was like looking down on it from the vineyards high on the hillside.

"Can we get down to the banks of the river from here?"

"Certainly," Claire said. "It's not really a river, you know, despite the name. It's an estuary."

The road down to the shoreline had been created for pony carts. It was steep, winding and narrow, and Claire negotiated it with extreme care. As they reached the rocky, rugged shoreline Kevin gazed out over the water, silent for a moment. Then he said, "I can see why my father fell in love with the lake country. From here, it's almost like being on our lake; about the same width, the same stone beach, the same hills rising up from the bank. It looks amazingly like home, only we get more sun. And more snow and ice, too, I'd imagine."

"America must be fascinating. I intend to visit after the war. I was there once, as a little girl when my mother was alive and Daddy was in the government the first time. But I remember so little of it."

"It's a big place," Kevin told her, "with tremendous variety from one locality to another. I've only seen a tiny part of the country. When the war is over, I'm hoping to take my wife and little girl and drive all over the country for three or four months. It'll be nice to get to know them all over again, and there are fellows in my unit from all over, so I'll have friends just about everywhere I go, if I decide to presume on them. And I will."

Claire said, "It didn't occur to me that you were married. I never think of any of Willie's RAF friends as having wives and children, probably because they never think of them either. I guess it's the war that does that."

"My little girl was just an infant when I left. Now she's a full-fledged toddler. I keep wondering how my wife is bearing up under the separation. We correspond, but Jane's not much of a writer. What I get from her are basically news bulletins—how Susan is doing in potty-training, that sort of thing. Susan is our little girl."

Claire frowned. "It must be very difficult for all you Yanks."

Kevin shrugged. "No more difficult for us than anybody else, I suppose. At least our homes haven't been bombed. And at least the war gives me the chance to see my father's home town free of charge."

"Yes. Well, just a few more kilometers now."

Labasheeda came up a few minutes later. The Austin rounded a curve, and there it was. Kevin was astounded. It looked nothing like what he had in mind from Liam's description. He was struck by the meanness of the place, by its smallness, by its very lack of distinction.

"This is it," Claire said. "Is it what you pictured?"

He shook his head. "Not at all."

"Unquestionably, your first stop has to be the church. It's a tiny place, and the priest will know everyone. I can drop you off."

"You're not coming with me?"

She laughed. "Having a Farrington in tow will open no doors for you. We're tolerated in the area, but we're not beloved by any means. Suppose I meet you down there at the dock at, say, four?"

Kevin looked at his watch. "Fine. What'll you do between now and then?"

"Shop a bit. I have errands to run."

He got out of the car and leaned in. "See you at four."

"Cheerio," she said, and drove off.

Kevin stood in the middle of the village for a moment, looking around. There were few people in the street, and they ignored him. The church, by far the most imposing building in the village, was down the street, and he walked to it, found the young priest and asked directions to his uncle Donal's house.

He found the it easily. This, at least, was just as his father had described. Kevin knocked on the door. In a few moments, a white-haired man, fleshy and unshaven, answered. His face was deeply lined.

"Yes?"

"I'm looking for Donal Brennan."

The old man's brow knitted. "Who's looking after him?"

"Kevin Brennan. I'm his nephew."

"Sweet Mary protect us," the old man said. "You're Liam's son?"

"Yes. You're my Uncle Donal?"

"I am," Donal said, studying Kevin closely. "I can see it now—about the eyes, mostly. You're shorter than your Da, and broader in the shoulders and chest, like Ma's side of the family. Come in with you, lad. We have to talk."

The house was dark, and the smell was of must and peat smoke and cooked food and sweat. Donal wasn't much of a housekeeper. They sat in ancient chairs in front of the dead hearth.

"The house is exactly as my father told me," Kevin said, "except for this planked floor. He told me it had a dirt floor."

"So it did—a lifetime ago. That's how long it's been." Donal motioned about him. "A place like this, I guess it isn't much to you, the way you live. How many acres does your da have?"

"About four hundred. Some of it is still wooded."

"Four hundred," Donal said, sitting back and imagining the vastness of it. "Lots of sheep and cattle, has he? We've been out of touch since Ma died, you know."

Kevin shook his head. "Only a few Holsteins now. We got out of the dairy business pretty much after Repeal. Most of the acreage now is wine grapes."

"Yes, yes," Donal said. "The wine. Me, I'll take a pint any time. Or a drop of whiskey. But a little wine never hurt. It never hurt at all. No, it didn't."

The old man sighed and stared into the hearth for a long moment. Kevin waited for him to speak, and when he didn't said, "Can you tell me about my aunt Kathleen and my aunt Anna?"

Donal, shaken from his reverie by the question, looked at Kevin questioningly for a moment, as if he were trying to place him. Then he shook his head and said, "Oh, no, no. Anna is in Galway. She's a nun, she is. Sister Joseph is the name she took."

"Do you see her often?"

Donal pondered the question a long time before he answered. "No, no. We write a little sometimes. The last time I saw Anna was just after our da died. She came down for the funeral. She was in Africa when our ma died, working for the propogation of the faith, she was."

Kevin nodded. "And Kathleen? She's in Australia, Pop told me."

"She married Gerry Donovan," Donal said, staring into the dead hearth. "He took her all the way there. I used to have an address for her. She was somewhere in Sidney, I believe. I don't know where the address is now. Kathleen was never one for writing. Worse on that score than meself." He looked up at Kevin. "I'm not much for writing. Your da can tell you that."

"I guess Pop isn't much for it, either."

Donal leaned back and stared at the ceiling. "Years, it's been. I often think of Liam. We fought as boys, you know—bitter against one another, we were. Well, that was then. God help us, that's all I can say. Can I offer you a touch to drink?"

Kevin nodded. "Yes, thank you."

Donal got up with an effort. He went to a battered cabinet along the far wall and came back with a jug and two chipped porcelain cups. He poured for each of them. Kevin sipped his while Donal shot his down and quickly poured another. The stuff was poteen, liquid fire. Kevin realized that Donal had already consumed a fair amount of it that day.

"I'd have thought you'd be out on the boat today," Kevin said, "going after fish."

Donal shook his head. "No, no, no. The boat's gone—sold years ago. I got too old to work on it meself. And with no sons, well, it was difficult, it was. So I sold it to the younger Rafferty boy. He put a motor in it, and he pays me a bit each month. That's enough to live on for a bit more. It's all I need. How's your ma? Helga, her name is?"

"No. Katherine."

"Ah, Katherine. That's right. Helga was the first wife. And what are you doing in Ireland?"

"I'm a soldier. A flyer."

"Ah, yes," Donal said. "The war. Foolish of me." He held up his cup. "Another?"

Kevin emptied his cup. "Please."

Donal poured each of them another drink. "So you're a flyer. All the way from America. Imagine that."

Kevin looked around the room. "You live here all alone, I take it."

Donal nodded. "Oh, yes. All alone. I had to care for my Ma, you know. I'd have liked to have married, but you can't bring a new woman into a home with your mother. Now, that you can't do."

Donal lapsed into another of his silences. After a moment he looked at Kevin and said, "Kathleen's in Australia, you know. Anna, she's in Galway, in a convent. She was in Africa for a while, working for the propogation of the faith. Sister Joseph, she calls herself. And Liam, he's in America, somewhere."

Kevin was startled. He hid it. "Ireland is very pretty. This is my first visit. The Shannon looks quite a bit like the lake we live on in America."

"Does it, now?" Donal said. "Well, one piece of water looks much the same as another, I suppose."

Kevin put down his half-filled cup and stood up. "I'm afraid I'll have to be going now."

"You know," Donal said, "things are hard for me. You might tell that to your da. A few pounds now and then from the rich brother in America . . . well, that would be a godsend. It truly would. You tell Liam that when you see him. I'm his brother, after all. Anna's all the way up in Galway, and Kathleen—well, God alone knows where she is. Australia, last I heard."

"I'll tell him," Kevin said.

* * * *

Kevin waited at the dock nearly an hour before Claire pulled up in her Austin.

"How was your visit?" she asked as he got in.

"Interesting. You know, I've been standing here I don't know how long, looking out at the water and wondering what my father would have become if he'd stayed here. My uncle is in terrible shape. I saw the priest after I left him. I'm going to have Pop send him money—but it'll go to the priest, not uncle Donal."

"Perhaps your father was fortunate to have left, then."

"Without a doubt."

Claire, catching his mood, tried to be cheery. "I'm taking you to dinner at a little inn over near the cliffs."

"The cliffs?" Kevin said. "Oh, yes, the Cliffs of Dooneen. Pop used to sing an old song about them. I'd like to see the cliffs."

"Then we'd best be on our way before it gets dark."

Kevin and Claire reached the Cliffs of Dooneen just as the sun was sinking over the Atlantic. They stood atop the huge rocky wall, looking down a sheer drop to the waves crashing in from the ocean.

Kevin shook his head. "Impressive," he said.

"And wild," Claire added as seagulls circled and shrieked above her and the wind from the Atlantic blew her black hair back from her face. She shivered and hunched her shoulders against the wind.

Kevin said, "You're cold. Let's go get something to eat."

The inn Claire had selected was eight or ten kilometers inland from the cliffs. It was a converted farmhouse nestled snugly under a stand of trees, a rare sight in a landscape where every available inch of woods had been cleared for farming. They were the only customers. The innkeeper was a smallish man of about fifty wearing a bow tie.

"Good evening," Claire told him. "We're here for dinner."

The innkeeper's face took on a pained expression. "I'm afraid that all we have is a bit of chicken. We don't get many visitors during the week, but I'm sure the wife could fix you up something grand."

"That'll be fine," Kevin said.

Claire went down the hall in search of the water closet, and the innkeeper disappeared into the kitchen. Kevin lit a cigar and wandered around the place. The downstairs consisted of a lobby, a small dining room and a parlor with a piano along one wall. He sat down at the piano and ran his fingers over the keys. He was delighted to discover that the piano was in perfect tune. It had been a while since he had last played, and his fingers were stiff. Kevin flexed them and rattled off the beginning of a selection from Chopin. He stopped, switched to some jazz for a moment, then he settled into "My Buddy." He began to hum the melody, then he played accompaniment and, very softly, began to sing.

"Nights are long since you went away," he sang in his rich baritone. "I think about you all through the day, my buddy, my buddy . . . No buddy quite so true . . ."

Then, from behind him, came a startlingly clear soprano.

"I miss your voice, the touch of your hand," Claire sang. "I hope and pray that you understand . . ."

They finished up together, their voices blending naturally in perfect harmony and pitch. "My buddy, my buddy, your buddy misses you."

"Well," Kevin said. "How about that."

"You play beautifully," she said, "and your voice is marvelous."

Kevin continued running his fingers over the keys, making up melody and accompaniment as he went along. "Only fair at both, I'm afraid," he said. "Tell you what, I'll play, and you sing. Try this."

Then Kevin launched into "The Sunny Side of the Street." Claire, sitting beside him at the piano, sang the song through.

"Play something else, and you sing with me, now," she said.

Kevin played "Beyond the Blue Horizon," and they sang together. Their voices were perfect together. From there they went into "Indian Love Call," and Kevin's baritone boomed while Claire's soprano rang sweet and true on the high notes.

When they had finished, Kevin said, "I could listen to you all night. You're good enough to be a professional."

"I was, for a brief while. I'll tell you about it over dinner."

"Here's the lady with the wine," Kevin said, looking over his shoulder.

"Play for me again after we eat, please," Claire said.

The innkeeper's wife was setting their table and opening the wine. "It was nice to hear that old piano again," she said. "My daughter used to play. She's in New Zealand now."

"It's in remarkably good tune," Kevin said.

"Oh, we keep it in tune," the woman said. "Every once in a while, someone stops in who plays, and the music is always grand."

Dinner was excellent, in marked contrast to the food prepared by Cecil Farrington's cook the night before. The chicken was moist, and the innkeeper's wife had prepared a white wine sauce to accompany it. The vegetables were crisp and fresh, and instead of the plain boiled potatoes they had been served the night before she brought them whipped potatoes with a hint of sharp cheese. Kevin and Claire went through the first bottle of wine, then a second and were working on a third when the coffee and tea came. They moved back into the parlor near the piano, Kevin feeling fine but Claire's speech a trifle thickened and her green eyes glittering.

"You were going to tell me about being a professional singer," he said to her.

"It was just a lark, really. I was sixteen. I'd just left school."

"That's pretty early to leave school, isn't it?"

She shook her head. "Not in Britain. Precious few English girls receive terribly good educations. We're meant for marriage and child rearing and all that. This is Europe, you know."

"That applies even to the daughters of baronets?"

"Especially to those of us in what some call the 'up-puh clahs-ses.' So there were no objections when I left school. Father objected strenuously, however, when I auditioned for and got, mind you, a good role in a traveling theater group. I spent the entire summer that year traveling about Britain imagining that I was a star. And performing every night. At first it was exciting. Then it became a dreadful bore, doing the same thing night after night. And I was really much too young to have all that freedom. I dissipated myself shamelessly. Finally, I just gave it all up and went home. I just wasn't cut out for it, I imagine."

"And what are you cut out for?" he asked.

"I wish I knew. It must be marvelous to be a man and to have all those choices arrayed before you, like fruit on a tree. You can be a barrister like Willie, or a flyer, like you."

"I'm only a flyer temporarily, thank you."

"Well, a vintner, then, or whatever you call it. At least you have choices."

"You could always find yourself some handsome earl or duke and get married. I can't imagine that there haven't been some opportunities along that line."

Claire lit a cigarette and sipped at her tea. "To be honest, there's one looming at this very moment. Not at this moment, actually, but not too far off. The chap in question is in North Africa. He'll be back soon enough."

"That doesn't sound all that terrible," Kevin said. "Is he a duke or an earl?"

Claire smiled. "Neither. Merely fabulously rich. And his father is a life peer, so the family is on the verge of being respectable."

"There, see?" Kevin said. "That doesn't sound too bad. What's his name?"

"Dickie. He's very nice. He's a bit of a bore, though—so 'veddy, veddy prawp-uh.' Respectability is comparatively new to Dickie's family, and he takes it so seriously."

"Well, you can't have everything."

"And why not?" Claire demanded.

Kevin sighed. "I wish to Christ I knew, but you can't."

"Sing to me, Kevin," she said suddenly.

"What do you want to hear?"

"Something outrageously sentimental. I feel like weeping."

"I know just the ticket," he said. "And it's appropriate."

With that he played and sang "The White Cliffs of Dover." His fingers were loose now, and his voice was rich and full. He sang the song slowly, drawing out the notes, modulating his volume. Claire burst out crying.

"I feel like such a fool," she said, sniffling and trying to stem the flow of tears. "I've drunk entirely too much."

She dropped her head on his shoulder and sobbed uncontrollably. Kevin merely played the piano softly. Then the innkeeper came into the parlor.

"Would you be wanting to go to your room, now?" he asked.

Claire's head came up quickly off his shoulder. "Yes, please," she said.

Kevin turned to her. Their eyes met for a brief moment. Hers were awash with tears, and her flawless skin was flushed about the cheeks. Kevin had never seen anyone lovelier. He dropped his eyes. Then he looked up at her silently.

"We can't stay the night," Kevin said.

"We'll take the room for only a few hours, then," Claire told the innkeeper.

The man reddened. "Well," he said stiffly, "that'll be up to you, now. Won't it?"

The bed was old and steel-framed with a hard mattress. Moonlight streamed in on it from over the Atlantic, painting Claire in a frostlike film as she climbed atop him. Kevin gazed at her in wonder—milky white, snowy white in the shadows, pearl white and almost translucent in the moonglow. She descended upon him like a warm fog, velvet and clinging. Claire moaned as he drove upward and penetrated. Kevin stroked her, his hands touching mist. She leaned forward, mouth meeting his, moistness and fire.

"Yes," she said to him. "God, yes."

For Kevin, it had been so long that he seemed to have no memory of the act. He behaved as his instincts told him—driving, stroking, kissing, caressing, driving again. When the eruption began to build, she sensed his urgency. Claire buried her fingers in his hair and pressed against him, searing him with her heat, quivering with her own passion.

And, when it was over, she lay in the cradle of his arms, breathing deeply. She reached a hand out to his cheek, stroking it with a feathery touch as delicate as breath. "Are you all right?" she asked him as she studied his face in the moonlight.

Kevin drew her even closer, powerful arms almost crushing her to him. He kissed her forehead. "I shouldn't be," he told her, "but I am."

* * * *

Given the fact that she and Kevin had arrived back at the house so late, Claire failed to come down for breakfast the following morning. Kevin, Farrington and his Uncle Cecil dined alone on sausages and french toast. They talked about Kevin's visit to Labasheeda, his uncle Donal and the war, of course, always the war.

After breakfast Kevin and Farrington changed into their uniforms and packed their gear. Cecil accompanied them to the field where the plane awaited. Farrington started it up, and the two flyers shook hands with the white-haired Englishman. As they climbed into the tiny aircraft, Claire came bursting out of the door of the house, through the gate and sprinted down the field. Farrington and Willie climbed back out of the plane, which sat there in the grass with its propeller whirling.

Claire shouted over the noise, "Be careful up there, Willie, you reprobate."

"I always am," Farrington lied.

She hugged him and kissed his cheek. Then she turned to Kevin and stuck out her hand.

"Goodbye to you, too, Captain Brennan," she shouted. "You must visit us again."

Kevin took her hand in his, and their eyes met briefly. Hers were wet again.

"Thank you for your hospitality," Kevin shouted out, and he climbed into the plane.

The weather observation craft, gassed up the day before by Willie and his uncle while Kevin and Claire were in Labasheeda, was in the air a moment later. Farrington took it up sharply, rising over the rolling Irish landscape. Kevin looked down for one more glance before they entered the clouds. He fixed the place in his mind. It was there forever, he knew—everything about it.

"Well, you Yank heartbreaker," Farrington laughed. "You appear to have made a conquest of my cousin."

"You have an overactive imagination, Willie."

Farrington laughed. "And a keen eye, my good fellow. A keen eye, indeed."

"Do you know what I'm going to do when we get back to base?" Kevin said.

"What might that be?"

"I'm going to figure out some way to get back to America for a few weeks. There has to be some way to hitch a ride on a dispatch plane."

Farrington looked over at him. "Why in the world would you want to do that, old man? We have a perfectly lovely war going right here."

Kevin frowned. "Just fly the plane, Willie."

Chapter 14

Her mother's curse had come true.

She could see her mother now—hair in wet, sweaty strings hanging in her flushed face, her faded housedress stained with baby food. Jane could close her eyes and smell their shabby, rented bungalow on Boydstown's south side, the air inside thick with the sour, acid stench of unwashed diapers.

"I hope you have a little brat who's as much trouble as you are," Jane's mother used to screech at her. "I hope you get a little bitch who never gives you a minute's peace."

And Jane had.

The radio was playing on the kitchen table in the shack, and the song was "Twilight Time," a new hit and one of Jane's favorites. She had settled down amid the sea of dirty dishes and littered clothing in which she lived and lit a cigarette. Susan had slept poorly the night before. Jane had managed only twenty minutes before to put her down for a nap. Now the music was flowing through the little house, and Jane was leaning back in the kitchen chair, catching her breath, preparing to go through the place like a whirlwind. It had gotten pretty bad, even by Jane's standards.

Then, from Susan's bedroom, it came.

"Mommy!" Susan called out insistently.

Jane clenched her teeth and ignored it.

"Mommmmeeeee!!!"

Jane jammed both palms up against her ears. "Shut up! Shut up! Shut up!" she shouted.

At that moment, Katherine came through the door. Jane looked up, saw her and groaned softly to herself.

Katherine stood in the doorway for a moment, hesitating. Then she said, "Jane, what's the matter? Can I help?"

From the bedroom: "MOMMMEEEEE!"

"I'll see after Susan," Katherine said.

"No," Jane said, leaping to her feet and flipping off the radio. "She'll quiet down in a minute. She always quiets down eventually. All you have to do is ignore her and let her scream bloody murder for a while."

"MOMMMEEEE!!"

"I'll get her," Katherine said firmly, and she went into the bedroom.

Jane moved out of the kitchen and to the sofa in the living room. The sofa was strewn with newspapers and magazines, and Jane swept them to the floor with an angry gesture. She sank to the sofa and buried her face in her hands. She realized she was weeping, and she didn't care. She didn't care about anything. She knew she was losing her mind.

Katherine came out of the bedroom with Susan in her arms. The child had her thumb in her mouth, and her lips were curled around a triumphant smile.

"Liam sent me down to see if you'd come up to the house for dinner," Katherine said. "We haven't seen you in days."

Jane lit another cigarette. "You haven't seen her, is what you mean."

"We want to see both of you."

"No, you don't," Jane said, the cigarette lodged in one corner of her mouth. "Let's not kid ourselves, Katherine. You want to see your son's child, not his wife. It's all right. I understand. I don't like it, but who cares about that?"

Katherine's face was beginning to flush. She spoke slowly and softly, but there was no mistaking the hardness in her voice. "You're welcome in our house any time, as you well know."

"Stop it!" Jane spat. Then, more quietly, she said, "Look, I know you're trying to be nice. I'd like to try to be nice, too. But I'm having my period; I haven't felt good for a couple of days, and the baby kept me awake half the night. I just can't put up with any more trouble. I'm a wreck, Katherine. Leave me alone, please."

Katherine held Susan close to her. "What can I do to help?"

Jane laughed bitterly. "Bring Kevin back to me. If you can't arrange that, then you can't help."

"Have you heard from him?"

"Not since last week. One letter a week, just like he sends you and Liam. That's my quota. And they get shorter and shorter." Jane drew deeply on her cigarette. "He has a woman over there. I know it."

"Jane!"

"Well, it's true," Jane said defiantly. "Men aren't like us, you know. I promise you he's not alone over there, not Kevin. But I'm alone here."

That was enough for Katherine. "I'm going to take the baby up to the big house."

"No, you're not," Jane said, her voice rising. "She's mine."

"You're too upset to take care of her properly today. Let her stay with us for a few days, until you've got a better grip on yourself."

"No!" Jane shouted. Then she burst out crying. "Oh, all right. Go ahead. I need the peace for a while. Go on, take her."

Katherine went back into the bedroom and gathered enough of Susan's things to last for a few days. When she emerged from the bedroom, Jane was sitting at the kitchen table, staring out the window at the lake, the radio playing the Andrews Sisters.

Katherine, the baby in her arms, left without a word. She climbed the hill with Susan, left her in the kitchen with Annette then went further up the hillside to find Liam in the vineyards.

"We have to talk," she told him. "Susan is with us in the big house. I went down there, and the shack is a pigsty. You couldn't imagine what it looks like. The baby was crying, and Jane is hysterical. You wouldn't believe the things she said."

Liam lit his pipe. "For instance."

"She hates us. She hates the farm. She's convinced that Kevin is keeping company with some English girl—and without a shred of proof, not a whiff of it. She said we hate her . . ."

Liam blew out a plume of smoke. "Well, we do, don't we?"

"Liam!"

"Well," he said, "I don't mean hate her, exactly. But let's be honest, my love, at least with each other. She's not what we would have selected if she had been ours to select, now is she? She's a wee bit too worldly for your taste . . ." he saw her redden at the accusation ". . . and mine, too," he added quickly. "And she's terribly lonely without Kevin."

"Liam . . ." she began in exasperation.

"All right," he said. "I'll go have a talk with the girl. I'll do it tonight, when she's calmed down. Right now, I'm hanging wire on this trellis."

"Now, Liam. The trellis can wait."

Liam Brennan surveyed the situation and declared himself the loser. He set aside his tools. "So it can."

He kissed his wife and walked off down the hillside, his pipe clenched tightly between his teeth. When he knocked on the door of the shack, Jane opened it a crack. Her eyes were red.

"You're a sight, girl," Liam told her. "Can I come in?"

"What do you want?"

He frowned in frustration. "To make whatever peace can be made. Don't be foolish. There's nothing to be gained from all this. Let me in."

Jane pondered his words, then let him in. Liam was appalled by the condition of the place, and his expression betrayed it. Jane saw his face, and she said, "I'm not much of a housekeeper. Kevin knew it when he married me. You might as well know it, too."

Liam looked around. "I've seen it worse. You should have seen this house when a man named John Hardy lived in it. Jane, I think it's time you got away for a while."

"I think it's time I got away forever," she said, lighting a cigarette.

He nodded. "I'm sure you do, right now. But I don't think you will in times to come. This is a hard time for you. The question is, what can be done to ease your load? Tell me, and I'll see that it's done."

Jane eyed him suspiciously. "What can you do?"

"I don't know," Liam told her. "What I can, I promise you that. We can take the child for a while, if that'll help. We can offer you our home, which, I'm afraid, we didn't do openly enough when Kevin brought you here."

Jane's expression softened. "I appreciate it. I do—really."

"I'm speaking for Katherine as well," Liam told her.

Jane laughed. "No, you're not. You may think you are. You may want to be. But you're not. Women know women in a way men never can. There'll never be any love lost between Katherine and me. If Kevin were here, we could hide it, because we both love him. But he's not, and we can't."

Liam nodded. "As you will, then. What can I do?"

Jane thought about it. "Nothing," she said finally. "I feel like I'm marooned. I can't stand it out here in the middle of nowhere. I have to see some people. I need to see some life. If Kevin were here I could stand it, I think. But even when he was here, even before the baby, it was hard. You men have your jobs, your work. Women have their men, and that's it. And when there's no man, there isn't anything."

"Women have their children."

"Yes," she said. "We have the dirty diapers, the temper tantrums. We have all the ugly parts of the children, the parts the fathers never see. I'm losing my mind. Look at me. I used to be pretty. Now I'm not even clean."

She went to the window and looked out at the lake. She stubbed out her cigarette and turned to Liam.

"I need to get out," she said, "and I can't leave. Not with Kevin gone and the baby here. I'm trapped. You want to know what's wrong, that's it."

"There are choices," Liam said. "Perhaps not good ones, but choices, nonetheless. Perhaps if you go away for a while each day. Take the truck. Take Kevin's Buick. Go to town. Katherine and Annette will watch the child."

"I don't know how to drive, remember? And if I did, where would I go? What can I do, wander the village every day? I can do that in ten minutes. Then what?"

"How about a job?" Liam said. "There's work to be done in the winery."

Jane shook her head. "Not the winery, please. God, not there."

"Then a job in the village. We could watch the child. What kind of work can you do?"

"Anything. You name it. Anything that would put me around people for eight hours a day."

Liam nodded slowly. "Then let me think about it," he said finally. "I'll talk to my friends in the village. There's a manpower shortage with the war. I'm sure there's something to be had. Give me a few days. Meanwhile, there's the child."

"I know, I know," Jane said. "Look, maybe you and Katherine could keep Susan for a day or two. Let me get myself together. I have to clean this place up. It's a horrible mess. I'll come up and get her tomorrow or the next day. I'll apologize to Katherine, too. It's just that I'm going crazy. I miss Kevin so much."

Liam nodded to her. "I'll do what I can."

Liam and Jane exchanged silent nods of parting. He left, and she could hear his footsteps going up the stairs outside. She stood by the front window for a moment, lighting another Chesterfield. Then she took a deep breath and looked around her.

Goddamn this war, she thought.

* * * *

Thomas Allen, Jr., was telling Jane, "I have to say, it never occurred to me that Liam Brennan's daughter-in-law would be looking for work, not with a young child at home. Why on earth do you want a job like this?"

"I need to keep busy, Mr. Allen."

Tom Allen's lips pursed slightly. He was a dark-haired man of medium height who tended to run to fat around the middle. He had come back from the Pacific after less than a year's service with a mild limp and a purple heart. Jane found him intimidating.

"You should know," he said, "that it's my personal opinion that there's no higher calling for a woman than motherhood—especially for a woman who can afford not to work."

"Then why are you bothering to interview me?" Jane asked.

"Out of courtesy to Liam, whom I've known since I was a kid and who was a good friend of my father's for thirty years. And, now that I have interviewed you, the job is yours—if you still want it."

"I do," Jane said. "Very much."

"Now," Tom Allen said, "I will insist that you be presentable at all times, which you most assuredly are today. And you must be punctual. The business day here begins promptly at 8:45. If, for any reason, you're not going to be here on a given day, you must call in no later than 8:46, so we can assign somebody from the secretarial pool to cover for you. When can you begin?"

"Well, I don't know. I have to arrange transportation. I don't drive. Liam brought me into town today, and he's picking me up, but he can't do that every day, obviously."

"Obviously," said Tom Allen. "Well, that shouldn't be a big problem. Bob Wright, our assistant sales manager, lives out on Lake Road well beyond Brennan's Point. He can pick you up in the morning on his way to work and drop you off at night. When he goes out of town, you'll have to fend for yourself. I'll let Bob know about the arrangement right away."

"If that's the case," Jane said, "I can start tomorrow morning."

"Don't you want to know your salary?"

"To be honest, I don't much care. You can pay me whatever you think is fair."

Tom Allen laughed. "You have no head for business, Mrs. Brennan. And that, incidentally, pleases me no end. I don't think a woman should have a head for business."

*　*　*　*

Helen ached in every bone in her body.

She dragged herself through the front door of the apartment and found Jack in the kitchen, packing his lunchbox. She sank into one of the two chairs at the kitchen table. "I need a beer right now or I'm going to die."

Jack reached into the refrigerator and pulled out a bottle of Old Ranger. He opened it and put it down in front of her. Helen drank a good third of it from the bottle in one shot. She put the bottle on the table in front of her and sank back in her chair like a thing of rubber. "God, I'm bushed," she said.

Jack filled his thermos with coffee and deposited it in his lunchbox alongside the wrapped ham sandwiches. "If you didn't work so much overtime, you wouldn't be so tired all the time. There's no need for that now, not with me working at the plant, too."

"We still need the money," Helen told him, "if we're going to buy a house."

"We do like hell. I'm bringing in more money than I ever did with the studio."

"That's because you're working a lot of overtime, too."

"You bet I am," he said. "I'm not going to be stuck on that assembly line forever. I've been studying the way the lines are supplied. I think there's a better way to do it."

"What do you mean?"

He sat down on the other side of the table. "Well," he said slowly, "you've noticed, haven't you, how at least once an hour at least one of the lines is shut down for a few minutes while one of the supply clerks goes running back for more parts?"

"So?"

"I was thinking, if you could get a gauge of everybody's speed, you could assign them positions along the various lines that would result in a reasonably even flow on each line. If you could do that, you could figure out in advance how many parts you'd need each hour of running time for each line, and you could supply the lines on a regular schedule in advance, at specified intervals. If it works, there'd be no down time. I think I might write it up and turn it in as a suggestion."

"You should do it, Jack. You have terrific ideas all the time, but you never do anything about them."

"I'll do something about this one," he told her. "If I have to work at a place like Potters, I want to be noticed. Maybe, if they like this, I can get on the same shift with you. With only Sunday off together, we end up seeing each other only one day out of the whole week. And we usually end up spending that day with your folks up at Brennan's Point."

"Where we get a good meal," she pointed out.

"Which we can afford to buy on our own, now. Look, I've got to run."

He bent over and kissed her. Then he was out the door. Helen sat alone at the kitchen table for a while after Jack left, sipping her beer and too tired to move. She leafed through that afternoon's copy of the *Boydstown Bulletin*, and after a while she got up for another beer. There was none left.

She faced two choices. She could walk downtown to the market and pick up a six pack or she could go next door to Peg Harper's and drink Peg's beer. Easy choice. Peg had drunk enough of the Ryans' beer.

Helen found Peg in her kitchen, feeding her new baby.

"Hi," Helen said. "Got any beer? We're all out, and I'm too tired to go out and get some more."

"No beer," Peg said. "But I have some sherry."

"Any port in a storm," Helen said. "I guess that applies to sherry, too."

Peg put the baby down and came back. She went to a kitchen cabinet and poured them each tumblers half full of sherry from a bottle she kept there. They settled down at the kitchen table. Peg looked at Helen carefully.

"You're really beat, aren't you?" she said.

"Dog tired," Helen said. "I feel like I've been hit by a truck. It's all that overtime. Would you like a cigarette?"

"Got my own. You know, I don't understand you. If your family is so well off . . ."

"Who says they're well off?"

"Jack did one night a couple of weeks ago. Don't you remember? And you agreed that they were comfortable. Am I sticking my nose into something that doesn't concern me?"

"Oh, that's all right," Helen said. "I do remember. I said they own a lot of land up on the lake and the winery and all that. But that doesn't mean they're well off. The fact is, my brother and I own probably half the land. It's in our names. Do I look well off?"

"No," Peg said. "That was my point. Why are you working so hard, then?"

Helen sipped her sherry. It was beginning to ease her aches and pains. "You don't know anything about the wine business, or farming, either. Kevin and I own a lot of land because of the way my grandfather set up his will. My father owns a lot of land on his own, and the house is his, too. Kevin and I are technically entitled to whatever profit comes in from the winery. But there's not much profit, not once my father gets finished paying all the help and doing whatever he does to improve his wines from year to year. He's always buying new equipment for the winery, and he's always clearing his own land to put in new grape varieties. That sort of thing takes a long time before it makes money."

Peg shrugged. "I don't know a thing about wine or farms. But it sounds like maybe he isn't charging enough for his wine."

"He probably isn't," Helen said. "But nobody's going to tell him. I know I'm not. He'd go through the roof if somebody tried to tell him how to run the winery. The fact is, I don't think he pays much attention to what he charges. He makes enough money to keep the place going. That's all he's interested in. Between what Jack and I make at the factory and what we get at the end of the year when what profit the winery does make is split up, we're managing to pay off the debts from the studio, but that's all. How many people do you know who have money in the bank? I know we don't."

"Us, either," Peg said. "I wonder what it would feel like."

"Well, I want to find out. We're going to buy a house as soon as the war is over. With the debts from the photo studio being whittled away, we're on the edge of doing okay. But I've got to keep working, and I want that overtime. I may even keep working when we get the house."

"Why, for God's sake?" Peg demanded. "Why work when you don't have to. Stay home and eat bonbons."

Helen laughed. "Like you? You work your tail off around here with that baby. I suppose that when we get the debts from the studio paid off, I'll quit and have kids. But I don't think I could stand sitting around the house all day listening to the radio."

"I like the radio," Peg told her. "Here, your glass is empty."

She refilled both glasses. Helen drank part of her second glass. "Thanks. God, I needed this."

When Jack entered the apartment at the end of his night shift, he was surprised to find it in darkness. Helen had to get up early every day, but she was nonetheless in the habit of staying up late, reading or talking on the telephone. The lights were always on when Jack came home from the night shift, but tonight he was forced to feel his way into the living room and turn on a lamp.

Helen was sleeping on the sofa, fully clothed, and she came awake, blinking, as the light went on. She seemed unusually disoriented, and he stared at her with some concern. "Are you all right?" he asked her.

She responded groggily, her speech thick. "I'm okay. I'm sleeping."

Jack sat down next to her, and he caught the odor rising from her. "Christ," he said, "you smell like your father's winery."

Helen put her face in her hands. "I had a little wine with Peg."

He looked at her strangely. "You had a lot of wine with Peg."

Helen rubbed her eyes. She couldn't seem to come awake. "I'm tired. I forgot to eat anything. What time is it? How long have I been here?"

"It's nearly one."

"God," she said, "I've been sleeping here since nine or so. I've got to get to bed. I've got to be up at six."

She got up shakily and staggered back to the bedroom, holding her arms out for balance. Jack followed, helping her into bed.

"You're half in the bag," he said angrily. "Christ, how much did you drink with Peg?"

"A couple of glasses. I don't know."

"You had too goddamn much," he said, irritated.

Helen sat up in the bed. "Why don't you just shut up? I'm sick of working. I want a baby."

Jack was nonplussed. "We can't have a baby until we get out of this hole from the studio," he said.

But Helen was enraged, and Jack was shocked to realize that she was out of control. "And whose fault is that?" she shrieked at him. "I want a baby. I want my own house and a baby."

He stood up and moved away from the bed. "You're drunk," he said.

"If I am it's because of you, you little bastard!" she screamed at him. "It's your goddamn fault."

Jack surrendered. He took his pillow and headed for the couch. "Go to sleep," he said. "We'll talk about it when you sober up."

Helen turned her back to him as he left the room.

* * * *

Bob Wright was dependable.

Every morning, Monday through Friday, he pulled up on the road at Brennan's Point precisely at 8:30. He had carefully timed the trip from the farm to the mill, a distance of seven and one-third miles. He knew that if he left the farm at no later than 8:31 or 8:32 he could drive the route and park his car and be at his desk with several minutes to spare, and that was important because Tom Allen abhorred tardiness.

Bob Wright had worked at Lakeside Mills ever since he had graduated from Lakeside Free Academy in the same class as Kevin Brennan. Never once had he been late for work. Never, that is, until he began picking up Kevin's wife.

Now every morning was another opportunity to arrive late under Tom Allen's disapproving gaze. Every morning Bob pulled his car to a halt on the main road between the big house and the shack, honked his horn and waited, wondering how long it would be before Jane came bursting out of either house, moving at a frantic dead run for the car. Sometimes he had to shut off the car rather than burn up the gas waiting for her. Gas was too dear during wartime to waste it idling.

It all would have been a trying experience for him but for one factor: he found Jane extraordinarily congenial, funny and unfailingly good company. He also found her so pretty that being alone in the same car with her was sometimes enough to make beads of perspiration appear on his forehead. His brief car rides with her were the high spots of his day. Still, he wished she could get out of the house on time in the morning.

One particular morning some time after Jane began work at Lakeside Mills, he pulled the car to a halt on the lake road and hit his horn. Inside the shack, Jane panicked. "Oh, God," she said. "There's Bob. I'm going to be late."

Jane turned to Susan, who was sitting at the kitchen table busily shoveling in her oatmeal. "I have to go, Sweetheart," Jane told her. "Can you finish up and go to Grandma's by yourself?"

Susan's face, her cheeks rounded and filled with oatmeal, took on a pained expression. She swallowed and said, "You take me to Grandma's."

"I can't, Sweetie," Jane said. "Mommy has to go to work. I can't be late. Have you seen my cigarettes?"

"Don't want you to go work," Susan said.

"Don't start," Jane told her as she dug through the house. "Where the hell are those cigarettes? Oh, the hell with it."

Jane hurriedly pulled on her coat and gathered her pocketbook. She ran over to Susan and planted a swift kiss on the child's cheek. "I have to go, Sweetie. You finish up your breakfast. When you're done, you go up to Grandma's, okay? Just put the dirty dishes in the sink, and be careful crossing the road."

The horn sounded again, and as it did Susan said, "I don't want you to go. Stay here."

"Cut it out, Susan," Jane said. "Just do what I told you. And look both ways when you cross the road."

Bob Wright was waiting patiently, as usual.

"Sorry," Jane said, climbing in. "Getting the kid ready to go up to her grandmother's slows me up."

Bob put the car in gear and they started in toward town. "You let that little kid cross the road herself?" he said in surprise.

"She's fine. She always looks both ways, and there's hardly any traffic out here anyway. Believe me, if ten cars a day go by the farm it's a lot, except in the summer.

"Even so," he said. "It would scare me."

"I don't get so easily scared," Jane told him. "Have you got a cigarette? I couldn't find mine."

He gave her a Pall Mall. She lit it and puffed at it nervously.

"Are you okay?" Bob Wright asked her.

"Oh, sure," she said. "It's always a riot getting out in the morning, with Susan and all. You're lucky. You've got somebody at home to get the day going with the kids."

He laughed. He was a big man, blond and ruddy, and he was outgoing and friendly. He had a ready laugh. "I'm lucky, all right," he said. You think it's tough with one kid, you ought to have three, like me. Every morning is a nightmare, trying to get going and get out on time. And Sally is a real bitch before she's had her coffee. The fact is, most days she's a bitch even after she's had it."

"Nice talk," Jane said.

"It's not just talk. Give you two or three more kids and you'll be one, too. I'm sympathetic. That still doesn't make it fun for the man."

"I know. Men always have it rougher. That's a laugh. Your wife should look at the bright side. At least she's got her husband around. I'll tell you, there's nothing emptier than an empty bed when you crawl in between the sheets at night. I worry about Kevin something fierce."

"Ah," he said, "Kevin'll be fine. Guys like him never have anything real bad happen to them."

"You sound jealous," Jane told him.

"Jealous of Kevin Brennan?" Bob Wright examined the thought. "Could be. My family used to own all this land that the Brennans have, you know. My great uncle sold it to old man Weidener. I've known Kevin all my life, and he's always had things more or less his own way. Guys like me, we bust our butts, and if we get anything we figure we're lucky."

"You don't like my husband much, do you?"

"Sure I do. Everybody always liked Kevin, me included. How do you not like Kevin Brennan?"

"I can tell you a few things I don't like. His mother, for instance."

"Well, when you're married, you don't just marry the person, you marry the whole family."

"Don't I know it," Jane said.

* * * *

"Hello?" Liam said. "Who? Who is this?" He turned to the women. "Be quiet out there. Yes, operator, put him on. Kevin, is that you?"

Jane and Katherine rushed to the phone, fluttering around Liam like butterflies. "Yes," Liam was saying in a loud voice into the phone, "we're all fine. Where are you?" Liam listened for a moment, then turned to his wife and daughter-in-law. "He's in New York. What the hell are you doing there?"

"It's a flying trip, Pop," Kevin said. "Listen, I don't have time to go into detail now, but I've got something I've been bursting to tell you. Do you remember that fight you had in the pub in Labasheeda all those years ago?"

"What?" Liam asked. "You don't mean the one back in 1908? That one?"

"That's the one," Kevin told him. "I met one of the guys you beat up—Cecil Farrington."

Liam was aghast. "Go on with you! I killed the man."

"Nobody was even hurt badly," Kevin told his father. "You're not as tough as you thought. Cecil and his brother were just banged up a bit, is all."

Liam said nothing, pondering the implications of the news. Then he said, "But, nobody ever told me. My da let me think . . ."

"He must have had his reasons," Kevin said through the static-laden line from New York. "Maybe he was afraid you'd come running back home. I met Donal, too. Be thankful you didn't go back to Labasheeda, Pop. I'll write you all about it."

Liam sighed deeply. "You're not joshing me, now, Kevin?"

"Nope. Cecil Farrington is just fine and sends his regards. Listen, is Jane there?"

Liam, pressed in by his wife and daughter-in-law, held out the two-piece phone with both hands. "Katherine, I've something absolutely incredible to tell you. Jane, say hello to your husband."

Her eyes aglow, Jane grabbed the phone. "Hello? Kevin?"

"Hi, Sweetheart. How would you like to sleep in a warm bed for at least one night?"

Jane was beside herself. "I can't believe it's you. When will you be here?"

"That's just it," he told her. "I won't. I'm only in the States for the rest of today and all of tomorrow. I have to fly back to England the next morning. I can't get up to the lake and back in time. But if you can get here tomorrow, we can have one evening together. And one night, if you're in the mood."

"If I'm in the mood?" she said. "I'll be there with bells on."

"Good. There's a train out of Boydstown at 8:48 tomorrow morning. You can be at Grand Central by late afternoon. I'll meet you. I've already got a room reserved at the McAlpin. We'll have dinner at the Stork Club. How's that sound?"

Jane was soaring. "Wonderful. You'll meet my train?"

"You bet. You make sure you're on the 8:48 to New York tomorrow, and I'll take care of the rest. You just bring a slinky nightgown."

* * * *

"So," Kevin said, "he put in a word with his Uncle Cecil, and Uncle Cecil put in a word with Churchill, for Christ's sake, and the next thing I knew I was on a B-17 heading home on courier duty. When we finally landed on U.S. soil I got rid of the papers and headed right for New York and a phone."

"What was in the papers?" Jane asked.

"Beats the hell out of me. All I know is they handcuffed a briefcase on my wrist in London and unfastened it here. Probably fish and chips for Roosevelt."

He was thinner, she noticed, and he was older, too. That surprised her, even though it had been more than two years since they'd last seen one another. Kevin's was not the only uniform to be found in the Stork Club, either, which told her that other couples were also spending big money on their reunions.

Kevin had been miffed that no Weidener or Brennan wines could be found on the Stork Club's wine list, and he had made Jane promise to mention it to Liam. He listened intently while she brought him up to date with news of home, including the death of Jack Ryan's father in the locomotive of his freight just outside Rochester. "They flagged down a passenger train to try to get a doctor to help him," she said, "and the only doctor on board was Jim Frazier. He was in the baggage car. He'd died the day before at a medical convention."

Kevin alternately enthralled and terrified her with stories of England and the war. When he was finished, she felt she had the perfect mental picture of Willie Farrington. "Errol Flynn," she said.

"Sort of," Kevin told her. "Not the kind of guy you want near your daughter. What's Susan like these days, by the way? She's got to be a full-fledged kid by now."

"Oh, Kevin. She's such a handful. I just can't deal with her sometimes. I hate to say it, but your mother is a tremendous help, her and Annette. I'd go crazy without them. They watch her while I'm at work, and—"

"You know," he broke in, "I'm not so crazy about the working."

"Why not?" Jane demanded. "I like working. I was working for a long time before I met you. I like getting dressed up and getting out. With you gone, work is the only thing that's kept me sane."

Kevin lit a cigar and sat back. "Just the same," he said somberly, "I'd feel better knowing you had your eye on Susan. Mom has raised her kids, and she's getting older, now. A little girl should have her mother around, especially when her father can't be there."

Jane's eyes narrowed. "I am around. I'm just not around every second, that's all."

Kevin said nothing.

"Look," Jane said, "I made a bargain when I married you. That's all right, I understood the bargain. It wasn't that I didn't love you, because I did and I do. But it's isolated out there. There's no Stork Club out on the lake. There's nothing out there except grapes and deer and fish and the lake—none of which hold for me the sort of magic they seem to hold for you. I needed that job, Kevin. I needed it for me."

He studied her carefully. "It means that much to you?"

She nodded.

"All right," Kevin said. "Tell me, what are you doing with the money you're making? I mean, Pop is still paying you my salary and my profit share, and I'm sending money back home. You've got more cash than you know what to do with."

"I'm buying clothes for me and Susan. I have to look right at work, and Susan is the best-dressed child in the state. The rest of it I'm just putting away. I have about three thousand in the bank, now."

Kevin grinned. "That's great. That's probably more than Pop has."

"I'm sure it is," she said, the tension between them evaporating. "Do you know what he did? He went out and bought a fabulous boat. It's a big Chris Craft, all mahogany and leather. It's like a millionaire's boat."

Kevin was stunned. He couldn't imagine Liam spending money on a luxurious toy. "Pop did that?"

"He sure did. He bought it for himself for his fifty-sixth birthday. He said he'd always wanted one, and he just went out and bought it. Your mother was furious, but he just ignored her. He and Henri built a boathouse down on the beach, and that's where they're keeping it until spring."

Kevin shook his head. "Pop must have gone nuts. I'd love to go out on that boat with them." He took her hand and kissed her fingertips. "You don't know how much I've missed you."

She reached over and ran one manicured hand through his hair. "Yes, I do," she said in a husky voice. "Believe me, I do. Let's get back to the room."

At the hotel, Kevin threw his jacket on the floor and loosened his tie. He sat back on the bed while Jane went into the bathroom. She came out in a negligee of the sheerest silk. He looked at her in the dim light of the single lamp that was burning, and he sat up on the bed.

"My God," Kevin whispered. "I'd forgotten how you look, how beautiful you are."

She came over to him, took his hands and put them on her. "You won't forget tonight," she promised him. "Not as long as you live."

In the morning, Kevin awakened first. He looked over at Jane, her hair spread out gloriously over the pillow.

He'd be all right now, he was sure.

* * * *

"You're still awake down there, aren't you, Brennan?" Farrington asked through the intercom.

Kevin, nestled in the *Fair Lady*'s Plexiglas nose answered back, "I'm cold and stiff. The combination is keeping me awake nicely, thank you."

Farrington laughed into the microphone. "You're having the time of your life, you faker. Look around. You'll spend an entire lifetime on that bloody lake of yours and never again see a spectacle like this."

Kevin glanced about him. It was bright, shiny daylight, the sun splashing down over bombers as far as the eye could see in both directions. Arrayed around them was all the mechanized air muscle of the Allied forces, flexing for a killing punch at a wounded enemy.

"You're right," Kevin said. "It's a hell of a sight. You could never get a sense of the size of the force on night missions."

"It's something to tell your children about in years to come," Farrington said, "especially the one that's on the way. If it's a boy, Brennan, you must name him William. Delightful name, don't you think?"

Kevin laughed. "And what if it's a girl?"

"Wilhelmina," Farrington said. "The important thing is the nickname— Willie. It has such a ring."

They had come this far without serious incident. Kevin had been struck by the weakness of the flak defenses as they came in over the coast. Looking around him, he hadn't seen a single allied plane struck by the sparse flak the Germans had sent up at them. The fighters, however, would be another matter. And even as the thought passed through Kevin's mind that they would have to be coming soon, from his perfect vantage point in the nose he spotted them coming out of the clouds. "Bandits at five o'clock," he shouted into his facemask.

The fighters buzzed toward them like angry hornets. The allied fighter escort planes engaged them instantly, and it was several more minutes before the first German attack planes broke through. One of them tore through the ranks of defenders close to the *Fair Lady*, and Kevin felt his heart pop into his mouth as it closed on them.

It was a Junkers 87B fighter, faster than the Stirling and with a higher ceiling. It had the capacity to pump shells from its three machine guns at a rate of 520 rounds a minute. As the plane roared by, he saw clearly the faces of its two-man crew. The sight left him shaken. After three years of aerial warfare, he finally had seen the face of the enemy.

Kevin heard the *Fair Lady*'s guns tail gun speak. He spun his head around to see what was happening, then heard the tail gunner scream into his facemask: "One's on our blooming tail, Willie."

Farrington instantly wrenched the plane hard to the left and dropped down quickly. Bomber discipline required that the planes stay in formation no matter what, but with a fighter on his tail, Farrington was violating that discipline, and Kevin was silently grateful.

He could hear their own guns firing, but he could also hear bursts coming from the Junkers 87B behind them, armor-piercing shells filled with a substance that burst into flame on impact. Kevin felt the shells hit his plane. The impact was jarring.

Even from his spot in the nose, Kevin knew the *Fair Lady* had suffered a serious wound. Farrington pulled her up and to the right, and then Kevin could see the German fighter coming at them. He could hear the Stirling's guns roar.

The Junkers burst into flame, and Kevin's eyes went wide. The Junkers stopped in midair at the impact of the Stirling's shells, and he watched in horror as one of the two crewmen went flying out, arms flailing, and disappeared into the clouds below.

As the Junkers went down, the *Fair Lady* suddenly dipped into a steep dive. There was no reason for it, and Kevin knew that Farrington had lost control of the aircraft. Kevin felt himself pressed up against the top of the bombing compartment. Then the aircraft began to spin, and Kevin prayed.

"Don't worry, lads," Farrington said coolly over the intercom. "We've got plenty of airspeed. I can get her back."

Up on the flight deck, Willie Farrington leaned on the rudder bar with his feet and jammed it as far as it would go. He was a strong man, and he gave it everything he had. The plane rattled and screamed, and Kevin could hear metal snap all around him. It took another ten seconds, but Farrington finally pulled the *Fair Lady* out of her spinning dive and brought her up level.

Kevin looked up through the nose, and he could see the tail end of the formation far ahead of them and high above. Farrington tried to pull the Stirling back up into formation, but the *Fair Lady* only groaned, and she wasn't climbing. He heard Farrington's voice over the intercom.

"Damage report," the pilot snapped.

One by one, the crewmen called in, including Kevin. Reported damage was minimal. Then Farrington said, "Tail gunner?"

There was no response.

"Brownwell," Kevin heard Farrington say, "go aft and see, will you, old man?"

A moment later, Brownwell reported back. "He's dead, Willie, and the tail is badly chewed up."

"All right," Farrington said grimly, "come on back up front. We've a bit of a problem here. The wireless is out, and I can't get her to climb."

"That's the tail damage," Brownwell said. "I can't fix it."

"Well, then," Farrington said, "I guess we're heading home, chaps. We can't very well drop bombs on Berlin in this condition."

"We ought to get rid of the bombs, Willie," Kevin said. "That's a lot of weight to lug all the way across the Channel, and it might give us more altitude."

"Good idea. Let them go."

Kevin did. He unloaded over a farmer's field, and he saw the field obliterated as they flew over. He thought of his father's vineyards and shook his head.

They made it through the German flak on the coast, and then they were out over the gray, choppy waters of the English Channel. The sight of the Channel gave Kevin an immense sense of relief. Only twenty miles to British soil. He climbed out of the nose and up to the flight deck.

"How's it going?" he asked.

Brownwell's face was grim behind his mask, Kevin could tell, but Farrington's eyes danced with their usual good humor. "It was a shame to miss the party, wasn't it?"

"Half the bloody damn instruments are gone," Brownwell complained. "I can't monitor anything in the engines."

Kevin shivered. "Well, at least we're close to home."

"Thank God for that," Brownwell said.

Then engine number one died.

"Goddamn it!" Brownwell said. He threw down his flight gloves in disgust. "I knew we'd lose one. Probably an oil leak from all that shaking up back there."

"We've enough to get back," Farrington said, adjusting his controls to fly with three engines. "It won't make landing any easier, though."

"We have faith in you, Willie," Kevin said. "Stiff upper lip, and all that."

The *Fair Lady* lost altitude on three engines. By the time they hit the British coast another engine was sputtering threateningly. An air of tension had settled over the crew.

"We'll have to put her down in East Anglia," Farrington said. "I don't trust her to make it back to our home base."

"I don't care where you put her down," Kevin said, "as long as there's a bar close by."

"My dear fellow," Farrington said, "I quite agree."

"I guess I'll get back to my station," Kevin said. He put a hand on Farrington's shoulder. "Good luck, Willie. Try not to screw this up, okay?"

"Oh, ye of little faith," Farrington said.

Kevin settled back into the nose and watched the countryside below grow ever closer. With a sense of relief, he saw an airstrip ahead.

"Now what the hell is wrong with the bloody flaps?" he heard Farrington demand of Brownwell.

"I'm giving you what I can," the flight engineer said. "The blasted things are frozen. We must have lost hydraulic fluid."

There was no more conversation after that. Kevin felt Farrington begin to pull back on the throttles, bumping the Stirling down rather than easing her down as he would have done with full flap control. The drone of the three remaining engines would die down as Farrington eased off the gas, then resume again as he straightened the ship out. They were quite low now.

"We'll be going in a bit faster than usual, chaps," Farrington said over the intercom, "because of the trouble with the flaps. I suggest you all find something to hold onto."

"Your balls, for instance," Brownwell suggested, and they all laughed, easing the tension a bit.

The Stirling came in very low over a field in front of the landing strip. No more than thirty feet below them, sheep scattered in terror. Another few hundred feet and the tarmac would be just below them.

Then another engine quit.

"Damn!" Kevin heard Farrington say calmly.

The Stirling dropped like a stone. With half its power gone, with its tail mangled and its flaps frozen, with the earth so close below them, there was no margin for error. No margin at all.

Kevin was watching from his box seat in the nose when they hit the soft mud of the sheep pasture at more than a hundred miles an hour. The tires dug almost instantly deep into the soft mud, and Kevin felt the world suddenly turn upside down. He was aware of a horrible noise— of crunching metal and slamming impact and the screams of men, including his own. He felt himself fly freely into the air.

After that, he felt nothing at all.

Chapter 15

Kevin's first sensations after the Stirling flipped over were of softness, of gentle hands touching him, moving with great care, slowly. He had the impression of bright lights and crisp, starched white fabric. He was floating, it seemed, and he knew not where, nor did he care. He realized at some point that the veil that surrounded his mind and his awareness was being lifted bit by bit, and before long he could feel pain coming up his spine and into his brain from his left side. At some point, he became aware that he was in a hospital ward. People there poked and prodded at him. They bathed and fed him, too, and they used his name constantly.

Later on, as they slowly cut back on the morphine, he came to realize that they were nurses. There was also a thin doctor with a craggy, lined face who spoke to him clearly and slowly and made notations on the chart at the foot of his bed. Kevin never spoke to any of them, although they regularly asked him questions about how he was feeling, how we were doing today and so on.

There was another person, too, a face and a voice he should know but could not place. Her face was framed in inky hair, and it bore an expression of deep concern. As he climbed out of the pit in which he found himself, he came to realize that this was Claire Farrington, and she was near him often, talking to him about the weather, about the other patients around him, about the war. She often read to him from the newspaper.

One day Kevin tried to speak to her, but he found that he couldn't form words. Claire called the nurse, who called the doctor with the craggy face, and he examined Kevin carefully. "He seems to be coming out of it now," the doctor pronounced.

"Will he be able to talk?" Claire asked.

"I should think so. Head injuries are strange, and the morphine hasn't helped him get his bearings. We'll cut back on it a bit more, and we'll see if that makes him more alert. If he has much pain, though, we'll have to up the dosage again."

After a while, Kevin said to Claire, "Hello."

She leaned over his bed. "Hello," she said softly.

"We crashed, didn't we?"

She nodded.

"How long?" Kevin asked her.

She understood the question. "Twenty-four days. You were in a coma. You're coming out of it now, and you're going to be fine, just fine."

Kevin shook his head weakly. "Hurt . . . down here."

"Yes. Your left arm and leg were badly injured, but they say they can fix them, with surgery. You're going to be fine, really."

Kevin was exhausted from the effort of speech. He wanted to know so much more.

"Willie?" he got out.

Claire sank her teeth into her lower lip. Then she said, "He's dead. The glass nose came off the plane, and you were thrown clear. You were the only one who lived."

Later on—he couldn't tell how much later; it could have been minutes, days—he asked her, "Why are you here like this?"

"I wanted to help you. I didn't want you to be alone with strangers."

"Why?"

She laughed and wept at the same moment. She would not answer him.

In all, Kevin was in the British hospital not quite ten weeks. The final three were spent in preparation for his return to a veteran's facility stateside. He insisted on being sent to Rochester so he could be close to his family. He signed papers by the sheaf, all brought to him by a spit-and-polish sergeant from headquarters, who stood there stiffly while Kevin plowed through the documents that would separate him from the Army Air Corps. During his last week, a major came in with the sergeant and awarded him the Purple Heart as he lay in his hospital bed. Kevin put the medal in his shaving kit.

For the last few weeks he got out of bed once a day and was put into a wheelchair. Because of the arm damage, even his movements in the wheelchair were limited, but Claire was there daily, and she pushed him around the halls and out on the hospital grounds. Throughout his years in England, the weather had, more often than not, been gray and dismal. But the island was visited during his last few weeks there by an unprecedented period of sunshine. He found it warmed both his body and his spirit.

Toward the end he told Claire, "You saved me. I don't think I would have come out of that coma if you hadn't been there. Before I knew who you were, I remembered your smell."

She smiled self-consciously. "How on earth could you know what I smell like?"

"From that night in Ireland."

"I smelled like wine that night."

He shook his head. "More than that. I read somewhere that a head injury can make your sense of smell more sensitive. I knew it was you even before I could think. That's how I knew."

"I'm going to miss you terribly," she told him.

"I wish I knew what to say to you. I'll never forget you."

"I'll think of you always, Kevin."

The last day she wheeled him out under a stand of trees on the grounds, some distance from the main building. He took her hand, and they sat there in silence for more than an hour. Then she wheeled him back, and she did not come again to the hospital.

The next day, Kevin was on a hospital plane back to America.

* * * *

Sylvan Weingarten, M.D., was a thickset man of twenty-eight with thinning black hair which grew in wild curls. He had powerful hands and eyes so weak that only his thick glasses could bring his vision up to twenty-twenty. He was only a few years out of his residency, and his perpetually furrowed brow was the only visible sign of the despair he felt over his work, which consisted of rebuilding to the best of his limited ability mangled human bodies. He began each day in surgery and ended each day in depression.

Weingarten was standing behind his desk as the Brennans entered. The doctor had seen them before: tall, rugged Liam Brennan; his wife and their daughter-in-law, a pretty woman who struck Weingarten as too intense to be really attractive. "The nurse said you wanted to see us," Liam said.

"Yes, I do. Please, everyone, sit down. I wanted to talk to you about your son, Mr. Brennan. He's been here just over thirteen months, and I think we're rapidly reaching the point of diminishing returns in terms of what you can expect us to accomplish."

Liam nodded. "Go on."

Sylvan Weingarten lit a Lucky Strike. "Our whole focus has been on trying to get him to walk again. As you know, the left arm will never be completely right. It's the left leg that's my big interest now. I've put in a new knee joint, but it can't approach what God gave him. The muscle tissue is permanently damaged, and most of the nerves are beyond repair. Still . . ."

"Still what?" Katherine said.

"He should be able to walk on it with a brace and crutch," Weingarten said, "and for some reason he can't. He's been an utter failure in rehabilitation. The problem with his body is bad, and we'll never be able to make it better. But if he's going to get out of that wheelchair, we have to find some way to overcome the problem in Captain Brennan's head. He's simply not making the proper effort."

Katherine said, "That doesn't sound at all like Kevin. He's seemed to be in high spirits every time we've seen him."

"You're right," Weingarten said. "He's not whining or carrying on. But he's not doing what we think he's physically capable of. He's an enormously strong man, Mrs. Brennan. The portions of his body that weren't damaged in that plane crash are remarkable."

Jane sat up. "Why do you think he's not trying hard enough?"

Weingarten said, "This is not an unusual phenomenon with strong, athletic men who suddenly find themselves unable to make their bodies do precisely what they want. The problem is this: we're going to have to release Captain Brennan before too long unless he puts his heart and soul into this rehabilitation. There's a waiting list for entrance into this facility. I've debated telling him myself, but this sort of message is usually best delivered by those who'll have to bear the burden of dealing with the invalid if he's not able to get himself back on his feet again. In that sense, this message is every bit as crucial for you people as it is for Captain Brennan."

"How should we handle it?" Jane asked.

"One way is for all of you to sit down with him and confront him with his failure to put all he has into rehabilitation. The confrontation will either be successful or it won't."

"I think he'd simply shut us out," Katherine said. "He'd blow up, then ignore us. Kevin has always reacted angrily if he thought he was being ganged up on. How else might this message of yours be delivered, Doctor?"

"The other way is for one of you—wife, father, mother or whomever he's most likely to listen to on a one-to-one basis—to sit down with him and carefully explain the sort of burden he'll be to the family unless he does his very best to get back on his feet. It shouldn't sound like an accusation. Bear in mind that he honestly thinks he's doing his best right now. He believes his body is broken beyond repair and that this whole matter is out of his hands."

"Which one of us should it be?" Liam asked.

"Me," Jane said quickly.

Liam and Katherine exchanged glances, then nodded to her.

"When should I do this?" Jane asked. "Any particular time?"

"Now would be nice," the surgeon said.

Kevin had spoken of those days in the British hospital to no one, nor did he plan to ever do so. But he thought of them often. He was thinking of them as he sat in his wheelchair in the veteran's hospital dayroom when his parents and his wife came in.

"Well, hello," he said. "I'd about given up on you."

Jane bent down and kissed him. "The weather was bad. It made for slow driving. How do you feel?"

"Not too bad. It's raining, but it looks warm outside. Almost planting season. I'd hoped to be home for planting, but the damned leg still isn't working right. Are Jack and Helen with you?"

"No," Katherine said. "They're watching Susan and little Willie at the lake. Henri and Annette went to New York for the week."

"Henri had some business with our New York distributing firm," Liam explained. "With the war in Europe over, business is starting to pick up. We're in the Stork Club now, you should know. Only with champagne, though. They won't touch any New York State dinner wines."

They talked for a half-hour, then Liam and Katherine excused themselves, and Jane and Kevin were left alone. Kevin took her hand as she sat next to him.

"You look terrific," he told her. "Nobody would guess that you just had a baby not very long ago."

"They would if they had a tape measure," Jane said. "I can't fit into any of my old clothes."

"Looks fine to me. I'm looking forward to getting home so I can get a closer look. When did Weingarten say he's going to let me out of here?"

"Not until you're up and around," she told him. "As soon as you're walking."

Kevin frowned deeply. "Christ," he said. "I can't walk. Doesn't he think I'd be walking now if I could?"

"The doctor says there's no reason why you couldn't get around with a brace right now, either with a cane or crutches."

"That's easy for him to say. It's not his leg. All I know is that I can't put the slightest weight on it without the pain knocking me right on my ass."

Jane eyed him coolly. "Is that your plan, then? Do you plan to spend the rest of your life on your ass—sitting in that wheelchair?"

Kevin looked at her in surprise. Then it changed to irritation. "Cut it out," he said curtly. "I'm not in the mood to put up with that sort of thing right now."

"You don't seem to mind much what I have to put up with. You've got me living out there in the middle of nowhere on that lake. I'm stuck with two kids, all by myself. You don't seem to mind that. And now you plan to do what? Come home in a wheelchair?"

"If I do, it's not my fault. Do you think I like it in a wheelchair?"

"You know what?" she said to him. "I think you do. I think you like being babied and pampered. I think you're looking forward to a life of that from me, and if you think that's going to happen, then you're sadly mistaken. You come home to me in a wheelchair, and I'll be out of there so fast it'll make your head spin. I didn't bargain for that, Kevin. I married a whole man."

He glared at her. "You're never going to get a whole man back, Jane. You'd better get used to that idea."

"Listen, that doctor can't figure out why you won't walk, but I know. I know you like nobody else knows you—not even your mother. And don't think that doesn't burn her up, either. Oh, you were the big ball player. And you went off to war to fly in bombers. It never really occurred to you that you could get hurt—that you were just like everybody else. Well, I'm sorry. We're all sorry. But that's the way it is. And I'm telling you, Kevin, if you don't get out of that wheelchair I'll be gone when you get back to Brennan's Point. You believe that, because it's true."

Kevin stared at her, his expression a combination of amazement, anger and pain. "This isn't just some kind of act, is it? You really mean it."

"I mean it," she said coldly. "I love you, Kevin. But I don't love you enough to spend my life pushing your wheelchair around. I don't love anybody that much. You think I ought to be like your mother, taking care of everybody no matter what. Well, sorry. I won't stay with a cripple."

"Jane!" he pleaded. "I can't help it. I can't walk."

Jane stood up. "Then you're on your own, Kevin."

She left without a backward glance. She found Liam and Katherine in the lounge at the end of the hall.

"How did it go?" Katherine asked.

Jane lit a cigarette, her face impassive. "He said he can't do it. I think he's probably right."

Katherine's jaw tightened. "I have to talk to him."

Liam caught her arm, steered her back to him. "No," he said softly. "I think that what had to be said has been said. Now it's up to Kevin. This isn't the time to show softness to him. He has to deal with this in his own way."

Katherine looked up at her husband, into his eyes. Then she buried her face in his chest. Liam held her for a moment as he watched Jane, cigarette in her mouth, wander to the lounge window and stare out into the rain.

* * * *

Liam looked up from his living room chair as Jack and Helen came in the door.

"Look at you," he said to Helen, "the budding madonna."

Helen blushed and smiled. "Hush, Poppy," she said. "I'm hardly even showing."

"You're showing, all right," Liam said, kissing her cheek. "I can see it."

"As can I," Henri piped in. "Of course, being French I notice every small detail of a beautiful woman."

"Henri," Jack said, slipping off his coat, "Charles Boyer has nothing on you. How's Kevin doing?" he asked, settling into the living room with Liam and Henri.

"He's fine," Katherine said, coming into the living room. "He'll be home in another month or two."

"It's true," Liam said. "He's in his wheelchair about half the time, on his feet the other half. The doctor is pleased."

"That's great," Jack said. "Where's Jane, by the way?"

"Down at the shack with the children," Katherine said. "I ought to go down and tell her you're here."

"I'll go," Helen said. "I haven't seen the inside of the shack for a while."

"It's not as neat as it could be," Katherine said. "You be careful going down that hill. There's some ice out there."

"I'll be careful. Jack, tell them about the house."

"You bought a house?" said Henri.

"Well," Jack said, "I'm an assistant production director now. We can afford it. It's a big old barn on Elm Avenue."

Jack described the place while Helen went down the hill to the shack. She found Jane in the living room. Little Willie was asleep, and Susan was playing with dolls in her mother's bedroom. The living room was a disaster, as usual, and Jane was putting on makeup at a tabletop mirror she had erected on the coffee table.

"How are you?" Helen said from the doorway.

Jane looked up. "Oh, hi. Come on in. The place is a mess. I'm sorry. But with a baby and a toddler and a job . . . well, you know."

"I will soon enough, I suppose," said Helen as she sat down. "I can hardly wait."

"You'll love it," Jane said, not enthusiastically. "How are you doing? You look great."

"I'm fine. I'm starting to burst out, and I'm tired all the time. I didn't think it was possible for anybody to have to pee so much."

Jane laughed. "If you think you're tired now, wait until the baby is born. Are you going to breast feed?"

"I haven't decided."

Jane put on rouge, gazing into the mirror. "I never could, you know. Willie is on a bottle. If you breast feed, you can't ever get away, not even for a few hours. Take my advice and don't do it."

"It does sound like a lot of trouble," Helen conceded. Still, . . . how's Kevin?"

"Oh," Jane said, "he's okay. I haven't seen him in a few weeks."

"No? Why not?"

"Well, it's tough to get away from work, and on weekends I've got a lot to do around here. Besides, he hasn't gotten over being mad at me for what I said back in the spring about not being here when he got back if he didn't start to walk."

"Doesn't he know you were just saying it to get him moving?" Helen asked.

Jane put down the eye shadow and looked at Helen. "He thinks I really meant it. Sometimes I think maybe I did, too."

"Oh, stop," Helen said. "Jane, you're being such a pill."

"I suppose I am," Jane said, her voice beginning to grow hoarse.

"You ought to be ashamed of yourself for saying those things—for even thinking them."

"I am ashamed of myself," Jane said, and now she was clearly upset. "But I don't think I'm wrong to want a life, too. I don't have any time for me, Helen. Kids take all your time. And without a husband around, believe me, it's no picnic. If I really thought Kevin would come back here in a wheelchair I couldn't take it."

"Well, he won't," Helen said. "Besides, it wasn't his fault."

Jane was in tears now. "It wasn't my fault, either. I didn't even want him to go away to that damn war. He didn't have to, either, not with a wife and kid. But he didn't care about me. Here I am with two whining, screaming kids living way out here, and my husband is going to come home and drag himself around on crutches—if I'm lucky, that is."

Helen sat down beside her sister-in-law. Jane's painstaking makeup job was ruined. "Come on," she said gently. "Get fixed up again and come up to the house later. I'll take the kids back up with me now so you can have some peace and quiet. You need to be alone for a while and get some rest."

"You're right," Jane wept. "I'm so damn tired."

Five days later, on a Friday morning, Katherine turned to Annette in the kitchen and said, "What time is it now?"

Annette consulted the watch she kept pinned on her apron. "A quarter before the ten," she said. "She is very late this morning, no?"

"Later than ever before," Katherine conceded. "I wonder if that Wright boy overslept."

Annette shook her head. "She would have brought up the children. She must have overslept, too."

Katherine went to the hall closet and got her coat. "Well, I'm going down there and make sure she's up. Those children will be starving."

"I will go with you and carry Willie," Annette announced.

The women made their way down the hill to the shack. The weather at the lake had turned cold, and a stiff breeze blew in off the water. Katherine bundled her coat around her and opened the door. Susan ran to her hysterically.

"Grandma!" she screamed. "Grandma!"

Katherine was overcome by a sense of disaster. She could hear Willie crying in his crib. She picked up the little girl and held her. "My God!" she said. "What's this? Jane? Jane? Susan, Sweetheart. Where's Mommy?"

Susan wept hysterically. "I don't know. I want Mommy."

Annette reached over and stroked the child's hair. "We will find her," Annette said.

Katherine comforted her granddaughter while Annette went into the bedroom. She emerged a moment later, her face ashen.

"Her clothes," Annette said quietly. "They are gone."

"What?" Katherine said. She handed the child to Annette and went into the bedroom. The bureau drawers were open and empty. Katherine threw open the closet. Kevin's clothes were untouched, but all of Jane's were gone, even her shoes. In the bathroom, all Jane's cosmetics were missing. Katherine came back into the living room, her brow furrowed.

"She's gone," she said simply.

Annette's eyes widened. "This cannot be. This must be the mistake."

"There's no mistake," Katherine said coldly.

Susan, hearing the words, began to howl. Katherine went to her and held her. Then she stood the child up on the coffee table.

"Susan," she said sternly, "now listen to me. Was your mommy here last night when you went to bed?"

Susan nodded her head frantically. "Mommy put me to bed. She kissed me goodnight and everything."

"Was she here when you woke up this morning?"

Susan shook her head vigorously from side to side. "No. Willie was crying. That's what woke me up."

"You're sure she wasn't here this morning," Katherine said, hoping against hope.

Susan shook her head.

Katherine turned to Annette. "Let's get them up to the big house. We'll get them settled, then I'm going to the winery and tell Liam."

Annette shook her head in shock. "This must be the mistake."

Katherine gathered up her granddaughter. "The mistake was made a long time ago," she said. "Now it's simply undone itself."

They took both children up the hill to the big house, fighting the wind and the cold. Katherine walked down the road to the winery and found Liam. Quietly, she told him what she had found in the shack. He was dumbfounded.

"Everything was gone?" he said. "You're sure."

"I'm sure, Liam," she told him. "There's no question about what's happened. She apparently left late last night or early this morning, while the children were asleep. She knew I'd go down there this morning if she didn't bring them up to the house on time."

Liam shook his head, dizzy at what had taken place. "But she has no car," he said. "She can't drive anyway. How did she go anywhere?"

Katherine shook her head at his naivete. "Can't you figure it out?" She demanded.

Liam picked up the phone and dialed Tom Allen.

"Hello, Liam," Tom Allen said. "How are you? Missed you at the Elks Tuesday night."

"My leg was bothering me a bit. I figured I'd stay home in front of the fire and read. Tom, is my daughter-in-law in at work today?"

"No," Tom Allen said slowly, sensing something. "She told me yesterday she'd need today off."

"Did she say why?"

"She said one of the children was coming down with something. Is there anything wrong, Liam? Can I be of help in any way?"

Liam looked over at Katherine, who was following the conversation. She closed her eyes and nodded. Liam turned back to the phone.

"Possibly," he said. "Can you tell me if that young Wright fellow is at work today?"

"No," Tom Allen said slowly, "as a matter of fact he's not. I've been expecting him for a while now. He's usually right on time, too."

"Tom, could you give me a call when he comes in?"

"I'd be happy to, Liam. As I said, whatever I can do. Are you at the house or the winery?"

"I'm at the winery now, but I'll be at the house in just a few minutes. You can reach me there. You have the number."

Liam and Katherine walked back to the big house side by side, neither uttering a word. Liam clenched his pipe tightly between his teeth. They went inside, and Susan, smiling now, leaped into Liam's arms. He tossed her in the air. Then he went into the kitchen and found Annette, holding Willie in her arms and crying openly. He was about to say something to her when the phone in the hallway rang. Liam picked it up.

"Hello, Liam. Tom Allen. After you called, I phoned Bob Wright's house. His wife said he went out to play poker last night, and she hasn't seen him since. She said she doesn't expect to see him, and, frankly, neither do I."

Liam sighed. "Thank you, Tom. I appreciate the call."

"Liam," Tom Allen said, "I want you to know that if what I suspect has happened has, in fact, happened, that son-of-a-bitch is finished here. He's out of a job, as of now. More than that, I have a bit of influence in this community—and you know that's true because you have considerable influence yourself—and I'm going to see that he doesn't work anywhere around here. Bob Wright is finished in the lake country, Liam, if that's any help, and I know it's not."

"You're a good friend, Tom. I appreciate it."

Liam hung up the phone and walked back into the kitchen. "The Wright boy is gone, too," he said. "Left his wife and kids."

Katherine's reserve melted. She burst out crying, and Liam took her into his arms. Susan looked on in amazement that grownups could cry.

"My God, Liam," Katherine wept. "How are we going to tell Kevin? How will we ever tell him?"

"I don't know," he said softly. "It never occurred to me that I'd have to go to my wounded son and tell him that his wife has run off with another man and left him with two small children. Of all the things I'd imagined . . ."

Katherine wept bitterly. "He deserves so much better than this. Nobody deserves what's happened to Kevin."

Liam Brennan stroked his wife's gray hair. "What you deserve in life and what you get often bear very little resemblance to one another."

* * * *

Fred Harper had red hair and a ruddy face that turned even redder when he was excited, which he was now.

In the admitting office of the emergency room of Boydstown General he started to turn to his wife for guidance, but then he recalled that she was three sheets to the wind and would be of no conceivable help anyway. Fred turned to Helen instead. He had to talk to somebody, even if it was a woman about to have a baby. "I hate this kind of thing," he said. "I didn't even like it when our kid was born. I'm going to try Jack at home again. If he's not there, Helen, do you have any idea where he might be?"

Helen, awaiting the next pain, shook her head. "What did they say at the plant?"

"They said he left with a bunch of fellows. Nobody knew where he was going."

Helen clenched her teeth as another pain came. Then, as they prepared to wheel her off to the delivery room, she suddenly remembered. "Oh, God," she said. "I know where he is. He's being inducted into the Seagulls tonight."

"The what?" Peg said. She and Helen had been drinking sherry when Helen's pains had begun. Peg had finished the bottle while waiting for Fred.

"The Lost Seagulls of Stockholm. It's a lodge. They meet upstairs over Harry O's."

Fred looked at her. "Is that the bar down on Railroad Avenue? I know that place."

Peg said, "Call down there and see if he's there."

"Hell, no," Fred said, sensing an avenue of escape. "I'll drive down there and pull him out."

Fred was gone in a flash. Harry O's, like everything in Boydstown, was not far away. He found Jack in an upstairs room with forty other men. His jacket was ripped, and his hair disheveled. He looked like he'd been run over by a truck, but he was celebrating.

"What is it?" Jack said when Fred came in, his expression grim.

"You're about to become a daddy," Fred told him.

"Holy shit!" Jack said.

By the time they got back to the hospital, Peg was waiting outside the delivery room.

"You've got a son," she told Jack, and the news was not delivered in particularly warm fashion.

Jack found the doctor.

"He's small," the doctor told him. "Six pounds, four ounces. He's a little premature, but he's fine, and so's Helen. I've had the baby put in an incubator. You can see him if you like."

Jack found his son, and he stared at him for a long time, thinking how his own father would feel if he could see the child. The baby would be named after Jim Ryan. He and Helen had agreed on that in advance. Then he found Helen in the recovery room. She was groggy but—predictably—angry.

"Jack," she mumbled. "I missed you."

He took her hands, kissed them. "How are you feeling?"

"All dopey. They gave me something just before the baby came. He's all right, isn't he? I can't remember for sure."

"He's fine—terrific. It's you I'm worried about right now."

"I'm all right. What happened to you? Your jacket is all ripped. You're dirty."

"I'm a Seagull," he said brightly. "I got inducted just before Fred found me. That's some ceremony, believe me."

"You look like a bum. What did they do to you?"

"I can't tell you," Jack said. "It's a secret ceremony."

Helen began to cry.

*　*　*　*

William Stewart, Liam's lawyer for thirty years, stuck his head through the door.

"She's here, Kevin," he said, "with her lawyer."

Henri, Kevin and Liam were sitting in a conference room in Stewart's offices in Lakeside. Like all offices in the village, it was modest. All three men wore suits and ties. A crutch rested next to Kevin's chair. The thick, stainless-steel brace that ran up his left leg from ankle to crotch was not visible.

"Send them in," Liam said.

Stewart came in the room and shut the door behind him. Since he and Liam had met on the deck of the shack after the *Iroquois Queen* disaster, Bill Stewart had gone bald and gained fifty pounds. His youth had vanished; his innate caution remained. "I've been talking to her lawyer," he said. "She's asked if she and Kevin can speak privately. Her lawyer and I both recommend it."

"Why?" Liam snapped.

"There are items to be worked out," Bill Stewart said quietly.

Kevin said, "I'll talk to her, Pop. Don't worry. Nothing terrible is going to happen to me."

Liam, red faced, stood up, and Henri rose to stand next to him. "It's already happened," Liam said. "Henri and I will be outside."

The older men left through the only door into the room. As Liam passed Jane in the outer office, he paralyzed her with a glare. Jane dropped her eyes. Then she entered the room and found Kevin sitting in a chair along the far wall. He was smoking a cigar. She closed the door behind her.

"You look good," she said. "You're thinner."

"I've lost some of the weight I put on in the hospital. Climbing up and down the hill is good exercise, especially on one leg."

Jane sat down on the far side of the conference table. Kevin eyed her in silence. "When did they let you out?"

"Right after you . . . uh . . . decided to leave. My parents came and told me one morning. Then, that night, I saw one of the nurses look at me and suddenly start crying. Like a fool, I thought she was crying because she felt sorry for me. So I decided to get the hell out of there the very next day. It wasn't until after I'd called down to Lakeside for somebody to come and get me that I found out the nurse had been crying because Roosevelt had died that afternoon. It was one more reminder that the world doesn't revolve around me. It also reminded me that being a cripple doesn't have to keep you from standing on your own two feet, so to speak."

Jane said, "Kevin, I'd give anything if all this hadn't happened. I seem to leave a path of ruin wherever I go. It's always been a talent of mine, I guess."

"Fine, fine," he broke in. "We're in agreement on that. I should never have married you."

"Don't cut me off like that, please," she said. "Look, I know you hate me. You have a right to—"

"I don't hate you, Jane," he broke in again. "I'd say I pity you, but that sounds so trite. The fact is, though, that I understand you. And I just can't seem to muster any regard for you—not knowing you the way I do."

Kevin leaned forward over the table. "There's something in you," he said, "some deep-seated revulsion you have for yourself, that's going to chew you up. You seem to have this uncontrollable urge to make yourself dirty, like a little kid dressed in his best clothes. And you absolutely insist on getting dirty, no matter who gets hurt, no matter how hard the people around you try to keep you clean. You're not happy unless you're unhappy, and I know that what prompted you to pick up and run wasn't what happened to me. It would have happened sooner or later, even if I'd never gone off to war. You're going to keep on doing things like this until something terrible happens to you or until you just fall apart. You're going to end up completely alone and real dirty somewhere, and then you'll finally have what you want." He sat back in his chair, and the silence hung between them like a cloud.

"Meanwhile," he said, "the reason we're here is to find out what you want now. What's the purpose of this family reunion we're having?"

"I want to marry Bob."

Kevin smiled. "That could be tricky. You already have a husband, remember?"

She looked at him, her gaze even. "I want a divorce, Kevin. Bob's wife has already agreed."

He nodded and lit a cigar. "There's only one ground for divorce in this state, my dear, in case you aren't aware of it."

"I'm aware of it," she said. "Adultery."

He leaned forward over the table. "And you're willing to go into court and announce that you're an adulteress? You are, as we both know, but it's one thing to live like a whore and another thing entirely to proclaim yourself as such in an open courtroom, in front of the whole world."

She flushed visibly. Then she lowered her eyes. "I . . . I was hoping that you would do it."

"Do what?"

"That you would say you'd committed adultery," she said in a voice so low he could barely make out the words.

Kevin sat for a moment in stunned silence. Then he burst out laughing. God, he thought, how Willie Farrington would have loved this. Talk about absurd.

"Me?" he said. "I can hardly walk, much less screw. Who's going to believe it? You can ask the nurses at the veterans hospital. I was a perfect gentleman all the time." He clenched the cigar between his teeth. "Forget it, Jane."

Jane was sure she was going to cry. "Kevin, please. I love him. He loves me."

Kevin frowned. "He might be foolish enough to love you. Nobody in the Wright family was ever very bright. But you don't love anybody but yourself. Here's the perfect chance to smear yourself with mud. I should think you'd leap at it."

"Stop it!" she shouted suddenly. Then she lowered her voice, which was trembling. "I can't stand it. Please, stop. Oh, Kevin. I couldn't help this. Honestly, I couldn't. You can call me anything you want, and I'll deserve every word. Only, don't keep me a prisoner. Let me go, for God's sake. I'm gone already. I do feel dirty, if it makes you feel any happier to hear me say it. I'll never feel clean again for leaving you. I kept asking myself, If you can't stay with him when he's hurt so badly, then what are you good for? And I don't have any answer for that. But please don't keep punishing me."

He stood up then, grabbed his crutch and began hobbling around the room, his face bright red. "It's not just me," he snarled at her. "You left your children." He leaned over the table, until his face was only inches from hers. "How can a mother leave her children? Tell me that?"

She turned her face away. "That's my punishment, too, isn't it? All they're ever going to know about me is what you tell them—you and your mother. Isn't that enough revenge for you? Kevin, you can despise me because I'm not strong enough to be what I honestly tried to be. But please—if you believe in God and his mercy—let me go."

Kevin Brennan sat down. He felt drained and weak, and his heart was pounding in his ears. He took a moment to collect himself. Then he said, "There are conditions . . ."

"What are they?" she asked.

He looked at her. "You can never use the Brennan name in any way. Before I put my name on any divorce document, I want every scrap of paper that links you to the Brennan family. I want every letter, every photograph. I especially want any picture of the kids you might have in your possession. When the cord is cut, I want every tangible piece of cloth or paper that ties you in any way to me and mine. That, incidentally, includes your wedding dress. That'll go right on top of the bonfire on the beach."

She looked at him, stunned by the depth of his hurt and anger, and yet knowing that she should not be.

"Oh," he added, "and by the way, not one nickel. You'll have to sign a waiver to any and all financial settlements. Understood?"

Jane Fellows Brennan sat motionless for a long moment. Then she said, "You really hate me, don't you."

"If you were me, what would your feelings be?"

Unexpectedly, she smiled. "If I'd been like you, this would never have happened, would it?"

Chapter 16

Jimmy Ryan's favorite program, "TV Ranch Club," came on every afternoon at four from WNBF in Binghamton. The show consisted of a local announcer dressed in jeans and a western shirt who did lead-ins for old western movies that dated back before the war. Jimmy, who was a great fan of Roy Rogers and who, in fact, owned the largest collection of Roy Rogers cowboy clothing and toys on the block, had become almost equally enamored of the more obscure adventures of such cowboy heros as Don "Red" Berry, Bob Steele and Lash Larue, not to mention Wild Bill Elliott, who wore his guns backwards.

After "TV Ranch Club," Jimmy would watch the "Mickey Mouse Club," which featured ancient cartoons and a bunch of kids wearing sweatshirts with their names printed across the front and little beanies with mouse ears attached. He could barely tolerate the cartoons, but he liked the serials. He delighted in the adventures of Spin and Marty and their friends at the Triple-R Ranch. He followed avidly the trials of the Hardy boys, who were enmeshed in unraveling a mystery at the nearby Applegate estate. He was entranced by the white German shepherd who starred in "The Adventures of Corky and White Shadow," although he thought the freckle-faced girl who played Corky overacted.

Jimmy Ryan was a quiet, bookish boy with a rich fantasy life and a touch of asthma. He was good in school, an avid reader of Tarzan books and Lone Ranger and Straight Arrow comics and the proud possessor of a Red Ryder Model Daisy B-B gun. He shoveled the walk at every snowfall, carried the empty garbage cans around back every week, rode fearlessly all around Boydstown's north side on his twenty-four-inch Huffy bicycle with the chrome fenders and slept restlessly at night in a small bedroom decorated in a western motif and distinguished by a small door leading to an attic that Jimmy suspected housed a monster.

He knew that President Eisenhower had been an important soldier a million years before, that Patti Page couldn't sing as well as his mother

and that the most beautiful and enjoyable place on earth was Brennan's
Point, where his mother's parents and his Uncle Kevin and his Uncle
Henri and his Aunt Annette and his cousins Susan and Willie lived on
Iroquois Lake. They had a gorgeous boat and a barn full of cats to whom
Jimmy was fiercely allergic. Jimmy caught sunfish off the dock, and his
grandmother and Aunt Annette cleaned them and fried them in butter
for him.

He had a little sister named Patricia, whom he considered a great
nuisance and whom he tortured at every opportunity. He brutalized her
dolls, called her names and tickled her until she cried. He was also fiercely
protective of her when they played outside, willing to lay down his life
to guard her against a wandering mean dog or the rough attentions of
the bigger kids in the neighborhood.

He came home one dreary January afternoon from the Nicholas O'D.
Lederer Elementary School a block away. He whipped through his two
pages of arithmetic (his best subject) and three pages of spelling while
his mother lay sleeping in the big downstairs bedroom and Patricia sat
at the kitchen table, humming and babbling blissfully to herself as she
scribbled in a coloring book. When he had finished his work, Jimmy
settled down in front of the television set in the pink-walled living room
for another half-hour session of "TV Ranch Club." He was deeply involved
in the movie when he heard from the kitchen in the rear of the house
a sound that approximated the falling of a tree. It was an immense crash
that rattled the windows. Jimmy Ryan leaped to his feet, deserting Rocky
Lane and his horse Blackjack, and rushed to the source of the disturbance,
which was also the source of a sudden, anguished wail from his obnoxious
little sister.

Helen Ryan, her hair plastered in tight little curls to her head with
the bobby pins she had worn to bed the previous night, sat on the kitchen
floor in her pajamas and robe in a pile of broken china. Her eyes were
glazed, and she looked around, confused. She struggled to rise, made it
part way up then fell back on the floor with a thump. Jimmy was terrified.
"Mom!" he cried out. "Are you all right?"

Jimmy put his hand on his mother's arm to help her up, and as he
did he was treated to a blast of Helen's wine-drenched breath.

"I'm all right," she told him thickly. "I jus' tripped."

Jimmy helped Helen up, and Patricia, still sitting at the kitchen table,
decided that the emergency was under control. She went back to humming
and scribbling in her coloring book. Jimmy was still shaken. "You broke
a plate," he said.

Helen, leaning against the sink, reached out and pulled the little boy to her. She hugged him tightly. "I didn't get hurt. Don't worry. Were you afraid I hurt myself?"

"Yes," the boy said shakily.

Helen hugged him more tightly. "You love me, don't you?"

Jimmy and Patricia answered in unison: "Uh-huh."

Helen bent down and awkwardly kissed the little boy's forehead. "I love you, too. I'm fine now. You pick up the pieces of the plate and throw it away for me. Don't cut yourself. I'm going to make supper in a minute. I want to go into the bathroom first and see if I have a bruise."

Helen lurched unsteadily into the downstairs bathroom, and Jimmy Ryan carefully picked up every shard of the broken plate and deposited it in the waste basket under the sink. Then, the crisis over, he went back into the living room and was in ten seconds once again caught up in the western, the incident forgotten. Patricia joined him, and the two of them sat on the floor in front of the TV set, lost to the world. About forty-five minutes later, as the Mouseketeers were singing "Why? Because we *like* you . . ." Jack Ryan came in the door from work.

"Hi," he said.

Jimmy, caught up in his program, merely waved in his father's general direction. Patricia said nothing. Jack frowned slightly. This was his usual greeting. Sometimes he wished he'd never bought the goddamn television.

"What are you watching?" Jack Ryan asked his children.

"Mouse," Patricia said.

"She means 'Mickey Mouse Club'," Jimmy explained.

"Where's your mother?"

"She went in the bathroom," Jimmy said. "She fell down in the kitchen."

Jack Ryan's eyebrows rose slightly. "Oh?"

He walked to the back of the house. Moments later, Jimmy heard his parents shouting in the kitchen. He got to his feet, and Patricia followed suit.

"Stay here or I'll bash you," Jimmy ordered.

Patricia sat back down as Jimmy moved cautiously into the dining room up to the kitchen door. Jack Ryan, still wearing his navy blue overcoat and gray fedora, was standing at the sink, pouring a bottle of wine down the drain. Jimmy's mother, still in her pajamas and her hair still imprisoned in the bobby pins, sat at the kitchen table, her face contorted with anger. "You goddamn fool!" Helen was shouting. "That's no way to treat me. That won't get you anything."

"It'll get you sober," Jack Ryan told his wife.

"I'll get more. You make me sick."

"This is what makes you sick," he told her, holding up the empty bottle before throwing it into the garbage. "You've got two children in there to take care of, and look at you."

"And you've got a wife to take care of," she shot back. "But you're too busy off being the big shot, aren't you? You're not here to keep this place clean. You're not here to do the cooking. You don't do a goddamn thing around here. I do it all."

"I bring home the money."

"And what do you do with it, huh? They called from the phone company this morning. The check bounced. They're going to shut off the phone. How about that, big shot production director?"

Jack Ryan's face was impassive beneath his gray fedora. "Well," he said more quietly, "there's some screw-up on that. I'll have to get that squared away with the bank."

"That's right," Helen Ryan sneered, "you get it squared away, big shot. You pour out my wine, and you get it squared away. But that won't make me love you, you little slob. You make me sick. You make me want to puke."

Jack Ryan spotted Jimmy in the doorway. "Go back in the living room," he ordered crisply. "Your mother and I are talking."

Jimmy moved into the living room like a shot and out the door, and then he was running in the cold without a jacket, up the street, down another, his legs pumping, the wind in his face, running, running until his breath gave out, until his asthma kicked in and then he was leaning against a huge elm tree, choking for breath. He sank down onto the icy ground, his skin scraped through his thin shirt against the rough bark of the tree. He gasped and wheezed for several minutes, tears pouring from his eyes.

Then, after a while, when he could breathe again, Jimmy Ryan walked back home.

* * * *

Kevin had begun his affair with Becky Ralston the night that Vinnie, her husband, had gotten so drunk at the annual Elks dinner that he couldn't be trusted to drive his new MG-TC home. Becky had cursed herself because she'd never learned to handle a standard transmission. Furious and embarrassed, she had asked Kevin if he would mind driving them both home, and Kevin had said he wouldn't mind at all.

The three of them had gotten into one of the big, navy blue Buick Roadmasters Kevin bought every three years, and by the time they pulled out of the Elks parking lot Vinnie had passed out cold in the back seat.

Becky, looking over at her husband from the front seat, said, "Why don't we take him down to the village dock and throw him in the lake?"

"He might drown," Kevin said.

"Wouldn't that be a shame."

They drove up the hill toward the house that Becky had inherited from her father, Spencer King, the dentist. Becky had short, dark red hair and a slightly underslung jaw that kept her from being a genuine beauty. But in early middle age she had style and poise and had retained the stunning figure that had made her such a spirited object of adolescent lust in high school, where Kevin had been two years behind her. After she went off to college in the Midwest no one was particularly surprised when she came back after her senior year with a husband. That was Vinnie—big, good-looking Vinnie, who had opened and closed several businesses over the years. The businesses had failed because Vinnie had been pegged early on as a blowhard and a snob and nobody in Lakeside had any particular interest in doing business with him. So, in rapid succession, he had gone through an insurance agency, a financial consulting firm, a marina out on the lake, a John Deere dealership and a restaurant that had served bad food at inflated prices. Now he was part owner of a food distributorship in Maryland. He spent three days out of every week in Bethesda watching his investment and chasing women.

Which was fine with Becky, as everyone in town knew. What no one knew was why she stayed with him. It certainly wasn't for family considerations. Becky's parents were long dead, and, thanks to an overanxious gynocologist in Rochester, she and Vinnie had no children. The doctor had performed a complete hysterectomy on her that Billy Frazier had privately assured Kevin had been totally unnecessary. The matter had been resolved with a malpractice suit that had only brought Becky and Vinnie more money, which they didn't need.

As the car pulled into the driveway of the old King family house, Becky said, "I'm afraid you're going to have to help me get him inside. I can't handle him myself."

Between the two of them, they had managed to drag Vinnie up the front porch, up the stairs and deposit him on his bed. Vinnie weighed over 200 pounds, and they were both puffing. He lay there in his plaid sport coat and snored loudly. Kevin and Becky went back downstairs. She offered him a beer, which he accepted. They sat at the kitchen table and talked.

"I don't think I've ever been in this house before," he told her.

"I've been in your house dozens of times. Not for years, though, not since Helen got married."

"Well, that's a long time, then. You ought to come out and stop by, Becky. I know my parents would like to see you."

She had looked at him. "How about you, Kevin? Would you like to see me?"

Kevin picked up the signal instantly, and was both startled and pleased. "What should I make of that?" he asked her flatly.

"How long since you've slept with a woman?"

Kevin laughed. "You're actually beginning to shock me, Becky."

"But you're still here."

"Yes. I'm still here. Now, the next logical question is—if this is the sort of thing you've got on your mind—why now and why me?"

She lit a cigarette. "Kevin, I've known you ever since I can remember. I had a terrible crush on you in high school, even though you were younger. I've been married nearly twenty years to a man I can't stand— a man nobody in town can stand. He has a woman in Maryland, and she's only the latest in a long string, although he's had enough sense somehow to behave himself in Lakeside. I've thought for a long time about how satisfying it would be to betray him, and I find myself tonight sitting with you in my own house while he's so drunk upstairs that he'd sleep through a nuclear explosion. Does that answer your question?"

"Yes," he said quietly, "it does."

"Now, answer mine. How long since you've been in bed with a woman?"

"The last time was in the McAlpin Hotel in New York City in 1944," he told her honestly. "June 12, to be precise, from roughly 11:15 until 12:30. Since then, I've just read a lot late at night."

"Good God," Becky King Ralston said.

Neither of them had ever before made love in a kitchen, but from the moment they embraced and their mouths met it was clear that they lacked the patience to make it to the living room sofa. He undressed her, marveling at the startling stiffness of her nipples and the compelling dark tuft at the bottom of her belly. She was stripped, however, not only of her clothing but also of her restraints. She had wanted Kevin for twenty-five years, and he had imagined a moment like this since the sixth grade. The fact that they looked ridiculous doing this in the kitchen and the presence of Becky's husband, snoring drunkenly on the floor above, inhibited neither of them.

Kevin's brace was a complication. He couldn't stand without it, and that limited the method of their coupling in such a setting. They pondered the problem for a moment as they groped at one another. Finally, Becky broke away from him and lay back across the heavy oaken tabletop.

Kevin, trousers around his ankles, stood next to the table and brought her legs up over his shoulders.

"I wish I had a picture of this," Becky said, grinning despite the excitement she felt.

"I can do a lot of things when I'm laughing," Kevin said, laughing despite himself, "but not this."

When he entered her, though, all humor ceased. They matched one another with stroke and counterstroke. They moved in utter harmony, each throb, each shuddering pause, each murmured endearment in perfect rhythm, a symphony they played together. Neither were children. They knew what to do for one another. In the end, when Kevin drove into Becky at the final moment and he felt her drawing the life from him, he could also feel the table shake precariously beneath them.

Then he gasped and leaned over her, feeling her tighten her legs around him. He kissed her gently. She smiled at him, her expression a combination of sexual abandon and mirth.

"This table," Kevin said hoarsely. "Where can I get one like it for Brennan's Point?"

Thereafter, on virtually every night Vinnie was out of town, Kevin visited Becky in the big white house on the hill overlooking the village. Often, they went to a restaurant in Rochester or Geneva first, and then they came back to her house. Several times in that first year they had been spotted by mutual acquaintances, and their affair became gossip in Lakeside. There was no doubt in either of their minds that Vinnie was well aware of their liaison, and he did nothing because he was so fond of the King money.

Kevin had often asked her why she stayed married to Vinnie, but Becky was a cool and self-possessed woman who would say only that she would wait for a better offer. Vinnie was in the habit, once or twice a year, of drinking too much and lashing out at her unexpectedly with a blow. Kevin had offered to take action on her behalf, but she had adamantly refused to permit him to intervene.

As they were both aware, their relationship was built upon sexual attraction, friendship and a mutual need for human companionship. Occasionally, she would tell him she loved him, and he would tell her the same. But these remarks came as part of the love-making ritual, and neither asked for reaffirmation when the lovemaking was through. Kevin discussed his relationship with Becky with no one, not even Billy Frazier nor Becky. He wasn't sure whom she talked to, although he suspected it was probably Lily Johnstone Stabler, who lived in Rochester with her husband, the principal of a junior high school.

"Sometimes I think we're too old for this," he told her one night as they lay in bed.

"Speak for yourself," she told him, "you're never too old to be in love."

"Is that what we are?" Kevin asked her. "Are we in love?"

She snuggled close to him. "Whatever it is, it's close enough for me."

* * * *

"How are the Yankees doing?" Liam asked as he entered the living room.

"It's four to three at the top of the sixth, Mr. Brennan," Art Dixon said. "The Yankees are on top."

Liam squinted at the set. He'd left his glasses upstairs. "Who's that pitching for the Yankees?"

"Whitey Ford," Art said, "but they're starting to hit him now. I think Stengel is going to take him out pretty soon."

As Art spoke, a Cleveland Indian drove a Ford curve ball high into center field, and a runner scored from second on the fly ball.

"I'd say," Liam said, and sat down.

They watched the rest of the inning in silence. Ford pitched himself out of trouble, and Liam watched the game out of one eye and Art out of the other. Another one, he thought. Liam, it sometimes seemed, had spent most of his adult life studying boys who came around to see his women.

This boy was a burly nineteen-year-old who had begun dating Susan the previous year, when both were students at Lakeside Free Academy. This mild July day in 1957 marked Art's first Sunday dinner with the Brennans. Susan had said that Art was usually outgoing, even rowdy, but on this extended visit to the Brennan household he apparently had held himself in check, listening quietly, laughing genuinely when it was called for and eating enough for two grown men.

Art Dixon was the youngest of three children from a working-class family in the village. His father was a machinist at Allen Mills. Art was acutely aware that the girl he was dating was from an established and, by the standards of the community, relatively well-off family. He was determined this first time in their midst for any length of time to make a good impression.

Art had the confidence that usually comes with being a good athlete and one of the more important figures in his high school. Susan, only a freshman at the time, had been ecstatic when Art Dixon, a senior and one of the school's in-crowd, had been attracted to her. Now, a year later, she was not at all deterred from netting him on a permanent basis by the fact that too little money and no decent offers of a football scholarship had kept him from going to college. Art would do all right, Susan knew. He had what it took, college or no college. Susan Brennan had every intention of marrying Art Dixon a few years down the road. He just didn't know it yet.

As the Indians were retired by a weary Whitey Ford, Liam said, "Well Art, now that you're out of school, have you figured out what you're going to be doing with yourself?"

Art shrugged. "I've got a job at Mike Wright's trucking company for the summer, and he'd like me to make it permanent. I'm just doing some maintenance work on the trucks right now, but Mike said he'd teach me the business."

Liam nodded. He couldn't recall just which of the many branches of the Wright family was represented by Mike Wright; there were Wrights all over Lakeside.

"Trucking is a good business, I suppose," Liam said, "what with the railroads going all to hell. We're shipping more and more wine by truck. You can't count on a good schedule with the trains any more."

"My father would be spinning in his grave if he knew," Jack said, entering the living room. "Have you seen Helen, by the way?"

Liam said, "When I went upstairs, she was in the kitchen with her mother and Annette cleaning up the last of the dishes."

"Susan is out there, too," Art said. "I think I'll go out and see if they need any help."

Jack laughed. "if you ever get married, you'll have a lot of opportunity to do dishes. Watch the ballgame while you can."

"Oh, I don't mind. My mom makes my brothers and me work in the kitchen all the time."

Art wandered off toward the kitchen just as a beer commercial came on television. Jack, who had had little opportunity to talk to his father-in-law all day, said, "So how have you been, Liam?"

"Oh, fine. I'm getting lazy in retirement. Billy Frazier says he'd like to see me take off forty pounds or so. Blood pressure. You know, I had that little stroke a few years back."

"You ought to listen to him," Jack said. "Blood pressure is nothing to fool around with. Helen's tends to run a bit high, too."

Liam nodded. "It's in the family. But she's young. I watch the salt, you know. That's the killer, the damned salt. How's business?"

"Good, actually. I keep thinking the bottom's going to fall out, but things are going great guns. We're putting on extra shifts. It's almost enough to make me vote Republican next time."

"Not likely," Liam snorted. "You're a dyed-in-the-wool Dimmycrat, just like Kevin."

Jack laughed. "I thought you said once that you'd voted for Roosevelt."

"Only once, the last time. The only Dimmycrat I would have voted for last time around was Kennedy, and they didn't have the sense to give him the nomination."

"Because he's a Catholic."

"And Irish," Liam added.

Henri came in from the dining room and sat down. "I am never playing cards with that boy again."

Liam chuckled. "Beat you, did he?"

"Brutally. Now, thank God, he's gone down to the basement to gloat, I'm sure. Kevin's son—your grandson, Liam—he has no respect for his elders."

After a while Jimmy Ryan came in. He was twelve now, small and wiry like his father and more pensive and withdrawn than Jack liked, although he was sure the boy would grow out of it.

"Where's your mother?" Jack asked him.

"She said she was going down to the beach for a swim."

"Alone?"

"I think so."

Henri said, "A fairly cold night for a swim."

"Ah," Liam said, "Helen is used to cold water. Don't forget, she grew up on this lake. She used to go swimming in April. I get blue in the lips just thinking about it."

"You're sure she went down alone?" Jack asked his son.

"Yeah."

Jack watched the game for a moment, his face grim. Then he turned to Jimmy, who was standing in the doorway. "Why don't you get your suit on and go down with her? She shouldn't be swimming alone in the dark."

Jimmy would swim anytime, anywhere. "Sure," he said, and quickly rushed upstairs to get into his bathing suit. Then he shot downstairs, a towel around his shoulders and into the kitchen, where he dived into the refrigerator for a coke to take to the beach.

Katherine, sitting at the table with Annette, Art and Susan, said, "And where do you think you're going, young man?"

"Down to the beach."

Katherine shook her head. "Not by yourself this time of night, you're not. Go get Willie to go with you."

Jimmy said, "He's down in the basement with Patricia showing her how to make model planes. I won't be alone, Grandma. Mom is down there. Dad said I could go."

"Your mother went down there?"

Jimmy nodded vigorously. "That's right. Dad said I could go."

"All right, then," Katherine said. "Go ahead."

Jimmy rushed from the room. Katherine heard the screen door slam. Annette was telling Art and Susan about life in Bordeaux when she had been a girl, and Katherine listened with only half an ear. Strange, she thought, that Helen should go off to the beach without mentioning it. Finally she stood up. "I think I'll go down to the beach for a while and watch Jimmy and Helen swim."

Annette shivered at the thought. "It's cold out there, Katherine."

"I'll put on a sweater."

Susan said, "do you want me to go with you?"

Katherine shook her head. "I think I can find my way. I've been walking up and down that hill for better than forty years now."

Forty years notwithstanding, Jimmy Ryan had the advantage over Katherine. He'd been going up and down the hill at a dead run for as long as he could remember, and tonight was no exception. The moon was a quarter full, and it threw only the dimmest light on the path, but Jimmy's bare feet knew every inch of the hillside. He shot down it as though it were high noon. He crossed the road and scampered lightly down the steps next to the vacant shack, his coke clutched in his hand and his towel snug across his bare shoulders.

At the bottom of the steps, he took off for the point, just barely visible against the black water. He could see Helen near the dock. As his feet crunched on the shale beach he could see her move, startled, and reach for her beachbag, jamming something into it. He was at her side in just a moment, and he saw her sitting on a beach chair, a towel wrapped around her torso.

"God, you scared me!" Helen shouted. "What are you doing down here in the dark?"

Jimmy laughed. "Dad said I could go swimming with you."

"Then go ahead. Just don't scare me like that."

Ordinarily, Jimmy would have been attuned enough to the rhythms and cadences of his mother's voice to realize that she was drunk. But the prospect of immersing himself in the inky lake had distracted him, and he had missed the slur to her words. As he disappeared off the end of the dock with a great splash, Helen pulled her bottle of sherry from her beachbag, unscrewed the top and took a long pull from it. Jimmy came up fifteen feet from the end of the dock in water ten feet deep.

"Whoo!" he called out. "It's cold as ice."

"The hell with it, then," Helen muttered, stuffing the bottle back into the bag.

Jimmy swam to the dock. "What?"

"Who gives a good goddamn?" Helen said.

Jimmy Ryan climbed up the ladder on the dock and, dripping in the fifty-degree night air, glared at his mother as she sat in her beach chair. He stood there a long moment, eying her.

"You're drunk," he announced.

"Oh, shut up," Helen said. "Mind your business."

Jimmy Ryan was furious. It was one thing for Helen to get drunk in their house back in Boydstown, far away from the prying eyes of Jimmy's friends and from the attention of Poppy and Grandma and the others. Here, it was something else entirely. He was enraged. "You're drunk!" he screamed at her. "I'm going to tell Dad."

"Go to hell," his mother said to him.

Dripping and shivering, Jimmy came in off the dock. Helen glared at him venomously. Before she could react, Jimmy had her beach bag in his hand. Helen grabbed for it, but the boy jumped back nimbly. "Give me that," she hissed.

Jimmy laughed. "It's in here, isn't it? Is this where your bottle is?" He reached in, dug it out, discarded the bag and held up the bottle of sherry. There was less than an inch of ruby liquid left. "Here it is! Here it is! Hah-hah!"

Helen lurched up unsteadily from the chair. "You think you're so clever, don't you? Just like that little bastard up in the house."

Jimmy responded with the words he had heard his father utter when confronted with a similar circumstance. He responded through rage and frustration and panic. "You're useless!" he shrieked at his mother on the shadowy beach, with the water lapping peacefully on the shore behind him. "You're as useless as tits on a bull. You're . . . You're rotten!"

Helen, her face set in her characteristic expression when the alcohol had numbed her brain and her facial muscles, lurched forward unsteadily. She fell heavily on her stomach, hitting the beach with aloud "Oof!"

It was then that Katherine stepped forward into the moon's pale light. Her face was a mask of misery, a study in despair. "Oh, Helen," she got out. "Oh, my dear God!"

Jimmy turned toward the sound, his eyes wide. He was stunned. His grandmother had heard him say "tits." He had to explain. He had to make Grandma understand. "She's drunk, Grandma," he said, the nearly empty bottle still in his hand. He held it up. "See, I've got her bottle."

Helen crawled to her knees. "I don't care," she rasped out. "There's more where that came from. Nobody can tell me what to do. Not you, not him. Nobody can tell me what to do." She climbed to her feet, stood there, swaying. A distant look came over her face. "I'm going swimming," she announced.

And she did. She staggered past Jimmy, who danced back thinking she was going for the bottle. But Helen, a large-boned woman despite her trimness, lumbered awkwardly into the lake. She hit the shallows, put her foot on the wet stones and went down hard, splashing and screaming unintelligibly.

Katherine, tears streaming down her face, said, "Jimmy, please get your mother up before she hurts herself."

Jimmy dropped the bottle and ran into the water. He was smaller than his mother, but he was strong. He half-carried, half-pulled her from the water while she raved and grunted, her arms flapping wildly. Katherine joined them at the water line and wrapped Helen in the blanket the younger woman had left next to her beach chair. Weeping, she wrapped her arms around her stepdaughter and drew her close.

"I'll show that bastard," Helen said, gasping for air. She reached up one arm and pointed a shaky finger at her son. "And that little bastard, too. I'll show both of them."

Jimmy, as horrified at the sight of his grandmother's tears as he was inured to the sight of his mother's drunkenness, said, "I'm going to go get Dad."

Katherine looked up, her sense of order taking over. "Only your father," she ordered crisply. "Don't tell anybody else—especially Poppy, do you hear?"

Jimmy nodded. "Yes, Grandma." He reached down to the beach, retrieved the bottle of sherry and handed it to his grandmother. "I'll leave this with you so she can't get it."

Then he was off in the darkness. She looked at the bottle in her hand, and she threw it as far as she could. She heard it smash on the rocks down the beach. Katherine wrapped both her arms around Helen, drawing the drunken woman near her. She stroked the long, golden hair, soaked now and in disarray, trying to smooth it.

"Dear God, Helen," Katherine said. "What's happened to you? You were the most beautiful girl who ever lived. You had everything anybody could want."

"It's that no-good bastard I married," Helen said, bursting into tears now. "I wouldn't drink if it weren't for that asshole."

By the time Jack Ryan appeared on the beach with Jimmy at his side, Helen had passed out on the shale, and Katherine was sitting next to her, stroking her hair and weeping silently. Jack saw them in the dim light, and he dropped to a squat next to them. Katherine looked up at him, her eyes filled with tears behind her rimless glasses. "I don't want Liam to see her like this," she said to Jack, pleading. "Drive your car down to the point. We can load her into it and you can get her home."

Jimmy said, "I'll get Patricia."

"Don't let anybody know!" Katherine ordered him sharply.

"I won't," the boy said. He disappeared up the hill.

"I'll get the car," Jack said.

He brought his Ford down the road near the gully, his headlights blazing, and parked it a few feet away. He and Katherine dragged Helen to the vehicle and got her into the back seat. Jack closed the door and turned to his mother-in-law. "Are you all right, Katherine?"

She shook her head, the tears flowing freely. "How long has she been like this?"

"Years, now," Jack told her. "She'll go months without any problem, then something like this will happen. I never thought she'd do it here, though. This one really caught me by surprise. I'm sorry you had to see this, Katherine."

"What are you going to do?"

"I wish I knew. I didn't want to lay this on your shoulders. I'd never have brought her here today if I'd anticipated this."

"What about the children?" Katherine asked him.

"They're used to it. They know how to live with it a lot better than I do."

Katherine shook her head. "Not Jimmy. I heard him talking to her. Jack, you have to do something."

He held out his arms in a gesture of hopelessness. "What can I do? Divorce her? What happens to her then? You know where she'd go? Right here. Do you want this going on in front of Liam? In front of Henri and Annette? Do you want to see something like this happen in front of Kevin and his kids?"

Katherine had no answer, and she had no time to formulate one. Jimmy and Patricia came down the steps to the beach. Jack turned to them. "Patricia, get in front," he said. "Jimmy, you get in back with your mother in case she wakes up. I don't want her falling out while the car is moving."

The kids crawled into the car in their appointed places as Katherine watched, still in shock. "Are you both okay?" she asked them.

"Sure, Grandma," Patricia said cheerfully. "We're fine."

Jack looked at Katherine. "See? It's a way of life with them. I'll be in touch, Katherine."

He climbed in behind the wheel, and Katherine looked into the car. Helen was wrapped in the blanket, her eyes closed. She lay crosswise on the seat. Jimmy sat next to her in his wet bathing suit with his towel wrapped around his shoulders. Helen was snoring.

"Take care of her," Katherine said to Jack.

"I try."

The Ford went up the road, its headlights illuminating the bank. Jack stopped at the main road, took a right and then they were gone.

Katherine stayed on the beach for nearly an hour. When she climbed the hill to the house, Art Dixon had departed, Henri and Annette had gone up to their house on the hillside and Kevin was on his slow and painful way upstairs.

"Good night, Mother," Kevin said.

"Good night."

Leaning on his cane, Kevin looked down at her from the landing. "Are you okay?"

Katherine looked up at her son and smiled broadly. "Fine," she said.

Kevin went on upstairs. Katherine found Liam asleep in his chair in the living room, his jaw agape, his glasses still in place. She turned off the television set, then shook her husband. Liam stirred. He slept deeply these days. It would take a minute or two to wake him and lead him to bed.

I can tell him that Jack and Helen went home after he fell asleep, she thought. She stroked her husband's brow.

Yes, she thought, I can make that story hold up.

* * * *

By 1959, the year Liam Brennan celebrated his seventy-first birthday, the winery had grown to more than seventeen employees, counting Liam, Henri and Kevin.

Brennan's Point now produced no crops except wine grapes. All the Brennan and Weidener wines were estate bottled—produced with grapes grown on the property. The winery was producing champagne, Johannisberg Riesling, Chardonnay, Chablis, Rhine wine, Vin Rose, Gewürztraminer and several sherrys. Henri was also turning out a variety of other wines with names and pedigrees unique to Brennan's Point.

The winery also produced several reds—a Burgundy, a Cabernet Sauvignon and a generic, moderately priced red table wine. But Henri was happy with none of them, being convinced that the lake country climate was simply too harsh for growing grapes for quality red wine. Kevin disagreed, and this was only one source of their growing conflict. But there was a palatable enough working relationship between Kevin and the chief winemaker for Brennan and Weidener wines to win medals in a number of state, national and international competitions.

Henri had become active in a number of professional associations, and was highly regarded among Americans involved with wine. He was a member of the American Society of Enologists, the Association of Official Agricultural Chemists, the Institute of Food Technologists and Les Amis du Vin, which had elevated him to the rank of Supreme Knight of the Vine. (Kevin delighted in infuriating him by continually comparing this rank to that of Eagle scout.) Henri also became known for his steadfast refusal to add water to his wines, thus polluting them with chlorine, flourides or chlorine byproducts. He also gained no small amount of notoriety by insisting on adding no cane or beet sugar to Brennan or Weidener wines, much less the corn syrup used by most other winemakers.

Kevin, too, had not escaped notice in wine circles. He was a member of the Finger Lakes Wine Growers Association and had published respected papers in trade journals on the growing of wine grapes. It was Kevin who had first advised other New York State vineyardists to cover graft points between *vinifera* cuttings and *labrusca* roots to protect the grafts from the region's hard winters. It was Kevin who urged his colleagues to avoid using Rupestris root stock and switch instead to Riparia so the wood would mature properly before the onset of severe cold. It was Kevin who popularized the practice of planning pruning so that the vines yielded no more than three tons per acre instead of the five or six tons most vineyardists had previously planned for, thus weakening their vines and making them susceptible to winter injury. It was Kevin who urged a good early spraying program for dead arm, mildew and rot sulfur. It was Kevin who was invited to sit on the New York Wine Research Advisory Board.

And it was Liam who supervised it all by keeping careful track of the company's finances, pouring every available nickel into improving the products, improving the vineyards, and enhancing the reputation of the Brennan winery.

The winery was, then, run by the three of them—none more important than the other. Each had his own area of responsibility, and each bowed to the other's expertise in specific areas. For Kevin, this collective leadership had been especially gratifying. He felt the winery should be a family business run by family members, but he fought hard to keep Helen's involvement to an absolute minimum. Kevin felt deep affection for his half-sister, but he had no regard for her judgment, and he harbored a deepening suspicion about her addiction to the product the family produced. He and Helen had clashed on several occasions over his refusal to let her become more deeply involved in the business, but Kevin remained adamant. Helen's appeals to Katherine had accomplished nothing. Katherine felt Kevin was right, and the joint influence of the two of them over Liam was enough to keep Helen frozen out of decision making.

Eventually, Liam's confidence in his son became so complete that he stepped back from his work in the vineyards and left that portion of the business exclusively to Kevin. "You're better than I am," Liam told him, "just as I became better in the vineyard than Christian was."

"I'm not better than Henri in the winery, though," Kevin pointed out.

"Nobody is better than Henri in the winery," Liam said. "Try to be as good. Keep the peace with him and pick his brain."

"He won't share anything with me or anybody else. He's an evil-tempered old son of a bitch, too, Pop."

"He's the best there is," Liam pointed out.

Although Liam no longer went to the winery on a daily basis, the three of them met formally every month. They would climb into Kevin's Buick on a Friday afternoon and head off to a restaurant near Ringlesport, where they would lunch well and discuss the company's direction. At one of these sessions Kevin presented a carefully thought-out plan that left Liam vaguely disturbed. He expressed reservations. Kevin, prepared for such opposition, pressed his case.

"We're being left behind," Kevin insisted. "Our production and per-unit profit are well behind Gold Seal's or Taylor's. That's because our equipment is outmoded and because the winery is so old it's crumbling around our ears. Unless we do what's necessary and get our cost per unit down and our volume up, our profits will continue to lag, and we'll eventually face real trouble. You know what the big wineries are turning out in terms of volume."

Liam shook his head. "This has gone beyond what I know. I don't fully understand how this would work."

Kevin leaned forward. "It's not that complicated, Pop. We'd need a good lawyer, somebody more sophisticated than Bill Stewart, I'm afraid, and a New York broker. They'd work out all the details. Going public is simply a new way of doing business. It's a way of raising capital we need."

"But all the federal regulations," Liam said. "We'd have the government looking over our shoulders every day. Isn't it bad enough with all the laws they have on producing wine, much less something like this?"

"Pop, we need to buy new bladder presses. We need to put in gyropallets in the champagne cellars and get rid of hand riddling. No operation our size does hand riddling any more. I need machinery for the vineyards. We might even think about a machine for harvesting the grapes . . ."

"No," Henri said. "Our grapes are hand picked."

"The machines are better now," Kevin said, "but, essentially, I agree with you. We should continue to hand pick as long as we can. And that's why it's essential that we modernize in other areas that don't affect the quality of the wine but make it easier and cheaper for us to produce, bottle by bottle."

Liam wasn't sure what frightened him most, offering some of the ownership of the family company to outsiders or simply the prospect of growing larger. He had always been afraid of growing too large, and yet now he found himself with a bigger business than he had ever envisioned and the need to grow even more to remain competitive. He was getting too old for this. "What do we need with more profits?" he demanded. "We all live comfortably?"

"It's not money for ourselves that I'm talking about," Kevin said. "You're right; none of us is rich, but we all make comfortable livings from the business. The issue here is the need to get per-unit costs down before we can no longer price our products competitively. We're going to start losing our market share not because our wines aren't good—they can compete anywhere in the world—but because we won't be able to sell them at competitive prices. That's the problem, Pop. I'd say let's do it by taking out a mortgage on the property, but that makes me nervous, and it would force us to actually raise prices to cover the cost of the loan. We could have done it that way five or ten years ago, but not with the market in the shape it's in now. This way we get the money we need, and it doesn't cost us anything."

Liam sighed. "I suppose. How would it work?"

"The only difference is that we'd have to share profits through stock dividends and account for the money more closely. We'd have to put out an annual report of where the money came from and where it went."

"You mean we would have to publish our salaries and bonuses?" Henri asked in horror.

Kevin nodded. "The stockholders will have a right under the law to know how management is paying itself."

Henri shook his head. "This I do not like."

"Would you like temperature control in your cellars?" Kevin demanded. "Would you like new, stainless steel vats? This is the price. We've always run this as a family operation. The equipment is old and failing fast. We can't keep pace with demand. The way I see it, going public is our only option. We need the cash to sustain long-term growth."

"I don't know," Liam said. "Does this mean we'll have strangers in here, telling us how to make wine?"

Kevin shook his head. "Not if we handle it properly. We can offer stock that amounts to only one-third or one-fourth of what the company is worth. We'd still maintain control. Between you and me and Helen, we'd control enough stock to do what we want with the company, and none of the other stockholders could force us to do anything we didn't want to do."

The two old men exchanged glances. They had been together for so long now that a good portion of their most serious communication was nonverbal.

"Henri needs new equipment," Liam said. "Let's look into it."

After lunch, Kevin drove his father and Henri back to the winery.

"I'm going into town to talk this over with Bill Stewart," Kevin said. "I might be back a little late."

"Will you be in for dinner?" Liam asked him.

"I don't know. I may stop in at the Elks. Tell Mother not to count on me."

Kevin drove the eight miles into the village and spent two hours with Stewart, who was instinctively cautious about such a dramatic change in the company's ownership. "It's a little like starting from scratch," he said.

"Starting from scratch isn't so bad," Kevin said. "It's starting without scratch that's tough."

After the meeting with Stewart, Kevin got a haircut, bought some shaving cream and blades at the drug store and walked the two blocks to the Elks hall. He played some pool and had a sandwich and some wine at the bar when some of the local members came in after leaving their businesses at closing time. By seven-thirty the faces in the Elks Hall began to change, the early people leaving for late dinners; the late people coming in after early dinners. Kevin walked down the street to his car and drove up Lake Street to Elm, and then up Elm to the top of the hill on the road that led to Geneva. As nightfall came, he pulled his car into the driveway of a large, white, Victorian house, drove around behind the building, parked and entered the house through the back door without knocking. She heard him come in.

"I'm in the living room," she called out.

Kevin, leaning on his cane, walked through the house and into the living room. Becky was watching television and reading a John O'Hara novel.

"How do you read and watch television both at the same time?" Kevin asked her.

"I can do two things at once. It's a gift. Do you want a drink?"

"No. Just you."

"Then let's go upstairs," Becky said to him.

* * * *

"Well, now," Liam said, "you're up early."

Standing at the stove in the predawn darkness, Katherine said, "It's barely four in the morning, Liam. You're up before the fish."

He came into the kitchen dressed in his tan work shirt and pants, his work boots, Kevin's leather bomber jacket and carrying his fedora. "That's the idea."

Katherine returned to making a pot of coffee for Annette, who would soon arrive, and cracking eggs into a bowl to begin her pancake batter.

"You don't have to be out on the lake this early this time of year."

Liam sat down at the table. "True enough. But I felt you get up, and I couldn't sleep. My back is stiff. I'm getting old, Darlin'. The pains of age wake me up now and again. Besides, I like to watch the sun rise over the mountain. It's an old man's pleasure, it is."

Katherine said, "Have you noticed how your brogue is coming back? It's been thicker ever since you had that stroke. Isn't that strange?"

He shrugged. "It could be that that little stroke made me forget how to sound American. Sometimes I can't believe I'm seventy-one years old. There are times when I feel like I'm twenty again, looking out there on the lake for the first time from the dock in the village. Sweet Jesus, the years have flown."

Katherine got up and poured him a cup of coffee. "Do you want some pancakes?"

"After I come in from fishing."

She sat down. "It's not the years so much. I can account for those. I look at this house and the children and their children. I look at little Susan, grown and married and a baby of her own on the way. No, it's the days that mystify me. Sometimes it seems as though I'm going to bed and I only got up an hour or two ago. But my brain works as well as ever."

"Kevin got his brains from you, my Darlin'," Liam told her. "I'm not very smart—just lucky, is all. And that, I'm afraid, I couldn't pass along to our son. His luck has been the worst a man could have."

Katherine nodded, her expression wistful. "I think Kevin is content, though. He loves this place, and he loves Susan and Willie so dearly. He's going to be absolutely wild about his grandchild."

Liam sipped his coffee. "He should have a woman. A man's not complete without a woman, not after he's lived with one. I remember when I had to do it. The feeling of loneliness you get when you don't have a woman any more. It would have destroyed me if you hadn't come along."

"Well," Katherine told him, "he has a woman."

Liam looked at her quizzically. "Go on with you! He has a woman, does he?"

Katherine threw back her head and laughed. "Men are so naive. Haven't you wondered where Kevin goes those nights when he goes into town?"

"I know where he goes," Liam said indignantly. "He goes to the Elks and has a drink or two."

"And then he goes right to Becky Ralston's house on the hill. He's been doing it for years now."

Liam blinked in disbelief.

"It's all over town, Liam," she told him. "I can't believe you haven't heard something."

"Not a word, not a word. You mean Becky King? She's a married woman, for God's sake!"

"Not a very happily married one, it would seem."

"That's an interesting reaction from you, my love. Have you forgotten how disturbed both of us were at another man fooling with Kevin's wife? And now he's doing the same thing with Becky King? And you making excuses for both of them?"

Katherine paused before she answered. "I'd say there are some differences. Kevin's forty-four years old, and Becky's even older. And there are no children involved. They know what they're doing."

Liam lit his pipe. "I guess you never get too old to be surprised. It's too early in the day to grapple with moral dilemmas. Dear God, though— Kevin and Becky King. Who'd have ever guessed it?"

"Everyone but you, my dear," Katherine said, leaning over and kissing his unshaven cheek. "You're the perpetual innocent, Liam, and I suppose that's one of the reasons I've loved you so long in spite of your nasty disposition."

He stood up, took her by the hands, pulled her to her feet and embraced her. Liam held his wife closely to him, then he released her and looked deep into her eyes. "And I love you, too, Katherine Cooley Brennan. I truly do."

They embraced again, an old couple in the privacy of their kitchen early in the day before the world came awake. After a while, they pulled apart, and Liam kissed Katherine gently on the forehead. "It's time to terrorize the lakers," he said, smiling. "I'm coming back with a big one for breakfast, so keep your skillet handy."

He went into the basement and gathered his fishing gear. He came up and Katherine walked out on the front porch with him. They found that the sun was already off the mountain on the far side of the lake.

"Well," Liam told her, "I missed the sunrise, but I enjoyed the conversation."

"So did I. You know, the house has always been so full of people that I realize at moments like this how little time we've actually spent alone over the years, talking like this. Not since Helen and Kevin were little."

"Not quite that long. We've had our talks. But not as many as I'd like. There's always been so much to do. What would you say to a trip this summer?"

Katherine was astounded. "A trip? What kind of trip? To Europe? Can we fly? I've never gone up in an airplane."

"Neither have I, and we will. But I wasn't thinking of Europe this time, unless you insist on it. I'd really like to see more of this country. You know, I've lived in America for fifty years, and I've never been outside New York State. Kevin and Henri have been all over for the wine competitions—even to Brussels and Paris and the like. How about a motor trip all the way across the country? We could sleep in motels along the way and take our time. And when we get to California, I'll take you on a plane ride over the orange groves? How does that sound?"

"Liam, it sounds absolutely wonderful. When can we go?"

He pondered the question. "I'd say mid-June. Maybe late June, after all the spraying is done and the new vineyard is planted.

"I'll get out the roadmaps."

He reached out and placed his large, horny hands on her ample breasts. "We'll go upstairs and spread the maps out in the bedroom. How's that sound?"

Katherine giggled, her first real giggle in years. "Liam Brennan, you're an old fool."

"I'll show you who's an old fool when I get back," he said, and started down the hill.

It was always chilly in the lake country early on April mornings. The sunlight was no match for the crisp wind whistling across the lake and ruffling its surface into whitecaps. Liam had his choice of two boats: his big Chris Craft in its heavy sling in the boathouse or the fourteen-foot aluminum rowboat with the seven-horse Mercury that was pulled up on the beach. He and Henri routinely used the smaller boat for fishing, but it looked rough out there today, and he briefly considered bringing down the eighteen-foot cruiser with its two tons of weight to keep him steady. Then he shrugged and tossed his gear into the rowboat. Bringing the Chris Craft down from its lift and out into the water was always a chore, and he felt too lazy for that much effort this morning. He pushed the rowboat out into the lake, got in from the bow and rowed off a respectable distance. He lowered the motor, pumped the bulb on the gas line leading from the remote tank to the motor, put the throttle in its starting position and pulled the starting cord. It took five pulls before the motor kicked into life. Then he put it in gear, gave it half-throttle and started out into the vast lake, his bow high out of the water and smacking against the rolling waves. In the middle, a half-mile from either shore, he cut the motor, dropped the line from his lake trout rig into the water and tried to light his pipe, but the wind had freshened and he couldn't manage it.

His pipe clenched tightly in his teeth, Liam Brennan drifted in the wind and on the waves of Iroquois Lake.

* * * *

"Every indication is that it's another stroke," Billy said. "We have to get him stabilized before we can be positive, but I'm sure that's what's happened."

Katherine looked at Liam through the plastic of the oxygen tent. He was a blurred image. She looked up at Kevin and Billy. "Can I be alone with him?"

"Certainly," Billy said. He and Kevin moved outside into the hallway where Henri and Annette were waiting.

The call from the hospital had been a stunning shock. Liam had been found, seemingly asleep, in the little boat when it had washed ashore at the summer home of a young Boydstown lawyer, who had called for an ambulance. The whole affair had been so sudden that Henri couldn't adjust to the idea.

"How long, Billy?" he demanded. "How long before you know if he'll get well?"

Billy shook his head. "I wish I could say, Henri. If he gets past the first two days, that'll be an important hurdle."

Katherine emerged from the room where Liam lay. Her face was calm. Kevin, who had taken the phone call from Billy, had expected hysteria at this point. Instead, Katherine looked momentarily confused, as if this were all some mistake.

"He seemed to know I was there, Billy," she said. "He made a sort of sound when I called his name."

Dr. Billy Frazier took her hands in his. "Then I'm sure he knew you were there, Katherine. We're going to do the very best for him we can."

"I know he's going to wake up," she said. Then her voice faltered. "Even if it's only to say goodbye to me, I know he'll wake up."

Annette moved forward now and took Katherine in her arms. "He is strong," Annette said. "He is very strong. He will survive this."

"He'll wake up," Katherine told her. "Wait and see."

Kevin couldn't sleep. He didn't even try. At two in the morning he was sitting in front of the fireplace of the big house. He had stoked up the fire and was looking through old photographs. Henri and Annette, both desolate, had gone up the hill to the winemaker's cottage. Katherine was sleeping fitfully upstairs, as was Willie, who had taken the news of his grandfather's stroke quietly and well. Susan, married to Art and conspicuously pregnant, was home in the village. Kevin hoped this wouldn't affect her delivery. Helen and Jack had come up from Boydstown and spent the evening sitting with Katherine, Henri and Annette at Liam's side. At one point in the evening, as word spread around town about Liam's illness, the entire family was in the room or just outside in the hall and virtual legions of family friends were appearing in the hospital corridors, one by one, to extend their prayers and good wishes. Kevin and Billy Frazier finally got the whole family into their cars and on their way home with plans to return the following morning.

Kevin was leafing through old photo albums when he heard a car coming up the gravel driveway. He put down the album and got up stiffly, leaning heavily on his cane. He reached the front door and opened it just as Billy Frazier, in fedora and overcoat, was coming up the steps. Billy stopped on the top step. The two men looked at each other from across the width of the porch. "You're out late," Kevin said softly.

Billy took off his hat and entered the house slowly. Kevin closed the door behind him.

"He died about twenty minutes ago, Kevin," Billy Frazier said. "His heart just stopped."

Kevin lowered his head, took a deep breath and looked up again. All the blood seemed drained from his features. He hobbled into the living room near the fire, where the albums were spread out on the floor near the hearth. Billy followed him.

"Normally," the physician said, "what the hospital does is have somebody call the family and have you come in and then somebody tells you there in the hospital. I just couldn't see any point in that. I've gone through this. I miss my father every day—and my mother, too. But it gets easier every day. It really does."

They heard soft footsteps on the stairs. Katherine, in her robe, appeared in the doorway.

"I heard a car," she said.

Kevin looked at her. "He's gone, Mother."

Katherine never wavered. Her eyes closed momentarily, and she took a deep, ragged breath. Then her eyes opened, and her lower lip trembled, but her voice was firm and clear. "Did he wake up?"

Billy Frazier said, "He did wake up, Katherine, just at the end. He said that he loved all of you, and he said goodbye. That's why I'm here, to let you know he said that."

Katherine nodded. She turned and slowly climbed the stairs to her big bed in her big bedroom that overlooked the lake. Kevin looked over at Billy, who looked back and shook his head. He had lied. Kevin was grateful for the lie. "Thank you, Billy. I have to call Helen now."

Billy Frazier put on his hat and walked to the front door. He opened it into the night, then he turned back to Kevin standing by the fire. "He was a good man," he said. "He was a truly fine man."

Billy Frazier went out into the night. It was crisp, in the forties. He wrapped his overcoat around him as he got into his Chrysler Imperial. As he drove home, he said a prayer for the repose of the soul of Liam Brennan.

* * * *

The custom was beginning to fade, but in 1959 it was still standard practice in older families, especially Catholic families, for wakes to be held in the home. Liam Brennan was buried not from McMartin's funeral parlor but from the living room of his own house.

The family received visitors at Brennan's Point on Wednesday afternoon and evening, Thursday afternoon and evening, and on Friday held a simple funeral mass attended only by close friends in the living room.

After the mass, as the assemblage moved outside to their cars to drive up to the burial site high on the hill, Katherine knelt next to Liam's casket for a moment, gazing for the last time on her husband's face, which had looked so different when it had been animated by the spark of his personality.

She stared at him and silently asked, What would I have been if it hadn't been for you? You gave me children, grandchildren. Now there's a great-grandchild on the way. You gave me warmth in our bed at night. You loved me and gave me a life to live. And now I have to live the rest of it without you. Liam, she thought, how could you have left me like this? I'll be with you again. She touched his icy hand. I'll be waiting for you to come for me.

"Mother," Kevin said from the doorway. She looked up. "It's time."

Katherine sighed deeply. She stared down at Liam, so much like a statue in his one good suit. Then Kevin was next to her, his arm around her shoulder. "Come on, Mother," he told her hoarsely.

Katherine never knew it, but there had been a mild dispute with the chief clerk of the Lake County health department when it had been learned that Liam was to be buried on his own property and not in Lakeside Memorial Park. The clerk had brought up the matter with the county health officer, complaining that Brennan's Point was not a legal burial site. He had been told to mind his own business, which he had done.

Several hours after the service high on the hillside, Jack mentioned to Kevin how impressed he had been with the way Willie had dealt with Liam's death. "The kid's been real good about it," Jack told his brother-in-law, and was overheard by his own son. At thirteen, Jimmy Ryan seldom cried any more, but now his eyes filled with tears, and he sprinted from the room and out the back door. Helen stubbed out her cigarette and followed him.

She found Jimmy, as she had known she would, on the dock at the point, looking out over the lake. Always when they were at the lake, he had fled there when he was disciplined, out of sorts or feeling unhappy and the victim of an injustice. The sight of the lake soothed him, as it had his grandfather.

"What's wrong?" she asked.

Jimmy, at the end of the dock, spun about. The tears were flowing freely, and they were both shivering in the bitter wind. Jimmy stared at her through watery eyes, clearly deciding if he should confide in his mother. Then he said, "I held up well, too."

Helen moved next to him. They were nearly the same height now, she realized. "Yes, you did. You did fine."

Then Jimmy was in her arms, clinging to her. He wept bitterly. "I loved Poppy, too. I loved him as much as Willie did. I loved him more than Willie. I loved Poppy more than anybody loved him."

Helen held her son tightly, her son who reviled her when she was drinking, who only the week before, as she lay drunk in her pajamas on the living room sofa, had told her he wished she would die. She kissed Jimmy's hair, stroking it.

"I know," she said. "I know . . ." Then, on the dock at Brennan's Point, with the slate-gray water rolling wildly in the wind and showing angry whitecaps, Helen Brennan Ryan clutched her growing son to her breast and comforted him and wept for her father lying under the soft dirt on the hillside above.

Chapter 17

Bluestone Park State Mental Hospital rose up against the gray December sky like a medieval castle, all stone walls and battlements and barred windows.

Billy Frazier's Cadillac Sedan DeVille pulled into the circular driveway and stopped under the portico in front. He turned and put his arm along the top of the front seat while he faced into the back. "I'll go in first," he said, "and get things set up. "Wait a minute and bring her in."

In the back seat, Jack Ryan said, "Should I bring her into the lobby?"

Billy thought about it for a second, then he nodded. "You give him whatever help he needs," he told the nurse he had hired for the occasion.

So, while Billy Frazier went into the hospital and sought out its medical director, a Dr. Walter Waverly, Jack Ryan and the hired nurse half-walked, half-dragged a heavily sedated Helen into the immense marble lobby of the huge building. Billy found Waverly's office and presented the necessary papers.

Waverly studied them and said, "Where's the patient now?"

"In the lobby with her husband and a nurse. She's sedated."

Waverly was a tall, lanky man of no more than thirty. He wore a baggy three-piece suit, and he was already balding. He studied the court order through thick glasses and pursed his lips. Then he looked up. "You realize, Dr. Frazier, that we won't be able to keep her long."

"How long is long?" Billy Frazier asked.

"We can't keep her here more than two or three weeks at the outside, enough time for her to dry out and to get her feet on the ground. Then we'll have to make room for patients who are truly ill. We'll certainly have to have her out before Christmas. You wouldn't want her to spend Christmas here."

Billy Frazier's eyebrows flew together. "Dr. Waverly, this woman has spent about three days drunk for every one sober for the past ten years. When she heard about the Kennedy assassination, she got drunk and

309

stayed that way for twelve straight days. As far as I know, she ate nothing in that period. During the course of that time she stabbed her husband in the left shoulder with a nut pick, superficially, fortunately. She fell down a flight of stairs. She smashed a kitchen window and managed to burn half the hair off her head trying to light a cigarette from a gas stove. She was hit by a car crossing the street in front of her house in a nightgown at two in the morning, and she sustained multiple cuts and contusions during that episode. I'm strictly a GP, and a country GP at that. I have no formal training in psychiatry. But I think, on the face of it, that the sort of behavior I'm describing constitutes evidence of a severe emotional abnormality. So did Dr. Rogers, who was the other physician who signed the committal papers."

Waverly sighed. "It's the behavior of an alcoholic, Doctor. This is a state mental facility, not an alcohol rehabilitation center. We can dry her out and talk to her, but we can't make her stop drinking. That's strictly up to her. Has she tried AA?"

"She refuses to try anything. She's convinced that all her problems would disappear if her husband disappeared. But she won't leave him, and he won't leave her."

Doctor Waverly studied the court order, as if there was something that had eluded him. He'd seen hundreds of such orders, and he knew the language by heart. He looked up at the face of the middle-aged country doctor he saw before him. "This is not an unusual pattern in these cases, Doctor, as I'm sure you're aware."

Billy Frazier was incensed now. "I'm aware of this: This woman is an old friend of my family's. She has a son away for his first year of college in Philadelphia. She has a lovely daughter of thirteen who spends most her time hiding in her room doing God knows what. She has a husband who has no idea of how to deal with her when she gets drunk and violent—which happens about half the time—and a handicapped brother and widowed mother past seventy who are in no position or condition to handle her if she leaves her household, where she simply can't stay any more."

Waverly said, "I'm sure that all you're telling me is absolutely correct, but it's not the province of the medical director of a state mental hospital. You know what kind of facility we are, Doctor. We're essentially a warehouse for people who think they're teakettles. If this woman sobers up and appears to have a reasonable handle on reality, then I'll have no choice but to release her because I simply don't have room for alcoholics. That's what the family is for. That's why AA exists."

"What you're telling me is that she's not going to get any treatment here."

"Not for alcoholism," Waverly said. "I can keep her until she's dry; beyond that, no."

Billy Frazier lit a cigarette. His hands were shaking. "You should be aware that it's my considered opinion as a physician who's observed this situation for a number of years that this woman is going to kill somebody one of these days if she doesn't kill herself first."

Waverly nodded. "If she kills someone and a court finds her insane, then I can keep her. That's the best I can do.

It was almost ten days before Jack came to visit. Helen met him in the patients' lounge.

"I want to get out of here," she told him.

"How do you feel?"

"Jack, get me out of here, please."

Jack looked at the floor. "We can't go on living the way we were. You know that."

Helen nodded. "We won't. Look, you've got to do some changing, and so do I."

"You can't drink any more.

"I'm not going to, believe me. Not after this."

"How are they treating you?"

"Jack, these people are crazy in here. I mean really crazy. You can't leave me here. Christmas is coming. You can't leave me here for Christmas."

Jack looked at her. "I don't know what to do, Helen. I don't know what'll happen if you come out now. Have you seen anybody? Has a doctor talked to you?"

"Doctor Waverly and I talked a little bit."

"And what did he say?"

"He said I can't drink any more. I already knew that."

"What else did he say?"

"He said I should join AA."

"And . . ."

"I told him I would when I got out."

"And will you?"

"Yes. Of course. God, please get me out of here. I can't stand it here. There's a girl on my ward, she screams all night. You can't believe what it's like."

Jack looked around. The lounge was a hard, cold tile floor and cheap furniture. Women in bathrobes wandered around. Their men, who were visiting them, studiously avoided one another's eyes. Nurses and orderlies went about their duties impersonally. This would be an unspeakably horrible place in which to be sane, Jack thought.

Helen was begging. "You've got to get me out of here. I'll do whatever you want."

"Go to AA. No more drinking."

"Yes," she said. "Yes. Yes."

The final interview with Dr. Waverly came a week before Christmas. He was almost perfunctory.

"You understand what you have to do to stay out of here, to stay on an even keel."

"I know," Helen told him. "I've had a lot of time to think about things, Doctor. Believe me, I've done a lot of thinking."

He nodded. "You have a husband, children. You have to think of them."

"We have a lot of problems in our marriage, Doctor."

"Every marriage does. You should also think about marriage counseling. Do you belong to a church?"

"Yes."

"You should see your clergyman. I can also recommend some professional people for you both to see back in Boydstown."

"I think we should. Doctor, when can I get out of here? I can't stand staying here."

A normal reaction if ever there was one, Waverly thought. "I'll see what I can do."

Two days later Jack received a call from Dr. Waverly's office that Helen was being released. He drove up to pick her up after work that night. Helen was bubbling and in high spirits all the way home. When she came into the house she hugged Patricia, who was delighted to have her mother back home. Everything had seemed so strange with Helen away in the hospital. Jim came home the next day on vacation from his engineering classes at the Drexel Institute of Technology. He and Helen were wary around one another, like strange dogs moving in circles.

On Christmas Eve, Jack took her shopping. She went off by herself down Main Street so he couldn't see the present she bought him, and she met him later, her arms laden with packages.

"You must have spent a fortune," he told her.

"No, I was careful."

"We have to get home and get these wrapped. We've got to be at my mother's by eight."

"Let's go, then. I have to wrap all these."

When they got home she carried her packages into the bedroom to wrap them. She emerged an hour later, in her pajamas, visibly unsteady on her feet, the gin on her breath rolling out in front of her.

"Helen . . ." Jack said.

"Fuck you," Helen said to him thickly. "And merry Christmas, Jack."

* * * *

The room was on the second floor of the Lakeside post office. It was shabby and worn, and the secretary who occupied the battered, gun-metal gray desk along the streetside window was a girl with whom Will had gone to high school. Her name had been Amelia Baddington, and now the black and white sign on her desk proclaimed she was Mrs. Roach. She was obviously quite pregnant, and if she recognized the tall, bearded young man with the shoulder-length hair as the classmate who had helped her through *Paradise Lost* in Mrs. Silber's sophomore English class, she gave no indication. She merely went through her paperwork and did her typing and tried to pretend that Will wasn't there, sitting in a hard wooden chair, waiting.

Finally, the door along the wall opened, and Bucky Coughlin, who owned the hardware store, stuck out his head.

"Come on in, Will," he said.

Will Brennan stood up and walked into the hearing room. He took a chair facing the members of the draft board that served Lakeside and adjoining communities. Sitting on the other side of a scarred conference table was a group of middle-aged men. Most of them Will had known all his life. They were friends of his father's and, like Kevin, pillars of the community. At the middle of the table was Tom Allen, the chairman and principal owner of Lakeside Mills, the father of Will's high school classmate Linda Allen and, if Will recalled correctly, a wounded veteran of World War II.

"Well, Will," Tom Allen said, "you know why you're here." He picked up a manilla folder. "You've applied for an exemption from the selective service system for reasons of conscience. You want to be permitted conscientious objector status, is that right?"

"That's correct, Mr. Allen."

Tom Allen looked at Will evenly. He was an imposing man, heavyset, self-possessed, with a full head of steel-gray hair, a perpetual air of controlled aggression about him. "How does your father feel about this?"

"He feels I have to follow the dictates of my conscience."

Tom Allen nodded slowly. Will knew that although he was with the draft board in a formal sense, he was actually dealing with Tom Allen, and the realization was not comforting. Tom Allen's Lincoln was parked outside, its Goldwater bumper sticker still defiantly displayed two years after the Arizona senator's defeat in the 1964 presidential election. "In your heart," it said, "you know he's right." Will remembered his father's response: "In your guts, you know he's nuts."

"Will," Tom Allen said, "I'm sure you realize there are some questions we have to ask you before we can rule on your request. Will, what's the philosophical foundation of your request? In what religious faith have you found principles that support your request?"

"Well, I was born and raised a Catholic, but I consider myself an agnostic. Or, at least, I don't think any particular group has a monopoly on spiritual truth. I subscribe to the beliefs of Mohandas K. Gandhi and to the nonviolent principles of Dr. Martin Luther King, Jr. I also believe in the principles outlined by Henry David Thoreau concerning the primacy of the individual human conscience over the demands of the state."

Tom Allen nodded slowly. Will wasn't sure whether he had understood any of what Will had said, and he was also pretty sure that if Tom Allen had understood it had gone completely over the heads of the other small-town burghers and farmers who sat with him on the board. This was not Cambridge. He was not taking his philosophy orals. He had to remember that.

"Let me ask you this," Tom Allen said. "If you were walking down the street and someone attacked you, would you defend yourself?"

"I would."

Tom Allen leaned forward across the table. "Would you kill to defend yourself, if you felt it was absolutely necessary?"

Will nodded. "Yes, Sir, I would. I'd do it reluctantly, but I would kill an attacker if it were absolutely necessary to preserve my own life."

"If that's the case, please explain to this board why we should grant you C.O. status?"

Will knew he was already sunk. The draft counseling center at Harvard had warned him that if, in this interview, he condoned violence under any circumstances, the board would leave his 1-A intact. But he'd gone into this determined to face the question honestly on his own terms, and this was his opportunity to outline those terms.

"I can't fight in this war, Mr. Allen," he said. "I object to this war in the deepest depths of my being. I think what this country is doing in Vietnam is wrong. I just can't justify taking another human life for the sake of what my country is doing there."

"Will," Tom Allen said slowly, "do you think that World War II would have been worth fighting in? Do you think this country was right in fighting Adolf Hitler?"

"Yes, I think the war against Hitler was a just war. My father came home wounded from that war, and I'm proud of him for what he did. But those circumstances were different."

Tom Allen said, "Explain, please, why a war against the Nazis was a just war and a war against the communists, with a similar idealogy of world domination, is not."

Will almost laughed. "There's a dramatic difference between Nazi idealogy and communist idealogy, Mr. Allen."

"They have common elements."

"And they have many more disparate elements. The distinctions aren't even subtle. Not that I'm defending communist idealogy, but I think it's largely irrelevant to this debate." Wasted breath, Will decided, looking at their faces. Maybe Tom Allen had heard of *Das Capital*, but none of the rest of them had, and Will was damned sure that whether he had heard of it or not, Tom Allen had never read even a review of the book, much less the volumes themselves. His was the best mind among them, and he had only the vaguest idea of what communism stood for. Will went on. "It's all very complicated—"

"Make it as simple as you can, please," Tom Allen said.

In other words, Will thought, screw you and the horse you rode in on. "All right," Will said, "I'll try. What was happening in Europe thirty years ago constituted a direct threat against all of Western culture, this country included. Hitler was an aggressor moving his armies across foreign borders for the purposes of conquest. What he did in Poland and France was reason enough to move against him—not even counting what he did to the British and to every Jew he could get his hands on. But to equate that war with Vietnam is misguided. What's happening there is essentially an expression of nationalism, and the communists are involved only because the Vietnamese had nowhere else to go for help in ousting the French. They certainly got no help from us. Yes, there's communist involvement. But where's the surprise in that? It's a country directly within the communist sphere of influence. Why is it surprising that the Vietnamese rebels should gravitate toward the dominant political philosophy in their part of the world and especially in a part of the world where democracy has no history and no tradition?"

"Will . . ." Tom Allen tried to break in.

You asked me, Will thought. "What's happening in Vietnam has no direct impact on the affairs of this nation," Will said, plowing on. "It's a matter for the Vietnamese, not us, to resolve. And, to a degree, it's a question of chickens coming home to roost. This is what we get for supporting governments like the Diem regime. It happened to us in Cuba. It's going to happen in Latin America. We'll back anybody who's not a communist no matter how bad and repressive a government it happens to be, and that's just bad policy. It's backfiring on us over there. Now, should we give the Vietnamese arms? Yes, I think so. It's the best of a selection of bad choices. Should we provide them aid? Sure. But, should we commit American lives? I think it's foolish and morally repugnant to do that. Where are the Red Chinese troops? Where are the Russian troops? If they were there, maybe I'd feel differently. But they're not there, and we shouldn't be there, either."

Tom Allen put his hands together, his fingers touching. "What you're suggesting is that you think you should have the right to decide which wars you would fight in."

"I'm saying that there are good wars and bad ones, and that an individual ought to be permitted to follow the dictates of his conscience in deciding in which he chooses to participate."

"You realize, of course," Tom Allen said, "that if that were permitted, there'd be damn few people representing American interests in Vietnam right now."

"I think that's possible, Mr. Allen, and that ought to say something about popular support for this war. If this country were in genuine danger, you wouldn't be able to hand out the uniforms and the guns fast enough."

Tom Allen sat at the table, his expression thoughtful. Will rejoiced that there was even a possibility that his words had made the older man think. The issue was so important to Will, and not just because the question of his military service was involved: he was a passionate young man, and he took his causes passionately.

"All right," Tom Allen said finally. "Let's assume you're right. Let's assume that there's not an immediate danger to, say, Lakeside from the communist threat in Vietnam. But what you overlook, Will, is the larger, global picture. First there's Vietnam. Then comes, let's say, Cambodia. Then maybe Japan. Lakeside would be on that list sooner or later. You just don't seem to grasp that."

"I grasp it," Will said. "I just don't accept it as a realistic enough premise upon which to base troop movements. Even if the theory has merit, the reality is something else entirely."

Tom Allen said, "Would you join the military to fight to save Japan, Will? The Japanese are our allies. How about South Korea? Would you fight for the South Koreans? Those countries are rather close to Vietnam in the global scheme of things."

"I'd have to know more about the circumstances, Mr. Allen. If those governments had been repressive and antidemocratic, it would be a tough call. It's a hypothetical case that I can't respond to without particulars."

Tom Allen fought back a smile. He'd fought this fight before, although not against as formidable an opponent. "Well, then, how about Hawaii, Will? How about California?"

"I'd fight without hesitation to protect American soil. Vietnam is half a world away from American soil."

Tom Allen shook his head wearily. The gesture struck Will as a trifle showy, and then he realized that Tom Allen hadn't listened to a word he'd said. His mind had been made up before Will had even entered the room. He didn't know why this surprised him, but it did. He should have realized that this was the only draft board he would ever have to face, but he was only one of hundreds of potential inductees who came before it each year. He had thought his ideas so important, but to Tom Allen and the others they were only obstacles to be overcome. This was not a marketplace of ideas. It was a draft board, and he was cannon fodder, nothing more, nothing less.

"I should think," Tom Allen said, "that a magna cum laude Harvard graduate would have a somewhat stronger grasp on world affairs than you seem to have, Will. I'm disappointed."

Will was annoyed. "That's bullshit, Mr. Allen. I have a fairly solid understanding of what's happening in Vietnam. I've read a great deal about it, and, as you might imagine, it's the number-one topic of conversation at colleges across the coun—"

"That'll do, Will," Tom Allen said.

Will knew he'd overdone it. Tom Allen was not a man accustomed to being lectured, and his displeasure with Will's outburst was written all over his face and the faces of the other board members.

"The board will consider your request," Tom Allen said, "and you'll be notified in due course of our decision. I think you should know, however, that your comments don't seem to indicate that you can meet the test for C.O. status. A man who can for reasons of religious belief or, in some cases, conscience fight in no wars is eligible; but somebody like yourself, who is willing to fight in some wars but not in others, is not, by any reasonable yardstick, a conscientious objector."

Will's face burned with embarrassment and a deep-seated sense of outrage. "This is a bad war, Mr. Allen."

Tom Allen's face darkened. "Will, being an American is a special privilege, and it carries with it special responsibilities. We're all that stands between the world and communist domination. We have an obligation to step in where a people is too weak to defend itself against aggression. Too many people your age have enjoyed the benefits of American citizenship without bearing its burdens. Your generation has had it soft. Now it's time to shoulder your share of the burden, as your fathers did, and you don't like it. I'm sorry, but there's no escaping your obligations. Now, if you'll be kind enough to have the secretary send in the next applicant. . . ."

Will opened his mouth to respond, but he caught himself. He wasn't about to convince anybody in this room about anything. He stood up and left wordlessly.

* * * *

Jack heard her before he saw her, and in hearing her he knew what he was going to see. But actually seeing her as the pajama-clad figure lurched unsteadily into the living room made his heart sink. Helen glared at him. "What are you staring at, you little bastard?" she demanded.

Patricia, sitting on the sofa with her nose in a science fiction novel, looked up and took it all in. At fifteen, she was a veteran of many such scenes. She went back to her reading, losing herself in it instantly.

"I should have known," Jack said, turning his gaze back to the television set. "You were twitchy all day. You were getting all wound up for this, weren't you?"

Helen made no attempt to sit down. "Little bald bastard. Not a hair on your head."

Jack was silently grateful that it was Patricia sitting on the sofa and not Jim, who was working at his summer job on the night shift at Potters. Jim had no tolerance whatever for this.

"Just go back in the bedroom and leave us alone," Jack told her. "Nobody's bothering you."

Helen made no attempt to move. "Where's your hair? Where did it go, that's what I want to know?"

Patricia looked up. "Mother, can't you leave us alone? We're not doing anything to you."

"Shut up!" Helen said. "You're going to go bald, too. You can thank him."

Patricia smirked. "Women don't go bald."

Helen glared at her and pointed a shaky, accusing finger at Jack. "You will, because *this* is your father—this little shit with his bald head."

Jack looked up at her. "Helen, just go away, will you?"

"Why don't you shut up, you little shit? I want to watch television. I paid for the goddamn TV set with my money from the winery. You don't pay for a thing around here."

Helen lumbered across the room and plopped heavily on the sofa next to Patricia. Patricia looked at her, curled her nose involuntarily at the stink of her gin-soaked breath, closed her book and got up. She walked across the room and kissed Jack on the forehead.

"Good night, Daddy."

"Good night, Sweetheart."

Patricia's room was a monument to pop culture. Its walls were covered with posters of Bob Dylan; Peter, Paul & Mary; the Rolling Stones; the Beatles; Jimmi Hendrix, Janis Joplin, the Jefferson Airplane. A huge peace symbol adorned the door. A fan magazine cover of Mr. Spock was taped above her bed. A hi-fi set, a birthday gift from Helen, took up a portion of one wall. In the bookcase beneath it was Patricia's extensive record collection. Now, anticipating trouble downstairs, she selected a Big Brother and the Holding Company album and slipped it on the turntable. She flipped on the music and settled down on her bed, engrossed once again in Ray Bradbury, the music no more than background.

Patricia Ryan was a high school sophomore, a natural whiz in the social sciences and better than average in the hard ones. That pattern was precisely the opposite of Jim's, who had excelled in science and math and was now studying engineering.

Patricia and Jim differed markedly in other particulars as well. Where he tended to be reticent among members of his peer group, Patricia was gregarious and outgoing in the company of those her own age. Where Jim had gone through high school with only two dates, his junior and senior proms, Patricia was popular with boys and enjoyed their company. She had, in fact, experienced her first sexual intercourse during her freshman year in high school. While she had later come to detest the boy, she decided that she liked sex, although she was extremely careful not to get pregnant. Patricia had no intention of ending up a housewife, changing diapers and washing dishes and slowly losing her mind. She'd seen what could happen to a woman facing that existance, and she was going to make damned sure that her life bore no resemblance to the one her parents were living.

She read Bradbury and, after a while, dozed.

It was hours before she came awake, suddenly and with a start. At first she was befuddled and fogged in, as she was always was when she was awakened suddenly. Then she heard the noise downstairs, and it was the sound of thumping and strange grunts and groans. Then Helen's high-pitched and ear-splitting scream came through. "Bastard! BASTARD! BASTARD! BASTARD! BAS—"

Patricia went downstairs to find Helen on the living room floor with Jack kneeling on her, holding a pillow over her face. He was drenched with beer, and an empty can lay in front of the television set. Helen struggled against the pillow, and Jack let it loose. Helen's head came up, lips flecked with foam and eyes rolling. She spotted Patricia on the stairs, over Jack's shoulder. "HE'S KILLING ME! HELP! HE'S KILLING M—"

Jack jammed the pillow back in place and looked over his shoulder.

"Go back to your room, Patricia," he said, puffing visibly. "I can handle this."

Patricia was less horrified than she was annoyed. "You can hear her all over the neighborhood. Mrs. Jones is going to call the police again."

Jack knew that was true. The Ryans knew it was the rotund busybody across the street who called the police every time Helen started screaming. Not that they could bring themselves to condemn Mrs. Jones. The blood-curdling shrieks emanating from the house directly across the street understandably unsettled an old woman's nerves.

"I can keep her quiet," Jack Ryan told his daughter. "Just go to your room."

Patricia went back upstairs and got ready for bed. She took a long, leisurely shower. Then she dried and combed out her long, ash-blonde hair. When the turned off the hair dryer, she realized that the house was eerily quiet. She walked halfway down the stairs and peered into the living room. Helen lay motionless and Jack knelt astride her, holding the pillow in place. They looked as though they hadn't moved in some time. Patricia went back upstairs. She closed her eyes and slept.

The crash awakened her. She sat bolt upright in bed, then she heard the sound of Helen's high-pitched voice downstairs, coming up through the floorboards. The illuminated face of her alarm clock told her it was nearly two in the morning. She'd been asleep since about twelve. She heard again the sound of thumping and shouting. Patricia leaped out of bed and ran down the stairs. Jack, in his underwear and robe now, sat in his recliner in the living room. Helen was raging around the room. The floor was a sparkling collection of fragments from the huge mirror that had adorned the space over the mantel. Patricia had adored that mirror.

"I hated that mirror, you little bastard," Helen was fuming. "I hated it because you bought it. It's the only goddamn thing in this house you ever bought."

Jack, clearly beyond the bounds of physical and emotional endurance, only said quietly, "Smash anything you like, Helen. I'm too tired to stop you."

Patricia heard the voice before she realized it was hers. It came out loud and shrill, louder than Helen's had been. "STOP IT!" she screamed.

Helen looked up at her daughter on the stairs.

Patricia yelled, "Stop it! Stop it! Stop it!"

Sober, Helen's reaction was predictable: hostility in any form seemed to unnerve her. Drunk, her response to any given situation was utterly unpredictable. In this case, she merely blinked her eyes a few times, then staggered off toward the downstairs bedroom, smashing with unconcern in her bare feet through the shattered glass on the carpet. Jack watched her go, then turned and looked up at Patricia, who came the rest of the way downstairs and collapsed, sobbing, on the sofa. "Daddy," she wept, "I can't stand this."

Jack sighed wearily. "I wish I knew what to do about it, honey. I really do."

"Get rid of her!" Patricia said. "Divorce her."

"And what would happen to her if I did?"

"Who cares?"

Jack was silent. He reached into the pocket of his robe, fished out a package of cigarettes and lit one. Then he said, "I took an oath before God. I said for better or worse."

"I didn't take any oath. Did for better or worse mean this? What about me? Don't you owe me anything?"

"Look," he told her, "you'll be out of here in a few years—like Jim."

"He's here summers."

Jack laughed. It was not a nice laugh. "And where is he right now? His shift at Potters ended more than two hours ago. He comes home summers, but he spends as little time here as he can, or haven't you noticed? And who can blame him. He's already gone, Honey, for all practical purposes. And you will be, too, before too long. I'm the one who's stuck. It's my decision."

Patricia lifted her face out of her hands and looked over at her father. He seemed so old to her. "You don't have to be."

"Sure, I do."

Patricia stared at her reflection in the dark window, and saw the police car, lights blazing and blinking, pull up in front. "Oh, God," she said with alarm. "Mrs. Jones called the cops again."

Jack stubbed out his cigarette and answered the door when the knock came. The police officers were young men in imposing uniforms. One was white, the other black. Jack motioned them into the living room, and they came in, their guns hanging on their hips like anvils. One of them carried a hand radio, and police calls crackled over it.

"We got another complaint about noise, Mr. Ryan," the white one said.

"I'm sorry," Jack told him. "I know you. You've been here before. You know what I'm dealing with here."

Patricia sat motionless on the sofa, looking out the window at the car. They had left the engine running and the lights on, and the bubbletop lights played off every house on the street. Why didn't you just turn on the siren, too, she thought.

Helen, hearing the voices, came lurching out of the bedroom. "It's that little bastard there," she said thickly, pointing a finger toward Jack. "He's why I drink. Just get rid of him, and I'll be fine."

The white cop said, "You've got to be quiet, Mrs. Ryan. You've upset the whole neighborhood, and people are complaining."

"It's that little bastard there," Helen insisted. "Get rid of that little fucker, and I'll be fine."

It was the black officer who spoke now. In a low, rumbling voice like a rich bass drum, he said, "You ought to watch your language in front of the girl, Mrs. Ryan. Now, look, you just go to bed and be quiet and everything will be all right."

Helen wasn't having any. "Why don't you arrest him? He's the little prick who's at fault. If he'd just keep his fucking hands off me . . ."

The white officer glared at her. "Mrs. Ryan, if I have to come back here, I'm going to arrest you for disturbing the peace, do you understand? Now you go to bed. Now!"

Helen opened her mouth as to speak, but the look in the young cop's eyes stopped her. She had seen that expression before, in the face of her son, and she didn't like it. She turned and walked unsteadily into the downstairs bedroom, slamming the door behind her.

The cop turned to Jack. "You're going to have to keep her quiet, Mr. Ryan."

Jack held up his hands in exasperation. "I'll do what I can."

"Why don't you just have her put away?" the black officer asked him.

"They keep letting her out. No psychiatrist will keep her in once she sobers up. Then she comes out and does this again."

The cop shook his head in sympathy. "Well, keep her quiet tonight."

They left. Patricia watched in relief as they got into their prowl car, killed the lights and pulled away. Just what we all needed, she thought. That was a big, big help. She got up and turned to Jack.

"I'm going to bed, Daddy," Patricia said wearily.

"Go ahead. I'm going to sleep here on the sofa."

"Do you need a blanket?"

"Just some silence, Honey," Jack said, settling down on the sofa. "I'll see you in the morning."

Patricia picked her way gingerly through the glass on the rug and went up the stairs. Jack heard her close her door, and he heard the music start a moment later—something loud and unintelligible she could hide behind. Thank God she had her shield. Jack had no place to hide.

* * * *

In the years following Liam's death, the number of family gatherings on Sundays at Brennan's Point declined somewhat. During the first few years Helen and Jack and their children made the long trip to the lake on a regular basis, but not three out of four weekends, as they had when the children were younger. Moreover, Helen's "problem," as Katherine referred to it, was no longer a secret after her hospitalization. As a result she no longer made the effort to sober up by Sunday to keep the truth from Kevin and the others. Once Kevin tried to speak to her about it. "If living with Jack is what makes you drink," he said, "then why don't you just leave Jack and knock off the drinking? The winery is making you enough money now that you should be able to live on your own."

"I'll leave when I'm ready," she told him. "Don't worry. Just as soon as Patricia is out of the house."

"Why not now?" Kevin demanded.

"I'm not sure I could get custody, and I don't want Patricia growing up without a mother."

It was clear, however, that neither of them was about to leave the other. It was also clear that general knowledge of her "problem" made Helen less eager to spend Sunday after Sunday at Brennan's Point. She much preferred staying home and drinking. Both Jim and Patricia loved the place, but as they grew older, and especially after Jim went off to college and Patricia began to develop stronger links to her teenaged friends in Boydstown, Jack felt less of an obligation to take them to Lakeside for such regular visits with their grandmother.

Moreover, after Liam's death, Henri and Annette were at the big house less often on Sundays. Annette was in the kitchen with Katherine virtually all day, six days a week. On Sundays she deferred to Henri, who wanted her company. Henri, never particularly jovial, had grown increasingly cranky, and although he got along with Katherine well enough, he saw more than enough of Kevin at the winery. The two worked together but without the warmth that had characterized Henri's relationship with Kevin's father. On Sundays Henri and Annette developed the habit of going off by themselves for dinner at one of the restaurants that were beginning to line the lake. Or they would go to a restaurant in Rochester or to a particularly fine restaurant in Boydstown Heights of which Henri was fond.

So it was that on most Sundays, the group at the big house had dwindled down to Katherine, Kevin, Susan and Art and their new baby, Liam Brennan Dixon, and Will.

Will had been home for more than a month after graduation. He was scheduled to begin in the fall as a Harvard graduate teaching assistant, but the draft had made that uncertain. The draft board had reclassified him 1-A a month after his physical in Boston. The Sunday after his hearing before Tom Allen and the others, Will left the dinner table. He went upstairs, slipped into his bathing suit and headed down to the beach, where he was lying on the dock when Kevin hobbled down from the big house to see him.

"What are you doing?" Kevin asked.

"Just watching the clouds," said Will, pointing upwards.

Kevin put down his cane and sat down heavily on a large wooden rocker that he had built with his own hands years before. He was puffing a bit. He'd been thinking of having a small road built down the bank from the main road and buying a golf cart to ease his passage back and forth from the beach to the big house. He had resisted the idea for a long time, but as he grew older the long journey up and down the hill became ever more difficult for him. He rocked back and forth and looked up at the sky. The clouds danced their graceful waltz high above the waves and the mountainside. Farther out in the lake, boats cut through the water.

"What are you going to do?" Kevin asked him finally.

Will sat up and stroked his shaggy beard, which Kevin detested almost as much as he hated his son's shoulder-length hair. "I don't know," he said. "I suppose I could have worn a pair of pink panties to the physical. I wish I weren't so damn healthy. You don't know what I'd give for a little heart murmur, or a big one, if it came to that. I suppose I can just refuse induction. The only problem is that you end up in jail with a bunch of ax murderers and rapists, and they spend all their time beating the shit out of you because they figure you're not a good citizen. I'm not sure how hard prison guards work at protecting people who refused induction. I honestly don't know what I'm going to do, Dad. My current thinking is to go back to Ireland and try to reestablish the clan."

"You wouldn't like it over there," Kevin said. "The food's rotten, and when the sun comes out it's so rare that people think it's a UFO."

"More seriously, I could go to Canada. Montreal isn't all that far away, or Toronto. I could sneak back now and again, I suppose. Or, when my draft notice comes, I could just go in and take my chances. Those seem to be about my only choices. I've thought about suicide, but that would seem to defeat the purpose of worrying about this to begin with."

Kevin lit one of his cigars. He looked down at Will, sitting on the dock. The boy looked so much like Jane it sometimes haunted him. Or, he looked like Jane used to look. She had shown up at little Liam's christening a few years ago, and Kevin had been shocked to note that she had gained perhaps fifty pounds over the years and had gone totally gray. "Will, is it because you're afraid that you'll get hurt or killed?"

Will looked up at his father. The question, Kevin could see, had wounded him. "I'm surprised that you asked me that. That's the presumption, isn't it, that if somebody's against the war it must be because he's a coward. I could feel that coming from Mr. Allen and those other guys on the draft board. I didn't expect it to come from you."

Kevin opened his mouth to apologize, but Will raised a hand and cut him off with a gesture.

"No, Dad," he said, "I'm not afraid of dying. Let me rephrase that. I am afraid of dying, but not inordinately so, not so much that I'd refuse induction to fight in a war I believed in. Were you afraid?"

"I was scared shitless," Kevin told him. "So was everybody else, except the ones with no sense."

"But you went anyway?"

Kevin shrugged. "We all went. That's what you did then."

Will nodded. "So would I if I could just convince myself that the war was worthwhile. I may end up going anyway. I just haven't made up my mind yet."

"I can't make your choice for you," Kevin said. "All I can tell you is that it won't help to resent what those choices are. That's beyond your control—and mine."

Will looked at his father in surprise. "Why shouldn't I be upset over the selection of choices that have been thrust on me? Why shouldn't I resent being forced into this position? Dad, did you ever stop to think how ridiculous the draft is in this society? We're supposed to be a free people, yet the mechanism we use to preserve that freedom is a form of slavery. From a historical standpoint there's no difference between this country's sending draftees to fight in Vietnam and the Roman Empire sending Nubian slave troops into Egypt. And I shouldn't resent that?"

Kevin knew from long experience that debates with Will could become disturbingly esoteric. In a few moments Will would be carrying on about patterns of injustice in the fertile crescent during the Bronze Age, and there'd be no reaching him with anything. "Listen, Will," he said, "let me give you a piece of advice. I know I'm always telling you what to think and how to look at things, and I know you think it's all sort of quaint . . ."

Despite his agitation, Will had to laugh.

"Nonetheless," Kevin went on, "I'm going to say something now that I want you to pay attention to. It's something my father never told me, probably because he never thought about it. He wasn't much for abstract concepts, and he lived comfortably for most of his life. He just never had to come to grips with the essential injustice of the human condition."

Will said, "That's a pretty big buildup. This must be some piece of advice you're working up to."

Kevin frowned. "It's very simple. You think you're the victim of an injustice, and you just might be. Get used to it. Get used to the bad choices, because you're going to face them for as long as you're breathing. That's what life is. It's an endless process of selecting from among flawed alternatives. And thrown in is the occasional cataclysmic event over which nobody has any control, like a bomber crashing on you and crushing your left arm and leg."

Will said nothing. This was the first time in his life that he'd heard his father make mention of the accident.

"There's never a perfect choice," Kevin told him. "Every one has warts. All you'll ever be able to do is pick the one alternative that's not necessarily good but merely better than the others. Now, you can let that paralyze you. You can spend your life sulking over that reality. Or, you can deal with it and make the best of things. Being an adult means you recognize that in most circumstances the best you can hope for is to make the best of things, and that there's no justice, that you're going to spend a lifetime suffering hardships you don't deserve. If you can live with that, then you'll probably be okay. If you can't, then, believe me, you'll end up self-destructing, one way or another. I've watched it happen to Helen. She couldn't face up to the choices she found facing her, and she's spent her whole life feeling sorry for herself, shaking her fist at those choices and driving herself and everybody around her crazy in the process."

Will was expressionless for a moment. Then he said, "Gee, Dad, you're always so cheery. Now I feel better about anything."

Kevin was frustrated. The kid was so bright, and it was so difficult to get him to understand anything.

"I'm not trying to cheer you up or make you happy," Kevin said. "Happiness is something you carry around inside yourself. It's your own responsibility—nobody else's. I just want you to know that whatever choice you make in this, I'll support you. I'll do whatever I can to help. I'll do that rather than lose my son. Those are my choices, and I'm letting you know which one I'm picking."

"I appreciate what you're saying," Will said quietly. "You disagree with me about the war, don't you?"

Kevin nodded. Then, just as emphatically, he shook his head. "It's a different kind of war. The fact that I've got a son facing induction doesn't do much to clarify matters for me. I'm confused, but your convictions on this are so strong that I can't argue with them. Would I be happier if you weren't in this moral bind? Sure. Do I think you're wrong for feeling this way? No. I support you for the sincerity of your convictions. Maybe I'm even beginning to share some of them."

Will gazed at Kevin. "Thanks. I need to be reminded every once in a while, but you're really not the worst old man in the world."

Kevin coughed self-consciously. "Well, I'm going back up to the house."

"I think I'll just stretch out here a while longer."

"All right," Kevin said, "see you later."

Slowly, he climbed back up the hill. Katherine and Annette were doing the week's baking in the kitchen. They would be so occupied well into the night. Kevin nodded in greeting, went to the cabinet and took down a tumbler. He went to the refrigerator, took out a bottle of Seyval Blanc, filled the tumbler and downed half the glass. Katherine and Annette exchanged glances.

"What's the matter, Kevin?" his mother asked him.

Kevin shook his head. "Nothing."

Katherine merely gazed at him. She was seventy-five years old, and he knew he wasn't kidding her. He said, "I'm afraid that my son is going to get himself killed in a war, Mother, and I don't know what the hell to do about it."

Katherine said nothing. Wordlessly, she took off her apron, laid it over the back of a kitchen chair, turned and left the room. They heard her footsteps on the stairs leading to her room.

"I guess I ought to learn to keep my mouth shut," Kevin told Annette.

"She will be all right," Annette said. "She is just remembering when she felt the same fear. And you should remember that her fears never came true."

Kevin sipped his wine. "No. They just came half-true."

* * * *

It took Jim Ryan slightly more than two hours to get Marci Roth up to his room in the fraternity house. They had been dating all winter now, and he was as captivated by her personality as he was by her body. Marci believed in flying saucers, ghosts and socialism. Her feet were planted firmly in the air, and her reaction to any given situation was never what Jim expected. He was insane over her, and tonight things were going well.

He had drunk a fair amount at the party downstairs. Once upstairs he was just about uncontrollable. Marci, who did not drink at all, had permitted him to remove her bra and to rub the clothing between her legs, but she possessed the control he lacked. Finally she sat up abruptly. "Uh-uh," she told him sharply. "That's enough."

Jim rolled over on the bed and struggled to catch his breath. "You're a cruel woman."

"A prudent woman, you mean."

"A prude?" Jim said. "Is that what you're saying?"

Marci laughed, and the tension between them evaporated. "You know better than that."

He sighed. "Where's all this free love they keep writing about in *Playboy?* To me, reading *Playboy* is like reading *National Geographic.* It's full of pictures of places I never get to visit. Come on, Marci. I've got a draft physical coming up. This may be my last . . . well, you know."

Marci fastened her bra. "Maybe you'll flunk."

"I hope so. I had asthma as a kid. I'm hoping it'll help." Jim struggled to rise, but he staggered and fell back down. "Shit, gravity works, doesn't it?"

She put out her arms to him. "Lie back down before you kill yourself."

He did, and she held him close. After a few moments of silence, she said. "You're really worried about that physical, aren't you?"

"You bet I'm worried. I'm going to get drafted. That'll put sort of a dent in my career plans—not to mention my plans to marry you."

Marci sat straight up on the bed. "Time out! What plans to marry me?"

Jim smiled at her. "Didn't I mention that? Damn, I knew there was something I'd meant to talk to you about."

Her expression was quizzical. "Is this your idea of a proposal?"

He shrugged. "Well, no. Not yet. I was kind of wanting to get my degree first, and a job. It would be nice to be able to support you, don't you think?"

She turned to him. "Jim, this is a big problem. You're Catholic, and I'm Jewish."

"So when our kids go to confession they can take a lawyer. Bless me, Father, for I have sinned. You can direct your questions to Mr. Shapiro, here." Jim had heard the line of television, and he had planned for months to use it at this very moment, when the question arose. He had expected her to laugh. She didn't.

"Look," she said. "My father is a Holocaust survivor. He's always been very protective of me—even before my mother died."

"So what's the big deal?"

She gazed at him thoughtfully. "You really don't understand, do you?"

Jim eyed her levelly. "Do you love me?"

"You know I do."

"Do you want to spend your life with me?"

"Yes."

"Then forget about your father. Let's jump off that bridge when we come to it. I have to get this draft business worked out before we can even talk about it seriously."

Marci seemed to Jim to be delighted to change the subject. "How do you know you're not going to fail the physical?"

"Are you kidding?" he said. "Look at this body. How can I fail?"

She laughed for the first time in a while. "Ha!" she said. "You ought to have a little sign printed on your underwear: Contents May Cause Drowsiness."

"How would you know?" he asked. "But I'm going to pass. It's the story of my life."

"What about the asthma?"

"Marci, it hasn't bothered me in years."

She came over and sat down next to him on the bed. "Didn't you tell me once you were allergic to cats?"

"Yeah, along with little Vietnamese guys with machine guns, I also hate cats. They're useless. When's the last time you saw a seeing-eye cat? And what has this got to do with anything?"

Marci said to him, "What would happen if you slept with a cat the night before your physical? Wouldn't your allergy pretty much duplicate the symptoms of asthma?"

He thought about it. "That's crazy. It would never work."

"Is it really all that crazy? Are you sure?"

He pondered it. This was an idea he hadn't thought of.

"Maybe not," Jim Ryan said slowly.

The cat belonged to a pledge. Under orders, the pledge brought it to the fraternity house from his home in New Jersey. The cat was a huge, orange tabby with an evil disposition and needlelike claws. The night before his physical, Jim took it to bed with him. He rubbed his face in its fur. By morning, he thought he was going to die.

He took the subway to city hall and switched to a bus that took him four blocks up Broad Street to the federal building, where he underwent his physical.

The doctor put his stethoscope to his chest.

"Take a deep breath," the doctor said.

Jim couldn't. He was delighted.

* * * *

"Hello," the man said. His voice was heavily accented.

"Could I speak to Marci, please?"

"Who's calling?"

"It's Jim?"

"Jim who?"

"I'm in her art history class. She knows me."

"Hold on. Marci!"

"Hello?"

"I failed the physical! The doctor told me they'd never take me! You're a goddamn genius! I love you!"

"That's very nice," she said primly.

"I know you can't talk. Look, don't think for a minute I'm going to let you get away. This is it. This is a formal proposal. I've always wanted to marry a prudent woman—as long as she's prudent enough to let me get my degree first."

"Well," she said, "that sounds like a good idea to me. Of course, there are arrangements to be made."

"I know," Jim said. "Your father. I'll talk to him. I'll bullshit him. You won't believe how I'll bullshit him. We're golden, Sweetheart, wait and see."

"I certainly hope so," Marci Roth said politely.

Chapter 18

Sam Roth was small, bent and lean, his face lined and craggy. He was not quite sixty; he looked older. He was animated in manner and nervous by disposition. Sitting in his comfortable chair in the living room of his brick rowhouse on Knorr Street in Northeast Philadelphia, he looked across the coffee table at the young man on the sofa. He sighed deeply. "I can't say I didn't see it coming," he said in his deep and heavily accented voice. "Marci always liked the goyishe boys. Every other boy she ever brought here was a goy. And now this." Sam sighed again.

Jim almost smiled. Marci's father was just as she had described him. He said, "Mr. Roth, I understand that this is a problem for you. I didn't understand at first how great a problem. Religion has never been particularly important to me—"

Sam looked up and broke in. "It's not just religion."

Jim nodded. "There's also a cultural question. Is that what you mean?"

"What do you mean?" Sam challenged.

"Well," Jim said slowly, "I mean that the whole question of intermarriage, as I understand it, is tied up with preserving a culture and a set of values and an identity that goes back five thousand years. I'll admit to you that it's all a bit ephemeral to me, but I think Marci has given me some appreciation for the implications."

Sam smiled and nodded. "Ephemeral," he said. "You're a smart boy. Smarter than me, when it comes to English. I don't know what that word means, for example. That word 'ephemeral'."

"It means—"

"I don't care what it means," Sam snapped. "You know this ephemeral and I know life. I'll take what I know, and you can keep what you know."

"Mr. Roth—"

"Quiet! Can't you be quiet? You come in here and say you're going to marry my daughter, and you talk my ear off. Aren't I entitled to say something?"

As Marci had predicted, he was angry. Jim said, "I'm sorry, Sir. What did you want to say?"

"I don't know what I wanted to say," Sam said. "No, I do know what I want to say." He looked toward the ceiling. "God, you've done it again to me, haven't you?" He looked back at Jim. "Only he's not listening because he isn't there to begin with. What are you majoring in at this college you go to?"

"Electrical engineering. I'll have my degree in another month, and I have a job lined up with General Electric in Schenectady."

Sam cocked his head. "Schenectady? Are there Jews in Schenectady? Not that it matters, with who she wants to marry."

"I'm sure there are, Mr. Roth. We've decided to raise our children Jewish, and we'll give them the right kind of religious education. You shouldn't worry about that."

"Oh," Sam said, gesturing expansively, "I shouldn't worry? Good, now I can relax. My daughter wants to marry a goy, and—"

"Marci tells me that's an insulting term," Jim broke in coldly.

Sam shrugged. "Not so insulting—unless you mean it to be insulting. I don't mean it to be, okay?"

"Okay," Jim said.

"But what's the difference?" Sam demanded. "Goy. Gentile. So what? What's what is that Marci marries a gentile and goes to Schenectady. And you say I shouldn't worry about it. What should I worry about, then? The Phillies this summer? I should worry about the Eagles this fall, maybe? I'll worry, if you don't mind. Schenectady, he says."

Jim watched him for a moment. Then he said, "Mr. Roth, Marci said this would be difficult for both of us. As usual, she was right. You and I both love her, and we both want the best for her."

Sam fixed Jim Ryan with a hard glare. "This is all very nice for you to say. You're a nice boy. You don't know anything, and you're a goy who wants to take my daughter to Schenectady, yet, but you're nice." Sam's jaw tightened. "The answer is no. I say no."

"Mr. Roth," Jim said quietly, "I want to say this with all respect, Sir, but I'm not here to ask you for Marci. I already have her. We are going to get married, Sir. I came here tonight hoping to get your blessing, but the marriage will take place with or without your blessing. You have to understand that."

Sam's lips formed a tight, thin line. "Oh," he said, "so you have a mouth on you. It figures. Marci has a mouth on her, too. Her whole life she's had a mouth. You'll find out. So you're telling me, is that right?"

Jim nodded. "Yes, Sir. That's about right. I'm sorry. I didn't want to have to put it that way."

Sam looked at Jim with appraising eyes. "So, I have to put up with this? Let me tell you, Boy, I've put up with more than you. I got out of Poland one step ahead of Hitler. I came here and built a life when everybody I loved stayed and died. I can handle you, Boy. You can't have her."

Jim looked into Sam Roth's face. He saw steel. He sighed and stood up. "I'm sorry you feel that way, Mr. Roth. I'd hoped it wouldn't be like this. I'd hoped Marci had exaggerated."

Jim started for the door and his Karman Ghia outside. As his hand touched the doorknob, he heard Sam's voice from behind him. He said, "Would you convert?"

Jim stopped, turned and looked at him. "I don't believe in organized religion, Mr. Roth. I don't believe in the religion I was born into and brought up in. It would be the height of hypocrisy for me to accept instruction in and become a practitioner of another religion in which I have as little belief as the one I now ignore. I'm sorry, I wouldn't."

Sam smiled a litte. "An athiest? Is that it?"

"No. I believe in God. I just don't believe in all the silly ways people worship him and the rituals that take the place of honest thought. To me, organized religion has value largely as a cultural experience, and that tends to be overvalued."

I see," Sam said. "Fine, I don't believe in religion either—not after what I've seen. I believe in people. I believe in tradition and in people loving each other. That's the important thing, don't you think?"

Jim, surprised at the sudden turn of the conversation, said, "Marci says that you and I would agree on a lot if we got to know each other. She thinks we're a lot alike. I'm not sure, incidentally, that she meant it as a compliment."

Sam laughed a warm and spirited laugh. "If you marry my Marci, you'll get used to that. She'll do what she wants. You'll do what she wants, too. Listen to me when I say this: Marci lives in a different world sometimes from the rest of us. Did she tell you I'm rich? Did she say that?"

Jim looked around the row house living room. This was a nice, solid house, a thoroughly middle-class dwelling. It was not the home of a rich man. "No. She told me you're a salesman."

Sam Roth rolled his eyes. "A salesman, he says. She doesn't know from salesmen. I'm a manufacturer's representative."

"Well, that sounds to me a bit like a salesman."

Sam Roth snorted. "I have my own company. I have six employees. I represent firms that sell technology to the government. Listen to me, Boy. I speak four languages. My English isn't the best, maybe, but I have a degree in physics from the university in Warsaw—an advanced degree, I have. She told you none of this, right?"

Jim shook his head.

"Marci, she doesn't care what I do. The money is just there, she thinks—like it grows in the front yard with the grass. She dresses like a Queen Elizabeth."

Jim said, "Maybe she doesn't think of you as rich."

"Well," Sam conceded, "I'm not rich—not like Rockefeller, I'm not rich. I'm well off, is what I am. I have a place in Florida. I have a good business. I have good investments. Understand?"

Jim didn't. This was one of the most baffling conversations in which he'd ever engaged. "I have the feeling," he said, "that you're looking for some kind of response from me—and I don't know exactly what you want me to say."

"What are they going to pay you in Schenectady?" Sam demanded.

"I'm starting at ninety-five hundred a year."

"I'll give you twelve thousand if you work for me," Sam said suddenly.

"What?"

"Thirteen. Not a penny more."

Jim shook his head. "I don't understand, Mr. Roth. My plans are made. I'm going to be an engineer."

Sam leaned across the coffee table. "If you're going to marry my Marci," he pleaded, "don't take her so far away from me."

* * * *

A bored voice over the Boydstown Airport's aged public address system rattled off a list of arriving and departing flights. Not a word was intelligible.

"I think that's his plane they just called out," Kevin said. "I couldn't actually make it out, but it's about the right time."

Katherine squeezed her son's arm. "I remember when your father and I waited for your plane to come in at Rochester. I feel the same way now."

Henri said, "I remember that. My God, the time goes by."

"Yes," Annette said. "The time, she leaps so fast."

"She flies so fast," Henri corrected.

"Jumps, flies, glides," Annette said with a frown. "It is all the same."

"There's his plane!" Susan called out. "See, Liam. There's Uncle Will's plane."

Will, in uniform, was among the first of the passengers to disembark.

"There he is," Art said, gazing through the glass. "He's trimmed down some."

As Will came through the door, the family surrounded him, smiling, pumping his hand, covering his face with kisses. He smiled and hugged his grandmother, his sister and Annette. Art shook his hand. Little Liam squeezed him around the neck. When Will put down little Liam he reached out for his father's hand. Kevin pulled his son close and held him. "Welcome home," Kevin told his son.

"Nobody ever said anything nicer to me," Will said.

Kevin had a table reserved at Cory's—Boydstown's best restaurant—and the family had been gathered around it to celebrate Will's return for less than twenty minutes when Jack, Helen and Patricia came in to join them. Jack looked much the same to Will—smallish, bald and smiling—and so did Helen, who even past fifty looked no more than thirty-five, but a hard-lived thirty-five, Will decided. There was a tightness to her face and an unhealthy flush to her cheeks.

Will was astounded in the change that had taken place in Patricia in just the fourteen months he had been away. She was seventeen now and had lost most of the baby fat that had marked her earlier high school years. Her hair was nearly waist length, and she affected a pair of granny glasses. She wore jeans and soft leather boots with fringe and a poor boy sweater. Her expression was one of consummate boredom.

Kevin had ordered a sumptuous dinner. As the courses arrived, various varieties of Brennan table wine and Weidener champagne were served. Art, long since at ease with his in-laws, kept the table convulsed with one bawdy joke after another.

". . . so the guy says to the *mohel*," Art said, finishing up one such story, " 'This wallet is worth every penny. If you rub it the right way, poof, it turns into a suitcase.' "

Everyone laughed except Annette, who had failed to grasp the joke. Then Kevin said, "You better be careful, Art. There are some people who might think that joke is anti-Semitic."

"There's nothing anti-Semitic about that," Art said, "a little raunchy, maybe, but not anti-Semitic."

Will, who had spent a lifetime hearing his family joke about anything and everything, said, "What's the sudden concern about anti-Semitism? Every joke I ever heard in this family would offend somebody. What am I missing?"

"This is all for my benefit," Jack said. "Your father just has his needle out. Jim is getting married in August. The girl is Jewish."

"That's great," Will said.

"You probably should be getting an invitation in a little while," Jack told him. "The wedding is going to be in Philadelphia. Jim says it'll be a real show. They're going to have a priest and a rabbi both."

"We'll be there for sure," Art said. "I've never been to Philadelphia."

Jack said, "Just picture a great big Boydstown where every other person you see is colored."

Art made a face. "Maybe we won't go after all."

"Jimmy's getting married," Susan said. "I feel so old."

"Oh, yes," said Katherine, who had turned seventy-eight the previous month, "you're a regular Grandma Moses."

While this conversation was taking place, Art turned to Will, who was sitting next to him, thoughtfully smoking a cigarette.

"See much action?" Art asked.

Will nodded. "Too much."

Art leaned back in his chair. "Christ, I feel sort of guilty sitting here next to you, in your uniform and all."

Will looked at him. "What for?"

"Well, you know, there's a war going on. Guys like you are getting shot at, and I'm sitting in Lakeside working at the trucking company. I feel like I ought to be doing something, you know? I'm only twenty-seven. In World War II I'd have had to go."

Will stubbed out his cigarette and lit another immediately. "This isn't World War II. Look, you're raising my nephew and taking care of my sister. That's plenty."

"I suppose," Art said. "Did you actually kill anybody?"

Will drew on his cigarette before answering. Then: "Yeah, I killed people."

"More than one?"

Will nodded. "I've got to go to the john. Excuse me for a minute, Art."

Will walked out of the dining room and into the restaurant's lobby. He looked out the door at the friendly North American night. He'd gone from Vietnam to Manila for final processing then flown directly home. It was still cold in upstate New York, more cold than he'd felt in thirteen months. He liked the look of the naked trees along the street and the leaden skies above. Bleak but familiar. He realized he'd left his cigarette in the ashtray back at the table. He lit another from the pack in his pocket.

"Got another one of those?" he heard someone ask.

He turned. His cousin Patricia stood next to him in her granny glasses and hippie outfit. He handed her a cigarette.

"Sure," he said, lighting it. "Jesus, everybody has certainly grown up while I've been away. Jim is getting married, and you're smoking. I hope you can handle a Camel."

"I like filters better, but I'll smoke a Camel."

She drew in on the strong smoke and blew it out expertly. As she did, Will studied her. She looked more like the Ryans than the Brennans. Patricia was small where her mother's family tended to be big. Her expression was essentially her father's. "Do your parents know you smoke?" he asked her.

Patricia took a drag on the Camel and blew out the smoke expertly. "There's lots they don't know. I smoke pot, too, sometimes."

"Do you, now? Well, I guess you have grown up."

Patricia eyed him levelly. He saw no touch of humor there. "You're making fun of me."

"Sorry. I guess I am, and I shouldn't."

"Do you ever smoke grass? In Vietnam, I mean?"

"It's the Vietnamese national flower. I've smoked a lot of these, too. I want to quit both now that I'm back. I used to run track in high school. My coach would be horrified to see me with this thing."

"It's bad for your health," Patricia agreed.

Will laughed. "The biggest immediate danger to my health has passed."

"Are you going to wear your uniform to Jimmy's wedding?"

"I'm not even sure I'm going to go yet. But if I do, I promise you I won't go in my uniform."

"Did you hate it over there?"

Will paused before he answered. Then he said, "Most of the time, yes. There were some good times, though. I had a ball in Saigon. The food was French, and it was great. Servicemen just owned that city— servicemen and journalists. I saw Walter Cronkite in the Caravelle Hotel."

"I think the war sucks," Patricia volunteered. "I hope the Republicans get elected this year so they'll end it."

Will looked at her quizzically. "So you think Nixon will end it—or Rockefeller?"

"I know Humphrey won't. And my father says Bobby Kennedy can't get the nomination, so what's left?"

Will drew on his Camel. "Nobody is going to end it, not for a long time. None of them really understands what's going on there. We're so arrogant. We got in there because we thought that the place was going communist, and we thought that if our troops showed up, those little dinks in black pajamas would run back into the jungle in terror. Only it didn't work that way. The whole goddamn country is against us there, except for the people who were coopted by the French twenty years ago and who still run the government in the south. Most of the country just wants to stay alive, and it's a real chore for a lot of them. What are you in school now, Patricia—a junior?"

"Senior."

"Are you going to college next year?"

"I got accepted at NYU. I got accepted at Syracuse, too, but I think I'm going to go to NYU. I want to live in New York City."

He nodded. "What are you going to take?"

"I don't have to decide on a major until I'm a junior. Will, what are you going to do now that you're back?"

He laughed. "Take it easy for a while, maybe work in the winery. This winter I might apply to graduate school again." He glanced at his watch. "We ought to go back in, I think."

"Yeah," Patricia said, stubbing out her Camel. "Could I bum another cigarette for later?"

He dug into his pocket. "Here, take the pack. I just quit."

* * * *

Art and Susan Brennan Dixon pulled their Mustang into the driveway of their modest house just off Lake Street in Lakeside at a little after three in the morning. It had been seven arduous hours from the Philadelphia catering hall where Jim and Marci had married.

Susan would have liked to have stayed overnight in the Marriot where they had spent the previous night, but the wedding had taken place on a Sunday, and Art had to be at work early Monday morning. As it was, he would be going in with only about three hours sleep.

Susan looked over into the back seat, where little Liam lay sleeping. "We'll have to carry him in and put him to bed."

Art rubbed his eyes, got out of the car and stretched, and then he reached into the car for his son. "Come on, little guy," he said, picking up the sleeping child. "Up and at 'em."

They went into the house and put Liam to sleep in his clothes. In their own bedroom, Susan changed into a nightgown and Art flopped on the bed in his shorts. It was hot. Susan opened the windows.

Art flipped on the television set. "Wonder what's on the late, late show."

"My," she said. "Aren't you brave. What time to you have to be in tomorrow—eight?"

"Some things are more important than sleep," Art told her, pulling her close. He buried his face in her hair. "God, woman, you're a goddess."

"You've got to be kidding," Susan said, yawning.

Liam called out in his room down the hall. Susan extricated herself from her husband's embrace. The boy was sitting up in his bed, crying. Susan sat down next to him and took him in her arms.

"What's the matter, Sweetness?" she asked, stroking the little boy's hair.

"How did I get here?" Liam said, crying piteously.

"You fell asleep in the car. When we got home we just carried you in and put you to bed. Here, let's get these clothes off, now that you're awake, and we'll tuck you in and you go back to sleep, okay?"

"No," the little boy said through his tears. It meant yes, Susan knew. Liam, awakened, was invariably whiny and uncooperative. She unbuttoned his shirt, undid his trousers and got him down to his underwear. As she was about to pull the sheet up over him, he rolled over on his other side, and she saw a large bruise on his thigh. It was purplish, swollen and the size of her fist.

"Liam," she said, turning on the lamp so she could study it, "how'd you do this to yourself?"

"I don't know."

Susan touched the bruise. "Does it hurt?"

"No. Go away, please? I'm sleepy."

Susan frowned. Then she said, "Okay, you go to sleep. See you in the morning." She pulled the sheet over the child, who was already asleep again. She flipped off the lamp and went back to her own room. Art was snoring in the bed. She sat down next to him and nudged him. "Come on, Don Juan," Susan said. "You're pooping out on me."

Art groaned. "I've got to get up early tomorrow."

Susan got up and switched off the television set and the lights. She crawled into bed and nudged Art with her hip. "Come on, move over to your own side."

He groaned and rolled over. Susan took a deep breath and closed her eyes, but all she could see was the ugly bruise on Liam's thigh. "Art?" she said in the darkness.

He rolled over toward her. "Hmmmm?"

"It was a nice wedding, wasn't it? Did Will seem a little strange to you?"

"Strange, how?"

"He's just been so quiet ever since he got back. He never seems to be able to enjoy himself any more."

"He had a bad time over there. We were talking that first day back. You know, he apparently killed a bunch of guys. You know that's the sort of thing that would affect him."

"I suppose. Liam has a nasty bruise on his leg."

"Kids get bruises."

"I suppose. Have you noticed how much Patricia is growing up?"

"The kid looks like a goddamn hippie, with all that fringe and those beads and her hair hanging down to her ass."

Susan said, "I bet she goes really wild when she goes away to college."

Art curled up against Susan's back. She felt his hand cup her breast. "Speaking of going wild . . ." he said.

Susan took his hand away. "Too late. You missed your chance. I'm going to sleep."

Art rolled over. "You owe me one. I'm keeping count."

* * * *

"Hello, Dawn," Sam said. "Is Otto in? He should be expecting me."

"Sure. Go right in, Mr. Roth."

Jim Ryan and Sam Roth entered a small, crowded office. At his desk in the corner, Otto Kruger, a balding, heavy-set man of fifty, was on the telephone, speaking in a clipped, German accent. He put his hand over the mouthpiece and motioned for them to sit down. "Hello, Sam," he said, "just a minute." Then, into the phone, he said, "I don't care about that. The shipment is four days late. I don't want the stuff next week. I want the stuff now. We have a contract, goddamn it!" There was a moment's silence as he listened to the voice at the other end of the line. Then he said, "I hope so. If it's not, you'll hear from me right away." He hung up the phone and spun around in his chair.

"Hello, Sam," Kruger said, extending his hand. "Jesus Christ, you try to get some sand delivered, and you'd think you were asking for gold dust."

Sam shook his hand. "It's gold when you're finished with it, Otto, you goniff. Otto Kruger, meet my son-in-law, Jim Ryan."

Kruger pumped Jim's hand. "Jim, how are you? So, you married that pretty daughter of his, eh? Well, I suppose that she's pretty enough that you can put up with this old bastard."

"Jim is in the business, Otto," Sam Roth said. "I'm going to be working with him, but he'll be the man who services your account."

"Oh?" Kruger said. "Well, do you know anything about printed circuit boards? Do you know anything about silicon chips? That's where the business is going to be in few years."

"I'm familiar with printed circuit boards," Jim said, "and I know a little about silicon chips. I took a course in them at Drexel."

"How'd you do in that course?" Kruger demanded.

Jim smiled ruefully. "I got a C. On the other hand, I graduated cum laude in electrical engineering, so I think I can pick up what I need to know to sell them."

"I hope so," Kruger said. "Drexel, eh? Well, that's not too bad. My son, he's in his second year at MIT."

Sam said, "Otto, since your account will be one of the biggest ones Jim is going to handle, I'd like him to spend the week here, watching what you do. How does that sound?"

"Fine," Kruger said. Then he picked up his phone and hit the receptionist's button. "Send Lee in here."

The three men sat and talked for a few minutes, then a youngish Chinese in wheat jeans and a sport shirt came in.

Kruger said, "Galen, you know Sam Roth. This is his son-in-law, Jim Ryan. He'll be handling our account. This is Galen Lee, our chief engineer. Galen, Jim wants to learn all there is to know about chips. He'll be here for the rest of the week. You teach him."

Galen Lee smiled, and Jim liked him immediately. "Fine. When do we start?"

"How about now?" Sam asked. "We came in separate cars."

"Fine," Galen Lee said. "Jim, just follow me."

The factory occupied a small building in an industrial park in King of Prussia, north of Philadelphia. As Jim and Galen walked along the hallway leading to the manufacturing facilities, Galen said, "Otto is a real putz, in case you didn't notice."

Jim laughed. "Sam told me he could be a bit difficult, but he seemed okay in there."

"Well, he's not. Don't get me wrong: he's a fairly good engineer and a damned good businessman; but he's a putz to work for. You'll see."

"What I want to see first is how this place operates."

Galen gave him a complete tour as they got acquainted. Lee was from Hawaii. He'd moved to the East Coast to finish his graduate work. He was several years older than Jim but didn't look it.

As they moved from the section that produced printed circuit boards and into the chip-manufacturing operation, Galen said, "Look, I'm going to pretend that you don't have any background in engineering. That'll make it easier for me to lay out for you what we do here."

"Fine, go ahead."

"Okay," Galen said, "you know what semiconductors are. They're nonmetallic substances—in this case silicon—that neither conduct electricity nor insulate but whose electrical properties lie in between. What we do here is dope silicon—infuse it with controlled amounts of specially selected elements called dopants—which we heat to gas along with the silicon and modify its structure by displacing a few of the silicon atoms. This forms conductive paths through the silicon through which electricity will pass more easily. Are you with me so far?"

"I understand the theory. I don't know much about the actual man-ufacturing process, though."

"Stay with me, because if you don't have the theory down cold you won't understand the manufacturing process. What we do here is create integrated circuits. Those are—"

Jim was getting impatient. "Multiple transistors, complete circuits in a miniature silicon chip. This much I learned at Drexel."

Galen nodded. "That's right. We're able here to imprint thousands of components in chips less than a quarter of an inch square. So far we're able to do it at a cost below anybody else in the country. That's our big selling point. We're cheap."

"What's Otto's trick? How does he do it at such a low cost?"

"One way is to hire kids like me, pay us peanuts and put us in charge. He's also a bear on buying materials. The fact that he's a putz keeps his costs down. Sooner or later anybody who's any good gets pissed off at him and leaves. Then he hires somebody else cheaper."

Jim smiled. It didn't sound like a bad technique. "Why are you still here?"

"My wife is in medical school at Penn," Galen said. "I probably won't be here in four more years. Anyway, let me go on with how this joint operates. We design integrated circuits to fit customer specifications. We're essentially a specialty shop. The customer provides detailed specs on what he wants, and we design and manufacture it. Right now, we're doing a fair amount of work for NASA, which is into miniaturization in a big way. They're not the bulk of our work, but they're our biggest single customer. We computerize the designs that come in from their consultants, then we manufacture the circuits."

"And how do you do that?"

Galen warmed to his topic. He was, Jim could see, extraordinarily bright, and he liked talking about what he did.

"What you have to do is melt the silicon into an ingot and slice it into a microscopically thin wafer into which you imprint the circuit."

"How do you slice them that thin?" Jim asked.

"We do it with little diamond-edged saws we buy from a company up in Springfield, Massachusetts. We buy a lot of saws because they wear out fast, and we need tight tolerances to do the job. Once you get the sliced wafer, you heat it with the dopant in a furnace that goes up to twelve hundred degrees centigrade to form your circuit. We coat the wafer with an emulsion that hardens when we expose it to ultraviolet light. We cover the wafer with one of the masks, and we zap it with ultraviolet light. That imprints the circuit. Then we . . ."

And as Galen talked, Jim took notes.

* * * *

The house was a rambling single story, white with green shutters. It had been built in the midfifties, Will guessed, and it was located on a side street in West Boydstown, which was a comfortable suburb of the city. There was a baby blue Lincoln in the driveway. He parked his own car, a new yellow MGB, behind it. Then he got out and knocked on the door.

The woman who answered was overweight and unkempt. A cigarette dangled from her lips. She wore a robe, even though it was nearly one in the afternoon.

"It's me," Will said.

Jane Wright cocked her head in confusion. The Will Brennan she had last seen at his sister's wedding had been shaggy and pudgy. This one was clean-shaven, short-haired, lean and tanned.

"I didn't recognize you," she said. "You look just terrific. Come on in. The place is a mess. I wasn't expecting visitors."

The house was nicely furnished, but newspapers, magazines and various articles of feminine clothing littered the living room. Three settings of dirty dishes rested on the coffee table in front of the television set.

"You just sit here while I pick up some of this mess," Jane said.

"Don't worry about it. Where's Bob?"

"He's in New York, on business for the newspaper. He went with the publisher, Mr. Farrell. Bob is the assistant national ad manager for the *Bulletin* now, you know."

Will realized as she sat down on the sofa across from him that his mother, even at this early hour, was a little drunk. Her words slurred conspicuously.

"I didn't know that," he told her. "I knew he sold ads for the paper, but I didn't know he was an executive."

"Well," Jane said, lighting a Winston, "he's only had the job for the past few months. He bought me that Lincoln outside to celebrate. We got a good deal on it from an advertiser. It's only two years old. When he got the job, I told him it was about time. He's been working for Mr. Farrell for damn near eighteen years now, and this is his first promotion.

That's why I didn't go to New York with him. I didn't want to mess anything up for him."

Will lit his own cigarette, a Camel. He'd found quitting more difficult than he'd anticipated. "Mom, you wouldn't mess anything up."

Jane laughed. "I probably would have. I always drink too much and run my mouth too much. But I guess you know all about that."

"It doesn't sound like any of my business."

"Oh, hell," Jane Wright said. "I know Bob calls Kevin and asks for advice on how to handle me. Kevin must think it's hilarious."

Will said, "He's never said a word to me about it."

"Well, that's nice, then. Your father's always been a nice man." Jane looked at her son carefully. "So, to what do I owe the honor of this visit? Not that it's not welcome. Come to think of it, I don't think I've seen you in . . . let's see, now . . . it's been a couple of years, anyway. You look different without that beard and long hair. You look a bit like your grandfather, you know."

"Nobody has ever told me that before. I just came to visit with you for a while."

"Well, good," she said. "I was so worried when you went to Vietnam. And then when I heard from Helen that you were back in one piece . . . well, I was thrilled. How's Susan? And my grandson? How's he?"

"Everybody is fine. You know that Susan had some kind of female problem last year, don't you?"

"Yes, Kevin called and told me. He hasn't called me more than three or four times in almost twenty-five years, so it was an occasion. He said she probably won't be able to get pregnant again. How's she taking that?"

"Pretty well. She says that little Liam is a handful all by himself. I think it bothers her, but she's not letting on."

"Well, good for her. She's always been a gutsy kid. Can I get you something to drink? We have some beer in the fridge."

"A beer sounds fine."

Jane got up and went into the kitchen. Will looked around. The end table next to him was covered with dust. The carpet, which was expensive, hadn't been vacuumed in some time. Jane came back in and handed him his beer, then she sat down again. "So," she said, "what are you doing with yourself now that you're back?"

Will shrugged. "I was going to go to grad school this fall, but I couldn't get it together. I'm just working a bit in the winery. Harvest is coming up."

Jane made a face. "I remember. How's your grandmother?"

"Okay. She had a mild stroke while I was away, but there was no lasting damage."

"I'm glad to hear that. I always admired Katherine—even though she didn't have much use for me. So, why are you here, Will?"

Will sipped his beer while he framed his reply. "Does there have to be a special reason? You're my mother, and I haven't seen you for a while."

Jane nodded slowly. "Will, it's been a couple of years now since I've laid eyes on you. I don't think you've ever been in this house. The last time you visited me we lived in a dump over on Second Street. I'm glad to see you and all, but you seem to have something bothering you. What is it? If there's anything I can do to help, then I want to do it."

Will was silent for a moment. "All right. I want to ask you a question."

"Go ahead."

"You might not like the question, and I'm not even going to tell you why I'm asking it. The only reason I'm doing it, frankly, is that I'm trying to work out something in my own mind, and I figure that any help you can give me is help I have coming."

Jane stiffened visibly. "Go ahead."

"I need to know how you felt after you left us. Not when you left us, exactly, but after you had made the decision and it was over and you had to live with it and there was no going back."

Jane didn't like the question. "Why do you want to know that?"

"I can't go into detail for you. You made a decision once, and it had consequences. I need to know how you dealt with those consequences. You're my mother—even though we haven't seen much of each other. Maybe the way you dealt with your decision can help me deal with a decision I made."

She lit another Winston. "Was I unhappy? Is that what you're asking?"

"No. I accept as a given that your decision brought you a certain degree of unhappiness. I need to know how you reconciled your decision with all the misery it caused you and everybody else."

Jane sat back on the sofa. The smoke from her cigarette rose in front of her bloated face in swirls. She was silent for a long moment. "I did what I had to do for me," she said finally, and her voice was brittle. "If it sounds selfish, then let it be selfish. Was I sorry about you kids? Sure, I was sorry. But I would have been sorrier if I hadn't left. Is that what you wanted to hear? Fine, then, you've heard it. You get one life, Will. It's in session right from the start. If you miss anything, then it's your own fault. I wasn't going to spend my life missing things."

He stubbed out his Camel and gazed at her coolly. "And you don't think you've missed anything?"

"Sure," she said, "I've missed a lot. But I'm not finished yet. I'm fifty-two. That may sound old to you, Kid, but I'm still a young woman.

I've got some living to do yet. I've got places to go, people to see, like the song says."

Will Brennan sat silently for several minutes. She sat silently across from him, drawing on her Winston and fixing him with a steel-hard stare. Finally, he put down his still-full can of beer and stood up. "Thanks," he said. "Look, I appreciate the beer. I've got to go now."

Jane made no move to rise and see him out. "Thanks a lot for dropping by. Stop by any time."

* * * *

"I saw Will the other day," Becky said.

Kevin, lying in bed next to her in the old King house, said, "Did you say hello to him?"

"Yes. It was strange."

"Strange how?"

"He was coming out of that bar down by the mill—the Unicorn. I looked at him and said hello. He looked right past me like I wasn't there."

Kevin shrugged. "Maybe he didn't recognize you."

"It wasn't just me he didn't recognize. He didn't know what planet he was on. He was in a trance, Kevin."

Kevin was was silent for a long moment. "I've seen that before. Ever since he got back, he's been sort of . . . well, he's had things on his mind."

"Is he all right?"

"As near as I can tell."

"Well, let me tell you, it was very strange."

"I'll show you something strange."

"Kevin Brennan! Stop that! You're such a pervert."

"Ha, ha," Kevin said. "I'll show you a pervert."

"Oh, no you won't. Kevin! You just . . . Yes. Yes, just like that, just like that. That's right. Oh, yes. Oh God, I love perverts. I love you! God, I love you, Kevin."

* * * *

The phone rang. Will, on his way down the stairs to the center hallway where one of the telephone extensions rested on a table, called out, "I'll get it. Hello."

The unfamiliar male voice with a heavy Brooklyn accent said, "I'd like to speak to William Brennan, please."

"This is William Brennan."

"Mr. Brennan, my name is Mark Costello. I wonder if I could come to your house and talk to you for a little while."

"Well," Will said, "who are you, Mr. Costello? And what do you want?"

"I'm a reporter for *Newsday*. We're a newspaper on Long Island. I'm in Lakeside, and I'm planning to stop out and see you, if I can."

Will was surprised and confused. "Can you tell me what it's about?"

"I'd prefer to go into the details face to face."

Will hesitated. "I'd kind of like to find out why you want to see me before I make any arrangements to see you."

There was a moment's silence from Costello's end. "I started out about five weeks ago doing a story on a guy from Long Island who came back from Vietnam and had a problem. He was a guy who served with you. His name is Richard Jackson. I'd like to talk to you about Jackson and . . . well, some of the things that went on in Vietnam when the two of you were there."

For a moment Will was afraid he was going to vomit. He felt his gorge rise, and he forced it back down. It left a sour taste in his mouth. His hands were shaking. "What kind of things?" he almost whispered.

"Well, Jackson's mother says he had a breakdown because of an incident in which some civilians were killed. Are you still there, Mr. Brennan? Can I call you Bill?"

"If you want to. Everybody else calls me Will."

"Then I will, too, Will," Costello said. "Look, I'm talking to just about everybody who was there that day. I've seen a half-dozen guys so far. I'd really like to spend an hour or so with you."

"I don't think that's a good idea," Will said.

"Well, look," Costello said, "I'm going to come out to your place and see you. You can throw me off the property if you like, but I really think we ought to talk in person."

"No," Will said quickly. "Listen, I'll meet you in town. There's a diner on Lake Street. I'll see you there in half an hour. How will I know you?"

"I should be the only guy in the place in a Hofstra T-shirt."

Will put down the phone. His stomach was churning, and for a moment he felt he was going to fall down. He leaned against the wall and cleared his head. His grandmother appeared in the doorway from the kitchen.

"Want some breakfast?" Katherine asked him.

"No. I've got to run into town."

"Without breakfast?"

"I'm meeting somebody."

"A girl?"

Will knew what answer she would like. "A knockout."

Katherine smiled. "Have a nice time, now."

Will found Mark Costello at the counter. They moved to a corner booth. Costello was a short, skinny guy with glasses an inch thick and curly black hair that shot off in all directions. He had a wispy moustache, and he wore corduroy jeans and a yellow T-shirt with red letters that spelled out HOFSTRA. He carried a khaki book bag over one spindly shoulder.

"Tell me about Jackson," Will said to the reporter.

Costello's voice had an irritating nasal quality. "He had a pistol—a target gun. One night he went nuts in a bar in Mineola, and he ended up shooting a Chinese aeronautical engineer. The guy was just sitting there drinking a beer. I did the initial story on the shooting, and when I talked to his mother she said that he'd gone nuts because of some incident in Vietnam when he and a bunch of other guys killed a bunch of civilians in a village near a place called Chu Lai. I got the names of other people in the outfit from the Defense Department. I've spent the past couple of weeks flying around the country talking to people who were there."

Will gazed into his cup of black coffee, as though it contained the secrets of the universe. Then he said, "What do you think you've got?"

"I don't know what I've got," Costello told him. "I think I've got a story about a lot of people getting killed, and nobody can tell me why. I think I've got a story about a lot of guys who've come back home and still can't figure out what happened to them. Do you know what Jackson's mother said to me? She said: I sent them a good boy, and they sent me back a murderer."

Will had difficulty thinking of Jackson as ever having been a good boy. He saw that pale face, and below it a dog tag chain filled with severed ears, like sadistic jewelry. "So what are you going to do with this story of yours?" he asked the reporter.

Costello sipped his coffee. "I'm going to go back to Long Island and write it. My editors have let me spend a couple of weeks running around the country, so I'm pretty sure they're going to print it. I still have to talk to a lot more guys, but the picture I get from everybody is pretty much the same."

"Then why do you need me?"

"I need to talk to as many people as I can."

"When is this story of yours going to run?" Will asked.

"A month or two, probably. I've got a lot of checking to do. At

Newsday stories like this get a lot of screwing around with from the editors."

Will looked at Costello across the table. The guy looked like a nerd. Clearly, though, he was smart as hell, otherwise he wouldn't have gotten this far with what he was doing.

"You look like you're about my age," Will told him. "Were you in the service?"

"Bad back," Costello explained.

Lucky you, Will thought. "So all you know about Nam is what you hear and read, right?"

"That's right."

"And what have you heard and read?"

Costello looked down at his coffee. Then he looked up again. "I read and heard that we were supposed to be the good guys."

Will laughed. "Yeah, that's what I heard, too."

Costello reached into the book bag beside him and pulled out a notebook and a battery-operated casette recorder. "So what happened?" he asked.

The interview had begun. Will knew he could stand up now and leave, and he entertained the notion for the briefest fraction of a second. What the hell, he thought. "It was a big search and destroy mission," Will said. "A couple of hundred of us were out from several companies. There was a lot of brass in the sky over us. They were in touch by radio. Jackson was in command of my unit. We found a village that showed signs of sympathy to Charlie."

"What sort of signs?" Costello asked, scribbling in his notebook.

"We found an AK-47 hidden there. Charlie had been there. Shit, Charlie had been in every village in the sector. Charlie was somebody's son or brother, and he went home, is all. It was the classic revolutionary situation, you know? You had a sympathetic peasantry hiding the rebels because the rebels were their relatives."

Costello nodded. Will came to the realization that he was discussing the topic in totally detached terms, as though he were back at Harvard talking about political science to a classmate. Either Costello was very good or Will's brain had gone soft. He couldn't be sure which. He should be running out of the diner like the demons of hell were after him.

"And . . ." Costello prodded.

"So we found the weapon, and Jackson got on the horn to the brass. He talked for a while. Then he told us to round up everybody. We put them next to the village well. Jesus, it all seems so strange now—sitting here like this."

"And then?" Costello pressed. "What happened then?"

"Then Jackson said to take care of them."

"What did he mean by that?"

"He meant to waste them—to kill them. He tried to make out like it was his own idea. That's basic military routine—the management procedure. You carry out an order like it's your own. That's what I think Jackson was doing. He was on the phone to his bosses. I'm convinced it wasn't his own order."

"Can you prove that?" Costello asked.

"No. He was the only one I heard give an order. Also, you've got to understand Jackson. That guy was the original good German. He'd do precisely what he was told and never question it. That's the kind of guy he was."

"So what happened then?"

"So, we shot them."

Costello scribbled that down. Then he looked up from his notebook. "Just like that? You shot them?"

Will was silent. "No. Some of us said we wouldn't. But Jackson kept yelling it was an order. So somebody started shooting, and then we all started. You've got to understand. It was combat conditions. Charlie was all over the place. My best friend in Nam was killed by a kid who couldn't have hit puberty yet. You can sit here and talk about it, but it was different when you were there. We were all half-nuts."

Costello scribbled. "Go on."

"I shot low the first time. I shot in the dirt. I emptied my first clip, but Jackson kept yelling. So I put in a new clip, and then I shot higher."

"You hit the people?"

"Yeah. I hit a few of them."

"You're sure you hit them?"

"Yeah. I shot higher the second time. I hit them. I saw some of them fall."

"How many?"

"I don't know."

"You killed them?"

"I don't know. Everybody was shooting. Yeah, I killed some of them. I must have. I shot right at them. They were only a few feet away."

"How many of them were there?"

"I don't know. Maybe fifty."

"How long did it go on?"

"Five minutes, maybe—could have been an hour. It's all a blur."

"And when you were finished, they were all dead?"

"No. One woman had hid her kid under her coat. Well, not really a coat. They don't wear coats. The kid couldn't have been more than three or four. The people were all lying around there, and this kid came crawling out. It was crying, and it took off across the compound."

"Was it a boy or a girl?"

"I couldn't tell."

"Did the kid get away?"

"Jackson started yelling for somebody to shoot it, only nobody would. So he grabbed a rifle and ran up behind the kid as it was running."

"And he killed it?"

"He blew the kid's head right off. You see, when you told me Jackson went nuts, I knew why right away. Jackson was a good German, like I said. But even Jackson would go nuts when he thought about that later. Anybody would go nuts thinking about that."

Costello scribbled in his notebook. They were silent for a moment while he wrote. Will sipped his coffee. This was all like a dream. Could any of it have happened? Could this be happening now?

Costello looked up. "As you look back on it, how do you feel about it?"

Will sipped his coffee. He looked at the casette in the tape recorder, turning silently. Then, in a flat, emotionless voice, he heard himself say, "Most guys went over there and handled themselves just fine. A lot of them got killed, but they never did anything like we did. I think about that a lot. I keep wondering why I deserved to come out alive after that— after what I did."

* * * *

New York City traffic didn't scare Jack Ryan. He'd driven in Manhattan two-dozen times in the past thirty years, and he knew how to handle himself. He'd go slow and easy and let the crazy people just go around him if they couldn't wait. "Almost there," he told Patricia.

At the next corner, Jack turned his Ford sedan down a one-way street, and, miraculously, found a parking space no more than a half-block down from the address Patricia had been given by the university. They got out of the car and walked back down the street until they were looking up at a Greenwich Village brownstone with stone steps. "Is this it?" he asked his daughter.

Patricia looked at the form in her hand. "On the third floor."

There was no elevator, of course. Jack had hoped for one, but he had not expected it. They climbed three flights of stairs until they stood before a heavy wooden door. Patricia knocked. In a moment a dark-haired girl with rimless glasses opened the door a crack and peered at them from the other side of the chain with an expression of city-wise wariness. "Yes?"

"I'm Patricia Ryan. This is my father. I'm supposed to move in here today. Are you Shirley?"

The door closed. They heard the sound of the chain being removed. Then the door opened, and the blonde girl stood there in jeans and a sweatshirt. "I'm Shirley Green. You're the girl from off-campus housing, right?"

"I'll go start bringing up your stuff," Jack said, starting back down the stairs with a sigh. Why couldn't she have gotten an apartment in a building with an elevator, he thought?

Patricia looked around the apartment. There was the main room, a kitchen off to one side and what she took to be a bedroom up a small flight of four stairs. The hardwood floors were worn, paint was peeling from the walls and she could hear the plumbing bang even as she stood there. She loved the place. It wasn't home. "This your first year?" she asked Shirley.

"I'm a sophomore. I lived in the dorms first semester, then I got my folks to let me move off campus second semester last year. I had to pull a three-O before they'd let me do it. You're lucky your folks didn't make you move into the dorms. Ugh! They're the worst."

"They wanted to make me live in the dorms, only they were full up. My father is all worked up that I'll be living so far off campus."

"Yeah, mine too. But I don't care. I'd have quit if they'd have made me live in the dorms. Want to see the place?"

Shirley led Patricia into the bedroom and then into the kitchen. It was quite possibly the dirtiest place Patricia had even been in. She liked it a lot. She also decided that she liked Shirley Green, who was friendly and laid back. They were talking about music when Jack came staggering in under the first load of suitcases and boxes. He dropped the baggage in the middle of the living room floor.

"Be back in a minute," he gasped, and disappeared out the door and down the steps.

Shirley laughed. "Looks like you've got your old man trained pretty good."

"He's a doll. I guess I better go help him."

"I'll go, too."

After two more trips, Patricia's gear sat in the middle of the living room like a miniature alp. Jack mopped his brow and said, "Well, who's up for dinner?"

The three of them ate at a corner table in a small Italian place in the east Village. Patricia, who had been watching her weight since her junior year in high school, picked at her veal, but Shirley, who was rail thin, consumed a massive plate of spaghetti and almost single-handedly destroyed an antipasto for three. Afterward, Jack drove them back to the brownstone. He circled the block three times before he gave up. "It doesn't look like I'm going to find a parking space," he said. "I guess I'm going to have to let you off here."

Shirley, sensing a goodbye coming up, said, "I'm going to go upstairs and get my own stuff put away. Nice to meet you, Mr. Ryan."

When Shirley had scampered up the steps and into the brownstone, Jack said to Patricia, "Well, Kid, this is it. Excited?"

Patricia virtually quivered. "I'm so excited I'm not going to sleep for a week."

Jack Ryan didn't even crack a smile. "It's tough to see your last kid go off to school. Especially your only daughter. I'm going to miss you, Sweetie."

Patricia leaned over and hugged him. "Love you."

"I love you, too," he told her. "When do you think you might get home for a weekend?"

"I don't know. I'm not even unpacked yet."

"Well, okay. You get settled, and keep in touch. You have any problems, you let me know right away."

She bounced out of the car. They waved at one another, then his Ford rolled off up the street. She stayed and watched until he went around the corner and disappeared. Patricia bounded up the stairs to the apartment and found Shirley sitting in the living room smoking dope. Patricia closed the door and flopped down on the sofa next to Shirley.

"Your old man is nice and all that," Shirley said, passing the joint, "but I didn't think he was ever going to leave."

Patricia took a long toke. "I'm with you," she said.

* * * *

The weeks before harvest were agonizing for Henri.

Always irritable, he became even more so. Always nervous, he became as taut as a violin string. He snarled and snapped at everyone with whom he had contact, even Annette. He slept poorly. He sulked.

Daily he ordered small bunches of grapes from each vineyard crushed. He checked the sugar level and a dozen other chemical yardsticks that he alone understood. Only when Nature had brought each vineyard to its finest state would he order a harvest, and Henri Le Barnot did not trust Nature. He trusted his laboratory. He trusted his yeasts. He trusted his stainless steel fermenting vats and his toasted French oak aging casks. Nature could not be trusted. She had turned on him too many times before. One never knew when she would decide to suddenly sweeten the grapes too much, or to visit a monstrous storm on the lake country that would blow down vines and ruin grapes.

Henri would not be at peace until the grapes were harvested and the juice in the vats and the fermenting process begun. Until then he would be a bear, and as he grew older, his annual mood grew worse.

"He is impossible," Annette told Katherine. "He is worse this year than any other. He will not even make the love."

Even after all these years, Annette was still capable of startling Katherine. "You still do that? Annette, Henri is pushing eighty."

"He is not seventy-six."

"And he's still . . . well . . . capable?"

"Is my Henri still capable?" Annette sniffed. "How can you ask?"

Katherine was truly nonplussed. "But Annette, you're past seventy. Don't shake your head at me. I know precisely how old you are. You're seventy-three."

"I am French. Age does not count in such matters when you are French."

Katherine went back to stirring her cake batter. "What a decadent people you are."

Henri raged daily about the winery, snorting and snarling, just looking for an argument. So it was that Kevin, sitting in the study of the big house working on the books, looked up and groaned when Henri came roaring into the room one fall afternoon.

"This must stop!" Henri roared. "We cannot have this!"

Kevin leaned back. "What's the problem, Henri?"

"Your son! He is smashing wine bottles," Henri said. "He is throwing them against the fermenting vats. We paid thousands for those vats, and he is throwing bottles at them."

Henri was right. At the winery, in the expanded room where the huge stainless steel fermenting vats loomed up high overhead, they found the shattered remains of two dozen bottles. They found Will in the winery office, reading the sports section of the *Boydstown Bulletin*.

"Hi, Dad," he said cheerfully.

"What's with the broken bottles?" Kevin asked him.

"The ones I smashed?"

Kevin felt himself losing control. "Yes, Will. The ones you smashed. Why'd you smash them?"

"They had something wrong with them."

"What the hell was wrong with them, for Christ's sake?" Kevin roared.

"I don't know," Will said thoughtfully. "Something, though."

Kevin sat down across from his son. "Look, if you find anything else that's . . . wrong—anything—you come and tell me. Do you understand?"

Will shrugged. "Sure, if you want me to."

Henri muttered a ripe curse in French and stomped off to his office. Will went back to the newspaper. Kevin sat there, baffled. "What the hell was wrong with the bottles, Will?"

Will looked up. "They weren't any good. I could tell that just by looking at them. The others seem okay, though."

Kevin stood up. "That's good. I'm glad to hear that."

There were other incidents. There would be moments when Will would be lost in thought, and other times when conversation with him produced no intelligible response.

"Aren't you going to eat dinner, Will?" his grandmother would ask him.

"I ate."

"You did? When?"

"On patrol."

"What?"

"I ate when I was on patrol."

The most disturbing incident to Kevin came during a drive to the village one morning. Will had been particularly distant at breakfast. As they rode into town, Will looked out the window at the lake.

"I talked to Jim last night," he said.

"Oh?" Kevin said. "When did he call?"

"He didn't call. I saw him down on the beach."

Kevin, who knew that Jim was living in Philadelphia and hadn't been near Brennan's Point in more than a year, was aghast. He drove in silence for a moment. Then he said, "Will, Jim wasn't on the beach last night. He's hundreds of miles away from here."

"No, he's not. I saw him last night."

Kevin shook his head. "What did he have to say?"

"He said he won't go. He'll leave the country first."

"Well, good for him."

"That's what I told him."

* * * *

"This is just plain weird, Billy," Kevin said as they sat at the bar at the Elks. "Most of the time he's just fine. But every once in a while, he starts talking and he makes no sense at all. It's the strangest shit you've ever heard. Yesterday he wouldn't eat the cornflakes Mother put out for him because they all looked alike."

Billy laughed.

"It's not funny, goddamn it," Kevin said. "One of the things that's always pissed me off about you, Billy, is that you'll laugh at anything."

"I had a wife who had that complaint once—among others."

"What do you think I should do?"

Billy looked at his best friend, and his expression was solemn. "I think you should get him to a shrink."

"Who do you recommend?"

"Let me check around. I don't get the opportunity to handle many psychiatric referrals. Folks around here tend to be disgustingly normal from an emotional standpoint."

Kevin looked into his old-fashioned glass and shook the ice around. "This is scaring the hell out of me."

"I don't blame you a bit," Billy Frazier said.

* * * *

As he was descending the stairs to the kitchen on a Saturday morning after harvest, Kevin found himself thinking about it. Well, go ahead and say it. Will had always been a bit strange. Not bad strange, certainly. Never angry or hostile. But Will had always been withdrawn, pensive— so different from the perpetually bubbling Susan.

Kevin had even been pleased when the kid had come home from college full of hot anger about the war. Well good, Kevin had thought. He's finally getting involved in something. To Kevin, at that point, student resistance to the war had been the moral equivalent of student fascination with the Spanish Civil War during his own time in college. Kevin had flirted with communism. Jesus, even Billy Frazier had for a semester. Damned near everybody had been caught up in the coming triumph of the proletariat. It had been stylish.

But now Kevin realized he had totally misjudged the depth of Will's resistance to the war. He hadn't realized how it would come to dominate all aspects of his son's emotional makeup.

"Just some coffee, Mother," he said, entering the kitchen and sitting down. "Has Will come down yet?"

"He came down a while ago," Annette said. "He say he was taking the big boat for the run."

"I wish he'd gotten me up," Kevin said. "I haven't been out in the Chris Craft since before the harvest."

His mother sat down across the table from him. "Did this doctor in Rochester say when this might get better, Kevin?"

Kevin bit into his toast and shook his head. "He said it's a deep-seated problem. Will's having trouble adjusting."

"You made that adjustment," Katherine pointed out.

"What I went through was apparently nothing compared to what Will went through, Mother. It was different."

"Maybe you were different," Katherine said.

Kevin downed his coffee and stood up.

"Where are you going?" she said.

"I'm going down to the beach to see if I can get a boat ride."

Will Brennan wasn't riding in the boat. He was sitting in the Chris Craft in the middle of the lake, smoking a Camel. The engine had been shut off for five minutes. He was listening to the transistor radio he'd brought along. He was listening, too, to somebody talk, and that freaked him out because he didn't know who it was.

The voice had started popping into Will's head a few weeks before, and Will had immediately known that was so weird that he couldn't tell anybody about it—not even the shrink in Rochester. They would put him in a rubber room if he told them that.

"So now what?" the voice was saying.

Will refused to answer.

"So, what are you going to do with yourself, now?" the voice asked him. "You're back here, and that newspaper story is going to come out any day, and then everybody is going to know. And even if the newspaper story never comes out, what are you going to do with yourself? Come on, Brennan. Get with it! I'm your friend, man. If you can't talk to me, who are you going to talk to?"

Nobody, Will thought as he smoked.

"Nobody?" the voice said. "You can't go on like that forever. You've got to tell somebody."

That's what annoyed Will most about the voice. It could read his thoughts. Will couldn't think about anything without the voice's wise mouth intruding into it.

"You know, Man," the voice told him, "You can't sit around forever. What happened to graduate school? Get off your ass, Man."

Christ, Will thought. I wish he'd shut up.

"Not yet, Man," the voice told him.

Will got up and walked the length of the eighteen-foot boat. He looked around him. It was late in the season. The summer people were still hanging around the lake, soaking up the last of the summer. The sun was hot for late October, and Will wiped the sweat from his forehead. He opened the engine compartment and the bilge fumes came rolling up. Will could smell gas. He left the doors to the compartment open to vent the bilge and sank into the leather-covered rear seat. As he glanced over at Brennan's Point, he saw his father hobbling down the steps next to the shack. Maybe he'd move into the shack for the winter. It hadn't been occupied for years, and the place was full of cobwebs and dust, but that kind of change of scene might be good for him. Something had to be.

"That won't do it," the voice told him. "You want a change of scene, do something dramatic."

Shut up, Will thought.

"Stuff it, Man," the voice told him.

Kevin came out on the dock. He motioned to the boat a half a mile away in the middle of the lake, and Will waved back.

"He wants you to go in and pick him up," the voice told him.

Will pondered it. Did he want to see his father just now? No, he didn't think so. And if he did, he'd have to wait until the bilge cleared itself of gas, anyway. He knew better than to start the engine when there was gas in the bilge. He could blow up the boat.

"Good thinking," the voice told him. "You could blow up the boat and end up dead."

Now there's a thought, Will said to himself. And he tossed the smoking stub of his Camel into the bilge.

* * * *

Of all the family, only Kevin ever suspected that the explosion had not been accidental.

Kevin had seen it, and although he wasn't completely sure that Will hadn't merely been trying to toss the cigarette overboard, his suspicions were rooted in the instincts of a father who had gazed into his son's tormented soul.

Even as the late-season weekend boaters went into the lake to rescue the floating accident victim—even as the young obstetrician from Syracuse who had been passing by in his sixteen-foot fiberglass runabout performed mouth-to-mouth resuscitation on Will Brennan on the deck of his boat, even as they brought Will ashore on the point and Kevin loaded him into the car and rushed him to Lakeside Memorial, even as the Korean emergency room physician tried and failed to bring Will back to life—Kevin knew in his heart that it had not been an accident.

It wasn't until a month after Will's burial, high on the hillside next to his grandfather and the memorial markers for Christian and Helga, that Kevin had spotted a small story in his mail-edition copy of the *New York Times*. There he read that *Newsday*, the Long Island newspaper, had printed an article in which a dozen servicemen had described the murder of an undetermined number of civilians in a Vietnamese village almost a year earlier. Kevin's clue was the military unit mentioned—Will's company.

Will's name did not appear in the *Times* account, which was on an inside page, but he suspected that it might have appeared in the original *Newsday* story.

Kevin entertained, just briefly, the thought of getting on the phone and obtaining a copy of the original newspaper in which the story had appeared. The *Times* version had been no more than ten or twelve inches long. But almost as quickly as the idea entered his head, he dismissed it. What purpose would it serve, he asked himself. If I find out that he was there—that this is why he did it—what would it accomplish? Would I tell Mother? Would I tell Susan? Aside from which, Kevin didn't really want to know.

Chapter 19

The burial service for Will had been conducted quickly and on a small scale. Becky had attended—conspicuously without Vinnie—and her presence there had been fodder for village gossip. Neither she nor Kevin cared much about that. Kevin, in fact, seemed to care about little. Becky wanted to comfort him, but she could find no way to ease his pain. She couldn't even get him to express it. Kevin avoided all conversation of Will. When they were together, he would grow stiff and cold when she tried to drain off his grief through talk.

In the end, Becky decided that all she could offer him was her companionship, her sex, her mute presence when he lapsed into the silences that had so marked his manner since Will's accident. A few weeks before Christmas she managed to lure him on a three-day trip to the Berkshires. They drove the six hours in Becky's Cadillac and stayed at the Red Lion Inn in Stockbridge, which was gaily decorated for the season. They toured the Old Corner House down the street, where were displayed the largest single collection of Norman Rockwell's paintings. They seemed to fascinate Kevin, who did some painting of his own. He paused and studied one particularly poignant image—a girl on the brink of puberty gazing at her image in the mirror, her expression wistful. On the floor next to her was a discarded doll. "I never saw this one before," Kevin said. "It reminds me of Susan at the same age. When she reached that point in life, I realized how useless I was to her. That's when she needed a mother. My mother ended up explaining everything to her."

"My father told me," Becky said.

Kevin looked at her. "He did?"

"If he'd had the grades, he'd have gone to medical school instead of dental. Medicine was sort of a hobby for him his whole life. He told me every detail of menstruation, and he explained the basic sex act. I had to learn about the variations on my own."

"How'd you react when he told you what went on?" Kevin asked her.

"If he hadn't made it all seem so clinical, I'd have thought he was kidding. I remember thinking, what a ridiculous thing for people to do. He neglected to mention orgasms, by the way. Once I had my eyes rolled back in my head once or twice I viewed it all in a new light."

"Who was your first?" Kevin asked her.

"Bucky Coughlin," she said thoughtfully. "Or maybe it was Billy Frazier, now that I think about it. Or Bobby Roach. I'm pretty sure it was somebody whose name began with a B."

For the first time since Will's funeral, Kevin laughed aloud.

Becky was delighted. "Actually," she said with exaggerated demureness, "you were my first, Kevin. Vinnie and I've always lived like brother and sister."

He put his arm around her as they wandered the museum. It was midweek, and they just about had the place to themselves. "One I know about for sure is Billy," Kevin said.

"How do you know that?"

"Hey," he told her, "we were boys. Boys brag about that sort of thing—especially when the girl is Becky King, with the best knockers in the history of Lakeside Free Academy."

"Great," she said sourly. "It takes more than thirty-five years to find out that Billy had a big mouth. Do you know how weird it's been going to see him as a doctor all these years—remembering what we did in high school? Half the time I'm afraid he might try it again right there in the office."

Kevin laughed again. It was so good to hear him laugh. Becky kissed him gently on the mouth. "Don't tell Billy I said that," she said.

"I won't. It might give him ideas."

"It's almost one. Are you getting hungry?"

Kevin looked around and slid a hand inside her open coat. "Not for food."

Becky smiled. "We did it last night. We did it this morning. You're pretty feisty for a guy past fifty."

Kevin clutched at the sweater-clad breast beneath her coat and kissed her. "Old broads turn me on," he said.

* * * *

"When do you feel this stuff?" Patricia asked.

Larry Engel, who looked like a young Jerry Lewis with a beard and shoulder-length hair, said, "You're not feeling it? You're shitting me."

"I'm not, honestly. I've always had a real high resistance to stuff—
to liquor or grass or anything."

Larry shook his head. He looked at the mixing bowl full of multicolored
pills and said, "You swallowed enough to bend a camel, for Christ's
sake."

"With what it costs to get you high," Shirley told her roommate, "we
could feed everybody in the east Village for a week. Don't you have any
compassion for the poor, Ryan?"

"The poor will always be with us," Larry said. "They're essentially
a zoning problem. That's what my old man likes to say, anyway. Of
course, he's a zoning lawyer, and he tends to see all social problems more
or less in that light."

Patricia laughed. She often laughed at Larry. He was the occupant of
an apartment on the next block and a badly failing philosophy student
whose fondest ambition was to do nothing at all. He had started out as
a casual friend of Shirley's, but he'd begun hanging around the apartment
on a regular basis ever since Patricia had moved in. He had a thing for
her, it was clear, and as long as he made Patricia laugh she was willing
to let him hang around and let him fool around with her a bit. And as
long as she was willing to do that, Larry was willing to keep the apartment
full of dope of all kinds. He was the ultimate candy man, with a book
bag full of grass and pills of all description.

Tonight he had shown up with a lid of Mexican gold. They sat around
smoking it and listening to music for an hour or so. Then he had gone
into the kitchen and poured his bookbag full of pills into a mixing bowl.
He'd said, "Hey, come on out here and check it out, ladies: Engel fruit
salad!"

The three of them had sat down at the kitchen table washing down
pills with bottles of Rhinegold and waiting to see what happened. That
had been an hour or so before. Now Shirley was more or less mellowed
out, and Larry was getting giggly. But Patricia was just yawning a little
and beginning to get indigestion. "I still don't feel much," she complained.

Larry Engel frowned through his beard. "You're a tough customer,
Kid," he said, reaching into a pocket in his leather vest. He produced a
vial with a prescription label on it and poured the contents out on the
table. They were tiny capsules, half white, half gray. "Pop a couple of
those and see what goes down," he told Patricia.

Shirley's glazed eyes brightened. "New goodies! Where'd you get these
goodies, Larry?"

"I took these out of my mother's medicine cabinet, if you want the
truth," Larry told her. "This is something called Fulene. It's a downer of
epic proportions. I shot down a couple a few weeks ago, and all my

bones dissolved. I turned into the Amazing Rubber Man. Great shit, really."

"Won't your mother miss those?" Patricia asked him.

He laughed. "She's got a medicine chest full of this shit. It's taking the best minds in the American pharmaceutical industry to get my old lady through menopause. She's stoned every waking minute, and thank God for it. Pop a couple. If these don't do it, I'm going to pack it in."

"What did I take already?" Patricia asked.

"Show me which ones you swallowed."

Patricia reached into the mixing bowl and brought out a duplicate of each pill she'd popped. Larry studied what she pulled out as a Jimi Hendrix solo blasted out of the stereo in the living room. "This one is a Seconal," he told her. "This is a Tranzene. This cute little thing here is Lithium. This one was a waste. It's a vitamin B tablet. How the hell did they get in there, anyway?"

Patricia was impressed. "You're a walking drugstore."

"Hey," he said with an exaggerated leer, "you ought to see my safety deposit box."

"Where do you get all this stuff?" Patricia asked him.

"Contacts. Most of this stuff I picked up the other night from a guy I used to live with at the dorms. He has a brother who's tied up with some kind of pharmaceutical house."

"Could this stuff kill you?" Shirley asked, not that she much cared at this point.

"Sure," Larry said, "if you take enough of it."

"How do you know if you're taking too much?" Patricia asked, washing down a Dexamyl.

"The tipoff is when your heart stops," Larry said.

"Oh, that's so funny!" Shirley said, bursting into gales of uncontrollable laughter. She lowered her head to the table and giggled for a good forty seconds. "When your heart stops. Oh, God!" She finished with a weak "Heh, heh, heh!" Then, in just a moment, she was snoring.

Larry looked at her and grinned. Then he turned to Patricia. "Well, that's pretty much the end of old Shirley for tonight. Come on, let's go into the living room."

Patricia got up, took Larry's hand and moved into the next room. She turned over the album and the music blared out. She settled down next to Larry on the sofa. "I never saw anybody laugh like Shirley tonight."

Larry wrapped a thin arm around Patricia. "It was the Mexican gold," he told her. "It turns everybody into Bob Hope."

"I hope that's not true," Patricia said, then she giggled.

"Way to go," Larry said appreciatively.

"Hey, now," Patricia said, fighting back another giggle. "I'm starting to feel something. My legs are beginning to tingle. Oh, that's weird!"

Larry rolled another joint and lit it. "Here, take another toke."

Patricia didn't need it. The stuff was beginning to kick in. She leaned back. "Oh, God. What a rush. I love it."

Larry Engel leaned back next to her and put his hand on her thigh. "We aim to please," he said.

* * * *

Billy Frazier, in the white coat he always wore in his office, opened the door and came into the examining room. "Hello, hello," he said jovially. He bent over and looked at little Liam Dixon. "And who's sick today, eh?"

"It's this little troublemaker here," said Susan, touseling her son's hair. "He's been running a fever for two days now, Billy."

"Really?" Billy said, straightening up. "Is that true, Liam? How do you feel right now?"

"Okay," the boy said.

Billy reached into the cabinet behind him and produced a thermometer. "Here, open wide."

As the boy wrapped his mouth around the instrument, Billy said to Susan, "Any signs of congestion? Any stomach upset?"

She shook her head. "No, just the fever. It comes and goes. It's the second one he's had this month."

Billy put his stethoscope to the boy's chest and listened. Then he looked in his ears and tapped his knees with a rubber hammer. When he had finished, he took out the thermometer and looked at it.

"Well," the physician said, "his temperature is normal now. I don't see anything too obvious. He looks a little pale, maybe, but that's about all."

He had the boy remove his shirt, and Billy examined Liam thoroughly. As he did, Susan said, "He's complained a lot lately of being tired, and he hardly eats anything any more."

"He must be watching his figure, right?"

"Right," Liam said. He liked Dr. Frazier. He always had.

Billy focused abruptly on an ugly bruise on the boy's left shoulder. It was purple in the middle, fading out to a grayish yellow at the edges. Billy's eyes narrowed as he studied. "How'd you get this?" he asked Liam.

The boy shrugged. "I don't know."

Billy turned toward Susan. "Did he have an accident?" he asked. "Did somebody discipline him, Susan?"

Susan shook his head. "Not that I know of. He's always bruised pretty easily. That one's pretty nasty, though."

"Yes," Billy said quietly, almost to himself. He peered into the boy's eyes, studying his retinas with a little light. "Is he sleeping all right?"

"Nothing out of the ordinary," Susan told him.

"How about it, Champ?" Billy asked the boy. "Are you sleeping okay?"

"Yeah," Liam told him.

"Is he getting to bed early?"

"The usual time," Susan told him, "about eight-thirty or nine."

Billy had the boy lie back. He felt carefully about his midsection. "Well, I can feel some swelling around the spleen. My guess is that he has a little infection. It's not uncommon, you know. There are a number of viral infections going around this winter. I must have had six people in here with one or the other of them the past few days."

"Can you give him anything to make it go away?" she asked.

"Well, Susan, there's not much you can do with a virus except let it run its course. They don't respond to medication the way a bacteriological infection will. The best thing you can give anybody to control fever is aspirin. If it comes back again, bring him back. But I suspect it's pretty much run its course by now. I'd keep him in bed today and inside the house over the weekend. Then, if he seems okay Monday morning, send him back to school to catch something else. That's where they get it, you know, all those kids crowded together indoors all day."

Susan looked down at Liam. He still looked too pale to suit her. "How's that sound?"

"I can't go out all weekend?" he complained.

"Nope," Susan told him.

"Heck," he said.

"I'd watch that bruising," Billy said. "If he shows any more of those, you give me a call right away. How's the family? I haven't seen your father for a few weeks."

"Grandma's still not right after Will's death. It was all a bit too much for her."

"Well," Billy said, "she's what, almost eighty now? A thing like that is difficult to deal with at any age, but when you get to be that old, it's tougher yet."

"She seems to be failing more every day. Tante Annette is with her all the time except in February, when she and Henri go down to Florida. This year I'm moving into the big house for that month, just to keep an eye on her."

"That's a good idea. I'm going out of town most of February myself.

I'm going down to my place on Saint Thomas. If you have any problems while I'm gone, Dr. Bonham will be covering for me."

"I don't know him," Susan said.

"He's a new man in town. We were lucky to find him and bring him in. None of these young doctors wants to practice in little towns like this any more, and those of us who're here are getting a bit long in the tooth."

Susan smiled. "You still look pretty spry to me."

"It's all a facade," Billy Frazier said. "Tell me, how are you feeling?"

"Me? Fine. Just worn down, is all. This little troublemaker here is wearing me out." Susan hugged the little boy. "Isn't that right, Troublemaker?"

"Oh, Mom," Liam said, embarrassed.

* * * *

Because of his childhood in a house where most fights seemed to begin—ostensibly, at least—over money, Jim Ryan was compulsively frugal. He knew at every moment how much he had in his wallet. He arranged his bills in order: twenties in the back, tens and fives next and then singles. If he ever found himself with a hundred or a fifty, he found a way to break it so the cash would fit neatly into the filing system.

He knew to the nickel how much he had in his checking account at any given moment. He kept records of the mileage of his new BMW 2002. He saved his loose change in a jar he kept on his bedroom dresser and put it into his savings account. He shopped for clothing only when it was on sale. He clipped food coupons out of the *Philadelphia Inquirer.*

He bought inexpensive cosmetics. He preferred the standard black phone the telephone company offered because it was a dollar cheaper every month. He added up his salary and Marci's during the first month of their marriage and put together a four-page monthly budget that was detailed enough to include how much they would spend for postage stamps. He was an orderly man with a reverence for hard-earned cash.

Marci, on the other hand, spent whatever she felt was necessary when the whim struck her.

"Do you like this?" she asked one night after dinner, swirling into the living room of their apartment in a new dress.

"It's okay," he said unenthusiastically. "How much did it cost?"

"Sixty something. I got it at Wanamaker's today after school."

"You did?" he said. "You know that coat and that sweater you got last week—and that bracelet? Do you know you went over the monthly clothing allowance for both of us on that trip alone? And now you're at it again?"

She glared at him. "It's my money. I need clothes to wear to work."

"You need something like that to teach a bunch of fifth graders in North Philadelphia? For sixty-some bucks? You could keep half your pupils on heroin for three days on what you spent on clothes just in the first two weeks of this month, do you know that?"

"It's my money, Jim!"

"It's our money. Just like what I bring in is our money. Do you see me spending money like that on clothes?"

"How about your car? That cost nearly four thousand dollars."

"It's worth every penny. I bought a car that'll last."

"For four thousand dollars. I spent almost fifteen hundred dollars less than that."

"Right—for a Plymouth Duster that'll fall apart inside of two years. For a piece of junk from Detroit."

"Oh," she said, "the hell with it, then. Let's buy a Rolls. Eighty grand, but it's a bargain, isn't it? You'll spend money on what you want to spend money on, but you give me a hard time when I spend money on what I want to spend money on."

"You want to spend money on everything. And you do."

"Don't scream at me, Jim. I don't like it."

"I don't like your cavalier attitude toward money."

"I don't like your cheapness."

"I don't give a shit what you don't like."

"And I don't give a shit what you don't like."

And so it went.

*　*　*　*

She knew she shouldn't, but Susan felt guilty about it. Billy Frazier had been the only doctor who had ever seen her or her son. But Billy was on Saint Thomas now, and Liam still wasn't right. He had to see somebody. Besides, Billy had said to see Dr. Bonham if there was a problem, and she was following that advice. Bonham turned out to be not yet thirty—lean and dark haired, with gold-rimmed glasses and dressed like the undergraduate he had been not many years before.

"Well, let's take a look," he said, beginning his examination of Liam. "How have you been feeling, young man?"

"Sort of tired," Liam said.

That was an understatement. The boy had been listless and weak for weeks now. He was perpetually pale, and the fevers had been coming and going with disturbing regularity.

"I'll bet you're not eating your Wheaties, are you?" Bonham said. He leaned close and studied a small bruise on the inside of Liam's upper arm. "How long has he had that bruise, there?"

Susan shrugged. "I don't know. That must be a new one. He bruises all the time now."

Then, as Bonham removed the boy's shirt, she saw another one along his ribs. This one was ugly, about the size of her fist and a deep, bluish-purple. "There's another one," she pointed out. "Liam, where did you get that bruise?"

"I don't know," the boy said.

Bonham stood up in front of Liam. "Let me feel around your ears here," he said. "Uh-huh." He pressed a hand against the boy's breastbone. "Does that hurt?"

"A little."

"Liam, I want you to stand up on this table here and undo your pants. Yep. Just like that."

The physician felt around the boy's abdomen for several moments. "There," he said finally, "That ought to do it. You can get your clothes back on now."

Bonham picked up Liam's chart and scribbled on it intently.

"Do you have any idea what's wrong with him?" Susan asked. "These sudden flash fevers are driving me crazy."

Bonham, writing, said, "I'm not sure yet. I think some tests are called for."

"It isn't anything serious, is it?"

Bonham looked up. "I quite truthfully won't know until we've had all the blood work done. The possibilities are so vast that I just can't say. I do want you to know, though, that there's no reason for you to become alarmed at this point."

Susan caught the phrase "at this point." She felt her heart turn over in her chest. She said, "Why didn't Dr. Frazier order tests like this?"

Bonham looked a little uncomfortable. "Oh, I can't say. Maybe he would have if he'd seen Liam this time. You just don't order expensive blood work for every childhood temperature fluctuation."

"But you're ordering them now," Susan insisted. "Why?"

"Well," he said slowly, "I think I need them for a complete diagnosis, is all. Look, I know this is difficult for you, but I'd really prefer to wait until I know the results of those tests before we get excited about anything."

Susan was already excited. "When do you think you'll be able to tell me more?"

"Oh, by the end of the week, I'd think. You'll hear from me. Promise. I'll call you the minute I have anything."

* * * *

"Quick, I need a beer," Art said.

Susan hadn't heard him come in. She was in the kitchen, preparing dinner, and she was tired. She'd spent the day with her grandmother out at Brennan's Point, and as much as she loved Katherine she couldn't wait until Henri and Annette got back from Florida. Maybe Annette could listen to interminable stories about the old days—the Depression and the war; both wars, actually—but Susan had only a limited tolerance for them. Susan suspected that Katherine was losing it a bit, and when Kevin had walked in the door from the winery, she had hurried home to her own house and her own life.

She got Art his beer as he settled wearily at the kitchen table. Art lit a Salem. "Jesus, I hate the trucking business. I hate it today, anyway."

"I had sort of a bad day of my own. I kept Liam home from school with a fever. I took him out to the big house with me and put him to bed in my old room."

"Where is he now?"

"Upstairs. Asleep."

"Have you heard from that doctor yet?" Art asked, sipping his beer.

"I'm supposed to hear from him by Friday."

"Did he say there's anything to worry about?"

"No."

"Then stop worrying."

"I wish I could," Susan told her husband.

Susan woke up Friday waiting for the phone to ring. It did, several times during the course of the day. One call was from somebody selling magazine subscriptions. Another came from a real estate agent, asking if she and Art wanted to sell their house. A call came from the volunteer fire company, looking for money. She took one call from a friend. By the time the phone rang at about two in the afternoon, she was near panic.

"Mrs. Dixon? This is Dr. Bonham."

"Are Liam's tests back?"

He was silent for a moment. Then he said, "Yes they are. I debated waiting to contact you until Dr. Frazier was back from vacation; but under the circumstances, I wonder if you and your husband could come in and see me today."

"Art's out of town for the day. Please don't make me wait until he's back. What's wrong with my son, Doctor?"

Dr. Bonham was quiet for a moment. Then he said quietly, "Mrs. Dixon, all the tests indicate that Liam has leukemia."

This couldn't be happening. Susan said, "Oh, my dear God!"

Bonham's youth betrayed him. He tried to sound reassuring and failed miserably. "Mrs. Dixon," he said, "let me say that the first thing you have to do is not to give up hope. We've made tremendous strides in treating leukemia in children. Your son has an excellent chance of survival."

Susan was sure she was going to lose her mind. "Are you absolutely certain?"

"There's really no doubt about it. He had all the classic symptoms: the easy bruising; the enlarged lymph nodes in the neck, armpits and groin. He feels mild pain over the breastbone. His liver and spleen are swollen. And the blood work shows a greatly enlarged number of white blood cells. In fact, the smear even showed Auer bodies. Those are red-staining rods in some of the white blood cells. It's considered conclusive proof of acute leukemia. In addition to that, his blood platelets are low, and he shows signs of anemia. That's because leukemia damages the bone marrow where the white blood cells—"

Susan cut him off. "I don't want to know all that." She knew she was getting hysterical and didn't care. "I want to know what you can do to keep my son alive."

His response was more quiet and subdued. "Well, there are drugs—"

"What drugs? What drugs can you give him?"

"It gets pretty technical, Mrs. Dixon."

"TELL ME!"

"We can use folic acid antagonists, corticosteroids and purine antagonists. There are also combinations—six-mercaptopurine, methothraxate. There've been some encouraging results with new compounds like L-asparaginase, vincristine and cystosine arabinoside. I'm sure none of this means anything to you, but the point is that we've had results with these drugs. Median survival time now exceeds three years. The latest literature lists more than a hundred and fifty patients who've survived more than five years. This is not at all a hopeless situation, Mrs. Dixon."

Five years. Her little boy may live five more years—if he was lucky. That's what this man was saying to her.

"Don't tell me any more," Susan begged him, whimpering into the phone. "Please . . ."

"Mrs. Dixon, I'd like to see you and your husband tomorrow."

"Yes, yes. What time?"

"I have Saturday rounds at the hospital until eleven or so. Can you stop by my office around noon? There are a good many things you have to know, so I suggest you have somebody watch Liam. It should take about an hour. I took the liberty this morning of making contact with Dr. Norman Sun at Boydstown Memorial. He's about the best oncologist upstate."

"Yes, yes. That's what we need. We need the very best."

"Well," Bonham said, "Dr. Sun is the best. I'll see you both tomorrow, then?"

"Yes."

"Goodbye, Mrs. Dixon. And don't give up hope."

Susan couldn't reach Art. He wouldn't be home until he returned from his run to Syracuse. When Liam came home from school at about three-thirty, he found his mother red-eyed and visibly shaky. But she had made him spaghetti and meatballs and french fries, too. Those were his favorites.

*   *   *   *

As Kevin came into the kitchen, Annette looked at him and smiled and said, "Good, you are here at last. Dinner is almost ready. Where is my Henri?"

Kevin Brennan's face was clouded with anger. "He said he'll be eating up at your place tonight."

Annette's smile never wavered. She untied her apron and said, "Well, in such a case, I suppose I must go make him something. Henri is not nice when he is hungry."

Kevin sat down heavily at his place at the kitchen table. "Or when he's fed, for that matter."

Annette nodded, her lined face weary. "He is merely getting old, Kevin."

Kevin looked at Annette and saw the hurt in her eyes. He felt a surge of guilt at having inflicted it. It took a saint like Annette to tolerate Henri. Kevin Brennan was no saint. "We're all getting old, Annette," he said. "I'm trying, but I don't know how you tolerate him."

"It is very simple," she told him. "I love my Henri. And now I must go. I must not leave him alone."

"Do you want a ride up the hill?" he asked her. "It's cold out."

"I like to walk in cold air. It is good for my lungs."

After Annette departed, Katherine removed the places she had set for her and Henri and silently put away the dishes and silverware. As she did, Kevin got up and poured himself a stiff jolt of bourbon, neat, from the bottle he kept in the kitchen cabinet. He sat down with it and sipped from the glass as his mother served dinner. Then Katherine sat down at her place and they began to eat in silence. After a while, she said, "What was it about this time?"

"Budget. He's gone over budget for the fourth month in a row. He just doesn't grasp the concept yet that we have stockholders now. He's got to pay some attention to how we spend money and when. And he's got to accept the fact that it's part of my job to rein him in. You should have seen the explosion when I showed him the figures. I thought he was going to have a stroke. I listened to it as long as I could, and then I just told him to get the hell out of the office."

"You got angry, then?"

He nodded. Kevin's temper was a frightful thing. He was, most of the time, a pleasant, gregarious and friendly man. But when provoked—and only Henri had the capacity to provoke him regularly—Kevin could be truly terrifying. Katherine could picture poor Henri, past eighty now and cranky as much out of habit as anything else, shouting and screaming as he did thoughtlessly and out of a lifetime of artistic habit suddenly confronting an enraged Kevin. She felt sorry for the old man.

"I suppose he can be irritating," Katherine said quietly. "You know, you can't imagine how different Henri was when he was young. He was always laughing and making jokes. He could be the funniest, wittiest man in the world. And he just adored your father, Kevin. He hasn't been the same since Liam died."

Kevin shook his head. "That's not it, Mother. Annette's right. He's getting old. He's slipping, and he knows it. He ought to think about retiring. I have the authority, as chief executive officer and board chairman, to make him retire—and don't think it isn't a temptation."

Katherine put down her fork. "You can't do that, Kevin. All he has in the world is the winery and Annette. You can't take half his life away from him. It would kill him."

"I'm going to kill him with my bare hands one of these days. The whole place is up in arms half the time because he's blown up at somebody. You just can't treat people the way he treats them. I have an obligation to my employees."

"Is he still a good winemaker?" Katherine asked.

"The absolute best. He always has been. When we were a little tiny company and Pop was around to keep him under control, he was worth all the crazy behavior and more. But now we have more than sixty employees, not counting the help at harvest time. It's not just a family winery any more. And Henri just doesn't have the temperament to work in a business organization."

Katherine could see that her son was still angry. This must have been some blowup.

"Kevin," she said, "Henri was your father's best friend. Ask yourself what Liam would have done in this situation. Would he force his best friend into retirement?"

"No, he wouldn't. He'd talk to him and get him under control. I'm simply not able to do that. Also, let me point out that during the last years that Pop was really active in the business, we were about one-fourth the size we are now. I'm not so sure that if he were around now, with so many employees and with stockholders to answer to, Pop would put sentiment first."

"Well, I'm sure," Katherine told him. "Your father, whether you realize it or not, was a very sentimental man. Nothing was more important to him than the people he cared about. If he were alive, he'd find a way to deal with the problem without the sort of solution you're entertaining."

Kevin smiled for the first time. "Are you speaking as my mother or as a heavy stockholder in the company?"

Katherine had inherited the stock Liam had collected each year as part of his executive bonus. It was far less than either Kevin or Helen held, thanks to the terms of Christian Weidener's will, but Katherine's holdings were large enough for her to cast deciding votes on key issues. She smiled back at her son. "Both. Let me ask you a question. How much of this trouble you're having with Henri is his fault, and how much of it is yours? I'm not saying that Henri can't be difficult. God knows that he can. But you're going through a particularly difficult time now . . ."

Kevin shook his head. "That's not a factor in this, Mother."

"You're sure of that?"

He began to argue with her, but then he held his words. She was old, but she still possessed a sharp mind. That's where Will had gotten his brains, Kevin had no doubt. It certainly hadn't been from him and Jane. "Maybe it is me a little bit," he said. "I'd be lying if I didn't admit that I'm worried sick all the time about my grandson. I talked to Susan on the phone this afternoon, and he doesn't seem to be getting any better."

"Oh, no," Katherine said. "He looked just fine Sunday. A little thin, maybe . . ."

"They've been taking tests down in Boydstown. Susan says that Chinese doctor they've been seeing down there wants to put him in the hospital for a week or more later this month to try some new combination of drugs."

"Why does he have to be hospitalized?"

"They expect the drugs to make him pretty sick, and he's already weak. They want to be able to keep an eye on him."

Katherine lowered her head and looked at her food. "I'm saying prayers twenty times a day."

"So am I," Kevin told her, "I can't believe that the kid isn't going to be okay, though. They can do all kinds of things today."

Kevin leaned back in his chair and downed the rest of his bourbon. He poked his fork through his food. He couldn't muster an appetite tonight.

"So maybe it is that—a little," he admitted. "But the biggest part really is Henri and his goddamn bullheadedness."

"He's an old man, and he was your father's closest friend. I want you to promise me you'll try."

Kevin sighed again. He looked at Katherine. "All right, Mother. I'll try. But I'm telling you, there's going to come a day when I'll reach the end of my rope with Henri."

"Well, when that happens, don't retire him. Just punch him one."

They both laughed.

Then Kevin said, "All right, I won't retire him, and I won't punch him, either—much as I'm tempted. But I wonder how he'd look with a cane up his behind."

* * * *

Jim Ryan opened the door of the new house he and Marci had bought in Huntingdon Valley and entered the front hall. He closed the door quietly and flipped on some lights. The downstairs was dark, although Marci's Duster was in the driveway. It was just after eight in the evening, and he was as mentally and emotionally exhausted as he could remember being in years. Dealing with Otto Kruger was a nightmare. Jim's mood was evil.

He was hanging up his coat in the hall closet when he heard it. It was faint but clear. It was coming from upstairs. It was Marci's voice. It was going, "Om, Om, Om, Om, Om, Om, Om, Om . . ."

Oh, shit, he thought. More yoga crap. He bounded up the stairs and into their bedroom. Marci, in purple tights, was hunched in the lotus position over an incense burner. She seemed unaware of his presence, although he had made enough noise coming up the stairs to shake the entire house. He stood in the doorway and glared at her.

She looked up, caught his expression and the expression of bliss on her lovely face was immediately replaced by irritation. "I'm busy," she told him. Then she lowered her head and resumed her chant.

Jim said, "Is there a chance you can tear yourself away from your search for cosmic oneness with the universe long enough to fix me some dinner?"

She looked up again, and her eyebrows were pressing together. "Downstairs," she said slowly, "in the kitchen, are two marvelous devices. One is a refrigerator, where food can be kept for long periods of time. The other is a stove, where it can be cooked and reheated. Now why don't you go down there and see what you can learn from those two devices and leave me the hell alone?" She closed her eyes and resumed her chant.

He rolled his eyes heavenward and entered the bedroom. "That goddamn incense is going to have me wheezing all night," he told her. "Do you have to burn that shit in this room?"

She looked up again. "Jim, I'm trying to meditate. Will you leave me alone?"

"Will you cook me something to eat?"

"Cook your own meal. It won't kill you."

He stalked across the floor and knelt down next to her, until his face was only a few inches away from hers and their eyes were at the same level. He said, "You wanted a new house. Poof, you've got a new house—which you crap up and which I keep clean. You said you wanted a bunch of labor-saving devices in the kitchen, and you got them. But the way they save you labor, Marci, is by your refusal to use any of them. Maybe you can live on nuts and berries and that health food crap you buy for yourself, but I need real food to eat. Now go down there and make it."

Her eyes blazed. "I'm not your goddamn maid!"

"You're not even your own maid. We're not in this house three months, and it looks like a slum in here. Castle Dracula is better kept than this place."

"Then hire somebody to come in and clean. You make enough money."

"I don't make enough to justify throwing it down the drain because you're too lazy to clean your own house. Make me something to eat. Now!"

She was on her feet at that, her voice as shrill as an air raid siren. "Don't you give me orders. Who the hell do you think you are? Nobody talks to me like that."

Somewhere, deep within Jim's brain, a tiny doorway opened—a doorway he struggled to keep shut because behind it were words and phrases delivered in a shrill female voice.

"You're not my boss," Marci was screaming at him. "You're not telling me what to do. I've taken all the shit from you I'm going to take."

Jim was pale and quivering. He started for the door, his lips drawn tightly. He didn't trust himself to speak. He didn't trust himself to do anything but leave that room at that very instant, or—

Marci's hand grabbed at his sleeve from behind. "Where do you think you're going, you son of a bitch?" she screamed at him. "You—"

The blow was delivered with his open hand. It caught her high on the left cheek. Marci, more shocked than hurt, staggered backwards until her legs hit the bed, and then she fell backwards. Jim was on her in a heartbeat. She moved to struggle beneath him, but then she felt a pillow close over her face, stifling her shouts of protest and shock and hurt and rage. She pushed against it, trying to get it out of her face, trying to get free so she could breathe.

He's trying to kill me, she realized in horror. He's trying to smother me. Marci screamed into the pillow—a shrill plea for help. He pressed down ever harder. He held her there for what seemed like an eternity, until she was too weak and exhausted to fight against him, and she stopped her screams and the pillow came away and he was there over her, straddling her, his face red and tears flowing from his eyes and whimpering. "Marci, Marci," he whined, "I'm so sorry, so sorry."

She rolled over, gasping for air. He wrapped his arms around her. "I'm sorry, I'm sorry, I'm sorry, I'm sorry . . ."

* * * *

Tiring as it was, the two hours of driving between Lakeside and Boydstown, once in the morning and once at night, were the best parts of Susan's day. She could turn on the radio and listen to the music and, if she was lucky, force from her mind the images of horror that lived there virtually all the rest of the time.

Tonight she had stayed at the hospital until nine-thirty, until Liam, so thin and so pale and such a good kid, finally drifted off to sleep beneath the crisp white hospital sheets. Then she had driven back home through the darkness, listening to a radio station out of Auburn with an unfortunate fondness for Skeeter Davis.

When she arrived in Lakeside, Art was in the living room with a can of beer, watching the "Sandy Duncan Show." Susan eyed him coldly. "It's nearly eleven," she said. "You said you'd call at nine."

"I had to work late. The clutch in Considine's truck has been slipping, and we had to pull the whole thing out and rebuild it. By the time I got in, I figured you'd already be on your way back, so I didn't bother calling. How are you, anyway? You look beat."

"I'm fine," she said, hanging up her jacket. "Why don't you ask about your son?"

He got up in his stocking feet and switched off Sandy Duncan. "You seem sort of nasty."

Susan turned on him. "And why not? I should think you'd have made it a point to call me instead of screwing around with a transmission—or whatever the hell it was."

"Susan, I was working. I've got to make a living, no matter what else is going on. Now cut it out and tell me what's going on with Liam."

She sank wearily down in one of the worn living room chairs. Not five years old, and they were shot. Cheap stuff to begin with, she knew. It was all they had been able to afford at the time. Hell, it was all they could afford now. "Doctor Sun is worried," she said quietly. "They've gotten the white count down, but they're still afraid he's too vulnerable to infection."

Art sat down across from her and chewed his lower lip. He took a swig from his can of beer. "How's he feeling?"

"He feels all right. He's tired all the time—very weak. When they're not working on him, he's just dozing. The real worry is infection."

"How much longer will he be in there?"

"I can't get them to say," she said. "I can't keep making that drive all the time. I liked it at first, but tonight I almost drove off the road at one point. If he has to stay there much longer, I'll have to get some kind of room near the hospital to stay in. I'm going to look for one tomorrow."

He shook his head. "I don't know where we're going to get the money for that."

She glared at him. "Well, we'll just have to find it, won't we?"

"Sure," he said. "Sure. Are you going to stay down in Boydstown on weekends, too?"

"What do you mean?"

"Well, there's a thing at the Elks Saturday. I thought maybe it would do you some good to get out."

She stared at him in open disgust.

"I just thought we'd spend a little time together," he said hurriedly. "Look, I really need to see you, Susan. This business with Liam is ripping me right up."

Susan closed her eyes. Maybe Art had been fixing a clutch and maybe he hadn't. Whatever problems he was having with his son's illness, he didn't seem to let it interfere with his regular drink with the boys after work, with his Tuesday bowling league, with his Saturday-morning softball games, with his fishing expeditions out on the lake on Sundays and—now, at least—his desire to participate in the social affairs on weekends at the Elks. "Liam is the one who needs me," she told him. "He might die, Art. Do you understand that? Our little boy might die."

"Don't say that!" he shouted at her. Then he got up and stalked across the room, pacing back and forth. "I don't want to hear that. Liam's not going to die, and that's that."

"It's time you faced it," Susan told him. "You're not there. I can see it in the doctors' faces. You can see them beginning to think they might not win this one."

"I won't listen to this!"

Susan got up and gathered up her purse. "I'm going up to bed. I'm tired. I'm getting a room in Boydstown tomorrow. When I leave I'll be taking some of my things with me. I don't plan to be back until they let Liam out."

"Are you coming back this weekend?"

"He can't come back this weekend, can he?"

Art looked at the rubber-backed carpet that covered the worn wooden floor of their house. "Look, it's just that . . . well, you know."

"Know what?" Susan asked as she put one foot on the stairs.

He looked at her awkwardly. "It's just that I was hoping we could do something together this weekend to take our minds off it for a while."

Susan sighed and glared at him. "And who's going to take Liam's mind of it, you selfish bastard?"

"Susan, I was just—"

"Oh, shut up!" she said as she went up the stairs. "You make me sick, Art."

* * * *

Billy Frazier's father had been a small-town doctor who'd worked himself to death with sixteen-hour days. He'd left his two children a four-year-old Olds with sixty thousand miles on the odometer, a comfortable middle-class house on Lake Street and two hundred dollars and eighteen cents in a checking account with Lakeside Trust. He had no left no stocks, no bonds, no savings accounts. Every penny he had ever brought in had gone to the support of his family and Billy's education. Billy had never expected more from his own life as a small-town GP.

When Lyndon Johnson capitalized on the memory of the slain John F. Kennedy to push through enormously expensive social programs to benefit the poor and aged, Billy and most other physicians in the nation opposed them bitterly. To most doctors the Great Society smacked of socialism—even communism. They lost that fight, of course, and Johnson won. But in so doing, he had created a mechanism for making doctors rich beyond their wildest dreams.

Thanks to Lyndon Johnson, Billy Frazier and the other doctors quickly became the surprised and delighted recipients of third-party payment programs. People who would never have gone to the doctor if they had been forced to pay for it themselves went regularly once government started paying for it. And the government fees were higher than Billy had been charging in his own private practice. Billy collected tons of money from Medicare and Medicaid. He collected ton upon ton of money from the improved private insurance programs employers were obligated to offer their workers simply because the unemployed and elderly suddenly had access to better medical care.

At the age of fifty-four, his tax accountant informed him, his net personal worth had just exceeded three quarters of a million dollars. Billy owned his father's house free and clear. He had a beach house on Saint Thomas that he enjoyed every winter. He owned several summer cottages along the lake that he used for rental income while their value rose. He owned the four-story building on Main Street in which his practice was located and he was doing quite well in the stock market. He was, in fact, only peripherally involved in the practice of medicine anymore, and that thought was very much in his mind as he drove his Lincoln Continental Mark IV along the Lake Road in front of Brennan's Point.

Kevin's office in the winery was a fifteen by fifteen room with a desk and two chairs for visitors and pictures of his family on the bookcase along one wall. When Billy stuck his head in, Kevin was leafing through a copy of the *Wine Spectator*. "You don't seem to be doing much," the physician said.

Kevin looked up. "It says here that there's an outfit out in Modesto, California, that's producing a bottle of champagne with only three pounds of grapes. We can't get it down below 3.4 even with our cheap stuff. I can't see how they do it."

Billy sat down. "I came here to tell you something. It's been bothering me. I wanted to get it off my chest now rather than later, when you're going to have too much on your mind."

Kevin looked at his friend carefully. "I think I know what you're going to say—"

"No, please. Let me get this out. I have to."

Kevin was silent. Slowly, he lit a cigar while Billy collected his thoughts.

Billy Frazier said, "I'm sorry that I didn't catch it myself. I should have. My only excuse is that when I saw the bruises I thought . . . well, never mind what I thought. The symptoms are easy to mistake, Kevin, and I was thinking about my vacation coming up. I'd been paying a lot of attention to my personal financial affairs. You know, I don't even see that many patients any more—just the old friends and the families I'm especially close to. And then all I do is give them some medication for colds and skin rashes and refer them to the specialists if it's anything more than that. Liam was a young boy, and there's no family history of this sort of thing. It just never occurred to me that it could be leukemia. I wasn't paying attention the way I should have been. And, well, after this business with Will, it just never occurred to me that something else could happen to the Brennans so soon. I just . . ." He began to weep. Kevin looked away from his best friend's tears. "Billy, you don't have to put yourself through all this. You did the best you could. Nobody's to blame, for God's sake."

Billy took out his handkerchief and blew his nose noisily. "I did do the best I could. And that's the worst of it. It just wasn't good enough to pick up what Liam had. That kid Jerry Bonham caught it right away. I'm not the world's greatest physician, Kevin. I'm certainly not the doctor my father was. I'm not even sure I should have become a doctor. My parents wanted it, so that's what I did. I probably should have gone into business. I'm pretty good at that, you know."

Kevin sighed heavily. "Billy, I'm not going to tell you what a great doctor you are. You might be terrific; you might be terrible. I have no way to judge. But you've been our family doctor just like your father was before you, and nobody has ever complained about the service. And would it have made any difference if you had caught it? Would anybody have been able to make him better if you'd caught it?"

Billy shook his head. "No, I don't think so. Nobody knows, though. Sometimes these things go just right. You catch it, you cut it out or you give the patient the right combination of drugs at just the right time and everything is fine. And then other times . . ."

"And other times nothing helps."

"That's right. It's God's will."

The two men sat in silence for a long moment. Each was in torment, and each was comforted, as they had been since childhood, merely by the other's presence. They had lived with one another through more than a half century of joys and heartbreaks, and now they could find solace just in one another's company.

"I had one of those phone calls the other night," Kevin said finally.

"From who?"

"Bob Wright."

"What did he want? The usual?"

"Advice on how to handle Jane. Can you imagine that? I was married to her for eight years, and I was away for half of those. He's been married to her for nearly twenty-five years now, and he still calls me for tips on how to handle her."

"The man's a jerk," Billy said. "What's she doing to him now?"

"Bob says she's been drunk in varying degrees ever since Will died."

"She's been drunk a lot longer than that, hasn't she?"

"Not like this, I guess. The weird thing is that she's spending hours on the phone a couple of nights a week with my sister. I can just imagine the two of them going at it. Can you picture what those conversations are like—raking husbands, and ex-husbands, over the coals by the hour? Jesus, the two of them. Who ever would have figured that?"

"You know," Billy said, "I don't think I ever saw a more beautiful woman than Helen. Or a more charming woman. She had everything in the world going for her."

Kevin frowned. "She's a little like Will."

"How do you mean?" Billy Frazier asked.

"Maybe a family weakness. When things get tough, you go hide. Helen does it in a bottle, and Will . . ." His voice trailed off.

"I feel terrible about the little boy, Kevin," Billy said, unwilling to let the subject go. "I'd have given anything to have diagnosed it correctly and to have been able to treat it successfully."

"They told Susan it should be over in a few days—a week at most."

"Are you going down to Boydstown?"

"I'll go to the hospital tomorrow and stay through the end. I've got a hotel room reserved. I want to be there with Susan. Art's down there now, but I get the impression that they're having problems."

Billy nodded. "Yes. That's not uncommon in situations like this, you know."

"I suppose. I just don't know what'll happen to them when he dies— or to Mother, for that matter."

"I can leave you some sleeping pills for her. I have some in my bag out in the car."

Kevin shook his head. "No, it'll be fine. Thanks for the thought, anyway."

Billy looked at him. "And you? How are you holding up?"

For the first time since they had known one another, Billy Frazier saw Kevin Brennan waver. Kevin's lower lip trembled. When he answered, his voice was weak and hoarse. "I'm waiting to die myself. I've gone on like this about as long as I can."

Billy was pitiful in his helplessness. He could picture Kevin doing something insane. He could see him going into the study and taking down his father's rifle and . . .

"Kevin . . ." he said.

But as quickly as it came, it passed, and Kevin Brennan was himself again. "No," Kevin said in a low voice, "I'm not going to do anything to myself. I have Mother to take care of. It's not my time yet—as much as I wish it were."

* * * *

"Hello."

"Hello, Vinnie. This is Dr. Frazier."

"Well hello, Billy. That's pretty formal stuff—Dr. Frazier."

"Yeah, I guess so. That's because I'm calling in my official capacity. Is Becky there?"

Vinnie Ralston said, "Yeah. Anything wrong?"

"Nothing much. I just got some test results back on her."

"Anything serious?"

Billy could have sworn he could detect in Vinnie Ralston's voice the heart-felt wish that there was something wrong. "No, he said, "nothing spectacular."

"I'll get her. Becky!"

Billy drummed his fingers on the top of his desk.

"Hello."

"This is Billy. Have you seen Kevin lately?"

"Excuse me for a minute. Vinnie. I'll take this in the kitchen."

There was a moment's pause. "I've got it, Vinnie."

Billy heard the phone click.

"He won't see me, Billy. He's just shut me out."

"But why?"

"It's the way he gets through hard times. He closes up on himself. It was bad with Will. It's worse now. I can't do anything about it."

"Call him."

"I did. He just hung up the minute I tried to talk about it. It happened twice. Billy, I know him as well as you do. He wants to go this alone."

Billy was silent. "If you can do anything . . ."

"Just pray for him. It's all he'll let me do."

Billy sighed. "Goodbye, Becky."

Becky hung up the phone and went into the living room. Vinnie Ralston sat in an easy chair watching "Star Trek."

"What was that all about?" he asked her.

"Yeast infection."

"Terrific," Vinnie Ralston said.

* * * *

Liam Brennan Dixon died in a brightly lit room in Boydstown Memorial

Hospital shortly after midnight. It was several days earlier than expected, but hardly a shock to his doctors.

His father was down the hall at the time. Art was in the men's room, staring through glazed eyes at his image in the mirror. He gazed at the stubble of his beard and at the beginnings of jowls and marveled at what was happening. He wondered when he would awaken from this nightmare and hear his wife humming in the kitchen and the ragged laughter of his little boy playing in the yard.

Susan was asleep when her son's heart stopped. She was slumped in an impossible position in a visitor's chair, exhausted after days of sleeplessness. She was dreaming of the lake in summer and the sun glinting off its waves. Within seconds of the sudden halt of Liam's breathing, she came awake with a start as an instinct deep within her voiced an anguished cry of alarm.

Her bleary eyes focused instantly on the small form on the bed before her. In place of her little boy, she saw a still, waxen figure. Susan sat transfixed, her own breath temporarily arrested. Then, slowly, she rose to her feet and tentatively crossed the room on shaky legs. She took her little boy's small, already cooling hand, and she knew without doubt that she was no longer a mother because she no longer had a child. Where had he gone? What had become of him?

She sank to her knees, pressing the limp hand to her forehead and moaning in a low voice.

That's how Art Dixon found her when he came back into the room. He froze in the doorway, his mouth opening and working silently, no sound emerging. Then a soft, hushed noise issued from Art's open mouth. It was a quiet grunt, as though he had been struck suddenly in the midsection and all the wind had been forced out of him. His broad shoulders sagged. His head spun. For a moment, he lost his balance entirely. He fell to one side and put out one strong hand against the doorjamb. Then he turned slowly and staggered out into the hallway, his head reeling.

Barbara Constantine had been a nurse for fourteen years. She was at her station when she saw Art stagger into the hall. She came smartly from around the counter where she had been working and marched up the hall, a model of starched, white efficiency. She marched past Art in the hallway. From the doorway of the room, she saw a woman on her knees, clutching the hand of a dead little boy on the bed. She saw the woman's head turn around, her eyes wide with horror and hurt and disbelief.

"Art?" Susan called. The word had been wrenched from her throat.

In the hallway outside, Art Dixon was sliding down the wall, hitting the floor and assuming a tight, fetal position on the ice-cold tile floor. The sounds of his noisy weeping bounced off the walls.

Barbara Constantine saw it all as she went to the child's body. She noticed the positions of the devastated parents almost unconsciously. They had told her about this earlier, that this child was dying, and she was the mother of two children of her own. She had lived through this before, and she knew what to do. She took solace in her routine, in her duties, and she did not think. Later, at home, she would think, and she would drink some vodka and she would go and hug her daughters in their room. But she would not think now. She would pick up the phone. She would make the call she had been programmed to make. And she would not think.

But she couldn't help but notice the positions of the devastated parents of this dead child. They were both too wounded to stand, too grievously hurt to do anything but settle into crumpled heaps and bury their faces. And she couldn't help but notice that they were some distance apart.

* * * *

Patricia didn't much like *Easy Rider*. The sound track was great, and she liked the guy who played the lawyer—Nicholson, his name was— but the two heroes buzzing across the country on motorcycles bothered her. She didn't know any freaks who had razor-cut hair, like Peter Fonda did in the film, and she thought the Dennis Hopper character looked too much like the bums she was constantly running into on the street.

Larry, on the other hand, loved the movie. They were arguing about it on a totally intellectual level when they got back to the apartment to find Shirley lying on the sofa, her eyes glazed dangerously. She was making strange sounds, sort of like a bird. "Cooooo," she was saying. "coo, coo, coo, coo. Coo-o-o-o-o-o-o-o . . ."

Larry looked at her in shock. It took a lot to shock Larry. "Holy shit!" he said.

Patricia's lips tightened as she bent down and examined Shirley. This was serious, and Patricia handled emergencies well. She'd had plenty of experience at that, especially after Jim left home. "Shirley, can you hear me?"

Shirley's eyes opened and met Patricia's. An expression of terror passed over her face, and she pulled back into a little ball on the sofa. "Don't touch me!" she screamed. "Don't fucking touch me."

"Oh, Christ," Larry said. "She's tripping. She's paranoid as hell. Come on, Shirley, let's get with it. We've got to get her to bed."

As they bent down to pick her up, Shirley informed them, "I can hear the moon."

"The moon?" Patricia said."

"Her brain is cornmeal mush," Larry said. "Here, get her legs."

They carried Shirley into the bedroom and laid her on the bed. She was moaning and cooing and babbling about the moon. Patricia was getting scared. "Her heartbeat is real fast. Maybe we ought to call somebody."

Larry pulled the covers up around her. "Like who—the cops? Do you want a search of this place? Let's just sit with her until she comes down. I wish I knew for sure what she took. I hope it wasn't acid."

"Has she done acid before?"

"Not this semester. She had a bad trip last year, though. Some people shouldn't take that stuff. She starts out okay, but then she freaks right out."

Patricia went into the bathroom and soaked a washcloth in cold water. She came out and put it on Shirley's brow and took her pulse again.

"Her heartbeat is up over a hundred," she told Larry.

"Ah, that ain't bad. You get up to 120, 130, then maybe you got a problem. She'll be okay. Won't you, Shirley?"

"It's green," Shirley replied.

"See?" Larry said. "She's fine."

Patricia remained unconvinced. "Shirley, do you want some water? How about some coffee?"

"Green, green. It's fucking green."

"She's cool," Larry told Patricia.

"What's green?" Patricia asked her.

"Who the hell knows?" Larry said.

They sat with her for forty-five minutes. Shirley would lapse into trances. Then she would emerge from them and babble nonsense. Sometimes she was animated. Sometimes she was almost comatose. Larry seemed to take it all in stride, but Patricia was unnerved. The phone rang just after eleven, and she took it in the kitchen.

"I've been trying to reach you all night," her father told her. "Liam Dixon died early this morning."

"Oh, God. That's terrible. How are Grandma and Kevin?"

"As well as they could be. They knew he wasn't going to make it. They just didn't share that with the rest of us."

"He wasn't even ten, was he?"

"Yes. He wasn't eleven, though. And he never will be."

"I feel so horrible. Poor Susan. Oh, my God. That poor little kid."

"They're going to bury him at Brennan's Point day after tomorrow. There's a wake tomorrow night."

"Do you want me to come home?"

"No," Jack said. "Frankly, it's something I don't want you here for. I guess Art's a complete mess. Susan told Kevin that the hospital orderlies had to hold him down so they could take the body away. You stay down there in New York and take your finals. How's the schoolwork going, by the way?"

"Fine, I guess. I think I'm going to get a B in finite math. There goes my four-Oh."

As she spoke, Patricia heard Shirley issue a blood-curdling shriek. "Hold on a sec, Daddy," she said, and hurriedly slapped a hand over the phone. The receiver had a long cord that enabled her to walk almost into the bedroom. Shirley was on the floor, flopping and rolling in her covers. Larry was on top of her, trying to hold her still. "You've got to keep her quiet," Patricia hissed. "It's my father."

Larry looked toward her. He was struggling with the howling, battling pile of sheets and blankets, and for the first time Patricia saw alarm on his face. "She's going nuts," Larry got out. "Get off the phone and give me a hand in here."

Patricia ran back into the kitchen and took her hand off the receiver. "I've got to go now, Daddy. Shirley's lost her key, and I've got to go down and let her in the building."

"Just get your studying in. I'm sending a mass card in your name. Say a prayer for your uncle Kevin."

"I will," she said, and hung up.

In the bedroom, Larry had managed to get Shirley up on the bed. Patricia, her eyes wide with fright, helped him hold her down.

"The bugs!" Shirley screamed. "Get the bugs away from me!"

"We've got to call somebody," Patricia told Larry.

"No, we don't have to call anybody. She's hallucinating. It'll pass."

"You've seen her like this before? This bad?"

"No," he admitted. "Not this bad. But it won't last."

Patricia glared at him, and he turned his eyes away. "You got the stuff for her, didn't you?"

"I didn't know she was going to take it when she was alone. How am I supposed to know she'd be that stupid?"

Shirley issued forth a plaintive and blood-curdling wail about bugs and the moon and a variety of other topics Patricia couldn't decipher.

"I'm going to call an ambulance," Patricia said.

"No!" Larry shouted, and it was the first time Patricia had ever heard him raise his voice. It caught her attention.

"Now listen, goddamn it," he told her, "if we just hold her down and keep her from hurting herself it'll pass."

It took more than ninety more minutes for Shirley to come down. Her eyes rolled, and she vomited twice. The sour stench of it turned Patricia's stomach, and she almost barfed herself. Finally, though, Shirley was just lying there, moaning softly and staring at the ceiling. She would not respond to Patricia's voice, but she seemed to hear some of what Larry said to her. It seemed to relax her. When her eyes closed, Patricia and Larry staggered into the living room.

"Jesus," Larry gasped, collapsing on the sofa. "I'm glad that's over."

Patricia took the chair. She sat with her face in her hands. "That was just plain scary."

"It was scarier for her, let me tell you. My first trip was very bad. I got paranoid as hell. I thought the room was full of snakes the size of fire hoses. I turned into a snake myself, at one point. Far fucking out, let me tell you. All the other trips were fine, though."

She looked up at him. "What's it like—acid, I mean?"

He sat up and stared at the ceiling, trying to find words to describe his experiences. "It's tough to describe. You see colors you can't see when you're straight. The world bends sort of funny, you know? Time is different. You can toss a pencil in the air, and it can take an hour to come down."

Patricia said, "I'd be afraid I'd get like Shirley."

"Not if you had somebody helping you along, like a guide. Also, Shirley is a little off the wall. She probably shouldn't use the stuff."

"If you thought that about her, why'd you give it to her?"

"Hey, am I her keeper? She's a big girl. Besides, you never know when somebody's going to have a problem and when they're not. I had one bad trip, and the rest were fine."

Patricia was unimpressed with that logic. Larry Engel was beginning to wear pretty thin with her, anyway.

The bedroom door opened and Shirley came out, her hand to her forehead. Patricia got to her feet.

"Shirley . . ." she said.

Shirley, her eyes closed, merely waved a hand at her as she staggered by. "I'm cool," she said.

Patricia watched as Shirley walked into the kitchen and opened the refrigerator. Patricia looked at Larry, questioningly. He shrugged.

"Is that it?" Patricia said.

"She seems okay."

Shirley took a container of milk out of the refrigerator and moved away toward the cabinet that contained the glasses. In so doing, she moved out of Patricia's line of sight.

"I ought to keep an eye on her," Patricia said, starting for the kitchen.

"Hey," Larry said, "Come here."

Patricia stopped and looked at him. He was smiling carelessly through his beard. "Crisis resolved. Come and sit next to me."

Patricia heard Shirley rummaging through the kitchen drawers. She started to say that she'd better get out there when she heard it—high and piercing, like a train whistle. Then she realized it was Shirley's voice, raised in an eerie howl. Patricia went for the kitchen like a shot.

Shirley was backed into a corner, her eyes rolling wildly. In one hand she held the container of milk. In the other she held a steak knife with a fake bone handle.

We just bought those knives at Macy's, Patricia thought stupidly. But by then Shirley was screaming again.

"Get them off me!" she screamed, looking down at her body, her eyes wide with horror. Larry came into the room and stopped, his own eyes wide and his mouth open. Then she dropped the cardboard milk container on the linoleum floor and drove the steak knife deep into her left thigh.

Patricia was unable to react for a good three seconds. She saw the pointed blade go through the denim into Shirley's leg. Then it came up and drove down again, piercing the denim in the harsh, overhead light. And then again. And all the while, Shirley was screaming and screaming and screaming.

By the time they got her down on the floor and wrestled the knife away from her, Shirley's upper left leg was bathed in dark liquid. The floor was slippery with blood. Patricia pulled off her belt and managed somehow to get around Shirley's thigh, near the crotch. She pulled it tight and held it there. With her other hand she held Shirley against the floor. She looked at Larry, who was clutching at Shirley's wrists. His face was ashen beneath his beard. "Now we'd better call somebody," he said.

Chapter 20

Kevin wasn't looking for it at the funeral—other things occupied him—but he could tell that Jim and Marci Ryan's marriage was not going well.

He liked Marci. She was gorgeous and funny and bright enough that she let only the slightest touch of her humor show through, considering the occasion. It was Marci's first visit to Brennan's Point. Although it was clear that she was a city person and regarded the wine country as a wilderness, it was also clear that she was perceptive enough to recognize the place's beauty. She was good with everyone: sympathetic with Susan and Art, respectful of Katherine, deferential to Jack and Helen, warm and friendly to Henri and Annette.

Jim, however, was distant and distracted. Kevin noticed that they did not touch one another. They didn't hold hands, for instance, not even during the walk down the hill from the graveyard. Marci sat in a chair in the living room even though the place next to Jim on the sofa was conspicuously vacant. They didn't speak directly to one another. And when they spoke of each other to the others, they didn't use the other person's name. When Jim spoke of Marci, it was "she"; Marci refered to Jim as "my husband." They were only small signs, and they seemed to escape the notice of the others, but not Kevin.

"How's business?" he asked Jim at one point in the afternoon when they found themselves alone in the study.

"Fine. Her father is a good guy. He's taught me a lot."

"So you're going to stay with it, then."

"Yeah. I like it. I never pictured myself selling, but it turns out that I like it—this kind of selling, anyway. I'm good at it, too."

"You like living in Philadelphia?" Kevin asked.

"We live in a suburb, actually."

"Got your own house?"

Jim nodded. "Spent a goddamn fortune for it, too. I put away a lot the first year we were married, and I'd hoped to get something cheaper and put the extra cash into the stock market. But it all ended up going into the house. It was the only way I could keep the payments down."

"How much did you spend, if you don't mind my asking?"

"I don't mind," Jim said "I spent seventy-two-five."

Kevin whistled in appreciation at the sum. "It must be a mansion."

"Hell, no. It's in a development. Nice neighborhood, but it's not any nicer than my parents' house in Boydstown, and Dad says that's not worth more than forty-five. Real estate is more expensive down there."

Kevin nodded. "I guess. Do you like it?"

Jim shrugged. "It'll do. She picked out the house. I just make the payments."

Susan was calm and restrained throughout the ordeal of laying little Liam to rest next to his grandfather on the mountainside. Kevin was not surprised, however, when she drove the Mustang out to Brennan's Point the next day, pulled out a suitcase and announced that she was staying for a while. Art phoned and talked to her for nearly two hours that night. The next afternoon, he phoned Kevin at the winery. "Can't you try to talk her into coming home?" he begged Kevin.

"Art, she's come running for a safe place. She'll leave it when she's ready to leave it. With what she's been through, you can't expect her to be thinking rationally."

"Her?" Art demanded. "What about me?"

"It's completely out of my hands. Art, look—all of us—we're just struggling to deal with this."

Art said, "Kevin, I'm so sorry for everybody. I'm sorry for Liam, for us. But I need my wife."

"I'll ask her to call you."

Susan refused. Several days later Kevin cornered her on the front porch. Spring was full upon the lake country, and buds were bursting in the trees and on the vines. "What are you going to do?" Kevin Brennan asked his daughter. "Don't you think it's time now that you went home to your husband?"

"Why?" she asked.

"Because he is your husband. Because you have a life together."

Susan looked at her father. Her face was drawn but strangely calm. Her calmness troubled Kevin. He could tell she wasn't acting out of grief or desperation.

"No, we don't, Daddy," she told him. "We had a life together, but that life is buried up there on the hillside. Whatever life Art and I had ended when Liam's life ended. That's if you can call what Liam had a life. Does ten years constitute a life? I don't think so."

Kevin lit a cigar. He was smoking a dozen of them a day now, and inhaling, too. "I don't think you're in any shape to make a decision like that—not right now. What you have to do when something like this happens—"

She turned on him, and the tone of her voice drove into his heart like an icicle. "Something like this? What's like this? My little boy's dead, I still have to go on living, and I don't want to. I want to go up that hill and dig up his grave with my fingers and crawl into the ground with him. And if I could, I'd do it in a second. He's up there under the dirt, cold and alone. Something like this? Jesus, Daddy . . ."

And then she wept. Kevin had never heard such a sound. For the first time since she was a little girl, her father reached out for her, held her, cradled her head in his arms. For the first time ever, he wept with her.

"Go home to your husband," he said at last. "Go home and love each other and comfort each other."

Her sobbing made her voice almost incomprehensible. "My child is dead. He's dead. He's dead. Don't you understand?"

"I understand," he told her, stroking her hair as the tears ran down his face. "My child is dead, too—tortured to death by something that happened to him. And there was nobody for me to turn to when it happened. My God, Susan, that's why people get married—to have somebody to share the pain with."

She looked up at him then.

"Why not Becky?" she asked him.

It was the first time she had ever spoken the name to him. It didn't surprise him that she knew. He hadn't been kidding anybody.

He shook his head. "She has a husband."

"She'd leave him in a second."

Kevin looked at his daughter, his eyes red and wet. "She hasn't, though, has she? Go home to your husband, Susan. He can do for you what none of the rest of us can do."

Susan cried for a while—silently and with a dignity Kevin found amazing.

Then she said, "I'll try."

She did, too. Susan spent two more months with Art Dixon. She made him breakfast and dinner. Sometimes they even joked with one another. But when they made love, she was reminded of the night she had gotten pregnant with Liam, on the sofa of the living room at Brennan's Point after everyone else had gone to bed. She could remember every detail of that night: Art's hands on her, his breath on her flesh, the stunning triumph of her orgasm. She could remember when she had first realized that life was growing inside her. She had known even before she had missed her period, and she had felt a joy and an awesome power that defied all she had imagined it would be. She remembered all that, and she contrasted that with how she felt now after they made love. She felt empty and dead inside. He would roll off her and she would feel nothing—not during and not afterward.

On a Wednesday in the ninth week they were back together, she walked him to the door and said to him, "Art, I won't be here when you get back from work."

He turned and gazed at her, his expression strangely calm and accepting. "I've been waiting for you to say that. I knew you'd say it. Where are you going to go?"

"Remember Julie Gauge? She was in my class in high school? She's living in Long Beach, California. She's married to a guy who runs an employment agency. I had her address from the sheet they passed out at my tenth high school reunion. I asked her if her husband's company could find me a job out there. She called back yesterday, and they found me a job in a supermarket. I'm going to go out there and take it."

He looked at her in surprise. "You're going to California?"

"It's as far away as I could think of—short of leaving the country."

He looked around the house. He hadn't expected this. "What about this place?"

"Sell it," she said. "Send me my share of the money. Or keep it. I don't care."

"How long are you going to stay out there?"

"I don't know. Until more of the hurt goes away, at least."

Art gazed at the floor. "Are you coming back?" he asked softly.

"I don't know. I just know I have to get away from here. I might come back. I might not."

Art's voice was a plea. "Susan, I need you."

"No, you don't. We thought we needed each other. We thought we could protect each other. But when the ultimate hurt came, neither one of us could put aside our own pain long enough to comfort the other. Each of us felt that was the time when the other person owed us, and the other person wasn't there. You'll be okay without me, Art. And I'll be okay without you. Really, I will."

"That's not true. We need each other. Especially now."

Susan was strangely at peace. She felt as though she were a million miles away from him.

"It's true," she said quietly. "You know it is."

Then she kissed him. It was a gentle kiss, one without passion, and they melted into one another, joining more closely than they had during all the time of their married intimacy. She held him tenderly in her arms, nutured him, loved him one last time. Then she stepped away.

"Go on," Susan told him. "Go to work."

Art tried to speak and found that he couldn't talk. So he went to work.

When he came home, Susan was gone.

* * * *

During lunch with Jim Ryan one rainy Friday at Old Original Book-binders, Sam Roth suddenly stopped talking and sat as still and silent as a statue. Jim looked at the older man in surprise.

"Sam? You okay?"

Sam Roth raised a hand and silenced him. Sam sat for perhaps forty-five seconds, staring at the luxurious paneling of the Presidents' Room, his expression blank. Then he said, "I think you maybe should take me to the hospital." Sam tapped his chest. "A dull pain, here. Down my left arm I feel it, too. Indigestion, maybe, but why take chances?"

Jim stood up. "You're right. Why take chances?"

It turned out to be a mild heart attack. The cardiologist at Jefferson Medical Center said that Sam Roth was alive, in all probability, because he was prudent. He had made it to the hospital's emergency room less than fifteen minutes after the onset of symptoms. Most men would have tried to ignore it for several hours, the doctor said. And a lot of them would have died.

Sam spent two weeks in the hospital. When he came out he moved in with Jim and Marci for another month. He watched the soap operas on television. He played for hours on end with his new grandson, even though he thought the kid had a silly name. Whoever heard of a Jewish kid named Eamon Ryan? But Jim had insisted, and, as it had always been, if it was okay with Marci, then it was okay with Sam. Sam had been thinking of Saul, which had been his father's name, but if it had to be Eamon, then he'd live with it. He just hoped the kid wouldn't get too bad a time at Hebrew School.

The kid was just two. Sam was crazy about him, and he almost didn't want to go off to Florida and leave him. But it was winter, and he was sick of the cold, and Florida was where he wanted to go to recuperate, even if Marci wasn't so wild about the idea.

"You shouldn't go down there by yourself," Marci told him.

"What makes you think I'll be alone? Florida is full of widows looking for old men to take care of."

Marci knew her father was going to do precisely what he wanted to do, so she decided not to make a production over it. Sam took Jim aside.

"You're in charge of the business now," he said.

"Only until you get back, Sam."

"Maybe I won't come back so soon. Anyway, while I'm gone, you're in charge. You got a question, call. Otherwise, make money."

And that was that. Six weeks after his heart attack, Sam got in his Cadillac and drove off for Florida, leaving Jim as the acting chief executive officer of Roth and Co. Jim spent a month steeping himself in the aspects of the business he hadn't yet learned. Then, with Sam's blessing delivered by phone, he took the opportunity to do something he'd wanted to do for a long time. He went to visit Otto Kruger and lay down the law to him.

"How's Sam?" Otto said when Jim called on him.

"I talked to him yesterday. He's got his golf game down to the high eighties."

Otto said, "I'd take a heart attack if it would help me break ninety."

"Otto," Jim said, "I'm getting some serious complaints from NASA about delivery problems. I thought it was time I came out here to see what I could do to help."

Kruger frowned. "These goddamn government people are on the phone all the time. I've got industrial accounts to worry about—people who have been my customers for electronics components for years."

Jim frowned. "Be that as it may, NASA is getting to be the biggest part of your business. This space program is just going to get bigger and bigger, and we have signed contracts with the government. I worked like hell to those specs written around your products, Otto, and now you're just not making the delivery dates. That's a good way to see to it that future contracts are written around somebody else's specs. I'll be honest with you; it worries me."

Otto Kruger stood up and paced. He was a perpetually rumpled and scratchy man in manner and outlook. "This plant is operating at full capacity. You don't just crank out semiconductors like they're postage stamps. Every one is complex. Every one—"

Jim had heard all this before. He wasn't in the mood to hear it again. "I know all that, Otto," he broke in. "I also know I'm losing credibility with your biggest customer. And not just your biggest customer, but mine, too. I represent other clients who do business with NASA. Your failure to deliver on time has the potential to damage my other accounts."

Otto Kruger's eyebrows raised. "So, that's the point, isn't it? You're not so worried about my business. You're worried about your other accounts, right?"

That was completely true—not that Jim was going to admit it. "I worry about all my accounts, Otto, and you should, too. When you make a deal with NASA, you've damn well got to deliver on time. These are guys you don't screw around with."

That was all Kruger needed. He was one of those people who couldn't wait for an excuse to explode. He delighted in conflict. He got bored when he couldn't have it. "Then don't make any more deals for me!" he roared. "If Sam wants to keep this account, let him come back from Florida and go back to work instead of leaving my business to a snot-nosed kid."

Chronologically, Jim Ryan was twenty-five years younger than Otto Kruger. He was generations older in cunning. That was why he remained cool while Kruger lurched around his office, sputtering. When Jim responded, his voice was so low Kruger had to strain to hear it. He said, "Sam's not coming back for a while. He's a careful man, and he doesn't think returning to work is worth another heart attack. The fact is, Otto, that I'm taking more and more responsibility in Roth and Co. Look, I'm not looking for a big fight with you. I came here today to tell you that these are problems that have to be solved. If they're not, we won't have NASA for a customer for very much longer, and that could end up endangering my company's other government accounts."

"Then the hell with NASA," Kruger fumed. "The hell with the whole government. And the hell with you, too, Kid. Nobody tells me how to run my own business. Do you know what I had when I came to this country in 1946? Nothing, that's what I had. Now I got a big house in Cheltenham and a kid in graduate school at MIT and three cars and I take three weeks in the islands every winter. And I don't have to kiss anybody's ass—not NASA's, not the government's and sure as hell not the ass of a punk kid three or four years out of college."

Jim stood up. He said quietly, "Otto, you just became too much trouble to do business with."

Jim started for the door, and Kruger shouted after him, "Go ahead! Get the hell out! There are plenty of reps around."

Jim turned back to him. He smiled, and the smile was cold and without mirth. "Not many that'll put up with you. You see, you've got something of a reputation. Would you like to know what that reputation is?

Kruger, quivering with rage, said nothing.

"The reputation," Jim volunteered quietly, "is that you're a putz, Otto."

Three days later, Galen Lee called Jim. "What happened between you and Der Fuhrer?"

"I quit. Or, I was fired. I'm not sure which. In any event, I don't represent the company any more."

"What the hell happened?"

"A little hassle over delivery to NASA. Otto may be able to screw around with his industrial customers, but Richard Nixon gets pissed off when his microchips don't come in on time."

Galen laughed. "Nixon has bigger problems than Otto right about now."

"Nixon'll ride it out. Talk about nine lives."

"I can't figure out who's a bigger asshole," Galen said, "Nixon or Otto."

"I'd say Otto. He's the Bureau of Standards asshole. Anyway, we've gone our separate ways. I told Sam about it, and he's with me all the way."

"Isn't the company a lot of billing for you?" Galen asked.

"It's a lot of billing. But we have other clients, and there are other semiconductor firms out there. A lot of them have rotten representation. We'll be okay."

"Listen, if you hear about a semiconductor company that needs a good chief engineer, let me know. Otto is impossible. I guess I don't have to tell you that."

"I'm just glad I'm through with him," Jim said. "I feel sorry for you, though."

Galen was silent for a long moment over the phone. Then he said, "Jim, I have an idea. I've had it for a while. Why don't we go into business?"

"Who? Us?"

"Yeah, us. You and me. Hell, I design and produce the goddamn semiconductors, not Otto. You sell the damn things. What do we need Otto for?"

Jim couldn't help but laugh. "Well, for one thing, he's got the factory. You see, Galen, there's this thing called money . . ."

"I've got some money—not a fortune, but some. And I've got a wife who goes into private practice next spring. Psychiatrists make a bundle. I'll have money."

"Not all that fast, she won't. And it takes some real cash to start up a factory—even a little one."

"I'm telling you," Galen insisted, "I've got money. My mother's family owns a decent chunk of real estate in downtown Honolulu."

"You never told me your family has money," Jim said, reflecting back on the weekly tennis games they played and all the times they had socialized.

Now it was Galen's turn to laugh. "It's funny, money is. No one person in my family has it, but the family does. Did you ever hear of a *kee?*"

"It opens doors, right?"

"No, schmuck," Galen said, "it's like a family corporation. All the holdings are joint. The *kee* produces money for kids to go off to college and get educations. And after they earn their educations, some of the money they earn goes back to the family *kee* to educate the next generation. I send back maybe a third of my take-home pay to cover the cost of my schooling."

"I never heard of that."

"It's an old Chinese tradition," Galen explained, "especially in Hawaii. We Chinese were brought in to work in the cane fields, and in two generations we ended up owning damn near everything worth owning in Hawaii. *Kees* are always open to good investments. I can come up with some money, believe me. The only problem is finding out how much."

Jim Ryan pondered the proposition. He'd never considered going into business for himself, and under no circumstances would he consider leaving Roth and Co., not with Sam sick.

"If you're serious," he said, "I might be able to come up with some cash. I don't know how much yet. But even so, we'd need some heavy financing. I can have Harold look into it."

Harold Warren, Galen knew, was Jim's friend and lawyer. He often met them for tennis.

"What do we need Harold for?" Galen asked.

"Two reasons: One, we're not going to be able to just go into a bank for financing. At least, not for all of it. They'll want too much cash, and the interest rates will be too tough. I want a lawyer in on whatever financial arrangements we make right from the start. Two, the firm Harold's with represents some guys who might be interested in putting up some venture capital."

"I've heard that term, but I don't really know what it means."

"Neither do I. That's why I want a lawyer working on lining up the financing for us. Also, Harold is a potential investor. He's always looking for something to do with whatever he doesn't spend on high living."

"I should have such a problem," Galen said.

"You and me both. You can't believe how fast Marci goes through money—especially now that she's not working any more. It's like being married to Jacqueline Onassis."

They discussed plans for the new company for a while, and finally

Galen said, "You know, this doesn't sound bad at all. I think we could pull this off."

"Let's see," Jim said.

* * * *

One of the stunning surprises of Jim Ryan's life was the discovery that the investment loan officer at Girard Bank turned out to be a high school classmate from Boydstown, David Collins. He was fresh out of the Wharton Business School, and he was about one-third the size Jim remembered.

He looked at the tall, well-set-up young man across the desk from him, and he said, "David, you must have lost two hundred pounds."

David smiled. "You're not far off."

"How?"

"I went on the world's strictest diet in college," David Collins said. "It took me four years, but I took it off, and I'm keeping it off."

Jim shook his head. "I'm astounded. Harold, look at this guy. You ought to get his diet."

Harold Warren, a telltale bulge of prosperity around his waist, merely said, "I'll stick with Weight Watchers."

"How are your parents?" David Collins asked Jim.

It was merely a courtesy, Jim knew. David had sprung from Boydstown aristocracy. He was the grandson of the late congressman J. Arch Gordon. His parents, both dead now, had always been members of the Boydstown Country Club. Jim's parents had never been asked to join.

"They're fine," Jim said. "My sister, Patricia, is almost out of law school up in New York."

"No kidding?"

"Yep. She's been law review all the way. She's always been as smart as hell, and about her sophomore year in college she just started to put it all together."

"Good for her," David Collins said, and he sounded genuine. Then he got down to business. "Now, I can't say for sure, but I'm pretty confident that the bank would be interested in supplying part of the financing—with mortgage rights on some of the equipment, of course. But I doubt that you'll get anywhere here looking for operating capital. It's just a bit too risky."

Harold said, "We'd expected to raise that on our own."

David Collins looked up from his papers. "Do you mind if I ask how?"

Jim thought he recognized something encouraging in David Collins's tone. he said, "Bank business? Or is that a personal interest?"

David Collins smiled. "I'm always interested in a promising investment. I'm not quite as conservative as the bank."

Jim was forever after astounded at how easy it was to raise the rest of the money. Harold had kicked in, of course, and he had brought Jim and Galen together with another lawyer, a red-faced man of fifty or so named Hewitt, representing venture capitalists.

"How will this work, exactly?" Galen asked Hewitt.

"Not simply," Hewitt said over lunch at Arthur's Steak House on Walnut Street. "The people I represent will go out and find an investor or a group of investors. They'll kick in their own cash. Maybe they'll also approach an insurance company or some other institution for more. Let's say that the institution puts up a sizable sum in exchange for, say, thirty percent of the stock you're going to issue in the new company. Then, with those two bundles of cash in hand, my clients will approach a bank and persuade them to take another portion of the risk. They'll want detailed proposals, of course, about what your plans are, about the market for your proposed product and so forth. If my people are successful— and they usually are in matters like this—the bank they find will loan you the rest of what you need for a variable rate of interest that's going to be probably two or three points above prime. That loan will be secured by the capital equipment you buy with the money you have from the insurance company."

"And if we default?" Jim asked.

Hewitt shrugged. "Then the bank has first claim on all the company's assets."

"And the insurance company?" Galen asked. "And your people?"

Hewitt smiled. "Then they take everything you two guys own or ever will own. You'll sign papers to that effect as a condition of the deal."

For the first time, Jim felt a thrill of fear buzz up his spine.

"That sounds fair," he said weakly. "Cruel, but fair."

The three of them ended up late one night sitting around the kitchen table in Jim's house, doing the math and weighing the pros and cons.

"The thing that scares me," Jim said, "is that I'd still like to have an extra fifty grand for the first year as insurance. If none of us tries to take anything out of the business the first year—except you, Galen, since you'll be full time—then we ought to be able to get through with the orders I have lined up. But I'd sure like that extra fifty grand for breathing space."

"So would I," Galen said. "As we sit here looking at this, I'm starting to get weak knees. We've got money in this from so many sources I can't keep it straight. I never really thought we'd be able to raise this kind of cash."

"Raising it is one thing," Harold said. "Keeping it is something else."

"I'd still like that fifty grand," Jim said.

Galen looked at him. "I've gotten all out of the *kee* I'm going to get. How about your family?"

"Good God, no," Jim said. "My father is always hurting for cash. My mother has some assets in her family's business, but they're not liquid. Besides, I have my own reasons for not wanting to ask for her help."

Harold shrugged. "Where then?"

Jim's expression seemed even more intense than usual. "I do have an uncle who might be interested," he said finally.

"So call him," Harold said.

Jim shook his head. "No, I'm going to get into the car this Friday night and go visit him. Give me a call here Monday night, and I'll let you know where we stand."

* * * *

"How much farther now?" Marci asked.

It was Saturday morning. Jim had planned on driving all the way to Brennan's Point after work Friday, but by the time they'd reached Binghamton, Marci had had it. They'd spent the night at a Holiday Inn, and they'd gotten off early for the last two hours of the trip. Eamon was in the back of the BMW, blissfully tearing a coloring book into confetti, and thank God he was occupied. He'd howled and whined all the way from Philadelphia to Binghamton.

"It's just down the road," Jim told her. "You were here a couple of years ago. Don't you remember?"

"I've blotted it out of my mind. God, that was a horrible thing. The little boy's parents split up later, didn't they?"

Jim nodded. "Susan got out of that marriage very quickly. My father tells me she's doing real well as a real estate lady in Orange County, California. I guess she and the broker she works for are something of an item."

Marci was silent for a moment. Then she said, "I suppose kids can hold things together when there isn't much else."

Jim glanced over at her. "I'd say so. Okay, here we are."

Katherine and Annette were in the kitchen, as usual. Kevin, hearing the noise downstairs, came down in a few moments. Jim was somewhat surprised at how he had aged. Kevin was heavier, his hair had grayed markedly and he was leaning on his cane with less steadiness. Eamon began ripping the place up right away until Annette gave him a bowl of cake icing to lick. He sat contentedly at the kitchen table rubbing his face in the bowl. The sight made Kevin laugh.

"It's good to see a kid around the place again," he said to Jim as the two of them took their coffee out to the front porch overlooking the lake.

Jim looked out over the waves, and he almost sighed aloud at the contentment he felt. Brennan's Point had always been the place he had loved most. "I wish I could get him up here more often," he told Kevin.

"It's not that far, is it?"

"From Philadelphia?" Jim said. "It's a good six or seven hours, depending on how many troopers are around."

"Are you going to see your parents while you're up this way?"

"Not this trip. I got up to Boydstown a couple of months ago, but I came up here to see you. How are you feeling?"

Kevin sipped his coffee. "Well, my back hurts. Billy likes to tell me that I'm reaching the point in life when my back goes out more often than I do. But you didn't come all the way up here to hear about my back. What's on your mind? Anything important?"

Jim sat back in his chair. He drew in a deep breath of the lake country air. "It seemed important until I saw the lake again. Jesus, I've missed this place. Some friends and I are starting our own semiconductor business."

Kevin looked at him in surprise. "You're going to quit your job with Marci's father?"

"No. I have a friend, a guy named Galen Lee, who's a better engineer than I am. He's going to run the design and manufacturing end. I'm just going to represent the company the same way I represent other lines. When I say I'm going to do it, I mean that Roth and Co. is going to do it, of course. What the new company is going to get out of me is some cash and free sales effort. Also, I'm going to be in on counting the money, of course—me and a lawyer named Harold Warren."

"Didn't I meet him at your wedding?"

"He was my best man. Harold is going to handle the financial end."

Kevin nodded. "That sounds great, Jim. I've got to confess something, though. I don't know what a semiconductor is."

"You don't? Well, if you don't know much about electricity . . ."

"If you can't drink it," his uncle told him, "then I don't know much about it."

"Did you ever hear of Lee De Forest?"

"Lee De Forest was where Robin Hood fooled around with Maid Marion, right?"

"That was Sherwood Forest," Jim said, smiling.

Kevin shrugged. "Well, I was close."

"Lee De Forest invented the vacuum tube back around 1905 or 1906. The vacuum tube was the universal method of conducting, modulating and amplifying electrical signals for decades. That's what was in radios back in the thirties and forties and when I was a kid in the fifties."

"I know what a vacuum tube is, then," Kevin said. "They're those goddamn things that were always blowing out in the television set."

"Fine," Jim said. "Well, as you know, the things had drawbacks. They were big and bulky, and they took too much power. And, as you mentioned, they burned out all the time. After a while, some guys who worked for Bell Labs came up with a better method of controlling electricity. They were working with nonmetallic substances, specifically, silicon. Silicon is a natural semiconductor. That means that it's not a terrific conductor of electricity—like metal—and it's not an insulator, like wood or rubber."

"Yeah?"

"Well, what these guys did was to discover that they could take a semiconductor like silicon, heat it to very high temperatures along with specially selected elements and that atoms of those elements would seep into the silicon by displacing some of its atoms. They could create a pathway for electricity to travel through, and that meant they could build electrical circuits that were smaller—much smaller—than the big, bulky vacuum tubes De Forest developed. Are you following me so far?"

"So far, so good," Kevin said.

"Well, what they did was invent the transistor. They got the Nobel prize for it because it had enormous implications for all sorts of tasks. Take computers, for instance. The first digital electronic computer, built with vacuum tubes, weighed fifty tons. The invention of the transistor meant smaller, more efficient and more reliable computers. Since those guys at Bell Labs did their work, industry has come up with ways to build multiple circuits into transistors. They're called integrated circuits. Today, you can put tens of thousands of electrical components into a little chip of silicon."

"You're starting to get over my head now," Kevin told him. "What's the net effect of all this?"

"From a scientific standpoint, the net effect is that you can take all the circuits on that first fifty-ton computer and fabricate them in a single chip of silicon that'll sit on your fingernail. And you can do it for a material cost of roughly ten bucks. This space shuttle that NASA is trying to build is going to be loaded with silicon chips, and little computer companies are springing up all over the country—mostly out in northern California and Texas, right now—who are desperate for companies who can produce sophisticated, quality integrated circuits. That's the sort of company we're starting up."

"It sounds like a pretty good business," Kevin said.

"It should be. I've drastically oversimplified the theory behind the product we're going to produce, and I'm not going to bore you with production details. But the point is that good engineers can produce a product like this with very little in the way of capital expenditure, compared to other manufacturing businesses. And there's a huge market for what we're going to be turning out."

Kevin looked out over the lake and thought about what he had been told. Then he said, "Look, I didn't understand two-thirds of what you were talking about. But you seem to understand it. That's the important thing. How much will it cost to get in on it?"

"You can get in for as little or as much as you want. You just buy stock. I'd like to raise another fifty thousand for the first year's operation. Your stock probably wouldn't pay a dividend the first year. In fact, I can guarantee it won't. But after that it should pay well. And its face value will rise once we get past the first year."

Kevin nodded. "I don't think I could come up with fifty thousand dollars on my own. Just about everything I own is tied up in the winery. But I've saved a few bucks from my salary and bonuses over the years. I could probably come up with ten or fifteen thousand. I suspect I could raise you the rest from some friends of mine here in Lakeside. I know Billy Frazier is always looking for some way to get rid of all that Medicare money your grandmother sends his way."

"That's great," Jim said. "Look, I'm going to have Harold get in touch with you."

"He knows where to find me," Kevin said.

Talk of business faded after that. Kevin talked about Susan's life in California. He hadn't met her boyfriend, but she had sent photos. The boyfriend was older, but that didn't bother Kevin. He thought that Susan needed an older man to keep her steady. He said he saw Art Dixon occasionally in town. Art was running his own business now, a discount liquor store, and he seemed to be doing pretty well. He was going with one of the Wright girls. Kevin couldn't remember which one. He just couldn't keep track of the current crop of Wrights and Baddingtons and Roaches and Coughlins.

Jim spent a pleasant day at the lake. He took Eamon out in the rowboat while Marci stood panic stricken on the dock, terrified that the boat would capsize. He caught a couple of rock bass off the point. As the sun set he felt more relaxed and more at peace than he could remember.

As he entered the house just before dinner time, he could smell Katherine's chicken and dumplings, and his stomach rumbled.

The phone rang during dinner, and Kevin got it.

"Yes," he said quietly. "Yes. All right. I'll get him. Jim, it's for you. Helen."

Jim took the phone. "Hi."

Helen said, "Jimmy, I called you at home first, but there was no answer. I didn't expect to find you at Brennan's Point. I called Patricia, and she's on her way home. Then I thought I should let Mother and Kevin know."

Jim felt a surge of alarm. "Know what?"

"Your father had a heart attack last night."

* * * *

By the time Jim gathered up Marci and Eamon and drove down to Boydstown from the lake, Patricia had arrived and was standing next to the kitchen sink when they came in. Jim raced into the house, leaving his wife and son behind. Helen sat at the kitchen table, staring, silent, unmoving.

Jim looked questioningly at his sister. Patricia's composure crumbled. "He died," she said, almost in a whisper.

Helen burst into silent tears.

Jim's first reaction was disbelief. "When?"

Patricia looked at the floor. "Just after I drove up from New York. Mother was waiting for me before she went back to the hospital. Before we left, they called and said he'd had a second attack. His heart just stopped."

Jim went over to his mother and put a hand on her shoulder. Helen looked up in despair. "I had things to say to him—important things."

"He knew, Mother," Patricia said.

Helen shook her head. "No, he didn't."

Jim heard Marci and Eamon come into the kitchen behind him. He turned to his wife, and she could tell from his face that Jack Ryan was dead. Marci went over to Helen and put her arm around her mother-in-law's shoulder. Jack, dazed, walked into the living room and stood by the front window that overlooked the street. Memories of the house—its sounds, its creaks, its smells—swept over him in a wave.

Outside, the sun shone down and a little boy of five or six came barrelling by on the sidewalk on a tricycle. Jim watched him, remembering doing the same thing in the same place—remembering Jack running beside him as he struggled to learn how to pilot a two-wheeler a few years later.

Everything looked pretty much the same on this street as it always had. How could that be? How could the world be the same without Jack Ryan in it? Where was the justice in a world that still contained an Otto Kruger but no longer had a place for Jack Ryan? If somebody had to die, why couldn't it have been one of the Ottos?

He felt a presence behind him. Without turning, he knew it was Marci. He felt his breathing change, felt it begin to come in great gulps, as though he were choking. He turned and fell into Marci's arms. She held him.

"Dad," he whispered, "Oh, Dad."

* * * *

Becky heard the Buick in the driveway. She was watching "An Affair to Remember" on television—absolutely the last movie she ought to watch, she reflected—as Kevin came in the door. He looked haggard.

"How did it go?" she asked, turning off the set.

"It went. Have you got anything to drink in this place? Irish wakes aren't what they used to be. I could use a shot of something with a kick to it."

Becky got him a few fingers of Vinnie's best bourbon. Kevin sat down wearily.

"I probably should have gone to the wake, at least," she said. "Helen was such a good friend when we were girls. But I've about had it with funerals. The next one I plan on going to is my own."

"It's just as well," Kevin told her. "Helen looked like hell. I used to think it was better to go quickly—like Pop did. But maybe if Jack had had some notice—cancer, maybe—he and Helen might have taken the chance to resolve a few things. All those years of combat. Jesus."

Becky gazed at the floor. "Marriage can be hard."

Kevin studied her. "What did he do now? Did he sock you around again? Becky, why don't you just let me kick the shit out of him when he pulls something like that?"

She shook her head. "He didn't touch me. He knows I won't put up with that anymore. I'd set fire to him in his bed. We're both getting too old for that sort of thing, anyway. What he did do, as he left to go down to Maryland and that woman he has down there, was mention you. For the first time in all these years, he said something about it."

"What did he say?"

"He said I should say hello to you for him. Isn't that strange?"

Kevin lit a cigar and frowned deeply. "I don't know what the hell that would be all about. I see him once or twice a week at the Elks, and we haven't exchanged a word since the second Eisenhower administration."

"He has something on his mind," Becky said.

"So do I," Kevin said, reaching for her.

They never made love in the master bedroom. Always, when they made love in the house where Becky had been raised, they either stayed downstairs or went into the guest room, which was the room Becky had lived in until she'd gone off to college. These days lovemaking was a leisurely activity for them most of the time. There was nothing they hadn't done together, and the urgency to know one another in new and intimate ways had long passed. Lovemaking between them had become almost a comfortable ritual.

Later, Becky got up naked and lit a cigarette. Kevin marveled at her. He had a roll around his waist that could have had the name of a ship printed on it. She was two years older, and she was built precisely as she had been in high school. Being spared the rigors of childbearing had helped, he supposed.

She stood against the dresser, smoking a Winston and gazing off into some imaginary distance.

"What's on your mind?" he asked, sitting up in bed and beginning to install the brace.

"Need some help with that?" she asked.

He shook his head, grappling with it. "I need to have this goddamn thing readjusted. That plastic knee joint they put in my leg all those years ago isn't worth a damn any more, and the way this brace is set up I'm not getting enough support to keep the knee locked."

She came over and helped anyway, and he was grateful. As she knelt before him and wrestled with the brace, he sat on the bed and stroked her hair,—once red but now more than half gray.

"There," she said.

Kevin stood and took a few steps. "Nice job. I never had a naked woman do that for me before."

She smiled. "This particular naked woman has done just about everything else for you."

"And very well, too," Kevin told her. "No complaints about the service."

"Do you have to go home tonight?"

"I ought to. I don't like the idea of Mother spending the night alone in the house the day Jack's buried. She always liked him. Even Pop, before he died, got to like him."

"How about you?" Becky asked. "You don't seem all that broken up."

Kevin looked over at her. "He was my friend for forty years. I'm broken up, all right."

"You don't show it, Kevin."

"I work hard at not showing things."

"Yes," Becky said. "How could I forget?"

* * * *

The phone rang in Jim's office.

"Jim Ryan," he said.

"You've got to come home right away," Marci told him, her voice sharp with irritation.

Jim groaned. "What's the problem now?"

"You know the problem," Marci hissed.

"What's she doing?"

He'd had to ask. Helen had been in the kitchen again, making some of her patented roast beef, and nothing had been put back in the right place. In fact, nothing much had been put back at all. What had been washed and put back hadn't been dried, and there was water in all the cabinets. On top of that, Helen had rearranged the refrigerator. Marci couldn't find her bean sprouts, and she couldn't find her unflavored yogurt, and she wasn't going to eat any red meat no matter who made it. If Helen didn't like it, that was too damn bad. Red meat made people too combative and nobody should eat it—especially not a woman Helen's age who smoked three packs a day. And those cigarettes were another thing. Why couldn't she just smoke in her own room? She knew how Marci hated cigarette smoke. Not only that, but she dumped her ashtrays in the toilet, and you had to flush the john a dozen times to get all the ashes to go down. Not to mention what those cigarette butts must be doing to the pipes.

Jim listened for nearly four minutes straight as it poured out of Marci— as it did almost on a weekly basis—then he said, "Why don't you have a talk with her and let her know how much this stuff is bothering you?"

"She's your mother. You talk to her."

Jim had tried. Helen always reacted the same way. She always drew herself up stiffly and said, "If you want me to go, then I'll go. It's your house."

And then Jim would have to calm her down as well as Marci.

It had been a losing proposition from the start. His marriage hadn't been in such terrific shape to begin with, and now it was worse than ever. Helen hadn't touched a drop of liquor, so far as he could determine. And if she did that, out she would go, no questions asked. But she bugged

Marci mightily. Marci was into her vegetarianism and her Eastern religions
and her EST classes, and Jim was into trying to singlehandedly keep Roth
and Co. going while Sam bathed in the Florida sun and worked on his
putting.

Jim was struggling, too, to keep the semiconductor company on an
even keel. The three of them had named it Achilles Technology, Inc.—
their private joke. The idea was that the company had only one weakness;
its principals hadn't the foggiest idea what they were doing. Business had
been excellent from the first, thanks largely to the space program. But
Achilles Technology took vastly more of Jim's time and attention that
he'd planned, and with all that was going on, he didn't have time and
attention to spare.

He got his new BMW out of the parking garage and drove home. It
took him fifty minutes, door to door, and he treasured the time. He'd
considered having a phone installed in the car so he could use the time
more profitably, but he'd decided against it. He needed the time alone.
During the course of an average ten-to-twelve-hour workday, his time in
the car was his only privacy. He had no time for it at work and no
possible way of having any at home. He'd even given up his Saturday-
morning tennis. He lacked the energy and time for it. It wasn't exclusively
because of Helen, but it was because of her in large measure. He still
couldn't believe he had done it, not after the nightmare that had been
his childhood. He'd sworn that once he left the house in Boydstown he'd
stay as far away from his mother as he could manage. No such luck. Jim
blamed Patricia for that.

After Jack's funeral, they had found themselves in the back yard,
walking over familiar ground that both had relegated to history the moment
they'd gone out the door.

"Mother seems to be holding up pretty well," he had said.

"I suppose," Patricia had told him. "When she called me in New
York, she was hysterical."

Jim said, "She was fine when she got me at the lake. Kevin seems
a little worn down by all this, though. So does Grandma. None of them
is getting any younger."

"Grandma's got to be, what—eighty-three or eighty-four now?" Patricia said. "And Kevin is almost as old as Daddy was. That has to be
on his mind."

Jim smiled ruefully. "I'm afraid that dying is the last thing on his
mind. Grandma told me that he hasn't played the piano since little Liam
died, not once. That must have been the real crusher for him. Patricia,
Mother is going to have to consider selling this house, you know. She

can't live here all by herself. Leaving this place after all these years would be pretty tough on her."

"I know," Patricia said quietly.

"Where are you going to practice when you graduate?" Jim asked her. "Are you going to come back home?"

"Not if I can help it," Patricia said.

"Why not? This is a good little city. I wish I could live here or up at the lake and make a good enough living."

Patricia shook her head. "It's not for me. You know, Mother has been so unhappy all her life that I decided early on that whatever I turned into, I wouldn't turn into her. If getting married and having kids did that to her, I certainly wasn't going to stay home and be the little housewife. I realize now that what happened to her would probably have happened to her whatever she'd done with her life. But living out mine in Boydstown, New York, has never been part of my plans. Besides, with the kind of law I'm going to practice, I can't work in a place like this any more than you can. I'm going to be specializing in public bond work."

"What's that involve?"

"Well, a bond counsel draws up a legal opinion for a governmental agency that issues bonds—like a school board or a water authority or any agency that borrows money for capital construction. The opinion certifies to the buyers of the bonds that they qualify for tax-exempt status. You can also get tax-exempt status on other types of bond issues, and that's when you need a sharp lawyer who can navigate the IRS code. It's like running an obstacle course, and it's fun. You do some good, too— get roads and schools built, that kind of thing."

Jim frowned. "Sounds thrilling."

"It's at least as interesting as microchips. That sounds like something that comes from little tiny cows."

"Why couldn't you be a bond counsel here?"

She shook her head. "You can't do it. The firms that do that kind of work are in the big cities. You'll find a few bond counsels in medium-sized cities, like Albany and Syracuse, but the big firms that pay the big bucks are in New York and Chicago and places like that. If I want to do bond work full time, and I do, then that's where I'll have to work. Jim, if I practiced here I'd spend most of my time doing wills and handling real estate closings and divorces. I'm really not interested in that."

Jim leaned against the big cherry tree near the garage. "Well, that presents us with a problem. Mother."

"I've thought about that."

"I don't know where the hell she's going to live. She'll get drunk and burn the place down some night without somebody to watch her.

And I can't let her go back up to Brennan's Point. Christ, can you imagine what a horror show that would be?"

"I know!" Patricia said, and her voice was harsh.

"She needs somebody to move in here with her," Jim said angrily. "Dad took care of her all those years, Patricia, but he's gone now. Somebody has to do this."

She looked at him evenly. "I could never live with her again, even if I could work in Boydstown, which I can't. You had your own troubles with her, I know. But I just can't stand to be around her. The things she used to do to me, to call me."

He shook his head. "We both took insults from her, and we both know it was just a lot of crap."

"Some things are different for women," Patricia told him.

The remark made Jim furious. "I'm not going to listen to a lot of feminist bullshit. I hear enough of that at home, thank you. You want special rules for yourself because you're a woman, and at the same time you want the same opportunities men get. You want more than the opportunity, when you get right down to it. You want a guarantee of equal success whether you can cut it or not. But equal responsibility? Not that. No, you won't take your share of responsibility. And your excuse is that some things are different for women. You really want it both ways, don't you?"

"I can cut it just fine," she said coldly. "My grade point average as an undergraduate was higher than yours. I keep track of things like that. Now, you can accept this or not accept it, but she did damage to me I'm not going to forget. If you want the truth, I think she was jealous because Daddy and I were so close. It would be all my nightmares come true to be shut up in this house again—just her and me. I won't do it, Jim."

Jim clenched his fists inside the pockets of his suit. "Well, then I don't know what the hell's going to happen to her."

Patricia never wavered. "Neither do I."

Marci was more than difficult about it. She was nearly impossible. It took a call from Sam in Florida—prompted by a call to Sam from Jim, pleading for help—before Marci would go along. And then only under certain, specified conditions, the first of which was no drinking. None. Jim agreed wholeheartedly. He'd never have Eamon subjected to what he had been subjected to. If it came to that, he'd throw Helen out into the street, he promised.

It hadn't come to that, however. After Jack's death, Helen went bone dry. Jim was suspicious, but she steadfastly maintained her sobriety. Drinking or no, though, Helen was a constant source of irritation to Marci. No small part of that irritation, Jim knew, was that Marci was no longer particularly wild about living with Jim, much less with his mother. This essential problem was exacerbated by Helen's relentless spoiling of Eamon; by her thinly veiled criticism of his Jewish upbringing; by Helen's subtle ridicule of Marci's fascination with EST, vegetarianism, Shintoism and the like.

It had become a serious situation. As Jim pulled the BMW into the driveway, he felt helpless and put upon. He wished the two of them would just shut up. Marci greeted him coldly, as usual, and Helen emerged from her downstairs bedroom only for a moment to say hello. Then, Salem in her mouth, she went back into her lair.

Jim went upstairs to kiss Eamon goodnight, but as he hit the steps he heard the phone ring. It was Galen. "I tried to get you at the office, but they said you'd gone home a little early. We've got a problem you ought to know about. I'm not going to be able to make delivery to Allied on time."

"Oh, shit," Jim said wearily. "Why not? They're good customers, Galen."

"The goddamn saws haven't come in yet. I can't meet the production schedule without them."

Jim Ryan sighed wearily. The diamond-edged saws were a crucial piece of capital equipment needed to slice silicon ingots into wafers. Because they operated to such fine tolerances, they tended to wear out quickly. The problem of the availability of saws had been growing now for more than a year.

"Who's the supplier?" Jim asked.

"Payne Machine Tool, up in Springfield, Massachusetts. They say they just can't make delivery. Jim, this is going to screw up the whole production schedule. I don't know what to do about it."

Galen never did know what to do about a problem, Jim had discovered in working so closely with him. He was a technical whiz, but he was not a manager, and more and more of the operating end of the business had fallen to Jim. Harold had his own practice, and he just didn't have the engineering background to understand what Galen was talking about. Besides, when they had started this thing, Jim had taken the title of president. It had seemed like a good idea at the time.

"Galen, did you talk to the top man? Did you tell him how badly we need the equipment?"

"I talked to Bill Payne himself. He said he can't do it. They're a small outfit, and they can't keep up with the demand."

"That's his problem. He's got a contract with us."

"He's willing to pay the penalty clause. Look, maybe if you gave him a call . . ."

"It doesn't sound like it'll do much good," Jim said. "Is there anybody else we can turn to?"

"Everybody else is locked up tight."

"Then I'm going to have to fly up there and see this guy face to face, and I don't know when I can do that. I'm going up to New York this weekend for my sister's law school graduation. We've got a big party planned. Next week I've got to be in Houston. Look, you get a letter off to Allied and tell them there's going to be a delay on delivery. Don't be specific about how long it's going to be. Meanwhile, I'll find some way to cut loose for a day or two and catch a plane to Springfield."

"Allied is going to be pissed," Galen said.

"Then let them be pissed!" Jim exploded.

"Okay, okay," Galen said. "Hey, man, lighten up."

"Do you mind if I go upstairs now and kiss my kid goodnight?"

"Be my guest."

"Thank you," Jim Ryan said, and hung up hard.

* * * *

Patrick Ryan, who drove a bread truck, had been to New York only twice before—once when the Army had put him on a troop ship to Italy and once when Lindsay had been mayor and Patrick had come down in a chartered bus with his Moose lodge to watch a mayor's trophy game at Shea.

He sipped his beer, looked around Danny's Hideaway in Greenwich Village and decided he liked the place. He decided, too, that he was glad his nephew was paying for this spread and not him. There was a mob here from Jack's wife's side—Kevin and Katherine and Henri and Annette. Then there was Patricia and Jim and his wife and kid and Helen and Patrick's brothers Dennis and Leo and their wives. This must be costing a bundle at New York prices. Patrick sipped his Heinekins. When Patrick Ryan had a good time on somebody else's money, he drank the good stuff. "So," he said to his niece, "when do you leave for California?"

Patricia looked up from her fillet of sole. "Next week. That's when my lease runs out here in New York."

Jim, two seats away, leaned over the table. He'd had a drink or two and was uncharacteristically jovial. "Patrick, did you hear who she's going to be working with? Charles Whittington."

"Hey, yeah?" Patrick said, impressed. "No kidding? He isn't still in Congress, is he? I thought he'd retired after Nixon beat him out for president in '68."

Patricia smiled. "He retired from politics. He practices law in Los Angeles now. Actually, all he really does is go to lunch."

"How so?" Kevin asked.

Patricia put down her fork. "The firm specializes in municipal bonds. That means we deal with elected officials from all over the country, and most of them are Republicans like Whittington."

"The country's got a hell of a lot more Democrats than Republicans," said Patricia's uncle, Dennis Ryan, who worked in Boydstown city hall courtesy of the Democratic party.

"That's right," Patricia said, "but most of the Democrats are in big cities. Most of the Republicans are in the suburbs and small towns. And every one of those towns has its own mayor and council and its own school board and its own sewerage authority, or something like that. There may be more Democrats in the country, but when it comes to local elected officials, the Republicans have them beat about five to one—maybe more."

Patrick turned to his brother. "Boy, are you a dope."

Dennis, who was a consummate dope, said, "I suppose so."

"Anyway," Patricia went on, "most of the time when a local government body or water district or something wants to float a bond issue, they go to local lawyers. But for a big bond issue, they like to go to a big firm. And they like the firm of Whittington, Gill and Haddon because they get to go to Hollywood and play tourist and they get to have lunch with Charles Whittington himself. That's a big thrill for a councilman from Peoria. So that's what Whittington does for a living now—he goes to lunch."

Kevin said, "I take it, then, that Whittington is worth whatever the firm pays him."

"I'd say so," Patricia told him. "He brings in clients. There are a lot of good bond counsels around the country, but only one of them has a man who was almost president available to go to lunch with you if you give his firm your business."

Kevin lit a cigar and smiled. "He never did get that close to being president, actually. The only one who had a chance of beating Nixon for the nomination was Rockefeller, and he didn't have much of a chance, either."

"Well," Patricia said, "then a former senator."

"That was back when you were a little girl, though," Kevin said. "Well, it all sounds pretty exciting. I hope you like California. Susan loves it."

"I was out there once," said Leo Ryan. "I thought it would be like upstate New York, only it's summer all the time. The place turned out to be a goddamn desert. And you can see the air, for Christ's sake. There's more crap in the air than you can shake a stick at."

"Leo," Jim said, "the air out there's no worse than it is in New York."

"The hell it's not," Leo maintained steadfastly. "I just about choked to death going around Disneyland. Even Mickey Mouse had a cough. And Spics? They had wall-to-wall Spics out there. That was worse than New York, too."

"Lots of Chinks out there, too," Dennis observed.

Jim smiled and shook his head at Dennis. "I never go to California unless I have to. I think Woody Allen's right. He says that the only contribution California's made to Western culture is the right turn on red."

"I like that, though," Patrick said, his face solemn. "That's handy. Did that start out there?"

"Who's Woody Allen?" Leo asked.

* * * *

When Patricia Ryan got to California, she bought a car—a silver Toyota Celica with black vinyl seats, which turned out to be a mistake. Every time she got in the Celica after it had been sitting in the sun, which was all the time in Los Angeles, the seats burned right through her clothes. She ended up with a towel strewn over the driver's seat and a heightened appreciation for cloth upholstery.

She found a one-bedroom apartment in a Torrance complex occupied primarily by single people roughly her own age. She was dating within two days of moving in. Patricia had dated more or less regularly in New York, but she had been careful to avoid anything that might resemble a serious entanglement. She found that a relatively easy task here. California men did little for her, she decided. She found a paucity of serious thought on any topic more pressing than the fortunes of the Dodgers. For company, she went to a pet store and bought a huge black cat, which she promptly had fixed and named Zorro.

She liked her work, though. The offices of Whittington, Gill and Haddon were on the twelfth floor of a sleek, glass-enclosed building on Wilshire Boulevard. It was a prestigious LA business address, and there was a pretty good restaurant on the top floor. The firm contained more than a hundred lawyers, and it had taken in a good-sized crop of new attorneys this year. Although Patricia was not herself in the business of writing opinions—the partners reserved that function for themselves—she was involved in the research necessary for those opinions, and she usually did the first draft. Patricia knew she was viewed as perhaps the brightest of the new associates.

She did not have her own office. That, she was told, would come in her second year with the firm. So she and eight new associates shared a bullpen in one corner. They worked shoulder to shoulder at desks that had been pushed together.

Patricia was one of only two women hired by the firm that year, and she did not particularly like the other woman, a corn-fed Midwesterner named Alice who seemed to think that Kim Novak hairdos were still fashionable. She got on well with all the other associates, however, with the possible exception of Dominic Fresina.

Dom was older than the others. He had gone into the service after high school and spent three years in the Marines before going to college. He was of medium height and wiry and dark, and he was given to corduroy jackets and cowboy boots in blatant violation of the firm's uniform, which consisted of conservative suits and wingtips. His hair was too long, and he seemed to view the practice of law as an enormous bore.

One afternoon, when just the two of them were in the bullpen, Dom Fresina took a sheaf of papers and threw them across the office. They floated down to the carpet in disarray.

"Why'd you do that?" Patricia asked him.

"AAHHH!" he shouted, stretching. "I'm getting so sick of sewer authority bond issues I can't see straight."

She looked at him over the top of her glasses. "Isn't that what you came here to do?"

"I hate bonds," he told her.

Patricia put down her own paperwork and removed her reading glasses. "Then why did you join this firm? This is eighty percent of what we do."

Dom Fresina smiled. Patricia had to admit he had a nice smile, even if he did need a haircut. "There's an old joke," he told her. "Somebody asks this guy, 'How come you're going out with that girl?' And the guy says, 'Because she's different from other girls.' So the first guy says, 'How's she different?' And the second guy says, 'Because she's willing to go out with me.' Get the picture?"

"Are you trying to tell me you couldn't get a job with another firm?"

"I sent fifty resumes around the country during my last semester at Yale. I wasn't law review, but this was Yale, after all. I thought I had it made. You know how many offers I got? Three: one in Atlanta, one in Dallas and this. My family's on the West Coast. So, voila! Here I am with sewer bonds."

"Why was it so tough?" Patricia asked him.

"I'm Italian," he said. "How many of the big, important law firms in this country have Italian names on the stationery?"

"I would have thought it would be easier if you're a member of a minority group."

Dom Fresina laughed. "Minority group? Listen, blacks are a minority. Hispanics are a minority. Italians haven't been a minority since Perry Como got a prime-time TV show. And when we were a minority, it was something that kept you out rather than got you in. Hell, women are a minority these days, even though there are more women than men. For you, that's a help."

"Are you implying," Patricia said coolly, "that I got my job here on any basis except merit?"

"No. I'm just pointing out that it's easier for a woman of any ethnic background to break into a blue-chip law firm than it is for any Italo-American male. You'll notice that of the eight new associates taken on this year, there's one black, one Chicano, three WASP males, two women and one lonely paisan—me. I just want to see how many of us are still around here in a few years when we're up for partnership. My guess is that everybody will have a good shot at it except me and Ortega. Our names would look funny on the letterhead. Too many vowels."

"My, aren't we defensive?"

He had caught the edge in her voice. "Not really. Just realistic. Listen, I'd be more upset if practicing law mattered much to me."

"Then why are you here?"

"My old man. The great dream of his life was that I'd be a lawyer— a learned man. He broke his butt for me to get through college and law school."

"Are you going to spend your whole life doing something you don't like doing just to make your father happy?"

"No. At some point, I'll go back home and get into some sort of business. A Yale law degree is always a nice thing to have on your wall. Maybe I'll work on the farm with the old man and practice a little on the side, writing appellate briefs, maybe. I'm pretty good at that. I'd hoped they'd give me a shot at that here, but no—sewer bonds. Jesus."

"Where are you from, Dom?"

"North of San Francisco. Ever been up that way?"

"No. I haven't been out of LA once in the past few months except to visit my cousin down in Newport Beach."

"You've got a cousin out here?"

"Yeah. She moved out a couple of years ago. She likes it here."

"How about you? What do you think of Southern California?"

She shrugged. "I like the job."

Patricia was somewhat surprised when Dom, a few days later, asked her out to dinner. She was reluctant at first. She didn't like the idea of dating men from her own office. But she was reasonably sure that nothing serious would develop with Dom Fresina. He liked to argue too much. It was sort of a sport to him.

Patricia often found herself locked in ferocious debate with him over issues like the nature of feminism, the economic system, the flaws of American education. Whatever position Patricia took, she could count on Dom to take the opposing viewpoint. After a while she came to believe that he was a man without a single deeply felt conviction. He could argue either side of any question equally well. It was a valuable trait in a lawyer, but it could be a nuisance in a dinner companion.

On their third date they drove down to Newport Beach in Dom's aged Triumph Spitfire to have dinner with Susan and her boyfriend, Roy Peel. Roy was a big, good-natured man in his late forties. He was quiet and pleasant, and he was clearly wild about Susan. After dinner at a seafood place on the pier, they went back to Roy's five-bedroom, Spanish-style rancher on a hilltop overlooking the Pacific. Patricia knew enough about Los Angeles real estate prices to realize that the house was probably worth close to a million dollars. They met Roy's two teenage sons, then the women sat in the living room and drank and talked while Roy, Dom and the two boys watched a college football game on television.

"Are you going to marry him?" Patricia asked.

Susan nodded. "It looks that way. He wants me to, anyway."

"You sound nervous about it."

"If you'd been divorced once, you'd be nervous, too, at the prospect of a second marriage."

"You know what my father used to say," Patricia told her. "He said one-third of marriages end in divorce and the other two-thirds end in death. He always said divorce wasn't so bad when you consider the alternative."

"How about this guy you're with?" Susan asked. "Anything serious?"

Patricia shook her head. "No, not really."

"He's cute."

He's a smart ass, though. I don't want to get serious with anybody, and I don't think he does either."

Susan said, "That's fine if you can keep it that way."

Patricia downed the rest of her Lite beer. "You watch me."

Later, as Dom walked her to her door, he slipped his arms around her and pulled her close. Patricia let him kiss her. She smelled his aftershave, felt his touch on her and felt a stirring down low. She hadn't been to bed with a man in months. Maybe that's why she'd been so cranky lately.

"Want to come inside?" she asked him.

"How'd you guess?" Dom said.

The ocean was a block away, but late at night, with the car traffic reduced, they could hear the surf through the windows. Dom undressed her in the dark. Patricia lay back on her bed while he sucked at her breasts, nipping lightly. He nuzzled her hair. His tongue flicked into her ear, as light as breath, leaving just the hint of wetness there. His fingers moved around her, settling finally where she wanted them, fondling her folds and crevices. After a while she began to ache. She reached for him, found him, felt him pulsate hotly in her hand. "Please," Patricia said.

She heard him moan as she encircled him, felt him thrust. With a technique born of instinct and practice, Patricia drew him in and released, drew him in and released, over and over. After a while, she felt her climax building. She worked for it, cried out when it arrived, savored it, then noticed Dom's breath and pace quickening. She arched to meet him, felt him drive into her, heard him gasp six times in rapid succession, then felt him relax on top of her. Patricia sighed as he rolled off and lay next to her.

"You want me to stay?" he asked after a while.

Patricia was warm and relaxed. She rolled over. "No," she said. "That'll do just fine. See you at the office, Dom."

* * *

"Hello."

"Kevin," Becky said, "I have to see you right away."

"What's wrong?"

"Nothing's wrong. Maybe everything's right."

Kevin paused. "Should I come to your house?"

"No. I'll meet you someplace. This time I'd rather not be seen."

"Well, this is all very cloak and dagger. Where do you want to meet?"

"Suppose I meet you on the beach at the college. Twenty minutes."

"Fine, I'll be there."

Kevin's Buick was parked in its usual spot outside the winery. Iroquois College was only six miles down the road toward the village, and he arrived there before Becky did. He got out of the car and wrapped his overcoat around him. It was beginning to get cold in the lake country. As he got older the cold seemed to bother him more. He made his way down the steps to the deserted beach and sat on the park bench they had chained to the tree on college point to discourage the college kids from throwing it into the lake. She arrived a few moments later in her white Cadillac. She wore a long black coat that went down to her ankles and had a hood attached. Kevin stood up as she came down the steps from the road. "What's on your mind?" he asked her.

"Vinnie. He left for Maryland this morning, and before he left he told me wants a divorce. He wants to marry that woman down there. He said he's reached a point in life when he can see the end of it, and he doesn't want to spend his last years in a loveless marriage."

"Did he mention you and me?"

"To his credit," Becky said, "he didn't. Of course, he didn't have to, did he?"

Kevin sat back down on the bench. "What are you going to do?"

She sat next to him. "Should I give it to him?"

He shrugged. "You and I both know you don't have much of a marriage together. Why not?"

She sat back and stuck her bare hands in the pockets of her coat. "The fact is, that I like having a husband. It's neat and tidy. You get invited places you wouldn't get invited to if you were alone. We don't have sex much together any more, but I like having a man in bed with me at night, if only for the warmth."

"Then I don't know what to tell you."

"I think I'm going to give it to him."

"Then give it to him. Let him go. Christ, you're better off without him, anyway."

Becky was silent for a while. She stared out over the lake, which was being kicked into a frenzy of white water and waves by the stiff fall wind coming off the hillside. Finally, she said, "I was hoping for a different response from you, Kevin."

"What kind of response?"

She sat up. "Frankly, I was hoping you'd ask me to marry you."

After all these years, Kevin thought. Finally, it's come out. "I don't know what to say to you," he told her. "We've seen each other for a long time, but we've never talked about marriage. It's never come up."

"It's come up. I've brought it up. I've never said, 'Let's get married.' I've never said it that way. But it's been on the table. You just never wanted to deal with it."

"And why not, do you think?"

"I have a lot of theories."

"Do you want to hear my reasons?"

"Sure. Go ahead. We'll see how smart I am."

"First of all, I'm sixty years old."

"You're fifty-nine."

"Sixty in a few months, then. I've been single for almost thirty years, and I'm not sure I could adjust at this point in my life to a change like that. I'm not sure I could live with a woman any more. I'm an old man, and I live a certain way."

"I'm older than you are, and I'm not afraid of a change."

"Well, I am," he told her. "Look, I've had a lot of things go wrong. I'm not about to put myself in a position where something else major might go wrong. If you want to divorce Vinnie, then go ahead and divorce him. Why does this have to be a factor in it? Why does it have to change anything?"

"It changes everything. You know that."

Kevin said nothing. He just looked out over the lake.

"Do you want to hear my theory?" Becky asked him. When he failed to respond, she said, "My theory has several facets. One is that you're a coward, Kevin. You've had some real heartbreak in your life, and I'd be the last one to deny that. But your response to all that has been cowardly. What you've done is to lock yourself up within yourself. I saw it when Will died. I saw it when your grandson died. You wouldn't let me near you. You wouldn't let me do what I wanted to do for you. And you didn't do it because you were afraid."

He stood up and leaned on his cane. "Becky, you're going to have to make this decision on your own. I can't help you."

"I've made it. I'm going to give Vinnie his divorce. Then I'm going to sell the house here, and then I'm going to go down to Hilton Head, where we have the winter place, and I'm going to live there year-round. And, if I'm lucky, I might find myself a husband. There are some people who need to be married, Kevin, and I'm one of them. There's nobody I'd rather be married to than you, but if you won't do it then I'm going to go shopping."

He looked down at her as she sat on the bench. "Don't do anything hasty."

"It's not hasty. I've had this on my mind for about thirty years now. Longer, actually. Kevin, I've been in love with you since we were teenagers. Now I'm an old woman, and I've been your mistress for twenty-some years. People still use that word, don't they? Mistress? It doesn't matter, I suppose. What does matter is that I've loved you every moment of that time, and what matters is that you've just confirmed the other part of my theory. Do you want to hear what that part is?"

"No, I don't."

"Well, you're going to, anyway. The other part of my theory is that you've never been in love with me, not for a single second. That's the hardest part of all this to come to grips with. And now that I've done that, I'm leaving."

He leaned on his cane wearily. "You'll never know what you mean to me."

Her face became contorted, and she put a fist to her mouth. She closed her eyes and tears squeezed out and rolled down her lined cheeks. "Yes, I do," she said, "and that's why I'm leaving."

Becky wept silently on the bench as Kevin climbed the steps to the road. As he got into the car and turned the key, he looked down at her. She was sitting, looking out over the lake. Her back was to him. She never turned around as he drove away.

BOOK 3

Chapter 21

The annual luncheon between the new associates and the senior partners of Whittington, Gill and Haddon didn't take place until four months after the associates had begun work. That was because Mr. Haddon, who was past eighty now, had broken a hip and hadn't been up to getting into a wheelchair until recently. Moreover, Mr. Whittington, whom everyone referred to as the Senator, had been on a tour of the Far East at the request of the Ford administration.

So the first time the associates got a look at Mr. Haddon, he had been wheeled into a private dining room of the California Club by his nurse; and the first time they saw Charles Whittington in the flesh, he had been nicely tanned from his months in Thailand, India and Singapore. Mr. Gill, who actually ran the firm, looked the way he always looked—harried and distracted. Mr. Haddon appeared to be only barely alive. And Senator Whittington looked marvelous. His hair was full and white. His waist was trim and encased in the vest of his navy blue suit. His perfect teeth almost sparkled as he talked.

And talk he did. He was captivating. "One of the things that always got to me about Rockefeller," Charles Whittington was saying, "was that he never carried around any money. Never a nickel. His aides got into the habit of carrying around big chunks of cash because when he saw a painting or something else he liked, he'd turn to one of his aides and say, 'Charlie or Fred or Bill, I'd like to buy this. You wouldn't happen to have a few thousand on you, would you?' And they'd damned well better have it."

Patricia, sitting directly across the table, asked, "Did he ever pay them back, Senator?"

"When he remembered. I'm sure he forgot often enough. People like Rockefeller don't look at money the way most people do. When he was governor of New York, I said to him once, 'Nelson, how much money do you have, really?' And do you know what he told me? He said,

BRENNAN'S POINT

'Charlie, I don't have the foggiest notion. You might as well ask me how many forks I have in the kitchen drawers at the governor's mansion. I could only tell you I have enough. That's how I am in the money department, too.' That's what he said. Gerry Ford was the majority leader in the house, then, and we were having lunch. I thought Gerry was going to choke to death. And now he's president and Nelson is vice president. Who would ever have guessed?"

Dom Fresina was sitting to Patricia's right. Next to him was Alice, the other woman associate. She was fairly gushing over Whittington. It made Patricia a little sick to watch it.

"It must be exciting to know the president so well, Senator," Alice said, a little too breathlessly for Patricia's taste.

Charles Whittington smiled, displaying thousands of dollars worth of dental work. "I've known every president since Eisenhower, Alice. I even thought for a while that I could do the job myself. Luckily, Dick Nixon had gotten the same thought earlier, and he knocked me out of the box before I even got to the convention."

Dom, his mouth half full, said, "Why do you say that? Didn't you want to be president?"

"Oh, I wanted it. I thought I was a better man than the other candidates my party had to offer. Nixon was too shallow and not totally trustworthy, and I thought Nelson had way too much ego. But I never really thought about actually doing the job after I won the election. Just the business with the missiles—whether you'd really use them if it came to that—that would be more than I'd care to deal with. No, I'm much happier practicing law than I would have been as president. Practicing law and . . .," he raised his glass, "drinking fine California wine at lunch. You've barely touched yours, Patricia, and there's another bottle on the way."

Patricia smiled self consciously. "I think I'll pass, Senator. Thank you, though."

"Not a wine drinker, eh? Too bad."

"No," Patricia said. "In fact, I love wine, especially with food. But I come from a wine family, and I guess I'm just a bit too fussy."

Dom Fresina looked over at her. "This is one of the best Rieslings California produces."

Just what she needed, Patricia thought, Dom badgering her with his penchant for debate in front of the senior partners. "That could very well be," she said in a low voice, "but it's a cut or two below what my family turns out."

"Your family?" Dom said. "I've heard of Rhine wine, but not Ryan wine."

428

Patricia's face flushed. "My mother's maiden name was Brennan—the Brennan Winery."

"I've heard about Brennan wines," Dom broke in. "They're okay, but they're not in this class."

She glared at him. "And where did you learn about wines?"

"I grew up in Napa," he told her.

"And that makes you an expert?"

Dom opened his mouth to reply, but Patricia turned back to Whittington. "The wines that come out under the Brennan label are not top quality. But the family also produces wines under the Weidener name. Weidener wines, especially the champagnes, beat anything that California turns out. More to the point, Weidener produces a Riesling that's vastly better than this." Then she realized that her anger at Dom Fresina had quite possibly embarrassed her. "No offense, Senator," she added lamely.

Whittington laughed. "None taken, believe me. I've had Weidener champagnes. I wouldn't go so far as to say that they beat anything my state has to offer, but they're good champagnes. I've never had their Riesling, though. Let's see if they have some here." He turned to one of his deputies. "Would you call the sommelier, please?"

Patricia felt she was boxed in now. She cast a smoldering glance at Dom Fresina. Then she turned back to Whittington as the sommelier arrived.

"If we're going to get serious about this," she said, "let's also get a bottle of Weidener Brennan's Point Chardonnay, 1968, if you have it."

"Very good, Madame," the sommelier said, and disappeared.

He came back with several Weidener wines and fresh glasses. Whittington took a sip of water, and then he compared the Weidener Riesling with that which had been brought to them originally. He also compared the Chardonnay. He did so expertly, swirling each glass with an appropriate flourish and cleansing his palate between each sip with mineral water. "You're right," he said finally. "The New York State wine is better. I have to confess that I'm rather surprised."

Patricia beamed. "My uncle Kevin would be very happy to hear you say that. I'm going to call him tonight."

"And give him my compliments," Whittington said. "I'm impressed. Actually, we're quite lucky that this wine was in stock. This club has one of the most complete wine cellars in the city. Most places out here, even the best ones, don't stock much in the way of New York State wines."

"That's also true in New York City, Senator," Patricia said. "I've heard my uncle Kevin complain about it quite a bit. California's state government has been much more supportive of its wine industry—of all its agricultural industries, in fact—than New York has."

"Really?" Whittington said. "I'll have to write to Governor Wilson
and straighten him out."

Patricia smiled. "You'd better hurry up. Hugh Carey is supposed to
beat him in the fall."

"Well," Whittington said, "I'll get a letter off right away then. You
just can't reason with a Democrat."

* * * *

After the first of the year the new associates had been freed from the
bullpen and assigned cubicles of their own. The cubicles were small, and
they were furnished in spartan fashion with gray metal desks and armless
secretarial chairs; but they had carpeting, and they afforded a measure of
privacy. Patricia had decorated hers with a poster of Robert Redford and
a huge sign bearing the motto Sue the Bastards! that she knew the senior
partners would never see because they never visited the associates' area.

The months of late 1974 and early 1975 were good ones for Patricia.
She boarded Zorro at the vet's and flew back East for Christmas at
Brennan's Point. Helen came up to join her, complaining about her
grandson being raised without benefit of a visit from Santa Claus, although
Jim always found an excuse to buy the boy a shamefully expensive present
about that time of year. Patricia was amazed at how well Katherine looked,
although she was eighty-something and her blood pressure was up and
down like a yo-yo. Kevin looked a little drawn, though, and he had
seemed quieter than Patricia had seen him since his grandson's death.
She suspected that it had something to do with the death of his ex-wife,
who had succumbed earlier in the month to the ravages of too many
cigarettes and too much vodka.

Despite all that, though, it was a nice Christmas. Patricia had helped
Katherine and Tante Annette with the cooking, and she had insisted on
cleaning up the kitchen herself while the two of them sat by the fireplace
worrying that she would do it all wrong. She had walked in the cold
along the lake, tossed flat stones from the beach into the rolling waves
and had felt more at peace than she had in a long time.

Several days later, she packed her mother into her rental car and took
her back to Jim's place in the Philadelphia suburbs. Patricia spent a quiet
New Year's Eve at the Ryan house, watching Guy Lombardo at the
Waldorf on TV. She insisted that she didn't want Jim and Marci to spend
New Year's Eve at home just on her account, but they each seemed
relieved at being able to avoid going out together. The whole family had
counted out the old year along with the crowd in Times Square, then

they had toasted 1975 with Weidener champagne. Patricia was pleased to see that Helen drank only lemonade.

Eamon was a delight. He was at the cuddliest of ages, and she had hugged him greedily until he fell asleep in her lap and she carried him upstairs to his bed.

Then it was back to LA and work. After the associates' luncheon with the senior partners, Patricia found herself actually writing a few opinions, and on several occasions she accompanied Charlie Whittington on luncheon engagements with local officials from the great heartland to explain the intricasies of the bonding process.

She became aware of and was not at all troubled by the fact that she was becoming known as Charlie Whittington's protégée. More important work that was coming her way was clearly at his direction, and she made it a point to do that work thoroughly and well. She consciously sacrificed speed for meticulous detail.

She was slowly and painstakingly writing an opinion one day in late April when Dom Fresina stuck his head in the door of her cubicle.

"Is that ready yet?" he asked brusquely.

Patricia never looked up. She and Dom now saw one another only rarely. They had experienced a bitter battle over his conduct at the associates' luncheon the previous fall, and Patricia had put the skids on their relationship not long afterward. They had dinner together once in a while, or sometimes a movie; they no longer slept together.

"I'm still writing it."

"It's been a couple of hours now since you said you'd finish up," he insisted.

Patricia looked up and removed her glasses. "What are you, now? The overseer?"

"Gill asked me to see if anybody's opinion was still out. Everybody else's is finished."

"Mine would be, too, if you'd get the hell out of here."

Dom frowned. "I've seen glaciers move faster than you write opinions."

"Will you leave me alone?" Patricia demanded. "What the hell is the matter with you? You've been absolutely rotten the past few weeks."

Dom moved into her cubicle and sat at the single chair she had for visitors. It was right next to her desk. He looked at her long and hard. "Call it an ethnic flaw. I guess I just lack the WASP polish of Senator Whittington."

Patricia looked at him in shock. "Are you losing your mind?"

"I haven't lost my eyes or my sense of humor. It's been a long time since I've seen anything as funny as that old man chasing you around and you just loving every minute of it. It's like a scene from a Marx Brothers movie."

Patricia reddened. She said, "Well, let's all get down on the floor and look for your IQ. You can't possibly be that stupid. Do you actually believe that?"

"I believe what I see. I see, for example, that you're getting all the important opinions to write. I see it, and everybody else sees it, too."

When angry, Patricia tended to shout. Her volume would go up with her blood pressure. This, clearly, was not the place for that. She was literally quivering with rage. But her voice was low and steady.

"What you see, Mr. Fresina," she said, "is a solicitious older lawyer who's taking an interest in the career of a younger lawyer. If I were a man, would you be saying we're queer for each other? The very implication that I'm getting the bigger, more important bond work because of Charlie Whittington's alleged romantic interest in me is just about the most insulting, most sexist remark anybody had ever made to me. Why don't you get the hell out of my office?"

"It's not an office; it's a cubicle. And you're either incredibly naive or incredibly calculating. I like you, so I'm going to choose to think it's naiveté. Let me explain something to you, since it's apparently eluded your notice. All factors considered, you're about the most attractive woman in the firm. Now, before you let your head get all swelled up, permit me to point out that, in general, this office is bowwowville, so your competition isn't all that stiff. The point is that Sen. Charles Whittington is now and always has been a notorious womanizer. Every year he sets his sights on one of the new associates and takes her under his wing, so to speak. Guess who's the lucky target this year? You. Now, if you're willing to use that to get ahead in this firm, then be my guest. Just don't try to pretend to me that you're Snow White and that the dwarfs are just good friends."

"Just who is it who says that Charlie's got the hots for the new women associates? I know it's not Alice, because if she thought it was true she wouldn't wear any clothes when she came to work."

He laughed. "I should tell you so you can go back to that geriatric Lothario and tell him? No thanks. Trust me; it's all over the firm. It's been going on for years, and it's no secret."

Patricia nodded grimly. "Man talk, right? There's good old Patricia Ryan getting ahead, so she must be screwing the Senator, right? It couldn't possibly be because she's good. No. We all know that if a woman does well it's either because of affirmative action or because she's performing unnatural acts on the boss. Now, you listen, and you listen good. There is nothing going on between me and Charlie Whittington. Nothing. Not now—not ever. Now, you get out of my cubicle or I'm going to start screaming."

He shook his head. "If he hasn't made a move on you yet, he will. You can count on it."

"Here comes the scream."

"Patricia, for Christ's sake! I'm trying to help you."

Patricia felt like going for Dom Fresina's eyes with her nails. She settled, though, for a scream that rattled the windows. Stunned, Dom was out of her cubicle and down the hall as though an earthquake had struck. The second he left, Patricia pounded on her desk top in silent fury. Her rage was almost boundless.

The chief stenographer from the secretarial pool was on the scene in only a few seconds. She was a perpetually befuddled middle-aged woman named Nina, and her expression was one of horror. No one had ever before made such a noise in the offices of Whittington, Gill and Haddon. "Are you all right?" Nina asked breathlessly.

Patricia looked up. "I just chased away a mouse."

Nine turned white. "A mouse? In this building? My God!"

"Actually, it was more like a rat. But it's gone now."

Nina was even more flustered than usual. "We'd better call an exterminator."

Under her breath, her teeth grinding, Patricia said, "Or maybe a hit man."

* * * *

One of Frank Brush's enduring disappointments in life had been his mother's politics.

She'd been a teacher and the first of her family with a college degree. She'd retained her lower-middle-class values all her life. She'd voted only for Democrats, and she'd named her son after the greatest of them all. Thus, Franklin Delano Brush, an officer of one of the most Republican banks in Maryland, had been forced to go through life using a shortened version of his name that made him sound like he'd been raised in a tarpaper shack instead of a middle-class home in Baltimore. Frank D. Brush. It sounded like the name of a redneck Georgia sheriff.

Brush sat near a window in an expensive restaurant in Rockville, Maryland, and downed the remains of his dry Rob Roy with a twist. Here he was facing disaster, and all he could think about was his long-dead mother and her screwy politics, which he did not share and never had. Herbert Hoover Brush. Herbert H. Brush. That wouldn't have been bad.

He pushed all that from his mind as he saw Peter Baldwin pull into the parking lot in his four-door Jaguar sedan. Baldwin was wearing a beige suit that matched the car's leather seats. Open collar, though, Brush noted. The son-of-a-bitch would wear a six hundred dollar, tailor-made suit, but he wouldn't wear a tie. He probably didn't even own one. Frank D. Brush owned thirty-two ties, and he hated every one of them. He hated Peter Baldwin more.

As Baldwin entered the restaurant, spotted him and came to the table, Frank D. Brush stood up and smiled broadly. "I was beginning to worry about you Pete. Great to see you."

Baldwin, tanned and fit at sixty, took the hand, shook it and sat down next to the younger man. He didn't even have to unbutton his jacket when he sat, and Brush hated him more for that. Baldwin's waist couldn't have been more than thirty-two, Frank D. Brush, at forty, had a gut that could have occupied its own chair.

"Sorry I'm late," Baldwin said. "I hope you're not too far ahead of me in the drinks department."

Frank Brush laughed appreciatively. It was something he had learned long ago to do freely in the presence of millionaires. "Only had one so far."

Baldwin nodded. "Well, we have a lot to talk about. You'd better switch to wine. It'll keep your head clearer."

Baldwin signaled to the waiter. He ordered a salad and a bottle of wine. As they waited for the food to arrive, Brush and Baldwin talked about inconsequential matters: Baldwin's absolute faith in the New York Yankees now that they'd signed Reggie Jackson, President Ford's chances in next year's election, Baldwin's small hotel on Saint Croix and the problems he was having about it with the tax people.

When the food came, Brush went through his quickly. When the coffee came, he said, "I'm sure you're curious why I wanted to see you."

Baldwin smiled. "I can guess. You're concerned because we're behind on the note."

Frank D. Brush nodded. "That's right, Pete. And it's not just that. It's also the fact that Consolidated isn't doing all that well. You know, I'm obligated to look at your financial reports as a condition of the loan, and there are things in there that are disturbing to the board. Your current ratio of assets to liabilities is way out of whack—much worse than it was when we increased the note last year. Your net profit ratio is down to less than a cent. Your return on equity is less than a nickel, yet you're still paying dividends. It's really that last part—the paying of dividends—that has the board upset. How the hell can you pay dividends on figures like that and not keep current on the note? That's what they're asking me, and I can't answer them."

Brush saw a small smile flash across Baldwin's face, and it infuriated him, although he didn't dare show it. Baldwin was amused at Brush's discomfiture. Inwardly, Brush boiled. Peter Baldwin was all Brush hated about the banking business. He was a clever, gutsy financial high roller, and he'd done well enough at it to live like a Middle Eastern potentate with four homes around the world while Frank Brush collected his six percent annual salary increases, his annual bonus and tried to make ends meet. And that wasn't easy with a daughter in boarding school and a house in Chevy Chase.

"It's all simple enough," Baldwin said, sipping his wine. "Paying dividends helps keep the price of the stock up. That is, after all, Frank, where my investment is. You'd be astounded at how many investors look only at dividends, especially older investors. They tend to look on the stock market as something like a savings bank, only with higher interest."

"But Consolidated can't afford to pay dividends," Brush insisted. "Look at your own financial reports."

Baldwin shrugged casually. Brush found the gesture infuriating. "I can't afford not to," Baldwin told him, "not if I want to maintain the value of my investment."

"And what about the bank's investment?"

Baldwin sipped his wine again. "The bank has a vested interest in keeping the price of the stock high."

Brush shook his head in frustration. "Look, Pete. You've got to get current on the note. You just have to do it."

"I can't," Baldwin said simply. "The money isn't there for both dividends and debt service. Something had to give, and it's had to be the note."

Frank D. Brush felt beads of perspiration pop out on his forehead. "I'm under big pressure to get this cleared up. And I mean big pressure, Pete. If we go another month or so without your getting current, the board is going to make me call the note."

"You realize how foolish that would be, don't you?" Baldwin said calmly. "If the note is called, then Consolidated just goes chapter eleven. When would the bank get its money, then? Besides, even if I were forced to liquidate the company totally, you'd only get about twenty cents on the dollar. You're not the only creditor, Frank. Your board would be writing off eighty percent of the note."

Brush was well aware of all this, which was why he'd avoided offending Peter Baldwin. The law was set up in such a way that Baldwin could default and none of the creditors could touch his personal assets or even his other business assets, which were tied up in such an intricate legal web that Baldwin himself probably didn't understand it all. If a note this size went into default and the bank eventually faced that kind of loss, then Brush would be back approving home-improvement loans at somebody else's bank. He knew it, the board knew it and, most infuriating of all, Peter Baldwin knew it. "Pete," he said weakly, "you've put me in a terrible spot."

"I know I have," Baldwin said. "I got you to push the loan through the board, and now I just can't pay. I'm in no position to without jeopardizing my own money. You're in a bad spot, Frank. If the company doesn't pay, you could be take a big loss on that Consolidated stock I talked you into buying. You're conflicted six ways to Sunday on this, and every option means a big financial loss to you personally. I feel sorry for you."

Which was a lie. Peter Baldwin felt no compassion whatsoever for Frank D. Brush or anyone else. Brush decided that begging might help. "It's more than a loss," he said. "Maybe you can afford a loss like this, Pete, but I . . ."

Baldwin emptied his wine glass and filled it again. And, as he did, he said, "Well, I wouldn't like it, but I could absorb it, yes. Consolidated is only one of a half-dozen companies I control. As much as I'd hate to see it fail, it would do very little damage to me personally. But it's a different situation for you, isn't it, Frank? They pay you a big salary to run that little bank, don't they? But in the final analysis, you're a wage slave. You have a mortgage and a payment on your Mercedes. I'd even bet that you're carrying a fairly hefty mortgage on that place over on the Eastern Shore."

"You're right on every count," Brush said, "but why bring it up? You've got something up your sleeve, don't you? What is it?"

Baldwin smiled again, Then, to Brush's astonishment, he said, "I want to take out another loan from your bank in Consolidated's name."

Frank Brush felt his heart turn over in his chest. Nothing to worry about, the doctor had told him. Bullshit. "You want to what?" Brush asked Baldwin. "You can't pay us what you owe us now. I couldn't get you another nickel. And if you get it, what the hell are you going to do with it?"

Baldwin stared down at the pale golden liquid in his glass. "Consolidated," he said, "is going to take over another company."

Frank D. Brush surprised himself by laughing out loud. It was a little rude, perhaps, but he was looking personal ruin squarely in the face. "You've got the biggest set of balls in the world," he told Baldwin. "Do you really think the board would come up with another penny to help you acquire another company? Consolidated can't even make a go of what it has now. Your liabilities are damned near equal to your assets. You couldn't get a loan anywhere."

Baldwin smiled again at Brush. "Actually, liabilities exceed assets, if you do the math right. I couldn't get a nickel anywhere else, that's true. On the other hand, nobody else has such a keen interest in seeing Consolidated get through this rather difficult period, do they?"

Brush wanted to sputter, but he lacked the energy.

Baldwin said, "You, in particular, have a rather strong interest, don't you, Frank? And you're the guy who got the board to approve the first loan, aren't you? And the increase?"

Brush swallowed hard. "All right. I'm listening."

Baldwin held up his wine glass. "Do you like the wine you're drinking?"

Brush had sipped his wine absently. He was a scotch man. "It's all right. What do I know?"

Baldwin swirled the wine in his glass. "Actually, it's rather respectable. Unfortunately, it's also overpriced for its class. It's a Brennan Rhine wine, from a medium-sized winery in upstate New York. I went to college with the fellow who runs the company. In fact, we were fraternity brothers at Cornell, back before the war. Kevin produces a rather nice line of wines, but he doesn't design his products for mass appeal, the way some of the big California outfits do. You, for example, would be a typical wine consumer, Frank. You might buy a bottle or two once in a while for a dinner party at home. Or you might ask a waiter to order you a decent bottle in a good restaurant. But, in the final analysis, you don't really knew a fine wine from an ordinary one, and you couldn't care less. Kevin Brennan ignores you as a customer, and as a result he can't produce in enough quantity to get his costs down."

Despite himself, Brush was getting interested. If there was one thing Peter Baldwin knew, it was how to make money—for himself, anyway. "You think your people at Consolidated could do it better?"

"Consolidated could certainly do it more efficiently and, without doubt, more profitably. The Brennan Winery is publicly traded. A quick glance at the annual report tells you a lot about the way the company does business. The stock is woefully undervalued. Unlike Consolidated, the company is stingy with dividends. They keep plowing cash back into the business so they can buy different grape varieties and the most expensive equipment. Aside from that, Consolidated has been the southeastern distributor for Brennan wines for fifteen years or so now, long before I picked up control of the company. Some of the people we have on board know the wine and liquor business well enough to be good wine-marketing people. Yes, from a financial standpoint, there's no doubt we could do it better."

"Are the Brennans ready to sell?"

Baldwin shook his head. "Oh no, of course not. On the other hand, neither were the people who ran Consolidated before I bought up a controlling share of the stock with the money your bank so thoughtfully loaned me."

"And which you can't pay back."

"And which I can't pay back, yes. But in the case of this loan, I'm willing to offer the bank a block of stock in Consolidated before I move against the Brennans. The stock will be offered in addition to interest on the loan, and the stock will be paid up front; call it points, if you like. We both know that Consolidated stock will go up once word gets out that we're making an acquisition like this."

Brush's lips tightened. It could be a way out. "And if the increase in price is only temporary?" he asked Baldwin, "What then?"

Baldwin sat back in his chair. "Well, I would certainly hope that the bank would have the good sense to sell off after the first surge. I'd certainly recommend that to anybody who owned a big block of Consolidated stock—somebody like you, Frank, for instance. If you were to pick up some more Consolidated stock after the loan went through, you could make a nice piece of change by selling, say, three or four days after news of the acquisition gets out. And it will get out, believe me. I've never seen an SEC hearing officer yet I couldn't outsmart. If they were all that smart, they'd be sitting on my side of the table."

"What are your long-term plans for Consolidated, Pete? Are you going to get out of it when the stock goes up?"

Baldwin shrugged his shoulders in his expensive suit. "I don't know yet. I might. The price would certainly make it tempting to take my money and put it somewhere else. But I've never run a winery before. In addition, the winery's assets include a lot of frontage on a lake that's going to be ripe for condos in a few years. I might just hold on to my stock in the new company until some developer comes along and takes it off my hands."

Brush smiled. He couldn't help it. He'd seen Baldwin do this sort of thing before, and it was beautiful. "And let me guess who that developer might be."

Baldwin held up in his hands, palms out, in innocence. "It'll probably be a purchase by an out-of-state corporation."

"And let me guess who'll control it. And in buying developmental rights from yourself, you drive up the price of the stock. Then you'll sell, right?"

"Then we'll see." Baldwin said quietly.

"You still haven't answered the basic question for me," Brush told him. "Even if I were to get a new loan for you, how would you go about getting control of the winery?"

"Well, about a third of the stock is in the hands of the usual investors—the institutional people. I can get a lot of that bought up very quietly in Consolidated's name. That shouldn't take more than a month or so from the time your bank hands me the cash. I'm also aware that about a third of the stock is in the hands of Kevin Brennan's sister. She's a widow. She lives with her son in a Philadelphia suburb, and even though she owns a lot of stock, she sees relatively little in dividends because the company has paid less and less in dividends the past five years or so. That also has the effect of keeping the value of her stock down."

"And you'll see to it that this is all explained to her?"

"She'll be told. I'm not sure how much of it she'll understand, though. From what I've been told, the poor lady has a very serious problem with alcohol."

Brush was, as always, rather amazed at the depth of Baldwin's research. "And where did you get all this information?"

Baldwin smiled again. "Well, things can fall into your lap, sometimes. One of the old stockholders in Consolidated gave me the lowdown on all this. The man is a small-timer named Vincent Ralston. Mr. Ralston turned out to be a fount of information about the Brennans, and he doesn't seem to be overly fond of them. Since I knew you'd be calling me up one of these days to have this little luncheon, I had the matter investigated. I suspect that Helen Ryan—she's the sister—would be willing to sell most or perhaps all of her stock if somebody offered her a price well above market value. I'm equally sure that the idea of a hostile takeover wouldn't even occur to her. If I can get the stock that's in the hands of the institutional investors and hers as well, I can pull this off rather easily. With a big portion of the outstanding stock diffused among a general investor ownership, I could effectively gain control of the company with a relatively small investment, provided, of course, that your bank has the vision to advance me the acquisition capital."

Brush considered the proposition carefully. Baldwin had it all worked out. He did not have the best record of running companies; the man was not a manager. On the other hand, he was a masterful stock manipulator, and that's what he was proposing—a stock manipulation. He would take a foundering company, use it to take over a healthy one and merge the two. Then he would sell off assets in the new company to other corporations he controlled. Eventually, the new company would fail, but by then Baldwin would have made his money by selling the stock whose

price he had driven up and by developing the assets he had sucked out
of the new company before it went down. Baldwin was a son-of-a-bitch,
Brush thought, but the son-of-a-bitch was smart. "It'll be a tough sell,
Pete," Brush said. "A very tough sell."

"If you think that's necessary, I'd be more than happy to appear
before the board and explain the advantages of aiding Consolidated in
such an acquisition."

"That might be a good idea," Brush said, tasting his wine. Not enough
punch in it to suit him. He ordered another Rob Roy.

* * * *

"You want to take me where?" Patricia demanded.

Dom looked sheepish, which was not his style. Despite herself and
despite their chilled relations lately Patricia found this small and uncharacteristic measure of humility in him strangely appealing.

"I want to take you up to see the California wine country," he told
her again. "Given where you come from, I thought you might find it
interesting."

"When?"

"This weekend."

Patricia didn't know what to make of the invitation. Dom had steered
clear of her lately, and just this morning he had, unsolicited, displayed
considerable displeasure at her regular trips to Charlie Whittington's house
in Bel Air. Her first impulse had been to go for his eyes. She didn't owe
Dom or anybody else any explanation on any topic, but Patricia nonetheless
had found herself explaining. She had told him that the trips were necessary
to deliver papers to Whittington and pick up others and to explain this
or that case to him. This was necessary because, she had discovered,
Charlie seldom came to work unless he had a lunch date. He simply
stayed home. In those circumstances, those cases in which he was involved
stopped, too, and Patricia wouldn't have that.

Dom had merely frowned deeply, as if he was doing her the favor
of considering her explanation. Patricia had turned on him coldly and
walked away to her cubicle. Then, a few hours later, Dom had appeared
in her doorway with his invitation. Patricia couldn't figure the guy out.
"I'm not at all sure why I should go anywhere with you."

He put his hands on his hips. He still looked cocky, but she could
tell he was trying hard not to. "Look, we've had some harsh words, okay?
We're still friends, right? I'm not talking about anything more than a
weekend trip up to San Francisco and the Napa Valley. We fly up, we
rent a car and we go. No big deal. I just thought it might be a chance

to make friends again. I liked it better when we were friends. Or do you have plans for this weekend?"

She didn't. "Dom, I appreciate the thought behind what you want to do . . ."

"If you're worried about sex, forget it. That's no big deal—no offense. I mean, we don't have to do anything. Separate rooms, the whole bit. I just thought it might be something you'd like to do, that's all. I like it up there. I think you might, too."

Patricia didn't know what to say. He seemed genuinely apologetic, at least as apologetic as he was likely to get. "Only if I pay my own way," she said finally.

"Hey, that's a condition of the deal."

They met at LAX and caught a Saturday-morning shuttle up to San Francisco. They were in a rented Olds Cutlass and on their way into the city by a quarter to ten.

"Do you want to go the fast way or the scenic way?" he asked her.

"Scenic," Patricia told him.

They had a nice drive. They didn't stop in San Francisco, but Dom took her through the city. From what Patricia saw of it she liked it very much. The Golden Gate Bridge was high but considerably smaller as a structure than the Verrazano Narrows Bridge that linked Bensonhurst, Brooklyn, with Staten Island. They stopped for an early lunch in Sausalito and dined overlooking the bobbing sailboats in San Francisco Bay with the skyline of the city off on the southern horizon. Then they went out to John Muir woods, where Dom showed her the towering Redwoods. He took her for a short stretch on Highway 1 where it ran just two lanes, high on a cliff overlooking the Pacific twenty-five hundred feet below. Dom loved the view. Patricia found the great height unnerving.

"Hasn't anybody around here ever heard of a guardrail?" she asked him nervously. Dom wheeled the big car around the hairpin curves almost casually. "Guardrails are for candy asses."

After ten miles of that, which was more than enough, as far as Patricia was concerned, he took the car up over the top of the mountain and headed for the Napa Valley. Within a few hours they were entering the California wine district.

It was very different from what Patricia had grown up with. The valley was split by a two-lane road that snaked along its floor. On each side were the rolling brown hills she had never quite grown accustomed to in California. On both sides of the road were vineyards. The vines grew on the flatlands here, not in the graceful terraces up the hillside that marked the Finger Lakes back home.

"What do they do about root drainage here?" she asked Dom.

"Not a big problem; the Napa Valley gets about fifteen inches of rain a year, compared to the eighty or so where you grew up. With only fifteen inches just getting the water is a problem. All these vineyards have artificial irrigation."

"What are those things?" she asked as they drove by a vineyard with a towering, two-story structure looming over it.

"Fans. They're used to keep the air moving if a frost comes along."

"Like in the orange groves in Florida."

"Yep. That doesn't happen very often, though. It's hot as hell here most of the time, especially in the summer. That's what makes the California reds so good—these long, hot growing seasons."

Patricia said nothing. She agreed that California reds were better than New York's. Not the whites, though, and not the champagnes, either.

They took two winery tours, one at Inglenook and the other, farther up the road, at the Christian Brothers Winery. Patricia was an avid tourist. She paid strict attention and asked the guides well-informed questions. As they left the Christian Brothers winery, she told Dom, "I really enjoyed that."

"Good. Tomorrow we'll hit a few more of the wineries. You might even more of a kick out of the smaller operations. They're less formal. Although, in a real sense, all this is small. The real big wineries—the ones that turn out the jug wines—are out around Modesto, over those mountains there. But here in Napa and in Sonoma, which is pretty close, this is where the quality California wineries are."

Patricia glanced at her watch as they got in the car. "I'm getting hungry again. Where are we going to eat?"

"Where we're staying," he told her.

"And where's that?"

"Right up the road. I think you'll like the place."

Three miles up the highway, Dom turned off down a long dirt road that threaded its way through rows of vineyard.

"What's this?" Patricia asked him.

"You'll see."

The large, white, clapboard house with its gingerbread trim at the end of the road, perhaps three-quarters of a mile off the main highway, looked like something out of a Norman Rockwell painting, despite its distinctly Western setting. A porch was wrapped around three of its sides. Behind the house stood a large stone building with a sign over its door that read Fresina Winery.

Dom saw the surprise on her face, and he smiled. "We're staying with my folks."

"Your family owns a winery?"

"A very small one. Mostly, my old man makes a living growing grapes for the big wineries. But he makes some wine himself, in limited quantities. It's good, too."

"You never told me about this."

"I wanted to surprise you."

"Well, I'm surprised, believe me."

As the rented Cutlass pulled in front of the house, a pretty woman of about fifty came out the front door. Dom got out and hugged her. "Mom," he said, "this is my friend, Patricia Ryan. Patricia, my mother."

"How do you do, Mrs. Fresina."

"Hello," Dom's mother said warmly. Then to Dom, "She's pretty." Then back to Patricia. "I feel better when the girls he sees are pretty. Some day he's going to get married, and what's he going to do if he has a little girl and she looks like him?"

Patricia flushed and smiled at the same moment. She had the feeling that Dom's mother was looking at her and thinking about china patterns.

"Patricia's already married, Mom," he said, and then he laughed as his mother looked at him with a poorly disguised expression of horror. "Got you," he told her.

Dom's father turned out to be a more mature version of Dom in khaki work clothes and an aged straw fedora. He was leaner and his face was cracked and lined from the sun, but the two men shared physical characteristics and even the same way of moving. Sal Fresina showed Patricia around the place while Dom went into the house to use the phone.

"He's calling his little brother, Mike," Sal Fresina told Patricia. "He's got his own place in Napa. Mike works with me here, but he doesn't live here. He likes the girls too much to live home any more."

"So you and Mrs. Fresina live here alone now?"

"Yeah, now. We raised two sons on this place, and it seems a little empty in the house sometimes. Although, I'll tell you the truth, we liked the quiet and the privacy the first couple of years after the boys left. Angela and me didn't wear any clothes in the house the first two weeks after Mike went away to school. Confused the hell out of the dog."

Patricia laughed.

Sal Fresina looked her approvingly. "Good: a sense of humor. You'll need a sense of humor if you see much of Dom. He's a good boy, but he can push real hard."

"I've noticed that."

"Don't hold it against him. He only pushes when he cares."

Dinner at the Fresina house was a warm and pleasant affair. Angela Fresina was a fine cook, and Dom's younger brother, who looked more like Angela, was likeable and solicitous of Patricia. Mike, it turned out, had a degree in government administration from San Francisco State, but he liked the wine business. "Pop and I are expanding the winery," he told Patricia. "We'll never be big, but we're making a small profit on the winery operations, and it's the part of the business that Pop really likes. He's doing more and more of that, and I'm doing more and more of the growing, which is where we really make our money." He slapped his brother's shoulder. "I keep trying to get my big brother to come home and help out, but he'd rather give advice to the East Jockstrap, Ohio, water authority."

"I don't have to wash my hands so often in that job," Dom said. "You're always kicking the manure off your shoes."

"You never bothered to kick it off before you came in the house," Angela Fresina said. "Stay in Los Angeles and shuffle papers. It makes it easier for me to keep this place clean."

After dinner at the house, Dom took Patricia into a bar in Napa called the Vintage, and they drank wine and listened to jazz. They got home just before midnight, and the house was still and quiet.

"They go to bed early here," Dom told Patricia. "That's life on a farm."

"I know about life on a farm," she told him.

The moon shone down brightly. There was never even a cloud in the sky this time of year in California, Patricia noticed. Hand in hand, they strode off into the vineyards. Several hundred yards from the house, Dom stopped and kissed her. Patricia had drunk some wine, and the day had left her feeling warm and relaxed. They made love in the soft, brown dirt. The vines loomed over them in the moonlight. When they had finished, Dom said to her, "Tell me you're not doing this with Charlie Whittington."

She jumped up and leaned against the upper wire of a trellis, her back to him. He gazed at her, her nakedness shining like alabaster in the moonlight.

"Well?" he demanded.

"I'm not," she told him, "and I'm not going to, either."

Not that the idea hadn't occurred to her.

* * * *

Kevin Brennan had begun to hate the telephone.

It had occurred to him that a good portion of the bad news he'd ever received had come to him over the telephone, with disembodied voices telling him things that tore him apart. Nowadays, when the phone rang, Kevin always braced himself for disaster. Disaster befell him that way one day, and he didn't even realize it until later. Disaster spoke to him in Helen's voice. "I want to move back home," she told Kevin.

He was sitting in his office in the winery. He leaned back in the chair and chewed thoughtfully on a cigar as she said it. "You haven't lived here in more than thirty years, Helen," he told her. "Why come back now?"

"I'm miserable, that's why. I can't stand that girl, Kevin, and she can't stand me. She's not all that wild about Jim either, if you want the truth. I just want to come home. I'll never be happy anywhere else."

Kevin sighed deeply. "Helen, if you want to know what I think, I don't think you're going to be any happier here than you are in Philadelphia or than you were in Boydstown. I don't think you're every going to be happy anywhere. From my standpoint, the question is Mother. She's pushing eighty-five. Annette isn't all that much younger, either, and, frankly, I've got more miles on me than I care to think about. None of us could handle the drinking."

"I haven't had a drink since Jack died. Ask Jim. Do you think he'd let me stay here if I had even one drink?"

"I don't know. I do know that you're suspect in that area, and I've got to look at the problem from a worst-case scenario. I just can't take a chance on Mother being subjected to what I have to view as a reasonable possibility if you were to move in here. I'm sorry, Helen. The answer is no."

Helen was livid. It came across clearly over the hundreds of miles of telephone line. "I own part of that place. You always kept me out of the business, and I let you do it. But it's my home, Kevin. Who the hell are you to tell me I can't move in there?"

"If you don't want to stay where you are, there are plenty of other options available to you. Patricia—"

"I'm not going to live way out in California. I've never even been there."

"That's up to you," Kevin told her. "But it's an option for you. You can get a place of your own, if you like."

"Where? I don't have enough cash to buy a decent place. I have some cash from the sale of the house and Jack's insurance, but not enough to cover a new house to live in."

"You have your dividend income," Kevin told her. "That would pay a mortgage for you."

"Yes," she said, "on a crackerbox. I'd have enough if you did a good job running the winery, but the dividends are peanuts. Besides, I can't drive a car. I couldn't live around here by myself. I couldn't live alone in Boydstown without a car. I couldn't even live in Lakeside."

"Then learn to drive."

"I won't learn to drive!" Helen shrieked. "I want to come home. I'm entitled to come home."

He said, "If it was just me, I'd chance it. But not with Mother."

"You're going to regret this, Kevin," she said furiously. "I promise you, you'll regret this. Nobody tells me what to do."

It was less than a week after Helen slammed down the phone in rage that she received a phone call from a lawyer representing a Maryland firm interested in buying her stock in the Brennan Winery. The lawyer told her that his client firm regularly invested in small companies that seemed to have possibilities and that he was approaching all the major stockholders in the Brennan Winery, offering them a premium price on their stock. He read off Helen's list of shares and their current book value. Then he offered her a price that was twenty percent above face value.

"Would you hold on for a minute?" Helen asked him.

"Surely."

She got out a pencil and a pad of paper and she took the figure he had given her for the total market value of her Brennan stock and multiplied it by 1.2. She looked at the figure for a long moment. Then she figured out how much she would have left over if she used the money to buy a small house on Iroquois Lake free and clear. Then she took what was left over and multiplied it by five percent, which was the amount of interest she expected she could clear after taxes if she invested the rest in savings certificates. She looked at the numbers carefully. Then Helen picked up the phone. "Are you still there?" she said.

"Oh, yes."

"I think we've got a deal," Helen Brennan Ryan told Peter Baldwin's lawyer.

* * * *

Henri Le Barnot saw Kevin come into the lab and looked up from his papers. Henri had his own office, but he insisted, as he had always done, on doing his paperwork on the bench in the lab. The lab was Henri's lair. The protocol between them dictated that Kevin not enter here without good reason.

"What is wrong?" Henri demanded.

Kevin's voice was hoarse. "I don't know where to begin."

Henri put down his fountain pen. "Begin at the beginning. This is always best."

"Henri, I've lost control of the winery." It was clear to Kevin from the old man's face that he didn't understand. "It's the stock," Kevin explained. "A big chunk of it has been bought up by one of the outfits that distributes our products in the southeast. They've also obtained proxies from some of the big institutional investors who hold our stock—you know, the banks and the insurance companies."

Henri's face was blank. "The stock?" he said, baffled. "I do not understand. I did not sell my stock."

Kevin shook his head. "They don't have yours. They don't need the piddling amounts you got as management bonuses. Look, Henri, it was all handled very smoothly, very professionally. The brokerage house that helped us go public in the first place got wind of it, and I had some lawyers look into it, but by then it was too late. An outfit called Consolidated Food Products had already gotten its hands on a lot of the stock—enough to give them control. I haven't heard a thing from them yet, but I will. They're clearly going to force a stockholders' meeting, and then they'll elect a new board of directors and they'll select new management. We're out, Henri. The battle was all over before I even knew there was one."

Henri was aghast. "This cannot be. It cannot! They have taken the vineyards, the winery, the houses—everything?"

Kevin shook his head. "No, not everything. There are some things they can't get their hands on."

"But how?" Henri insisted.

"I've had the lawyers look over the company's holdings. It turns out that a good portion of what's there was in Pop's name. After he died, it passed to Mother, me and Helen. Pop never bothered to make out a will, you know, and in this state when you die intestate your property is divided into thirds. What Pop apparently did, before he married Helga, was to buy a big chunk of land from Christian Weidener. It included the land on which the house now sits and some of what today is the best vineyard—the *vinifera* grapes we make our Weidener wines from. We also still have the shack and the point, although there's only about four hundred feet of lakefront instead of the two thousand feet we've always thought of as part of the place. Consolidated can't touch that four hundred feet of lakefront, the shack, the big house or the vineyard where we've planted the best grapes. But they can and will control everything else, including this winery and most of the vineyard and the management of the company."

Henri's mind was reeling. "But how?" he asked again. "How did they get the stock? You said that no one could ever get control away from the family."

Kevin sat down on a lab stool. "It all goes back to Christian Weidener's will. I've seen photocopies of the papers on file at the courthouse. Pop couldn't inherit any of the farm's holdings. All he had was what he bought while Christian was alive. Half of what was originally Christian's— the family stock—was in Helen's name, and half was in mine. When we went public, we took forty-nine percent of that family stock and offered it on the market. All Pop ever owned was the land he had bought outright and, like you, what he got in bonus shares out of the other fifty-one percent. When he died, what stock he had was split up between Mother, me and Helen. Helen had as much equity in this place as I have. She has had—all these years."

"So?" Henri said, still mystified.

Kevin sighed deeply. "She sold her shares to Consolidated."

At first Henri thought his ears had betrayed him. "She sold her stock?" he whispered.

Kevin nodded. "Yes. I had an argument with her a little while ago about her coming here to live. She was mad, Henri. And she apparently didn't realize that by selling such a big chunk of stock to these people that she was giving away family control."

"Can't we sue? Can't we buy back the stock? Kevin, what can we do?"

He looked out the window at the lake. "I don't know about suing. The lawyers don't seem to think we'd have much of a case. Maybe Helen didn't understand she was giving away control, but she's not incompetent. She should have understood it. She never checked with a lawyer. Hell, she never even checked with Jim. She just took the papers they sent her in the mail and went to some bank somewhere and signed them in front of a notary. If we sue, the issue will be whether Consolidated made the purchase in good faith. As for buying back the stock, where would we get the money? We all live comfortably, but everybody associated with the winery has somehow avoided getting rich. Plus, there's no evidence whatever that Consolidated wants to sell. What they seem to want is control, which they have."

Henri was in tears of rage. "She sold her stock," he hissed. "She did this thing. How could she do this thing?"

"She got upset," Kevin said. "When she gets upset, she's capable of just about anything."

Henri's fist thumped down on the lab bench. "She has sold my life. Sixty years of my life are gone."

"Henri . . ."

"That bitch! That drunk! She has done this to me. Damn her! Damn her soul!"

"I can take care of you," Kevin broke in. "You can take retirement today, and they won't be able to touch your pension."

Henri would not be consoled. He wept and raged. "That drunken fool. She has ruined me. She has killed me. She should rot in hell for what she has done."

Kevin, who was having problems with his own anger, said, "That's about enough, Henri. She—"

"She's a devil," Henri snarled. "She is a leech who sucks the blood. She has done this terrible thing. She should die screaming."

That pretty much did it for Kevin. Henri was on the verge of hysteria, and Kevin had run out his string. His own anger was immense. He had held it in at great cost, and he could no longer do so. "That's enough, Goddamn it!" Kevin Brennan roared. "She's sick. She just didn't understand."

Henri was beyond all intimidation. He was shouting at the top of his lungs. "Am I to forgive her because her mind is soaked with drink? Am I to forgive you? I told you this stock business would be our ruin. It was you who convinced Liam to issue the stock."

"If we hadn't, we'd have gone under a long time ago," Kevin shouted back. "If we'd kept up profits instead of spending a fortune on every harebrained lab and winery trick you came up with maybe we could have headed this off. You've got better equipment than any other winemaker in the world, and you've got bells and whistles on every piece of it. I warned you years ago that you had to learn to control your spending. That's what got us into this fix as much as anything."

Henri just stood there for a moment, his lips moving soundlessly like the mouth of a fish out of the water, searching for words to express the depth and intensity of his anger and grief. His English was not good enough; his hurt was too deep. Finally, he said simply and quietly, "You have taken my life—the two of you."

Looking at the bent and ancient little man, Kevin felt a surge of profound pity. He wanted suddenly to reach out and to crush old Henri to his chest. The old man was wounded beyond imagination. "Henri," Kevin said softly. "Stop it, please."

Henri stood next to his lab bench. He ran his eyes over his beakers and his gas burners and his test tubes and his eye droppers. He looked, it seemed, at every detail of his beloved laboratory—peering through his glasses, his lower lip sucked inside his wrinkled mouth. Then he looked back at Kevin. "I am going back to France," he said shakily. "Annette and I must leave this place now." Then his rage flared up once again. He shook a gnarled finger an inch from Kevin's nose. "You have driven us away!"

"Oh, bullshit!" Kevin exploded. "Do any goddamn thing you want. Go back to France if you want to. Do you think you're the only one who feels pain here? You see the whole world from one perspective—your own. You're a selfish, vicious, evil-tempered old man. I've listened to you rant and rave my whole life. I've watched you snarl at that saint you're married to like she was a dog. I've had enough of you, Henri. I've heard enough from you today—that's for sure."

Without another word, Henri took off his lab coat, folded it neatly and placed it on his stool. He took his nylon jacket off the wall rack, put it on, zipped it up to his neck and walked out of the room. Kevin heard his steps as he went down the stairs. Kevin sat on the lab stool for perhaps ten minutes, trying to regain his own composure. He hadn't meant to lose his temper. He'd tried not to. But Henri had always possessed the capacity to enrage him. Finally, he got down from the stool, climbed down the stairs and out to the road. He walked along the road, his leg stiffer than usual, looking out over the lake. When he climbed the hill and entered the house, he found his mother and Annette in the kitchen. Their eyes were wet. He stood in the doorway, staring at the two old women. "I see he told you both," Kevin said. "I was hoping to break it to you more gently than I suppose he did."

"They're leaving tomorrow," Katherine said.

"What?"

Annette, sitting at the kitchen table, looked up. On her face was an expression Kevin had never before seen. Only Henri and Katherine had seen it before, and then only on a few occasions, most notably the deaths of the two Liams. She said, "We are going to France tomorrow. Henri has gone to pack."

"That's crazy," Kevin said. "He didn't mean it."

Annette nodded sadly. "He does mean it. He is wounded to his death. He is going home to France to die. He will die now, don't you see? There is nothing that can be said to him."

Annette's lower lip quivered. Kevin was shaken, but he was also still angry. He crossed the room and sat at the table across from her. "Stay with us," he told Annette. "If he wants to go, then let him go. But you stay here with me and Mother, Annette. This is your home. This is where you belong."

Annette was silent for a long moment. Her long, gracefully manicured fingers were wrapped around a drenched handkerchief. She looked up at Kevin. "I cannot part from Henri," she told him softly. "He needs me now."

'He's never had a kind word for you," Kevin told her. "You've cooked for him and cleaned for him and slaved for him. You don't owe him a thing. Stay with us, please."

Annette shook her head. "There were kind, loving words once, when we were young. The years have made him the way he is. I could never let him go alone."

Annette stood slowly. Katherine uttered a small, tortured sound. The two old women embraced and wept silently while Kevin sat at the kitchen table, staring at the linoleum floor. "You have been my dear sister," he heard Annette tell his mother. "My heart will always be with you. We will meet again in the hands of God."

Annette Le Barnot got her shawl from the hook on the wall and draped it over her head and shoulders. She walked out the back door, down the rear steps and started up the hill toward the winemaker's house.

Katherine turned and walked out of the kitchen. Kevin got up and followed her. He found her in the living room, sitting in a rocker and staring blankly into the cold fireplace. "Don't worry, Mother," he said. "Nobody's going anywhere. This is all Henri's big talk. He might be a lot of things, but he'd never be a big enough bastard to uproot Annette out of here after all these years and to take her back to a France that doesn't even exist any more."

Katherine said nothing.

That evening, for the first time in nearly sixty years, Katherine did not prepare dinner in the big house at Brennan's Point. Kevin made sandwiches for each of them. Katherine barely touched hers, and she went to bed early. Kevin fell asleep in front of the television set. He awakened as the Syracuse station played the national anthem, ending broadcasting for the day. As he hit the wall switch in the kitchen, he looked out the window, up the hill toward the winemaker's house. The little building was brightly lit, and it was long past the hour when the Le Barnots usually retired. Kevin stood in the darkness, gazing up at the house. Then he went off to bed.

In the early morning he awakened and splashed water on his face in the main bathroom. He dressed, grabbed his cane and climbed the hill to the winemaker's house, where he knocked on the door. There was no answer. He peered in the window. The house looked as it always had, the antique furniture gracing its interior. Kevin walked over to the garage that had been added to the house during the fifties. Peering in that window, he saw that Henri's aged Renault was gone.

He rapped on the front door of the house sharply, and when, after several minutes, there was no answer, Kevin broke the window with his cane and entered. The Le Barnots' most intimate personal possessions—their cosmetics and the best of their clothing, the photographs and keepsakes of two lifetimes—all were gone. Everything that would fit into suitcases that could be carried by a little old man and his aged wife had been cleared out. Kevin could imagine it: a drive to the airport at Syracuse or Rochester, a flight to New York, a wide-bodied jet to Orly, with Henri grim-faced and Annette in tears every inch of the way. Their passports had always been kept up-to-date. If they had left shortly after Kevin had gone to bed they could even be in the air at this very moment. Henri would send for the furniture; he might leave the old car at the airport and let it rot.

Kevin went through the little house, looking at the things they had left. He wondered how anyone would decide in a few hours which bits of his or her life would be carried off in the dead of night after sixty years?

He went out to the porch and looked up at the vineyards that were no longer his. Then he looked down at the big house gleaming white in the rising sunlight. He would have to go back down and break the news to Katherine that Henri and Annette had gone. Then again, of course, she had known they would.

Chapter 22

The only good news that month came from Susan.

She phoned to tell Kevin and Katherine that the weekend before she and Roy Peel had driven his Buick Riviera to Las Vegas, married and spent their honeymoon at the MGM Grand Hotel. "Not only am I a wife again," Susan said as both Kevin and Katherine held extensions in different rooms, "but I'm a mother to two teenaged boys."

"Who are crazy about her," Roy said from his own extension in the house in Newport Beach.

"That's grand," Katherine said. "That's just grand. I'm so happy for both of you."

"I'd like very much to meet you, Mrs. Brennan," Roy Peel said, "and you, too, Mr. Brennan. I've heard so much about both of you. If you don't mind, we're planning to fly in next Friday and spend a few days with you both. And the boys would like to come along."

"Tell them to bring their fishing gear," Kevin said.

The following weekend turned out to be one of the most pleasant in Kevin's memory. Roy Peel was bluff and hearty, and he laughed at Kevin's old jokes, even though Kevin suspected that there was hardly a joke Roy Peel hadn't heard. Both Kevin and Katherine liked him. They conveyed that message individually to a delighted Susan.

The boys, sixteen-year-old Ronald Peel and fifteen-year-old Brian, were classic California beach boys. They spent every daylight moment splashing in the lake and roaring around in the Boston Whaler that Kevin had bought to replace the Chris Craft.

On Saturday night Kevin took the whole squad into the village for dinner at the refurbished Lakeside Hotel. The Peel family flew back to California the following evening. When Kevin got home from the airport, Katherine went up to bed.

Just after midnight, as Kevin sat only half-awake watching an old Charles Laughton movie, the front door opened and closed. Kevin came awake with a start. He saw Art Dixon standing in the doorway to the living room. Art swayed drunkenly.

Kevin, thoroughly surprised, said, "Hello, Art. How are you?"

Art didn't answer. He glanced over at the photo Kevin kept on the table near his chair. It was a picture Jack Ryan had taken of Art, Susan and little Liam. The boy had been about six at the time. His cheeks were ruddy with good health, and his smile was full and fine. Kevin followed Art's eyes, and he saw the expression of abject misery on the younger man's face.

Art slipped into a chair on the other side of the room. He looked at Kevin with bleary eyes, then he cried. Kevin found it incredibly painful to watch. Art wept with a hopelessness that Kevin would never have imagined was in the man.

After a few minutes, Art finally managed to compose himself. He wiped his eyes and blew his nose. He walked over to the picture resting in its gold frame and stared at it long and hard. Then he bent down and kissed Kevin Brennan on the forehead.

Art Dixon left without a word.

* * * *

"Where's Eamon?" Jim Ryan demanded as he came in the door.

Marci's mouth was set in a grim line. "Watching TV in our room. He has no idea what's going on. He thinks she's sick. What are you going to do about this?"

He sat down. "I don't know. The first thing I'm going to do is to stay up until she sobers up later tonight or early this morning. Then I'm going to talk to her."

"When you do," Marci told him, "tell her to pack."

"I'd love to. I just don't know where to tell her to go."

Marci leaned down until her face was close to his. "She can go any damn place she wants to. The one thing she can't do is stay here any more. You may be used to this, but I'm not. I want that woman out of this house tomorrow."

"Do you mind if I sober her up first?" Jim asked.

"I don't care what you do with her as long as she's out of here tomorrow. If she's not, Eamon and I will be on the next plane to Florida."

"You go upstairs and watch TV with Eamon," he told his wife quietly. "I'll stay down here and keep an eye on her. If I have to sleep on the sofa, then I will."

"You bet you will," she told him, and she stalked up the stairs.

It was just after midnight before Helen emerged from her downstairs bedroom. Jim, dozing fully clothed on the family room sofa, heard her in the kitchen and went out to see her. Helen was dressed in a wrinkled robe. Her hair, still bleached a vivid shade of blonde in a poor imitation of the color of her youth, stuck out in all directions. Without the protection of makeup, her face showed lines and a fine network of wrinkles around the eyes. She was standing by the sink. She was unsteady and sick, he could tell.

"You must have put on some show today," he told her coldly.

Helen looked at him through bloodshot eyes. "I don't feel good. Just let me make some coffee and leave me alone."

"The 'coffee' you're looking for isn't there any more. I found your bottle in the tank of the downstairs toilet. Do you think I've forgotten that trick?"

Helen glared at him through veiled eyelids. "Aren't you clever?" she said acidly.

Jim walked into the kitchen and stood next to her. She was a large woman, and he was a smallish man. They stood almost eyeball to eyeball. "I'll show you how clever I am," he told his mother. "Tomorrow morning I'm taking everything you own—and you—and I'm very cleverly putting you out of this house. I'll take you down to the Bellevue Stratford Hotel in Center City and get you a room, and I'm leaving you there. From then on, you're on your own."

Helen looked at him and saw the resolve in his face. It startled her. "Oh, Jim! Cut it out."

"Don't 'Oh, Jim!' me," he said angrily. "You've made a major miscalculation. You seem to have confused me with my father. Bad mistake. Spend tonight packing or I'll pack for you first thing in the morning. Either way, you're gone by noon, even if I have to drag you out of here screaming."

He meant it, Helen saw, and the realization terrified her. "Where am I going to go?"

"Go wherever the hell you like. You've got more money than you know what to do with now that you've sold your whole family down the river."

Helen blinked uncertainly. "I didn't know they were going to take the winery away from us."

"What the hell did you think they were after?" Jim exploded.

"I just wanted some money so I could live on my own," Helen told him. "But I can't spend any of it now, not with what it did to the winery. Besides, where could I go? There's nothing left back in Boydstown—no friends. Peg Harper's dead. Jane's dead. And Kevin won't take me back at Brennan's Point, especially not now. You can't throw me out, Jim. I've got no place to go."

"Get on a plane and go out to California and live with Patricia, although I don't think she'll put up with your getting drunk in her house and more than I will."

"I can't go to California," Helen said. "I've never been to California."

"Here's your chance," Jim said quietly.

Helen looked at him in horror. "You can't throw me out. I'm your mother. I gave life to you."

He glared at her. "That distinction is yours only by right of biology. You long ago forfeited any right you had to a mother's love and respect. I brought you here out of a sense of obligation—misplaced obligation, as it turns out. It certainly wasn't because I owe you anything. I'm not willing to have Eamon subjected even for one day to what I had to grow up with. Pack, Mother."

He turned to leave. As he did Helen sank to the floor. He turned back and watched her burst into tears. She was racked by sobs. He watched for several moments, unmoving. Then he said, "Thank you, Helen Hayes. I'm singularly unimpressed."

Helen rolled over on the cold floor and stretched out. She buried her face in her arms. "Where's Jack? He'd never have let this happen to me. He was the best friend I ever had."

That was too much for Jim. He came back and stood over her, looking down. "I can't believe you. You dedicated forty years of your life to making him miserable. You called him every name you could think of. You spent every waking moment chronicling his failures and rubbing his nose in them. And now you have the brass to say that you miss him?"

"It's true," Helen sobbed noisily. "I just . . . I just didn't think he'd go and die like that. I thought we'd work out everything one of these days. And then one day he wasn't there any more. I didn't want the husband I had, and now I want the husband I can't have. I'm so lonely. I don't have anybody to talk to."

"You don't talk to anybody. You talk at them. Your whole life has been one long, plaintive wail of complaint. If you're looking for an audience for that, then you're out of luck."

"I just want to die."

She wept terribly then. Jim stood there and looked down at the old woman weeping piteously on his kitchen floor. Despite all his experience and all the bitterness burned indelibly into his consciousness, he felt remorse for her. "You need professional help, Mother," he told her.

"I know," she said in muffled tones through the folds of her robe.

"Then what are you going to do about it?"

"I don't know what to do. I think about killing myself. God, why can't I just die?"

Jim knelt next to her. "If I make arrangements for you to get help, will you take it? Will you go to a psychiatrist?"

Helen shook her head. "I don't want to see a psychiatrist."

Jim stood up. "That's up to you. You can always pack."

Helen buried her head in her arms again. Then she said, "All right."

Jim sighed. Then he bent down, took her arm and helped her to her feet. "Fine. Then you go to bed. And if you take one drink—if you just sniff the stuff—you'll be out of here so fast it'll make your head spin."

He led her back to her room, put her to bed, shut off the downstairs lights and climbed the stairs to his own darkened bedroom. He undressed and climbed naked beneath icy sheets. He shivered, but he knew better than to roll up against Marci's back for warmth.

"Well?" she said.

"She's sober," Jim told her. "She's agreed to get some therapy."

"I don't want her in this house."

"I can't bounce her out without giving her this last chance," Jim Ryan said angrily. "You may not like it, but this is the way it's going to be."

Marci was only a dim bulge in the covers on the other side of the bed. She never moved. But she said, "You're going to be sorry you did this."

"Is that a threat?" Jim asked her.

"Yes," Marci told him.

* * * *

Charlie Whittington's house occupied a choice site in Bel Air. It was a large two-story structure of white stucco that sat atop a mountain overlooking the Pacific. He and his wife lived there alone, except for a maid-cook and butler-driver team who took off on Tuesdays and Wednesdays.

Patricia had driven to the house an average of two days a week for more than a year now. Usually she had left the necessary papers with the butler or maid and driven back to the law offices on Wilshire Boulevard. Today, though, she arrived with legal papers during the servant couple's annual month-long holiday, and she knew that Charlie Whittington was suffering from a slight case of the flu. She parked her Toyota in front and let herself in the front door. "Charlie?" she called out.

"I'm in the library," she heard him call back.

Patricia followed the voice and found Charlie Whittington in his walnut-paneled, book-lined library sitting in pajamas and a robe on a beige leather sofa. A box of Kleenex rested on the coffee table. "The Dating Game" was on television. He turned off the TV set with a remote control device and said, "Hello, Patricia. Forgive me for not rising."

"If you have a fever," she said, putting the papers he had requested next to his box of Kleenex, "you shouldn't even be sitting. You should be in bed."

He sneezed and said, "The fever is gone now. Besides, I've already spent two days in bed. I'd have come to the office today, only Eleanor threatened to throw a fit if I did. So I stayed home, and she went out. How's that for sympathy? These are the papers for the Dayton bond issue?"

"These are the ones you asked for. If you have any questions, just give me a call. I'll be in the office all afternoon, and I've enclosed my home number in case you have any questions later."

Whittington dug through the papers. "Your home number? Well, that was thoughtful." He looked up at her as she rose. "Do you have to go back right away? Would you like a cup of coffee with me?"

"Well . . ." Patricia said.

He stood up and snapped his fingers. "I know. You sit right down, and I'll be back in only a second."

Charles Whittington padded out of the room in his bedroom slippers as Patricia sank back into her chair. The man amazed her. She knew he was nearly seventy. Even in his robe, pajamas and slippers, she thought, and even with his black-rimmed glasses perched on the end of his nose, Charlie Whittington was one of the handsomest men she had ever seen. He came back into the room a few moments later carrying a bottle of Weidener champagne and two tulip-shaped glasses.

"I've laid in a supply of that champagne you introduced me to," he told her, popping the cork. "I had a little trouble finding it in the cellar. Pablo has his own system down there, and I have a hell of a time locating anything when he's off."

Patricia accepted the glass and sipped at it gingerly. "Do you mind if I tell you something?" she asked Whittington. "This is the only house I've ever been in that had a butler."

He smiled. "Oh, well. That's an old Republican tradition. One of many. Would you like to hear some others?"

Patricia nodded. "Please."

He scratched his chin. "Well, let's see if I can remember. First of all, Republicans sleep in twin beds; Democrats usually don't. That's the primary reason why there are more Democrats than Republicans."

Patricia giggled.

He beamed at her appreciation. "There's more. A fellow once read into the Congressional Record a whole list of items that differentiate Republicans from Democrats. Let's see, now . . . Democrats give their worn-out clothes to the less fortunate; Republicans wear theirs. Republicans have governesses; Democrats have grandmothers."

"I can vouch for that last one."

"Democrats name their children after people who are well known in sports or entertainment or politics; Republicans name theirs after their parents or grandparents—depending on where the most money is. Now, what else was there? Republicans tend to keep their shades drawn, although there's damned little reason why they should; Democrats ought to, but they seldom bother. Democrats eat the fish they catch; Republicans hang them on the wall."

"My grandfather Brennan was a Republican and a fisherman," Patricia said, "and he ate every one."

"A statistical aberration," Charles Whittington told her. "Finally—and this is the last one I can remember, although there are a few others— Republican boys plan to marry Republican girls; but they date Democratic girls because they feel they're entitled to a little fun first."

Patricia broke up. "That's funny," she told Whittington.

"Do you know how you can spot a Republican, by the way? Republicans are the people you see coming out of wooden churches."

Later, when they had killed the entire bottle of champagne, she said, "Charlie, you've cheered me up. Thank you so much. This is just what I needed. I got a call last night from my older brother. He and his wife are talking about splitting up. It made me feel just awful."

"Well, that's too bad. But these things shouldn't be much of a surprise, I suppose. That's sort of a craze these days—divorce."

"I've always been the crazy one in my family," she said, "not Jim."

He smiled. "You don't seem at all crazy to me."

She leaned back in her chair. The champagne had relaxed her. "I was, believe me. When I was in college, I did every drug you can imagine. I'm lucky I didn't burn my brain out. Or maybe I did and don't realize it. It was the thing to do back then."

Whittington sat back on the sofa and put his hands behind his head. "My own view is that you're either responsible for what you do or you're not. Unless you're clinically insane or demonstrably impaired in some other fashion, then—by definition—you're responsible."

"That's why you're a Republican," Patricia told him.

"I make no apology for it. I certainly make no claim to being a paragon of virtue. I'm sure you've heard stories about me. You don't have to answer that, by the way. My point is that I take full responsibility for everything I've done or failed to do. And that's not a purely Republican point of view, by the way. Dick Nixon never acknowledged any personal responsibility for anything that happened to him. That's why I never had any respect for the sanctimonious son-of-a-bitch, despite his intellect."

"It strikes me so strange to hear somebody speak so lightly of a president. Dick, you called him. I hear you say that, and suddenly I remember who I'm talking to."

He smiled self-consciously. "You're talking to Charlie Whittington, colleague and—I hope—friend. But go on. You were in the process of making excuses for becoming a drug fiend."

"I wasn't a drug fiend, exactly. And, incidentally, Charlie, I hate to be the one to tell you, but that's not a term you hear much any more."

"A shame. It always seemed so appropriate. Go on. Why did you adopt that particular lifestyle, then? Did you grow up surrounded by drug fiends?"

"No. It's . . . it's difficult to explain. My mother . . . she's always lived this terribly traditional life. She never worked after we were born. She grew old in the kitchen and pushing around a vacuum cleaner. She was so miserable that she made all the rest of us miserable, too. Actually, she turned into a terrible drunk, if you want the truth. I didn't know then what I wanted to be in life, but I knew didn't want to become my mother. So I became something else. I guess that's how I fell into that way of life in college."

He sat there for a moment, digesting all that. Then he said, "You know, it's truly amazing. Years ago, when I was in the Senate, a bill came to the floor that I cared about passionately. I don't even remember what it was now, but it was important to me at the time. Lyndon Johnson managed to shift four votes overnight, and I never knew it until it was too late. So I went to him afterward, and I said, 'Lyndon, how do you do it? How do you manage to line up votes so effectively?' He took pity on me—I was a new senator, then—and he said, 'Charlie, it's simple. Know your members. Know who they are and where they come from. Know where their parents failed in their lives. Once you know that, you know how to appeal to them to vote your way.' And he was dead right. We're all slaves to the failings of our parents—men to their fathers' failings and women to the failings of their mothers. You've just proven that point to me again." He sat back on the sofa. "All right," he said, "that's how you got into it. What changed you?"

"My roommate," Patricia told him. "Shirley took too much of something one night and went wild. She took a kitchen knife and stabbed herself in the legs. She didn't die, but it was very close. There was blood all over. It scared the living shit out of me, Charlie, if you'll excuse the expression. I've never touched anything else since."

He nodded. "You have my congratulations on your redemption."

Patricia looked down at her hands, which were folded in her lap. "I've never told anybody some of the things I've told you today. I can't believe I've been so . . . I don't know."

"Honest?"

She looked up. "I guess you could say that. I let my guard down. I haven't done that in years."

He moved to the end of the sofa, sitting closer to her. "It's not good to cut yourself off from people—or from the truth."

Patricia studied his handsome face, framed by his carefully styled white hair. "Sometimes it's hard to face up to what the truth is," she said.

Charlie Whittington took her hand and kissed it. Patricia looked into his blue eyes. Then, slowly, she got up, walked to the door and closed it. She turned the key in the lock.

Patricia walked back across the library and sat down next to Whittington. He put his arms around her and kissed her, his tongue probing into her mouth. Expertly, he removed every stitch of her clothing, nuzzling and stroking and kissing as she quivered. He entered her and made love to her on the sofa. Her bare flesh squeaked against the leather as he moved on her, stroking with skill and patience.

Afterwards, she said to him, "Is this the sort of thing Republican boys do to Democratic girls?"

He kissed her breasts gently. "Every chance they get," Charles Whittington said.

* * * *

Dr. Mai Lee was tiny and delicate and looked far younger than her thirty years. She dug through the manilla folder on her desk and told Jim Ryan, "There's no doubt that she suffers from a physical addiction to alcohol. But that's not her only problem. Aside from that, she meets just about every clinical test for serious depression and classic alienation. That's vastly more difficult to deal with than the alcoholism, and the one feeds on the other. She suffers from depression, and she drinks to feel better. Then she gets depressed because she's drinking. It's not just that she's unhappy. It goes well beyond that. She suffers from a totally pervasive sense of joylessness virtually all the time. She derives no satisfaction from any sort of social interaction. And it may just be that she's no longer emotionally or physically capable of being helped in any way."

Jim nodded slowly, digesting it all. "What you're describing is the pattern of her life ever since I can remember. What about AA? Could that help her?"

"It couldn't hurt," Mai said, "but I think her problem is largely biochemical—a shortage of neurotransmitters called endorphins. Her brain chemistry creates her chronic misery. I'm going to prescribe some drugs, but they must be taken with extreme care. And she has to avoid alcohol at all costs while she's taking this medication."

"Does she know that?" Jim asked. "And she's willing to take the medication?"

Mai nodded. "She says she is. The problem here is that it'll probably be a while before we hit on the right combination of drugs to combat her depression, and I'm afraid that during that period of trial and error she's going to experience some spectacular highs and lows. The danger is that she might turn to alcohol again during one of those lows to make herself feel better."

Jim frowned. "Nobody has ever been able to keep liquor away from her if she decided she wanted it. She's going to be in a senior citizens apartment complex in Cherry Hill. There'll be a lot of people around, and she'll get very good care, but during the week she'll essentially be on her own."

Mai's lips pursed. "Have you considered having her stay with you a bit longer?"

He shook his head. "Apartments in places like this are tough to come by, and if she passes this one up, God alone knows how long it'll be before anything else becomes available."

Mai Lee said, "It's your choice."

* * * *

"Brennan Wine Company," the operator said.

"Kevin Brennan's office, please."

"One moment, please."

"Kevin Brennan."

"Mr. Brennan, my name is Baldwin. I'm the chairman of Consolidated Food Products."

"Well, I've been waiting to hear from you. What's taken you so long?"

"There was really no need for us to get in touch with you until the annual meeting was coming up."

"No, I suppose not. And now you're calling me, I surmise, to inform me that there's really no need for me to go to the annual meeting."

"Something like that. We're circulating our own list of nominees to the board of directors to the stockholders. You can expect that Consolidated people will be moving into key positions in the winery on, say, Monday the sixteenth. That's the Monday after the annual meeting."

"All right," Kevin said. "I'll inform my employees who plan to stay. A good many of them don't, by the way—especially the higher-ranking people."

"They would have been replaced, anyway."

"I have a question I'd like to ask you."

"Go ahead."

"Well, Mr. Bellwin, I'd like to know why—"

"That's Baldwin."

"Whatever. I'm curious as to why you picked my company. If you had to make a run at somebody, there are a dozen wineries in this region that are bigger and more profitable than mine."

"You mean you don't know who I am by now?"

Kevin was silent for a moment. "All right, I give up. Who are you?"

"You don't remember me—Peter Baldwin?"

"Where do I know you from, if you don't mind my asking?"

"From Cornell," Baldwin said quietly. "We were enemies, Brennan. Don't tell me you don't remember that. I've never forgotten it."

There was silence from Kevin's end of the line for a long moment. Then he said, "Baldwin, you poor, sick bastard. I can't even remember what you looked like. Your face hasn't spent a second in my mind in the last forty years."

Baldwin, startled, began to respond angrily, but then he realized that the phone had gone dead in his hand. He slammed it down hard on its cradle. He got up and began pacing in his spacious office, trying to bring under control the rage that had him quivering. Somehow, that conversation had not gone the way he had envisioned.

* * * *

The end had come, Jim knew, when Marci announced that she and her friend Sonia had become Jews for Jesus. "Have you gone totally nuts?" he asked her in disbelief.

"I'm not going to lose my temper, Jim, no matter what you say to me," Marci told him. "I don't need the sin of anger in my life now. I have only love—for you and for everybody. We're all the children of Christ."

The entire affair was surprisingly simple and painless on both sides. Marci was too full of new-found Christian virtue for recriminations. Jim moved into a center city apartment. He would go out to the house on Friday nights and pick up Eamon and take him to his place, and he would bring him back on Sunday nights. He would send Marci a check every two weeks, and they would file for a no-fault divorce. Neither, by legal agreement, would be permitted to cohabit with a member of the opposite sex on those days when they had custody of Eamon. And that was it.

Sam Roth was enraged at Marci's latest religious aberration and heartbroken over the marital breakup. He insisted that Jim continue running Roth and Co. "Who could have guessed this?" he said. "Jews for Jesus, already. How did this happen to me?"

"You're right, Sam," Jim told him. "She'll get over it."

"And then you'll get back together?"

"Not a chance," Jim told his father-in-law.

If Sam Roth was torn up by the separation, Helen Ryan was not. If anything, she seemed relieved, because it meant that Jim was now living half an hour to forty-five minutes closer to her high-rise apartment on Route 70 in Cherry Hill, New Jersey, in a complex that would accept only tenants over fifty-five. To Jim, who now visited his mother one evening during the week and every Sunday with Eamon, she seemed more relaxed now, and he attributed that to the drugs Mai had prescribed for her. She also, however, seemed a little distant on occasion, and she seemed to have far less energy than she had exhibited before.

"How are you feeling?" he asked her one Sunday as they sat at her small kitchen table. Eamon was gleefully engrossed in a showing of "Doctor Doolittle" on Channel 48 and couldn't hear the conversation.

She shrugged. "I don't get worked up over anything. I don't feel bad. I don't feel good. Most of the time, I don't feel anything."

"Do you like that?"

"I don't not like it."

On a spring Wednesday night Jim arrived at Helen's complex weighed down with Chinese food. He rang the buzzer for fully ten minutes before he realized that she was not going to answer. He sought out the building superintendent. They went up to the twelfth floor and let themselves into Helen's apartment.

Helen was lying fully clothed on the living room sofa, sleeping, breathing peacefully and regularly. Jim was unable to awaken her. He left the bag of Chinese food on the kitchen table. With the help of the super he carried her to the elevator, then out into the parking lot and into his BMW. He raced to Cherry Hill Medical Center. An Indian physician on duty in the emergency room told him his mother had suffered a stroke.

Jim got on the phone. Galen and Mai were on hand within a half hour. Mai went in to examine Helen while Galen and Jim sat in the waiting area. She came out forty minutes later, her face grim.

"When will she wake up?"

"I can't tell. Nobody can. She might awaken in five minutes or five months or not at all. There's no way to predict."

"Is she in danger of having another stroke?"

Mai's lips pursed. "A neurologist would be a better source of information for you. But, yes, statistically she's at greater risk for the first two weeks after a stroke—especially the first forty-eight hours."

Jim shook his head in shock. This all had such an unreal quality to it. "What caused it? Could it have been the drugs?"

"Not the drugs by themselves. Her blood shows that she'd been drinking. She's been a heavy smoker for forty-five years. She's had blood pressure problems. There's some family history, too. Also, Jim, she's coming up on sixty-five years old."

Jim ran his hand over his face. "I've got a lot of people to call. I can hardly wait to tell her brother and my grandmother. This is just what they need. Mai, what was her blood alcohol content?"

".14."

Jim sighed. "That's pretty drunk, isn't it?"

Mai nodded.

Jim sat at Helen's side for about an hour. Her eyes fluttered open several times, and she looked around the room, but she made no attempt to speak, and Jim wasn't sure how much she understood about what was happening to her. When he got home late at night to his apartment on Spruce Street, he phoned Kevin and broke the news to him. He left a message on Patricia's machine.

Patricia called at about two in the morning.

"I hope I didn't wake you. I just got in. What's wrong?"

"Mother's had a stroke."

"Oh, God! Is she . . ."

"No. She's alive, but she's comatose."

"I'll catch a plane back first thing tomorrow morning."

"Well, let me know when you're getting in so I can pick you up."

"I'll get back to you as soon as I can. How are you?"

"I'm fine. Get back to me, though."

Patricia hung up, and Jim walked into the kitchen for a glass of milk. The phone rang. Patricia, he thought. He answered it.

"Hello."

"Jim, this is Mai. The hospital just called me. Your mother has had another stroke."

* * * *

The second stroke drove Helen more deeply into her coma, but it became obvious by Saturday that she was probably going to live.

The neurologist was just what Jim would have ordered. He was big, self-assured and a dead ringer for Peter Graves, the actor. His name was Cronin.

"Her eyes will begin to open occasionally," Cronin told Jim and Patricia, "mostly when she's disturbed. It'll happen when she's moved or bathed. Nobody can tell you what she'll know or won't know. My own suspicion is that she's not now aware of anything."

"Doctor," Patricia asked, "what would your guess be? About her prognosis, I mean."

Cronin looked at her. "Well, she could go on for a long while."

"How long is a long while?" Jim asked him.

The neurologist shrugged. "It could be years. Patients like this have a spasm at some point and vomit up some of the liquid food we shoot into their digestive tracts. Then they aspirate it and develop pneumonia. Then they go very peacefully. That's the usual pattern."

Both Jim and Patricia were silent. This was the first time they had been told outright that Helen would not recover.

Jim said, "She could go on like this for years?"

"I said she could," Cronin told him. "She won't necessarily. She could suffer another stroke. The process I described could happen sooner than that. The thing to remember, Mr. Ryan, is that she's not really aware of what's happening to her. She doesn't know anything."

After six weeks in the hospital, Helen was transferred to a skilled nursing facility. She shared a room with a much older woman who seemed to suffer from senile dementia. When Jim came to visit, the woman constantly mistook him for someone from her past named Arthur, and she moaned and groaned until the nurses came in and pulled the curtain around her bed. Jim visited his mother every Saturday morning for six straight weeks.

In August, after a business trip had kept him out of town for twelve days, Jim drove out to the nursing home on a rainy Saturday morning. Helen had grown thin on the liquid nutrients she was fed through a tube in her stomach. Jim sat next to her and to the night table he had decorated with photos of Eamon.

"Hello, Mother," he said softly.

Helen opened her eyes and looked directly at him.

For a moment, Jim thought he would pass out. He felt his heart turn over in his chest. He ran for the nurse. "My mother," he said, gasping with excitement. "She's awake!"

The nurse said, "This happens a lot with patients in comas, Mr. Ryan.

They often have their eyes open, but they're still comatose. They don't know what's going on.''

Jim went back to the room. Helen lay quite still, unable to move anything except her lips and eyelids. The senile woman in the next bed howled about Arthur. Outside the window behind Jim rain slanted down from a leaden sky. Tubes hung from beneath Helen's covers. Her lower lip was raw and swollen from where she had chewed on it. Her blue eyes were open, and Jim looked directly into them with a growing sense of horror. It began in his middle and spread upward, choking him, forcing the air from his lungs and the saliva from his mouth. Helen Ryan stared out at her son from the prison that was her body.

Sweet Jesus, Jim Ryan thought. She knows.

Chapter 23

More than anyone else it was Charlie Whittington who got Patricia through the first year of her mother's coma. She found in his breadth of experience the capability to come to grips with the feelings of guilt and self-loathing that Helen's illness had forced out of her.

The very closeness of their relationship highlighted the difference between their ages. Charlie, who was older than Patricia's mother, routinely dredged up some fact from his frame of reference that meant nothing to Patricia; she was too young. She noticed the difference in their ages, too, on the tennis court. Charlie hit the ball masterfully, but he had no legs.

Legs were not necessary in the bedroom, however, and there Charlie never disappointed her. No small part of that was that their relationship was only partly physical. They spent most of their time talking. Charlie knew more and thought more than anyone Patricia had ever encountered.

One Tuesday afternoon when Charlie's wife was in Washington and the maid and butler were off, they were sitting alone in the library of the Bel Air house. Patricia complained casually that some of the men in the law office viewed women primarily as sex objects.

"That's not unnatural," he told her. "I don't mean that it's proper for a man to view a woman merely as a major appliance with sex organs, but it's perfectly natural and even biologically desirable for a man to first be attracted to a woman because of her physical attributes."

"By that you mean what?" Patricia asked him. "That women should first be viewed as sex objects and secondarily as thinking, feeling beings?"

"Well," he told her, "there are fundamental differences in the way men and women view sexual relationships, and those differences can't be written off as merely the product of the socialization process. They represent differences in basic biology—all according to God's great plan."

"You and God have discussed this at length, I presume," Patricia said.

He laughed. "No, not yet. But I'm more or less looking forward to the conversation. At my age, the prospect of discussing such matters with God actually has some appeal. I was an atheist until I began to come to grips with aging, at which point I became a fervent believer. Just in case there really is a God up there, I don't want to irritate him any more than I absolutely have to."

"Are you sure that He isn't a She?"

"I hope he's a she. I always ran better with women—or so the pollsters told me."

Patricia said, "Tell me more about Whittington's doctrine of divinely inspired sexism."

"Well, it's more Darwin's theory than Whittington's. Darwin taught us that desirable traits are passed on and that less desirable ones die out with the animals that possess them. Now, among the higher mammals the male can impregnate a female virtually daily. The female, on the other hand, can produce only a certain number of young each year. In the case of human beings, as opposed to, say, dogs, only one or, rarely, two young are produced with each birth; and there's a long gestation period, to boot, not to mention a long period of growing up with the mother caring for and educating the young creature so it can survive on its own."

"So what's your point, Charlie?"

"Here's the main point: Because the human male can produce more young than the female, it's not necessary for the male to be particularly selective in his amorous activities. In fact, it's his biological obligation to be nonselective—to spread his genes around as liberally as he can manage. The more females he impregnates, the more of his genes he passes along, which is his job, according to Darwin."

Patricia frowned. "And the female? What makes her different in her approach?"

"Again, natural selection. The female is biologically obligated to select only the best genes for her young. Therefore, she's much more selective in choosing a sex partner. Whereas the male will mate with virtually any female, the female will mate only with the best, most dominant male she can attract. That's her biological job."

"And that," she said, "explains why some men will screw mud if the mud is willing?"

His eyebrows raised. "Essentially."

"Even if I accept what you're saying, does that make it right?"

He shrugged. "Right and wrong cut no ice in biology. The double standard is, with very few exceptions, an integral part of every culture on earth, especially Western culture. Even women look down upon another woman who's not selective sexually."

"I just don't accept what you're saying, Charlie."

He said, "The very fact that you're here with me is proof of my thesis. What is there about me that you find attractive?"

"Your mind. You're brilliant. You're famous. You're fabulously successful."

He nodded. "What you're saying is that in our culture, I'm dominant—not in a physical sense any more, of course. In all probability, any man in the office under forty could beat the hell out of me. I couldn't hold on to you in a primitive society. But by the standards of our culture, I'm dominant over those younger fellows. I'm richer. I have more status. I have more power. And the fact that you're here with me instead of out running around with one of them makes my point for me."

"Has it occurred to you," she said, "that I have to be back in the office before five and we've done nothing but talk today?"

He looked down at her, an amused expression on his face. "Do you have a better idea?"

"Yes," Patricia said. "Show me how dominant you are."

He undressed her with the agonizing slowness that had become part of their ritual. Then, as she lay back on the sofa, he took off the custom-made shirt, the carefully cut trousers, his socks, his underwear. Only when he was totally nude could she see the signs of his age, and by then it never mattered. She held her arms up to him.

"Come here," Patricia Ryan whispered to Charlie Whittington.

After a while, he suddenly withdrew from her and sat up on the leather sofa. Patricia sat up with him.

"Charlie?" she said. "Are you all right?"

He touched himself on the chest with a clenched fist. "I'm feeling some tightness—right here." He was ashen beneath his tan.

Patricia snapped to her feet and stood next to him, leaning over him, touching his forehead. "You're having chest pains?"

"Without question," he said quietly. "Could you go over to the bar and pour me some scotch? That might help."

She went to the bar and brought down a bottle of Johnny Walker Black. As she poured, she looked over at him. He was still holding his fist to his chest, and he was staring off into space, concentrating on his body and what was happening inside it.

"Do you want me to call anybody?" Patricia asked. She was beginning to get alarmed.

He looked up and smiled weakly at her. "And wouldn't we look marvelous—both of us sitting here naked? No, just give me a stiff drink and let me catch my breath."

She started back across the study. "Should you drink if you're having a problem?"

"Alcohol expands the blood vessels," he said. "I've read that—" And then Charles Whittington's eyeballs bulged. He gurgled something unintelligible and slid over sideways on the sofa.

Patricia dropped the tumbler of scotch to the floor. "Charlie!" she shrieked. "Charlie! My God!"

* * * *

"Dom Fresina."

"Dom, it's Patricia. You've got to help me. I'm at Charlie's house in Bel Air. He's collapsed. I think he's dead."

"Jesus Christ! Did you call an ambulance?"

"No, I couldn't. He's . . . He doesn't have any clothes on."

Dom put the phone down on his desk top. He took a deep breath and picked it up again. "Well, for Christ's sake get his clothes on him and call an ambulance."

"I can't. He's too big. I'm too shaky to do it. I can't even get my own clothes on."

"Then the hell with it. Just call an ambulance."

Patricia was wailing over the phone. "Everybody would know."

Now that the situation was sinking in on him, Dom discovered that he was furious. "You're worried about your reputation at a time like this? Are you nuts?"

"No," she wept. "I'm worried about his. This would get into the papers. The ambulance people would tell somebody. And . . . It doesn't make any difference, Dom. He's dead. He's not breathing, and I can't get a pulse. He's turning blue, for God's sake. Please come out here and help me. I need you, Dom."

He smashed his fist hard on his desk. "I'll be there as fast as I can," he said through tight lips, and he slammed down the phone.

At the other end, Patricia sighed a deep sigh of relief. She was still half undressed. Her shaking fingers fumbled futilely with her clothing. She looked over at Sen. Charles Whittington's naked corpse on the sofa and headed for the bar. She poured herself a drink from the bottle of Johnny Walker Black, downed it, then downed another. All it did was make her feel like throwing up. She went over to Charles Whittington and ran a hand gently across his cooling brow. "Oh, Charlie," she wept. "Poor, sweet Charlie."

Dom pulled up in his red Triumph Spitfire half an hour later, having broken every speed limit in Los Angeles County. She let him in as she fastened the rest of her clothes. His face was both grim and angry. "Where is he?" Dom snapped.

"In the library. Over here."

Dom bent over Whittington and felt for a pulse. Then he held a hand under Whittington's nose. He looked over at Patricia. "He's dead, all right." He went over to the desk and picked up the phone.

"What are you doing?" Patricia asked him.

"I'm calling Gill. I want some advice on how to handle this."

She shook her head. "Can't we just get him dressed and call an ambulance?"

Dom held the phone in his hand and looked at her, his expression anything but friendly. "Look, Patricia. Sen. Charles Whittington just died in your arms. I suspect the firm might view this as something of a public relations problem. I'm getting the advice of a senior partner before I do anything. I should have done that before I ever came here, but I didn't have time to think it through." He looked over at Whittington's body, and his face softened. He put the receiver back on the hook. "I don't want to use the phone in here. I'll use the one in the hall." He stalked out of the library. "Don't go away."

She heard him talking out in the cavernous foyer, but she couldn't make out what was being said. All she could do was look at Charlie Whittington and wish that it had been she who had died instead. He had been such a dignified man. To see him lying there naked, with all the unlovely parts of his aged nakedness exposed for all to see—Patricia turned away.

Dom came in a few moments later. "Help me get him dressed."

She obeyed. "He feels so cold," she said.

Dom struggled with Whittington's shirt. "He's not uncomfortable. Take my word for it."

"I thought I heard you make another call."

"I called the police emergency number. That's what Gill told me to do. He's coming right out. As soon as we get his clothes on, you get the hell out of here. Gill and I will handle it from here."

It took both of them to get Whittington's shirt on. Patricia found his socks and pulled them up over his bluish feet. Dom picked up the trousers and shook them out. Then he looked around anxiously.

"Where the hell are his shorts?" he asked anxiously.

She glanced around the area near the sofa. "I don't know. They should be here with his other clothes."

Dom bent down and searched the floor. "They're not here."

"He must have thrown them somewhere when he took them off."

"This must have been some party," Dom said, standing up. "Where the hell did he throw them?"

"I don't know!" Patricia shrieked at him.

Charles Whittington's shorts were nowhere to be found. They spent precious minutes looking for them. Finally, Dom said, "We're out of time. The cops and the ambulance are going to be here any second. Let's just get his pants on, and his shoes. Then you take off."

She was desperate. "You can't leave him without his underwear."

"The man's beyond embarrassment, Patricia. Help me with his legs here."

"They'll undress him at the hospital. It'll look funny."

"It'll look a hell of a lot funnier if he's not wearing any pants at all," he snapped. "There's no more time. Now help me, goddamn it!"

He was right. There had been no more time. Before Patricia could get out the door, a patrol car rolled up in front of the house.

"Oh, shit," Dom said. He turned to Patricia. "Look, you just keep your mouth shut and let me do the talking."

There were two police officers, a uniformed black man of about thirty and a bulky plainclothes officer past fifty. Patricia saw them through the window as they got out of the car and rang the bell. Dom answered the door. "Where's the senator?" she heard the older man say.

"In the library. It looks like he's had a heart attack."

The ambulance arrived outside as the three men entered the library. The older man spotted Patricia. He stopped and looked at both of them. "Who're you two?"

"I'm Dominic Fresina. I'm an attorney with the senator's law firm. This is Patricia Ryan. She's a lawyer with the firm, too."

"Which of you was with the senator when he came down ill?"

"I was," Dom said. The only problem was that Patricia said precisely the same words at the same time. It came out as a chorus. Dom rolled his eyes heavenward.

"We both were," Dom told the detective. "We came out here to go over some papers with the senator. We'd been here only a few minutes, and he just keeled over."

"How long ago was this?"

"Just before I called—ten minutes, maybe."

The detective nodded. The emergency team was already working on Whittington.

"Why don't you two go into the living room?" the cop said. "I'll be in there in a minute."

As Dom and Patricia left the room, they heard the detective ask the head of the ambulance team, "How is he?"

"Stone dead," came the reply. "Rigor is beginning to set in."

Patricia and Dom exchanged glances.

"Rigor mortis?" the cop asked. "Pretty quick, isn't it?"

"Not really," the ambulance attendant said. "I'd say this man has been dead a little while now. Here, feel how cool the body is."

"I'll take your word for it."

Dom and Patricia sat in silence in the living room until Gill arrived a few moments later in his chauffeured limousine. His face was as gray as his suit. As Gill came into the living room, the detective came in after him. Gill introduced himself. The detective made no attempt to shake his hand. "I've got some questions for all of you," the cop said ominously.

Henderson Gill immediately took command of the situation. He was an innocuous-looking man in his early sixties who had actually been running the firm for years because one of his partners was too old to function and the other had spent the bulk of his time pursuing other interests—Patricia, for example.

"Why don't you sit down here with us, Officer?" Gill said cordially. "This chair here is quite comfortable."

Patricia noted and filed it away. It was a pleasant gesture, but it served to remind the cop that Gill was a frequent guest in this opulent house, that he was very much at home here, that he was in effect the host and the detective was the guest. It was subtle, and it had effect. The cop sat down in the chair Gill indicated.

"When's the last time you spoke to the senator?" the detective asked Gill, his tone more respectful now.

"I talked to Charlie on the phone this morning. I just can't believe he's gone. Damn." Gill spoke calmly, but his color was only slightly better than Whittington's had been.

The detective turned to Dom. "Now you, young fellow. You said the senator collapsed about fifteen minutes ago, right?"

"Well, about that—yes. I can't say for sure."

"And you called the emergency number the minute it happened."

"There might have been a few minutes delay. We were flustered."

"And you, young lady," the detective said, "is that what happened?"

Patricia only nodded dumbly.

The head of the ambulance team appeared in the doorway and motioned to the detective.

"Excuse me," he said.

The cop left the room. Dom, Patricia and Gill continued to sit in silence. In less than thirty seconds, the detective came back in and resumed his chair. "Mr. Gill," he said, "you're the senator's law partner, is that right? You were pretty good friends, were you?"

"Charlie Whittington was the best friend I ever had in my life," Henderson Gill said quietly.

"Can you tell me if he was in the habit of wearing underwear?"

Patricia felt her stomach turn over. Dom rolled his eyes and leaned back on the sofa.

Henderson Gill said, "What?"

"Did the senator wear underwear? You know, did he wear shorts under his pants?"

"What kind of question is that?" Gill demanded.

For the first time, the detective smiled, revealing tobacco-stained teeth. "The senator's body is fully dressed, Mr. Gill, but he isn't wearing any undershorts. Also, his shirt isn't buttoned properly. It's all one button off. Now, maybe he liked to wear it that way, but . . ." The cop let his voice trail off. The four people in the living room were silent for a moment.

Then the cop reached into the pocket of his suit jacket and brought out Charlie Whittington's undershorts. "One of the attendants just found these over behind the drapes." The detective looked directly at Patricia. "None of you would happen to know how they got there, would you?"

Henderson Gill stood up. "We have no more answers to give you at the moment, Officer."

The detective stood up and eyed Gill levelly. "That's all right with me, Mr. Gill. You don't have to say a word to me. But you're going to have to answer these questions sometime, either for me or in front of a coronor's jury."

For the first time, Henderson Gill permitted himself a small show of temper. "Officer, my best friend has just died. My two colleagues and I are quite shaken. We're going back to our offices now, and I'm going to call Eleanor Whittington in Washington and inform her of what's happened. Now, if you don't mind . . ."

The detective seemed to smirk. "We'll be back in touch, Mr. Gill."

Henderson Gill loaded Dom and Patricia into the back seat of his white Cadillac limo. He gave his driver a wordless gesture, and the big car pulled out. "I'm afraid this is going to be very bad," he said grimly. "I'm going to make some phone calls when we get back and try to get that cop under control."

"I screwed up, Mr. Gill," Dom said. "I'm sorry. I just couldn't find the goddamn undershorts."

"There's nothing that can be done about that now. Patricia, we're going to drop you off at your apartment. I suggest that under the circumstances you stay away from the office until further notice."

She nodded. "My car is back at Charlie's. I'll need it."

"So's mine," Dom said.

"Give me your keys, both of you. I'll see that the cars are picked up and delivered."

They rode the forty minutes to Patricia's apartment in a silence that was broken only by Patricia's directions to the driver. Dom got out of the car with her and walked her to her door. "You did fine, Patricia," he said gently. "It's going to work out all right."

Patricia said nothing. She let herself into her apartment and closed the door behind her. Zorro was sleeping on the sofa. Patricia picked him up, and he purred contentedly. She took him to the bedroom and collapsed on the bed. Cats were great for crying on, Patricia had always thought.

* * * *

Patricia was totally shot.

She wept and wept and the big black cat purred and purred and finally she fell asleep. She awakened in darkness. Her illuminated alarm clock told her it was nearly midnight.

Groggily, she flipped on some lights and made her way to the bathroom. Then, in just her robe, she went to the kitchen and poured a glass of orange juice. She looked out her apartment window at her parking space. The Toyota was nowhere to be seen. She was heading for the shower when the phone rang.

"Miss Ryan?" a woman's voice asked. "Patricia Ryan?"

"Yes."

"Miss Ryan, I'm sorry to be disturbing you so late. My name is Linda Chapman. I'm a reporter for the *Herald-Examiner.* I'm calling you because we're putting together an obituary on Senator Whittington, and the police report said you were with him when he died. I wonder if—"

No way, Patricia thought. "I'm sorry. I can't talk now. You can call me tomorrow at my office."

"Your office said you wouldn't be in until further notice, Miss Ryan."

"Who said that?"

"Somebody who answered the phone. Her name was Alice something."

Figures, Patricia thought. "Well . . ." Patricia began.

"Miss Ryan, I've just spent the past ninety minutes calling everybody with your name in Los Angeles County. I just have a few questions to ask you, and I'm right in the middle of a deadline."

"I'm sorry. I can't."

"Miss Ryan, we've been told that the senator wasn't completely dressed when he was found. Can you explain why that might be?"

Patricia was rattled. "I don't know. I don't know that he wasn't dressed."

"You don't know that he wasn't dressed? Is that what you said?"

"I don't know why he wasn't wearing undershorts," Patricia said, then she realized immediately that she should have said nothing of the sort.

"What was the nature of your relationship with the senator, Miss Ryan?" the reporter asked. Over the phone line, Patricia could hear the woman's fingers tapping at a word processor.

"I worked for him," Patricia said. "Look, I really can't talk."

"Did you have a romantic relationship with him, Miss Ryan."

Patricia hung up the phone. That's what I should have done right away, she thought. She called Dom and told him about the reporter's call.

"I don't know what to do," she said to him. "They'll be banging on my door next."

"They're already banging on mine. I chased a guy from the LA *Times* away from here tonight. I'm thinking about getting the hell out of here and going up to my folks' place in Napa. I'm going to talk to Gill about it tomorrow."

"This is a nightmare," Patricia said.

"I'm afraid it's going to last a while. The coroner—what's his name, Yashimoto—he's a publicity freak. He'll probably milk this one for all it's worth. Whittington's death was on the eleven o'clock news, but they didn't have anything except that he died of an apparent heart attack at his home in the afternoon. I'm afraid both papers will have a lot more tomorrow."

"I can't stay here," Patricia said. "The reporters will be all over here tomorrow. Can I stay with you?"

"Patricia, I'm the last person on earth you want to stay with. They'll be after me, too."

"I guess I can call my cousin in Newport Beach. I could stay there. But I don't have a car. Nobody ever came and delivered it tonight."

Dom chuckled. "I got my car, but it's somehow reassuring to know that Gill is fallible. Look, you call your cousin and let her know you're coming. I'll drive you down."

They pulled up in front of Roy Peel's Newport Beach house just before two in the morning.

"The lights are on," Dom said. "It looks like they're expecting you."

"I guess," Patricia said. "Susan doesn't watch the news. She doesn't have the foggiest notion of why I asked to come down here and spend a few days. I don't know how I'm going to tell her this." Without warning, Patricia Ryan burst into tears. Dom put his arms around her and pulled her close. He stroked her hair while she sobbed uncontrollably. In a few moments, she had regained a semblance of composure.

"You'll get through this," he told her. "We both will."

She looked into his face with wet eyes. "I want you to know something. At the time you asked me, it wasn't going on then. It's only been the past year or so."

"You don't have to make excuses to me," he told her.

The front door to Roy Peel's house opened, and Susan stepped out in a robe and slippers. "Hey," she said, "are you going to come in and let me know what's going on, or what?"

Patricia clambered out of the Spitfire. Dom said to her, "I'll call you tomorrow. From now on, I'll take care of you. Promise."

She smiled through her tear-stained face. "Yeah? And who's going to take care of you, tough guy?"

* * * *

Patricia was awakened the next morning by Susan nudging her in the guest room of the Newport Beach house.

"There's something on TV you should see," Susan told her. "Come on out, quick."

Patricia was in her robe and in the family room with Susan and Roy in only a few seconds. An earnest-looking young Asian woman was doing the local news segment in between sections of the "Today Show." She was saying ". . . circumstances surrounding Whittington's death. The medical examiner refused to comment on printed reports that Whittington's body was only partially clad when medical assistance arrived."

"He was completely dressed except for his undershorts," Patricia said aloud.

"Shhh!" Roy Peel said.

". . . coroner's inquest is scheduled for two tomorrow afternoon at the Los Angeles County Courthouse," the woman on television said. "Expected to be subpoenaed are two young lawyers from Whittington's firm who were allegedly with him at the time of his death. They are Dominic Fresina of Studio City and Patricia Ryan of Torrance. Whittington's butler, Pablo Arguente, told "Action News" last night that Miss Ryan, a junior bond specialist with the Whittington law firm, had been a regular visitor at the Bel Air mansion for more than a year . . ." As the woman spoke, the image of Patricia's law school graduation picture flashed on the screen behind her.

"Oh, shit," Patricia said.

The woman said, "In other news . . ."

Roy Peel, dressed in a suit and ready for work, turned to Patricia and shrugged good-naturedly. "Well, you're a celebrity now."

Patricia was aghast. "I can't believe this. He had a heart attack and died. Why are they making such a sideshow out of it?"

Roy stood up and picked up his briefcase. "That's the way Dr. Yashimoto likes it. Any time he can get his mug on TV, he pulls out all the stops."

"Screw him," Patricia said angrily.

The phone rang in the kitchen and Susan got it. "It's for you," she told Patricia. It was Dom.

"I'm home," he said. "I just got served with a subpoena to appear at a coroner's inquest tomorrow. I imagine you're on the list, too."

She shook her head. She was exhausted. She had slept hardly a wink all night. "Isn't there any way out of this? We're going to be all over television and the papers."

"Doesn't look like it," Dom told her. "I just got off the phone with Gill. He said, basically, that we're on our own."

"I'm on my own, you mean. You weren't even there when it happened, and that's what you're going to have to tell them."

"Not necessarily. Maybe we can work out a story that both of us were there."

She shook her head, even though she knew he couldn't see the gesture. "Dom, it won't work. Look at how we screwed it up with that cop. They'll catch us if we lie any more, and it'll just look worse. I'm just going to have to tell the truth at the inquest."

"That's going to be pretty embarrassing."

"I'd rather get embarrassed than get nailed for perjury," she said. "They can't take away my license because I'm an adulteress, but they can if I lie under oath."

He laughed. "I can't remember that last time I heard that word— adulteress."

"It doesn't come up in conversation much these days, does it? I'm just glad they don't stone us anymore."

"No," Dom said. "They just plaster your picture all over the front page. That's the modern day equivalent. Gill wants us to stay away from the office until further notice—at full pay, of course."

"Did he say anything about legal representation at the inquest?"

"The firm doesn't seem to be volunteering, no."

"I suppose we ought to hire somebody—a criminal guy, maybe."

"That'll just make you look bad," Dom said. "You go out and hire some high-powered criminal guy, and the papers will make it look as though you need him because you did something illegal. You're a lawyer.

You know legal procedure and what your rights are. All Yashimoto wants is a big show. Then he'll proclaim to the cameras that Charlie bought the ranch while he was flagrante delicto, as they used to say."

"With me."

"Well," Dom Fresina said, "that's show biz."

* * * *

Patricia hadn't been in a courtroom since her second year of law school, when she'd taken a course in trial procedure. That courtroom had been in an ancient building in lower Manhattan. This one was sleekly modern and jammed, as Dom had predicted, with reporters. Dr. Daniel Yashimoto, the coroner, was a trim, smallish man who was balding and struggling to hide it by combing his hair sideways over his naked skull. He occupied the high seat behind the bench. He clearly enjoyed all the fuss.

Patricia had dressed for this session in a quiet gray suit. She had pulled her hair back severely and pinned it into a bun. She had left her contact lenses home and wore instead a pair of black-rimmed glasses. The last thing she wanted was to look alluring. She was also having second thoughts about having given in to Dom on refusing to hire a lawyer. The questioning was being handled by Yashimoto's assistant, a chubby, dark-haired young man in a glen plaid suit. His name was Levitt. His job allegedly was to solicit from each witness simple facts, but he was coming on very much like a prosecutor. He whipped through the testimony from the assistant medical examiner who had performed the autopsy on Whittington and determined that death had been caused by a myocardial infarction. Then he called the obnoxious detective who had arrived with the ambulance. The detective described the scene in detail, especially the finding of Whittington's undershorts.

Levitt put Dom on the stand and seemed distinctly disappointed when Dom so readily admitted that he hadn't been present when the senator died. "You lied to the police then, Mr. Fresina. Is that correct?"

"That's correct," Dom said evenly.

"Why did you do that?"

"I was interested in preserving reputations."

"Oh," Levitt said in mock surprise. "And whose reputation, precisely, were you interested in preserving?"

Dom's eyes narrowed. "I think that's obvious."

"Just answer the question, please," Levitt said.

"You must answer the question," Yashimoto said from the bench.

"I was interested in preserving the senator's reputation," Dom said, "and Miss Ryan's."

Levitt nodded in satisfaction. "And the reputation of your law firm, of course."

"Yes," Dom said, "that, too."

That was the end of it. Dom was told to step down. When that happened, Patricia knew that the hard questions had been reserved for her. She took a deep breath when she was called to the stand. She felt her heart thump wildly as she was seated in the witness box.

Levitt got right to the point. "What was the senator doing when he collapsed, Miss Ryan."

Patricia was startled. She had expected him to lead off with questions that established her identity, whether she had seen Whittington that day and so forth—questions designed to lay a foundation for tougher questions.

"Did you hear the question?" Levitt demanded.

"Yes. He was sitting on the sofa in his study."

"How was he dressed when he collapsed?"

"Did I say he collapsed?" Patricia asked innocently. If he was going to ignore procedure and push her around, then maybe it would do him good to be reminded that she'd gone to law school, too.

"Just answer the question please," Yashimoto said from the bench.

"He was nude," Patricia said quietly. It was foolish. She had no way to fight back. She would just have to take this.

"He was nude, did you say?" Levitt asked, although he had clearly heard her response.

"That's right."

"I see. And how were you dressed at the time?"

Bastard, she thought. "I was dressed similarly."

"You were nude?"

"If he was nude and I was dressed similarly, then one could say that I was nude, right?"

Levitt was not all intimidated by her anger. There was no doubt in Patricia's mind that this charade was not designed to determine whether the circumstances surrounding Charlie Whittington's death had contributed to that death. The pathologist had already testified that the man had died of a heart attack and that he had found nothing unusual. The clear purpose of the hearing was to enable the media to titillate their readers, listeners and viewers. And—not coincidentally—to get Yashimoto's name and face on television and into print. Levitt not only understood his role, he relished it.

"So," he said, "you and the senator were nude together."

Patricia sighed. "We were."

"Was anyone else present at the time?"

"It wasn't that kind of party," Patricia said.

"Just answer the question, please," Yashimoto said from the bench.

"No one else was present."

"Why were you and the senator undressed together?" Levitt demanded.

Here it was. She answered it as calmly as she could manage. "We'd been making love on the sofa when he became ill."

"You'd been making love?" Levitt said. "Do you mean you were engaging in sexual relations?"

"I already answered that," Patricia told him.

"And the senator collapsed?"

"Yes."

"Did you call for medical help?"

"Medical help was called."

"Immediately?"

"No, not immediately."

"And why not, Miss Ryan?"

Prove this is a lie, she thought. Then she said, "I administered CPR and I tried to revive him. When I realized he was dead, I called the firm for help. Mr. Fresina came over, and then we called for medical assistance."

"How long did all this take?"

"Maybe a half hour."

"And the senator was unconscious all this time?"

"The senator was dead."

"Oh?" Levitt said. "And how did you determine that? Were you able to administer an EEG to check brain wave activity? Did you administer an EKG to check his heart rhythms? What medical school did you attend, Miss Ryan?"

Now they were getting to her. Patricia had determined that she wouldn't give them the satisfaction of seeing her break down, but it was getting progressively tougher. When she spoke, her voice was on the verge of breaking.

"He . . . he had no pulse. He wasn't breathing. He had no color. I knew he was dead. Anybody would know he was dead."

"And what if he wasn't dead at the time, Miss Ryan? What if you had called for help immediately, and what if your speedy phone call had resulted in Sen. Charles Whittington being revived by experts and being alive today?"

That got her. Patricia burst into tears. "Charlie was dead," she choked out. "I did the very best I could."

"You did the best you could to save your reputation. Isn't that what you're saying? Isn't that what motivated you?"

"I don't have to answer that," Patricia shouted at him.

Levitt almost smiled then. When he responded, his voice was low and calm and sounded extremely self-satisfied. "Yes, you do have to answer it, Miss Ryan. But I won't insist on it. The answer seems obvious. I have no further questions."

It was over then. Yashimoto didn't even bother to retire to consider his verdict. He simply ruled, predictably, that Sen. Charles Whittington had died of natural causes, and no compelling evidence had been presented that his death had been preventable. When Yashimoto banged down his gavel, Patricia was up and heading for the door with Dom and Susan behind her.

Television cameras had not been allowed inside the courtroom, but they were in abundance in the hall. Patricia was blinded by the glare of harsh lights. As the reporters crowded around her asking questions about the nature of her relationship with Whittington, she felt a strong hand take her by the arm. Dom was dragging her down the hallway. Roy Peel was next to him, and he had his big arm wrapped around Susan. The four of them walked down the hall a few hundred feet, then Dom made a sharp right turn, opened a door and shoved Patricia into a small room with a worn sofa, a table and chairs and a battered black-and-white TV set. Roy and Susan came in behind them. Dom closed the door and leaned on it. "I made arrangements for us to hide here for an hour or so," he said. "By that time, they'll get tired and go away."

"How?" Patricia asked him.

"I gave twenty bucks to a court attendant. This is a lounge for those guys."

Susan had been badly jostled by the mob. She straightened her hair in a mirror along the far wall. "How are you doing, Patricia? You did a great job. That son-of-a-bitch."

Patricia shook her head. "It was worse than I'd expected. Poor Charlie. He'd be mortified."

"I wouldn't bet on it," Dom said. "I think he'd love the idea of going out with such a virile image. Christ, I'll bet they couldn't even get the coffin closed."

Patricia glared at him. "That's a rotten thing to say."

He shook his head. "I'm never going to feel guilty about anything I ever say about Sen. Charles Whittington—not after this."

Patricia was livid. "Then why don't you just get the hell out and leave me alone."

Dom's eyes flashed. "You know what? That's a great idea."

Then he turned, opened the door and stomped out, slamming it behind him. Patricia was stunned. She hadn't meant it.

She turned, and Roy Peel's face wore a disapproving expression. That troubled her, too, because she realized that she valued Roy Peel's approval. "It's been tough on him too, Patricia," Roy said gently. "He's nuts about you."

Patricia broke down. She felt alone and sullied and hopeless. She burst into tears, and Susan came over to her. Susan glared at Roy. "She has her own problems right now."

Patricia struggled for control. She held up her hand to prevent a fight between Roy and Susan.

"I'll be all right," Patricia said. "Just give me a minute."

"We have to get you home," Susan said.

Patricia laughed a brittle laugh through her sobs. "Home? Where's that? Where can I go now—after this? The house I grew up in is gone. Daddy's dead. Mother's in that nursing home. Jim is living through a divorce. I can't stay here. Where can I go?"

Susan put an arm around her cousin's shoulder. "I know a place," she said.

* * * *

Henderson Gill called her the day after Charlie Whittington's funeral, which Patricia had possessed the grace to miss, to inform her that returning to the firm was simply out of the question. "I hope you understand," Gill had told her over the phone. "Charlie's widow is deeply wounded by all this. I've known Eleanor Whittington nearly forty years. Between that and all the damned publicity, there's no way I could have you back in this office. Your separation pay will be a year's salary plus an estimate of what your bonus would have been. We'll keep your health benefits alive for six months. I'm sorry, Patricia."

Patricia had merely sighed into the phone. "I understand. The firm can't have the scarlet woman around, can it?"

"Please," Gill told her. "This is very difficult for me. You're a fine attorney. I'm sure you'll have other offers."

"I have no doubt of that," Patricia told him. "I had a phone call this morning from *Hustler* magazine. I have no idea how they found me here in Newport Beach. They want me to do a nude photo spread for them. They offered me twenty thousand dollars, Mr. Gill. Do you think I should do it? They seemed very enthusiastic."

Gill coughed nervously into the phone. "That's not quite what I had in mind."

"Neither did I," Patricia said. "What I had in mind was practicing bond law. Just deposit my check in my payroll account, Mr. Gill. And thanks for everything."

The trip across the country marked the first time since childhood that she had not been a slave to a schedule. She could go where she pleased and at the rate she pleased. She was carrying several thousand dollars in cash. She had her gold American Express card and her Diners Club card. She had a fat bank account in Los Angeles and enough identification to cash a check in any good-sized city in the country. She had a class-A car and a cat carrier for Zorro. For the first time in her life she was embarking on a tour of that part of America that people on the coasts never see from ground level. She'd been only a day's drive from the ocean during her childhood and only a few minutes from it in New York and California. She was surprised by the vastness of the North American continent as she crossed it. She had no fear of solitude. At this point she welcomed it.

From Los Angeles she headed first to Las Vegas. On the advice of Susan and Roy, she stayed at the MGM Grand. She lost four hundred dollars in the slot machines and saw every show in town. She also fought off every conceivable variety of lounge lizard, and she was delighted that her notoriety had been relatively short-lived. If anyone recognized her, no one indicated it. Then it was northeast to Salt Lake City, where she studied the vast expanse of the Great Salt Lake and the strange monument the Mormons had erected to the seagull. She drove through the grandeur of the Rockies, along roads that made the stretch of California's Highway 1 to which Dom had treated her seem like child's play. She visited the Black Hills of South Dakota and the scene of Custer's Last Stand. She spent two days in Minneapolis, watched a Twins game and drove for twenty straight hours to Chicago. There she spent a luxurious eight days in the Palmer House, treating herself to room service dinners and every movie in town. She saw *Star Wars* twice. From there she cut south to Indianapolis and Louisville, which she found unimpressive, then east to Virginia and from there into Washington. There she spent five days in the Hay-Adams, seeing all the capital had to offer. From Washington it was a straight shot of only seven hours up through Maryland and Pennsylvania. Jim had called her in Newport Beach one of those first nights, when he had caught her image on network television in Philadelphia. When she had told him her plans he had urged her to stop and visit him when she passed by. She had promised to do so, but this close to her goal she decided to plow on. She made her way to the rounded, green-encrusted hills surrounding the Boyd River valley.

She pulled off the highway and checked into the Holiday Inn along the Boyd River. The next day she walked all around Boydstown. She walked from downtown out to the house in which she had been raised. She found that it had been repainted. The house that had been barn red in her childhood was yellow now, with green shutters. Children's toys littered the front yard. She walked back downtown, ate lunch alone in the hotel dining room while leafing through the *Boydstown Bulletin*, and then checked out.

She drove to the cemetery on the city's south side to visit her father's grave. She talked for nearly an hour to Jack Ryan, who lay silently beneath the gravestone. It bore his name and the dates of his birth and death, and next to that was Helen's name. Only her birth date was enscribed there; Patricia knew that the blank space would be filled in soon enough. Nearby, no more than four rows away, lay Jack's parents. And not many rows of headstones away from that were the graves of her great grand-parents. Here, where rested the bones of her antecedents, was home in a very real sense.

Slightly more than an hour later she pulled the Toyota into the driveway of the big house at Brennan's Point. Katherine, who looked startlingly old, tiny and frail to Patricia, sat on the porch in her wheelchair as if she had been waiting. Patricia opened the car door. Zorro leaped out, free after a journey across the continent. As Katherine struggled to rise, Patricia came up the steps. She dropped to her knees in front of her grandmother's wheelchair and put her head into Katherine's lap. Then, her long journey behind her and her travail a continent away, she wept.

"There, there," Katherine Brennan told her, stroking her granddaughter's hair with a gnarled hand. "You're home now."

Patricia clutched at her grandmother. She knelt on the wooden porch, her head in Katherine's lap, purging her soul of pain and hatred and anger.

Chapter 24

Katherine and Kevin looked older—markedly older, Patricia noticed. The people they had hired to help them were disturbingly unfamiliar in this most familiar of places.

Maggie was the cook and maid. She was timid and efficient, and she seemed to live in terror of Kevin, although he never spoke a harsh word to her. Moreover, Maggie's manner was in direct contrast to that of Linda Nelson, the outgoing live-in nurse who had been hired to care for Katherine. Linda was a busty woman in her midforties. She was capable and exceedingly glad to be caring for an old woman who had her wits about her instead of emptying bedpans at the Lake County Nursing Home.

On Patricia's first night back at Brennan's Point, she insisted that Maggie leave early. Patricia would clean up, she promised. Maggie was surprised and pleased, and she drove her old Plymouth down the driveway only minutes after serving the roast.

At dinner Katherine said, "I can't get over how much you look like Helen as you get older."

Patricia was pleased. "Don't I wish I could look like she did. She was so beautiful."

Kevin, sitting behind a glass of Brennan white table wine, said, "Mother's right. Now that I look at you, you do look like Helen. It's strange I never noticed that when you were younger. It's still hard for me to think of you as being the age you are now. You were always the baby of the bunch. I always think of you as a little girl, Patricia."

"So do I," Patricia said. "That's what gets you in trouble. You keep thinking that you're still a kid and that somebody is going to bail you out if you get into trouble. Only when trouble comes there's nobody there. Actually, that's not true. Susan was there. I suppose she told you all about it."

Patricia knew that they had probably seen some of it on the network news, as Jim had, but Katherine only smiled and said, "She told us you

489

needed a place to stay for a while. I said we want to have you here as long as you want to stay. We haven't seen enough of you since you went away to college. The sleeping arrangements are a little strange, though. I sleep in Liam's old study because I can't make it up the stairs any more. Kevin has moved into the master bedroom, and Linda has Susan's old room. Kevin is using his old room as an upstairs study. Will's room is vacant, of course, but we've been using it for storage. It'll take a few days to get it cleared out. Meanwhile, I did have Maggie go down and sweep out the shack so you'll have a place to stay until we can get you up here in the big house."

"The shack is fine, Grandma. Jimmy and I used to love it when we could sleep overnight there with Will and Susan when we were kids. I wouldn't mind staying there all the time I'm here."

"Whatever you like," Kevin said. "I just hope it doesn't rain too hard until I can get somebody out here to patch that roof. How old is that building, Mother?"

"Well," Katherine said, "let's see . . . It's the original building on the property. I'd say it goes back a hundred and fifty years, anyway. I have special memories of that little house. You'll have a grand view of the lake from there."

"We'll get the place fixed up for you," Kevin said, "and it's yours for as long as you want to stay with us. Frankly, I hope you stay here forever. It's just nice to have you back home again."

Katherine said, "You ought to give Jimmy a call. He's been worried sick about you ever since you left Los Angeles. We all knew you were driving across the country, but nobody knew exactly where you were at any particular moment."

"I know. I just took the opportunity to see some of the country. I needed the time to be alone after all that flap in LA. I ought to call Susan, too."

"I already took care of that," Kevin said, "while you were talking to Mother. She said she'll be in touch with you."

"She was a godsend," Patricia said. "She and Roy, too. He's a really nice man."

"I like him," Kevin said. "He seems like a fine guy. He and Susan and Roy's kids spent a weekend with us. They're real fireballs, those two kids. I was afraid they were going to sink the Boston Whaler. You ought to take it out, Patricia. The damn thing goes like a rocket."

"Okay, I will. I guess I ought to give Jim a call now and let him know I've landed safely."

"You should do that," Katherine said from her wheelchair. "You just give me a kiss goodnight, now."

Patricia phoned Jim from Kevin's second-floor study.

"How are you holding up?" he asked her.

"Now that I'm here I feel like the weight of the world is off my shoulders. How's Mom?"

"No change."

"Now that I'm back east, I ought to drop down and see her."

"Don't worry about that. She won't know you. You just worry about taking it easy. I think I'm going to drive up to Brennan's Point this weekend."

"Jim, that's a long haul."

"I have Eamon this weekend, and he's old enough now to have some fun at the lake. Besides, I just picked up a new car I want to try out."

"What did you get?"

"A Porsche 924. It was overpriced, but it goes like a bat out of hell."

"Did you trade the BMW?"

"No. I gave it to Marci. You remember that old Plymouth Duster she was driving? It finally quit at a hundred and ninety thousand miles. I didn't think it would go fifty, but I went through two BMWs while that piece of junk just kept rolling. It went finally, though. Even all the I Love Jesus bumper stickers she plastered all over it couldn't save it."

"How is Marci? How's her father?"

Jim Ryan sighed into the phone. "Marci's Marci. She and Jesus go shopping together every Saturday. Sam could handle everything but the Jesus bit. He's given me a forty-nine percent interest in Roth and Company, and he did the same thing for Marci. He kept two per cent for himself so he can break a tie between us on any major decisions."

"Who gets the two percent when he dies?"

"Me. He doesn't trust her and Jesus to make the right decisions if he gives her control. Tell Kevin and Grandma that I'll be up late Friday night. Eamon will just love to see his aunt Patricia again."

After the phone conversation Patricia went back downstairs. Kevin was in his living room chair, watching television and smoking one of his cigars. "Jim's coming up this weekend," Patricia told him.

"Good," Kevin said. He killed the TV set with his remote control. "How are you, Patricia? How are you feeling after all this?"

She sat on the sofa. "Sort of in shock, still. It's wearing off. Just being here does that for me."

"You'd be surprised what you can get through. There's a limit, but you're young yet."

"How's Grandma doing? She doesn't look good."

He shrugged. "Well, she's pushing ninety, but she still has all her marbles, as you can see. She can get up out of that wheelchair, but not easily. And with her blood pressure problems and that stroke she had a couple of years ago Billy doesn't want her doing any more than she has to do physically. Maggie is a good sort, and she lets Mother sit in her wheelchair in the kitchen and order her around, but Mother misses Annette. That was real hard on her."

"Do you hear from Henri and Annette?"

"Annette and Mother exchange letters twice a week, but it's not quite the same as having her around. They're living in that little village in Bordeaux where they were both born, but I can't tell you how well they're doing. The last time I heard from Henri was when he sent me a nasty little note with a check in it asking me to send his furniture to them. They shouldn't have any financial problems. Henri has his pension, and he sold every share of his Brennan stock when it was high, right after the merger."

"I've told you how I am," Patricia said. "How are you?"

"Getting by," he told her. "I'm catching up on a lot of reading these days—that and TV. I've become the world's greatest living expert on the Flintstones now that I don't have a job to go to any more."

Patricia shook her head. "Isn't there anything you can do to get back control of the winery?"

Kevin drew on his cigar. "Not a thing. I've explored it from every legal angle. I just lost control of the company. It happens all the time. That doesn't bother me nearly as much as what they're doing to the wine. Pop must be spinning in his grave up there on the hill."

"What are they doing?"

She saw Kevin's eyes flash. "They're turning out swill. All the wine we produced here was always from our own grapes or from grapes we bought from contract growers we'd known and done business with for years. We made one hundred percent New York State wine from varietals and hybrids. But these bastards from Consolidated are bringing in California wine by railroad tank car to mix with the juice from grapes grown in this region. You can produce a wine with up to twenty-five percent of the juice produced somewhere else and call it New York State wine. The consumer never knows that you're diluting the native grapes with inferior and distressed wines from California or somewhere else. They're putting the Brennan and Weidener labels on that crap. They're destroying the family names among people who know and care about wine."

Patricia sat up. "Is the California wine they're bringing in that much worse than what's grown around here?"

"What they're bringing in is rotgut," Kevin told her. "They're doing it to lower costs. The other thing is this: there are no federal inspections of tank cars at either end, so the tank car that carries wine today could have carried fuel oil yesterday or insecticide and nobody would be the wiser. That's what they're putting into bottles with Brennan and Weidener labels."

"But couldn't people taste fuel oil?" Patricia asked him.

"Not necessarily. They can add corn syrup or concentrates. There are a lot of things you can do in the manufacturing process that can alter the taste of foreign bodies in wine. Only somebody who knows wine can tell the difference. Most people could be drinking polluted wine and they wouldn't know the difference. Aside from which, I know that they're adding crap to the wine right here. They're adding cufex and casein. They're adding fumaric acid, gum arabic, sodium carbonate. They're adding yellow dye to the whites. It's a goddamn disgrace."

"That's terrible," Patricia said.

"It's criminal," Kevin said. "On top of that, they're producing what they like to call 'American' wines. That means—under the backward laws of this state—that the wine can be made up of grapes from anywhere in the country. People who know wines have bought our wines for years and have been happy to pay premium prices. Now that quality customer is gone."

"How do they stay in business doing what they're doing?"

Kevin stubbed out his cigar. "They've laid off a lot of people who worked for us for years, and they've cut production costs that way. They've lowered prices since they can afford to now, and they're reaching a new customer, the casual wine drinker. From a marketing standpoint they're absolutely right, but what they're turning out under the family names is just plain shit. I'm sorry, but there's no other word to describe it. Haven't you seen the new Brennan light wines?"

She shook her head.

"Well," Kevin told her, "They're out there on the shelves. What they do is they turn out a wine with fewer calories by diluting the stuff with water and using unripe grapes. The stuff is a disgrace. Diet wine, for Christ's sake. Do you know that under federal law you can add up to almost fifty-four percent water to wine? People are paying for a bottle of wine at about seventy percent of what our real wine used to go for, and they're getting fifty percent water. Of course the company is more profitable. The fact that adding water means adding chlorine and flourides from public water supplies is just fine with these bastards. It makes me sick just to think about it."

"And there's nothing you can do about it?"

"Not a thing," he told her. "I have my stock, but it's nowhere near enough to get control back. I not only have to sit by and watch this happen, I have to collect my dividend checks, too. I actually profit from the crimes they're committing. And they are crimes, if not in a legal sense, in a moral one. I've never had such a sense of powerlessness, not even when I was in the hospital after the war and was learning how to walk again."

Patricia was silent for a long moment. Kevin's fists were clenched, and his jaw was tight. Then he summoned forth his ferocious sense of self-control and was himself again. "Hey," he said, "I'm the one who's supposed to be feeling sorry for you. I'm curious about what really happened out there. You don't have to tell me if it's too much for you or if you think it's none of my business."

"I don't mind talking about it," Patricia said. "Simply put, I just had an affair with a much older man. He was handsome, charming and captivating. He'd seen more of the world than I'll ever see and from a perspective I can only imagine. I paid no attention to anything in my life except my work and the affair. And then he just died in my arms one day—figuratively, anyway—and under embarrassing circumstances. I don't know what you saw in the papers or on TV here—"

"Very little. It was mostly a local story out in California. You were on TV from Rochester once, I think."

"Thank God for that. It was a horror show out there. There was no way I could stay after Charlie died, not after that coroner's inquest."

"He was a lot older than you," Kevin noted. "Hell, he was even older than me."

"I didn't think much about that," Patricia told him. "Charlie was a young man inside.

Kevin smiled. "Honey, we all are."

"Then you know what I mean."

"Yes," he nodded. "Most people your age wouldn't understand that."

"I wouldn't have understood it if it hadn't been for Charlie."

"You loved him, then?" Kevin asked her directly.

Patricia thought about the question. "I don't know. We never told each other that, not even once. I don't even know if I believe in romantic love. I think it's just glands, if you want the truth. First it's glands, then it's habit. And it's habit only if you're lucky. My parents were in love at the beginning. Look what happened to them."

Kevin said, "They were always in love, right up until the end of your father's life. That doesn't mean they should have gotten married, though. They should never have done that."

"What do you mean?"

"Jack stayed with Helen because he couldn't imagine facing life without her, no matter how miserable she made him. After all those years, they had so much life experience in common that separation was unthinkable.

Whatever else happened, they'd be together. I knew Jack pretty well, and that's the way his mind worked. For a man, Patricia, that's love."

She nodded slowly. "I'll buy that—in part, anyway. But what about her? Why did she do what she did?"

Kevin leaned back in his chair and folded his hands atop his head. "If you asked Helen—and if she could tell you—even she couldn't answer that. What I think it was was this: Helen expected Jack to be a rock, like Pop, and he wasn't. That made her scared, and it made her mad. The reason she was angry was that she loved him, and she'd expected him to protect her from every unpleasantness. Both of them always acted as if they had unlimited time to work out their problems. They didn't accept each other's mortality—the fact that it was all going to end when one of them died. They just ran out of time, Patricia. Everybody always figures that they'll always have a second chance. A lot of people never realize that life is in session from the opening bell."

Patricia listened to Kevin, and she sank her teeth into her lower lip as he spoke. Then she said, "If that's love, then I don't want any part of it. I'll just get through this life on my own."

"It's possible," her uncle told her. "I know, because I've pretty much done it. But it's better if you don't try."

"Why is it better if you depend on somebody else?" Patricia demanded. "They'll just let you down, like Mom and Dad let each other down all those years."

Kevin looked over at her. He said slowly, "Let me tell you something. There was a woman . . ."

"Aunt Jane."

He shook his head. "No, not Aunt Jane. Now, that was glands. I know you think of your Aunt Jane as an old bag with liquor on her breath. You didn't see her forty-some years ago."

"Then who was it?"

Kevin was silent for a long moment. Then he said, "I won't give you a name. For one thing, she was married at the time. For another, she still lives here in Lakeside for part of the year. When Will had the accident—and when little Liam died—she got me through it. She doesn't think she did, but without her I would have lost my mind. I should have told her then how much having her meant to me, but I didn't want to be in love with her. I was afraid of having one more thing to lose."

Kevin turned to his niece. Patricia was almost hypnotized by his voice. He said, "That's what love is for—to get you through living. And when you don't have it, you're not really alive. Sometimes I think that when it's taken away from you, it's all according to the big plan. A man gets so he likes to do certain things, and he gets close to certain people. Then the things he likes to do are taken away from him, and the people he's close to go away. They either die or they just go away, and then you're by yourself. I think that's what nature—or God, if there is one—does to prepare you for dying. When things and people are taken away from you one by one, you don't really mind when it comes time for you to die. You're alive only when you have somebody to cling to. You see, Patricia, you don't really know yet—you're too young—all the heartaches you're going to be called upon to endure. Don't write off love, as you seem to be doing. Love makes life possible, bearable. Do you understand what I'm saying?"

She studied his face as he spoke. Kevin was looking at her but he wasn't seeing her. He was staring into his own thoughts. "I think I do," Patricia Ryan said.

He smiled sheepishly, embarrassed now. "It doesn't matter. If you don't know now, you will at some point. Just cling to every bit of love you can find in life. Treasure it. It gives you a place to hide, and there ain't that much of it around that you can afford to squander it."

Patricia rubbed a hand across her face. She was exhausted. "I'll think about it. I promise."

Kevin put his hand on the cane that rested against his chair. He forced himself to his feet. He yawned. "I'm so tired I'm punchy. That's why I'm preaching."

She smiled at him. "I like the preaching. And the jokes. That's why you've always been my favorite uncle. Philosophy with a punchline."

Kevin chuckled. "No punchlines tonight. I'm going to bed. You can still find your way down to the shack, I hope. Take your cat. He's lounging on the front porch, I see through the window."

"I'll be fine," Patricia told him.

He said, "Of that, I have no doubt. You're Liam Brennan's grand-daughter."

* * * *

Jim did not appear Friday night. It wasn't until the following morning, as Patricia lounged on the sun-washed dock in her favorite two-piece, that a red Porsche pulled up in front of the steps leading to the beach. Eamon Ryan, in T-shirt and shorts, bounded out, down to the point and into Patricia's arms. "Aunt Patricia!" he said, hugging her.

She hugged him back. "How are you, Killer? What's new?"

"New York," Eamon told her. "New Jersey, too."

"You forgot new math."

"What's that?" Eamon asked, distressed. That had never been part of the joke.

Patricia kissed him. "You look great."

"What's new math?" he insisted.

"Confusing," Jim told him, joining them on the dock.

"Can I go swimming, Dad?" Eamon asked.

"Go ahead," Jim told him. "Your suit is in the gym bag in the back seat, on top. You go up to that big house up there and get in your suit and come back. And be careful crossing the road. Look both ways."

Eamon zipped away, running with joyful abandon. Jim watched him go, then he hugged his sister. He pulled off his shirt and collapsed in the sunlight. City life had left him pale.

"I thought you said you'd be in last night," Patricia said to him.

"I ended up working late. I didn't pick up Eamon until almost nine. I thought I could still make it, but by the time I realized I was going to fall asleep and kill us both it was too late to call. I pulled off at a fleabag around Waverly, and we got up at dawn."

Patricia looked up at the Porsche. "Nice car."

"I think I liked the BMW better."

She laughed. "Oh, you're so casual about it." She mimicked him: "I think I like the BMW better."

He smiled. "Cars are my one vice. I don't smoke. I don't drink much. I don't take dope. I don't overeat, and I don't play around. Or, at least, I didn't when it counted for something. I think next time I might go for a Jag."

"How about a 'vette?"

"Bite your tongue," Jim Ryan told his sister. "Now, an Alfa? Maybe."

He looked around at the lake. The summer people were out in force. Teenagers were waterskiing. The vast expanse of the lake was dotted with colorful sails. He gazed at the summer homes going up on either side of the point.

"What's going on here?" he asked. "Cottages this close to the point? Who's doing the building?"

"That's a long story. Kevin will give you the details when you go up to the big house. That's the land the family lost in the takeover."

"This was part of the company holdings? Jesus, I always thought this was all family land."

"Nope," she said. "The new owners just sold it off—at eight hundred bucks a front foot."

Jim frowned. "They're right on top of us."

The houses were several hundred feet away.

"Well," Patricia said, "not quite. We've got a lot of lake frontage, but you can see your neighbors now."

Jim's brow knitted. "Will and I used to pop beer cans with twenty-twos all along the point. This is starting to look like the Jersey shore."

"It's not quite that bad."

"Close enough," Jim Ryan grumbled. "So, how are you? Did *Playboy* call you up to do a spread for them?"

"No, but *Hustler* did when I was in LA."

"Seriously?"

"Seriously. Twenty grand."

"Hold out for *Playboy*. More prestige."

"That's what I figured," she said.

He looked at her. "Well?"

"I'm fine. A few more days of lying here next to the lake and I'll figure the whole thing was just a bad dream."

He stretched. "This is the place for it. I wish to Christ I could live here. This is the only place I ever wanted to be."

"You could always move up here."

He sat up and wrapped his arms around his legs. "No, I couldn't. First, I've got a business to run. Second, I used to have a wife who wouldn't have lived here no matter what, and now I have a son I need to be close to. Maybe when Eamon grows up I could think about it. I guess I ought to be looking for a summer home up here on the lake, now that I think about it. Of course, at eight hundred bucks a front foot I'd have to give up thoughts about the Jag or the Alfa. How are Kevin and Grandma?"

"You'll see for yourself. Grandma looks a hundred years old."

"She is, damn near."

"Poor choice of words," Patricia said. "She looks . . . so frail, I guess. And tiny. Here comes Eamon."

The boy was standing on the far side of the road in his bathing suit. He was carrying several towels.

"Look both ways," Jim called.

Eamon did. When he had crossed and come down to the dock he handed them both towels.

"Uncle Kevin says to give you these. He says he'll see you when you decide to get off your asses and come up to the big house. Can I go in, Dad?"

"Go to it," Jim said.

Eamon went off the end of the dock uttering a blood-curdling shriek.

"Don't go out too far," Jim shouted to him. Then, to Patricia, he said, "How's Kevin doing?"

"He's bitter over losing the winery. He's tired; and a little defeated."

Jim frowned. "That's too bad. You know, you contrast him with Mother, and you can't help but wonder at the forces that shape people. She always had a relatively comfortable life—a husband who loved her, whatever his other failings. She always lived in good neighborhoods. There was always enough to eat, no real hardships. Her two kids may have had their faults, but we've turned out respectably enough."

"Speak for yourself," Patricia said.

"Oh, all this bullshit will pass. You had a guy die on you in bed. Big deal."

"A famous man," she reminded him. "A married man."

"A man," he told her. "It'll pass. My point is, you compare her life with his—and her reaction to it with his—and you see the difference in people. The same environment. The same genes. And look at the difference in them."

"Not quite the same genes," Patricia said. "They had different mothers. Speaking of Mother . . ."

"No change. She lies there with her eyes open half the time and closed the other half. She's down to about a hundred pounds now."

"Oh, God. Do you think she has any idea what's happening?"

"I don't know," he said quietly, his eyes on the little boy swimming near the end of the dock. "I think at first she did. They kept telling me that she didn't, but they were lying, since they couldn't do anything about it. Now, I don't think she knows. I think she lost whatever mind she had after the stroke. If I had to guess, I'd say she's living somewhere in her memory now, that she's blotted out the present. I imagine she went through a lot of self-examination first, though."

When Patricia spoke her voice was choked. "It's like hell. It's worse than hell."

"Purgatory, anyway. She's serving her time right here on earth. I just wish I didn't have to watch it. You know, sometimes when I'm alone in that room with her, I think about just taking a pillow and holding it over her face and smothering her. It would be the greatest kindness I could ever do anybody. I find myself struggling to fight back the urge to do that, sometimes. That's one of the reasons I don't see her so often any more. One of these days I'm afraid I'm going to do it. I don't think I could help myself if I saw her more often."

"It's been a long time now. When do they think it'll end?"

"They don't know," Jim told her. "The total tonnage of what doctors don't know is terrifying. I just hope she gets that pneumonia they promised pretty soon."

Patricia was disturbed by his mood. She said, "Let's talk about some-thing more cheerful. How's business?"

He laughed. "That's your idea of cheerful? Actually, it is pretty cheerful. We've got more business than we can handle. We bought a specialty machine tool shop up in Massachusetts a couple of years ago, and this week I got a call from a guy named Stayments, who's some kind of vice president for Allied Industries. I'm having lunch with him when I get back to Philadelphia on Monday. I think they want to start buying equipment from us. They were big customers of the machine tool company when we bought it, and we had to cut them off to manufacture the capital goods we needed for the microchip end of our business. Now, if we can get them to pay enough for the equipment we need, we'll take a loan and expand the machine tool outfit and we'll clean up. To answer your question succinctly, business is booming."

"How much are you making out of it?"

"You never asked me that before. That's considered bad form, you know."

"Call me nosy," Patricia said. "You're my big brother, the industrial tycoon. How much do you bring home?"

He thought for a moment. "This year I ought to take about ninety-five grand out of the various businesses, once we sort it out. Plus the car. That's owned in the company's name."

"Not bad."

"Well, not terrific, either. We're plowing a lot back in, so my take could be a lot higher—maybe double that—if we were just trying to stay even in the market. I also made the mistake of marrying a woman with marvelous taste in lawyers. I pay Marci two grand a month out of that for child support and another thirty-five grand a year alimony. After taxes that leaves me about forty a year clear. That's okay, but it's not anywhere near what I really make."

"Your take-home was about what I was making gross at the law firm."

"I'm older," he said. "I've been at it longer. Besides, you're only a woman. Hey! Stop hitting me like that, or I'll toss your butt into the lake. I'm only kidding."

"Ha, ha," she said.

"How about you? So what are you going to do here? Are you going to work?"

"I'm not going to go into a courtroom or advise clients. But I think I can get some work. The legislature passed a law not long ago that set up industrial development agencies in every county and any municipality that wants to set one up, and they can all issue bonds. It's a bonanza for a lot of small-town lawyers, and they don't know much about bonds. So I think I'll be able to get a lot of work from other lawyers writing opinions and things like that. But I'm not going to knock myself out for a while. I have a big chunk of cash in the bank, so it's not an immediate problem."

"That must be a nice feeling," Jim told her. "I make a lot of money, but if I miss one monthly check my entire financial house of cards comes tumbling down. You're in much better shape than I expected. I think maybe I underestimated you."

"I'll be okay. I had my doubts until I got here, but I'll be fine. I'm more worried about you, actually—this business with Marci and Mother and all. How are you holding up, Jim?"

"Remember the Hans Conreid character on the old Danny Thomas Show? Uncle Tunoose? That's me. I'm strung like bool."

"Seriously," Patricia said.

"Seriously? Well, it was tough for a while. When I was a kid, I always thought that once I got out of that house and out on my own that I'd have control over my own life, that I'd be able to control my own happiness. That turned out to be true only to a very limited extent. When the thing with Marci disintegrated, I came to realize that. It took a long time to get used to the idea that things can go wrong even when you think you're guarding against them going wrong. Some things are just beyond your control, no matter how hard you try. I'm getting used to that now. I have a friend whose wife is a psychiatrist, and she put me in touch with a guy—a shrink. I've been seeing him for a couple of months now, and I'm starting to realize how much we're all shaped by events we think we've left behind us. Eamon growing up like he is helps me feel better. He makes up for other disappointments. I'll tell you what not having a wife makes me afraid of, though. It makes me afraid of getting old. The idea of being old and alone just scares the hell out of me."

"I wouldn't have thought of anything ever bothering you like that."

He smiled. "Wait until you start to go bald like this. Or, in your case, when you start to get gray hair and your boobs sag. As bad as it can be to be with somebody, it can be worse to be alone. Watching Mother near the end showed me that."

"Do you think you'll get married again?" Patricia asked her brother.

"At some point. I don't know about you, but I think I need somebody with me over the long haul."

"You're just like Dad," she told him.

"Hopefully not—not exactly, anyway. It's interesting, but that's another thing I admire about Kevin. He's been able to go it alone."

Patricia thought back to her conversation with Kevin, and she began to respond that he hadn't always gone it alone and that he didn't seem to like it much when he did. But something stopped her. Certainly, she had not been pledged to secrecy. As she thought back on their talk, however, she decided that it had been a private discussion between the two of them and that Kevin had opened up to her to make a point. So she said only, "I think I can go it alone, too. I've been giving it a lot of thought. No shattered expectations, no disappointments—or, at least, not all that many."

He told her, "For you that could be. Good luck with it. I ought to go up to the house and see everybody. Then I'm going to come down here and go swimming. I haven't been in this lake in a long time. Will you be kind enough to keep an eye on my son and heir for me? He can swim fine, but I don't want him trying to go across the lake."

Patricia stood up. "I'm not only going to watch him, I'm going in with him."

And with that, she executed a smooth dive off the end of the dock into the water next to the splashing Eamon.

Patricia's nephew screamed with delight.

* * * *

Jim left Brennan's Point right after "Sixty Minutes." The three of them watched from the porch as the low-slung Porsche tore down the driveway, sending gravel flying, and disappeared toward Lakeside.

"He's going to get back down to Philadelphia awfully late," Katherine said.

"Well," Patricia told her, "he's well rested now, so he should be able to make the whole trip in one shot. Also, his first appointment isn't until lunch tomorrow, and Eamon doesn't have to be back with his mother until Tuesday."

"If that's the case," Kevin said, "why didn't he stay and leave tomorrow at dawn instead of driving at night?"

"The luncheon appointment," Patricia said. "It's with some big wheel from some big company. My brother is becoming a captain of industry."

Kevin looked out over the growing darkness beginning to enfold the lake. "You know, I think maybe I'm going to take the boat out for a little while and see if there isn't a laker or two prowling around out there."

"Just be careful going down the hill," Katherine warned.

Kevin smiled. Because the walk up and down the hill to the beach had finally grown too much for him, he had purchased a second-hand golf cart from the Iroquois Country Club. Katherine lived in constant fear that he'd turn it over and maim himself further.

"Don't worry, Mother," he assured her, "I'll keep it under fifty-five."

Patricia and Katherine sat on the porch and watched him drive the golf cart down the road to the beach. He went into the boathouse. A few moments later he backed the Boston Whaler out of its stall, flipped on its running lights and was gone for the center of the lake.

"He has a tape player in the boat," Katherine said, "He's listening to big band music out there. I hope the trout like Glenn Miller."

"It's getting close to your bedtime, Grandma," Patricia told her. "Do you want me to go get Linda to help?"

"Oh, a little later, maybe. That Billy Frazier wants me in bed every night early, but doctors don't know everything. If they did, they'd all live to be as old as I am, and not many of them do. Let's just sit here and watch it get dark. Liam and I used to do that in the summer. Listen, and you'll hear the crickets come out. The owls, too. They live in the big trees along the beachline."

"I haven't heard them since I've been here. I wonder if all that construction along the beach scared them away."

"Could be. It would have scared away a lot of the field mice and chipmunks the owls live on, so the birds may have just moved up the hillside."

"That's a shame," Patricia said.

"A lot of things have happened that are a shame," her grandmother told her. "At least they couldn't touch this house and the point and that vineyard up the hill where Liam planted those fancy grapes all those years ago. This year they'll all just rot. Kevin won't sell them to the Brennan Winery, and none of the other wineries on the lake buy enough *vinifera* to make them worth harvesting. Most of the places that make quality wines are estate bottling or dealing with contract growers they've had relationships with for years."

"How many acres are left in your name?"

"Let's see . . . They got the winery building, most of the lakefront, most of the older vineyards—the ones Christian Weidener planted—and the winemaker's house. What we have left is a touch more than two hundred acres, but a good third of that is still taxed as forest. It's not all in my name, either. Kevin, your mother and I each have a third. I guess that with Helen sick like she is, you and Jim actually control her share of it—the vineyard. It's just about the best hundred and thirty acres in the lake country."

"Grandma, isn't there anything you can do?"

Katherine patted Patricia's hand. "You're a lawyer. You ought to know better than anybody how these things work. I talked to Kevin about building a new winery on our own land up on the hill back there, at the top of the vineyards. He said it's just way too much money, even if we sold all our Brennan stock and put everything we had into it. And the truth is, Patricia, Kevin is running out of fight. If Will were alive or if Susan were still here in the lake country, I know he'd never have given up. But he has, and I can't blame him. There's a limit to what one person can endure."

"It must have been very hard on you all these years watching these things happen to him, one by one."

Katherine took a moment before responding. Then she said, "I've lived way too long, seen too much. When little Liam died, I thought to myself, Why did he have to go and why did I have to stay? I've lived so long, and he never had a chance to live at all. Kevin has never been right since that happened. Up until we lost the winery, I was praying that I wouldn't have to go along much longer. Now that it's gone, and I see that Kevin can't fight back, I feel the urge to stay on until I see how this is resolved. I don't want to die knowing that everything Liam built up is crumbling."

"The house is still here," Patricia pointed out. "The point is still here. Those things will always be in the family."

"Will they?" Katherine asked. "I'm an old lady who's lived way past my time. Kevin is almost ready to collect social security. Will is gone, and Susan can't come back here; there are too many memories for her. Jim has a life of his own down in Philadelphia. You're going to have to go off one of these days to live your own life. Who'll be here? Who'll put it all back together?"

"I hadn't thought about it that way."

"It's all I do think about," Katherine said. "I didn't think enough about it until we lost the winery. It's not just that I see the end of my own life coming—I see the end of the life we've all had here, generation after generation."

"Grandma," Patricia said, "you're depressing me."

Katherine smiled. "Sorry. I haven't had anybody to talk to since Annette left. I go on too much."

"Kevin tells me you correspond with her. How are they?"

"Henri has been ill. Annette is a little vague about it, but I showed her letter to Billy. He said it sounds as though he's developing congestive heart failure. It means that your heart doesn't pump efficiently any more, and you get a buildup of fluid in your lungs."

Patricia shook her head sadly. "That's awful. I always loved Henri and Annette so much."

"I always loved Annette. Henri could be harder to love, especially when he started to get old. But he was always good to you kids. Liam always loved Henri, too. He and Annette saw a side of him that the rest of us never got to see, I suppose."

"I always thought you liked Henri."

"I got along with Henri. He was always good to me because I was Liam's wife, but Henri never seemed to have much use for anybody in the world except Liam and Annette. The man gave of himself sparingly."

"Are they ever going to come back—even for a visit?"

Katherine shook her gray head. "Not at their age, and not with him so sick. I miss Annette, but we enjoy writing to each other. That's a lost art these days, you know. Everybody phones."

"I always just phone," Patricia admitted. "That's how Jim and I keep in touch."

"It's not the same. With letters you always have something to look at. I have every letter I've ever received. I take them out every once in a while and go over them. They take me back years when I do that. I wish I'd begun to keep a diary when I came here. You ought to start one, Patricia."

"Maybe I will. I'm not sure I could stick with it, though."

"Well," Katherine said, "I think I'll go to bed. I want to be fresh tomorrow morning when I show you how to fry trout."

"Maybe we'll get lucky and Kevin won't catch anything," Patricia said, wheeling her grandmother into the house.

"Kevin never comes back from the lake empty-handed," Katherine told her.

* * * *

Every nice day Patricia's first act upon awakening was to slip on a robe, go out to the end of the dock, drop the robe and dive nude into the lake. She was confident that none of the new neighbors flanking the point could see her clearly—not that she particularly cared.

Her swim finished, she went back inside the shack and dried her hair. Then she put on cutoffs and an Iroquois Lake T-shirt she had bought at one of the shops in the village and started up to the big house. She went up the steps from the shack to the road and stood at the edge of the pavement to make way for a car that was barreling down the road from Lakeside. It shot past her and stopped dead in the middle of the road, amid a screeching of brakes and rubber.

Dom Fresina, the top down on his red Triumph, jammed the little car into reverse and rolled right in front of where Patricia was standing. "Hey, Lady," he said, "Is this the road to Encino?"

Patricia was astounded. Dom was growing a beard. It was in its Yasir Arafat phase.

"What are you doing here?" she demanded.

He pulled to the roadside, shut off the little car's engine and got out. "I drove straight through from LA, day and night, sleeping in campgrounds when I started falling asleep at the wheel. Right now, I'm embarked on a desperate search for a place to take a leak."

"Dom," she said, annoyed, "how did you find me?"

"Susan gave me directions," he said casually. "Hey, nice tan. You look all mellowed out. Good for you."

Patricia looked at the Spitfire. It was covered with dirt. "I'm surprised this old wreck made it all the way from LA."

"Hey," Dom said with mock indignance, "this is a vintage British sports car in the finest tradition. Unfortunately, it's a little rough on the kidneys at high speeds. I really do have to pee."

"Follow me," she said, and led him down to the shack. Dom disappeared into the bathroom. When he came out the shack was empty. He looked through the front windows and saw Patricia sitting out on the dock, staring out at the azure lake rolling and glittering like a huge gem in the sunlight. He went into the refrigerator, found a half-empty jug of Brennan White Table Wine, dug out two glasses and walked out to join her.

"Pretty spot," he said, pouring each of them a glass.

"This is my ancestral family home, as they say," she said. "My grandmother and my uncle live up in that house up the hill."

Dom nodded appreciately. "Tara with beachfront. Not bad."

"So?" Patricia demanded.

"So? So what?"

"You are really beginning to get me pissed off. What are you doing here?"

He smiled. "I came to see if you're okay. Here, have some wine. It'll loosen you up."

"It's too early," she said. "I haven't even had breakfast."

"I did. I ate greasy eggs and sausage at that diner in town. Man, that's roach country safari, for sure."

She laughed slightly. "For sure. That's the first time I've heard that expression since I left LA."

"This part of the country is culturally deprived." He sipped his wine. "Not bad."

"You came all the way just to see how I was doing?" she asked him.

Dom Fresina shrugged. "I was a little worried about you. I'd never driven cross-country before. This seemed like a good excuse to do it. So, here I am. Thanks for the use of the john. Now, how are you fixed for a place to crash?"

"For how long?"

"We'll play it by ear."

"What about your job?"

"Oh, that," he said. "I told Gill to take his job and shove it, just like in the song. I'm afraid I didn't handle it with all the aplomb I'd planned on. I started out dignified and ended up screaming so much that I began to foam at the mouth—literally. By the time I got it all out, I looked like I had rabies. It scared the hell out of Gill."

"You quit?" she asked. "Just like that?"

"I ought to get an Oscar for that resignation," he told her. "Your good friend Alice was in the next office, and I'm pretty sure she just about wet her pants. So, I figured I'd hop in the car, drive three thousand miles and spend a little time with you—separate bedrooms, of course."

She frowned. "Unfortunately, there's only one bedroom in the shack. You'll have to sleep on the couch."

"No sweat," he said, smiling.

Patricia shook her head. "You're too much, Dom. You'll never get a decent reference out of the firm if you really did what you say you did."

"It was fun, though. Jesus, I loved it."

"What are you going to do with the rest of your life now that you've blown your legal career?"

"Live it. I admit that the details are still a little fuzzy now, but I'll work it out. How about you? Have you figured anything out?"

"I've figured out that I never want to be more than a day's drive away from this place. That's about it."

His expression turned serious. "How are you, Patricia?"

She kicked at the top of the waves with her bare feet. "You want the truth? I feel better than I can ever remember feeling. I think it has something to do with being here, where all the good memories of my childhood were born. I can sit here and look out over the lake and nothing has changed. I do that for hours every day—just look at the lake and watch the water move, and the clouds."

Dom looked around. "It's a nice lake. I went by Lake Tahoe on the way east. That's gorgeous, too, but it's different. I saw all the vineyards growing up and down the hillside coming in here this morning. This is a lot greener than Napa—and hillier."

"It's colder, too. This is about as hot as it ever gets around here.

They don't even need air conditioning up in the big house. You have to come up and meet my grandmother and my uncle."

They walked back to the shack. Patricia put the wine in the refrigerator, and they started up the hill together.

"You don't look right here," she said to him. "You're supposed to be in Los Angeles. There you looked okay."

"I didn't feel okay there. I'm a farm boy. Who lives in that little house over there?"

"That's the winemaker's cottage. It used to be part of the family property, but now it belongs to the company that took over the winery."

"Your family sold the winery?" he asked in surprise.

"It's a long story," Patricia said as they reached the steps. "Ask my uncle Kevin. It's his favorite topic."

Linda Nelson, the nurse, had the day off, but Patricia and Dom found Kevin, Katherine and Maggie, the timid cook, in the kitchen. Patricia made the introductions.

"You drove all the way from Los Angeles?" Kevin asked.

Dom nodded. "Drove every inch. Saw everything I wanted to see, from Yellowstone to Niagara Falls. I didn't see any place in the country as pretty as this, though."

"That's because there isn't any place as pretty as this," Katherine assured him. "I never saw Yellowstone National Park, though. I always wanted to."

"Well, Mrs. Brennan," Dom Fresina smiled, "why don't we just go out and pile in my Triumph, and we'll go together."

Katherine beamed. "I might just hold you to that," she warned.

"You think she's kidding," Kevin told Dom. "She's not. Give Mother half a chance and she'll turn into Auntie Mame."

"That's better than being Tugboat Annie," Katherine said. "Your father said once that I reminded him of a landlocked version of Tugboat Annie. He was trying to make a joke."

"Making jokes was never Pop's strong suit," Kevin said. "He could make wine, but not jokes."

Dom said, "Patricia tells me you sold your winery."

Kevin frowned. "Not quite. We lost control of it in a stock deal."

Kevin explained the history of the winery and how it had been lost as Dom drank three cups of coffee. Kevin omitted details of Helen's drinking problems, contenting himself to say that she had merely sold her stock without realizing the consequences. Katherine and Patricia, who knew the story so well, held their own conversation at their side of the table, and Maggie involved herself not at all. Toward the end of his story,

Kevin complained bitterly again that the new owners were ruining the wine and his family's name in the trade.

Dom said, "Well, that's too bad. What kind of things are they doing that bother you?"

"It gets pretty technical," Kevin said.

Dom smiled. "Try me."

"Do you know what the hydrogen-ion exchange process is?"

Dom said, "It's a method of eliminating potassium bitarate sediment from wine. You use sulfuric acid or hydrochloric acid as a regenerator."

Kevin was impressed, and so were Katherine and Patricia. Their conversation came to a halt as they decided to listen.

"Where'd you learn about that?" Kevin asked Dom.

"I grew up in the wine business in California."

"Then you know the problems with the process."

"I know it can act like a water softener on wine—strip it of minerals."

"That's right," Kevin said, "especially natural potassium and vitamin B. They're using the hydrogen exchange process, and it's affecting the taste of the wine. They're also using the cation exchange process."

"What's that?" Patricia asked.

Dom looked at her. "You don't know? I thought you grew up in the wine business, too."

Patricia frowned slightly. "Not like you did, apparently."

Kevin smiled. "Tell her, Dom."

"That's where you use sodium chloride as a regenerator. That affects the taste in a big way. It's adding salt. For some people, it's a health problem."

"When we ran the winery," Kevin said, "we never used any of that stuff. We'd chill the wine for a few months at about twenty-eight degrees. It worked damn near as well, and it didn't screw up the wine. That takes too much time for these people. Everything they do is designed solely to cut costs."

"What else are they doing?" Dom asked.

"They're filtering champagne through asbestos, which we'd never do. We used to filter all the wines and champagnes through natural cellulose filter sheets. It was more expensive—"

"—About twice as expensive—" Dom said.

"But we weren't putting crap into the wine," Kevin pointed out.

Patricia's eyes were beginning to glaze over with all this. So, too, she could see, were Katherine's. "Look," she said, standing, "you two seem to have found a ready audience for each other. I'm going to wheel Grandma down to the dock for a while. I don't understand anything you guys are saying, anyway."

Dom told Kevin, "Patricia's conversation is generally limited to municipal bonds and the Rolling Stones."

"What's a rolling stone?" Katherine asked.

Patricia sighed and grabbed the handles on Katherine's wheelchair. "Come on, Grandma. I'll explain it to you."

Kevin said, "See if you can explain to me some day what a municipal bond is."

Patricia told Dom, "He's on the school board, so I think he might have some idea of what a municipal bond is."

As Patricia rolled her grandmother down the driveway, Katherine said, "He's a nice boy. I hope he doesn't mind Kevin bending his ear like that."

"It'll be a contest as to whose ear gets bent further. You'll find that Dom Fresina is an expert in all matters—even those he knows nothing about."

"Then he and my son ought to get along just splendidly."

* * * *

At Brennan's Point time had a tendency to slip by almost unnoticed. Patricia had arrived in June. Dom had followed a few weeks later. Nearly a month went by before Patricia realized that Dom was becoming a fixture around the place. He was fitting in so well it made her nervous. He and Kevin had hit it off tremendously. Kevin found an audience for all his old jokes, and Dom possessed a seemingly endless supply of the truly tasteless cornball gags Kevin most admired.

The two men fished together daily. Kevin dragged Dom into the Elks Club to meet all his drinking buddies. Billy Frazier, in semiretirement now, liked Dom fully as much as Kevin did. In fact, Billy and Dom managed to bring down an out-of-season deer high on the hillside during Dom's second week at the lake, and the two of them had cheerfully butchered it in the barn in blatant violation of state hunting laws. Patricia wrote the whole thing off as a male bonding ritual, but the she had to admit that the venison was good.

Dom continued to sleep on the sofa in the shack. He and Patricia spent a fair amount of time together, but she had made it clear that she would welcome no romantic advances, and he made none. She continued, however, to rise every nice morning to go to the dock and plunge naked into the lake. She suspected he watched her routine regularly from the shack. They had never shared the same roof before for more than a night, and although she had no immediate interest in sex with Dom or anyone else, she perversely enjoyed being the object of his voyeurism. There was something distinctly pleasurable in making Dom Fresina squirm. So she continued to drop her robe on the dock every morning, stretch her smooth body just a trifle longer than necessary, and plunge into the water, laughing to herself.

She also found herself annoyed after a while when he abandoned her to go out in the Boston Whaler with Billy and Kevin. One day in August she insisted on going along. The four of them found themselves drifting in the dusk with their lines down deep beneath the boat. Billy managed to bring in one six-pounder. He put it in the live well and sat back in his chair, drinking a beer.

"You're never going to catch another laker unless you put your line back in the water, Billy," Patricia told him.

"You fish," Billy Frazier said. "I'm just going to relax."

"What happened to all that energy you used to have?" Patricia demanded.

"Medicine is hard work," Billy said.

"So's law," Dom said. "That's why I don't do it any more."

"Too bad," Billy said. "Kevin could use a good lawyer. I'd like to see you sue those bastards, Kevin."

Kevin looked up from his line. "I keep telling you, it was all legal. I just lost—and before I ever knew I was in a fight."

Billy Frazier frowned. "There ought to be something you can do."

"Why don't you just open a new winery?" Patricia asked. "Grandma says she's been pushing you to do that. You've got the land up on the hillside to build one. You've sure got the vineyard."

Kevin shook his head. "It's not practical."

"Why the hell not?" Billy demanded.

Kevin smiled, and not good-naturedly. "Money, for one thing. I'd have to put up new buildings. Do you know what one stainless steel fermenting tank costs? Then I'd have to put together a payroll. I'd also need a winemaker."

Billy gestured toward Dom. "Let him be your winemaker."

Dom laughed. "I'm not remotely qualified except for the fact that I'd work cheap."

Billy laughed. "From what he's saying, that's a pretty important qualification. Shit, Kevin. Why don't you just do it?"

"I'd have to liquidate every share of stock in Brennan, and that's what I'm living on. And even then I'd come up way short."

"You might be able to get some investors," Dom offered.

Kevin turned to Billy. "How about it, Billy? You got an extra half-million in Medicare money laying around?"

Billy's bluff had been called. He was notoriously conservative with his investments. "Well," he said awkwardly, "not a half-million. But I do have some money I could kick in, yes."

"Keep it," Kevin told him. "It doesn't matter if you have a million."

"It might be less than you'd think," Dom offered. "A lot of little wineries in California get going on not much at all."

Kevin said, "Look, let's fish, all right?"

When they brought the Boston Whaler back in, Kevin and Patricia took his golf cart up to the big house while Dom and Billy walked up the hill.

Dom said to Billy, "You made some sense out there about the winery. I don't see why he doesn't do it if he's so upset about losing the other one."

"I do," Billy told him. "We've known each other all our lives. He's reached his limit, is all."

Dom gazed up at the golf cart going up the driveway on the other side of the road. "He must have really been something a few years back."

Billy laughed out loud. "Kid, we all were something a few years back."

* * * *

On a Wednesday afternoon in early September, Patricia said to Dom, "Why are you so quiet? Are you sulking?"

They were lolling in the sun in their bathing suits. She sat in a lounge chair, slathered with suntan lotion; he was stretched out on the dock, his dark skin even darker after several months at Iroquois Lake in prime season.

He sat up. "I've been here all summer. I think maybe it's time I got rolling."

She took off her sunglasses. "Why?"

"Patricia," Dom told her. "I just can't lie around here in the sun forever and do nothing."

"What's wrong with doing nothing for a while? That's what I'm doing."

"You've got a ton of money in the bank. The firm wasn't quite so generous with me. It probably had something to do with my making that comment about Gill's sexual preference when I quit. I've got just about enough to get me back to the west coast—if nothing goes wrong with the car on the way. Besides which, you're a woman."

He could always be counted to make some crack like that. It maddened her. "So?"

"So a woman who chooses not to work is pursuing one of her options.

A man who does the same thing is a bum. Even women think so. Aside from which, I need to come up with some money."

"You don't need any money here," she argued. "There's food, a place to sleep. There's a wine cellar in the big house that'll last well into the next century—even with you around. And I have money for anything else."

"That's your money. It's not mine. If you have think I'm going to let you support me, you're in for a big disappointment."

"So you just drop in for a few months then you go back to California?"

Dom said, "I came here to make sure you were going to be okay. You're doing fine. Now I've got to get on with my life."

"Yeah?" she challenged. "And what are you going to do with it?"

He looked out over the lake. "Something. I don't quite know yet."

When Patricia responded, her voice was gentler. "Then stay here until you figure it out. I've gotten sort of used to having you around, even if you do hog the bathroom."

He gazed into her face for a moment. Then he lay back down on the dock. "For a while longer, then."

"All right," Patricia Ryan said, "only for a little while longer."

* * * *

It began just before bedtime. At first, Kevin barely noticed it.

He had been sitting in the living room, thumbing through an old photo album and sipping a bottle of Weidener '68 champagne he had brought up from the cellar. Katherine was sleeping in what had formerly been the study. Linda Nelson, the nurse, had gone to her room to watch television.

Earlier in the day he had attacked the flower beds in front of the porch. Using the pitchfork from the barn, he had overturned all the beds and planted fresh tulip bulbs. When he became aware of the pain high in his back, he had attributed it to the heavy labor. He had done little of a physical nature since the winery had changed hands.

The pain had gone away when he quit working. Tonight, though, it had returned, joined by indigestion. He washed down several antacid tablets with a glass of fine champagne and then climbed the stairs to his bedroom, bone weary and carrying his album. Kevin slipped between the chilled sheets and flipped on the radio, hoping to catch one of the Rochester talk shows that came in clearly on summer nights.

As he lay totally at rest, the pain in his back subsided, and the lump he had felt in the region of his upper stomach seemed to go away. But Kevin still felt shaky, and he knew that sleep would come hard. He turned off the radio and turned his attention back to the album. It was his most treasured possession: sixty-four pages of photos spanning an era from his college days until the period just before Will's death.

On the first pages were photos of Liam and Kevin in the fields and in the winery with Henri. There were several shots of Kevin and Billy with some of Billy's cars. A series of six pages contained shots of Kevin and Jane and the children, and after that some photos of Liam and an incredibly young Katherine. There were three pages of photos Jack Ryan had taken of a party on the beach at night with everyone gathered around a raging bonfire. There was Liam in his leather jacket and fedora, a pipe clenched between his teeth, and Katherine sitting benignly beside him, a coat wrapped around her and a scarf over her head.

The next series was photos that Kevin had taken in England, shots of Willie Farrington and the others in the RAF bombing crew with which he had flown. There was one shot of Willie, his uncle Cecil and Claire Farrington in front of the bungalow in the southwest of Ireland. It was a shot Kevin had taken with an old Argoflex. He had lost the negative long ago, and now the print was fading badly.

There was a shot of Helen and Kevin, taken after the war. Helen had been gloriously pregnant with Jim. There was page after page of shots of the children: Susan holding baby Patricia, Will and Jimmy in mock combat on the front lawn with boxing gloves. The photos from the 1960s of the children dominated the album, and now they were in color, so vivid and so immediate, as though they had been taken yesterday. There were shots of Will, looking so hard and muscular in his Army uniform, holding little Liam. There were shots of Kevin and Art Dixon, cigars jammed jauntily in their mouths as they stood on the dock with the lake behind them. There was a single, stunning portrait of little Liam that had been taken by a commercial photographer in Boydstown.

Resting loosely in the album—he had never glued it in—was a snapshot of Becky Ralston that Kevin had taken in the snow outside the Red Lion Inn in Massachusetts. Kevin studied that shot a long time.

With a sigh, Kevin closed the album, shut off the lamp and drifted off to sleep. It was several hours before he was awakened by the pain in his back, which suddenly sharpened as he came out of his hazy sleep. As he lay in the dark stillness of the old house, he felt the pain walk up and over his shoulder and center directly on his chest. In just a second or two, he felt as though an anvil were resting there, pressing down on him, taking his breath away.

Kevin Brennan felt a brief surge of fear. It was purely reflex. He knew what heart attack victims felt when the flow of blood to the heart muscle was cut off. He felt his pulse rate quicken and the perspiration bead on his forehead. A sensation of clamminess crawled over his flesh, stroking him with damp fingers. The tightness in his chest grew worse. He could feel it spreading down both arms, reaching toward his elbows, finding them, then stretching to his wrists. The pain was very bad.

The great danger of a heart attack, Kevin knew, was that many victims refused to acknowledge what was happening. They waited too long to call for help. After a while, the heart, starved for blood, would beat erratically, and then it would lose its capacity to pump blood at all. What followed, he knew, was a sudden drop in blood pressure, a deprivation of oxygen to the brain. Death came with a blackout. The brain, starved of nutrition, simply shut down like an electric lightbulb when you hit the switch.

Help, Kevin knew, was very near. Dom and Patricia had gone off to a movie in Geneva, but they would surely be back by now, and the shack had its own phone. Linda Nelson was a nurse, and she was sleeping just across the hall. He could summon any of them for aid. They would either call the rescue squad or load him into the car and take him to the hospital in Lakeside, only fifteen minutes away at most. Then the emergency room staff would summon Billy Frazier and they would administer drugs and they would stand by with a machine to shock the heart back to its proper rhythm if the attack progressed. Kevin raised his head and eyed the phone's shadow in the darkness. For only a brief moment, he toyed with the idea of picking it up and dialing the number of the shack.

Then he lay back against his pillow, which was soaked almost through with the sweat he was generating. He had felt greater pain, long ago after his injuries in the plane crash. Not even the morphine they had given him had protected him totally from that pain. By comparison, this was easily bearable, although his body rebelled instinctively against his growing difficulty in breathing. Soon, he was gulping every breath, his chest heaving mightily against the imaginary weight that bore down on it.

Time passed; he had no idea how long.

Kevin knew what he was doing. His mind was as clear as it had ever been. He thought back to the touch of Jane, to her feel and her smell. He thought of little Liam, the way the boy had moved and laughed. He recalled Will's vacant expression those last few weeks. He thought of Becky, and he felt guilt.

Then he felt his heart turn over in his chest, as if it had somehow slipped loose from its moorings. He felt it sputter and start and sputter again, beating wildly, desperately. He gasped for air, but none came.

As Kevin Brennan sank down into darkness, he had only one thought. Well, he said to whomever was listening, it's about time, isn't it?

Chapter 25

It was an unpleasantly pleasant day, Billy Frazier thought as he sat on the front porch at Brennan's Point and looked over the shimmering lake at the multicolored hillside beyond.

Early fall in the lake country always had a special quality. The wet heat that sometimes appeared in late July and early August had been replaced by feather-light daytime warmth and crisp nights. Maples up and down the hillsides had donned their fall colors. The vineyards were bursting with sugar-filled grapes. The water, bathed in sunlight all summer, was even warmer than it had been in early July. The sun popped over the far side of the lake every morning and smiled down all day long, vanishing in modesty only occasionally behind rolling cumulus clouds. It was the kind of day Kevin had loved, and Billy thought it unfair that such a day should be when Kevin no longer was.

The injustice of it would have made him angry if he had let it. He knew the anger would come anyway. For now he felt mainly shock and a sense of loss, but later there would be rage, then deep depression then, finally, acceptance. He'd read the literature. He knew what he'd experience. He wasn't looking forward to it, though. He'd never been through a bad experience in his life without Kevin Brennan to turn to. Kevin had been there through the death of Billy's older sister Ellen, through his two divorces. Billy wondered how he'd manage to get through this alone.

It had been a day of surprises. Becky Ralston—now Becky Fletcher—had shown up at the graveside with her new husband and had wept openly in front of the mourners, confirming widespread local suspicions of many years' standing. So, too, to Billy's shock, had Linda Nelson, Katherine's nurse. He didn't know who else had noticed it, and maybe Linda Nelson's reaction to Kevin's sudden death had been only natural. Still, Billy had known Kevin, and it had made him wonder. He kept his wondering to himself. The only person with whom he had ever been able to share that sort of gossip had been Kevin.

518   BRENNAN'S POINT

Billy turned to Katherine. Sitting in her wheelchair on the front porch several hours after Kevin had been laid to rest up in the family graveyard on the hillside, she was wearing, Billy would swear, the same black dress she had worn so many years before when Liam had been buried.

"I'm going to have to be going, Katherine," he said at last. "If there's anything I can do—anything at all—you just give me a holler."

Katherine took his hand. "It was nice of you to come, Billy. Thank you."

"How could I not come? I'm going to miss him terribly, Katherine. For every day I have left, I'm going to miss him."

Billy's voice grew hoarse as he spoke, and Katherine patted his hand. "He wouldn't want you to feel too badly, Billy. You know that. Kevin's at peace now."

Billy said, "He would never have left you willingly."

"He was tired," Katherine said quietly.

The crowd was thinning out. Perhaps a hundred had attended Kevin's funeral. Of those, fewer than a half-dozen could reasonably have been classified as close family friends. They were the last to leave Brennan's Point. The family—Susan and Roy, Jim and Patricia—had gathered on the porch to say goodbye. Dom was also there. He wasn't quite family, but he was sharing Patricia's quarters, and Katherine supposed that in this day and age that was close enough.

"I guess I'll be going now," Billy Frazier told Patricia. "I said goodbye to your grandmother. She's holding up pretty well, I'd say."

"When are you going down to your place in the Caribbean?" Jim asked.

"Tonight. I'm flying out of Boydstown, switching at Newark. I'll be in Miami by sunup, and then its off over the Bermuda Triangle. I don't believe all that stuff about the Bermuda Triangle, do you?"

"I think it's all nonsense," Jim said. "You look good, Billy. Taking it easy seems to agree with you."

"Lots of golf," Billy said. "Some deep-sea fishing. I stay down there until the snow melts up here, then I come back from spring until the end of August. That's it. I like it better here, but I can't take the cold any more. I've got a touch of high blood pressure, and I'm through pushing myself."

Dom said, "I hope you'll be back in the spring for trout season."

"Wouldn't miss that," Billy Frazier said. "I'll be out here at the house April first at seven in the morning. You have the boat ready."

Dom smiled. "If I'm still here, you can bet on it. It won't be the same without Kevin, though."

"Are you planning to go somewhere?" Billy asked him.

Patricia said, "He doesn't know yet."

"I've got to go to work sometime," Dom explained.

"Well," Billy said, "why don't you and Patricia start up that winery we were talking about? That'll give you plenty of work to do."

"What winery is that?" Jim asked.

"It was just some talk," Dom said. "We were trying to talk Kevin into it, but he never expressed much interest.

"Well," Billy said, "just remember, if you're interested, I'd be interested in pumping in some money. That offer still goes."

Dom shuffled his feet uncomfortably. "Well, we'll have to see."

Later, when the house had been cleared of visitors and the family was seated around the kitchen table drinking coffee, Jim said, "What's that winery idea all about—the one Billy was talking about?"

"What winery idea?" Susan asked.

"Oh, that," Patricia said. "Billy and Dom were trying to talk Kevin into building a new winery to do battle with the people who own Brennan's now. It was all sort of a pipe dream to get him going again, but he wasn't really interested."

"I think it's a good idea," Jim said.

"Who's going to do it?" Patricia demanded. "It would take a fortune to get it rolling, and I don't know anything about the wine business. Dom knows a little about winemaking—"

"I know a fair amount about winemaking, in fact," Dom corrected. "But I costed it out. The construction and the equipment would run over three-quarters of a million. And then there's payroll and a lot of other costs. And we wouldn't produce any wine—no revenue—for a couple of years. Kevin was right. It would be too steep."

"Well, hell," Roy Peel said, "you could get some financing. You don't have to come up with all the cash."

"We could get financing for part of it," Dom said, "but not all that big a part. The banks are leery of new wineries now that the big corporations are getting into the business. Coca-Cola owns Taylor's now. Those guys who took control of Brennan's are a pretty good-sized outfit with a lot of other interests. You'd be surprised at how little financing there is for beginning wineries to take on big companies like that."

"There's private financing," Jim said quietly. "Billy expressed some interest."

"Yeah," Roy Peel said. "I might even come in for a little bit, depending."

"You could lose every nickel the first year, depending," Patricia told him. "We wouldn't really have any idea of what we were doing."

Susan laughed. "Listen, don't worry about Roy. He never loses."

"Fact is," Roy Peel said, "I'm looking for a little something to invest in. Even if I lost a little, it would help me taxwise."

Dom sat up, interested. "How much are you talking about?"

Roy Peel shrugged. "Twenty-five thousand, fifty, maybe. Could be a bit more, depending on what sort of package you could put together."

Patricia shook her head. "Roy, we got to playing around one night before Kevin died, and even if we could find ten people like you and Billy to come in for amounts like that we'd still be short by hundreds of thousands of dollars. It just isn't practical."

"I could finance whatever you need," Jim Ryan said quietly.

Patricia looked over at her brother. "You could finance a million dollars?"

He nodded. "Yep."

Dom and Patricia exchanged glances. "Are you serious?" Dom demanded.

"I'm serious," Jim Ryan told them.

Silence fell over the table. Katherine, sitting quietly in her wheelchair, said nothing. She had said nothing since the conversation began. But Jim could feel her eyes boring into him like drill bits.

Susan broke the silence finally with a good-natured laugh. "It sounds like you're doing better than I'd thought."

Patricia said, "Jim, you told me what you make when you were here early in the summer. You're doing great, I know, but where would you get that kind of money?"

He looked over at her, uncomfortable under such scrutiny. Then he said, "All right, we're all family here, and we're all talking about going into business together. I'll tell you where I got the money as long as I have everybody's personal assurance that it doesn't go beyond this room."

There were murmured assurances. Jim sat back in his chair, every eye on him.

He said, "You know that some partners and I started a little company a few years ago that manufactures semiconductors. In fact, Kevin had some stock in it, Susan, so that means that with his death you're going to benefit from what I'm going to tell you. Well, to make microchips, one of the tools you need in your factory is a diamond-edged saw to make precision cuts. We're talking about very fine tolerances, and you go through a lot of those saws in any given month. We bought all our saws from a machine tool outfit over in Massachusetts. The machine tool company's other big client was Allied Industries. The Massachusetts company was having trouble servicing us both, so we offered to buy them out so we could have a ready supply of the saws we needed. They agreed, and we made the deal a couple of years ago. Earlier this summer Allied bought us out—semiconductor company and all—primarily to get its hands on the plant that makes the saws."

Roy Peel had been listening closely. "How much did you get from that deal?" he asked quickly.

"It was mostly a stock transaction," Jim told him, "and, to be honest, I don't really know what I got. I won't know until four-and-a-half years from now when I'm able to sell all the stock. If the stock goes up—and there's every indication that it will—it could be quite a nice piece of change. The point is that the stock just split, and I can sell the initial block at the end of this year. If current prices hold over the next few months, I'm going to end up with just under two million dollars with the sale of the first block of Allied stock."

There was a moment of silence around the kitchen table. Jaws dropped, and for the first time since she had learned of Kevin's death, Katherine smiled slightly. Somewhere, she was sure, Kevin was listening to this conversation and laughing uproariously. She could almost hear him. She could feel him in this house, just as she had felt his father's presence all these years.

"You're kidding," Patricia said quietly. "Two million? What's the total value of the deal going to turn out to be?"

Jim permitted himself a small smile. "It could go as high as ten million over the five years, according to my lawyer, who's also a partner. The point is that I'm fixed for life. I'm sinking most of it into tax-free municipals—primarily in several trusts for Eamon. But I could lose this whole two million and never feel a twinge of pain. There's nothing I'd rather do with it than get a winery going on this land again. I think I owe it to my ancestors, if nothing else."

No one knew what to say. Patricia gazed at her brother, almost in a trance. "You're not kidding, are you?"

He smiled and reddened visibly. "Hey," he said, "I'm loaded."

Patricia clenched both fists and brought them down on the table with a crash. She whooped like an Indian on the warpath. "My brother the millionaire!" she shouted, her face alight with mirth. "I wish Dad were alive to see this."

"I just fell into it," Jim said sheepishly. "Anyway, the money is there. You tell me what you need to get it rolling, and after the first of the year, I'll just write a check."

Roy Peel said, "Under the circumstances, consider me in for a hundred grand. I don't want to look like a piker."

* * * *

In the shack that night Patricia told Dom, "You've got to stay to help me get this rolling."

Dom stood by the sink, tie loosened, jacket open. "You don't need me," he said. "You can afford to hire the best winemaker money can buy. In fact, you'd be crazy to bring me on as winemaker. I'm not qualified."

There was an urgent note in Patricia's voice. "This isn't the law. There are no entrance requirements in the wine business. We can learn together. Of course we'd hire a winemaker. But somebody has to know enough to know if the winemaker knows anything. I don't. You do. You have to stay for the first year, anyway."

He frowned. "Patricia, a year is a long time."

"I'll pay you," she insisted. "You can go on salary. You can be executive vice president or something. We'll put you on the payroll for forty thousand the first year plus a share of the profits. You won't do that well with any law firm in the country."

Dom Fresina, drinking a glass of water, leaned back against the sink. She was standing in the main room of the shack in her funeral dress and her stockings. Her shoes had, as always, been thrown in different directions the moment she had come through the door.

"First of all," he told her, "there won't be any profits the first year. Or the second, for that matter. Or the third, probably. Maybe—just maybe—you'll break even the fourth year. But not if you load up your payroll with people like me whose contribution will be marginal at best."

She seemed agitated to him. She paced the room in her stocking feet. "You wouldn't be marginal," she said to him. "I couldn't do this without you. Dom, I need somebody to talk to."

Dom cocked his head. "Somebody to talk to?"

Patricia Ryan turned and looked at him squarely. Her expression was just this side of plaintive. He'd never seen that before, not even during the deepest moments of her travail in Los Angeles after Charlie Whittington's death.

"Somebody to talk to," she said to him slowly, "and somebody to sleep with."

He said nothing. He only studied her, unmoving, expressionless.

"We haven't made love since the Napa Valley," she said to him softly.

"I'm well aware of that."

"That's why you're leaving, isn't it? It's because we haven't done it together."

Dom Fresina smiled. His was a cockeyed smile, and it always had a quality of irony even under the best of circumstances, which these weren't. "That's something of an oversimplification," he told Patricia.

"Bottom line?" she said.

He turned and poured his glass of water into the sink. Then he turned back to her. "Bottom line, that's part of it. I haven't been with a woman in a long time now—months."

"You haven't come near me."

He frowned deeply. "It was my very distinct impression that you didn't want me to. I'd never try to force myself on you, Patricia. I figured that when you and Charlie started, that was pretty much it for you and me that way. You never gave me any sign once I came here that anything had changed. We've been pretty good friends. We've been roommates. But it's seemed pretty clear to me that you haven't had any interest beyond that."

"And that's when you began to talk about leaving?"

Dom didn't answer at first. He looked down at the floor, then he looked back in her direction. "What the hell do you want from me, Patricia?" he asked finally.

"A year of your time," she said. "At the end of this month next year, you can go wherever you want. I need somebody with me to get this started. I need a friend, Dom."

"Don't you have any other friends?" he demanded.

Patricia walked over to him. She took his hand, lifted it up and held it to her lips. "None I'd be interested in sharing my bed with," she said. "You don't want me to try to start up a winery when I'm all hung up with sexual tension, do you?"

He looked into her eyes, and they were bright with mirth. Dom laughed. He put his arms around her. "I've always been open to just about any possibility," he said, "but somehow I never pictured myself as a wine pimp." He kissed her, long and hard. Then he said, "At least I'm finally off that goddamn sofa."

* * * *

From the beginning the new winery was different from the old in every significant detail.

The buildings, constructed high on the hillside, looking down on the lake, were stark and modern in appearance. They were built of steel beams and concrete blocks and were covered with off-white stucco and dark brown wooden trim. Patricia complained that the new winery complex looked more like something you might see in the Napa Valley instead of the Finger Lakes, but Dom had taken complete control of the physical plant and would not be deterred. As the project neared completion, Patricia was forced to admit she was pleased.

The enormous fermenting tanks were stainless steel. The aging casks were made of the finest imported French oak, toasted and constructed in the Old World by skilled craftsmen. The lobby, designed to attract tourists, was decorated with newly reframed color photos of the lake country taken by Jack Ryan many years before. Oil portraits of Liam and Kevin, done from photographs by a professor of fine arts at Syracuse University, hung along one wall. Smaller portraits of Henri and Christian Weidener had also been commissioned, and they adorned a hallway leading to the small but comfortable executive offices. Patricia also had a full kitchen installed next to the concrete patio to serve food to paying visitors.

Most impressive, however, were the winery's laboratories. Jim Ryan had taken a personal hand in this. The basic laboratories were modern and antiseptic, but Jim also insisted on installing computers for a wide variety of tasks. Personal computers handled standard business functions such as payroll, purchasing and inventory control. But Jim brought in a team of consultants from Texas who designed computerized machinery that would take over the task of hand riddling the champagnes that the new winery would produce. They also set up computerized weather stations along the mountainside to continuously record soil and air temperatures, wind speed and rainfall.

"Henri would go wild if he could see all this," Patricia told him.

"He'd go wilder yet if he saw the rest of it," he said. "Did you ever hear of a nuclear magnetic resonance spectrometer?"

"A what?"

"It's a machine that bombards a substance with radio-frequency pulses and gives you a computer-detailed map of the substance's molecular structure. I'm making arrangements to rent one and get it in here."

"For what?"

"For wine. Look, our big job here will be to make wine as well as Henri did. We have a basement full of his best stuff, and we have his notes. But with this gear I'm leasing we can take a sample of Henri's best and run it through a liquid-chromatography instrument that'll break it down into all its chemical components. Then we can zap it with nuclear magnetic-resonance equipment and feed it all into the computer. That'll give us a graphic fingerprint of Henri's wine. Then we can then go to work on figuring out what aspect of the wine-growing and winemaking process was responsible for each chemical component in it. That'll give us a leg up on producing wine identical to what Henri turned out. Once we come up with something that has the same fingerprint, we'll know to a scientific certainty that we've produced precisely what Henri produced—down to the last molecule."

Patricia shuddered. "That's creepy."

"That's science. I explained to Dom how the equipment works, and he's all for it."

"Well," Patricia said, "it's your money."

Jim smiled. "And if Dom had thought it was a dopey idea? How would you have felt about it, then?"

"Oh, I'd be all for it, then," Patricia laughed.

Dom and Patricia fought. They argued viciously over every detail of the new winery. But Patricia found herself deferring more and more to him as he supervised the construction and the beginnings of the winery's business operations. Despite the battling, they grew closer. They even reached the point where he could joke about Charlie Whittington.

"You know," he told her one night, "what happened to Charlie proves an age-old mathematical principle."

"What's that?" she said, snuggling closer to him in the darkness of the bedroom in the shack.

"Just this: Sixty-nine into twenty-five won't go."

She punched him.

"Poor Charlie," Dom giggled. "He didn't know whether he was coming or going."

She punched him again.

"He went out as the senator erect," Dom said, and collapsed in laughter.

Patricia sat up in bed. "That one wasn't even remotely funny," she said, grinning.

By the following September they had hired a staff and were preparing for the harvest. Jim called Patricia one night for a progress report.

"How's Dom?" he said.

"He's Dom. Just as sweet and easy to get along with as ever. I'm being sarcastic, in case you hadn't noticed."

"Are you two ever going to stop shacking up and get married?"

"I have no intention of marrying anybody, as you well know. And very high on the list of people I have no intention of marrying is Dom Fresina. How about you? What's going on in your life?"

"Well," Jim said slowly, "there is this woman . . ."

"Is there, now? Tell me about her."

"Her name is Carole Murray. She's a schoolteacher. I met her when we were both doing volunteer work for the Reagan campaign."

"You're working for Reagan? Yucchh! Dad would do a back flip in his grave if he knew that."

"All us millionaires work for Reagan. Wait'll that winery starts turning a profit, and you'll see who you like better."

"I just never thought of you as a conservative."

Jim laughed. "You'd be surprised at how your political convictions change when you realize that you've got something to conserve. Anyway, I met her when we were stuffing envelopes together. She's divorced, and she's got a couple of kids. We've been skirting around the corners of talking about getting married."

"Don't marry anybody until you bring her up here and give me a chance to check her out."

"Funny you should say that," Jim said. "I've been thinking about driving up for a weekend with her and her kids and Eamon, just to say hello."

"With a mob that size, you'd better start thinking about getting a bigger car."

"I've already gotten one. I have a Mercedes now—a four-door sedan, just like the Fords Dad used to drive."

"Not a Cadillac?"

"I'm not that Republican," Jim said. "I do want to come up to Brennan's Point, though. I'd like to see Grandma again. I don't know how many more chances I'm going to get. I've also decided to buy one of those houses next to the point for a summer home. I'm going to have one of the local brokers handle it."

Patricia said, "What if the people who own it don't want to sell?"

"They'll sell. The location is important to me. I'm sure I can offer them a price that'll interest them."

"It would be nice to have us all together again up here," Patricia said.

"That's what I'm thinking. I want to do it before Eamon gets too old to want to spend time up there."

"Once this place gets into his blood, he won't want to be anywhere else."

"That's what I'm hoping."

"You sound happy to me," Patricia told her brother. "I can't remember you sounding so relaxed."

"Well, I guess I am reasonably happy. What's more, being happy doesn't scare me like it used to. That's a sign of growing up."

She laughed into the phone. "I'm going to have to grow up, too—one of these days."

"You'll get there," Jim Ryan assured her.

That fall and winter the new winery produced its first products. Quality wines were put into storage for proper aging, but medium-level vintages were issued under the label of the Brennan's Point Winery. Consolidated Food Products immediately filed suit, claiming that the Brennan name belonged to the Brennan Wine Company, which they had bought and paid for. The suit was filed in New York State's court of original jurisdiction, which for reasons known only to the framers of the state constitution was called State Supreme Court. Each side filed briefs, and oral arguments were heard in Boydstown. Patricia and Dom retained a Boydstown firm, Merrill and Merrill, to represent them, but the justice who heard the case ruled in favor of Peter Baldwin's firm.

While Patricia appealed the case to the next higher court, the Appellate Division of State Supreme Court, she also ordered all the Brennan's Point Wine labels modified. They now read B—————— Point Winery, and she included a new slogan at the bottom of each.

"They may have taken our name," the slogan read, "but not our . . ." And there, at the end of the printed message, was a drawing of a donkey, skillfully executed by Dominic Fresina, Esq., who had taken an art course or two as an undergraduate.

Consolidated Food Products filed suit over that, too, but Patricia would not be deterred. She wrote and phoned the *Boydstown Bulletin*, the Rochester *Democrat and Chronicle* and the *New York Times* to tell reporters the story of how her fledgling winery was battling a food industry giant for the right to use the family name that was hers by right of birth and tradition. The *Wall Street Journal* was so intrigued by the story that it devoted a full column to it in down the middle of its front page. Business picked up markedly after that, and Patricia, acting on Dom's suggestion, bought an aged donkey and tethered it in front of the winery to the delight of tourists who came through the lake country to visit wineries. She named the donkey Mr. Gill.

* * * *

Katherine's stroke came just after dawn.

About nine, Linda Nelson came into the study turned bedroom to awaken her. She found Katherine stretched out on the floor, unable to speak, her eyes rolling wildly. Linda phoned the rescue squad and the winery, in that order. By the time Dom and Patricia had come down the hillside to the big house, the ambulance was already there, and Katherine was being carried out on a stretcher.

She spent several weeks in Lakeside Memorial. Billy Frazier had flown in from his winter home on Saint Thomas to supervise her care. When it became clear that Katherine Brennan would survive this stroke, although badly impaired, Billy felt it his duty to speak to Patricia about a nursing home. "She needs skilled nursing care," Billy said. "Linda might be able to handle part of it if you decide to keep Katherine out at Brennan's

Point, but it's a twenty-four-hour-a-day responsibility. Linda's going to need help."

"If we keep Grandma with us," Patricia asked, "what would we need?"

"Two more nurses. A respirator. You ought to have a defibrillator on hand, if you're serious about it. She's a very old, very sick woman, Patricia."

Dom and Patricia exchanged glances. They understood one another. "If my grandmother's going to die, Billy," Patricia said, "she's going to die at Brennan's Point."

Billy Frazier nodded. "I'm so glad to hear you say that."

The expense was immense, but Jim Ryan had immense resources. Susan insisted on contributing as well, but it was largely Jim's monthly checks that kept the house running. Katherine was unable to move or speak, but there was no question in Patricia's mind that the ancient woman knew and understood all that went on around her. Patricia could see it in her eyes.

When warm weather came Katherine was wheeled out on the porch daily. She spent much of the day there, sometimes dozing, more often staring out over the lake.

On a day in early May, Patricia took Dom's Spitfire and drove into Lakeside. When she returned, top down, she pulled the little car directly in front of the porch. She came up the steps to her grandmother and knelt in front of her. "Good morning, Grandma," Patricia Ryan said. "How are you today?"

Katherine answered with her eyes.

Patricia lowered hers for a moment. Then she looked up and said, "Grandma, I have something to tell you. I haven't told anybody yet—not even Dom."

Katherine listened intently.

"I'm pregnant, Grandma," Patricia whispered. "Dom and I are going to have a baby."

Slowly, and with great effort, Katherine Brennan nodded in approval.

Patricia's voice turned hoarse, and her eyes filled. "Dom wants me to marry him," she said. "He's been after me for months now to make up my mind. I'm going to do it."

Again, Katherine nodded almost imperceptibly.

Patricia clutched the old woman's aged, bony hand, so devoid of life and movement. "I'm going to have a girl. I can feel it. I just know. I . . . I want to name her Katherine, after you—Katherine Ryan Fresina. That'll be her name, and she'll know all about you and Poppy and my mother and my father and Kevin. I'll tell her who she is, Grandma. I promise you I'll do that."

For a moment—just a moment—Patricia was sure she felt the slightest touch of pressure from the old woman's fingers. She was sure she felt Katherine try to squeeze her hand. "I'm going to try to raise her to be like you," Patricia said. "I want her to be strong and loving and full of life, just like you've been all these years. I want her to love this place, just like you've loved it. I . . . I'm babbling, but I can't help it. I'd been scheduled to go in to see the doctor for a couple of days now, but when I woke up this morning I knew I was carrying a baby. I just knew it. He only told me what I'd already sensed. And I know it'll be a girl. It's the strangest thing. Did that happen to you with Kevin? Did you know he would be a boy?"

Katherine's head moved ever so slightly. But tears welled up in her eyes, behind her glasses, and Patricia was alarmed. "I'm upsetting you," she said.

With enormous effort, Katherine shook her head. It was the most minimal of gestures, almost invisible unless you knew her so well, as Patricia did. Katherine's mouth turned up in a faint grimace that Patricia recognized as a smile.

The younger woman stood up and hugged the frail, ancient creature in the wheelchair. "I'm going to go in and have Maggie make me some breakfast," Patricia said. "I don't know why I bother. I'll just throw it up again. I'll see you in a little while. I love you, Grandma."

Patricia squeezed Katherine's hand. Then she was gone, inside, the screen door slamming behind her with that familiar sound.

Katherine sat in her chair. It was a truly glorious day in spring, a morning alive with light breezes. It was the kind of morning Katherine had always loved, that had filled her with joy and a sense of well-being beyond description. She gazed through aged eyes out over the lake, its waves rolling and pinpoints of gleaming sunlight dancing on them. Beyond the vast expanse of water was the mountain, alive with hard, green grape buds awaiting the heat of summer. The cotton-candy clouds rolled by, stark white against the stunning blueness of the sky, casting giant shadows that crawled across the lush landscape. Katherine raised her eyes and stared at the clouds.

Liam, she was sure, was resting atop one of them, looking down benignly on the lake and the land. She could almost see him. But then, as she gazed, she became aware that he was suddenly there. Katherine could see him clearly, down on the point. Yes, it was Liam. There was no doubt about it, and it didn't strike Katherine as at all strange. He was coming up the steps from the lake, crossing the road. She could actually see him as he came up the path in the sunlight—the familiar stride, the pipe clenched firmly in his teeth. Liam's hair was reddish-brown, his waist trim and tight. He walked with a lilt to his step, up the driveway toward the porch.

Katherine saw him coming, and she felt her heart quicken dangerously with excitement. She raised a hand in greeting. He waved back, smiling and stepping up his pace toward her.

Liam Brennan was so young, she realized, as he came up the steps to the porch and Katherine felt his hands lovingly encase her own.

Then again, she thought as she rose up easily to greet him, so was she.

THE END